MAHARANI
THE FIRST AUSTRALIAN PRINCESS

CHRIS KUNZ

Set in 11pt Book Antiqua on 13.5pt
Typesetting by Excell Printing, Pambula, New South Wales, Australia

National Library of Australia
Cataloguing-in-Publication entry:

Creator: Kunz, Chris, author

Title: Maharani – the first Australian princess:
                a novel based on a true story / Chris Kunz

ISBNSs: 9780648014119 (paperback)
                9780648014157 (ebook)

Subjects: Princesses--India--Fiction
                Princesses--Australia--Fiction
                Biographical fiction
                Historical fiction
                India--Queens--Fiction
                India--History
                Australia--History

Dedicated to the memory of my great-aunt:

Elsie Caroline Thompson
Maharani of Tikari

The first Australian princess

and also to

Myrtle McLeod and May Maxwell

The author acknowledges the following for assisting him in his research:

The late Dr Coralie Younger, author, who bequeathed me her notes on Elsie
The late Sita Carter (née Binstead), Elsie's goddaughter

and

Linda Albertson, Bega Council Librarian, NSW, Australia
Natalia Bazhenova, tour guide, natalia-tour.com, St Petersburg, Russia
Pauline Brockett, Librarian, Epilepsy Foundation of Victoria, Australia
Andrew Dawrant, Trustee, Royal Aero Club, Leicester, UK
Deena Diamandis, Freedom of Information Officer, Dept of Health, Vic.,
    Australia
John Fasal, author and expert on Rolls-Royce cars, UK
Nick Forder, Museum of Science & Industry, Manchester, UK
Terry Glebe, Librarian, Fort Street School, Sydney, NSW, Australia
Dave Harris, Co-ordinator, Midlands Railway Study Centre, UK
F. G. Hart, Chief Clerk, Privy Council Office, London, UK
The late Ron Hickman and wife Helen, Jersey, Channel Islands
Benjamin Hollister, Genealogist, Roots and Branches, Adelaide, Australia
Dr Elisabeth Kehoe, author and historian, London, UK
Dr Pundarik Mukhopadhaya, Associate Professor, Macquarie University,
    Sydney, Australia
Greg Phillips, Building Manager, Lordsgate Properties Ltd, London, UK
Brian Riddle, Chief Librarian, National Aerospace Library, Farnborough,
    UK
Jennifer Sabin, Historian, Federation Internationale de l'Automobile, Paris,
    France
Lt Col Vidya Sharma, author, Gaya, India
Franco Svampa, Italian language teacher, U3A, Tura Beach, NSW, Australia
Frank Van Straten, Official Historian, Live Performance Australia

as well as

National Library of Australia (Trove)
National Library of New Zealand (Papers Past)

and importantly

My late parents, my brothers and cousins, and especially my wife Lana.

About the Author:

Maharani - The First Australian Princess is Chris Kunz's first novel.

It is an epic historical work based on the remarkable life of Elsie Caroline Thompson, his great-aunt on his mother's side. Elsie was a beautiful Sydney-born singer, actress, dancer and comedienne, who became the first Australian to marry overseas royalty.

Chris was a teacher, then an expert in ethnic groups and countries with the Australian Bureau of Statistics. His previously published books, *Brainstrains: Creative Problem-Solving and Logical Thinking – International and Historical Themes, Books 1 and 2* (1991 and 1994), are used by schools in Australia, New Zealand and the United States, mostly as a resource for gifted and talented students.

Important note:

This novel is the result of many years of detailed research into the remarkable life of my great-aunt. While it does reveal previously unknown facts, some parts are purely fictional linkages between known occurrences.

All newspaper reports included in this book are genuine and reproduced here with their original spelling and wording.

Similarly, quatrains from the *Rubáiyát of Omar Khayyám* are reproduced here exactly as they were published by Macmillan and Co. (London) in the 1890 version that Elsie memorised.

Letters by Elsie, Raji, HSL Polak, Willie Hathaway, Myrtle McLeod and my mother are reproduced here exactly as they were written. They originally came from Privy Council case records or our family's holdings.

Other letters by Elsie, May Maxwell, The Public Trustee, various institutional staff as well as clinical reports and notes are recorded here with the spelling and wording as they were originally written. They were obtained under Freedom of Information.

Occasionally, some parts of newspaper reports, letters, legal documents and clinical reports and notes have been omitted. This has been done because they do not add anything to the reader's understanding of Elsie's story.

Contents

Contents

Contents

Chapter 1

Sydney 1897

When all is as it's meant to be, and nothing's to behold
Small stones transform to diamond ones, and copper plate to gold,
When all's told as it should be told, clocks stand the test of time
And minute hands make hourly pans, around their dials in rhyme.

"Tick tock, tick tock, time to take ya little clock … remember lads, just like I learned ya: bump, but not too 'ard, then twist, pull 'n' split—seez ya back in Sussex Lane in a few ticks!"

The four huddled figures then melted into the Saturday morning streetscape. The tallest ghosted into passing pedestrians, while the three boys crossed the cobbled street through the traffic, holding a thin mattress, temporarily on high—heading on a collision course with their elderly victim.

Seconds later, the youngest one was off like a startled rabbit—gold fob watch in hand.

"Stop him! Thief! He's taken my watch!"

The youngster ducked in front of a passing horse and buggy.

"Whoa!" the driver cried, pulling hard on the reins as the figure scampered away.

"I'll catch him, Father!" a young man, preparing to dismount from the passenger position, told the driver.

"No you don't, Jonathon! Stay right there! He will see more darkness than light in his shortened life—and I want you to have a long one in the sun! Besides, we are nearing Thompson's now."

Reluctantly, Jonathon settled back down, but peered through the canopy searching for the fugitive.

The horse and buggy turned up Erskine Street and soon halted outside James Thompson, Bookseller and Stationer, on Erskine's north side.

"Now you may get out young man … Jonathon? Jonathon! I do not intend to be known as the only master in Darlinghurst to have a dolt for a son. Step down right now!"

"Father, I am really not that interested," he started to protest, but his father's withering look changed his mind.

The shop doorbell tinkled as it gave way to the will of one of the entrants.

A middle-aged man looked up from the counter where he had been sorting books for the stacks with the love and care others reserved for more animate beings. "Mr Battersby, sir!"

"James, good to see you once more! I've brought my son Jonathon. He really is settling into good reading habits."

"Excellent! Nice to meet you young sir—now what would you like? Homer? Shelley?"

Alas, Jonathon's attention had strayed to the pair of petite boots balanced on a ladder behind the shelving to his right. The owner of the boots was desperately trying to watch him, too.

"Jonathon! Mr Thompson has the graciousness to give yourself his valuable time and attention—you could at least have the decency to return in kind. Dickens ... Dickens will do, James—which do you have?"

"Most of them, sir. *The Pickwick Papers, David Copperfield, Oliver Twist ...*"

"*Oliver Twist* sounds just fine—and especially appropriate given the incident on Sussex Street, earlier!" James' quizzical look elicited more. "Jonathon was about to chase a young thief, though I assured him he had plenty of years left to be a hero!"

The boots on the ladder shifted from their flat and safe distribution to a more ballet-like pose as their owner struggled for a better view through the satirical work of Swift.

"Jonathon! Come forward, please! Is this what you would li ... this would be good, would it not?"

Jonathon, who could not differentiate *Twist* from a turnip, inched forward with minimal enthusiasm. The owner of the boots tried to follow his visage from the ladder—but leaned too far when passing volumes of Voltaire.

As Jonathon's hands reached out to grip Dickens' classic, the boots' owner overreached and lost hers—there was a scream and an almighty crash.

"Elsie! Elsie! Oh, my girl!" James cried, as he and his customers rounded the end of the stack to be greeted by a scene of chaos: the fourteen-year-old's figure lay stretched doll-like over the ladder, as books still tumbled, Emily over Charlotte Brontë, from the shelving above.

For a moment, all seemed to freeze: James, in anguish and fear for what had happened to his much-loved and only daughter; Mr Battersby in sheer surprise; while Jonathon—well he was just—transfixed.

His seventeen-year-old heart had been captured by the twisted but pretty young form that lay before him: the cute boots, the flowing and colourful dress—but most of all, the beautiful face.

Elsie opened her eyes just enough to see her audience—and check that Jonathon was watching. Even in the dappled light between the shelving space, he could see that her eyes were amazing—they looked violet.

Then she sighed, a sad and pained sigh that triggered the others—except for Jonathon—into immediate action.

As James moved in to nurse his daughter's head, Mr Battersby bellowed out instructions, while gesturing to the south-east: "Jonathon! Get Dr Devorin—he is up around the corner in Kent Street!" But Jonathon was just staring at Elsie, with his mouth open. "Boy! Get going, NOW!"

"Yes … Father," he muttered haltingly, turning, tripping over the edge of the ladder, stumbling into a stack and somehow, just making the door. Thankfully, his father did not see him try to push the inward-opening door, out.

The minutes that followed seemed like hours to all: Jonathon scampering from doorstep to doorstep on Kent Street; Mr Battersby wondering why God had burdened him with such an incompetent son; and James caressing his daughter's head in his lap while praying for help to come soon.

"Does it hurt any place in particular, my darling?" James asked in desperate hope of a negative reply.

Elsie, who had been silent and frowning, thought not, but twinged in pain as she turned slightly to answer his query. "Owww!"

"Better to be careful in moving her, James—she may have injured her neck!" warned Mr Battersby.

Eventually, the tinkling doorbell heralded the return of Battersby junior with a panting Dr Devorin in tow.

The doctor studied the scene for a moment, then asked: "Is there a room with a table here?"

"You may use the counter if you wish, doctor," replied James.

"I will need to do a full examination—such a thing should not be done in public view!"

"You can use my office at the back—I will clear the desk," James offered. "Mr Battersby, would you mind holding my daughter's head in the meantime?"

"Certainly, James," he responded, spreading his strong hands under her hair. Elsie thought they smelt of the sea, though how she could have discerned this, as the former ship's captain had not journeyed on the waves for years, was a mystery.

Her father was soon back and Dr Devorin gave the order to carefully carry the patient into the office. Jonathon lifted her feet and excitedly touched her legs briefly, just above the ankle stockings where her skin felt like silk. Dr Devorin then advised: "Thank you, gentleman, this may take some time—I must be sure of her condition."

With that, the others were ushered out of the office and Dr Devorin closed the solid wood door that contained only a small pane of frosted glass. Unbeknown to Elsie, he placed his heavy doctor's bag against the door opening, then, turned to face her.

The sole window to the back laneway was covered with the grime of an industrial city, but permitted enough light to ensure the examination proceeded without artificial exposure. Tick tock, tick tock—that was all Elsie could hear for a few moments, as the French marble clock on the office fireplace mantelpiece insisted it should not be ignored.

Then, Dr Devorin spoke, though Elsie noted a slight quiver in his voice not present earlier—*maybe he is cold*, she thought.

"I … I am going to check your limbs … first."

Slowly, he undid the lacing on her boots sliding each off with care—and then her stockings. He ran his long, gaunt fingers over the tops of her feet, then his thumbs moved down under their base—a touch that would normally have encouraged tickle-triggered laughter—though Elsie felt no such reaction.

"Lift your right leg," the doctor requested. Elsie did so

without problem. "Now your left." This time Elsie grimaced—a reaction noted by the doctor.

He moved around to her side and the procedure was repeated with both arms—this time the right producing a wince rather than the left.

"Please stand by the side of the desk," he said, reaching out a helping hand to ease her to the floor. She grabbed it for support, immediately noting it was sweaty.

Dr Devorin rotated both her arms and then struggled a little with his words. "Pl … please t … take off … your dr … dress … and shift."

Elsie was feeling less at ease as time progressed, but he was a doctor, so she did just as he requested.

Standing there on the bare stone floor, with feet to match and just her drawers to barely cover her from the waist down to just below the knee, Elsie was feeling close to naked.

Dr Devorin could feel the warmth radiating from her body as his large hands reached for her shoulders. He turned her around so her back faced him. "T … tell me if it … if it hurts when I press," he asked. His fingertips moved from one point to another, never leaving her silky-smooth skin.

She could hear his breathing clearly now.

"Lie back on the … the … d-desk … on your b-b-back on the desk … El … Elsie," he said, helping her back up.

She was happy to do this—at least she could close her eyes and not see his gaunt, bespectacled features leering over her.

Meanwhile, just outside the bookshop's office window, an argument had erupted between a group of figures over the value and possession of a gold fob watch. The Sussex Lane Gang were squabbling over their latest trophy.

The participants in each encounter were far too focussed to note the presence of the other group, a mere few feet away.

As the doctor moved closer once more, Elsie noticed his breathing was even more rapid and his fingers were trembling. Standing behind her head, he pressed on her shoulders, then, ran his fingers down past her collarbones to her firm, pert young breasts.

He seemed to struggle for breath, then, shuffled around

the desk to her left side, where he continued his in-depth examination of this part of her anatomy.

Elsie was petrified. She closed her eyes tightly, as if hoping to expel these moments from reality.

The doctor's breathing was becoming frantic now and hands more sweaty, as his left one slipped over her navel and caressed the smooth curve of her stomach.

She felt something wet dropping onto her skin, opening her eyes only briefly enough to see his mouth agape and dribble leaking from one side.

His fingers slid with urgency into her drawers and sought out and explored her pubic hair, before heading further down. His breathing now shifted to near hysterical, just as the minute hand on the French clock reached its apogee and the first of eleven chimes exploded into the tension of the room. Elsie uttered a voiceless scream that failed to halt the doctor's assault.

Outside, in the main body of the bookshop, the other three waited anxiously, with James pacing nervously, fearful of his daughter's condition. It was to be a few more minutes before the doctor emerged, looking worn out and frazzled.

Closing the door firmly behind him, he breathlessly informed James and the Battersbys that Elsie had bruising to her right shoulder and lower left back, for which he would prescribe Gartner's Ointment—but otherwise, physically, she was fine.

"Oh, thank the Lord! Dr Devorin, you have been most diligent!" cried James, greatly relieved. "Please, how much do I owe you?"

"Mr Thompson, sir, I shall be content with your daughter's … your daughter's patronage … at times when she pleases … or is in need—that, sir, shall suffice," the doctor offered, as he began to recover his composure.

"Dr Devorin, you have been too kind. And I thank my good friend, Mr Battersby, for alerting me to your expert services!"

"Ah … there is one more thing, Mr Thompson. Your daughter … she has suffered severe shock and trauma. It is an unfortunate side effect of such occurrences that … that victims often become distraught, frequently hallucinate and appear certain of imaginary … and unlikely events. Your daughter has been so afflicted. She will … will need regular warm baths and care, for some time yet."

"Her mother and I shall ensure it, doctor. Thank you again!"

With that, Dr Devorin eased open the office door, picked up his bag and motioned for Elsie to emerge. A dishevelled, though now fully dressed and tearful young lady, eased herself into her father's arms—leaving Jonathon wondering if his turn with such an angel, might ever come.

As all three visitors departed, James prepared to close the shop early, hastily writing a sign stating:

Shop Closed Early Due to Accident—Apologies
All Stock Half Price on Monday

"Come on, El, we're going home. We'll go by hansom cab rather than the ferry or the tram, as it will be quicker."

He looked up and across Erskine Street, spying a single horse-drawn carriage sitting idly on the other side—just down from W V Bond Chemist at No. 47.

James carefully guided Elsie across the road, then up the hill and into the chemist.

"William, old friend, do you have a tin of Gartner's Ointment?"

"Most certainly do, James! Another patient of Dr Devorin, eh? He must have shares in that company!"

Tin in hand and arm around Elsie, James approached the cab, whose driver was snoozing under a hat tipped over his eyes, as the morning sun warmed the back of his neck.

"Birchgrove Road, Balmain, my good man!" James instructed, as the driver, perched up behind the black cabin, struggled to wake from his morning nap.

As the cab set off, with Elsie tucked within her father's protective reach, she spoke not an audible word—though thought many dark thoughts. She wondered just how different things would have been if she had not exaggerated her condition. "It's all my fault," she muttered to herself. "It's all my fault!"

Chapter 2

The Girl with Golden Hair

In youth there springs a hope that brings, with little to compare:
A friendship wrapped in dance and song, with a girl with golden hair.
Think naught of failing consequence, fear not the broken heart
For riding in relationship, beats loneliness apart.

The wheels of the hansom cab bumped and slipped over the cobblestones, causing James to tighten his grip around his daughter. He was now feeling her pain. Perhaps the familiar ride on the Balmain ferry, he pondered, though departing later and travelling slower, may have been the better option.

As the horse turned obediently at the bottom of Erskine Street, and the cab headed left, the full quayside panorama that was Darling Harbour came into view.

Steam-powered vessels jostled with square-riggers for the privilege of disgorging their cargoes to nearby warehouses and into Sydney and the colony's growing populace—hungry for everything this industrial age could produce.

Trolleys, carts and drays of all description ploughed the harbour front, laden with barrels, sacks and other containers guided by tough men and youths. Their exertions, exhortations and gesticulations filled the daylight air and later accompanied them into the nearby taverns, boarding houses and brothels of the night-time world.

There was an intoxicating lure about the scene that even Elsie, in her reflective state could not resist. She sneaked a peak at the living, moving landscape, as her father sought to distract her thoughts to the land side, sprinkled with sandstone shops and the occasional patrolling shopkeeper.

"Look, El! There is Mr Harding's store. You remember the colourful parrot he had in the entrance and how it talked to us when last we walked past?"

Elsie smiled, though just briefly at the memory, as she loved animals.

The cab soon swung right on to the long and straight Pyrmont Bridge that crossed Darling Harbour. The wheels slapped over the bridge's timber slats—except when they passed through the inevitable horse droppings scattered periodically along its length.

Around halfway across, James noticed a less usual sight emerging at the other end. "El, can you see the bullock train coming this way? It must be hauling something heavy!"

Elsie looked forward and counted the bullocks … two, four, six, eight … as they approached with a slow but purposeful gait, under the watchful eye of the whip-wielding bullocky.

"Sandstone!" James exclaimed as the dray drew alongside. "Sandstone blocks from the Pyrmont quarries—the same as used to build the Town Hall—heading for a building in the city centre, no doubt. Oh, how quickly this city is growing!"

The cab headed up Union Street, turned left into Miller, then right onto Bank Street before crossing the bridge over Johnstone's Bay and on to Glebe Island. It was a route that both occupants knew well, though both preferred the slow churn of the picturesque harbour ferry run.

James opened the trapdoor and called instructions to the driver sitting behind and above: "No. 12, Birchgrove Road's south end, please, sir!"

As the cab entered Weston Street, Elsie's head turned on her father's chest to study the streetscape to their left. James knew why, and just stroked his daughter's hair. "How are you feeling now, princess?"

Elsie's reply was not immediate, as she was lost in a mix of thought and concentration on the passing scenery. "A bit better."

"You will have to rest up for a while, El," he cautioned, unsure if his words would be heeded.

The cab halted outside 12 Birchgrove Road, a medium-sized stone cottage. James alighted first and paid the driver more than the trip's worth, acknowledging the care the driver had taken.

"Why thanking you most kindly, sir!" said the driver.

"Is that a Midlands accent I discern?"

"Your ear ain't half good sir, Stoke. I left work there in the potteries near three year ago now … and must say I don't miss them winters, sir!"

"I must rush my daughter inside, but take care in your travels!" James responded, after Elsie had squeezed his hand.

"God bless you and your family, sir!" the driver called, as he turned the cab around in search of another valuable customer.

The sound of voices outside the cottage had alerted Mary Ann Thompson to her husband's early and unexpected presence. She rushed out the front door calling: "James, what's wrong?"

"Nothing too serious, Mary Ann. El fell off the ladder in the shop and Dr Devorin says she has bruising and needs a bath and rest."

"Oh, my darling!" Mary Ann exclaimed, reaching for and cuddling Elsie a little more gently than she normally did. "Come inside and I will make up a bath."

As preparations were made, Mary Ann could not help noticing that James seemed deep in thought. "James, is there anything you want to talk to me about?" she eventually asked of her husband, who had waited obediently outside in the kitchen. There was however, no immediate reply.

"Mumsie, can you wash my face again with the facecloth?" Elsie pleaded in a trembling voice, interrupting any possible response as she sought a repeat of her favourite bath time experience.

She closed her eyes as the warm water streamed down her face and splashed into the soapy sea below. At that moment, Elsie and her mother could hear James moving to the front door, a muffled conversation and then the door closing. Elsie sat up with a start—and a splash.

"Who was that at the door, Father?" she called.

"Nobody really important, darling," he uttered awkwardly, for he knew that the girl with golden hair he had just turned away was Elsie's very best friend.

"Father!" Elsie exclaimed indignantly, for she had never known her father to lie.

"Very well, yes, it was Emma! I told her you had an accident and if she were to come back tomorrow, she might well be able to see you."

"But Father!"

"El, darling, there is no point in her seeing you now," her

mother added. "We will wait and see how you are bearing up tomorrow. Perhaps Emma can see you then."

Some time later, a rugged-up Elsie began her regular evening ritual of reading out aloud, as her father sat with eyes closed in his armchair, listening attentively:

WAKE! For the Sun, who scatter'd into flight
The Stars before him from the Field of Night, ...

James sighed deeply as Elsie continued:

Drives Night along with them from Heav'n, and strikes
The Sultán's Turret with a Shaft of Light.

Before the phantom ...

"Elsie!" James interrupted, as he could bear it no longer. "Why have you chosen a translation of Persian poet Omar Khayyám's *Rubáiyát,* when ..."

"James, please! The poor darling is unwell!"

"I well appreciate that, dear, but the English language has so many great and more easily interpretable poetic pieces, such as Coleridge's 'The Rime of the Ancient Mariner' and ..."

"Elsie, my darling! You need to sleep in any case. Off to bed now and I shall come in and rub that Gartner's Ointment into your back," her mother said, motioning her daughter to the door.

Once Elsie had left the room, Mary Ann turned back to her husband. "There is something wrong, is there not, James? We shall talk in a few minutes."

By the time she returned, James was pacing the room and muttering to himself.

"What is it, James? ... Tell me!" she demanded.

"Well ... I ... I placed a sign on the shop door this afternoon, stating books would be at half price on Monday, due to my early closing," he admitted, though still clearly agitated.

"So why is that a problem?"

"No, no! Mary Ann, you do not understand! Monday morning is when the rare book collector David Mitchell peruses Sydney bookshops for a bargain. He shall do me out of some of my finest for a pittance!"

"Will the sign be showing when he arrives?" Mary Ann asked pointedly.

"Well, no ... but ..."

"So that is it then—he will know nothing of it!"

"No, I simply cannot do such a thing. My word is my bond!"

"Oh, James, sometimes you are far too decent for your own welfare. Yet, surely there is more than this small matter?"

James sighed and put his arm around her as they moved to sit on the couch. "Why is that women so often hear what men cannot say? Yes, I have had much to occupy my mind these last few days."

Mary Ann tucked her arm protectively around him and rested her head gently on his shoulder as he continued: "Twice, in just the last week, Mr Ives, the Mayor of Sydney, has paid me the honour and courtesy of a visit, seeking my agreement in becoming the Returning Officer for the Division of Lang."

"And would there be good recompense for such a move?"

"Oh, yes, and I would of course be able to maintain the shop, though it is not the money that so interests me—it is the honour. I sense we are entering momentous times, Mary Ann, with talk of a possible federation of the colony's states. To be in charge of the voting process in arguably the most important division of a new nation's first city—that would be a very great honour indeed!"

"Then you must take the opportunity, James!"

"It is not that simple, my dear. It would mean leaving our home here in Balmain, our proximity to your dear and ageing parents, as well as Elsie leaving Emma, for a move into the city centre."

A silence enveloped the room as both parties struggled with their thoughts: Mary Ann on how she might cope with the physical distancing from her parents in Booth Street, as well as any change for Elsie; while James mostly sought to interpret how his wife was feeling.

In her bedroom, Elsie had heard the murmuring of distant conversation, but was blissfully unaware of its consequence.

"As the head of this household, I have already made enquiries as to possible suitable accommodation in the heart of the city." Heartened by no immediate negative reaction, James continued: "There is an apartment at 52 Carrington Street of some sizeable proportions. Our neighbours would be some of the finest professionals in the city!"

"Carrington Street is by Wynyard Park, is it not?"

"Yes, the apartment overlooks the park from the east side and is just across from the top of Erskine Street. We would be most central and close to the bookshop! I would be much happier if you were further away from the factories of Rozelle, Pyrmont and Balmain, Mary Ann. They do nothing but exacerbate your asthma."

* * *

A few evenings later, James asked a recovering Elsie to join him and her mother for a discussion.

"Princess, I have something very important to tell you!" he started, though annoyed with himself that he felt somewhat nervous, anticipating her likely response.

"As I am now a justice of the peace, I have been most kindly asked by the mayor of Sydney if I would consent to becoming the Returning Officer for Lang Division, in the city. After consulting with your mother, I have agreed to accept."

There was silence for a few moments as Elsie tried to comprehend just what this might mean. "Will you have to give up the bookshop, Father?" she asked, concerned.

"No, I have been informed that it should be possible to combine both jobs, though your assistance in the bookshop after school shall be needed and appreciated more than ever. There are, however, a couple of changes that will need to be made ..."

James hesitated, as Elsie struggled to think of what these changes might be.

"The first," her father continued, "is that from now, you must not talk about or imply what my opinion is on any public issue whatsoever. As the person to be responsible for all voting within the division, it is essential that I be seen as impartial. Yes, it is true that I have spoken privately, and often, of my admiration for the late Sir Henry Parkes and his idea of a federation of states of Australia. It is also true that I have written and sent articles to my mother in London on that same subject. However, from now on, your relaying of my attitude in relation to any public or private matter must cease. Do you understand, Elsie?"

"Yes, Father." She was now very concerned, as she had rarely known her father to sound so serious about anything, even though he was not the most jovial of men.

"I have this day written to your brother Walter's boarding school to inform them that we will be moving to Carrington Street by the end of the month."

There was silence, as Elsie tried desperately to think of the implications. So, her father continued: "The apartment is, by quite some measure, larger than this cottage and we will be very close to the bookshop El, so you will have just a short walk to Fort Street School and back, each day."

Elsie wanted to raise the issue of Emma and the impact that such an arrangement might have on their relationship, but dared not, lest raising the matter might in some way hasten the relationship's demise. Displaying typical Anglo reservedness, neither of her parents ventured any related comment, either.

* * *

That night, Elsie drifted off into a nostalgic semi-sleep, remembering fondly how she had first met her best friend …

She had seen her before, though mostly on a Sunday afternoon, riding a horse slowly down Birchgrove Road, the soft breeze and her gradual progress accentuating the flow of her long golden hair.

One particular Sunday, a couple of years ago, Elsie, determined to make her acquaintance, concocted a plan. She rushed around her front garden pulling out spring flowers and piled them into a basket.

Then she waited impatiently at her front gate, watching intently the bend and entrance into Birchgrove Road. *Surely she will come today*, Elsie thought, *she must!*

Eventually, a brown horse ridden slowly but comfortably by a young girl with golden hair came in to view. Elsie waited till they were about level with the block of their next-door neighbour, Mr Read, then, spun into action—literally.

She twirled her way onto the road and briefly towards the approaching horse, tossing out flowers into its path, before spinning back towards her gate.

Elsie smiled and pulled the bed blankets closer, as she remembered what happened next …

She had turned to see the girl with a big smile on her face, and, as their eyes met, she felt certain they would be friends for life.

"My name is Emma, Emma Bellamy. But you must not spin like that! I will show you how to do it!" the girl said as she dismounted.

It was only then that Elsie realised something else for the first time—the girl had been riding bareback, with no bridle.

"And I am Elsie Thompson, though my parents call me El!" she said, unsure whether to offer her hand or the basket.

Emma took the basket and took control.

"Keep your feet moving and keep spinning smoothly," she said, demonstrating Elsie's ambush with a level of finesse far beyond what Elsie had exhibited.

"Now!" said Emma. "We will try it together. Hold my hands and make sure to keep turning with me."

Elsie hesitated briefly, looking at the horse.

"Don't worry about Daisy," Emma said confidently, "she will not leave me—we've grown up together. Now, let me start …"

The girls twirled around and around on Birchgrove Road, Elsie noting that Emma's hands were smaller than hers and Emma appreciating just how big and pretty Elsie's eyes were. Soon the twirling was getting faster and faster and they were heading for an inevitable crash.

As they fell onto the road's grassy verge they collapsed into each other's arms, laughing.

Elsie smiled again at the memory and pulled the blankets even tighter, as if they were Emma herself …

Time seemed to stand still as they lay there, together, neither wanting to move lest some spell be broken and their lives and relationship might return to the way they had been before they met.

Eventually, it was Daisy who broke up the embrace, as she came over to nuzzle Emma, checking on her wellbeing.

"You must come riding with me on Sunday next, El. I will bring a horse for you. You can ride a horse, can't you?"

Fearful that their relationship might end before it had barely begun, if she had replied in the negative, Elsie blurted: "Oh yes, of course!" She neglected to admit she had only ever been on horseback once, when placed there by her father as a baby.

"Great! I will choose a horse for you from my father's stables and be here at 2 pm. We can go for a ride. I have to rush now. I have to be at my sister Mary's house further down Birchgrove Road. She married Andrew Tulloch two months ago and I visit them each Sunday afternoon."

With that Emma kissed Elsie on the cheek and rose. She looked around and noticed the thick posts that bordered the Thompson's gate. "Watch this!" she demanded, as she started to clamber up their side.

Elsie rushed to offer a hand but Emma managed to balance on top on her own—just. "Daisy! Come here!" she called to her horse, which had been munching grass. As the horse came over, Emma swung herself onto its back and in moments they were trotting down the road.

Tears started to well in Elsie's eyes. Emma turned back and called: "2 pm next Sunday—remember, El!"

Elsie was so happy, that she could not speak. All she could do was just frantically wave her acknowledgement.

The tears that now ran down Elsie's face as she recalled these times, sank slowly into the sheets and blankets cradled around her. "Oh, no! But …" she called out aloud as she remembered what was to come …

She could not wait to see Emma again, but how could she tell her that she could not ride a horse?

Around one o'clock on the Sunday, Elsie was startled to see Emma ride past, holding the reins of a second horse—a black one. She had not stopped or looked at No. 12—just headed straight on down Birchgrove Road.

For an hour Elsie fretted over her possible rejection. *Has Emma found another young girl as a companion?*

Then, as the mantelpiece clock in the Thompson lounge room

whirred its approach to a two o'clock chime, Emma was there—as she promised.

"Emma!" Elsie called as she rushed outside, relieved that her fears were groundless.

"This is Bella, El. Just come and talk to her quietly."

Elsie was still gasping with relief when she reached the black horse's side. Bella lifted up a hoof and plonked it down, straight on the toes of Elsie's left foot. "Oww!" she screamed.

In an instance Emma swung off Daisy and whacked Bella across the top of the left foreleg, screaming: "Off, Bella!" at the same time. The horse lifted its hoof and Elsie pulled her foot away.

"Oh! That is so sore!" Elsie was as stunned as much by Emma's forcefulness and control of the horse, as the pain from her toes.

Emma used the stirrups to climb up on Bella and ride her around slowly, calming her down. "You may climb up now, El!" Emma called, already sensing Elsie was less familiar with horses than she had hoped. "Put your right foot in the stirrup and climb up here, behind me."

Elsie's left toes were throbbing with pain, but she tried her best to be strong. She had seen others mount horses, so it could not, surely, be too difficult. With her right foot in the stirrup, she swung her left over Bella to the other side, as Emma rose to let her sit behind in the saddle.

"Bella, to Daisy!" Emma called as she pulled Bella towards her horse. Then, in a feat of gymnastics at which Elsie marvelled, Emma leapt off Bella, and onto her own.

"My father has a saying about horses, El:

> Give them love and guidance
> Give them praise when due
> Yet always let them know that
> They are not the boss of you!

I do try to remember this every day, though I have known horses all my life. Let's go Daisy!"

On that command, Emma dug her heels into her horse, and they were off.

Elsie, who was struggling to adjust to sitting in the saddle, let alone coping with any movement, tried to copy her. "Go Bella!"

she called and dug her heels in as she had seen Emma do. Bella immediately took off in hot pursuit of Daisy with Elsie clinging on for dear life.

It may only have been at a moderate canter, but Elsie was terrified that she would fall off. As they headed down Birchgrove Road, she felt herself swaying from side to side, desperately trying to stay on.

She saw Emma slowing ahead but was so focussed on keeping her balance, she hurtled right past her. "Elsie! Pull back on the reins!" she heard Emma scream, but all she could do was try to keep her balance.

Elsie tossed in her bed remembering the panic she felt …

Just when she thought the nightmare would only end with her lying in a heap on the dusty road, Emma was by her side with Daisy, grabbing Bella's reins and calling: "Whoa, Bella!"

Eventually, the two young girls dismounted—though Elsie more awkwardly—and sat together by the roadside. Elsie was still shaking and started sobbing. Through her tears she tried to explain: "I never had ridden before … but wanted to ride with you as I was afraid … afraid that you … might not … might not want to see me again … if … if I said I couldn't ride …"

Emma leant against Elsie and put her arm around her. "You did really well, El!"

"I … I did? But I was scared—really scared!"

"Nobody that I know could have held on like that on her very first ride, El. I thought you were great!"

Elsie tipped her head so that her darker hair mingled amidst Emma's golden locks. They just sat there for some time as Elsie calmed down. She was full of admiration for this strong young girl who was mature beyond her years.

Eventually, it was Elsie who spoke first. "Where do you live?" she asked.

"In Weston Street, Rozelle, No. 48. On the corner with Graham Street. I ride down Darling Street to get here." Elsie felt sure that from now on, even the sight of the Weston Street sign would make her think of Emma.

As they sat side by side in the September sunshine, Emma explained that her father Michael Bellamy, a farrier by trade, provided the drays and horses that hauled wool and other cargo to and from the wool stores and the harbour. They had stables in the backyard, housing mostly Clydesdales, as they were powerful, though not fast.

She was ten years old—though soon eleven—born on 20 January 1885. Elsie felt some embarrassment in admitting she had just turned twelve, being born on 2 August 1883.

Emma told her she played the piano and competed in dancing competitions, often with her brother, Arthur. *Emma may not be truly beautiful,* Elsie thought, *but she is soooo talented!*

Elsie volunteered that she loved singing, then added: "We could use the rehearsal room on the corner of Birchgrove and Darling—it has a piano. I know Mr Cohen who has the key!"

"Only after riding first, El. You need the practise!"

"Can I call you Em?"

"Yes, El!" came the immediate reply and they both laughed.

And so it was that El and Em fitted perfectly together, and just like neighbouring letters of the alphabet, it seemed they would be forever linked.

Elsie drifted off to sleep, once again cherishing that thought.

* * *

At the breakfast table the next morning, Elsie looked tired and sullen. James knew he had to raise the subject of Emma. "Your continued use of the rehearsal room on Sunday afternoons for dancing and singing sessions, El, will be rendered impractical, but Emma may ride in to Carrington Street with Bella each Sunday if she so wishes."

James could see that his beloved daughter was struggling to see the positive aspects of his announcement, so he added with a reassuring smile: "The girl with golden hair will always be welcome in our household!"

Chapter 3

Fort Street School 1898

For a time not of one's choosing, on a track to right through rule
Runs a line most surely scripted, to a place called Fort Street School
Where 'The Fortian' bears witness, to the pain, the pride, the joy
Of this salutary sequence, shaping every girl and boy.

Miss Ellwood, headmistress of Fort Street Girls, strode out of her office near the top of the grand staircase, turned to her right, then hesitated.

She gazed left over the staircase railing and down at the kaleidoscope of light that flooded through the magnificent stained-glass panels backing the stairs' upward twist. In all her years at the school, she had never failed to be inspired by the image before her.

Taking a deep breath, she drank in the scene like an alcoholic would savour a first bottle in days, before moving her large, matronly frame purposefully down the corridor, with religion teacher, Miss Bothroyd, well in her wake.

She could hear the murmur of voices emanating from behind the closed sewing room door ahead—yet with just a turn of the handle and a creak of the door, the room fell silent—for as every girl and indeed staff member of Fort Street well knew, Florence Ellwood was not a woman with whom to trifle.

Elsie and the fifteen other girls rose quickly to their feet and in fervent unison greeted her with: "Good morning, Miss Ellwood!"

"Say good morning to Miss Bothroyd too, girls!"

"Good morning, Miss Bothroyd!"

The headmistress scanned the group of girls in white dresses. She seemed to be counting, for she soon said: "Sixteen—excellent! Sit down!"

Everyone did—except Stella Hancock. She just stood there seemingly unable to move. Elsie studied her for a moment, then to her horror noticed Stella's large eyes rolling to the top of her head. Her knees started to buckle and her body started to sink towards the schoolroom floor.

Elsie dived out to try and catch her, only just managing to cradle her head before it could strike the hardwood floor between the desks.

A number of the girls started to scream in sympathy and shock, just as Stella began shaking uncontrollably as she lay on the floor with Elsie's hands under her head.

"It is the sign of the devil!" cried Miss Bothroyd, at last finding her voice. "The devil has possessed her!"

"She's having a fit, you stupid woman!" Sophia Geeves chimed in, though the second half of her comment was muttered quietly lest its target might hear. "My cousin, Richard, has them occasionally."

"That is what comes of lascivious thoughts and actions!" Miss Bothroyd persisted.

Miss Ellwood now took control as Stella continued to convulse on the floor. "Elsie! Return to your seat immediately!"

"But Miss Ellwood, she needs someone with her," Elsie protested, as she continued to hold Stella's head above the floor.

"Place her head down carefully and return to your seat, Miss Thompson!" Reluctantly, Elsie did as she was told.

It took quite some minutes for Stella's convulsions to cease and then for her to regain consciousness. When she did, Jane Gibbs and Katherine McKay helped her to her feet and back in to the seat next to Jane and across the isle from Elsie.

By this time, Miss Ellwood had already written the surnames of the girls in the class on the blackboard, in groups of four:

> 1: Brown, Newling, Hunt, McCarthy
> 2: Gibbs, McKay, Howe, Norris
> 3: Isaacs, Geeves, Lambert, Noble
> 4: Hancock, Vivian, Thompson, Craig

Miss Ellwood was about to explain things, when she heard a voice at the back of the room. "Ophelia Howe! If you have something to say, I presume it is of great importance, and as it is, then we all should hear it. And stand when I speak to you, girl!"

Ophelia stood nervously, clearly not anticipating such a large audience.

"Well, what is it?" Miss Ellwood demanded.

"I … I was just telling Margaret about my brother, Andy, being chosen for the Sydney Selection to play the miners of Joadja in the annual challenge …"

"Play what, Miss Howe?" asked Miss Ellwood, feigning momentary interest.

"Association football, Miss Ellwood. We won the Atkinson Price Challenge Cup 2-1 last year … and …"

"We have heard enough and you have wasted our time, Miss Howe! When the lunch bell rings, you are to report to the desk outside my office where you shall write five hundred times: I must not waste time in class! Now, does anybody else have anything to say?"

Unsurprisingly, there was silence, so Miss Ellwood continued: "Miss Bothroyd and I are keen to see what dramatic talent there is in this group, with a view to performing a short Christmas pageant. You will now have twenty minutes to break into the four groups I have outlined on the board. Each group must devise a short play or skit lasting no more than five minutes, which you shall present before this session closes. You may gather and practise in the corners of the room. Well, what are you waiting for?"

This was just the sort of activity that Elsie really enjoyed. She quickly took charge, herding the blonde and petite Annie Craig, the larger and red-haired Sarah Vivian and the still groggy brown-haired Stella Hancock—who was told of Elsie's assistance, and thanked her profusely—to the back right of the room. "I have an idea! Well, we could be tortoises!"

"And slowly come out and move around until …" started Stella, before Elsie interrupted to suggest that Stella could be an Aborigine, who would hunt them and cause them to flee.

"We could pretend we are scared and run away!" chimed in Sarah.

"And then escape and hide in our shells!" added Annie.

"Ok, let's practise. Just follow me!" Elsie urged, as Miss Ellwood passed on after hovering around briefly.

As her group's performance time neared, Elsie was confident that she would lead them in triumph. When their turn came, Elsie milked her lead role for all it was worth: cowering, ducking, scampering and weaving her way from timidness to exuberance, then fright and flight as they were hunted.

The reaction from the onlookers made it plain that the final performers in the drama challenge, group four, had won.

"Thank you, girls! You may all head to lunch, with the exception of Miss Howe, who I will see outside my office in a few minutes," Miss Ellwood decreed. Then, much to Elsie's surprise, she added: "Miss Thompson, stay behind please as I wish to speak with you!"

Elsie waited nervously as it had never, in her experience, been a good thing to be asked to see Miss Ellwood.

The headmistress motioned for Elsie to sit near her at the teacher's desk, as the other girls and Miss Bothroyd vacated the room.

Everything went very quiet as Miss Ellwood, her elbows on the table, brought her hands together, as if in prayer. Her fingertips touched her lips as Elsie held her breath.

Eventually, Miss Ellwood said: "Miss Thompson, will you be returning to Fort Street next year?"

"I believe that is what my parents intend, Miss Ellwood. Just one final year."

"Good—I am very glad that is the case, Miss Thompson." Hearing these words, Elsie breathed a quiet sigh of relief. *But why is she asking?* she wondered. The answer came soon enough.

"Miss Thompson, I knew you could sing well, but I didn't realise quite how well you could act. I have it in mind that we shall do a Gilbert & Sullivan production next year as our annual concert—jointly—with the Fort Street Boys. Perhaps *The Pirates of Penzance* or *HMS Pinafore*—I have yet to decide, and will talk with Mr Turner about this. Irrespective, I would like you to play one of the lead roles, as I think you would be well suited to comic opera."

Elsie could hardly believe what she was hearing. As she tried to take it all in, tears came into her eyes as a smile broke across her face. She bit her lip to try to stop herself from crying, but it did not help.

"Well, are you interested, Miss Thompson?" the headmistress asked, though she could plainly see from Elsie's emotional reaction, that such a question was, in this circumstance, entirely unnecessary.

"Oh, yes, Miss Ellwood … oh yes!"

"Well, in that case you had better compose yourself, for I want your word that you will not mention anything of this to your schoolmates."

Like any excited person, sharing one's happiness was a major part of the fun, so as Elsie stood to leave, a feeling of disappointment crept slowly through her being. "Yes … I promise."

It was something that Miss Ellwood noticed, so she added: "Don't worry, Miss Thompson, you are going to be a star!" as Elsie headed towards the door.

It stopped Elsie in her tracks and she turned to face Miss Ellwood, open-mouthed, as now those tears ran down her face. Through them, she thought she could make out a smiling Miss Ellwood, though such a thing and this last minute of conversation were not occurrences that Elsie could ever have believed possible.

Chapter 4

The Palace

I closed my eyes most tightly, to escape the world I knew
The monochrome reality, the drabness of the pew
I found colour in its curving, and a beauty in its art
And a style that sung of Eastern, with the Palace at its heart.

James Thompson picked up the day's copy of *The Sydney Morning Herald,* but his gaze initially fell, not upon its printed pages, but on his beloved daughter.

In the days since she had informed her parents with great excitement of her promised role in next year's Fort Street School production, both James and Mary Ann had realised that Elsie had never seen a professional theatre show.

James had always been—as his father had too—devoted to the book, the written and printed word in its multiplicity of variations, as well as its collection and sale.

Mary Ann, for her part, had dedicated herself to ensuring the household functioned as smoothly for her family as could be wished. She had ordered her world as most women of her age had done, by Mrs Beeton's *Book of Household Management.* It contained everything from recipes to dining rules to servant etiquette and child rearing, though nothing, as far as she could recall on the necessity to attend popular theatre—though she had to admit that she had stage dreams of her own, once.

James had never seen the need for frequenting the theatres of the colony, as so many of the masses did, for what at times was coarse entertainment.

As he watched their daughter read in silence in their Carrington Street apartment, James made the mental commitment to ensure she appreciated the environment in which she would perform. The theatre was not his world, but he felt it would be unwise to limit her horizons within his restrictive boundaries. She had a talent, and who was he—even though her father—to be selfish enough to refuse its flowering, be it merely for just a school musical.

He turned back to *The Sydney Morning Herald* edition of Wednesday 7 December 1898 and quickly found the section containing theatre advertisements. They were there in their inevitable page two spot, though it was usually one he bypassed.

He looked up again and seeing Elsie still engrossed in her book, whispered: "Cissie!", his pet name for his wife, while pointing in the direction of the kitchen.

She followed him there and they studied the theatre listings. "The Alhambra, Her Majesty's, Criterion or the Palace—which do you think Elsie would like best?"

Mary Ann did not need time to mull over the choice. "The Palace! Definitely the Palace! After all, a princess belongs in a palace!" she said with a smile. "It is in Pitt Street and not far from here, and has that spectacular Indian-domed front. I have heard it is wonderful inside!"

"That being so, if you could go to Palings tomorrow, darling, purchase five tickets for whatever show is on Saturday of next week, then we all can go, together. As Walter is returning home from his school year in the mountains on the Friday evening, it can be a celebration for all of us!"

"Five tickets? Why five? There will just be four of us," Mary Ann responded, puzzled.

"Emma! Remember Cissie, this is really for Elsie and who else would she want to have with her on a special night? We will make it a surprise. I will contact the Bellamys and assure them I will escort Emma back to Rozelle after the show."

* * *

To Elsie's great delight, Emma had joined Elsie's older brother Walter, as an addition to the usual complement in the Thompson household.

As the late afternoon of Saturday 17 December slipped towards evening, Emma revealed that she had a surprise. She proudly passed a green and gold book to Elsie, who did not recognise the title, *Melbourne House*, by S. Warner.

"Look inside the cover, El!" Emma whispered.

Opening it, Elsie noticed there was an inscription next to the title page:

It was not just that this was a prize Emma had been given, but the date that surprised Elsie. "Oh, Emma, congratulations!" Elsie exclaimed, giving her a hug and kiss. As today was the 17th, Emma had been presented with the prize just over a fortnight ago, though in her usual modesty, had not informed her best friend.

As Mary Ann was clearing the table, James warned the others that they should change quickly as they all had to leave for the Palace Theatre in thirty minutes. To both Elsie and Walter this was astonishing news, though one received it with far more enthusiasm than the other.

"Spending more than two hours listening to American tarts warble is not my idea of fun," Walter said pointedly.

"Walter, please!" his mother pleaded, while his father just stared at him, then closed his eyes and shook his head. And this was just his first day back home.

Walter had always been one to say what others only dared to think, and this had brought him in to conflict with his father on many occasions in the past. While his parents had hoped that his boarding at The School in Mount Victoria would help his asthma, they had been more certain that the separation would have the side benefit of significantly improving household harmony.

As James looked at his seventeen-year-old son with a mixture of disappointment and apprehension, he wondered whether he had matured as much as his growing height hinted.

During the short walk to the Palace, James did his best at 'small talk' to thaw the frosty restart of their relationship. "One of your old Fort Street classmates was in the shop last Tuesday and asked me to pass on his regards."

Now this was a comment Walter could not ignore. "Who was that?" he asked, genuinely intrigued as anyone returning to their former stomping ground after some time away, would be.

"Douglas Mawson. He has nearly exhausted my supply of natural history books!"

"Douggie, yeah, we used to joke he'd marry a penguin!" came Walter's reply, just as the Palace Theatre came into view across Pitt Street.

Elsie squeezed Emma's hand as they took in the glistening lights of the covered entrance, with the arches above leading to a French-style roof topped by a glowing Indian-looking dome. It was an unusual mix of styles that translated into exotic in their eyes.

Mary Ann already had their tickets, so they started to head inside—when Elsie stopped in her tracks. In fact, they all did, as they gazed in wonder at the magnificence around and above them. Tall and ornate lamps with crowns of lights illuminated the foyer area. The lighting added a soft touch of seductive naughtiness as it caressed the scantily clad female figures seeming to float on the ceiling.

"Told you we would see tarts here!" Walter quipped in a deadpan voice.

This would normally have brought a rebuke from his mother, but she was too entranced by her surroundings to react.

As they moved towards the stalls entrance, they could see marble staircases leading up either side of the baroque-style vestibule. These led to boxes hidden beyond, where the rich and idle took their seats.

Handing over the tickets to an usher, they were taken forward from semi-light into the cavernous wonder of an auditorium that opened up before them, like a picture book with folded illustrations.

After the usher indicated the general seating area, Walter, less fixated than the others in the party, opted for a location nearer the back, where he could study the bulk of the audience before him.

If what they had seen outside had made them gasp, what was around them now was simply breathtaking. They all followed Walter into the seating as if in a trance—first Mary Ann, then James, Elsie and Emma.

"Oh Emma, Emma, Emma!" was all Elsie could say at first.

"Isn't it beautiful, El!" Emma exclaimed, as she scanned the dream-like vision around them.

There was peacock blue and gold everywhere. The boxes at the side were capped with golden domes, like turreted features on an Indian fort. A golden statue of Buddha perched high above the stage, while beneath him hung the most exquisite curtain patterning, akin to the most intricate Persian carpet ever made.

The dome-outline surrounds made the silk mosaic curtain look like a glistening silhouette that hinted at further riches to be revealed.

"Of course, I heard it opened two years ago," said James in wonder, "but I never thought it would be quite as remarkable as this." After a pause to contemplate, he added: "What do you think of your palace, princess?"

Elsie was so excited and overawed, that at first she could not find the words to respond. She wondered, for a few moments, what it would be like to perform in this most beautiful of theatres and of the different artists this setting must have seen come and go. Then she responded in a way not even James would have predicted:

> Think, in this batter'd Caravanserai
> Whose Portals are alternate Night and Day,
> How Sultán after Sultán with his Pomp
> Abode his destined Hour, and went his way.

"What was that?" asked Emma, as James raised an eyebrow, knowing full well its origin.

"*Rubáiyát of Omar Khayyám,* Quatrain …" Elsie said, as she struggled to allocate it in its appropriate sequence. "Quatrain 17!"

Meanwhile, Walter had been assiduously studying the seats in front of him and the patrons entering. "Ah ha!" he exclaimed with considerable pleasure, as he focussed on a group settling many rows in front. "I shall be back soon—maybe!" And with that he rose, sidestepped across the row, then hurried down the isle towards his target.

The others watched him go with varying feelings. Mary Ann was concerned in case he got himself into trouble; James was delighted to be relieved of his presence—though it had barely been a day since his return from months away at boarding school; while Elsie only wanted to know who he was meeting, just as any busybody sister would.

She craned her neck and looked intently at the figures greeting each other warmly. "It is his friend, George Bretnall!" said Elsie triumphantly.

There were other young men in the group and two young ladies, one of whom turned around as Walter turned back to indicate the Thompson party. "It's the Hancocks! Mumsie, you remember I told you about Stella, the girl who had an epileptic seizure at school."

"Hancocks?" said James. "They must be Randle Hancock, the letter-carrier's children. He drops into the bookshop most regularly."

Stella waved at Elsie, and Elsie reciprocated enthusiastically. "The others must be Stella's sister, Amy, and her brothers, though I don't know their names. I don't think Walter will be coming back to sit with us," Elsie predicted.

James greeted this possibility with some satisfaction and he turned to Mary Ann with his son in mind. "Darling, Walter must get a job, an apprenticeship or something that will allow him to live independently."

"He could always work with you in the shop, James," Mary Ann suggested, more out of obligation than realistic hope.

James turned his back on Elsie and spoke to his wife in as forceful a way as one could in a crowded theatre: "I am NOT having my son working with me or eventually taking over my business!"

"You could always find a job for both Walter AND George Bretnall, Father," Elsie, who could not avoid eavesdropping, suggested. "If the two were to be together, I think Walter would accept."

James was not pleased that Elsie had joined in the discussion, but her contribution did, he had to admit, make considerable sense.

"I shall make enquires on Monday," he conceded, as the theatre lights dimmed and the show featuring the fourteen artists that made up M'Adoo's Original Jubilee Singers, began.

"Imagine, Emma, if only it could be us out there on the stage and in the spotlight!" Elsie whispered excitedly, as the lighting illuminated the portly figure of Madame Mattie Allen M'Adoo, 'The World's only Lady Tenor'.

As the evening progressed, the girls pretended they were the ones performing on the Palace stage, reaching notes far beyond their own capacities and receiving the cheers from the packed thousand-strong audience.

As they departed, still somewhat transfixed by the occasion of their first Palace Theatre experience, the girls were adamant that they wanted to return—and soon.

"And how did you enjoy the evening, Walter?" Mary Ann asked, as her son eventually caught up, while they ambled off into the Pitt Street night.

"It was great to meet up with George," he responded, then realising that she expected a comment about the performers, added: "but I didn't mind the look of that big piccaninny!"

"That was Miss Susie Anderson, 'America's Black Melba'—or so she is called," his mother corrected. "I think we were privileged to hear her."

James immediately made a definitive mental note to exclude Walter from any future Thompson theatre excursions.

On the Monday afternoon, when Elsie dropped into the shop on her way home from school, her father had news.

"I have spoken to Bill Mullarkey of Alex. Cowan & Sons. As a customer of longstanding for Cowan's paper and stationery, he was happy to listen to my request in regards to your brother and George. I will tell Walter that he should see Mr Mullarkey for an interview."

"No, Father!" Elsie insisted. "He will not listen to you!" Then she thought for a few moments. "But … I think I just might have a far better idea!"

* * *

It was the early evening of Wednesday 21 December 1898, when a firm knocking alerted the inhabitants of 52 Carrington Street that there was a matter of importance at their front door. Walter, who had spent much of the last five days since his return from the Blue Mountains, wallowing in boredom, saw the door-opening event as a tiny respite from his torture.

To his considerable surprise, the neatly dressed figure sporting a fine greying moustache standing before him, was familiar.

"Mr Hancock, sir!" Walter exclaimed. "What brings you here?"

"A matter of significant import—in fact one that concerns you, young man!"

At this point Walter began to fear he may have done something wrong and Mr Hancock could see the concern on his face.

"There are details of which I am unaware, but rest assured that these matters are most positive and should be welcomed. Mr William Mullarkey, manager of Alex. Cowan & Sons, has asked me to personally pass this letter on to you. He told me he looks forward to meeting you very soon."

"What is it, dear?" said Mary Ann, who had just emerged in the hallway, shadowed by James.

"Good evening, Mrs Thompson and to you too, James!"

"Won't you come inside for a few minutes, Randle?" James asked.

"Thank you kindly, sir, but I have yet some important business to which to attend, though I must say this one is of the most import. I consider Master Thompson to be a lucky young man. My best wishes to you all for the season ahead!"

With that Randle Hancock nodded respectfully, pivoted and was gone, leaving Walter holding an envelope in his hands.

"Bring it inside, darling, and we can all look at it," Mary Ann said, like a child anticipating her first present of a Christmas procession.

They headed into the lounge room where Walter studied the envelope's front, its Alex. Cowan & Sons imprint and addressing to:

Walter Thompson Esq.

"What beautiful paper!" James exclaimed, as Walter opened the envelope to reveal a page with luxurious weave of the type that a stationer like James would drool over.

"Read it out, Walter!" urged his mother.

Walter looked down at the contents and read it slowly and thoughtfully:

Walter Thompson Esq.
52 Carrington Street,
Sydney

Dear Sir,

Alex. Cowan & Sons is a firm at the apex of the paper and stationery industry in the colony. As such, we are always searching for persons of quality and character.

I have been assured that both you and George Bretnall are of the type who would represent this company with the distinction it deserves.

We are growing rapidly, with new offices being established across Australasia, and would welcome an interview to ascertain the appropriateness of appointing both of you to our main Sydney office.

I have taken the liberty of making time available on this Friday, December 23 and look forward to meeting both of you at 11 am in our Wynyard Square head office.

With regards and best wishes for your futures in this great company.

Yours faithfully,

W. J. Mullarkey
William J Mullarkey, JP
Manager
Alex. Cowan & Sons
37 Wynyard Square, Sydney

It was clear that Walter was stunned by what he was reading.
"Isn't that wonderful!" Mary Ann cried, delighted for her son. "This is such a great opportunity for Walter, don't you think, darling?"
"Yes," James had started to say, when he noticed Elsie violently shaking her head from side to side in the background. "Yes, it may seem on the surface to be good," James continued,

desperately trying to match Elsie's direction, "but it is not a company I would wish you to join."

On hearing this, Elsie raised her arms in the air miming applause, so James continued: "In any case I would caution you against joining any company in tandem with George Bretnall."

Now Elsie was ecstatic, though silently so, while Mary Ann was close to distraught. "James, how could you try to block your own son's hopes and ambitions?"

The conflicting emotions caused no confusion for Walter. "That is that then! I'll be joining Alex. Cowan & Sons—with George Bretnall! I'm off to see George right now!"

With that, he rushed out the front door, letter in hand, as the others waited till the fast patter of footsteps were swallowed by the sounds of the Sydney summer eve.

"Oh, El, my darling El!" James said, addressing his daughter with as much admiration as he could muster. "How did you know things would end like this?"

Elsie sighed and just shrugged her shoulders in a pitiful attempt to avoid adoration. "Female intuition I guess, just female intuition!"

Chapter 5

The Push

There are eyes that strip you naked, there are hands within the crowd
There are gangs within the backstreets, there are pitfalls for the loud
Foolish heroes boast in daytime, but wiser men say "Shush!"
For the creeping world of night-time, spreads the shadow of The Push.

"I shall find her—she can't be far!" Walter had called out, nearly half an hour ago.

James paced up and down his lounge room, alternating his glances between the fob watch in his hand and the receding light of Wynyard Park outside.

Elsie had promised to be at the shop before its Saturday five o'clock close, yet it was near six now and there was no sign of her.

A fast-moving brown blur caught James' eye and he headed straight for the front door. Unfortunately, it was a solitary and panting Walter.

"I checked the shop area and asked some of the other shopkeepers, but nobody has seen her."

"If only Mr Merriman had the telephone connected. Sometimes these modern inventions are a blessing, not a curse," James observed with regret.

Elsie had gone to spend the afternoon with Julia Merriman, an old childhood friend and one-time neighbour in Argyle Place, Millers Point.

The Merrimans still lived on the corner at No. 18, while the Thompsons had rented No. 16 next door. It was there Elsie had been born in 1883, sixteen years ago.

"I will take a hansom cab down to Argyle Place and bring her back!" Walter volunteered.

James was just beginning to see elements of maturity and responsibility in his son, which he put down to his job with Cowans. He knew Walter would have needed to be faster than the veritable Flying Pieman, to have made it the mile or more down to Argyle Place on foot—and had any chance of returning before dark.

"Here are some coins to cover the fare—and take care. I will give her a good talking to when you return."

"Argyle Place, sir!" Walter commanded of the cab driver waiting on the fringe of Wynyard's green.

As they headed west down Erskine Street, the last rays of the setting sun disappeared below the western horizon. Once they had swung right on the long straight ride down Kent Street, the occasional gas lamp provided the only relief from the enveloping darkness that had started to replace the shadows, but not the growing unease.

The lights of a building would normally signal safety in a sea of darkness, but not those of The Lord Nelson Hotel. For years it had been a watering hole for gangs of English-born youths and criminals from the meaner streets of London, Manchester and Liverpool, who had no great liking or respect for native-born colonials, but even less for the Irish.

As The Lord Nelson loomed larger, the driver studied the streetscape carefully. In his nervousness, he doubled the reins around his wrists, before turning the cab right to Argyle Place.

"No. 18, please!" called Walter, with a sense of urgency.

Reaching the corner outside No. 18, the driver stopped, then twisted in his seat, checking the street around him warily.

"Just wait—I will be back in a minute!" Walter alighted and headed for the black door with brass numbering.

A few thumps of the lion-head doorknocker drew a response from inside, but no opening.

"Who is it?" an older male voice queried.

"Walter Thompson, sir. I am here to pick up my sister."

With that a bolt was slid and the door opened, but hesitatingly, until the light within splashed on Walter enough to illuminate his features.

"Walter! It has been quite some time!" said Mr Merriman, offering a hand. "My! You have grown!"

"Hello, Mr Merriman. It is good to see you, but I must take my sister back now. Our parents have been concerned."

Mr Merriman looked puzzled. "Elsie? Why, she was here around two o'clock, but said she had to leave before three. I offered to get her a cab, but she insisted she would be fine."

"Oh, no!' said Walter, as he leaned with one hand against the

Merriman's front wall, trying to think what he should do next.

"Come on!" the driver's gruff voice urged from the street outside.

"Walter, you must be careful. This area can be as docile as a lamb by day, but it can eat a wolf alive at night! The Push can be anywhere and everywhere!"

"I have that cab waiting for me—though, thank you. Do you recall which way she went, sir?"

"Oh, that I cannot say."

The stirring of horses behind him, roused Walter into action as he bid Mr Merriman farewell.

"My kindest regards to your parents—and be careful!" were Mr Merriman's final words as he closed the door and slid the bolt across for good measure.

Walter barely had time to turn, when the neighing of horses and the slapping of wheels signalled the immediate departure of his transport—without him. The driver had chosen to race through the dangerous area of The Rocks rather than risk another passing of The Lord Nelson.

"Damn it!" Walter cried in exasperation. He lent back on the black rail fence outside No. 18 and tried to review his options, as for the first time, he noticed that an odd sea mist had rolled in, cloaking the air in a veil of mystery.

He turned and looked right, and could still see the lights of The Lord Nelson and hear the raucous utterances of its objectionable patrons. *Surely, she would not have headed there!*

Then, he turned left, peering through the mist towards the Argyle Cut. *And surely, Elsie would not have headed down there, either, so where could she have gone? I cannot return home without her!*

As he had this depressing thought, he was conscious for the first time of his fingers running backwards and forwards across the vertical rails of the fence. There was something most comforting about it … but what?

He did it again and again and then he realised he was drifting back to his childhood.

He and Elsie had run their fingers—and sticks—along this fence many a time. Often she would say … she would say … and then it came to him …

"Race you to The Steps!" she would say, as the two would run off, out of Argyle Place and head up left across Argyle Street. On they would charge, to the large stone steps that rose like the processional way of a Mayan temple, high towards the grass of Observatory Hill.

As he looked up, he could just make out the lower few steps as the gas lamps fought with the gathering mist for control of the night-time array.

Walter checked to the right and left again, but could not see anybody, yet The Steps seemed to lure him on.

He took a deep breath and pushed off the fence rail. *Maybe,* he thought, *if I move quickly, nobody will see me!*

As he crossed Argyle Street with The Steps looming, the giant Moreton Bay fig trees seemed to grow even larger, towering above like protective parents over the grey stone slabs.

The light of the gas lamps faded to an apologetic spatter as he reached the once familiar footing.

For a moment, he wondered if he should call out Elsie's name, then immediately dismissed that idea for fear of attracting attention. For, as Mr Merriman had said, The Push could be anywhere and everywhere.

He twisted around and looked back, up and down Argyle Street, searching for movement in the shadows—but there was nothing.

"One, two, three ..." he whispered to himself as he climbed each step "... four, five, six ..." and then he stopped.

The shadows from the trees were blocking what light there could have been on this part of The Steps, so he had to tread carefully, "... seven, eight, nine ..." and then he stopped again, as a tall figure to his right momentarily caught his eye.

He dared to look in the figure's direction again, his heart pounding and his mouth going dry—until he realised with relief, as he peered into the darkness, that it was only a tree.

He waited on the ninth step, trying to slow and quieten his breathing. Just a few more, he thought, and then, "... ten, eleven, twelve ..." as the short patch of ground above The Steps before Watson Road loomed.

Many times, as children, they had raced across Watson Road

and further onward, up the grass banks of Observatory Hill, to roll and tumble.

Watson Road seemed as still and silent as a tomb. Perhaps he should turn back now towards the relative safety of the gas lamps? Yet something drew him on …

As he stepped onto the grass of Observatory Hill his gaze lifted up across the rising bank ahead. Through the mist, there seemed to be a patch of white among all the darker colours.

As he moved closer, the image metamorphosed from the night-time landscape.

He could see two figures lying together in each other's arms—and one of them, he would recognise anywhere.

"Elsie!" he cried, in a combination of relief, frustration and anger, shattering his self-imposed code of silence.

"Oh! … Oh! … Walter?" came the startled reply, as Elsie tried to recover her composure. "Walter … this is Liam from Fort Street Boys … we are in the musical *HMS Pinafore* together and we were just … we were just practising!"

"Elsie! How could you!"

Just then, some laughing could be heard from higher up the grass slope. Liam rose quickly to his feet as three figures materialised menacingly out of the mist. As they came closer, Elsie and Walter both noticed that the smaller central one had rippling, tattooed muscles that popped out from a Union Jack waistcoat. He twirled a walking stick with an arrogance that showed clearly he was the boss.

"Oh, 'ullo, dis looks most intrestn', lads!" he said, with more than a hint of a cockney accent.

Liam did not hang around and took off as fast as he could down The Steps and towards The Rocks.

"Liam!" Elsie yelled, as he disappeared into the darkness.

"Irish, eh?" the centre figure proclaimed with some relish. "Oh, I do so like a good Irish stew!"

The other two thugs moved in slowly and deliberately to surround, forming a triangle from which the siblings could not escape.

"Ow 'bout we bash 'im Billy, an' take the girl?" one said.

"Yeah, why not! I'll just soften 'im up first!" said Billy, as he slowly circled Walter, spinning his silver walking stick that had a heavy steel grinning skull for a handle.

Walter was so terrified he could barely move, as Billy sidled around him feigning to let loose with the stick, laughing with each attempt by Walter to brace himself for the impact.

"Leave 'im alone!" Elsie cried, as she desperately tried to imitate his cockney accent. "'E's dun nufin' to ya!"

Billy hesitated, throwing Elsie a puzzled glance, then continued. After more than a minute of shadow boxing, he grew tired of the pretence and seemed to relax for a moment and turn away, before whirling around and sending the skull end of the stick thudding into Walter's stomach.

"Aargh!" he cried out, as he doubled over in pain.

Fearing that the next blow would be for Walter's head, Elsie attacked.

"Ow dare ya treat us cockneys like dat!" she cried, as she shoved Billy back, catching him off guard. "You oughta be ashamed!"

"Bu' … ay, wotchit!" Billy retorted, regaining his balance just as Elsie stopped, for she had heard a somewhat familiar sound.

It was faint at first, then quickly louder, but she knew well from her international dancing lessons with Emma, the sound of bodhráns—Irish drums.

Billy heard them too, and the pounding of running feet. He turned to see shadowy figures racing quickly through the night towards them. "Bleedin' Irish Push, lads! Back to Nelson!"

The other two had already fled by the time Billy turned on Elsie. "We'll meet again someday, strumpet!" he said, grabbing her roughly by the chin. "Den we'll do some dancin'… t'gefa!" And with that he was off and in a great hurry, as the first of the Irish boys reached Elsie and Walter, club in hand.

Liam was not far behind and headed straight for Elsie, who was tending to a buckled and gasping Walter on the ground.

"I'm sorry!" Liam said, still panting. "But dey will get dat scum, soon enough!"

Chapter 6

The Comic Opera

If you sail the ocean blue, on a saucy ship—a beauty
Know your part—its words and hue, for your role is all your duty
Never tarry on command, nor neglect your dress and grooming
Captivate your boss and crew—and a rise in rating's looming.

The events of that September 1899 evening around Observatory Hill had severely disappointed James and Mary Ann—and for quite some days they considered whether it would not be better to demand that Elsie withdraw from her role in *HMS Pinafore.*

In the end, a mutually acceptable compromise was reached, which was always James' preferred option in matters of disagreement: Elsie agreed to not see Liam outside of their role in the musical.

She told them both, individually, that she would not and they expected her to keep her word. Further, she most humbly (and tearfully, if the truth be known) apologised for not keeping her appointment with her father and for causing Walter so much trouble, and indirectly, injury.

Injury was something the boys of Fort Street could contemplate if they managed to get on the wrong side of Mr Turner, head of Fort Street Boys and headmaster of Fort Street School. It was rare for any one of the thousand boys to spend their schooling at Fort Street without having joined the queue for Turner's cane on at least one occasion.

That said, John William Turner was universally respected—caning or no caning—and referred to with some degree of devotion as 'The Boss'.

By 1899, the year proclaimed as Fort Street's fiftieth anniversary, Mr Turner had presided over the school's operation for almost a decade. Certainly no pupil—and most probably no staff member—could imagine Fort Street without him.

Even the students of the Girls School, which ran a parallel operation with separate playgrounds and a deliberately independent curriculum, knew Mr Turner both by sight and reputation.

It was therefore no surprise that on this late September Thursday afternoon, the line of Fort Street boys curling its way through the esteemed corridors of their alma mater like a snake, moved with discipline and purpose, mindful of the venom at its head.

Mr Turner stopped outside the main room of the Girls School, reviewed his retinue with a firm but evaluative gaze, then, with a quick wave of the hand, signalled for them to enter.

As they did so, the more than twenty girls inside studied each boy, their eyes feasting on them like one would in starvation when tempted by forbidden fruit. There was an inevitable sexual tension about this coming together, and both school heads knew that the performances could only benefit from its presence.

Miss Ellwood was aware that there was one girl in her group who could take maximum advantage of the situation, but had refused—publicly at least—to single her out, leaving that to Elsie's own talents.

Mr Turner's sturdy but medium-height frame joined Miss Ellwood's at the front of the classroom, as the students stood around the room's fringe, just inside the line of desks and chairs that had been cleared specially for the rehearsal.

"Welcome to another rehearsal of *HMS Pinafore*—though I intend that it shall be anything other than 'just another rehearsal'!" Miss Ellwood exclaimed.

Most of the students had been surprised by a couple of aspects of this year's chosen concert.

Firstly, the direct involvement of Miss Ellwood—she had not been involved in any school production in the past, to their knowledge.

Secondly, why Gilbert & Sullivan and their comic opera *HMS Pinafore* had been chosen. For years, Fort Street had performed Shakespearian plays as their annual gift to the thespian gods. These were believed to be Mr Turner's preferred choice, so why the change—especially for a jubilee concert?

Yet there were reasons, and Mr Turner wished that they might merely be guessed, not confirmed.

He had been a music teacher by training and *Pinafore* presented a most welcome opportunity for major involvement by the school orchestra he had nurtured. Any attempt to accommodate them in Shakespeare would have appeared token and effectively 'much ado about nothing'.

"So, you have all memorised your lines, have you?" Miss Ellwood queried with all the inoffensiveness of a scorpion—for there was always going to be a sting in the tail.

"Rogers!" she cried, indicating one of the older and taller boys. "Perform the first verse of 'When I Was A Lad'."

Russell Rogers had not anticipated such a singling out and struggled to organise his thoughts enough to remember the lyrics:

> When I was a lad … I served a term
> As office boy in an attorney's firm …
> I cleaned the windows … and I swept the floor
> And polished up the handle on the big front door …

Rogers gave a sigh of relief as he finished.

"So that is it, is it, Mr Rogers?"

"Well, they are the words, correct as I remember them, Miss Ellwood," replied a mildly indignant Rogers.

"Mr Rogers! I did ask you to PERFORM! That is the operative word! I say this now, not just to you, but to everyone else here!" Miss Ellwood emphasised this by moving out into the middle of the room and turning to cast her gaze across all the students before her.

"What role are you in the opera, Mr Rogers?"

"Ah … Sir Joseph Porter, Ruler of the Queen's Navy, Miss Ellwood."

"Well, act like a ruler of the Queen's navy, speak like a ruler of the Queen's navy and move like a ruler of the Queen's navy, Mr Rogers! Just memorising the lines is simply not enough. I want each of you to bring your characters to life, and if that means you have to transform yourselves into persons far different from your own natures, then that is exactly what you do! For that is performing, and I will accept nothing less from every one of you! Do you understand?"

"Yes, Miss Ellwood!" they all cried in unison, as some of them began to think that Miss Ellwood knew just a little more about the acting profession than they had believed possible.

"Well, let us see just how much you have understood ..." Miss Ellwood hesitated; then pretended to search randomly for her next victim, forcing each cast member to urgently reappraise their role and future performance. "Perhaps ... Miss Thompson! ... Miss Thompson, perform the first verse of 'Oh Joy, Oh Rapture Unforseen', please."

"May I have the musical introduction, please, Miss Ellwood?" Elsie requested, knowing that an acceptance would give her valuable extra moments for contemplation.

"Very well. Orchestra, please form over here to my right."

Mr Turner set about ensuring that the boys and girls of the orchestra were set up in their correct sequence. This was followed up by a tuning check, giving Elsie about four minutes to reprise her task.

"Speech, facial expression and movement, then be her," she whispered to herself as she stepped her way mentally through the verse.

"Right, I think we are almost ready," Mr Turner began. "Oh, Watkins, that instrument is a violin not a drum, and as such should be stroked not belted! Ready? I will count you in ... one, two, three."

As the orchestra began their introduction, Elsie rotated into the middle of the floor—an unnecessary addition, though Elsie was determined to add her own spin to her part.

She twisted and turned, gesticulated and showed all the emotion one could hope for in a sequence that would normally have been shared with Liam as Ralph Rackstraw.

Elsie's classmates were most impressed, but more importantly, so was Miss Ellwood, who had hoped she could rely on Elsie to get her message across, that there was more to performing than just saying words.

It was a seminal moment for the production's development, but one that was followed by weeks of industry in rehearsals.

The whole school, or so it seemed, was contributing. Students in carpentry, a subject only introduced to Fort Street's curriculum in the last decade, worked tirelessly on creating the sets and props that would be painted by the school's art classes.

Each cast member was measured up for their outfits, which were made by the girls in sewing classes.

When Mr Turner announced that the twelve-year-old Her Majesty's Theatre—on the corner of Market and Pitt Streets, and the largest theatre in Sydney—had been booked for the performance on the evening of Saturday 18 November, as well as morning dress rehearsals during the week before, the effort and excitement escalated.

* * *

On that Saturday, all three levels of the theatre were filled to overflowing, with a total of more than one thousand seven hundred excited spectators for the jubilee concert.

The Thompsons, with Emma happily in tow, settled into their plush and crimson seats—though nowhere near the back row where Walter preferred to be.

Emma looked up at the massive gas chandelier that glistened above her from the auditorium's central dome, then around at the throng taking up every vantage point. *Oh, what a remarkable setting for a theatrical debut!* she thought to herself, as she crossed two fingers superstitiously, promising to keep them that way until her dear friend's voice had completed her first solo successfully.

Mr Turner's mounting of the stage induced a hush to spread rapidly through the packed theatre. He began addressing the crowd from a lectern, placed at the stage's right edge by two senior boys.

Although he had a sheet of paper in front of him, the headmaster gave no sign that he needed its assistance whatsoever. Instead, he expanded the spread of his gaze to take in the full width, depth and height of the audience before him:

"Ladies and gentleman, boys and girls, friends and members of the Fort Street community! My name is J.W. Turner ..."

Here he hesitated for the inevitable laughter and applause, as he knew he needed no introduction.

"... and I have had the great honour and privilege of being Fort Street School's headmaster for a full decade.

That is, as you will agree, a considerable length of time, yet it pales into fractional insignificance (one fifth to be exact) of the fifty years since this great school's founding. In that time Fort

Street has operated proudly and most successfully as Sydney's Model School—training and moulding the great teachers of the future.

Our school's Latin motto—*Faber est suae quisque fortunae*— Each one is the maker of his own fortune—encapsulates the responsibility each of us should feel in developing our potential in this great and different land.

We are gathered here to witness the jubilee concert. There most certainly have been many wonderful individual contributions to making tonight happen, from the scene enablers: the many teachers who gave their time and efforts enthusiastically; the scene builders and painters: those who created the stunning sets, lighting and costumes you will see, and those who apply the make-up; to the scene stealers: the actors who play the individual parts, the chorus groups and the wonderful orchestra arranged at my feet—all, have made their contributions, proudly, as Fortians!

My time has expired, and your time for enjoyment has arrived! Without any more ado, I give you Fort Street's jubilee concert performance of Gilbert & Sullivan's *HMS Pinafore!*"

As he finished these words, greeted by a great roar of approval, he raised his arms, the orchestra erupted into life, theatre lights dimmed, the curtain rose, stage lights shone and the show began. Elsie, like everyone else in the cast was nervous, but so very excited.

Some two hours sandwiched around an intermission later, the show ended to a long, standing ovation and calls of "Encore!"

Mr Turner mounted the stage and raised his arms, appealing for silence.

"I have taken the liberty of anticipating the possibility of an encore," he said, and then continued: "The play's six key individual performers: Mr Russell Rogers as Sir Joseph Porter … Miss Penelope Noble as Buttercup … Mr Warren Green as Captain Corcoran … Mr David Paterson as Dick Deadeye … Mr Liam Byrne as Ralph Rackstraw … and Miss Elsie Thompson as Josephine … will each sing one of their solo pieces."

As each name was mentioned, the performer stepped forward on stage in front of the rest of the cast, to rapturous applause from the audience and cast alike. Only in Elsie's case there was something else as well—wolf-whistles. The Thompsons were embarrassed to hear them emanating from young and not so young men in their vicinity, and beyond.

Elsie heard them as well, and blushed, but they could not take the smile off her face.

"However," Mr Turner continued, once relative calm had been restored, "they will not sing alone, for you will sing with them!" Another great roar went up, before the headmaster added: "To ensure you know your lines, we have arranged for students to distribute lyric sheets to each row, which they should do, now!"

If anything, the applause resulting from the singalong was even greater than at the opera's conclusion.

The final piece to close the encore sequence brought all the cast and audience together, as they sang a variant of the lyrics from 'I Am the Captain of the *Pinafore*':

> Now give three cheers and one cheer more
> For the hardy Captain of the *Pinafore*!
> So give three cheers and one cheer more,
> For … the Captain of the *Pinafore*!

The effect of nearly two thousand people singing—more like chanting those words, together—was astounding.

Elsie was floating. She had felt herself swept along by an exhilarating tide of emotion and support. She had felt the electricity, togetherness and camaraderie of working as a triumphal team with the other students; she had felt her own power, when on a couple of occasions she had deliberately hesitated, causing the audience to wait for her with bated breath; and she had felt them all surging with her, singing her on to exaltation in the encore—and she wanted more.

It was well over half an hour after the curtain had finally come down, that Elsie emerged from a straggle of remaining well-wishers to greet her parents and Emma—for Walter had long ago found reason to head home.

"You were just wonderful, darling!" Mary Ann cried, greeting Elsie with a big hug.

"We are all very proud of you, El—you were great!" Emma said, holding Elsie's hand and not wanting to let go.

"Oh, Mumsie, this is what I want to do. I just love being on stage!" Then Elsie added, almost as an afterthought: "However, I did make a few mistakes ..."

"You may well have done, princess, but we didn't notice them!" James joined in. "I am just not so sure I will get used to having an acclaimed performer for a daughter!" he added, far more honestly than the others realised.

That night, Elsie slept not a wink, for she was so elated, reliving over and over again in her mind, the way the evening had progressed.

A couple of days later, it was announced that due to the outstanding success of the jubilee concert, it would be repeated the following Saturday afternoon as a matinee.

As Elsie's time at Fort Street came to a close and a new year beckoned, the Thompsons insisted that she greet 1900 by working with her father in the shop. However, they did agree to allow her to dabble in productions with a local amateur company in the hope that it would satiate her desire.

Chapter 7

The Message

If people talk in muffled tones, and look askance at you
Don't think the worst—pretend the best—is just what you should do
For fretting much and wondering, creates a fearful mind
And paranoia surfaces, when all was meant as kind.

As she sorted the books on the counter in front of her, in early November 1900, Elsie caught sight of two figures walking outside the bookshop out of the corner of her eye, though she paid no particular attention.

On the ringing of the bell attached to the back of the front door, however, she lifted her head immediately. One figure she recognised instantly.

"Miss Ellwood!" Elsie said with some surprise, as she could not ever recall her visiting the bookshop, not even on a Saturday morning like this one.

Just then, the figure behind the headmistress moved into full view. He was a middle-aged man of some size and from his dress, seeming respectability, though she was pretty sure (and she was always proud of her visual memory) that she had never seen him before. He was looking at her most intently.

"Miss Thompson," Miss Ellwood queried, "is your father available?"

"Yes, he should be, Miss Ellwood. He is doing the accounts in the office," Elsie explained. As she was turning to go there, she felt certain that the gentleman's gaze had not left her.

"Father, Miss Ellwood and a gentleman wish to see you," she said, as she leaned just a little against the office door she had opened.

James Thompson looked up, but was lost in thought about the accounts he was scrutinising.

"Father, they are at the counter to see you!" By the time this second approach had concluded, James was back in the real world, and getting quickly to his feet—and heading towards the counter.

"Miss Ellwood! How nice to see you! Are you after books for

the school?" he said, far more in hope than in any expectation, for, as far as he could remember, Fort Street had never made a bulk order through James Thompson, Bookseller and Stationer, of any kind.

"Mr Thompson, I would like you to meet Mr William Hawtrey. We are, in fact, here to speak to you about your daughter."

James hesitated for a moment, surprised, disappointed and a trifle concerned. "Ah … then you had better come in to my office." He ushered them into the back room and closed the door with its frosted glass.

Elsie had watched them go and noticed that William Hawtrey was still looking at her as he passed. She felt uneasy. *Why should my former headmistress and a man I have never previously met, want to see my father about me?*

Naturally, the same question occurred to James, as he quickly drew two extra chairs up to the office desk.

When James looked up, he could not see the twisted dark outline through the frosted glass, which would have indicated that Elsie was standing at her usual place at the counter. In fact, she had grabbed a few books and moved into the stack nearest the door, hoping to eavesdrop on the conversation. All she could discern, however, was a dull rumble of sound.

Seeing that James looked concerned, Miss Ellwood sought to ease his apprehension.

"William is manager of his own comedy company," Miss Ellwood started, dominating conversation as most teachers tended to do, until she was cut off.

"Hawtrey! Yes, the name is familiar—are you by chance related to Charles Hawtrey, the famous English actor?" James queried.

"You are certainly well read, Mr Thompson! Charles is my brother, and a major reason why my plans are as they are."

"And, what are your plans, Mr Hawtrey, and where is my daughter involved?"

"You see, Mr Thompson …" Miss Ellwood started, before she was interrupted again.

"I think I should explain this, Florence! I returned from England only last week, after having negotiated with my brother for his long-running London hit *A Message From Mars* to be staged in this country for the first time. We have brought over the scenery and most of the cast, though not all."

At this point, Mr Hawtrey looked at Miss Ellwood, as if seeking permission for something, but perceived no objection.

"It is not well known here, Mr Thompson, that Miss Ellwood was, quite some decades ago, a star on the London stage—and great assistance to my brother in his early career. As such, her opinion has always been highly respected, and she has assured us that your daughter has considerable acting and performance talent. We have a juvenile role of 'A Little Girl' that Florence insists Elsie could fulfil most expertly."

Mr Hawtrey then hesitated as he could see James was looking concerned, though silent with his thoughts.

"Let me assure you, Mr Thompson, that *A Message From Mars* does not contain a single element that can be construed as vulgarity or improper suggestion!"

"And I can assure you, Mr Thompson, that Mr Hawtrey here, is a man of the finest character and would ensure Elsie's safety and happiness during the production!" chimed in Miss Ellwood.

"Thank you Florence, though I feel I should give you more detail, Mr Thompson. I plan that the company will start with the play in Sydney at the Palace Theatre on Saturday 22 December, then move on to Queensland at the start of winter, before moving to Adelaide for three weeks from July, then either Melbourne or New Zealand. We start rehearsals at the Palace on Monday. I can promise your daughter payment of five shillings for each performance!"

Seeing that James looked as concerned as ever, Mr Hawtrey increased his offer.

"One pound, then!"

"Mr Hawtrey, money is of relatively minor import. My daughter is barely seventeen years of age. What you have placed before me, are matters of much significance, though they are matters upon which, I, as head of the Thompson household, could independently adjudicate. However, on matters affecting my daughter, I would always wish to seek the opinion of both my dear wife and essentially the child herself, for I would never want to place her in a position in which she was unhappy. I shall discuss these matters with them over the weekend and let you know on Monday at 10 am."

"I must be at rehearsal at that time, sir, so if I was to meet you here at 9 am, would that be suitable?"

"9 am it is then, though I cannot promise you a decision that will please."

The two gentleman rose, shook hands and then, joined by Miss Ellwood, exited the office.

Elsie waited impatiently, hoping that she would be informed, though she did so in vain, as the two visitors exited without another word, departing with just another glance from Mr Hawtrey.

"Father, what did they want?"

"Nothing of consequence, princess. They had a message to pass on. We shall discuss it this evening," James said, as he returned to his accounts in the office.

"But Father, they were talking about me!"

"I have said that we will talk this evening. It can well wait till then!" James emphasised.

Elsie realised there was no point inquiring further, and she would just have to wait for the evening.

The hours passed agonisingly slowly as Elsie struggled to think of what it all could mean. What she had not appreciated was that her father was battling far more with the positive and negative aspects relating to the message, than those that stared back at him from the ledgers.

After dinner that evening, James was relieved to broach the subject, though still uncertain of his own position.

Predictably, Elsie was most excited about her possible involvement, but when her father mentioned that the show would be performed at the Palace, of all places, she was ecstatic.

"What do you think, Cissie?" James asked of Mary Ann. "Any change would likely affect you at least as much as me."

Mary Ann had been quiet to this stage, but as a relatively young mother, she could identify with her daughter's excitement and dreams. "I think that this is an opportunity she should take. She could always come back to the bookshop if things do not work out for the better."

James could see in what direction the decision was heading, but he still had at least one major concern.

"Elsie!" James said, addressing his daughter unusually formally. "If you were to become a professional performer, I would not want you to do so under the Thompson surname. We are a family with a reputation to protect. I have the bookshop, am a justice of the peace and a returning officer, and there is such stigma associated with young women on stage. From what I hear, there are far too many common and unsavoury stage productions. So if we decide that you may take this path, then you must choose a stage name."

"If I really have to, Father," Elsie said, disappointed, though appreciating that if this was the only price she had to pay for permission, it was worth it.

"So where does my daughter see herself in five or ten years if she chooses to go on stage now?"

"Given that she cannot see the forest for the trees, that is a pretty unreasonable question, Father!" Walter chimed in from the background.

"Oh yes I can!" Elsie snapped back.

"Well, in that case you should call yourself 'Elsie Forest'!" said Walter smirking.

"Elsie Forest … Elsie Forest," she said. "Father, isn't there a Western Australian premier by the name of John Forest?"

"Yes, there is, princess, he was a famous explorer too, though his surname is Forrest with two 'r's."

"Elsie Forrest with two 'r's? Yes, I think I quite like that! … Then all my fans will be 'Forrest creatures'!" she said with a laugh.

"More like fungi or toadstools!" Walter sniped.

"Oh, shut up, Walter!" she snapped back.

As head of household, James felt obliged to play devil's advocate and continue to work his way through the labyrinth of issues. "Now, it was said that the play would likely tour the other colonies—though we shall all be calling them collectively Australia from 1 January next year—and I must say that I am not keen for my seventeen-year-old to travel without a chaperone."

"I agree totally, James, but what if I accompanied her? I have yet to go to Brisbane, Adelaide or Melbourne and perhaps it would give me a break from the polluted Sydney air," Mary Ann suggested.

James sighed. He could see how this might work, though the

world as he knew it would be turned upside down. There was the shop, meals and goodness knows what else to consider. Silence enveloped the room for quite some time, until Elsie could stand it no longer.

"Please, Father!"

"Well, I suppose if it has to be, it has to be. That is it then! I shall tell Mr Hawtrey on Monday morning that my daughter, as … Elsie Forrest … shall be joining The Hawtrey Comedy Company forthwith—though it is a lot of change and complication for just one pound a performance!"

"Oh, thank you, Father!" Elsie exclaimed as she gave him a hug and a kiss. She was just about to do the same to her mother when Walter interjected.

"You could always tell him that Elsie will strip on stage for three!" he exclaimed from the background, showing that his mouth moved quicker than his brain.

What subsequently occurred was unprecedented in the history of Thompson household relationships. Suffice to say, the upshot was that Walter, given that he now had a paid job of his own, had a week to find accommodation elsewhere.

After a weekend of emotional turmoil, James opened the shop to a beaming Elsie, Mr Hawtrey, and Mary Ann, at 9 am on the Monday.

The company manager had noticed Elsie's beautiful big eyes and the smile that made them glisten like searchlights, and knew before even a word was said, that he and they had made the 'right decision'.

"I will just need you to sign the contract, if you don't mind, Mr Thompson. Unfortunately, there are formalities. *A Message From Mars* is stated here, along with another play *Tom, Dick and Harry*."

James studied the paperwork carefully, as he knew he should. He returned to the Elsie Caroline Thompson name at the top and inserted:

to be known by the stage name 'Elsie Forrest'

"As long as you accept this change, we have a deal, Mr Hawtrey … I suppose I can call you William? I pray both parties will benefit."

"I must say that it is an unusual request—but, we have a deal, Mr Thompson. Ah … James," Mr Hawtrey said with a smile, before adding a flowing and unsurprisingly theatrical counter-signature.

As Mary Ann, Elsie and Mr Hawtrey set off for the first rehearsal at the Palace and the shop door closed behind them, James felt a door closing on the predictable and conservative existence he had known.

He slumped into his chair in his office, as a feeling of melancholy swept through him. He was sure his life would never be the same.

Chapter 8

The Man in the Shadows

He lurks within the darker realms, but surfaces anon
He follows me from place to place—he's on the tram I'm on
I wish I could describe him, though my memory's not clear
I see him when he's not there—for his name is Mr Fear.

Just returning to see the Palace Theatre again after almost two years was enough excitement for one day for any seventeen-year-old, let alone having to meet new cast colleagues and review an unfamiliar script.

Mary Ann did what she could to make Elsie feel comfortable—by being there, but never too close. She sat midway back in the seating; watching without watching too closely; listening without listening too attentively, but invariably knitting.

Elsie could not wait for her first walk on the Palace stage, so as the cast milled around the wooden structure, she wandered in and out of the dome outline stage surrounds, soaking up the gold and peacock blue-tinged atmosphere that she pretended shone just for her.

There were a dozen other single females in the cast, so she was never short of easy conversation. Everyone seemed to be very kind and going out of their way to make her feel comfortable.

Miss Winifred Austin, who Elsie was assured was one of those most familiar with the play and the demands of the theatre, was quick to take Elsie under her wing.

"Just enjoy it," she said, "and always remember that this is supposed to be a comedy."

Remembering lyrics for a performance such as *HMS Pinafore*, where there was musical accompaniment and invariably rhyme to aid memory, was one thing—recalling lines and associated actions in relative isolation, was entirely another.

When Elsie's first time to make a contribution arrived, she was so determined to make an impression that she jettisoned the script, literally, on the side of the stage and launched into her lines with gusto—only to realise part way through that she had used the wrong words and approached the wrong character.

In an instance she retracted her words, retraced her steps and flung herself into an extravagant but correct rendition that drew laughter and applause from her fellow cast members.

As she retreated, embarrassed, to the side of the stage, Mr Hawtrey was keen to not let the moment pass without more formal acknowledgement.

"I think you may now all appreciate just why I have asked Miss Thompson to join us!"

The cast, were not the only ones impressed. As Elsie turned to glance at her mother sitting in the theatre, her gaze swept over a male figure standing in the shadows on the theatre's left side.

When Elsie looked back that way, the man seemed to be staring intently at her.

Elsie turned away to be greeted by Winifred. "You will be just fine!" she said, squeezing Elsie's hand.

"Wini!" Elsie said, turning her back in the direction of the man in the shadows. "If you look over my … my right shoulder—can you see that man by the wall? Is he still looking at me?"

Winifred squinted past the stage lights. "Yessss …" she said slowly, "I can see a man in a high white collar in the shadows—and he does appear to be looking in this direction—but that is what we as actresses would hope for. The moment people stop wanting to look at us, we are finished!" she said, with a laugh and another reassuring squeeze of the hand.

Elsie was only mildly mollified by Winifred's assurance and the presence of 'the man in the shadows' worried her enough to mention the matter to her mother as they headed off to lunch.

Mary Ann admitted that she had not noticed anyone.

At the next morning's rehearsal, Elsie was so focussed on ensuring she remembered her lines in the correct sequence, this time, she had not thought about 'him'. It was only after successfully completing her entry to the play that she threw a glance towards the theatre's left side—but there was nobody there.

A sense of relief washed over her and she turned towards her mother in the centre of the auditorium with a smile. What she saw shocked her.

There, sitting right next to her mother and talking to her, was 'the man from the shadows'—the man with the high white collar. Elsie could see now that he looked to be in his forties.

Surely, her mother must know with whom she was conversing.

Elsie turned her attention back to the play trying to concentrate on her role. A minute or so later, 'the man from the shadows' had vanished and her mother was sitting alone, knitting as usual.

As they left the Palace that day, Elsie had only one thing to ask her mother.

"Mother!" Elsie said in a state of some annoyance, choosing to use the less familiar form of address rather than her usual 'Mumsie'. "That was 'the man from the shadows'!"

"Oh, was it, darling?" Mary Ann queried.

They kept walking and turned down King Street on their way to the bookshop in Erskine Street, without Mary Ann saying any more.

"Mother!" Elsie cried in frustration. "Who is he and what did he want?"

Mary Ann could see that Elsie was determined to find out more.

"Well, his name is Henry Lee. He is an American and he runs his own theatre company, called …" and here she stopped and reached into her purse, producing a card "… called Lee & Rial's World's Entertainers."

"And?" Elsie asked, half in frustration and half in curiosity.

"He said he was in Sydney to assess the Palace Theatre as a possible venue for his company's Sydney season later next year. However, I assured him that no matter what he wanted—acting, comedy, dancing or singing—you could do it! He didn't argue with me!"

"Mother! I have only just started rehearsals for my first professional performance and you are trying to move me to a troupe called 'World's Entertainers'!"

"Calm down, darling! I told him you had a contract with Hawtrey and would be heading to Brisbane in May for a season. He merely asked that you make contact with him after his company opens in Sydney in August next year. I told him that you would have just turned eighteen by then. All he asks, he says, is that he sees you at an audition."

This was not the news that Elsie wanted to hear, just as she was struggling as a perfectionist to master her new role. They walked on in silence, with Elsie feeling confused and unsettled.

As the weeks of rehearsals merged with public performances of *A Message From Mars* at the Palace Theatre from Saturday 22 December 1900, Elsie began to forget about 'the man in the shadows'.

A Message From Mars was playing to packed houses and receiving great reviews. These reviews had been summarised in an advertisement in *The Sydney Morning Herald.*

"Listen to this, El!" said Emma, picking up the Thompson's copy of the paper of Wednesday 26 December. "This review is by the *SMH* itself:

> There was a large and fashionable audience, and at the close of the last act the curtain had to be raised several times and the stage was covered with handsome floral tributes.

And from the *Australian Star:*

> Richard Ganthony's story, as told on the stage of the Palace Theatre on Saturday night, is not only a comedy with a wholesome moral, but it goes further, and appeals to the deeper feelings of our common humanity. It preserves a bright vein of humour that sparkles throughout.

And, there is more, from the *Evening Post:*

> At the Palace Theatre on Saturday night there was produced the best play that Sydney has seen for many a day. And not only was the play so good, but it was acted and staged suitably to its excellence. If the Palace Theatre is not crowded for weeks to see "A Message From Mars", then the higher theatrical taste of Sydney, which has not usually gone wrong in the past, will certainly belie its reputation.

See, El, you are a star!" Emma cried, dropping the paper and falling into Elsie's lap in the Carrington Street lounge room armchair.

Elsie smiled as Emma gave her a kiss. "I don't feel like a star—it said Elsie Forrest, not Elsie Thompson in Saturday's paper and in the theatre program," she said, taking a peak around Emma towards her father—but James, deliberately, did not react. "In any case, I don't have a big part—I just do what I can, as well as I can."

"Sydney may have to wait until she joins World's Entertainers!" interrupted Mary Ann.

"Mother! Please don't talk about that! I really have not thought about 'the man in the shadows' for quite a while. The whole thing seems like a world away."

A Message From Mars continued to play to large and enthusiastic crowds at the Palace Theatre in Sydney, until Friday 22 February 1901.

The cast then changed to performing another comedy, *Tom, Dick and Harry,* until they found themselves in May in the Queensland state capital of Brisbane.

Chapter 9

The Challenge

My future is my own preserve — and not what others writ
If I listened to my critics, I would not have done a bit
Their damning is a challenge, and their distain, a spur
To create the me I want to be, and not the me they were.

Hotel Daniell, on the corner of George and Adelaide Streets in the Brisbane city centre, had just seen significant improvements and a refurbishment, courtesy of its owner, Charles W. Daniell.

As Elsie bought a postcard of Hotel Daniell from its reception desk, she could honestly say that she was starting to feel at home in both the building and the warmer climate of New South Wales' northern neighbour. She found a pencil, turned the card over and started to write to her very favourite person:

11 May 1901

Dear Em,

Mother and I share a room here — and it is nice! AMFM going well, but may be starting TD&H soon. Ruby Ray has a publicity photo card with a kitten that is really cute — will bring you a copy! Hope to see you in a few weeks!

Lots of love — miss you heaps!
El XOXO

Mary Ann insisted that Elsie was not to follow the common practice of sending postcards in their raw and open state through the mail, so Elsie asked for an envelope at hotel reception. They gave her one, and for two pence a Queensland, Queen Victoria Patriotic Fund stamp to cover the postage to Sydney, which they said could take about a week.

Elsie wrote the address on the envelope:

Miss Emma Bellamy
48 Weston Road
Rozelle, Sydney
NEW SOUTH WALES

Then she added the stamp, before slipping the postcard inside, sealing it and adding a kiss.

* * *

When it was announced to the cast and crew on Tuesday 21 May that the next evening's show would be the last Brisbane performance of *A Message From Mars*, before changing to *Tom, Dick, and Harry*, Mary Ann grew agitated.

She well knew that Elsie's role would be reduced in the weeks to come—and frankly, had started to miss the comforts of home and the familiarity of James' presence.

The contract that had been signed included the possibility of subsequent tours to Adelaide, Melbourne and even New Zealand, though Mary Ann was struggling to see how much more Elsie could gain from reprising her roles with The Hawtrey Comedy Company, yet again.

That next evening, as the cast celebrated the end of the run of *A Message From Mars* in Hotel Daniell, Mary Ann was determined to take action. Seeing William Hawtrey in the hotel lounge talking with musical director, David Cope and stage director, Percy Walshe, Mary Ann approached them with a force that none would have anticipated.

"I must speak to you, and right now, Mr Hawtrey!"

William was quite taken aback and at first sought to delay any interaction. "I am talking about tomorrow's arrangements, Mrs Thompson, can it wait half an hour?"

"No, it cannot, sir!" Mary Ann insisted, standing her ground in front of the trio of gentlemen.

William's mind whirled quickly through the array of possibilities that could explain her presence and manner, though each seemed to lead back to sexual indiscretion when dealing with the careers of young and attractive actresses.

"If you wouldn't mind excusing me for a few minutes gentlemen … Mrs Thompson, I think we should move to the back of the bar." He was hoping his apprehension over what was likely to come, was not being clearly broadcast.

They moved to a couple of facing stools as William readied himself for the onslaught.

"Yes, Mrs Thompson, how can I help?"

Mary Ann for her part was unsure how to proceed, only knowing that their discussion should end with Elsie's release from her contract.

"Elsie cannot keep going on the way she has!"

"Why, what is wrong? Has she been injured or offended in any way?" He sensed from the comment that she had just made, that perhaps his concerns were unwarranted.

"Injury and offence can occur in many ways, Mr Hawtrey!" Mary Ann seized on his words to describe issues that clearly might concern him.

She hesitated, desperately seeking the appropriate words that would signal a smart move in what was rapidly developing into a game of chess.

"She has not been given the opportunities that her talent deserves!" … Moving a pawn forward …

"Mrs Thompson! Elsie is just a young girl, and while I do not deny that she has considerable potential, there are many in the cast who have spent decades honing their skills in minor parts in preparation for more meaningful roles. Just what were you anticipating?" … Retaliating with an equivalent move …

Here, Mary Ann took a gamble. "Elsie, not Ruby Ray, should be playing the part of Minnie Templer!" … Check …

William was stunned and sat open-mouthed for a few moments. "But … Miss Ray has a great many years of experience and Minnie Templer is one of the play's most important roles! Surely you do not think such a move would be wise or even possible?" … Moving in a pawn to block check …

It was at this point that Mary Ann pondered whether she should mention Elsie's hoped-for audition in Sydney for World's Entertainers, though wisely decided that her real motive should remain hidden. "Either the Templer role or release her from her contract!" … An aggressive move offering a face-saving way out …

"Never! I could never contemplate such a role for Elsie at this stage of her career! Throughout—and I say this with much regret, Mrs Thompson—your constant presence has been unsettling for all. Yes, I feel, even for Elsie! Have you not knitted enough tops to supply the whole New South Wales Rum Corp?" … A thinly disguised counterattack …

"How dare you question my motives and commitment to my daughter!" Mary Ann rose to her feet in a gesture that made William feel his 'opponent' might upend the chessboard at any moment. She was not sure that he had actually done either of what she had claimed, but she felt it might put him on the back foot—at least temporarily.

She was right—William struggled to explain himself. "Perhaps then, you are too committed?" Though as Mary Ann still stood scowling down at him, he added: "I cannot give her the Templer role, so if you insist, then a release from contract is the best, and I feel, only option." … Demonstrating that he was prepared to sacrifice a minor piece to save his Queen …

With this he rose and walked to the bar to get a piece of paper and pencil. He sat down, took a last look at Mary Ann, who was still standing, and wrote:

I, William F Hawtrey, do release Elsie Forrest (Elsie Caroline Thompson) from her contract with The Hawtrey Comedy Company.

William F Hawtrey
Wed 22 May, 1901

As he handed Mary Ann the piece of paper, he could not resist a parting shot or two. "You realise, Mrs Thompson, that one pound a performance is all but unheard of for someone of Elsie's age." He waited for a reaction, but there was none. "For a third of that money—or even less—there would be many young ladies of potential, eager to play her 'A Little Girl' role."

"Fine! So you will have absolutely no problem replacing her!" Mary Ann said, with no hint of disappointment or regret.

William could sense he was being made out to be the loser in this battle. "It is a shame really, she is such a nice, young girl with fair ability. Now she will just slip back to the anonymity of amateur dramatics, never to be seen again!"

If he was seeking a reaction, he now got it. Mary Ann

wrenched the paper from his grasp and gave him a final glare as the fire of her distant Irish and Roffey heritage burned within and through her eyes. "Really, Mr Hawtrey? Well, WE shall see!"

As she wheeled away it was plain to both of them that the challenge had been issued. And, it had been accepted.

A shocked and upset Elsie was told they were leaving the next morning by train for Sydney.

Chapter 10

Courting the World

I dreamed that I was on a stage, and all the world was there
The theatre it was packed each night, with fans — all debonair
Then I awoke to solitude — for spider scuttled hence
To dream his dream of eating bugs, while perched upon a fence.

James Thompson welcomed home his wife and beloved daughter, feeling sure that this was the first and last occasion that they would be parted for so long.

He most apologetically dispensed with the hired help of Mrs McIntyre and gradually slipped back into the more familiar environment characterised by cooking, banter and moments of affection that only the two closest women in his life could provide.

Moreover, his princess was back in the bookshop. There were times when James would look at her in wonder, contrasting the image of today with yesterday's little girl who would struggle to lift a volume from one shelf to the next.

As August 1901 approached, Elsie noticed that her mother became more interested in *The Sydney Morning Herald* than she had ever seemed before.

James had noted this too, as it would only take a brief absence, for him to find on his return a ruffled paper or his wife still perusing its contents.

It was on one such occasion — Wednesday 7 August — that Mary Ann found exactly what she was looking for.

"Here it is, on page eight! Listen to this:

THE WORLD'S ENTERTAINERS

Mr Henry Lee, the noted American actor and character impersonator, arrived here safely from San Francisco this week with an entirely new company formed for the presentation of "polite vaudeville" in this city. This new company entitled the "World's Entertainers", will open at the Palace Theatre, under the direction of Messrs Rial and

Lee, on Saturday evening. Mr Lee's "Great Men, Past and Present" will be a feature, and Messrs Kelly and Ashby (acrobats), and Josephine Gasmann and her Louisiana Piccaninnies, Charles Sweet (musical comedian), the Mahr Sisters (dancers), Arthur Nelstone (comic singer) and many other artists will appear. The plan is now open at Elvy's.

We must go there tomorrow morning, Elsie, and convince Mr Lee that you should join the troupe!"

Elsie was horrified. "Mother! These are international stars from overseas and I am an Australian who has … just … just been in a couple of plays! Why would anybody want to see me perform on my own?"

Elsie looked at her father for support and he was quick to provide it.

"Elsie is right, darling," he started saying, but stopped when he saw Mary Ann looking witheringly at him. He got up and walked to the window to look out over Wynyard Park, for what seemed a very long time as the others waited. Finally, he banged his fist on the windowsill and turned to address them. They both knew that such an action was most uncharacteristic and meant that his decision had to be accepted.

"Well, there is something to be said for finishing this matter properly, so it is not raised again. Clearly, your mother is insistent, so I can see that it is best you go with her tomorrow morning—then we can all get on with our lives, as if nothing has happened!"

* * *

As Elsie followed, just a pace behind her mother's determined stride towards the Palace Theatre, she was mulling over how embarrassing parents could be for teenagers. *How is Mother going to handle this?*

The theatre was open, so they walked through to the doors to the main auditorium, where Mary Ann stopped a young man in a hurry.

"I am after Mr Lee."

"Look, I don't think he will have time to see anyone—we are all flat out right now!" he responded, about to head away.

"Tell him an old friend needs to see him urgently!"

The young man hesitated, looked unsure, but then headed off towards the stage. *Oh! How embarrassing!* Elsie thought to herself.

Around a minute later, a well-built figure Elsie remembered as 'the man in the shadows' appeared in front of her mother.

"Henry! It is so good to see you again! I have returned with my daughter Elsie, just as you asked me to do when we met last year!"

Henry Lee was not at all impressed ... until he glanced past Mary Ann at Elsie.

"Well, I'll be!" he said in his American accent. "She sure is beautiful! And how old did you say she was?"

"Eighteen, Mr Lee—and, she can dance and sing with the best of them!"

Elsie felt like reminding her mother that she had only just turned eighteen, having had her birthday six days before.

Lee turned towards the stage and called to a dark-bearded figure in a brown coat: "James! Can you come over here for a moment?"

He then turned back to Mary Ann and Elsie. "Look, there is absolutely no way anyone can even contemplate joining up with World's Entertainers without seeing our show. You have to appreciate the quality of the show and the standards we demand. Then of course, there is the not too small matter of whether she really has the talent—and whether we can take on an Australian in the company. We don't have one yet!"

By then, the man in the brown coat had joined them.

"James Rial, I would like you to meet ... ?"

"Mary Ann Thompson, I am Elsie's mother!" Mary Ann said, offering her hand.

"James is my partner in the company, Mrs Thompson. James, would you have a couple of tickets for Saturday's opening night? Mary Ann and her beautiful daughter, Elsie, can then see exactly what the show is like."

"No problem at all!" James said, removing a bunch of tickets from his pocket and handing two to Mary Ann.

"If you bring her back here at 8.30 on Monday morning we can run her through an audition—though I must caution you that it is most unlikely she will get a gig," Henry warned.

"Well, thank you very much gentlemen! It was lovely to meet you both. We will enjoy the show and make sure we are back at 8.30 am on Monday!" Mary Ann responded.

As they walked down Pitt Street somewhat more relaxed than they had arrived, Elsie asked her mother what a 'gig' was. Mary Ann replied that she was unsure, but that it was no doubt an Americanism. "I think we should stop in at Elvy's and get an additional ticket for Emma, don't you think, darling?"

There was no need for Elsie to respond.

On that Saturday night, 10 August 1901, the Palace Theatre was packed with Sydneysiders eager to see what this new troupe of Lee & Rial's World's Entertainers had to offer.

Mary Ann led the way into the seating, with Elsie comfortably sandwiched between her mother and Emma.

From the talk around them, it was plain that everyone thought this was solely an American show despite the appellation hinting otherwise.

This feeling was reinforced at the start, by the American accent of the formidable and talented impersonator, Henry Lee. His sequence of Great Men, Past and Present began a procession of rapturously received acts that seemed to delight everyone, except Elsie.

She was desperately trying to see herself fitting in to the show—but was failing utterly. What could she provide that would cause this audience to rise to their feet, cheering at the conclusion of each act?

Perhaps, she mused briefly, Walter's crude comment about her stripping on stage might be her only chance. However, as soon as her thoughts toyed with the possibility, the natural shyness of a teenager intervened as she quickly realised that nobody would be interested. Well, certainly not in this 'polite vaudeville' extravaganza, as the show was promoted.

Emma could tell that her best friend was struggling to appreciate and enjoy the show for what it was. She reached over and held Elsie's hand, but noticed as the acts passed that the hand became clammy.

After the dancing Mahr Sisters had followed the spectacular acrobats Kelly and Ashby, Elsie said she was not feeling well, and by the time Charles Sweet, the 'Musical Burglar' had completed his comical repertoire, Elsie said she had a terrible headache and felt ill.

Intermission could not arrive too soon as Elsie rushed to the ladies' room, followed by a concerned Emma. She only just made the handbasin before throwing up, to the shock of an elderly lady who was about to wash her hands.

Emma managed to steer her back to her seat, but it was clear she was exhausted. She recovered only marginally as the second half of the show began with the 'Man with the Laughing Legs', Arthur Nelstone, and his hilarious performance of 'The Animated Doll', followed by the coin tricks of Allan Shaw.

The audience was absolutely enthralled by the appearance of Josephine Gassman and her two little piccaninnies, as black Americans were rarer than hen's teeth in this part of the world. Even Elsie was fascinated and distracted by the cute children, the trained pig that accompanied them and their Southern Songs performance.

The show closed with a stunning visual presentation utilising Thomas Edison's invention, the Projectoscope, showing scenes of everyday life around the world.

A standing ovation continued throughout the reappearance of the whole cast and Mary Ann, Elsie and Emma left under absolutely no illusion about the challenge facing Elsie if she was to ever become a part of World's Entertainers.

When Emma dropped around the next afternoon having ridden Daisy, with Bella in tow, she heard Elsie was still in bed and unwell.

"I don't think she will be attending the audition tomorrow, Emma. She is very down," Mary Ann whispered, having just emerged from Elsie's room with a basin and face cloth.

Emma stood at the door and looked in at the figure lying in the bed but staring out through the window across Wynyard Park.

Her dark hair contrasted magnificently with the white pillowcase and sheets.

Emma stood there and watched her for quite some time, all the while reminding herself how much she loved her friend.

Eventually, Elsie turned to look towards the door as she had a feeling that she was being watched. "Emma!"

"Hello, beautiful!" Emma responded, rushing to her side, kicking off her shoes and throwing back the bed sheets as she moved in to Elsie's embrace.

They lay there for a while just holding each other, with neither thinking that there was another place they would rather be.

Gradually, Elsie's focus drifted back out the window and into the distance, thinking about events and possibilities yet to come.

"I cannot give World's Entertainers anything it doesn't already have, Em," she said, in a sad and resigned voice.

"Rubbish!" Emma cried defiantly, as she tossed back the sheets and sat up on Elsie's nether regions, pinning her to the bed. "Now you listen to me, Elsie Caroline Thompson! You are beautiful and talented!"

"But, you are a better dancer than me!" protested Elsie, with a laugh that was limited by Emma's weight on her stomach.

"And what is more, you have a wonderful voice—and can make people laugh—which is something I can never do!" Emma continued. "How many people get an opportunity like this? If I were you, I would be there at 8 am tomorrow, waiting on the doorstep. You don't know how lucky you are, El!"

"Do you really think so?"

"Absolutely!" Emma cried, emphasising her insistence by pushing her hands down on Elsie's shoulders. "You … are … going … to … that … audition … tomorrow!" Emma swayed from side to side as she leaned over Elsie, causing her long golden hair to brush Elsie's face with each word.

Elsie laughed and Emma realised she had at least cheered her up. "But what if I mess it up?"

"If you do, then at least you will be able to say you did your best and tried—not ran away!"

This last comment made Elsie become reflective, as she certainly did not want to be seen as a coward.

"Now, to make sure everything will go your way, I made you this," Emma said, reaching into her pocket to remove a white handkerchief with 'EMMA LOVES ELSIE' sewn onto it.

Elsie did not know what to say.

"You are to take this with you to the audition, as a reminder that I love you and that I am always with you! I have kissed it," she said, placing it on Elsie's face, "and so has Bella!"

"Oh, no!" shrieked Elsie in a muffled voice, imagining her horse slobbering on the handkerchief.

Emma tried to keep the handkerchief on Elsie's face as the two rolled backwards and forwards across the bed laughing, eventually tumbling together onto the floor with such a crash that Mary Ann and even James rushed to see what was happening.

"We are fine!" gasped Emma reassuringly, as the girls lifted themselves from the floor. "Elsie IS going to the audition tomorrow—and she IS going to make us all proud!"

* * *

The sight of the Palace Theatre stage the next morning brought a mix of excitement and apprehension to Elsie. She felt for the reassuring ripple of embroidery that was Emma's love and best wishes secreted in her pocket.

The now familiar figure of Henry Lee was moving towards them, but there was another and unfamiliar gentleman, next to him.

"Good morning, Elsie! Good morning, Mrs Thompson!" Lee said in greeting. *Well, so far, so good,* Elsie thought.

"I trust you enjoyed our show on Saturday night?"

"Oh, yes! It was excellent, Mr Lee!" Elsie said with genuine enthusiasm.

"Very good. Then you will appreciate the high standards we set. As I believe I explained to you before, we are a touring company of international artists and do not have an Australian in our ranks. This has not been by chance. Quite frankly, we have seen nobody of the quality here to make the grade!"

This brutally honest assessment of her nation's artistic positioning was something that Elsie could have done without. Her fingertips played nervously with the embroidery—though Emma seemed to be saying to her 'do not waver!'

"Nevertheless, we have arrived at this point, so we will move forward," Lee continued. "To assist me in evaluating your performance, I have asked Mr Arthur Nelstone to be present.

He brings a wealth of experience in the fields of dance, comedy and song, none of which are my specialities—in fact many would be churlish enough to suggest, that I have none!" he added, with a laugh to his self-deprecating aside.

Beginning to realise that his audience were not present for a personal homily, he changed tack. "Before we start, do you have anything to say, Mr Nelstone?"

"Nothing other than to wish the young lady well and remind her that we are looking for something out of the ordinary," Nelstone said in what both Elsie and Mary Ann easily recognised as an English accent. So they were not all Americans, after all.

"Good! Mrs Thompson, I must ask that you take a seat at the very back of the auditorium, and that you do not communicate with your daughter. Mr Nelstone and I shall position ourselves in the middle. Elsie, move to the centre of the stage and await further instruction."

Mary Ann gave Elsie a kiss and a squeeze and they went their separate ways.

As she climbed the steps to the stage, Elsie's fingertips danced across the embroidery—and Emma seemed to answer back that she would be dancing with her. *What will I be asked to do?*

Mary Ann crossed her fingers in the back row as Elsie placed herself in the exact centre of the stage.

"You will have two minutes, Elsie, to perform a routine," Lee said. "I will call out a countdown from five for you to start, then when you have one minute and later thirty seconds to go. Now, on the side of the stage you will see there is a pair of butterfly wings. Pick up the wings and return to the centre of the stage for the countdown."

A routine of two minutes on being a butterfly! Elsie thought to herself. *Quick, think of what you must show—what happens in the life of a butterfly? Birth, flying, friendship … danger, injury and death. That is six things in two minutes—six into sixty seconds is ten, times two is twenty seconds—so twenty seconds on each.*

She took a deep breath and tried to repeat the six phases in sequence: *birth, flying, friendship, injury, death …* then realised she had forgotten one as that was five. She tried again: *birth, flying, friendship, injury, danger—no! Danger, injury and death!*

As she repeated the six a final time she tried to quickly think how she might show each, but realised that she would have to do so 'on the run'.

With a butterfly wing on each arm, she stood at the centre of the stage then sank to the floor curling the wings over herself.

"Five, four," Mr Lee began.

Birth followed by flying, Elsie said to herself—just twenty seconds for each …

"… two, one, start!"

Slowly, from a curled position the butterfly wings quivered, then gradually extended—but shaking and seeming nervous, as if unsure about their position in this new life.

Halfway! Elsie thought, *I must be just over ten seconds … extend the wings out on each side … slowly rise to face the world with a triumphal smile! Twenty seconds gone … now flying …*

Elsie moved her wings a little and then reacted with delight as she seemed to glide—so tried it again, but with bigger flaps of the blue, purple and black-rimmed wings. Soon, she was gliding gracefully around the stage.

It must be about time, she thought, so she came to a sudden halt for friendship, where she leant tentatively towards a pretend friend, then backwards, coyly curling her wings protectively around her body in feigned shyness, only to extend them in friendship and then seem to move in mirror response to this invisible new-found companion.

Keep going, she thought, *until he calls out the halfway point.*

"One minute!" came the call from the floor.

Danger, Elsie said to herself as she once more moved to extend her friendship, but reacted with shock and alarm at an invisible threat.

"Oh, she is damn good, Nelstone—far better than I had expected!" Lee whispered.

Elsie retreated in fear to one side of the stage but her pursuer was determined and she ducked and weaved as she sought refuge.

Time for injury, she thought, as she arched her back and shook a wing as if in pain and staggered across the Palace stage.

"She has hurt herself!" cried Nelstone in more than a whisper as he rose to his feet, totally caught up in the storyline of the performance.

Elsie's wings began to droop. *Hurry up,* she said to herself. *Make the thirty second call!*

Lee had now joined Nelstone in standing. *This is an act, is it not?* Arthur thought. *Yet, it is so convincing.*

Elsie was struggling to work out how to extend the injury phase. *Make the call!*

Lee suddenly realised he had been distracted from his timekeeping task.

"Thirty seconds!"

Another ten seconds of injury, thought Elsie, *but it can't be too motionless, as it will be followed by death!*

She struggled to make her wings flutter as they had, but it was no use, and she limped into a downhill spiral that brought her back to the centre of the stage, where over the final twenty seconds she displayed increasingly less sign of life, before ultimately sinking into the position from which she had started.

Lee, who had seen no need to call an end to the performance, just shook his head and muttered: "Remarkable!"

Elsie could not hear this, so remained curled up on the stage. Mary Ann, who was desperately trying to eavesdrop on the two gentlemen, could only discern muttering.

"She moves so well—and has such a good figure!" Nelstone whispered in admiration.

"Very well, thank you, Elsie," Lee called out, trying not to give away his feelings. "Mr Nelstone has a song he would like you to perform."

Arthur Nelstone reached into his pocket and took out a piece of folded paper, unfolded it, looked at it for a few moments, then to Lee's great surprise scrunched it up and threw it on the floor.

"What are you doing?"

"I have a much better idea!" Nelstone responded. "I will be back in just a jiffy!"

With that, he sidled down the row, mounted the stage and headed in to the backstage dressing room area.

Elsie felt in her pocket once more and her fingertips traced across the embroidery … E M M A … and then L O V E S … as she waited …

After a short break, Nelstone emerged at Elsie's side. "Here, have a read of this first. Then see what you can do as you sing it!" Nelstone said, passing Elsie a page.

Elsie studied the contents:

The Animated Doll

On a shelf at the top, in a large toy shop
In the midst of the Lowther Arcade
By the side of the famous Tin Gee-gee
I was there once displayed
Only four D is the price of me, said the ticket upon my chest
I was cheap, I suppose, as I'd very few clothes
And wasn't wax like the rest
As the years unrolled I remained unsold
And did nought but pine and sigh
Till one fine day, in the month of May
I happened to catch the eye
Of a dear little girl, who to her Papa said
'That is the one I'd choose …
For I really believe I could love that doll.'
And directly I heard the news—

Chorus:

I commenced to hop all over the shop
First I was here then there
In starts and fits began doing the splits
Frightened the rest of the dolls into fits
My joints flew out, I danced about
With a kind of spasmodical jerk
And as soon as that little girl touched the spring
The figure began to work.

I was carefully packed, and in paper wrapped
In her doll's house found a place
She told me the name she would call me by
And having washed my face
Gave me some jam, then with an old lamb,
Who was minus his tail and head
A duck who quack-quacked, and some tea-things all cracked

I was instantly put to bed
And then every day she and I would play
And as soon as she older grew
I'd play the part of her sweetheart
And I liked it, twixt me and you
When e'er I did wrong she would box my ears
And sulky for hours remain
But directly she kissed me and made up
Then I'd feel my feet again.

(Chorus)

I was happy and gay, till there came a day
I received the worst of shocks
For the lamb, the duck, and poor little me
Were all put in a box
She had found new joys, got too big for toys
And the dear little artful miss,
Had hit on a plan, then to have a young man
Instead of a doll to kiss
I went off my head, and the toys all said
As they laughed at me, 'Oh! Oh!
You should be sent up to Parliament
Where the wooden-heads mostly go!'
So now I'm left, all on my own
Which to me appears a crime
With no one to love and nothing to do
But think of the good old time.

(Chorus)

Elsie was surprised, but a little grateful that the song was something she had seen—and loved—on Saturday night. But singing and performing actions associated with the lyrics was always going to make her look well and truly second-rate, when compared to those of a genius like Arthur Nelstone.

Holding the sheet in her left hand, she sought solace and encouragement from the embroidery in her pocket. *Oh Emma, I wish you were here to help me,* she thought, as she took a deep breath once more.

"Are you ready, Elsie?" called Lee.

"Yes, sir!" Elsie responded, with far less confidence than she wished to possess, as she frantically studied the lyrics and sought to imagine actions she could create to accompany them.

"Five, four, three, two, one!"

On a shelf at the top, in a large toy shop …

Elsie started but was interrupted by a commotion on the floor.

"Arthur! What are you doing? This is your trademark!" Lee exclaimed in surprise and annoyance.

"Everything will be fine. Let us just see how she does things!"

Henry Lee studied Arthur Nelstone for a few moments. "We shall be discussing this when the audition has finished. My apologies young lady! Please start again!"

Elsie tried to do her best to demonstrate not only her vocal skills, but also her ability to move backwards and forwards into different character rolls. When she was the doll, she was variously stiff and then disjointed in her movements. As the girl, she was child-like and seemingly entranced. When moving from one to the other, she would twirl around three hundred and sixty degrees and immediately adopt the appropriate mannerisms and posture.

Elsie had made it to about halfway through the second verse when she was stopped.

"That will do!" Lee bellowed. "That is enough thank you, Elsie! Mr Nelstone and I will now adjourn to a back room for a discussion." He rose to his feet and was followed by Nelstone, as they walked down the row, up on to the stage and into the back room area.

Elsie sighed. She thought she had done the best she could, and if it was not good enough for them, there was nothing more she could do. Why had she been given such a hard piece, and one that would test any artist to their creative limit?

She folded the lyrics up and disconsolately headed off the stage towards her mother, still seated at the back.

In a back dressing room, the door was slammed behind two figures, at least one of whom was not happy at all.

"What the hell do you think you are doing?" demanded Lee. "You are thirty-three years old!"

"No, I am thirty-one!" the Englishman indignantly corrected his boss.

"Who gives a damn! She is only eighteen years old. Eighteen—do you get that, Arthur? You have Agnes Mahr assisting you until Amy Stirling arrives this week, and already you are seeking to dump them!"

Nelstone did not know what to say.

Meanwhile, Elsie had made her way to the back stalls and slumped in a chair next to her mother. "You were very good, darling!" Mary Ann said, greeting her with a kiss. "If things are not to be, they are not to be!"

Elsie looked up and around at all the glory of the Palace, trying to take her mind off the inevitable.

It was some minutes till Henry Lee made his way through the auditorium, though there was no sign of Arthur Nelstone.

"Sure hope this was not too much of a trial for you, Miss Elsie," he said, trying to reassure her upon seeing her frowning countenance.

"No, Mr Lee, it was fine—I enjoyed it," Elsie said, trying to be as positive as possible while her fingertips stroked the embroidery.

"Well, I am afraid that I cannot give you any good news." Elsie's heart sank. "Well, not right now, in any case. We were both very impressed, in all honesty far more than we expected. However, we would like to see you audition once more. In three weeks time, we would like you to perform the butterfly dance and one other …"

"Oh, please, can I perform one of my own creations?"

"I do not think that would be appropriate, Miss Thompson!" Elsie noted he had not used her first name in responding, but persisted.

"Please, Mr Lee! My best friend Emma and I have written it and I am sure you will like it!"

"Elsie! You heard Mr Lee!" Mary Ann interjected.

"Please, Mr Lee!"

Henry Lee was perplexed. Here he was, offering a lifeline to a young lady to have a real chance to be the only Australian in an international touring act, yet she was seeking to sabotage her one opportunity.

"And … and what is this piece called, Miss Thompson?"

"It is called 'Snugglepoke', Mr Lee!" Elsie exclaimed with delight, though this was not something that was reflected on Mr Lee's face.

"Snug … gle … poke?" he said incredulously, shaking his head.

"Oh, yes, and you will just love it!"

"Well, I guess either it is a knockout—or you will be—knocked out!" He was still shaking his head as he took out his diary. "Three weeks from today, which is … Monday September 2nd, at 8.30 am—here!"

"Oh, thank you, Mr Lee!"

"Yes, thank you, Mr Lee. Elsie, we shall talk, outside!" Mary Ann said, most firmly.

Under other circumstances, the walk home might have been close to a triumphal stroll, but Mary Ann seemed determined to turn it in to a walk of shame, as she was furious with her daughter.

Well before they had left Pitt Street, Elsie decided to run on ahead, as her mother simply did not understand.

Chapter 11

The World is Your Oyster

If you act and if you think, just like what you suppose
Your character is meant to be — and stay well on your toes
And don't clam up like others might, in this artistic sea
The world might be your oyster — or it has you for its tea.

The atmosphere at the Thompson dinner table that evening was far from usual.

"I have done everything I can to support you," Mary Ann argued. "Everything! I have been your chaperone to ensure things ran smoothly with *A Message From Mars*. I have encouraged you to have an audition with Lee & Rial's—and just when there seems to be a real chance—and you are offered an opportunity by Mr Lee, you slap him in the face by insisting on this 'Bubblebloke' stupidity!"

"It is 'Snugglepoke', Mother!"

"I don't care what it is. It is not what Mr Lee wanted, and what Mr Lee wanted, Mr Lee should have got! Sometimes, Elsie, you are your own worst enemy, as you get carried away. I am telling you right now that if you insist on doing your own stupid piece, then I will be sparing myself the embarrassment, by not attending your audition! And, that is final!"

"Cissie, please!" James intervened. He had remained silent till now, but it was clear that something had to be done to try to break the impasse.

"I shall be asking Emma to join us for dinner on Wednesday," James continued. "She is a smart girl, and one not prone to falsity or exaggeration. She knows this Snuggle thing and I am sure her opinion would be most valued."

By Wednesday, Mary Ann's position had not shifted one iota. As she ladled out the potatoes, she asked Emma for her opinion.

"Well, if it was me in Elsie's shoes, I would have gone with what Mr Lee wanted, as that would have been the sensible thing to do."

"See! I told you, didn't I, Elsie! You should listen to your best friend!" Mary Ann was heartened that at last someone shared her concerns.

"But, I am not Elsie, Mrs Thompson, and I do not have her talent," Emma continued.

"So, tell me, Emma. What is this Snuggle thing like? Is it too childish?" James asked.

"Childish?" Emma repeated, looking at Elsie with a smile that was quickly reciprocated. "No, Mr Thompson, I don't think you could quite call it that!"

"Well, perhaps you could perform it for us now," James suggested.

"You will do no such thing!" Mary Ann stated emphatically. "You should not even contemplate doing anything other than what Mr Lee wants. Either go tomorrow to Mr Lee and beg his forgiveness and guidance, or do things your own way—though if you do, I refuse to be there to share the embarrassment!"

With that, Mary Ann picked up her chair and put it firmly in against the table, making it clear that her dinner would remain uneaten.

"Cissie, please!" James pleaded again, as he followed her to the bedroom, only stopping briefly to appeal in gesture to Elsie before disappearing.

It was some minutes before James returned to a cold meal and a pair of anxious girls.

"Your mother and I have agreed that the choice is yours, as it is your potential career. She will not be attending the audition. I shall be escorting you there, Elsie, but then leaving for the bookshop." James then hesitated, and the girls could tell he had more to say, so they waited in silence. "Furthermore, I shall be asking Mrs Bellamy for her permission for Emma to be present to provide you with some moral support."

"Father!" Elsie cried, as she rushed to hug him in delight, but his lack of enthusiastic response showed her he was still anguishing over the whole matter.

"Well, Elsie, you must take every opportunity to practise. I am sure Emma will insist it is at a high standard for the audition."

"Don't worry, Mr Thompson, we will do everything to make sure she has a real chance!" Emma assured him as she took Elsie's hand in hers.

* * *

A few minutes before 8.30 am on Monday 2 September 1901, James introduced himself to Henry Lee at the entrance to the Palace Theatre auditorium.

"If you should need it, sir, here is my business card," he uttered, far more in hope than expectation.

He then exchanged good luck kisses with Elsie and Emma, asking them to head to the bookshop once the audition had finished.

Elsie motioned Emma to sit at the back of the theatre as she simultaneously felt for the comfort of the embroidered handkerchief, to ensure Emma's spirit and strength stayed with her.

As she climbed on stage, she noticed that the butterfly wings were in position.

"Butterfly, butterfly, concentrate and become," she whispered to herself.

When she looked up, she noticed that Mr Nelstone had joined Mr Lee in the theatre's heart. Looking beyond them, Elsie could just make out Emma.

"Countdown from five, Miss Thompson!" called Mr Lee.

As she worked her way through the sequence, she tried desperately to complete each part better than she had in the first audition.

At the end, she was greeted by applause—from the back of the theatre. However, it was the reaction from those in the centre that really mattered.

"Well done, Elsie!" Mr Nelstone called out. "I think your transition between sequences was better than your previous attempt!"

Mr Lee had not commented, which unnerved Elsie. Perhaps he was having second thoughts already—and he had not even heard her made-up song.

"Time for this song of yours. I presume it is a song, Miss Thompson?"

"Yes, Mr Lee, 'Snugglepoke' is a song!"

"Ah yes ... 'Snugglepoke'!"

Elsie moved to the front centre of the stage and felt for the embroidery as she looked out at Emma in the distance.

Emma for her part had grabbed the back of the seat in front of

her and was squeezing it as hard as she could and whispering
to herself: "Come on, El—you can do it!"

Elsie shifted her focus to the two gentlemen in the centre. *I
have to make them feel as if I am singing about them!*

"Countdown from five, Miss Thompson!"

"Tune, voice, actions," Elsie whispered, just before she began
singing:

> When I was a cute young girlie
> And I needed care
> I would Snugglepoke with little Lambi,
> Bunny and the Bear
>
> Now I'm just a wee bit older
> And my taste has changed
> I'll Snugglepoke, with special people
> —It can be arranged!

"Clap with me in this chorus!" Elsie called out, raising her
hands:

> (Clap, Clap) me and (Clap, Clap) you and
> (Clap, Clap) moi et vous
> Snugglepoking's what I dream of
> In my dreams with you!
>
> (Clap, Clap) you and (Clap, Clap) me and
> (Clap, Clap) me and you
> Snugglepoking's what I dream of
> Make my dreams come true!

While she was into the second verse of the chorus, she noticed
that Emma was on her feet and clapping.

> Chandler 'neath a candelabra
> Minister in mime
> I'll consider propositions
> Each one at a time!
>
> Said we came from Eden's Garden
> Or from Noah's Ark
> Either way we were configured
> —Snugglepoke's our spark!

(Clap, Clap) me and (Clap, Clap) you and
(Clap, Clap) moi et vous
Snugglepoking's what I dream of
In my dreams with you!

(Clap, Clap) you and (Clap, Clap) me and
(Clap, Clap) me and you
Snugglepoking's what I dream of
Make my dreams come true!

This time, she was sure that Mr Nelstone was on his feet and clapping along too.

Hansom cab or village haystack
You just choose the place
Open up your heart and feel
The warmth of my embrace!

What's this then? You say you're married?
Oh this cannot be!
Well, she can join us in a troika
—Snugglepoking three!

(Clap, Clap) me and (Clap, Clap) you and
(Clap, Clap) moi et vous
Snugglepoking's what I dream of
In my dreams with you!

(Clap, Clap) you and (Clap, Clap) me and
(Clap, Clap) me and you
Snugglepoking's what I dream of
Make my dreams come true!

Now I live at Guv'nor's Pleasure
Within these prison yards,
Yet none can stop me Snugglepoking
With the prison guards!

When I take that black maria
To my resting ground, they'll
Chisel deep into my tombstone:
'Fun To Be Around!'

"One last chorus, slowly!" Elsie urged:

(Clap, Clap) me and (Clap, Clap) you and
(Clap, Clap) moi et vous
Snugglepoking's what I dream of
In my dreams with you!

(Clap, Clap) you and (Clap, Clap) me and
(Clap, Clap) me and you
Snugglepoking's what I dream of
Make … my dreams … come true!

"Brilliant, just brilliant!" Mr Nelstone called out, rising to his feet as Emma kept applauding in the background.

Elsie could not help smiling as she felt she had done well and had certainly impressed Mr Nelstone.

What she had not seen, however, was Henry Lee's hand pulling down on Arthur Nelstone's jacket, forcing him to curtail his enthusiasm and resume his seat.

Still frozen in her finishing pose, Elsie turned her attention to Henry Lee. It was then she noticed that he was not so much looking at her, as looking through her. He seemed to be concerned, and not at all the delighted and welcoming joint company proprietor that she had hoped he would be.

After a few moments of thought, Lee stood up. "Elsie, thank you, but I want you to stay there. I will be back soon."

With that, Henry Lee headed down the row, up on to the stage and through to the backstage rooms. Elsie could hear him calling out "James! James!" as he went.

She looked out towards Arthur Nelstone, who seemed to have read her mind.

"Don't worry, luv," he assured her in his English accent. "Things will be all right. Just make sure that if you are asked to do it again, you really emphasise the fun. Let us see and really feel it!"

In the backstage area, Henry Lee had finally found his friend and joint proprietor of World's Entertainers, James Rial.

"James, I want you to come and look at young Elsie's performance."

"Is there a problem?"

"Look, I don't doubt her quality—she is pretty damn good— but I am just concerned that it may not fit in with our 'polite vaudeville' theme, that we use to differentiate ourselves from some of the low-class rabble out there."

As they turned back to the stage, Lee continued: "I want your honest opinion. I don't want us to be seen to be encouraging juvenile prostitution."

Rial looked at his partner in surprise that such a thing should be mentioned—clearly the performance would be interesting.

As Elsie briefly turned at the sound of footsteps approaching from offstage, Nelstone interrupted from the floor, causing her to turn back.

"Hey, Elsie! I think you are absolutely smashing!" he called out in a loud whisper with a thumb raised and a smile.

Emma was sitting on the edge of her seat at the back of the theatre trying to decipher the comings and goings and hear the comments.

"Miss Thompson! I have brought Mr Rial out to watch your performance. Could you repeat your song for the benefit of all of us, please."

With that the proprietors joined Mr Nelstone in the centre of the auditorium.

"Countdown from five, Miss Thompson!"

"Fun and exaggeration," Elsie whispered to herself. "Make this the performance of your life!"

Eventually, when she came to a final standstill, Elsie was sure that this was her best performance yet. However, it was not to be her decision.

"What do you think, James?" Lee asked his partner.

"It's catchy, has audience involvement and she is cute! Her voice is good and timing is excellent. Sure, the piece is a bit risqué, but she has real personality—and it comes across with a lot of humour."

"So … should we sign her up?"

"Absolutely! I think that she would add something to the company that we do not have. Sign her up, Henry!"

Lee rose to his feet and called out loudly enough for even Emma to hear clearly: "Well done, Elsie! 'The World' is your oyster! Welcome to Lee & Rial's World's Entertainers!"

Elsie's feelings on hearing these words were a mixture of delight and relief, given the recent tensions with her mother.

A few tears ran down her face as Mr Lee and Mr Rial reached her. Mr Nelstone wanted to be there even faster, but felt that it might be better if he held back, just a little.

Meanwhile, Emma was jumping up and down in the background with the excitedness of a jack-in-a-box.

"I have your father's business card and will be dropping around to Erskine Street tomorrow morning to work out the details of your involvement," Lee said, reaching into his pocket and producing a handkerchief.

"It's all right!" Elsie assured him, as she pulled out her own and felt the lettering stroke her face.

"You realise, Miss Thompson," Mr Lee said, "that you will be the first Australian to join World's Entertainers!"

Chapter 12

The Pairing

The isolate did speak out loud—but no one really heard
Not the passing crowd of folk, nor the fleeing, flying bird
In pairing there is sacrifice: you act more as a twin
Each giving something of themselves, to take a little in.

James Thompson made sure that the name on this, the second of Elsie's contracts, was to be 'Miss Elsie Forrest'. He felt this was for the best, though, as he had still not heard 'Snugglepoke', he had no real idea just how important such a decision would prove to be.

For her part, Elsie was careful never to remind her mother of her reluctance to support her daughter's dreams. Some things were better left unsaid. And in any case, her relative generosity may need to be remembered at some later time, as she had the maturity to already know that life might not always be a smooth, one-way ride.

Over the following month, leading up to her planned solo debut with World's Entertainers on Tuesday 8 October 1901, Elsie threw herself enthusiastically into her new life in the company.

On her first morning of rehearsals, it was Arthur Nelstone who was quick to grab Elsie's hand and introduce her to each member of the company, individually.

Elsie was delighted to meet all these talented artists, most of whom she had only admired from afar.

Everyone was most welcoming—though with one exception.

"Arthur, I don't think you need to hold her hand!" Amy Stirling snapped when Elsie was introduced.

As Arthur Nelstone's assistant and performance partner, Miss Stirling had noted with increasing annoyance his fawning over the company's new recruit.

"I think she is old enough to stand on her own two feet—at least for a while!" Miss Stirling added, with a feigned smile in Elsie's direction.

As Elsie wandered around the Palace Theatre backrooms,

she noticed just how hard the performers practised, leaving nothing to chance. These people were real professionals.

Even the transition between acts was rehearsed and timed. The last one of a reshuffled sequence between the pair of acrobats Kelly and Ashby and the Projectoscope's moving pictures was particularly problematic.

Quite a deal of equipment needed to be rushed off stage quickly but carefully, while the curtains were closed. As the Palace Theatre's electric lights, powered by the recently installed generator, came on, Henry Lee would appear in front of the curtains, to assure everyone that one final performance would follow, lest patrons thought that the whole show had concluded.

As he did so, the Projectoscope operators would move their equipment into a pre-determined position within the audience.

It was into this environment with an expectation of excellence that Elsie stepped, admittedly nervously, on her Tuesday debut night.

She was well aware that neither of her parents had seen her perform 'Snugglepoke', but she was comforted to know that Emma would be there as well, this time accompanied by her widowed mother, Elizabeth.

Whenever nerves would surface, Elsie pretended that she was about to perform privately, just for Emma.

Arthur Nelstone had arranged for her appearance to precede his, meaning that she was third act on stage, immediately after Miss Frances Gwynne and her *Illustrated Songs*.

As she waited in the wings, trying not to think too much about the packed theatre she could glimpse through the scenes and sidelined curtains, a hand reached out and stroked her arm.

"You will kill them sweetheart, I know it!" Nelstone said, adding a reassuring pat. He had not noticed until he turned away, that his assistant, Miss Stirling, was glaring at him with a look that could kill.

The strains of Frances' final song 'Tommy' echoed through the theatre and signalled a deep and extended breath from Elsie.

So much of her focus and emotional commitment to date had been on 'Snugglepoke', though she first had to perform the butterfly routine.

The applause for Miss Gwynne was still ringing through the theatre, as stagehands laid out the butterfly wings either side of the centre of the stage.

Elsie took another deep breath and spun her way out from the side of the stage to sink in its centre, with arms stretching out and hands grasping each wing.

The ripple of chatter that ran through the audience was soon transformed into enthusiastic applause as Henry Lee strode onto the stage and announced: "Ladies and gentlemen! I have great pleasure in introducing to you, the first Australian to ever perform with World's Entertainers, Miss Elsie Forrest!"

Elsie quickly switched into performance mode, making sure she had her timings of the six, twenty-second sections correct. The hearty applause when she had finished indicated that she had done well, but Elsie knew that she had performed better many times in rehearsal.

In the back stalls, Mary Ann Thompson was busy telling anyone who might want to listen that Elsie was her daughter. James conserved his countenance, sensing that 'Snugglepoke' was the key to how his daughter would be perceived.

Henry Lee moved back onto the stage once more as stagehands removed the wings and Elsie had spun temporarily out of view.

"Miss Forrest will now present a song of her own creation, 'Snugglepoke'!"

Elsie appeared once more, though this time in a long blue nightgown, but her own introduction to 'Snugglepoke' was nothing that the other cast members had ever seen her rehearse before.

Standing in the centre of the stage, Elsie appealed to the audience. "When I hold my hands out like this," she said, holding them apart in front of her, "I am about to clap. That is a signal for you to get ready to clap with me. Now, I want you all to hold your hands like this, and be ready to clap, everyone, on the count of three: one, two, three!"

Clapping, though a bit fragmented, echoed around the theatre.

"Come on, you can do much better than that!" Elsie urged. "We will try again, but this time, watch my hands and listen to the count. One, two, three!"

This time the clap was much more in unison. "Well done everyone—well, nearly everyone. I did notice a man in a brown suit in the back stalls who didn't seem to be in unison." The audience laughed, unaware that Elsie was indicating her father. James, for his part, was mortified.

"So let's do the clapping in sections. We will start with the stalls. So stalls people, get ready. One, two, three!" A loud and virtually simultaneous clap boomed out from the most populated section of the theatre.

"Excellent stalls people, you are so clever! Now, let's combine the family circle, dress circle and those of you up the back there in the cloud seats in the gallery. One, two, three!"

"Terrific! Now, that only leaves one part of the theatre," Elsie said, peering mischievously in turn at the ornate boxes on either side of the theatre to her left and then to her right, as the balance of the audience laughed knowingly.

"Oh, I agree with you too! I think there are some very loud clappers in those boxes and we have not heard the best of them yet!" she said to more laughter.

"Come on box people, you may have the expensive seats, but the rest of the theatre want their money's worth from you!" The rest of the theatre laughed and cheered. It was a typically Australian reaction to wish that the more affluent and pretentious were brought down a peg.

"One, two, three! Well, that was not too bad at all."

"To think she is only eighteen!" Henry Lee exclaimed in wonderment, shaking his head as James Rial joined him. "She already has the audience in the palm of her hand!"

By this time, other members of World's Entertainers had gathered at the sides of the stage, hoping to witness this piece of unique theatre.

"Now we need to put it all together—yes, everyone together—ready? One, two, three!" A single clap thundered through the theatre.

"Fantastic!" Elsie cried, "except for the young man up there in the gallery who was staring into the eyes of his beloved!" The audience turned to scan the gallery, searching forlornly for the pair Elsie had described.

"At least you could look at me, a poor and lonely eighteen-year-old seeking love and attention!" Elsie complained in mock distress, as a mixture of laughter and sighing rang through the audience.

In the back stalls, Emma had a big smile on her face and tears welling in her eyes. What she was seeing was classic Elsie, and she knew that once the Elsie train had left the station, it was not going to stop any time soon.

"In this song I am about to sing, I will need your help. There are three points in each part of the chorus where you will need to clap, with a pair of sequential claps, in this way: clap, clap, with that rhythm. Now we are going to try this most difficult sequence. Only this time I am not going to count. You just watch my hands and get ready to clap!"

The claps that rang through the theatre were not as distinct as Elsie liked, so she demanded a repeat. This time, it was syncopated. "Very good everybody, but can you do it when I am hiding?" she said, racing out to the left side of the stage and hiding behind the curtain.

The audience watched intently for Elsie's hands to appear and when they did, the sequence of claps followed Elsie's movements.

"Wonderful! However, I will just test your abilities one more time," she said, as she scampered across to the right side of the stage and hid behind the curtain, making sure to be seen to slide in on the floor as she did so. Then she waited for a few seconds, feeling the power she had to make the audience hold its breath, till she reached her hands out just above floor level and clapped—twice.

Now, she reasoned, she was able to take them with her. She disappeared temporarily beyond the curtain, where she removed her nightgown, emerging back in the centre of the stage in a long white nightdress, to a collective hum of appreciation from the audience.

"Remember to watch my hands!" With that Elsie began her song. When she reached the chorus for the first time, her hands went out and the audience reacted just the way she had hoped.

"Well done! You did it!" she cried out, pausing before heading in to the second section.

As ecstatic as Emma was, James Thompson was concerned, and by the time Elsie had reached the part about 'proposition' in the third verse, James simply uttered "Oh no!" and put his head in his hands. This was not quite the little girl he liked to recall.

The mention of a 'troika' sent a mixture of gasping and giggling through the audience, though Mary Ann dabbed a handkerchief against her mouth as if she had wished she could have stopped her daughter's words from ever emerging.

The ovation Elsie received at the end—and it was a standing one from quite a few male members of the audience, complete with wolf-whistles—left her parents with no doubt that others had received her performance well. They looked at each other and well appreciated that neither would have let her go to Mr Lee had they known this song's content, but as they well knew now, the filly had already bolted.

Lee and Rial were troubled. Her appearance, voice, movement and timing had been as good as they could have wished. True, they had witnessed and been seduced by these at audition and rehearsal, but her manipulation of the packed audience, had taken her performance to a different level. She had generated an atmosphere of 'animal magnetism' that they feared was incompatible with 'polite vaudeville'.

"That was just fantastic, Elsie!" Nelstone enthused, as he gave her a big hug and kiss as she entered the backstage rooms. "The way you worked that audience was just remarkable!"

"Arthur! Get back here now!" Miss Stirling called. "We are on in a moment!"

Elsie felt herself float through the minutes and hours ahead. What concerns she had about her ability to be an accepted part of World's Entertainers had vanished.

As the traditional closing act, the Projectoscope films, completed their display, the whole cast gathered on stage to be greeted by a standing ovation—and a couple of curtain calls. *This is where I belong!* Elsie thought to herself.

* * *

Not a smoker himself, as he felt it affected the vocal chords, Henry Lee had banned the practice from the backstage rooms. For this, Elsie was most grateful. Neither of her parents smoked and she was irritated by the taste and smell.

Lee had insisted that any smoking be done outside the backstage door in the narrow alley between the Palace Theatre and the Tattersall's Hotel with it's famed Marble Bar.

Blonde-haired Allan Shaw, known as 'The Emperor of Coins', emerged from the alley having finished a cigarette and returned to the backstage celebration. "There are a couple of young men out there who want to see you, Elsie!" he called out with a laugh.

"Oh, that must be my brother Walter and George Bretnall!" Elsie said, moving away from Nelstone and towards the door.

As she headed out, Nelstone called out: "Elsie, be careful!"

"Will you just leave her alone!" Amy Stirling snarled.

Arthur glared briefly at his assistant then started for the door in pursuit of Elsie.

"That is it!" screamed Amy. "I have had enough! You can find another person to be your dogsbody! Why don't you take her as your assistant? You are all over her as it is!"

The yelling had silenced the room and temporarily stopped Arthur.

Outside, Elsie had reached the bottom of the steps and heard the door close behind her. She peered through the half-light created by distant street lamps. She could make out a figure to her right, nearer Pitt Street. "Walter?"

The person, silhouetted in the lamplight kept coming closer. She grew increasingly unsure that it really was Walter—or even George.

"Miss Forrest!" the figure finally said, in an unfamiliar, slurred voice. "We've been waiting for you! We want to take you up on your proposition, in your song!"

We? thought Elsie, as she swung around only to see another man appear behind her, cutting out her retreat back up the stairs to safety.

As she turned back again, the first figure reached out and grabbed her roughly, pulling her towards him. She kicked out with her right knee, catching him in the groin. As he exhaled with a groan, his alcohol-fuelled breath suffocated the evening air.

The man behind then dragged her away and was pushing her towards the theatre wall, when the backstage door opened.

Arthur Nelstone's head was still spinning from the verbal assault he had just received from Miss Stirling, so he took a few seconds to register what he saw in the alley below.

"Leave her alone!" he shouted, as he rushed to Elsie's defence.

Elsie's first assailant, still cowering from the pain in his groin, was in no shape to stand and fight, so shuffled off as quickly as he could in the direction of Pitt Street.

The second man pivoted and swung a fist at the fast-approaching Nelstone, catching him fair in the face, before racing off after his friend.

"Arthur, are you all right?" Elsie gasped, as Nelstone struggled to stay on his feet.

By now, Charles Sweet and Allan Shaw, who had heard Nelstone's yell, even through the closed door, had reached the bottom of the steps.

Together they guided Elsie and the unsteady Nelstone back up and into the backstage area, where the mood had changed markedly in less than a minute, from celebration to concern.

Under the electric light, everyone could already see swelling around Nelstone's right eye. Elsie stayed by his side and held his hand as Josephine Gassman brought a towel, bowl and water to dab his face.

Lee and Rial stood together in urgent but whispered conversation. Their earlier misgivings—reflected they felt in the incident that had just occurred outside—as well as Miss Stirling's flight, necessitated change to the program. Exactly what, would be determined by a meeting the next morning.

At 10 am the following day, Elsie was summoned to meet with Lee, Rial and a still sore Nelstone in a backstage room.

Lee started by acknowledging that Amy Stirling had quit the company, and as a result, Arthur had no assistant. Additionally, the audience reaction to 'Snugglepoke' and the subsequent fracas involving Elsie and Arthur, had caused him and James considerable concern.

Elsie immediately thought she knew what was about to be proposed, and after the feeling of elation that followed her solo debut the previous evening, this was not exactly where she wanted her career path to lead.

"Couldn't Agnes Mahr take over the assistant role, just as she did in the days before Miss Stirling arrived?" Elsie asked.

"Agnes has most reluctantly agreed to fill in, but only temporarily," Mr Lee said. "As you know, she has been a longstanding member of this company and an exceptional dancer and solo performer. As such, we have agreed that she will assist for the next two nights, but that you, Elsie, should take over the assistant's role from Friday the 11th of October."

Sometimes, even the inevitability of a situation does not make bearing it more palatable, Elsie thought, feeling deflated.

Silence enveloped the room for a few moments as everyone felt the awkwardness of their own position. Finally, it was James Rial who broke the impasse.

"Elsie, you were just fantastic last night, we all know that—and we were all so darn proud of you! You worked the audience real well and you are a terrific talent. 'Snugglepoke' is a great and catchy song, but it encourages the sort of reaction that does not fit with this company. We cannot afford to take that sort of risk again—but we do want you to stay in this troupe."

Elsie's head dropped, so Rial moved in close to her and put a hand comfortingly on her shoulder, then added: "You have to remember that you are just eighteen, still a young 'un, and Arthur is thirty-one, and the best in the world at what he does. There is no finer comic dancer. It is absolutely no disgrace to be partnered with Arthur Nelstone!"

"Elsie," Arthur said, looking her straight in the eye. "From the moment I first saw you, I realised that you were more than just a pretty face, luv! You can dance and sing, but most of all you are smart—and have a sense of humour."

"But I have never partnered a one-eyed English Dalmatian guard dog before!" Elsie said, reaching to give Arthur a thank-you hug.

"See!" Arthur cried, as he held her at arms length and started shaking her. "You have a rare ability to ad lib! You and I will practise for the next two days, then on Friday night we pair up.

We will do 'The Animated Doll' and other interplay together."

"Alas, I never could resist a hero!" Elsie said, pretending to bang her head against Nelstone's chest.

"Elsie! We are going to be a truly smashing team!"

Lee and Rial looked at each other with a sense of relief. They had thought this process was going to be far harder than it had turned out to be.

And so it was, that on the evening of 11 October 1901, the pairing of Arthur Nelstone and Elsie Forrest made its successful debut as part of Lee & Rial's World's Entertainers, at the Palace Theatre in Sydney.

Chapter 13

The Luncheon

Life's a luncheon spread and more, across a table wide
The more you taste of difference, the less you wish to hide
Rejoice in mix and ample choice, refuse—and feel the pain
A narrow mind and shallow heart, can never feast again.

In the middle of October 1901, just after Elsie had teamed up with Arthur, Henry Lee announced to the assembled company that they would be moving in a fortnight to Adelaide and later Melbourne. As the Sydney season had been such a success, they would in all likelihood, return in three to four months.

For most performers, this was just another cycle on the performance treadmill; however, for the Thompsons, this was a time—inevitable though it was—that they had dreaded.

Mary Ann well knew that James did not want her to leave him once again for an extended period, as she had done when *A Message From Mars* had headed north to Queensland.

For her part, Mary Ann was adamant that Elsie, who was still just eighteen, must have a chaperone if she was to stay in places beyond her motherly care.

This chaperone needed to be a woman who could be trusted. If Elsie liked her, that would be a pleasing bonus.

"I want you to tell us who you think such a chaperone might be. Your father has kindly agreed that she should be remunerated for the task."

Such a prospect had not occurred to Elsie and she had mixed feelings about not having her mother with her. She would be without the support she had always known, but on the other hand, she knew there would, most likely, be fewer constraints.

Elsie did not need to think for very long. "Josephine Gassman!" she said with excitement.

"What? The Negress?" Mary Ann said in surprise.

Elsie noticed her father raise an eyebrow—though only briefly. What she could not have perceived were the lewd images of Southern whorehouse practices that momentarily flooded his mind until they were washed away by the guilt of a very religious upbringing.

"Are you absolutely sure, princess?" he asked, after a short delay for self-flagellation, that Elsie interpreted as serious questioning of her chosen option.

"Oh, absolutely sure, Father!" Elsie blurted out with such enthusiasm, that both her parents wondered if there was not indeed some illicit liaison already afoot.

"Well, that being the case, I shall be writing to Josephine Gassman—and Arthur Nelstone, separately—to request their presence at a special farewell luncheon we will host."

"Father, Bill and Irene must come too!" Elsie added.

"Who are Bill and Irene?" James queried, concerned that his generosity was being stretched.

"They are the piccaninnies, Josephine's children!"

"Oh well, I suppose they must be included. There isn't anyone else, I trust?"

"Only Grunter!"

"Grunter?"

"Grunter is the pet pig that appears with Josephine and the piccaninnies. Remember?"

"Now, Elsie, I am not going to pay for a pig to attend one of Sydney's better eateries!"

Elsie thought about asking him if it would be a case of 'too many snouts in the trough', but wisely withheld her humour. It was best, she thought, that her parents did not see too much delight with a chaperone option that excluded her mother.

"I will miss you, Mumsie!" she said to cover her tracks. "But where are we going for lunch?"

"It will not be anything too formal, just a relaxed meal," James insisted. "Your mother and I think the Refreshment Room at the Botanic Gardens would be nice. They always have a few tables they set aside."

The near midday sun of Sunday 27 October flickered through the varied vegetation that lined and overhung the curving paths of the Sydney Botanic Gardens.

These gardens had always been a special place to Elsie, and somewhere her parents had often brought Walter and herself since their very early childhood.

They had rolled down grassed slopes, tossed acorns into ponds and played hide 'n' seek amidst the trunks and boughs of a great variety of nature's ornaments. She had grown to love every visit to this oasis of tranquillity that lay close to the heart of Australia's first city.

"I have booked a table for seven," James said to the attendant at the Refreshment Room door. "The name is Thompson."

"Yes sir, the table in the far corner. The waiter will be with you shortly."

Elsie studied the table setting and wondered where she should sit, then wisely thought she should station herself next to her mother until the others arrived.

She had barely taken a seat, when she noticed a figure darting backwards and forwards from the trees to the glass of the arched windows. How very odd, she thought at first, then quickly recognised the individual. "It's Arthur!" she cried.

A few moments later the attendant was pointing him in their direction.

"Oh, it can be so very hard to get the audience's attention!" Arthur Nelstone said, still panting hard from his outside exertions. "You must be Mr Thompson, sir!"

"Please, just call me James, Mr Nelstone!"

"And me, Arthur!" came the response with a laugh.

"You must be Elsie's mother, madam!" Nelstone said, reaching out a hand. "It is a great pleasure to meet you too!"

Realising that Nelstone was at this moment alone with her family, Mary Ann tried to make the most of this brief opportunity. "Mr Nelstone, I must insist that all your dealings with my daughter are entirely honourable!"

"Oh, Mrs Thompson, I wouldn't even know the meaning of the word 'dishonourable' let alone how to spell it!" Nelstone quipped with a smile, though this did not exactly assuage Mary Ann's fears.

"This is a serious matter, Mr Nelstone! My daughter is only eighteen!"

Arthur was about to offer words of comfort when a commotion erupted at the entrance. The attendant could be clearly heard saying: "No! No Abos allowed in here! Out you go!" as he herded two young children and a woman, back out the door.

"Father! It is Josephine and the children!" Elsie appealed, but James was already on his feet and moving with a speed and determination towards the attendant, the like of which Elsie had rarely seen.

"Excuse me, young man! These people are my guests!"

"Sorry sir, but we have our rules. No Abos allowed in the premises!"

"They are not Abos, as you call Aboriginal people. They are American Negroes, and I repeat, they are my guests!"

By this stage, the ruckus had attracted the attention of the manager, to whom James turned. "My name is James Thompson. I am a justice of the peace and the Returning Officer for Lang Division. This woman and her children are Americans and are my personal guests. If you refuse them entry I shall take my party and custom elsewhere and ensure that the papers are made aware of this matter and that your establishment is prosecuted with the full force of the law!"

"Ah … look … let me apologise, Mr Thompson," the manager stuttered, while pulling the attendant away from the doorway. "We don't see many niggers in these parts! Please, come in madam!"

Josephine and the children entered hesitantly and it took quite a few hugs from Elsie for them to settle and seem, ostensibly at least, to put the incident behind them.

After the food arrived, accompanied by some drink, Josephine was quick to expound on her relationship with Elsie: "She be my friend, and lord knows we Negroes ain't got too many friends!"

The earlier incident, while a case of mistaken identity, had clearly touched a raw nerve and made Josephine just a bit more talkative in her nervousness, than she otherwise would have been.

"Elsie helps look after the children and I help look after her! Specially when you are around, you naughty Englishman!" Josephine said, wagging an admonishing finger at Arthur, who was going red in the face trying to think of what he had done to justify the 'naughty' tag. He had mentally exhausted virtually every possibility of deviancy when Josephine added to his great relief: "Nah, only joshin'! Miss Elsie ain't got a bad bone in her body, Mrs Thompson! And I can tell you, Mr Nelstone, that she has a nice body too! … Woops, oh my, I'm sorry—forgot my company!" Josephine said with a nervous laugh.

Just as Mary Ann was becoming a little confused as to whether she could really entrust Elsie's care to both Josephine and Arthur, she received a reassuring pat on the hand from James. He seemed to read her mind. "It will be all right, Cissie! It will be all right!" he whispered.

When Elsie lent over and helped the children by cutting up their meat into bite-sized pieces, it was plain to everyone how much they and their mother welcomed Elsie's presence.

The rest of the luncheon passed without incident and at its conclusion, the parting of ways was accompanied by firm handshakes, hugs, kisses and assurances. The Thompsons appreciated that they were farewelling the closest family Elsie would have over the next few months.

While strolling west and homeward, through the winding pathways of the Botanic Gardens, James, noticing that Elsie had moved a few paces ahead, whispered to Mary Ann: "Let go Cissie, you have to learn to let go."

Chapter 14

The Matinee Idols

*It takes a bit to shine a bit, amid a youthful group
A little bit of laughter, and involvement by the troupe
Reach out and offer welcoming, to each and every hand
And be repaid with faithfulness, where idleness won't stand.*

On the last day of October 1901, the southbound train carrying World's Entertainers, pulled into the New South Wales regional city of Goulburn. Their first performance outside Sydney would be that night at the city's Oldfellows' Hall, in front of a crowded house. It was an early start the next morning, as the train headed for Melbourne, then west to South Australia.

On Saturday 2 November, World's Entertainers opened its season at Adelaide's Theatre Royal before another packed audience.

Publicity circulated to the local newspapers, described Arthur Nelstone as a 'versatile comedian and grotesque dancer', something he was keen to exaggerate at ever opportunity. As his assistant and performing partner, Elsie was at times caught between playing the perfect nymph-like foil and the desire to follow Arthur down his path of exuberant craziness.

To Arthur, Elsie and the other twenty-five performers who made up World's Entertainers—as, no doubt with stage performers anywhere—the most important thing was the crowd reaction on the night.

However, each and every one of them would have been lying if they said that they did not care what theatre critics wrote about their exertions.

The critics ranged across a spectrum. The bookend on one side was the 'Theatre Mole', who would praise any and every performer, irrespective of true quality. The Mole's sole focus was to maintain and if possible increase the patronisation of the craft and its hosting establishments.

The great tragedy of the Mole's analysis was that, once having been identified as such, a critic's assessment contained so little in terms of comparative merit, that it was rendered as useful as the material churned out by each company's publicist.

At the other extreme, was the 'Historical Cynic', for whom nothing and nobody lived up to expectation.

If anything was cast in stone, it was that the Cynic's verdict was as unreliable as the Theatre Mole's, though it was obvious which one a performer would wish to read.

Thankfully, most theatre reviewers sat between these two extremes, though they did so, often under a pseudonym: 'The Watcher', 'The Dress Circler', the bland 'Theatre Critic', and even 'Lear's Whore'.

Rarely was the writer personally identified, which was not surprising given the sensitivities within the theatre industry.

On occasion, a Monday-published review of a Saturday opening night performance only carried the bare minimum of headline, such as the venue, with no by-line. This was the case with the one titled 'Theatre Royal' that appeared on page seven of Adelaide's *The Advertiser* on Monday 4 November 1901.

Frances Gwynne was the first to grab a copy of the paper as the company decamped from breakfast to the lounge of Hindley Street's Adelaide Hotel.

"Oh, listen to this!" she cried, as others jostled to read over her shoulder:

> Somewhat of a new departure was made at the Theatre Royal on Saturday evening, when the "World's Entertainers", an American vaudeville company, under the direction of Messers. Henry Lee and J. G. Rial, made their first appearance in Adelaide. Much was expected of the company, in consequence of the high reputation that had preceded them, and the fact that they just completed a phenomenally successful season of twelve weeks at Palace Theatre in Sydney. Great as were the expectations, however, they were fully realised, and the boast that the combination is composed entirely of "star" artists was amply justified ...

Frances scanned down the page looking for her name, then hesitated as she quickly checked that the comments were 'suitable' for broadcast. "Here we are!" she called, above the murmur and tangle of inquisitive heads:

> ... Miss Frances Gwynne, a tall and graceful young lady, also won a hearty welcome in her illustrated songs, "The Roses" and "By the Silvery Rio Grande." As the vocalist, who has a soprano voice of excellent quality ...

And here Frances put great emphasis on the words 'excellent quality'. She continued:

> ... sang the songs, a series of beautiful and appropriate pictures were thrown on a screen, the effect being both novel and striking ...

Henry Lee and James Rial sat back in lounge chairs away from the excited throng, like doting grandparents. Unbeknown to others, they had already made themselves familiar with the article, having instructed hotel management to deliver *The Advertiser* early to their rooms.

It was at this time that Elsie glanced at them, noticing James leaning forward to Henry and clearly making a suggestion, to which Henry first shrugged his shoulders, then thought for a moment before nodding repeatedly.

Elsie had no idea what the matter was, but she was to find out soon enough.

For now, Elsie sat back with Arthur. He was never one to rush to see the latest review—though it was not because he did not care—more, that perhaps he cared too much.

In her time with the company, Elsie had realised that while it was easy to presume that comedians were the happiest of people, the opposite was much more likely to be true. She had known from her school days that the class joker was often the child with the saddest home life and would use every opportunity to bring laughter and peer acceptance into their world. Now, she too, as in part a comedienne, had joined this cavalcade of clowns.

"Arthur!" Agnes Mahr called from the newspaper huddle. "You've been given some bouquets!:

... Mr Arthur Nelstone, an eccentric and original comedian, who introduced himself in song as "The howling millionaire," sent the audience into convulsions of laughter. His grotesque dancing, his rapid and excruciatingly funny "patter," and his diverting by-play, speedily placed him en rapport with the audience who greeted his witty sallies with uncontrollable merriment ...

Elsie could see that Arthur was pleased with the review so far and gave him a hug as he jostled her hair and said: "You were great too, Sis—you were great too!" Agnes meanwhile, continued reading:

... Mr Nelstone, who was assisted by Miss Elsie Forrest, is certain to become a great favourite during his stay in Adelaide, and deservedly so, for his entertainment is exceedingly bright and clever ...

Arthur could feel Elsie's disappointment as she physically sagged next to him. "You were my star, Sis!" he muttered, as he stroked her neck.

In the press, she had only been mentioned in passing, though as she well knew, she was not the true star of the pairing. *Ah, the trials of a performer,* she thought to herself. *You feel either crowned with a wreath of laurels, or stabbed in the heart with a dagger!*

Just as she was wallowing in a well of self-pity, Josephine called to her: "Miss Elsie! Mr Henry wants me and the children to host a reception for the audience after the 2.30 pm matinee on Wednesday."

"And you would like me to help? Of course I will!" Elsie said, suddenly forgetting the newspaper review. "In fact, you speaking to me, is a good reminder that I must send a postcard to my parents!"

With that she was off to the hotel's reception desk where she bought a postcard of the hotel and wrote:

Dearest Mother and Father,

Adelaide is a quiet and pleasant place where we have all been very well received. Adelaide Hotel is in Hindley Street and not far from our Theatre

Matinee shows always had a different feel to the standard evening performances. The preponderance of children inevitably led to certain parts being received with greater audience response than others.

Like all the performers, Elsie was eager to receive and reinforce any audience response—and she knew children liked the dramatic and unexpected.

As a large group, children were outgoing and raucous, but individually, each was often quite a different sort of beast.

And so it was, at the conclusion of the Wednesday matinee. Mothers and their children spilled out into the Theatre Royal foyer, to be greeted by tables of drinks and cakes with only Elsie, Josephine and her two little piccaninnies 'blocking' the way.

The chatter quickly died as the two groups faced each other in a most uncomfortable silent standoff, given they were supposed to mingle enthusiastically.

Eventually, it was an older girl who broke the impasse, reaching forward and rubbing four-year-old Bill's face in a bid to remove the boot polish she felt certain hid a disguised truth.

Instantly, Elsie knew she had to react. The whole purpose of the exercise had been to expose the children of 'small-town' Australia and its prejudices to the culture of the American Negro—and right now it did not seem to be working.

"Billy!" Elsie called, reaching forward and grabbing his left hand. "Hold on to my waist!"

With Bill in tow and five-year-old Irene quick to join in, the Elsie-led conga line started to dance its way through the foyer, picking up participants from the local juvenile population as it went.

Elsie deliberately twisted and turned, forcing those behind to follow, raising squeals and laughter and encouraging others to join. By the time she returned to where she had started, the atmosphere in the foyer had changed completely.

"Billy! Peel off to the end!" Elsie ordered, as one by one those holding Elsie's waist momentarily peeled off to join the end of an ever-lengthening line.

Next, Elsie zigzagged through the line of tables causing chaos for the waiters trying to stock the refreshments. As she did so, Elsie looked up to see that Josephine was talking to a group of mothers. *A couple of more circuits,* she said to herself.

After the children had tucked into the drinks and cake, Josephine thought it was safe to retrieve Grunter, the pig, from the care of a stagehand at the rear of the stage, and introduce him personally to his many young admirers.

The belated but welcome success of the post-matinee interaction was not lost on Henry Lee when he rose to address the company at lunch the next day. "Unaccustomed as you know I am to speaking," he started to the accompaniment of guffaws. "Seriously," he continued, "most seriously, I must, on behalf of my commercial 'pardner' James and my good and modest self, thank all of you for all the darn good work you have done to make Lee & Rial's World's Entertainers the great popular and commercial success it has been over these past few months."

His audience had quietened considerably, as each realised they had not heard Henry speak quite like this before.

"The full houses we have continually enjoyed have been both a great motivation for us all, as well as a boon to our finances, as our treasurer, Mr Broun, will attest. You are all under individual contracts, however, both James and I believe that we should share some of our providence collectively. To such an end, we have had confirmation that Melbourne's finest hotel, The Grand, can accommodate us all for as long as we perform in Melbourne—and shall do so at our expense!"

A hum of excitement and appreciation spread around the tables.

"Excuse me, sir!" Fitzroy Tobin, part of the master musician pairing 'The Tobins' with his wife Lotta, interrupted: "When are we due to depart for Melbourne?"

"Our current thinking is a few days after we close here at the end of next week, Fitzroy. All things going well, we anticipate being in Melbourne till at least Yuletide."

"What is Yuletide?" whispered Elsie to Josephine, sensing it was might be an Americanism.

"Christmas, Miss Elsie! What you folk call the Christmas season!" she responded, just happy she could help Elsie out for once.

"Thereafter, most likely, we shall be back in Sydney," Henry added.

"Will there be any change to the performing list?" asked the English-born Victor Kelly, part of the popular Kelly and Ashby acrobatic combination.

"So funny you should ask, Victor. We were considering leaving behind a certain Kelly and Ashby duo in Adelaide, but we realised you would miss us all, way too much!" Henry teased to general amusement.

When the schedule was confirmed, Elsie bought a postcard of Adelaide's William Light Square and wrote to Emma:

Dearest Em,

Our final performance here in Adelaide is on Saturday 16 November. All is going well and Arthur and I are working on new pieces. We open in Melbourne at the Bijou Theatre in Bourke Street a week later. Henry and James are paying for us all to stay at Melbourne's finest hotel— The Grand, in Spring Street!!!! Should be ~~grand~~ great! Tell mother and father we are likely in Melbourne past Christmas.

Love to all,
El XXXOOO

Chapter 15

The Grand

A building soaring gracefully, with rich and regal lines
With polished brass and crystal glass, and porter dressed to 'nines'
High teas with the bee's knees—all class, you understand ...
We were heading into Spring Street, and its icon called The Grand.

The Adelaide Express train pulled in to the relative chaos of Melbourne's Spencer Street Station, just about on its early afternoon scheduled arrival time.

Having been well rested in sleeping cars during their overnight journey, the World's Entertainers were keen to disembark and prepare for the next leg of their Australian tour.

The platform was already buzzing with passengers alighting by the time Henry Lee and a porter, wearing a jacket with Grand Hotel emblazoned on its pocket, made contact.

Not only were the members of the troupe and their private luggage to be transported, but also a whole train wagon full of costumes, props and scenery—none of which hotel management had, evidently, anticipated.

It was soon obvious to everyone that the three large covered and logoed Grand Hotel drays were totally insufficient to satisfy transportation requirements, something that infuriated Lee, who clashed publicly with troupe General Manager, James Love—in full view of a growing audience on the station platform—over what he termed 'a lack of basic planning and simple foresight'.

It was to be an omen for times ahead, though at that stage, nobody could have foreseen the troubles that lay in wait, especially given the atmosphere of bonhomie and generosity that had established their rendezvous with The Grand.

After some heated discussion, it was agreed that the troupe and its private luggage was the priority and that the balance from the goods wagon would have to wait for later loading by station attendants onto separate drays.

Elsie and most of the company caught their first good glimpse of a most impressive Melbourne city centre, as the drays crossed the city from west to east.

More ordered and imposing than Sydney, were Elsie's first thoughts, while Bill and Irene were more focussed on peering south to catch occasional glimpses of the Yarra River, as they held on to the open-mesh cage that was Grunter's travel home.

The pig seemed content with Bill and Irene close, even more so when they offered occasional scraps of fruit and vegetables, with apple his current favourite.

The days when Irene could comfortably pick up and carry Grunter had now passed and his cage had been modified with a handle on each side, so the children could share the load.

As the drays pulled up in front of the hotel in Spring Street, all could see the large, bearded and partly balding gentleman in a dark suit and tie, who stood dominatingly in the middle of a truly grand hotel entrance.

Above him were a pair of beautifully carved reclining figures: Plenty (a male) and Peace (a female) holding the respective shields of the Victorian and British Coat of Arms. The words 'The Grand' were emblazoned immediately below.

The troupe spilled out of the drays and collected reverently with their luggage on the ground before the entrance steps.

Henry Lee was the one to break ranks, moving cautiously forward and offering a hand upward to the large figure, standing imperiously at the top of steps.

There was something about the man that caused even Henry to baulk at joining him.

Instead, he remained two steps below the top, his hand still outstretched. Cautiously, the figure reciprocated and they quietly exchanged pleasantries, before Henry stepped back 'into line'.

The man at the entrance slowly and very deliberately scanned the group in front of him from his left to right, where his critical gaze fell upon Grunter.

"Henry! I was not informed about THAT!" his index figure pointing derisively at Grunter, who was chewing away on a slice of apple Bill had provided, oblivious to his sudden notoriety.

Henry wheeled around to briefly glare at Love, whose responsibility it was to communicate such matters, then realised, as 'head prefect', that he would have to take at least the initial rap.

"He is our performing pig … sir …" Henry muttered, shocked at his own sudden and most uncharacteristic subservience.

'Sir' meanwhile, had signalled to one of the porters. "Take it around the back to the stables. It can be kept with the horses!"

The porter wrested the cage and Grunter from the protesting children's grasp and hurried him away to their right up Spring Street, not daring to stain the hotel's foyer and its elite patrons with his cargo's presence.

With Grunter's departure, everybody's attention shifted back to the figure in front of them.

"Welcome to The Grand! My name is William H Burgess and I am the manager of this establishment," he said, somehow managing to replace the scowl with the hint of a smile. His audience, hung on to its promise, much as a gladiator greets another sunrise.

"You may have noticed the large building diagonally across Spring Street," he continued, gesturing over the group to everyone's right. "That is the Commonwealth parliament building, where the members of our recently elected first Federal Parliament meet. I am proud to say that many of those honourable gentlemen frequent this establishment. Please follow me inside to the hotel foyer where I shall introduce you to your new home."

With that he pivoted with an aplomb of which Arthur Nelstone would have been proud, and headed inward. World's Entertainers followed with a mix of great anticipation, excitement and particularly awe, as they arrived in the cavernous foyer of the hotel.

"Impressive, isn't it! It's no wonder that we call it The Grand!" Mr Burgess boasted, following up on the inevitable 'oohs' and 'aahs'.

Elsie had already seen the words 'Grand Hotel' featured above the building's fourth floor, then, just before entering, the words 'The Grand' above that imposing entrance. She had then spied the words 'The Grand Hotel' on the notepad on the reception counter. *Does this establishment have a minor identity crisis?*

Meanwhile, Mr Burgess had continued, though in a much quieter voice, now that he had everyone's attention again: "I would ask all of you to respect the privacy and tranquillity of all your fellow guests." Turning to stare pointedly at Bill and Irene, he added: "And there is to be no running or shouting inside the hotel!"

Seeing that the children appeared to fully understand (though Bill and Irene merely held Elsie and their mother's hand, respectively, even more tightly), he continued: "Please leave your baggage over here to my left and your right, next to the luggage room. We shall be back here after a short tour."

Mr Burgess waited until all the bags were where he wanted them and everybody was focussed on his next word. Elsie felt this 'schoolmaster' was more a puppeteer than an educator, though, like everyone else, she followed his direction.

"If you were to venture along to your right, you will see a hairdresser, a tobacconist, a dentist and finally a chemist to the right of the entrance door. Further along the inside corridor, you will find the café and men's smoking room. Over here to your left, is something quite different. If you would all come this way," he motioned, walking a few paces to the left of the lobby and past the base of the grand staircase and a dark metal structure.

"Oh, my!" Elsie exclaimed as she looked ahead and beheld an exotic lounge area.

As if on cue, Mr Burgess chimed in: "Our spectacular Moorish lounge is available to guests whenever they choose to relax and enjoy its luxurious couches and chairs."

While most of the group followed Mr Burgess back towards the lobby, Elsie burst into verse in admiration for the Moorish scene:

> And we, that now make merry in the Room
> They left, and Summer dresses in new bloom,
>   Ourselves must we beneath the Couch of Earth
> Descend—ourselves to make a Couch—for whom ?

The puzzled look from Josephine was always going to elicit a response.

"Quatrain 23, *Rubáiyát of Omar Khayyám*," Elsie said with a smile.

The now recognisable boom of Mr Burgess' voice had already begun to filter back from the lobby, so the four made haste to join their colleagues.

"So, if you should need, we have specific luggage as well as mail and telegraph rooms located opposite the reception desk. Follow me, please!" he ordered as he strode straight ahead and past the reception desk to a pair of grand doors. He opened them to much admiration from those who followed, as they scanned the extended vista. Already laid dining tables sat immaculately beneath chandeliers that hung from a sequence of large coloured glass ceiling domes that ran down the spine of the room. A trio of arched stained-glass windows highlighted each distant end. The room was flanked by arched doorways and hung with luxurious curtaining.

"I give you our grand ballroom, more commonly used as the grand dining hall, ladies and gentleman!" Then he added, without a hint of apology and looking straight at Bill and Irene: "It is hotel policy that all children are fed by nurses in the children's dining room to the side!"

Elsie and Josephine looked at each other, both now wondering whether The Grand was such a good option.

Meanwhile, Mr Burgess had pivoted and headed back to stop in front of a wrought-iron structure just around the corner from the grand staircase.

"Can I have four volunteers, please?"

Though there was no indication what they would be volunteering for, World's Entertainers were an adventurous lot, so Gwynne, Ashby, Shaw and Sweet were selected from a larger group who raised their hands.

"Before I ask these four to step forward, I want you to note the bell-like buttons here on the ironwork frame: one, indicating 'up' and the other 'down'. When its button is pressed, at least one of the two new lifts is summoned from wherever it is in the hotel, to this very spot."

A whooshing sound could be heard as a lift came down from above. "When the lift has arrived and stopped, you merely slide across the metal screen and enter," he said, motioning the four volunteers to move inside. "Now close the screen and press the button with number one on it and we shall meet you at the first floor."

With that, the four disappeared in a vertical direction and Mr Burgess ushered everyone up the grand staircase to the first floor. By the time the rest of the group had scaled the steps, they were greeted by a rather smug-looking 'fabulous four', standing outside the lift well in the middle of the first floor's twelve-foot wide grand corridor.

From that moment on, there was no doubt about what anyone's preferred method of progression from one floor of The Grand to another was, though Mr Burgess did have a warning. "Naturally, children are never allowed to push any of the lift buttons or travel within the facility, alone!"

Mr Burgess walked south down the corridor with his flock in hot pursuit, until, with the wave of his hand, he bade them all to stop. Walking on, he peered around a door to his left, then, waved everyone closer. "This is the ladies' drawing room. Ladies, you may utilise the room at anytime. There is also a writing room next door."

Everyone stepped forward to peek in turn admiringly at the drawing room's luxuriously upholstered furniture, circular divan and elaborate ornamentation that crowded its expanse. "Oh, I love the piano!" was all Charles Sweet, 'The Musical Burglar', could say when he spied the white grand piano that sat invitingly open, near the window.

"Ladies only, sir!" the manager admonished.

"I shall just have to play you a tribute from a distance, Charles!" Agnes Mahr consoled.

"Oh, how very sweet!" quipped Allan Shaw, only to be greeted by a scowl from Charles who had spent years being tortured by his surname.

"Are you quite sure, Allan?" added Arthur Nelstone to groans.

"That is quite enough!" called Henry Lee. "Let's move along! We are all looking forward to our rooms, Mr Burgess!"

Mr Burgess wheeled the group around and back towards the staircase, and as he did, Elsie simply could not help herself. "We're heading leeward!" she cried.

What followed was a general mix of chuckles and calls of

"Oh, shut up!"

Mr Burgess halted at the foot of the stairs and pointed north down the grand corridor. "You will also find a library and reading room down this way. Please feel free to utilise them." As he had earlier sensed a slight impatience, that was given voice by Henry Lee's remark, he added: "Your rooms are not on this floor. The rooms here are suites and are mostly occupied by long-term tenants. We shall head up to the third floor, where your rooms are located."

As the group trudged up the flights of the grand staircase towards their new home, each made a mental note that they would be doing this upward staircase journey for the last time.

From the third floor grand corridor, they headed right and around the back to a much smaller corridor where the World's Entertainers' rooms lay.

Mr Burgess outlined the modern facilities in each room. "You will find you have both an electric button and a telephone. If you wish to summon a member of hotel staff to your room, press the electric button. If you wish to call a number outside this hotel, just lift the receiver. You will go through to a switchboard that will give you access to thousands of Central Melbourne subscribers. If you wish to speak to reception by telephone from anywhere in Melbourne, just ask the switchboard operator to connect you to number 695."

Almost apologetically, he continued: "Unfortunately, there are no private toilet facilities on this floor. However, there are large marble bathrooms at the end of the grand corridor, with the ladies' to this southern side and the men's to the north."

Turning back to the grand corridor, Mr Burgess then stood quite deliberately with his back to the lift and his large arms outstretched. "Now, if you would all head down the staircase and back to the lobby, you will find your room allocation and key at the reception desk. Both myself, and my staff are at your service—should we not anticipate, you need only ask. We all wish you a long and happy stay at The Grand!"

Maintaining his arms at their full extent, he walked forward, herding World's Entertainers like a flock of sheep down the grand staircase. As the last one started down, he pivoted, but could not resist a smile as he headed back towards the third floor lift.

However, unbeknown to Mr Burgess, the acrobat Richard Ashby had vaulted over the railing to the second floor and pressed both second floor lift 'down' buttons before the manager had reached those on the floor above.

It took quite some time before all the cast and support crew had journeyed down to the lobby via the lifts they had commandeered.

It took even longer before the lift door opened at the lobby, spewing forth a red-faced and frustrated Mr Burgess.

Chapter 16

The Next Animal Star

Grunter's size was beginning to be an issue. Though much loved by Bill and Irene, both Lee and Rial recognised that a replacement—or at least a stand-in—needed to be found. They gave Elsie two pounds and their blessing, to accompany Josephine and the children in the search for World's Entertainers' next animal star—as long as they were back by 4 pm.

Alfred, at The Grand's reception desk, was quick to indicate where their search should most likely start and end. "The Eastern Market is just around the corner, a short walk away down Bourke Street, where it joins Exhibition Street. It's a large stone building that looks wonderful from the outside, but it has struggled for years. There are a fair number of empty stalls and simply not the custom that the Queen Victoria Market has across town. If you ask me," Alfred added, leaning forward and whispering, "the terrible murder there just two years ago, did not help!"

"Terrible murder?" Elsie repeated in shock, then turning to check that Josephine and the children were still sitting some distance away on a couch in the lobby, whispered back: "What happened?"

"An astrologer savagely murdered another shopkeeper, who had ventured into his room. You would think he might have foreseen the matter! In any case, madam, there is a sizeable animals section on the Eastern Market's southern side. Just make sure anything you return with can stay in our stables!"

Outside the Market's stone edifice in Bourke Street, Elsie took a deep breath, for that side of Bourke Street had taken on an eerie complexion. There was no way she was going to relay the tale of the astrologer's escapade to Josephine and now she tried to forget about it herself.

Finding the Eastern Market building was not difficult, but selecting a potential animal star will be a challenge! Elsie reflected.

They entered through an archway to be greeted by the occasional empty shopfront and a central courtyard of scattered tables upon which sat various goods. In fact, there seemed to be something of everything, but one, in abundance—customers.

Consequently, many pairs of eyes followed them as they weaved their way through the tables. Elsie could feel their gazes fondle her approvingly, but treat Josephine with disdain, and the children, well, piccaninnies were all but unknown in this backwater.

As a bootmaker reached out to Elsie with a pair of boots, even she could smell the 'farmyard' through the leather.

"Miss Elsie!" cried Irene, pulling her forward.

"Bill and Irene! Just remember that the animal should choose you, not you choose them!" cautioned Elsie, though she smiled at the prospect of an upcoming animal encounter.

The children raced off to the straw-covered southern side of the building, with Josephine and Elsie ambling, though within protective visual reach.

As Bill and Irene picked their way through the area past calves, lambs and puppies, Elsie noticed that something seemed to be following Irene.

"Josi!" Elsie whispered. "See that rooster? It is staying at Irene's feet. Irene!" Elsie called out, gaining her attention. "Sit on the bench over there!" The others watched as the rooster happily followed Irene to the bench.

Irene looked down and laughed, then ran over to a barrel—and the rooster followed.

Irene reached down and stroked its orange and red chest. Surprisingly, the bird did not run away.

Josephine was about to say something when somebody grabbed the back of her dress.

"Oh, my!" she cried out, as she wheeled around to see two very large brown eyes and long eyelashes blinking at her playfully. It was a camel.

"These camels, madam, are the descendants of those that carried Bourke and Wills!" a man in dirty overalls, whose standard sales pitch, this clearly was, explained.

"Famous Australian explorers," Elsie whispered, as she knew that her friend was ignorant of most things antipodean. "Possible, I suppose, though I thought all the camels died on the expedition," she muttered to herself. Then she added out aloud: "What do you think of the rooster, Josi? It would be a lot easier to carry than Grunter!"

Josephine was about to ask Irene what she thought, but she noticed that her daughter was cradling the bird in her arms.

"Three pound for the rooster!" the farmyard salesman crowed confidently.

Before Josephine could say anything, Elsie jumped in: "Three pounds! That is outrageous! Come on children, we are going!"

With that Elsie reached for Irene's hand, forcing her to drop the rooster. She started to cry, but Elsie was firmly steering her away.

"Two pound then, madam!"

Elsie did not hesitate as she headed out of the farmyard area. "There are other farmyards in this city!"

Josephine was dumbfounded, as she had never seen Elsie behave like this.

"One pound then! A bargain at one pound!" pleaded the salesman, causing Elsie to suddenly stop.

"One pound, but only if you throw in that cage over there!" Elsie said, pointing to a beautiful iron piece she had admired earlier.

"But that cage, madam, is my best!"

"All right! Fine! Let's go children!" was Elsie's firm response, as she pulled a crying Irene further away towards the main northern entrance.

"But … oh, very well! One pound then for the rooster and the cage!" exhorted the salesman, desperate for a deal.

Elsie slowed then stopped, and as she turned past Josephine, her friend could swear that she winked.

"Irene! Go and pick up Mr … Rusty and put him in that cage over there."

The salesman was still mopping his brow when Elsie handed him a pound from her purse.

And that was how Rusty the Rooster joined World's Entertainers.

Chapter 17

The Ghosts of the Bijou

I am old but I am timeless, I am death upon the rise
And when you think you've seen me, I will drift into disguise
I will hasten in a hallway, I will glide on past a post
For I've seen a thousand past times, in my spectre as a ghost.

The telephone in Henry Lee's room rang just before 4 pm. It was answered almost instantly, as by now Lee had lost faith in James Love competently performing his role as general manager. He would show Love how things should be done.

The props, scenery and costumes that had been unloaded from the train wagon at Spencer Street Station, now sat compliantly in two drays outside The Grand.

"Tell them to wait for five minutes and we will all be down. We will go straight to the Bijou!" he told reception.

Putting the receiver down, he realised that he had not yet rung out. He picked up the receiver again and waited … there was a crackling sound, and then a faint female voice answered: "Central Telephone Exchange—number please?"

This was not what he was expecting. "Ah …" he said in frustration, as he searched fruitlessly through his pockets for the card of the manager of the Bijou Theatre. "Look, I don't know what the hell the number is! Just put me through to the Bijou Theatre!"

"How do you spell that, sir?"

"B I J O U!" Lee bellowed into the telephone.

There was a pause far longer than Lee was prepared to tolerate, so he interrupted the silence with: "What is the goddamn problem, woman?"

"Connecting you now, sir!" she said, just relieved to pass the rude American to another poor soul.

"Bijou Theatre, Jackson speaking."

"Phillip! It is Henry Lee—thank God I can speak to somebody with a brain bigger than a bee's! We are all in town now. Can we come over in the next half an hour with the props and scenery?"

"No problem at all, Henry! I will ask our caretaker, Mr Urquhart, to wait for you at the Bourke Street front entrance. You sound a trifle flustered."

"Yeah, only a trifle! Even if you tipped in this goddamn country, I would still be holding on to all my money!"

"I was half expecting James Love to make contact," Jackson said.

Lee hesitated for a moment, unsure that he should allow internal bickering to spill into the broader domain, though his pride got the better of him. "Well, you know the old saying: if you want things done properly, you do things yourself!"

Much scurrying and many more raised voices eventually resulted in a scene that might have been misconstrued for a funeral procession.

The two drays headed north on Spring Street, followed closely in their wake by World's Entertainers on foot. They then swung ninety degrees left on to Bourke Street and headed west towards the Bijou Theatre.

A gaunt-looking but smiling man in an ill-fitting suit stood respectfully under the central curved arch of the roof at the front of the Bijou, and when Lee approached, arm outstretched, the man reciprocated.

"Mr Urquhart, I presume?" Lee said, not doubting his greeter's identity.

"Samuel Urquhart, sir!" he qualified, as he scanned the group and waited. "If you would move in closer please, World's Entertainers."

Mr Urquhart waited, like an experienced actor, until he had everyone's attention.

"On behalf of Mr Jackson, the manager of the Bijou, I welcome you all to our special place—to the new Bijou Theatre!"

"What happened to the old one?" Frances Gwynne asked.

Mr Urquhart hesitated, before his eyes became wide and distant, as he seemed to look right through the group. Suddenly, he closed his eyes tightly, dropped his head and seemed to struggle with his emotions. For a few moments his lips moved but no sound came forth. Then, gradually, but painfully, he began: "She was a beauty ... old Bijou ... I was there ... a memory forever ... April 1889 ... poor Charles Williams fell thirty foot … terrible … it was too fierce … the fire … just terrible …"

The World's Entertainers stood there transfixed. For all their acting and performance training and experience, this was raw and real drama and emotion playing out before them.

"I tried … I did try my best!" he pleaded to his audience, as tears ran down his face.

Elsie bit her lip, trying to hold back her tears, while Arthur dug a thumbnail into a finger in a bid to control his own.

"Captain Parsons from the fire brigade … the wall fell … nothing could be done … their spirits are still here …"

"You mean it is haunted?" a voice from the back queried.

"Some say so … oh, dear! Oh, I am so sorry!" Mr Urquhart whimpered. "I have tried to forget about that night for so long!"

"Samuel!" Henry uttered, as he wrapped an ample arm around the caretaker. "We understand! All theatres have their histories, characters, stories and charm. Sometimes the walls seem to speak. Now, we have a job to do and need your guidance!"

"Of course, my sincerest apologies to one and all! Once inside, take the scenery to the left and costumes to the right."

As the troupe headed for the drays, James Love took a folded set of papers from his pocket and was opening it, when it was wrenched from his grasp by Henry Lee.

"I'll handle the checklist and get it done quickly and efficiently!" Lee barked. "You help with the unloading!"

Over the next hour, scenery was sorted and stored and costumes were checked, ordered and hung, in a process familiar to all the performers.

It was nearing 5.30 pm, when some of the troupe assembled on the stage to take in the view of the three levels of seating—dress circle above stalls and gallery above dress circle—that they first heard it—a clanging, though brief, like a dull ringing of a fire engine's bell. Then, it stopped before anyone had the chance to remark upon it, before reoccurring a few seconds later.

"There it is again!" said Josephine, her eyes wide as she turned to look backward and upward in the rough direction from where she felt the sound originated.

"Remember what Mr Urquhart said—the captain of the fire brigade, he died in the fire!" Agnes Mahr added, vocalising what nearly everyone else was thinking.

"Why, it surely be a warning to us!" Josephine muttered, the urgency in her voice bringing Elsie to her side to give an embrace and words of comfort.

"No, Josi, no! There must be a simple explanation for it," though at that moment, Elsie could think of none.

As the days passed, and their Melbourne opening on Saturday 23 November 1901, was nigh, Lee was as concerned and intense as the troupe had ever known him to be, that all should be perfect to ensure another sequence of packed houses.

On two further occasions, the clanging sound interrupted rehearsal and on the second, Lee, seeing what impact it was having on the troupe, reacted: "Damn you!" he cried, his arms stretching up towards the theatre's ceiling, and then the roof of the backstage area, in a gesture that seemed half threat and half appeal. "We come in peace to glorify this arena! We are on your side!"

The troupe around him was stunned and silent—and the silence held for perhaps ten seconds—till a mournful cry echoed through the theatre, causing screams from more than just the women present. Lee instantly knew he had a potential crisis with just one day before opening night.

"Down there!" Lee yelled, gesticulating towards the nearest empty seats. "I want everyone down there and sitting in that goddamn front row! Now! And that means EVERYONE! That means performers, backstage crew—EVERYONE!"

It took what seemed minutes for all to be seated and accounted for. Lee meanwhile was circling his prey, prowling backwards and forwards on the stage's edge, like a lion preparing to strike.

"All of you know that I respect your talent and abilities. Each one of you has stood up each and every night and delivered to audiences in towns and cities across this country. Each of you has played a crucial part in ensuring we play to packed houses, each and every night! Tomorrow night, and the next night and for the nights to come after, know that they will be no goddamn different! NOBODY and NOTHING will change that, because you are, and want to remain, the very best in our business!"

This was classic Henry Lee. For all their recent anxieties, the company responded as Lee had wished. At first in dribs and drabs, then universally, they applauded and rose to their feet.

"So, see," Lee continued, as he mopped sweat off his brow, "we are all together! Tomorrow, TOGETHER, we shall capture Melbourne!"

The euphoria that resulted from Lee's speech dissipated as the hours passed, and some began to worry if the Bijou Theatre itself might be a false sanctuary for their art.

Little did the Saturday 23 November audience realise that what might have seemed opening night nerves, was more apprehension at the possible reappearance of the ghost, or ghosts.

Still, the success of that opening night and the one after, seemed to have calmed things, though it was apparent to everyone at meal times, that not all was well.

"Have you noticed how James Love no longer sits at the Lee and Rial table?" Elsie said rhetorically to Arthur.

"Elsie! Shhhhh!" Arthur said, emphasising the point by placing a finger lightly against Elsie's lips. This only tempted Elsie to playfully bite him.

"Hey, watch out! I need them for the performance! Seriously, Sis, I have noticed that Love now sits with Kelly, Ashby and Miss Roberts, and if he wants to sit with the acrobats, well, that is his choice. But they don't pay our wage, Lee and Rial do. SO WE AIN'T GETTIN' INVOLVED—you understand?"

"Anyone care for today's paper? You can read about the real star of our show!" Charles Sweet said with a grin, as he tossed a copy of Monday's *Argus* onto the table in front of them, interrupting any possible response to Arthur's lecture.

Elsie had no trouble finding the article, as Charles had left it open at page six. Under the Bijou Theatre heading was the subtitle 'The World's Entertainers', followed by a review, which Elsie began to read out loud, selectively:

In a performance so uniformly meritorious it is difficult to
discriminate between the artists, but possibly Mr Charles
R Sweet, the musical burglar, scored the greatest of this
succession of successes ...

Elsie turned to look at a table to her right, and sure enough,
there was Charles, grinning at her like a melon minus a slice.
So, she read on:

... Mr Henry Lee's imitations of great men differed from
anything of the sort previously seen in Melbourne from the
facts that he conducts the whole of his changes and make
up in full view of the audience ...

Elsie looked up to check if Henry was following her recital,
but noticed that he was in deep conversation with James Rial,
so she continued:

... One of the most original turns was that of Miss Josephine
Gassman ...

Elsie paused. "Josi!" she called out, when she realised her
great friend was focussed on how her children were faring in
the neighbouring dining room. So she picked up the paper and
walked over and continued reading:

... Miss Josephine Gassman, a handsome 'yellar' girl,
as are read about in the southern states, and tiny little
children, coloured a shade or two darker. Miss Gassman
first rendered a couple of plantation songs, then across the
stage rushed the two tiny black figures, the youngest, a
child of about three, bearing a rooster in her arms ...

"Well, heck, I did promise Grunter the night off—just a pity
the paper missed him!" Josephine explained, as Elsie read on:

... The two piccaninnies afterwards did an imitation of a
cake walk, to the intense amusement of the audience, to
whom the novelty of a tiny mullato with rolling whites to
her eyes was a source of laughter itself ...

Elsie continued scanning the article as she moved back to her
table, then stopped in front of Arthur:

... Mr Arthur Nelstone, is a comic man of a sort different to
Mr Sweet and approximates closer to the English type ...

"That is because he bloody well is English!" interrupted
Arthur loudly to considerable laughter.

... The dialogue between him and Miss Elsie Forrest is
clever and amusing, and there is a series of original gags
and stage tricks that provoke laughter from the most blase
patrons of variety entertainment ...

It was a nice way to begin another week, though nobody
suspected what that night would have in store, in The Grand.

* * *

Not long after Elsie had rolled over to sleep on that Monday
night, she heard a squeaking sound from near her door. She
held her breath and listened, then turned around to face the
door.

There was another squeaking sound and Elsie switched on
the lamp next to her bed.

Looking through the semi-gloom, she could see that
something or somebody was turning the door handle. She
raced out of bed and rotated the key in the door lock, pushing
a hand and shoulder against the door as she did. She waited
and listened, but heard nothing, then walked backwards to her
bed, watching the handle as she went.

As she lay in bed, with the lamp light still on, she could
almost hear her heart pounding. She watched the door handle
and waited ... and waited ...

It must have been half an hour or more and she was starting
to dose off, when she heard a squeak again and the door handle
started to turn.

*It's all right! I have locked the door! But could a ghost pass through a
locked door? Oh! What would Emma do? Emma would stand up and
not be afraid! That is what she would do!*

With that, Elsie stepped out of bed and strode once more,
back to the door. She put one hand on the door handle and the

other on the key, took a deep breath, turned the key, and then the handle.

There was nothing and nobody immediately outside her door, so she looked down the dimly lit corridor to the right—nobody. Then left—and that is when she saw it: a white sheet was gliding down the corridor. She could just make out bare feet underneath.

She raced to Josephine's door and turned the handle, but the door was locked. Inside, Josephine was cowered in the corner of the room with both children in her arms, terrified.

Elsie turned to Arthur's door. She just had to tell somebody. The handle to his door turned and she pushed, and met with no resistance. "Arthur! Arthur!" she urged in as loud a whisper as she could muster.

Through the near darkness she could just make out his bed and a writhing, complaining figure that lay upon it. "No, no I am not going! … What? What? … Who is it?" he demanded, as he sat bolt upright. He fumbled for the light and squinted through its dazzle. "Elsie! Sis, what are you doing here?"

Elsie looked back at the open door and raced back to close it, then sat on Arthur's bed.

Arthur looked at her and marvelled at her beauty, just as he had on so many occasions before. Yet, at this moment she seemed more beautiful than ever, in just her nightdress, with her long dark hair and those beautiful, wide violet eyes.

"I saw it!" Elsie exclaimed. "The ghost, or something like it, in what looked like a sheet, and with bare feet!"

"Whoa, whoa … hold on! Where did you see this thing?"

"In the corridor!"

"Well, I am no expert, but I doubt ghosts go around under bed sheets and in bare feet!" He pulled Elsie towards him to comfort her. She lay there with her head on his shoulder as he ruffled her hair, realising with each successive stroke just how much he loved and wanted her.

For some minutes they remained there: Elsie most content to be within his protective embrace and Arthur marvelling at the intense warmth of her body—while also recalling his promise to her parents that he would look after her. After all, she was barely eighteen years old and he was a full thirteen years her senior.

"Sis, I think you should go back to your room now," he said, though not really wanting this time to end. "Here, I will take you back!"

As he rose, he hoped she had not noticed the erection that distorted the smooth line of his nightshirt.

He opened her door and switched on the light. "See, Sis, nothing and nobody! You will be fine. You can tell Henry in the morning!" With that he kissed her on the top of her head and she shuffled back to bed, before heading back to lock the door.

"Thank you, Arthur! You have been very sweet!" she called softly through the door.

She could just hear him reply: "You know where I am if you need me!" as she turned the key.

That night, both of them had difficulty sleeping, though for different reasons.

As World's Entertainers drifted down to breakfast, Elsie sought out Henry, who was talking with Charles Sweet.

"Mr Lee, sir, may I have a quick word with you?"

"Certainly, Elsie—don't tell me your door handle was turned in the night, as well?"

Elsie gasped. *So, there were others apart from me? I was not the only one?*

As if reading her mind, Henry added: "You are the third young lady to mention this to me this morning!"

"But Mr Lee, sir, there is something else," she said, turning to check that nobody else was listening. "I saw a figure in a white sheet, with bare feet!"

"Really? In a white sheet? That is very interesting! Charles! I think Elsie might have seen the culprit!"

"Yes, as you know it is dim in the hallway, but that is definitely what I saw!"

"We shall have to catch this son of a bitch, Charles, before he destroys this company!" Henry said, gnashing his teeth in anticipation of the pummelling he would hand out.

"Piano wire!" Charles whispered.

"What are you taking about, man?"

"We could use some of my spare roll, string it across the corridor and trip him up!"

Henry frowned, so Charles took him and Elsie aside.

"You see, Henry, Elsie's room is just across the corridor from mine. If we both tie the ends of a length of piano wire to the upper part of the leg of a chair in our rooms," he said demonstrating on a chair just where it should be tied, "then rotate the chair clockwise till the line is tight and … are you following me?"

"Ah, I think so," said Henry, still unsure.

"And sitting on the chair at the same time, while of course the wire passes through the small gap between the closed door and the wall—and then cabush! We have our trap! Now, what time did you see this 'ghost', Elsie?"

"It must have been near midnight."

"Yes, that is about what the others said, Charles."

"Hmmm," Charles thought for a moment. "We don't want to set it too early, nor too late—perhaps 11.15 pm will do. I will tap on your door at 10 past, Elsie and we can set our trap!"

"But I can't get out the door without standing up and unwinding the chair, once the trap is set!"

"Precisely! That is why Henry will be waiting to pounce as soon as our trap is successful!"

"I like that idea—I like it very much!" Henry enthused, thumping a fist into a palm.

And so, that night, the trap was set …

Elsie yawned as she sat on her chair against her door. The lack of sleep from the night before was taking its toll, and though she tried very, very hard, she was soon fast asleep.

The wrenching of her chair, the loud cry of "Ah, bloody hell!" and the crash of a body in the corridor outside, shook Elsie awake, though she could not be certain as to the sequence in which these occurred.

"Get him!" someone cried from outside, as Elsie turned the chair anticlockwise and opened her door to a chaotic scene in the dimly lit corridor.

A figure in a sheet was struggling to its feet, as men closed in from all sides to bring it down.

A right hook from Henry soon floored the 'ghost', as all prepared for the unveiling.

As Henry dragged the sheet away, there was an audible gasp from the assembled company.

"Victor Kelly! You son of a bitch!" Henry yelled as he laid in to Kelly, though he was restrained from inflicting serious injury by Rial and Shaw. "Of course! I should have realised!" Henry seethed. "Only an acrobat could have climbed up into the rafters of the Bijou!"

"Henry and I shall see you at 9 am in the office of the manager of The Grand!" Rial ordered, though unsure he wanted to involve Mr Burgess in proceedings.

At 9 am the next morning, a sorrowful and sore-looking Kelly, sporting facial bruising beyond a swollen jaw, struggled in to Mr Burgess' office, where his fate had already been sealed.

Burgess had wanted him thrown out of the establishment for being disruptive, while Lee had wanted him out of the company altogether, but as Rial cautioned, the trio of acrobats—Kelly, Ashby and Miss Roberts—were among the show's most popular acts, and a suitable replacement leading into the Christmas-New Year period would be difficult to find.

In the end, a compromise was reached and Ashby and Miss Roberts, as well as Kelly, were shifted from their comfortable rooms on the third floor, to the hotel's most cramped accommodation on the fourth. The punishment needed to be collective, for as Lee explained, the other acrobats must surely have known of his pranks.

As Kelly left the manager's office, head bowed, Lee turned to Rial and asked pointedly: "And who do you think now sits with those three at meal times?" The answer suggested that all their trials were not yet over.

* * *

Just before 3 pm on Wednesday 18 December 1901, the telephone rang in Elsie's room, shattering her afternoon nap. Nobody had ever called her before, so she struggled to respond appropriately, knocking the receiver off the telephone base and sending it whacking into the bedside table.

She squeezed her eyes tightly, shook her head and breathed deeply, before reaching down for the receiver that hung limply but was twisting slowly near the floor. "Oh, I am sorry ... is anyone there?"

"Reception here, Miss Forrest," came the reply. "We have a package for you!"

"A package? I shall be down in a couple of minutes."

Replacing the receiver more carefully than she had dislodged it, Elsie headed first to the washbasin, throwing water over her face, then, patting herself with a towel as she studied her still sleepy image in the mirror. "Pretty enough for a swine, perhaps, though Grunter has rejected me before!" she joked as she turned towards her door.

The lift was, even over four weeks into their stay in The Grand, a source of minor thrill. As she pressed the 'lobby' button, she wondered who might be sending her a package.

The answer was soon at hand, in the form of a long, firm but thin package tied up by string. On the front was Emma's unmistakable handwriting.

Elsie grabbed the package with greater enthusiasm than courtesy and headed straight to the Moorish lounge, finding it, thankfully, unoccupied.

Selecting a plush armchair in the corner, she plonked herself down beneath a hanging eastern lamp and a domed screen that bore an uncanny resemblance to the upper stage set of Sydney's Palace Theatre.

Having unknotted the string, she was most careful not to tear any of the paper where it bore her best friend's handwriting, as if it might bode ill for the fracturing of their close relationship.

Removing the paper, revealed a letter on top of a copy of a magazine called *The Million,* which was dated 12 December 1901. "But that is just last Wednesday!" Elsie exclaimed to herself in surprise, then turned her attention to Emma's letter:

Dearest El,

I am missing you very much, but was delighted to see this issue of The Million. You know how they always have photos of actors, actresses and performers on page 13 ... well you are there—at the top!

Elsie put the letter on a side-table and opened the magazine to page thirteen ... and there she was in a pose captured at Sydney's Talma Photographic Studios. Underneath the photograph were the words: 'Miss Elsie Forrest—With Lee and Rial's World's Entertainers'.

Elsie turned her head from side to side critiquing her smiling image. "Acceptable, I suppose," she said with a sigh, before turning her attention back to Emma's letter:

> *You will also notice that Mr Lee is down the bottom of the page ...*

She had not noticed, so turned back to the magazine, and sure enough, there was Henry, looking his severe and upright self, captioned: 'Mr Henry Lee—A star turn with and part proprietor of the World's Entertainers Show, now appearing with great success at the Bijou Theatre, Melbourne.'

> *I have heard a rumour on very good authority that your brother Walter has hung the large cover photo of Mademoiselle Cavalieri from the 28 November edition at his workplace, and what is more, has a photo of another famous French actress, Anna Held, in his bedroom! I must admit that both are very beautiful!*
>
> *Mama sends her love. I have been helping her as much as possible since Papa's death, while my brothers are working hard at managing the family transport business.*
>
> *We are all looking forward to seeing you back in Sydney—hopefully some time in the New Year.*
>
> *Lots of love,*
> *Em XOXOXO*

Elsie placed the copy of *The Million* carefully on the coffee table and curled up in the armchair with Emma's letter clasped to her breast. It was not easy as an eighteen-year-old, spending months that included Christmas away from her best friend and family. However, her maturity and natural pragmatism combined to help her appreciate that it was her professional family of performers who were her priority now.

Still, at that moment, only one person mattered, so Elsie turned over in the armchair, closed her eyes and pretended that she had her best friend with her, safe and warm within her embrace. She soon slipped off to sleep in the dream-like surrounds of the Moorish lounge.

* * *

When the telephone in Henry Lee's room rang just after 8 am on the morning of Thursday 26 December, it was not immediately answered. A few Christmas drinks from the day before had slowed his awakening and rendered him a little less than his normal coherent self.

"Who? … What? … Yes? …" was about as good as he could manage as a frustrated Phillip Jackson, the manager of the Bijou Theatre, tried to get his point across.

"Sing? … Well … we can all sing it!" Lee exclaimed, gradually dragging himself into reality. "Mr Love? Forget about him—I will handle everything!"

Before the morning's rehearsal at the Bijou, Lee gathered the whole cast and crew together for an urgent meeting.

"We will be having very important guests to our New Year's Eve performance next Tuesday night. Mr Jackson has informed me that Australia's Governor-General, Lord Hopetoun, together with his wife, Lady Hopetoun, will be in attendance. Additionally, it is quite possible that the Prime Minister, Edmund Barton, may choose to join His Excellency in the Bijou's royal box."

Lee paused, as he wanted the significance of the upcoming event to sink in.

"Irrespective, we shall all, as if we were a choral group, lead the singing of 'God Save The King' when the Governor-General arrives at 6.50 pm. We need to rehearse this singing, now, and then polish up our acts so that they are performed at your very best on Tuesday night!"

Tuesday 31 December 1901 at the Bijou, was always going to be a special night—and Henry Lee was determined that it should be the World's Entertainers finest night yet. The Bijou was packed, just as it had been each evening of their Melbourne shows. All the cast felt the tension build on this special evening as the curtain opened, after Henry Lee announced from the stage's edge: "Ladies and gentleman, boys and girls, would you please be upstanding for the entrance of the Governor-General, His Excellency, Lord Hopetoun and Lady Hopetoun!"

With that, the curtain opened to reveal the whole troupe on stage, awaiting a signal to acknowledge the official party's arrival in the royal box. Elsie caught a glimpse of the young Lord Hopetoun casting an approving eye over them, as the orchestra started the national anthem.

As the evening progressed, Henry Lee was even more flamboyant and creative than usual in his introduction of each act. Elsie was introduced as 'the lovingly luscious little lady from Liverpool, Sydney'—which she was not, well not from Liverpool—while Arthur was 'the laughingly lithe and leaping lunacy from Liverpool, England!'

With the show now close to its conclusion, Henry mopped his brow, but could not wipe the smile off his face, as he headed out past the stagehands putting the final touches to the trampoline-surfaced billiard table prop for the Kelly and Ashby acrobatic show.

"Ready!" called the lead stagehand and Henry nodded in response. Then he took a deep breath as he stepped through the curtains to introduce the final human act before the Projectoscope's pictures closed the show.

He paused, till he heard that the audience was hushed and focussed on him. He turned momentarily towards the royal box and noted that even there, eyes were looking at him. He smiled, strode to the middle of the edge of the stage and announced: "Ladies and gentleman, boys and girls! For our final human act tonight, I give you the courageous Kelly, the athletic Ashby and the reckless Roberts in their comedy acrobatic act!"

Henry shuffled sideways to his right, as his left arm remained raised towards the now open centre stage. He knew through months of performance that the pounding sound of Kelly's feet striking the stage floor, having just vaulted onto and then off the billiard table's spring-loaded surface, should have been heard as he had made his fifth sideways step ... but there was nothing—just silence, and a solitary billiard table.

"There are always twists when acrobats are involved!" Henry jokingly assured his audience, as the curtain closed. Hearing the pounding of running feet behind the now closed curtain, he was sure things were at last right to go. "Finally, they are ready. I give you the amazing acrobats: Kelly and Ashby!"

Henry could hear and feel the centre of the curtain shake behind him, briefly open a little and then close, as a breathless and anguished Agnes Mahr whispered just loudly enough from the other side of the curtain: "Mr Lee, sir. The acrobats and Mr Love, they have left the theatre!"

She need not have completed her sentence, for Henry had already realised just what was going on—he had been stood up.

Sweat instantly materialised on Henry's forehead and seeped from his hands, as his mouth, for once, hung open without emitting a sound and with breathing suspended. As he stood there, frozen, disquiet spread through the audience—and Henry's humiliation was complete.

The ghosts of the Bijou had taken their revenge.

Chapter 18

The Saviour

When you know him you will love him, and believe that you've struck oil
J.C.'s fame it is a vestige, of long days and nights of toil
While his knowledge is outstanding, his height suggests aloof
Yet the saviour of the theatre is a man who knows the truth.

"I saw one! I saw one!" Allan Shaw called out, as he scampered towards members of the troupe gathered in The Grand's lobby.

"Saw one what, Allan?" Rial queried.

"A horseless carriage! I had just turned into Bourke Street on my morning walk, and there it was!"

"Pardon me, for interrupting, sir!" Alfred called out from behind the reception desk. "Was the motor you speak of brown?"

"Ah … well I'll be a raccoon! Yes! Brown it was!" Shaw replied after initially struggling to recall.

"Then that would have been Mr Chandler, the hardware merchant, in his chain-driven petrol Tarrant!"

The whole group turned and looked at Alfred in surprise, and he was happy to bask in their admiration, shrugging his shoulders, smiling and then explaining: "You have to know such things if you work in this establishment! It seems it is all the members of parliament who stay here, talk about!" He paused, then seeing he still had everyone's attention, added: "If you want to see another motor, there is the steam-powered Thomson one. He always drives it from Armadale into the city each morning. I am reliably informed he leaves home at 9 o'clock and crosses Prince's Bridge outside Flinders Street Station around 9.15."

"Thompson with a 'p'?" asked Elsie.

This was not a question that Alfred had expected—vehicle specifications were his specialty, but spelling was not. He bit his lip momentarily before visualising a newspaper headline. "Without a 'p'—definitely without a 'p'!"

"And what colour is the car, Alfred?"

"Green, Miss Forrest," he answered with some hesitation,

unsure why a young woman should ever be interested in such a manly pursuit.

"Quick, Arthur! We can get a hansom cab to the station and catch a glimpse!" Elsie called out as she headed for The Grand's front door.

"But we have rehearsals at 9.30! It is … already 9.04!" Arthur pleaded, after glancing at his fob watch. However, he quickly realised his protestation was useless and followed Elsie out the door.

They reached Flinders Street Station at 9.13—according to the station clock.

For quite a while, Elsie peered intently down the length of Prince's Bridge towards the constant variety of transportation that emerged from St Kilda Road. They seemed to rise into view on the bridge's surface like an understage platform being raised to prominence: horse-drawn carts and trolley buses of all descriptions, even a tram running on the rails, but no green motor.

"Oh, Elsie, come on! It is already 9.20 and Alfred said that green thing goes past around 9.15!"

"Perhaps he is running late!" she responded defiantly.

"Perhaps he was running early and we have missed him!"

Elsie gave him a look that needed no words to interpret. This young lady was not for turning. He held off for a few minutes till in absolute desperation he tried logic. "You know how Henry is so insistent on us being on time for rehearsal—he has been through so much in the last few days, we must not let him down."

Elsie turned and looked at the station clock, which glared back uncompromisingly with 9.26.

She sighed and was about to hail a hansom cab, when she saw something green and extremely unusual materialise. It rose into view like a portent of things to come.

Elsie had taken just a brief glimpse, but already she was smitten. She held on to her hat with her left hand, gathered in the length of her ribboned dress to join with her parasol and purse in her right—and headed across the end of Prince's Bridge, into the path of the green motor.

"Elsie! Watch out!" Arthur screamed, but it was too late for her to hear him. She had already dodged the Simonds Milk delivery dray, sidestepped a passing tram and was standing straight in front of her fast-braking target.

Thomson blasted his horn and gesticulated furiously, as passing modes of yesteryear took their opportunity to hurl abuse at their stationary nemesis.

"What the hell do you think you are doing, young lady?" Thomson yelled above the expletives.

Elsie moved close in to the front of the vehicle. "I am the 'p' for whom you have always been searching!" she said with a wicked smile.

Thomson was unsure if he had heard what he thought he had heard, which in any case, had made no sense at all. He leaned forward in his driver's seat and wiped the dust from his driving goggles in the hope of a better view—then decided that removing them altogether was the best option.

The young lady in front of him was as charming in appearance as any he had ever encountered.

"You will give me a lift to the Bijou Theatre in your beautiful motor, won't you, Mr Thomson?"

Given her positioning, attractiveness and his total lack of passengers, Thomson had very little choice.

Elsie opened the passenger side door and pushed herself up into the vehicle's interior.

"Sit down in that side seat and let's get going!" Thomson barked.

"Oh, Mr Thomson! You wouldn't kidnap me and leave my father behind, would you?" With that, Elsie stood up and called out to Arthur: "Come on, Daddy, we are waiting for you!"

Thomson was just reliving the wisdom of his late father's advice to never trust a beautiful woman, when Arthur arrived on board, having ducked and weaved his way through a line of assorted transports and dodged numerous horse droppings with the skill of a professional dancer.

"Daddy?" Thomson queried, realising that the figure now ensconced on his back seat was barely likely to have fathered anyone who had progressed beyond lollipop stage, let alone a fully grown seductress.

"He was a mature boy!" Elsie quipped with a smile, as

the spinning of the green motor's Dunlop tyres signalled its departure up Swanston Street in hot pursuit of its many detractors, who had initially left it anchored in their dust.

Elsie loved her position in the side bucket seat, looking straight at the driver. As the motor picked up speed, she took off her hat and unpinned her hair, bathing in the admiration that the combination of her long flowing locks and the novelty of the flashy green motor, garnered from those she passed.

After turning right into Bourke Street, the vehicle chugged its way to the north side of the thoroughfare, eventually turning in behind a Shetland pony-drawn dray that was unloading barrels of beer, immediately opposite the Bijou.

"Thank you, Mr Thomson. I really don't know who or what is more beautiful, yourself or your motor!" Elsie oozed with syrupy emotion, as she squeezed a gold sovereign into a left hand that still showed traces of the oiling he had applied to his 'baby' that morning.

"Elsie, come on! We are running very late and Henry, poor man, will be most unpleased!" Arthur warned, as he helped Elsie step down to the less glamorous level of Bourke Street.

Henry Lee had not only been humiliated on New Year's Eve, but the press had reminded him of the company's travails, for the last three successive mornings. Worse still, James Love was threatening legal action and claiming that his contract was with James Rial, rather than the troupe's front man. And then there was the issue of hiring replacements for Kelly and Ashby.

The signing of The Lottos, a four-person cycle track act, who fortuitously were holidaying in Melbourne at the time, would, under most circumstances, have seemed enough to arrest this sudden downward spiral. Yet, everyone in World's Entertainers knew that it was going to take a major jolt from a circuit breaker to jump-start enthusiasm for the enterprise once more.

As Arthur guided Elsie across Bourke Street, neither knew that their 'saviour', just might have already arrived.

"Perhaps we could sneak in the main entrance, work our way quietly down the side of the theatre and slip into seats at the side of the front," Arthur suggested, as they stole under the central arch of the Bijou's entrance. Then he stopped and held her firmly by the arm and spoke to her in a way he never had before: "Elsie Caroline Thompson—do not EVER force me into a chase for a motor before rehearsal, again!"

"Oh, Arthur, I am so, so sorry," Elsie pleaded, as a hint of tears welled in her eyes.

"We are now nearly nine minutes late! We had better go and face the music!"

He grabbed her hand and led her up to the theatre entrance doors and halted to peer through the glass. Both could vaguely see a male figure on stage. They well knew the way all rehearsals started. In a performance that would last around fifteen minutes, Henry would stand on stage with the troupe scattered around the front rows. He would lecture all on their shortcomings from the night before, then toss in the occasional piece of praise, just to keep his troupe motivated.

Arthur, stooping and keeping his head down, eased open the door as quietly as he could and led Elsie to the right in the less than semi-darkness of the back stalls. Elsie glanced towards the stage momentarily and glimpsed a tall male figure. Exactly what she expected. She continued on tiptoes, guided slowly by Arthur around the corridor, but the sound coming from the stage made her look up. That simply was not Henry Lee's voice. It was American in origin, but softened at the edges.

"Arthur!" she whispered, while at the same time firmly pulling him to the left and into the back of a seat.

"Oh, God!" Arthur exclaimed out aloud in pain, as his knee struck the back of an armrest.

Elsie froze as the figure on stage stopped talking and looked up and out in their direction. He looked to be in his fifties, sported a moustache and was good-looking. Almost instantly, she realised she had seen him before.

"Mr Nelstone and Miss Forrest!" the figure boomed from the stage in a voice that rolled like a tidal wave across the empty seats and crashed into the walls at the Bijou's rear. It was a voice well used to performing on the biggest of stages—and being obeyed.

Arthur and Elsie moved slowly out of the shadows and into the centre of the Bijou's seating as the rest of the troupe turned to witness this unscripted execution. The pair then stood motionless and silent.

Elsie suddenly felt weak, as if her legs were going to give way at any moment, for she was now sure, from theatre visits and newspaper images, exactly who stood before her.

There was a pause for a few moments as the man on stage appreciated he could toy with his audience and that everyone's attention was guaranteed. He also understood he had been given the perfect opportunity to impart a valuable lesson that could cement his authoritarian reputation.

"Do you know who I am?" he asked in a quiet and controlled way.

"Yes, Mr Williamson, sir!" Elsie responded.

James Cassius Williamson, commonly known as J.C., was the doyen of Australian-based theatrical managers and entrepreneurs. For more than two decades he had hired and fired performers and launched productions in theatres he had bought, across the country.

"And do you think J. C. Williamson tolerates tardiness?"

"No, sir! It was all my fault, sir!"

"That may be," Williamson insisted, "but any repeat and I can assure you, Miss Forrest and Mr Nelstone, you shall never work for a company I manage! As I have just explained to your colleagues, given this company's recent issues, Mr Lee and Mr Rial have requested that I join them in co-managing World's Entertainers. I have agreed, subject to completing due diligence on the finances and reviewing all acts."

At that point, he motioned to Arthur and Elsie to join the group, then continued: "I have already watched each of you perform and will do so again before passing judgment on your suitability to continue with World's Entertainers at the conclusion of an interview. My new production, *Ben Hur*, opens at Her Majesty's Theatre in Sydney next month, so your company's move to Sydney in February is perfect timing. Let us see just how many of you continue with World's Entertainers, there!"

With that, Williamson shook hands with Lee and Rial, and then left, stage right. Elsie and Arthur were left wondering if they would still be part of the enterprise.

* * *

Over the next week, they both did everything they could to ensure that their act had never been better. This period had started most positively for Elsie, as she received her first piece of 'fan mail'—a letter from a Miss May Maxwell of Jolimont, who said she had been greatly impressed by Elsie's performances.

Coincidentally, Miss Maxwell described herself as an actress and comedienne. Sensing a kindred spirit, Elsie immediately made contact and the pair met up at The Grand before the week was out. Elsie was surprised to find that May was seven years older than herself, but she promised to keep in touch.

* * *

As the time for interviews with J.C. approached, every member of the troupe, irrespective of reputation and experience, became edgy.

The instructions were clear. Each interviewee had to be at Melbourne's Princess Theatre box office ten minutes before their stipulated interview time. Elsie was not going to be late, so took the few minutes walk up Spring Street from The Grand with Arthur, who was scheduled for interview half an hour before her 'grilling'.

The Princess had been chosen as Williamson had paid for its construction in 1886 and still maintained an office on its upper floor. This, together with its proximity to The Grand, made it an ideal venue for the interviews.

Elsie had often seen the majestic outside of the three-towered building, with PRINCESS above a coat of arms, shining out at night in illumination, from below the front of its central dome. Yet, she had never stepped inside—until now.

A marble floor with a statue-lined marble staircase spread before her. *It's beautiful!* she thought in wonder to herself, as Arthur headed to the box office counter to announce his arrival.

It was just before 2.20 pm and Elsie, knowing she had plenty of time to spare, set off to explore. She started by climbing the long marble staircase that turned upward to the right. As she reached the next level she looked around her: statues punctuated the vivid scenes and ornate stained glass ringed the area leading to the elaborate entrances to the theatre's dress circle and boxes.

Trying to take it all in, Elsie looked behind her and found a chair up against a column. As she sat down, she looked up and noticed beautiful frescos covered the ceiling. "Oh, wow!" was all she could say as she leaned back, gently resting her head against the column's solid certainty in this time of uneasiness and stress. *I have plenty of time,* she thought to herself, as she soaked in the atmosphere around her. She felt the images wash over her and she closed her eyes and smiled at the soothing comfort they provided, and within seconds, she was asleep.

Arthur emerged exhausted from his interview at 2.57 pm, and it took him a few moments in the theatre's foyer to understand what was wrong: Elsie was nowhere to be seen.

He scanned the extent of the foyer, but could not see her anywhere. He wheeled around to the box office window and asked the attendant if he had seen Miss Forrest. But after reviewing his interview list, the young man confirmed that she had not appeared, and was already eight minutes late.

In panic, Arthur searched the foyer again and this time focussed on the grand marble staircase. He raced upwards and only paused at the top long enough to look past the column into what was a clearly empty upper level.

He turned dejectedly and headed back down the stairs, the thwack of his footsteps stirring Elsie.

Arthur had feared that something like this might happen: Elsie had panicked under the pressure and fled back to The Grand. *How could she do this when we have been a partnership for so long!*

Elsie winced as she woke, then blinked her eyes a couple of times before she realised where she was and exactly why she was there. She rose, then raced as quickly as she could down the staircase. As she neared its base she looked ahead, to see Arthur who had just exited the theatre's front door, holding his head in his hands. This could only mean one thing.

She wanted to rush outside, but turned briefly to check the time on the theatre clock above the box office. It was one minute to three. She was nine minutes late already and her appointment was just one minute away.

She turned in frustration and anger towards the attendant, who told her that Miss Seberry would be with her in a moment.

As she waited, she fumed. *How could Williamson reject the greatest comic dancer in the English-speaking world! As he hasn't accepted Arthur, then he can't have me! And, what's more, I am going to tell him!*

An older lady wearing spectacles appeared from a side door. "Miss Forrest? I am Miss Seberry, Mr Williamson's secretary. Follow me, please!"

Elsie wound herself up as she made her way up the internal staircase to Mr Williamson's wood-panelled office.

"Miss Forrest is here, Mr Williamson!" Miss Seberry said, after knocking briefly on the door, before allowing Elsie to enter the room first.

Elsie noticed there was a grand desk with its chair backing a window, though Mr Williamson stood in front of one of four leather armchairs, arranged two on each side of a coffee table.

"Please be seated, Miss Forrest!" requested Mr Williamson, indicating one of the armchairs, though Elsie was having none of it.

"I will not sit in the company of someone who rejects a talent like Mr Nelstone, the finest comic dancer ever to set foot in this country!"

J. C. Williamson, Australia's leading theatrical manager, was dumbfounded—so surprised, that he was temporarily speechless.

"Miss Forrest!" gasped Miss Seberry. "Nobody speaks to Mr Williamson in that manner!"

"Shirley, it is okay!" Mr Williamson urged, before he paused for a moment, composing himself and thinking carefully about what he should say next. "I fear Miss Forrest has made a severe misjudgement—not a situation unusual in those of limited life experience."

"But … you mean …" Elsie started to say.

"Arthur Nelstone WILL be heading to Sydney with World's Entertainers!"

The wave of anger-driven emotion that had thundered on to Elsie's beach had suddenly halted, then ebbed and was now in full retreat, leaving her as unsure and disorientated as flotsam and jetsam.

Williamson noticed her swaying and quickly steadied her

with his big, strong hands, guiding her into an armchair. "Shirley! Get Miss Forrest a glass of water!"

"Oh, sir, I am so sorry, I am so sorry!" Elsie sobbed, as Mr Williamson settled in to the armchair next to her.

"Miss Forrest, let me assure you of this: nobody works for J. C. Williamson unless he sees ability and value in their maintenance. And, in you Miss Forrest, I see now a broader range of abilities and possibilities than even I had perceived! You will be joining Mr Nelstone and the troupe in Sydney!"

Elsie was shocked. She started sobbing even more audibly. "I don't deserve to work for you!"

Mr Williamson reached in and gently raised Elsie's chin so that he was looking into her big, teary eyes. "Did anyone tell you that you are even beautiful when you cry?" he asked rhetorically, as Miss Seberry returned with a glass of water, which Mr Williamson pressed to Elsie's lips.

She took a couple of sips and dabbed her cheeks and eyes with a handkerchief that Miss Seberry offered.

They waited patiently for Elsie to recover her composure and it was nearly a minute before Mr Williamson spoke again in a calm and fatherly manner: "Exactly how old are you?"

"I am eighteen … well, nearly eighteen and a half. I was born Elsie Caroline Thompson on the 2nd of August 1883," Elsie whimpered, as Miss Seberry scribbled notes in the background.

"You are younger than I had thought! Now, I must ask you something personal, Miss Forrest: are you in love with Mr Nelstone?"

"In love with him, sir? He is nearly fourteen years my elder!"

"Well, let me assure you, Miss Forrest, there is many an older man who has his heart stolen by a much younger and beautiful lady."

"He treats me like a much-loved little sister, sir, and I greatly respect him for that, but …"

"But what, Miss Forrest?"

"But he is an Englishman! If I marry, I would hope it is to an Australian!"

Mr Williamson laughed. "I am on my second marriage, Miss Forrest, and I can assure you that love does not discriminate purely on the basis of nationality. There are charming and good people everywhere, though not everyone is charming and good! Still, as an American who has been in this country for over two decades, I think I understand the difference you perceive. Now, you have reminded me of one of my favourite pieces from *HMS Pinafore*—'For He is An Englishman!' Do you know it?"

"Oh, sir! I played Josephine in the Fort Street School production in 1899."

"Really? And did the school seek my permission?" he said with mock indignation. "Do you know, I have held the rights to *HMS Pinafore* in the colony from the time I first played Sir Joseph Porter in the production I staged here in 1879?"

"Oh, I guess then we might have staged it illegally!" she suggested, as the hint of a sheepish smile peaked through her previously sad countenance.

Miss Seberry had already settled in her armchair and put her pencil and paper down, appreciating that she was at least surplus to, if not interfering with the relationship that was blossoming before her. She reached forward and picked up the near empty glass and escorted it into the neighbouring bathroom, reflecting on the fact that rarely had a glass so empty ushered in one so metaphorically full. As she rinsed the glass in the sink, two voices sang together:

> He is an Englishman
> For he himself has said it
> And it's greatly to his credit
> That he is an Englishman! ...

The singing cheered Elsie significantly. "I did see your play *Australis, Or The City of Zero*, sir, and thought it was very funny and imaginative!" she said when they had finished.

"Well, I am glad you enjoyed it! Not all the critics did!"

"I particularly laughed at the notion that Australia would be led by a former trade union leader in the year 2000, but I thought the idea of having a great bridge from Circular Quay to the North Shore is a wonderful one, though I doubt it shall ever happen!"

"The future is near impossible to predict with any certainty,

Miss Forrest, though if you continue with the same passion and ability you have demonstrated to date, you will prove a great asset to any company. I do, however, think you should have singing lessons with my friend and stage manager, Henry Bracy, who is a Welsh tenor of note. I shall arrange for these to start in Sydney. Additionally, as a former comedian, I feel you have particular talent and further potential as a comedienne. I would like to see you incorporate even more comedy in your performances."

"Yes, sir," Elsie said before pausing for thought, trying to take in all he had said. "Thank you for your guidance."

"Now, I feel there is a certain Englishman waiting nervously for your return to The Grand. You had best leave!"

Oh, this man has everything! Elsie thought. *He is tall, good-looking, powerful, intelligent and talented, and despite his intimidating reputation, a real fatherly figure, who is so kind and understanding!* Their eyes met as she searched for a reciprocation of the love and admiration that shone from hers. For a brief moment, she wondered whether she could kiss him, but he may have read her thoughts, and motioned her towards the door.

"Thank you, sir!" She caressed him with her eyes and smile, then, turned towards their future, in Sydney.

It may have been childish, and just perhaps unrequited, but she had fallen deeply in love with a man in his late fifties, who was the most powerful figure in Australian theatre.

Chapter 19

A Plague on Both Your Chariots

The theatre world's composed of folk, of many different yards
From carpenters to costume queens, and lighting lads to bards
Most active in the daytime, rarely visible at night
They build the sets and paint the scenes that others set alight.

After two nights performing at the port city of Geelong's classical Mechanics Institute, World's Entertainers' long train journey from Melbourne to Sydney was punctuated by a one-night show in the New South Wales regional town of Wagga Wagga. Unlike any of the other performers, in going back to Sydney, Elsie was returning to her home city, and had been given special permission to stay with her family, as long as she ensured she was punctual for rehearsals and productions.

As they sat on the late afternoon tram gliding up George Street towards the vicinity of 52 Carrington Street, Elsie noticed that her mother was on edge and seemed unwilling to touch the tram's seats or bars. When Elsie had placed a steadying hand on the back of the seat in front, her mother had been quick to admonish her daughter.

"Mother, what is wrong?"

Mary Ann looked around to check that no other passengers were paying attention, then leant in to her daughter, whispering in her ear: "The plague—have you not heard? The bubonic plague is back!"

Once home, Elsie was told to wash her hands thoroughly with soap.

Her father was delighted to see his dear daughter after months away, and told her to leave her suitcase and coat in her bedroom.

Coat in hand, Elsie opened her cupboard and screamed in shock and surprise at the morgue-like figure standing, smirking amidst her outfits—then squealed with delight as she hugged and kissed a giggling Emma.

At the dinner table, James Thompson explained that the situation was indeed quite serious. "I have had the bookshop fumigated and have seen more rat-catchers in lower Erskine Street than potential customers. Sadly, its proximity to the wharves of Darling Harbour means that the plague may be the death of me before any vermin are exterminated!"

"Near every week brings news of more deaths from this pestilence in the city, so your father and I do not wish to take any chance until this plague has run its course," her mother explained. "We wash our hands regularly and are most careful where we go and who we meet."

After dinner, the girls retreated to Elsie's bedroom, threw off their shoes and cuddled up on the bed together.

It did not take Emma long to sense that her dear friend was holding something back—though Elsie was not keen to let 'the cat out of the bag' too quickly.

"I am in love!" she finally admitted in exasperation and exhaustion after Emma had tickled her until she surrendered.

"Who is he?" Emma demanded.

"Oh, that I cannot say, but I am sure you know of him!"

"It isn't Arthur is it? I thought there may be something between you after all the time you spend together!"

"No, it isn't Arthur," Elsie insisted, waiting for her inquisitor to try again.

"So … it isn't Arthur Nelstone … and you said I 'know of him'. You didn't say 'I know him'! Have I met him?"

Elsie's reply of "You may not have!" seemed calculating and was met with another round of tickling as the two rolled back and forth over one another.

"Does he have a job?" Emma queried. "There has been so much unemployment in recent years, it would be unwise to marry anyone without good prospects!"

"Who said anything about marriage? I just said I was in love … though I suppose marriage could be possible …"

"You have not answered my question, El!" Emma insisted, while at the same time tickling her again. "Does he have a job?"

Elsie was silent for a moment, contemplating just how she should respond. "Well, sort of …"

"Have you kissed?" Emma demanded, trying another tack, as she was becoming frustrated with what she thought was Elsie's deliberate evasiveness.

"No, only in my imagination!"

"Oh, El! You have a crush on someone who I know, but whom I may not have met, who 'sort of' has a job, but who you have never kissed! What type of relationship is that!"

Again Elsie hesitated, wondering just what she should add. Then quietly and calmly, but with a sincerity that Emma knew she could trust, Elsie stated: "You are my best and dearest friend, Emma Mabel Bellamy, and I promise I will introduce you to him soon!"

All the talk around Sydney from early February 1902 seemed to be about *Ben Hur*, J. C. Williamson's expensive and ground-breaking production that was set to open at Her Majesty's Theatre on Saturday the 8th. Her Majesty's had been the venue for Elsie's final Fort Street performance in *HMS Pinafore*, so returning there—let alone for a show like *Ben Hur*—was bound to be a memorable experience.

It was certainly the hottest ticket in town, and Elsie made sure that she had four for opening night. With World's Entertainers not opening till a week later at the Palace, the timing was perfect for Elsie to have a very rare Saturday night off.

Excitement and expectation were high with the advertising calling *Ben Hur* 'The Most Important Theatrical Event of the Year' and 'Mr J. C. Williamson presents The Greatest Spectacle of Modern Days', though in truth nobody knew exactly what to expect beyond the promise of witnessing four hours of 'The Most Elaborate and Expensive Production Ever Attempted in Australia'.

Elsie, her parents and Emma emerged from their dress circle seats at interval, still gushing with enthusiasm for the spectacle they had only seen partly completed: four hundred participants from the leading dramatic societies of Britain, along with camels and horses, but with the grand highlight yet to come.

In the theatre's foyer, Elsie wanted to head to the counter with the ice cream, but Mary Ann insisted that as she would be paying, they would turn towards the boy at the fresh fruit stand instead. "I have noticed that you have put on a little bit more weight than you should be carrying, Elsie, so we shall all have fruit!" She paid the lad for four apples, which were soon devoured between comments on the glorious costumes and stunning scenery.

The second session promised much and delivered more, with a remarkable four-horse chariot race between Ben Hur (with a chestnut and three black horses) and a Roman officer (in a scarlet chariot drawn by four greys) staged on a giant treadmill with the scenery turning in the background. It was breathtaking and unforgettable.

At show's end, the audience stood and applauded, again and again. Finally, Mr Williamson himself was called on stage.

"That is him!" Elsie said to Emma.

"Yes, I know! I have seen his picture in the paper before!" she responded, oblivious to Elsie's hint.

"Come on, Emma!" Elsie ordered, as she grabbed Emma's hand and dragged her downwards, towards the stage. They bobbed like corks against the theatre-exiting tide for some minutes before eventually making their way into the backstage area.

Elsie craned her neck above the milieu of performers and stagehands. *He must be here—somewhere!* Then she spotted J.C. congratulating a group of Roman soldiers. "Mr Williamson! Mr Williamson!" she cried insistently.

He turned briefly, but that was all the encouragement Elsie needed. "Mr Williamson, this is my very best friend in the world—Miss Emma Bellamy!" she said, thrusting Emma forward.

"A pleasure to meet you, Miss Bellamy. I trust you and Miss Forrest enjoyed the show?"

"Oh, it was fabulous!" They both gushed simultaneously, then laughed at their synchronisation.

"James, the press would like a word!" one of his assistants cautioned.

"Excuse me, ladies!" J.C. bowed apologetically as he turned away.

"Isn't he wonderful!" Elsie sighed, as they walked back towards the foyer and her parents. "I did promise I would introduce you!"

Emma stopped in her tracks in shock. "Elsie Caroline Thompson! Are you telling me that the person you are in love with is Mr Williamson! Why, he is easily old enough to be your father—nearly your grandfather!"

Elsie said nothing in response, as she was still basking in the warmth of their brief reunion.

* * *

On Tuesday 11 February, Elsie was passed a note by James Rial at rehearsal, stating she was to meet the Welsh tenor, Henry Bracy, that afternoon at 2.30 pm at Her Majesty's.

She approached the theatre quite unsure of what to expect, for she had never met Mr Bracy, nor had any clear idea of what the session would involve.

At Her Majesty's box office, she was told to head inside to the stage. Entering the theatre brought back sensations from the excitement of Saturday night, though as she progressed down the central aisle towards the stage, she was conscious of the absence of the more than two thousand souls who had packed every vantage point.

A sizeable gentleman sat on the edge of the stage, staring at her with considerable interest. "Miss Forrest?" he asked, and seeing that she nodded her acknowledgement, he rose to his feet demonstrating considerable height. Despite his slicked, dark hair, Elsie guessed he was around J.C.'s age.

"Please join me up on stage," he added, in what Elsie appreciated was a lilting Welsh accent. When she stood at his side, he turned her attention to the back of the theatre. "See those doors at the back? I want you to make them move! Sing whatever you want, but opera would be good."

Elsie struggled to recall the detail of anything beyond Gilbert & Sullivan comic opera, so chose 'Never Mind The Why and Wherefore' from her old favourite *HMS Pinafore*.

As she was about to begin, Bracy placed his hand on her abdomen, causing her to catch her breath in surprise. He left his hand there throughout her singing and only removed it when she had finished.

"You did well, Miss Forrest, without battering the doors. It is, however, just as J.C. had suggested to me: your breathing is too shallow. You must learn to breathe from deeper down

154

and to project your voice even more. I want to expand your knowledge and experience to include the works of Puccini, Verdi and others. After a few Tuesday sessions, I am sure you will be a more versatile and capable performer."

This was not quite what she had expected to hear, but Elsie swallowed her pride and became determined to learn from the tenor's knowledge and experience.

She was soon to put any changes into practise, as World's Entertainers were due to debut back at her much-loved Palace Theatre that next Saturday night, albeit with a slightly changed line-up.

Just before 7 pm, World's Entertainer's new business manager, Harrie Skinner, a J.C. appointment, wandered through the backstage area in an exultant mood. "Sold out! We are already sold out!" he cried.

While all the performers were well used to playing to packed houses, the fact that the evening had sold out before doors had even opened was unusual, particularly as *Ben Hur* was in town.

It took 'The Emperor of Coins' Allan Shaw, to be the man on the money with an explanation. "There are hundreds outside seeking a seat for our show. I heard some say they had tickets to *Ben Hur* tonight, but Her Majesty's Theatre has been closed due to the plague!"

"Oh, gosh! I hope we are not next!" said Arthur, as the atmosphere changed from elation to concern.

The spread of bubonic plague was casting a pall over the city and causing newspaper editors to set aside regular column inches to its insidious progress, just as was done the following Monday …

"Oh no! Oh, dear, dear me!" James Thompson exclaimed as he read the Monday edition of their newspaper in the lounge room of Carrington Street in the late afternoon.

"James, darling, what is it?" Mary Ann called from the kitchen.

James did not respond immediately, for he was reading ahead. By the time Mary Ann had moved in to the lounge room, she found James staring out the window.

"James, is something wrong?"

"Today's newspaper carries news that concerns us all—and it isn't about the Boer War," he said somewhat cryptically, then returned to his armchair and read out aloud:

> A suspicious case of sickness was reported to the board yesterday, and upon investigation it proved to be plague. The patient was a boy named G McIntyre, residing at Surrey Hills. It was reported that McIntyre had been engaged in selling fruit, and that he had been following his avocation nightly at Her Majesty's Theatre ...

Elsie, who had seemed to be dozing in an armchair in preparation for the evening's theatrical exertions, suddenly shot to life. "Mumsie! We could all have the plague!"

"I would think that most unlikely, my dear!" James cautioned.

"My stomach hurts!" Elsie cried, as she sought to begin a description of a range of ailments that had transformed her instantly from healthy eighteen-year-old to within a footstep of death's door.

To distract them both, James kept reading:

> ... This discovery led to a decision by the authorities that the theatre should be closed till it had undergone thorough disinfection and fumigation. No performance of Ben Hur could be given on Saturday, and this resulted in great inconvenience to the public, who did not know of the theatre being closed till they arrived at the door ...

"I am now sweating too, Mumsie!" came the mournful commentary from a figure slowly sinking into a ball in an armchair.

"Elsie, darling, I think we should all be fine," Mary Ann suggested without any great conviction, as she went to dampen a face towel to ease her daughter's fears.

"Mr Williamson has made a statement," James continued, but then paused as he realised that Elsie's complaining had ceased while she waited to hear just what Mr Williamson had said. Gradually, though intermittently, James continued reading:

> ... The closing of the theatre, said Mr J. C. Williamson, is singularly unfortunate, because in the first place the

patient is not employed by him, and secondly because it
has interrupted the run of a very expensive production ...
the loss will be very heavy. The outlay before the curtain
went up was over 6,000 pounds. An announcement relative
to the early reopening of the theatre will probably be made
today or tomorrow ...

"Oh, poor Mr Williamson!" Elsie cried.

In fact it was to be a week till the theatre reopened and *Ben
Hur* resumed its spectacular run.

Meanwhile, World's Entertainers continued to perform in
Sydney up to Wednesday 19 March. The next day, they headed
to Brisbane by train for a brief three-night sequence at His
Majesty's Theatre, before touring regional Queensland. On
arrival in the state capital, Elsie sent off a postcard to May
Maxwell in Melbourne.

Tucked up in her comfortable bed in the familiarity of
Brisbane's Hotel Daniell, after another successful evening
performing before a full theatre, on Saturday 22 March, Elsie
had no inkling of the drama that was to unfold under the cover
of darkness, many miles to the south.

* * *

It was only after the cleaners and fumigators had departed
Sydney's Her Majesty's Theatre around 5 am, that night
watchman Robert Hanigan allowed himself the luxury of
wallowing in the grandeur of *Ben Hur.*

He had not seen the extravaganza, unlike it seemed, much of
Sydney, though he had heard of its magnificence. Yet, unlike
nearly everyone else, he had golden-key access to its treasures.

It was that beguiling time when the night had all but retreated,
though the day had not quite the courage to dawn—an occasion
long drawn-out by the sleepiness of a Sunday morn—when
Hanigan sat in Ben Hur's chariot in the room behind the stage.

He could have turned the electric light on, but chose to dream
of his own rise to prominence in the gloom of a room crammed
with props, canvas stage scenery and costumes, lest the harsh
light of reality destroy his delightful delusion.

As the time drifted towards 6 am, he lit a cigarette while resting on the floor of the chariot. Soon after, he thought he heard something—a knocking sound—though it soon ceased. Shortly after, he heard it again, this time, louder: 1, 2, 3, 1-2.

He knew that knock pattern well—it was his wife's on the theatre's side door.

He tossed his still lit cigarette in the direction of the room's sandbox, as his wife did not like him smoking, and hurried towards the side door.

There, they talked for a couple of minutes: she explaining that she had been up caring for a sick neighbour and would head off around the back to Gaffney's Bakery—one of the few shops open on a Sunday, let alone this early and on Palm Sunday—for a fresh loaf of bread.

Hanigan ambled back towards his favourite chariot, though even before he reached the room, he sensed something was very wrong: first he heard a whooshing sound that seemed if anything to be getting louder, then he saw a flickering light emanating from the back room.

He rushed to the entrance only to see the room well alight. *The bucket and water! I must get the bucket and water!* was all he could think, as he blundered through the backstage area and found the bucket placed near the tap in case of fire. He filled it as quickly as he could, looking fearfully over his shoulder at the growing glow behind him.

By the time he reached the back room again, he could see things were well out of control: smoke and flame had consumed the room and were spreading upwards and outwards.

He raced to the telephone to call the fire brigade, but could not get a tone on the line to speak to the operator.

In his panic, he neglected to do the one thing that might have helped—lower the asbestos drop stage screen that had been installed as a fire safety measure when the theatre was constructed in 1887.

With the telephone not working, Hanigan rushed outside to the fire alarm box on the corner of Market and Pitt Streets.

Mrs Hanigan had not long departed Gaffney's Bakery with the loaf, when the air became filled with the cries of warning from staff and patrons from the hotels that bordered the theatre: the George and Her Majesty's.

Within minutes, the clanging bells of the fire brigade added to the morning cacophony, though it soon became clear to Superintendant Webb that 'Big Ben', their most formidable weapon—along with many more fire units—was desperately needed.

Belle Pye, a twenty-seven year old domestic servant and her three-year-old son William, had been roused in an upper back room of Gaffney's Bakery. Belle, whose job it was to clean the bakery after working hours, had just enough time to dress herself and her son, before joining the growing crowds bordering Market and Pitt Streets.

It was only while she waited amidst a mix of half-dressed travellers and curious locals, that Belle realised she was missing something precious. A legal document, detailing her rights and entitlement following her husband's death a couple of years earlier, had been left behind in the kitchen.

Belle looked around and could see a woman near her, and that the nearest policeman seemed preoccupied with crowd control on the Pitt Street corner.

"Please, mind my son for a minute!" she said, passing her son's hand to that of an older woman.

In a flash, Belle was gone, off across Market Street, jumping the anaconda-like snakings of fire hoses that were fighting a losing battle to save Sydney's grandest theatre.

"Eh, you! What do ya think yar doin'!" called one firefighter, as he saw Belle from the corner of his eye. But it was too late, as she had already disappeared into the laneway leading past the back of the theatre.

Smoke and flame now rose from the roof of the theatre and it was clear, to even the most naïve amongst the many suited and hat-wearing men who constituted the bulk of the onlookers, that the best that could be done was to contain the fire's spread.

A few minutes later, the roof of the theatre caved in with a tremendous crash, bringing down with it the boxes and dress circle. Shortly after, the northern and eastern walls collapsed, the latter over the back of nearby shops. It was quite some hours more before Belle Pye's body was found, crushed under a pile of bricks, but protectively grasping the document she had so prized.

* * *

News of the disaster did not reach World's Entertainers until the next morning's breakfast at Hotel Daniell. It was Arthur who broke the story to everyone, while brandishing a copy of the Monday edition of *The Brisbane Courier* and its headlines:

BIG FIRE IN SYDNEY

HER MAJESTY'S THEATRE

ONLY THE WALLS LEFT STANDING

A YOUNG WOMAN BURIED IN RUINS

ORIGIN OF THE FIRE UNKNOWN

The troupe were shocked into silence, as Arthur continued:

Other features of the disaster are:- That three firemen were slightly injured; that a loss of about 35,000 pounds has been sustained; that the leading playhouse of Sydney has been demolished; and 600 people engaged in the production of Ben Hur have been thrown out of employment ...

Charles Sweet, to satisfy his own curiosity, had grabbed a different newspaper nearby, and started reading out aloud:

Mr Vincent, Mr Williamson's associated manager, arrived on the scene shortly after the outbreak. Every stick and every stitch, in fact everything belonging to Ben Hur has gone, and the loss is tremendous. To add to the great loss, the whole of the properties, effects, scenery, machinery, &c., were uninsured, with the exception of the two dynamos used for working the electric light machinery ...

Elsie pushed her breakfast away, for she now had no appetite. Charles continued:

... A telegram conveying the disaster was sent to Mr Williamson, who is in Melbourne, and Mr Vincent received the following reply:-

"Terrible disaster, but thank God it did not happen during the performance. I am sorry for my company and the people who suffer with me."

Performances generally that night in Brisbane were the 'flattest' that any of the troupe could recall. It seemed as though everyone was preoccupied with any implication the disaster might have for their own performing careers, now that they too were part of the J. C. Williamson stable.

For Elsie, everything came to a head as she lay in bed that night. *How could such bad things happen to such a nice man like Mr Williamson? First, the plague closed down the theatre for a week, and now the theatre itself has been burnt down and the most expensive stage production in Australian history has been destroyed! Poor Mr Williamson!*

As her tears tracked down her face and collected onto her pillowslip, she was sure she could see him, standing alone on a balcony, outside a double set of open doors that she could reach via a long corridor. She started running towards him and calling out: "James! James!"

He turned to see her approaching, her dress flowing behind her and black ribbons of mourning following the line of her hair backwards, as she raced onward. He opened his arms as she passed through the double doors and she rushed into his embrace. "I am so sorry, James darling—so sorry!" she cried as she sobbed hysterically against his chest.

He bent over and kissed the top of her head, but within seconds she felt teardrops seeping through her hair. She turned and looked up at him in shock, for she had never expected that a man, so rich and powerful, would cry.

"It is all right, Elsie! It is all right!" he assured her. "I may have lost a lot, but we have found each other!"

Chapter 20

The Land of the Long White …

I have heard folk speak about it, though have not traversed its downs
Scaled its snow-capped peaks in season, mingled much in its quaint towns
Dwelt within its northern fern land, stepped inside a Maori pa
So a voyage east to find it—is a journey not too far.

The hansom cab wound its way past the residences of Sydney's great, good and successfully avaricious, on its way down Elizabeth Bay Road.

Elsie peered out the window with a mixture of excited fascination and foreboding—the former because of whom and what she might encounter, and the latter due to her parental companions and their anticipated intent.

The driver well knew to stop outside No. 106, and even the horse seemed to acknowledge the familiarity of his destination with a nod and a shake. In this neighbourhood, everyone knew where J. C. Williamson lived.

James Thompson inspected his fob watch as Elsie admired the wrought-iron gates and chiselled stone pillars—one of which bore the brass nameplate inscription TUDOR—that guarded the entrance to a lifestyle that none of the Thompsons had ever experienced.

"It would not do to be too early, nor fashionably late," James advised. "Another forty seconds and it shall be 11 am and the time of our appointment. I shall open the pedestrian gate at exactly 11!"

James was careful and respectful by nature, but ever more so when dealing with those of actual or perceived higher status. He waited, fob watch in one hand, as the other rested on the gate latch. At the moment the second and minute hand pointed to their apogee, he pressed forward, leading two other members of his family into a different world.

They paraded down a paved pathway flanked by manicured lawns towards a flowing fountain. Elsie could not stop smiling as she soaked in the beautiful surroundings.

The trio passed the fountain and crossed a circular driveway that curved under a porte-cochère, where Elsie visualised elaborate coaches or even motors might regularly pause.

As they reached the large cream-painted front double doors, Mary Ann grasped Elsie's hand as James reached for the lion doorknocker.

Two respectful thumps triggered the shuffling of shoes, on what Elsie felt from the sound, was almost certainly marble.

A perfectly attired gentleman servant opened the door and was greeted by an immediate explanation from James: "James, Mary Ann and Elsie Thompson to see Mr Williamson, sir!"

"Welcome, sir and ladies! My name is Richard, Mr Williamson's butler. Mr Williamson is expecting you. Please follow me."

Elsie was still smiling, but now her eyes were wider, as she looked to the left and right as they glided down a central corridor lined with beautiful paintings. Everywhere she looked there was style and good taste.

The butler eventually halted at the entrance to a large wood-panelled library. "The Thompsons, to see you, sir!"

As they entered, Elsie was surprised to see two men already inside.

"James Williamson, Mr Thompson," Williamson said, extending his hand. "I am very glad to meet you!"

"Please call me James, James!" said Elsie's father.

"You know James Rial, don't you, Mr Thompson?" Williamson said, to which Mr Thompson responded with a nod and a handshake. "Well, three Jameses in one room—remarkable!" J.C. added.

"No, four!" Elsie interjected, ignoring the rebuking squeeze on her hand from her mother who was encouraging and expecting her silence. Williamson looked at her questioningly and her smile was reflected in her glistening eyes, as she pointed to a red leather-bound book in the large bookshelf that covered a whole wall of the room. "A King James version of the Bible!"

"You know, young lady, that is one of the things I really like about you. You are quick—mighty quick! Please, be seated on the couch!" Williamson urged.

As the three Thompsons sat together on the couch, admiring

the view out of the wide and full-height window to the lawn that ran into the watery panorama of Elizabeth Bay, J.C. continued: "My understanding is that you asked for this meeting, Mrs Thompson, as you are concerned about your daughter being part of the planned World's Entertainers' overseas tour to New Zealand and then the United States."

"Mr Williamson, she is still only eighteen, she has never travelled abroad, and it is a long way to journey without a chaperone!"

"Mrs Thompson, let me first state that I have made my fortune by selecting the right shows and the right performers. I am not renowned for backing failures. Your daughter has proved a great success with the company, even though nobody recognises her as its only Australian! How does her partner, Arthur Nelstone, feel about the situation?"

Mary Ann was going to say that she really did not care, but thought it might not be tactful.

J.C. picked up the receiver of a telephone from a side table and dialled. "Richard, could you tell Mr Nelstone that we can see him now."

What followed was a sequence of affirmations, promises and a partial compromise that was only proffered when it was confirmed that Miss Gassman was continuing with the troupe.

"But only New Zealand!" Mary Ann warned. "My daughter will not be going to America!"

Arthur was elated that their partnership would continue, for now, but could see that a choice about his future would have to be made in New Zealand.

"Elsie, you will be in World's Entertainers No. 1 troupe, a grouping that includes Kelly and Ashby—though I appreciate that not everyone has wholeheartedly accepted my decision to invite them back," J.C. admitted. "Henry Lee will stay on the Australian mainland with the No. 2 troupe, so your New Zealand tour will be led by James Rial. James," J.C. added, turning to his financial partner, "please ensure that Elsie shares a cabin with Miss Gassman on the journey to New Zealand."

"Certainly!" Rial responded, making a note in his journal.

* * *

On the morning of Saturday 3 May 1902, the No. 1 troupe of World's Entertainers joined the excited throng of other passengers, relatives and friends that milled about the Sussex Street Wharf, in front of the green and white steamer *Waihora*.

Josephine, her children, Grunter and Rusty were there, but so too was a third animal—a sulphur-crested cockatoo in a cage. "Miss Elsie, ain't he beautiful!" Josephine exclaimed.

"Josephine is beautiful!" it squawked in response, as its owner proudly showed Elsie, her mother and Emma. James Thompson had to remain in the bookshop, just up the road, though Elsie had said her fond goodbyes to her father a few minutes earlier.

At 11 am the captain stood at the top of the gangplank and called for silence. "I am Captain William Farmer of the SS *Waihora*. At midday we depart on a five-day journey to the New Zealand capital of Wellington; then a day trip on to Lyttelton near Christchurch on South Island; then Dunedin, Bluff and back to Sydney via Hobart and Melbourne. Today we shall be carrying 47 passengers in saloon class out of a capacity of 138, as well as 32 out of a capacity of 84 in steerage. So there will be plenty of room for all! You may start boarding now in an orderly fashion, making sure that your name and details are correct on the passenger list."

James Rial corralled the troupe before they joined the 'sheep run' up the gangway. "It is good that we have everyone present, bar Allan Shaw. Allan, is unfortunately most unwell, and will not be making this journey with us, but hopes to meet up with us in Auckland in two months time." Noticing that everyone seemed keen to board, he quickly added that lunch would be a selection of sandwiches and refreshments at 1 pm in the saloon dining room. "I trust that by then we should have well cleared Sydney Heads!"

Elsie gave a last hug and kiss to her mother and to Emma—and then reminded the latter that she would send a postcard, as soon as they had settled in the 'Land of the Long White Cloud'.

At 12 noon sharp, the *Waihora* sounded its horn and smoke rose from its funnel, as it plotted its way carefully off the Sussex Street Wharf and out through the maze of masts and funnels that dotted the Darling Harbour inlet.

Elsie stood with Arthur, Josephine and the children, waving to those of ever decreasing size on the wharf. Briefly, she thought she spied J.C. himself waving and smiling back at her—though perhaps this was just the product of youthful and wishful thinking, egged on by a most fertile imagination.

As the ship turned east into the main harbour channel, passing Elsie's birthplace of Millers Point and the Rocks to the starboard side, Elsie suggested they could all get a better view at the prow of the ship. A desperately quick race to the front to have a better view and glimpse of Admiralty House on the port side, only resulted in Josephine's hat being blown overboard in the freshening breeze. This, and the sudden onset of showers from an overcast sky, saw the group retreat all the way back to the stern. There, they squeezed under the shelter of the saloon deck's canopy as Circular Quay bade farewell to the south, and the convict-cut stone of Fort Denison loomed just ahead, to starboard.

This isn't the most beautiful of days, but Sydney, surely, Elsie reasoned, *still has one of the world's most beautiful harbours!* There were spectacular abodes balanced around beautiful bays in every direction, from Mosman Bay in the north, to those on the south.

"I know what that is!" Elsie cried triumphantly. "Can you see Mr Williamson's mansion in Elizabeth Bay?" she asked Bill, as she hauled him up onto the railing in front of her. "It is that one there," she said pointing, "the big one on the waterfront!"

Perhaps, she thought, *Mr Williamson has just made a mad dash home and is at this moment peering through the large copper telescope I saw in his library. Perhaps he is focussing on me right now, in which case I had better wave!* She raised the one arm that was not protectively wrapped around Bill and blew kisses with her fingers in his supposed direction, just in case he might be distressed by her distant apathy.

Elsie had been on ferries on the harbour before and she loved the flowing, cresting, churning, turning mix of white and blue and green that signalled a boat's passage through its heart.

As a capable swimmer, she had often scoffed at those who welcomed the relative security of terra firma, or claimed seasickness at the slightest rock of a boat. While she had never journeyed to sea, she was certain the ocean held no fear for a water baby such as she. What she did not know was that the hours ahead would severely test her confidence.

As the *Waihora* turned forty-five degrees to starboard to align with the gap that was Sydney Heads, the waves that had glided like small mounds past her sides, transformed into hills and valleys. The *Waihora* noticeably rose and sank from prow to stern, as it surfed the swell towards the headlands.

Elsie gazed out at the sea, though it seemed to stare back at her with a deepness, darkness and mercilessness she had never anticipated. At the moment *Waihora* crossed the line between North and South Head and left the embrace of the harbour, she longed for the land and life she was leaving behind. She tried to focus on the excitement of new lands that lay ahead and their seemingly inevitable arrival.

There was now no turning back—neither physically nor psychologically—and she would meet what lay ahead in the Tasman Sea as she had faced each challenge so far in her young life: with enthusiasm and courage.

Lunch was served in the saloon dining room, with Elsie noting the tables with raised-rim edges and initially pondering their significance. The repeated dip and sway of the boat seemed to have little impact on the other members of the troupe, who were seasoned seafarers. They had journeyed by ship from the United States to Australia, at least, in the first place.

Elsie, with Bill and Irene in tow, managed to persuade the chef to part with a bucket of leftovers, and headed to the back of steerage where Grunter, Rusty and Cocky were domiciled.

Each seemed happy to see them, with Irene insisting Cocky say "*Waihora*" before being fed some grain. He turned his head sideways then raised the sulphur crest plumage skywards, as he battled to understand—but he soon grasped the pronunciation of the ship's name, much to the children's amusement.

As darkness fell, the wind intensified and the rain that had only masqueraded as occasional showers in Sydney Harbour, beat upon the ship's deck with a vengeance, as if insisting it should not be ignored.

By the time the passengers had gathered to dine on soup in

the early evening, there were worried looks all around, even amongst the crew.

"Nobody, absolutely nobody is to go out on deck for the foreseeable future!" Captain Farmer commanded. "We are heading into a storm and I ask you all to remain in your cabins. Rest assured that *Waihora* is a fine and strong ship. She has survived far worse conditions than we shall encounter tonight, so she will see us all through safely."

Elsie, Josephine and the children hurried to their cabin, holding on to the handrails as they progressed. Their cabin had two pairs of bunk beds and the adults had sensibly reserved the upper one of each for themselves, with Bill below Elsie's.

Once changed into their nightclothes—an operation that took far longer than it should have thanks to the lurching of the ship—any idea of each sleeping in their own bed was abandoned as the first lightening strike illuminated an angry sea. The resulting thunderclap struck with such immediacy and ferocity that both of the children started crying in fear of what might yet come.

"Oh, my, Miss Elsie!" is all Josephine could say, as she gathered Irene in her arms and they joined Bill and Elsie to cuddle together on Bill's bunk.

"I will tell you a story," Elsie began, desperately trying to distract the children's attention from the gathering tempest. "It happened long ago, but the mouse and the rabbit never forgot it, and how it made them the best of friends ..."

The increasingly sharp rise and fall of the ship was starting to have a nauseating effect on everyone, and it was not long before Irene's little body began to heave in anticipation—Josephine only just managing to stagger with her to the room's handbasin as Irene disgorged lunch and dinner into its pristine white expanse.

Bill had seemed to be coping till that moment, but cries of "Mamma, Mamma!" pre-empted upheavals to come. He soon joined his sister at the basin.

The hours that followed were terrifying, with Elsie trying not to look out the cabin porthole, with each flash of lightening exposing mountainous seas rising, cresting and then crashing across the *Waihora*, submerging the porthole glass in the process.

For the most part, Elsie closed her eyes, held on to Bill and tried to think of being safe and sound with Emma and her own family on the stable surface of Sydney sandstone.

She even promised to become at least, a temporarily believing Christian, if only the powers that be could halt the storm.

Exhausted, she must have fallen asleep, for a tugging on her nightdress took a few moments to awaken her to reality.

"Miss Elsie!" Josephine whispered insistently, indicating at the same time the bunks above. Elsie slowly soaked in the changed atmosphere: the boat was only rocking gently and there was no pounding rain, lightening or thunder.

She tucked Bill into his bed and like Josephine, Elsie scaled a ladder to her own bunk above. Within a few seconds, she was fast asleep in the comfort of her own bed.

It was the running of water in the room's handbasin that caused Elsie to stir and turn toward the sound. Morning light had started to flow through the room's porthole, illuminating the face and figure of Josephine via the basin's mirror. Perhaps she was just dreaming, thought Elsie, but Josephine's face looked unusually white, until she applied a brown substance from a container. As Elsie squinted through tired eyes, she thought she saw her friend quickly transform into the Josephine she knew.

Elsie yawned and turned away towards the cabin wall, to sleep.

It felt like an eternity before she woke, this time feeling relatively refreshed. The morning light had seen the nightmare of the previous hours and its swell and storm, transformed into a placid Tasman Sea. It seemed to chide Elsie for ever believing it to have been a savage beast, though at last Elsie knew differently. She had learnt to respect the sea and appreciate its better moods.

The four days steaming that followed, saw more sun than clouds, and plenty of card games and relaxation after the terror of that first night.

At noon on Thursday 8 May 1902, the *Waihora* anchored in Wellington Harbour, exactly five days after departing Sydney.

Elsie and the other passengers had many hours to appreciate the hills of New Zealand's capital, sprinkled with houses and buildings down to the waterline. The *Waihora* was not due to berth at Queen's Wharf till 9 pm, so the troupe spent the afternoon watching activity on the shoreline of a country only James Rial had visited before.

Well after the cloak of night had descended, the *Waihora* hauled up its anchor and turned, heading for the wharf. Everything seemed to be going smoothly until there was a loud cry and gesturing from one of the crew at the prow: "Back! Go back!"

Soon, crew were running backwards and forwards with long poles that they rammed through the shallow waterline, as the steam engine worked as hard as it could, but it was no good—the prow of the ship was rammed firmly in the mud off Pipitea Point.

Eventually, an exasperated and apologetic Captain Farmer called the passengers together and announced that there would be an attempt to re-float the vessel in the early hours of the morning, on the rising tide.

In the meantime, he called in a tender to enable those who had planned to disembark at Wellington, to leave the stricken ship at the earliest possible time.

As the troupe was staying on board till Dunedin, there was nothing to do but submit themselves to the standard cycle of shipboard life. So, they all slept until woken by a revving engine and the calls of celebrating crew as the *Waihora* slipped back and then sideways, away from its muddy captor and towards a 2 am docking at Queen's Wharf.

In the morning, provisions and extra passengers were loaded, though unfortunately, there was no time allowed for the troupe to explore New Zealand's capital.

As the *Waihora* put to sea once more—this time on the short trip down New Zealand's south-eastern side to Lyttelton, the port for the major city of Christchurch—James Rial called the troupe together.

For so long, Rial had played the 'silent partner' in World's Entertainers management to the outgoing and voluble Henry Lee. Now, for the first time, he was free from Lee's considerable shadow and was blossoming in his time in the sun, in his own quieter (and Elsie thought, most un-American) way.

"I have resolved that we should change the sequence in which we perform. While I know this is a new country, word still travels far faster than we ever can and the papers are often full of detail and critique." Rial hesitated momentarily, and most deliberately, as his gaze drifted across the performers before him. When it settled, it did so on Elsie—and she swallowed, even though she had only known him to be a kind and fair man.

"Tell me, Elsie, why did you change your skits with Arthur from those you so successfully performed in Melbourne's Bijou, to the ones in Brisbane?"

Elsie could feel herself tensing and surely, she thought, going red in the face. "But Mr Rial, we had to! You can't keep on performing exactly the same piece every night and expect the passion to still be there! Humour needs freshness and currency to make a real impact, and ..."

"Calm down, Elsie!" Rial said. "I asked you because I felt you appreciated what was required, as you are so damn new to the profession. Unfortunately, too many who have been around the stage for too long rely on their past to generate their future and it ain't always gunna work! Sure we fill theatres, and I know they don't know us intimately here in New Zealand, but we know ourselves. That's what concerns me. We need to freshen and mix things up!"

The troupe listened carefully, but Elsie could sense that some were wishing he had spoken these words four days earlier, when the odd card game could have been ditched overboard in favour of intensive experimentation.

Rial then leaned forward and pointed, first at Arthur and then Elsie as he spoke: "We will be starting our Dunedin shows with Awkward and Elegant, so you guys will be first cab off the rank and can set the tone for the evening. I will let you all know the rest of the sequence this afternoon." He stopped for a few moments and looked at his watch, knowing full well that all eyes were still on him and that nobody had moved. Then, he stood up with a smile on his face. "Go on! Get lost, in your rehearsals!"

By the time the *Waihora* had berthed at Port Chalmers, it was well into the morning of Saturday 10 May. Eight miles from Dunedin, the port was the southern outpost's drop-off point for larger passenger ships.

It took well over an hour to unload all the luggage, costumes and scenery, even with many extra hands seconded from those hanging around the dock. Eventually, the waiting train was filled, though lunchtime had passed and been sorely missed.

Rial had long realised that any possibility of World's Entertainers opening as planned and advertised that night at Dunedin's Princess Theatre, was an absolute impossibility. He had already cabled ahead to that effect, stating Monday 12 May would now be opening night.

The troupe was most relieved, with many doubting whether Henry Lee would ever have entertained the thought of such a practical compromise.

It was nearing four o'clock and the sun was beginning to contemplate a night-time nap, as a line of drays pulled up outside The Grand Hotel, on the corner of Princes and High Streets. *Not quite equivalent to its Melbourne namesake*, thought Arthur, *but still pretty nice.*

"Sure is one stylish town, ain't it!" said Rial as he alighted— and there was not a person who disagreed with his assessment, given the many fine buildings they had passed. "We will have something to eat quickly, then some time around seven o'clock, we can take a look at the theatre."

Members of the public were still milling around the main entrance of the Princess Theatre, studying the postponement notice when the troupe was ushered in a side door. Rial well understood the need for performers to visualise in advance the environment in which they would perform, and he was not going to make an exception at the start of 'his' tour.

As the troupe entered the theatre, everyone could see that it was unlike any they had performed in before: six tall and sculptured posts that balanced on the railing of the dress circle, supported a star-studded dome from which a large but solitary chandelier hung over the massed rows of bench seating beneath. At a glance, Elsie estimated that about 150 persons could be accommodated in the individual seats and boxes upstairs, with more than double that number in the stalls below.

As Elsie strode the stage, under the swag-edged curtain, she imagined how it would feel when they opened on Monday night—and she and Arthur were to be the very first act on the very first night of World's Entertainers' very first tour of New Zealand.

By Wednesday, World's Entertainers had comfortably settled into the rhythms of New Zealand's 'southern belle'.

Elsie had bought two postcards of The Grand Hotel and written to Emma on the back of one:

Dearest Em,

I miss you very much and wish you were here so that you could see this beautiful place with me. Dunedin has many grand buildings (apart from the one we are staying in) and a stately central area called the Octagon —most unusual!

Arthur and I open the show here and we have all had great support and reviews. Tell Mother and Father that Josi is looking after me.

Love to all,
El XOXO

PS: Drawing of Arthur from the Otago Witness enclosed.

She slipped the postcard and the image from the newspaper into a Grand Hotel envelope, kissed and sealed the contents, addressed it to Emma and passed it over to hotel reception. The second postcard was later sent to May Maxwell, in Melbourne.

A week later, the whole troupe had well and truly adjusted to the slow swing and style of Dunedin and was looking forward with some reluctance to their departure for the bigger city of Christchurch, just up the east coast, where they were due to open on the 26th.

As the stragglers were finishing breakfast in the hotel's dining room, Charles Sweet noticed a bellboy deposit that day's issue of the *Otago Witness* on a table near the entrance door. Unable to resist, Sweet sidled quickly but quietly through the maze of tables and snaffled that newspaper of 21 May 1902 before anyone else could get near.

He retreated to a corner to quickly scan each page before eventually halting at page fifty-six. He was reading so intently, he had not realised that his occasional laughing, bobbing and nodding, not to mention his nearly continuous grin, had attracted the attention of others.

"Hey, you! Charlie!" called out Richard Ashby. "Share it with the rest of us!"

Charles meandered back to the group, stating that the review was a near full page and admitting it was really quite good. He started reading out aloud and with considerable theatrical over-emphasis:

> No company in present writer's recollection can carry their reputation so gracefully or with so much dignity than can the World's Entertainers, and no company has a better right to the title "All Star" vaudeville.

This statement was greeted with much self-congratulatory applause and he was urged to continue:

> Each turn is done with a finish and grace only to be expected from artists so high up in their branch of business as are the members of the World's Entertainers. There is not a dull moment in the whole show from the appearance of Arthur Nelstone and Miss Elsie Forrest to the "ring down" on Big Casino, Little Casino, and Queen of Hearts.

"Next!" called out tenor, George Lyding. "Your turn Florrie!" he added, as he motioned Florrie Mahr to take over, temporarily. With Charles indicating her starting point, she read on with a flourish:

> Arthur Nelstone is a grotesque dancer ...

"Very grotesque!" interrupted Victor Kelly, to much laughter.

... and patter comedian, clever enough to remain on the
stage many minutes over the time allotted to him by the
stage manager. This artist is ably assisted by Miss Elsie
Forrest, who is responsible for much that is good in the
performance.

A round of applause and congratulatory urgings greeted the
last sentence, something that Elsie really appreciated.

"Next!" cried Lyding again, looking around for another
victim.

He spotted James Rial, who was quick to respond: "Oh, no!"

"Oh, yes!" said Lyding defiantly, and Rial could see that even
he had to join in the fun. Quite reluctantly, he rose and Florrie
Mahr showed him where to take over:

Charles Sweet, the Musical Burglar, occupies the stage
for fully 40 minutes, the whole of which time he has the
audience in a constant roar of laughter.

The bearded and tubby Sweet beamed in severe satisfaction
from his seat, as Kelly and Ashby spontaneously broke out in
chanting:

He's got them in stitches
He's got them in snitches
You'll soon find him up
Lady Singleton's britches!

The resulting laughter was curtailed by an icy look from
James Rial, who continued reading:

Sweet entertains solely alone, assisted by a piano, a ladder,
a dark lantern, and a cornet. Altogether Chas. Sweet is
the best single-handed entertainer this writer has ever
listened to.

After much raucous applause from the breakfast audience,
Lyding called out: "Next! ... Elsie!" and Elsie took a deep breath,
determined to project herself enthusiastically with whatever
confronted her in the paper. Rial pointed to where she should
start and she was off:

Not generally known that Miss Josephine Gassman, the
talented coon warbler of the present World's Entertainer's
Company, in Dunedin Princess, is a white woman.

As she read the words, their meaning slowly dawned on Elsie
and she continued, though quieter and slower, in disbelief:

The popular belief is that Miss Gassman, by reason of
her copper-coloured skin, is a quadroon, an octoroon, or a
"roon" of some description; and this belief is further given
effect to by the appearance of her two little Louisiana
piccaninnies, "Bill" and Irene. Miss Gassman's colour is
due to an excellent preparation of brown grease paint ...

Elsie could no longer speak and Arthur had stood up and
asked if she was all right. She read silently and quickly on:

... which she applies so artistically and so delicately to her
skin that one can scarcely detect its presence, even when
standing close beside her ...

There seemed much more, but Elsie had seen enough. She
dropped the paper on a table and raced off towards her room.
Josephine asked Frances to mind the children and headed after
her, in hot pursuit.

By the time Josephine reached Elsie's room, she was sprawled
out on the bed, crying. She approached slowly, before carefully
sitting down next to her, and stroking her hair softly.

"You know that is another thing that I really love about you,
Elsie—you are so trusting and accepting of others!"

Elsie could tell from the hand that stroked her and the
breathing that this was Josephine, but there was now no "Miss
Elsie" or southern black speech, just a standard west coast
American accent.

"I loved you for who I believed you were, Josi, even though I
thought you were a Negress!"

"And I love you even more for doing that, Elsie! Most people
treat me badly, but to you, my colour didn't matter! Here, turn
around beautiful!" Josephine turned Elsie over and lifted her
up till her head rested on her lap. Now, as she stroked her hair

again, she could see the tears tracking across Elsie's nose.

"Did the others know?" Elsie murmured.

"They have all known for a very long time, but accept it is the way I want to be."

"Oh, I feel so, so stupid!"

"Well, you shouldn't! You may think this has been a long white lie, but it is even longer than you think! I have been playing and living this part for years. Though I am really a white girl with a bit of a tan from San Francisco, I am a Negress in everyday life, so when I go on stage I have a better chance to play her to perfection!"

"And Bill and Irene, they call you Mamma."

"Bill and Irene are both black orphans. I found Willie Brown in Pittsburgh and Irene Gibbons in St Louis." Josephine then hesitated, wondering whether she should admit something. "They are," she said slowly, "my seventh pairing."

"Seventh pairing!" exclaimed Elsie, raising her head from Josephine's lap in astonishment.

"Yes, seventh. All the others were black orphans too! I chose them from orphanages. How many other poor black children in that situation would ever get the chance to travel and be schooled in the discipline of the stage? I teach them and raise them, and then they are ready to be adopted by a good home."

"Bill and Irene—will they be leaving soon?"

"They will stay with me during our upcoming tour of the States, but during that tour I will be on the lookout for my eighth pairing. And the cycle will continue."

"Do Grunter, Rusty and Cocky know?" Elsie asked, as a cheeky smile broke across her face.

"I suspect they understand far more than we appreciate! Well," Josephine said, taking a deep breath, "Miss Elsie, me thinks 'tis 'bout time yuz and me go back to dat breakfast area and rejoin our troupe, before wez are really missed!"

* * *

After performing in Christchurch and later in Wellington on North Island, the World's Entertainers found themselves in the provincial town of Feilding, north-east of the capital.

It was in the heart of farming country and the livestock

markets were right in the centre of town. Rather than a classical luxury theatre, the venue for their single, Wednesday 18 June 1902 performance, was the Drill Hall, a sizeable though not overly large, rectangular wooden building.

A marquee had to be erected as a change room, with performers led into the hall from outside as their turn to appear arrived. Elsie and Arthur brushed away the flies as they prepared to enter, but what was inside was to have greater impact.

Climbing the stage, they noticed that the hall was packed, mainly with men: farmers and farmhands, many of whom had been smoking in anticipation of the opening act. In a very large theatre, such a practice was annoying but might be endured, yet in a small venue such as this—for Elsie at least, it was a nightmare.

She felt ill before she settled on stage and struggled to continue at times during the ten-minute piece. Not that the audience seemed too concerned with her dialogue, their attention focussed more on her appearance and movement, much as a meat worker studies the attributes and relative merit of portions of carcass dangling before him.

At the conclusion of her performance, Elsie staggered from the hall and fell to the ground coughing, spluttering and gasping for the fresh, fly-ridden farm air that circulated around her.

* * *

On departing the Feilding Hotel the next morning, Josephine told everybody that she had a special function to perform.

Taking a piece of paper from her pocket, she directed the line of drays to a farm just outside the town. Grunter was probably the last of the travellers to recognise the property as a piggery. The truth was, he had physically outgrown his role.

Grunter was removed from his travel cage and put on his leash. He always enjoyed these moments, and even more the fond farewell pats that everyone showered upon his personage.

A last squeeze and kiss from Bill and Irene and he was off walking happily by Josephine's side towards a new life.

Pig farmer, Milton Black, stood waiting at his gate. He had assured Josephine that Grunter would remain as the family's special pet, but who can predict the future, especially when his kind are sold for slaughter on a daily basis.

* * *

With Saturday 12 July 1902, World's Entertainers last night of performance in New Zealand looming, an intensity and desperation that had not characterised Elsie and Arthur's relationship before, surfaced.

She well knew she was heading back to Sydney alone, while Arthur was destined to sail with the rest of the troupe to San Francisco.

On the evening of 8 July, there was a late night knocking on Elsie's door.

"It is me, Arthur! I must talk to you!"

Elsie opened the door and without a word, they embraced and held each other for a while. Arthur had wanted to do this for quite some time, but, as an archetypal Englishman, he had not known how to ask.

"The truth is, I cannot now imagine performing without you, Elsie! We are such a good foil for each other!"

"Arthur, that's so sweet! But you are the very best in the world at what you do. World's Entertainers are a great and reliable outfit, and, besides, there are many girls who could 'pretty dance' like me!"

"There's nobody as beautiful as Elsie Forrest, and I don't want to perform with anyone else! I only want to perform with you!"

They sat on her bed as Arthur explained his plan.

"My mother will kill me!" said Elsie, somewhat relishing the prospect of taking a course of action that might elicit such promised retribution.

"Tomorrow morning then, at 10 am!"

The next morning, Arthur, with a page from the *New Zealand Herald* in hand, escorted Elsie to Auckland's City Hall.

"I am after Mr Percy Dix," Arthur quizzed a cleaner.

"You can find him down that corridor, in the office round the corner! Mind you, I would be careful, he is not in a good mood!" she warned.

A baby-faced man was slumped over a desk covered in

accounts. His carefully constructed theatre empire that had spanned New Zealand's four major cities of Auckland, Wellington, Christchurch and Dunedin with permanent venues and full-time shows under the banner of Dix's Gaiety Company, was in decline. He had to shut down his operation at Dunedin's Alhambra Theatre just a few weeks before, as part of a desperate cost-cutting campaign to keep his dream alive.

"Excuse us ... Mr Dix? We were wondering if you would take us on as part of your show?" Arthur said respectfully in his English accent.

Dix glanced up momentarily, but he was in no mood for distraction from the maudlin task before him. "No, bugger off! I cannot take more acts, what I need are more patrons! Go and annoy the Fullers—those bastards will probably take you!" he said in an undeniably Australian accent that had barely been chiselled by years in Kiwiland.

Then he paused, frowned and slowly looked up again, in great astonishment, his cherubic mouth wide open. "You ... you are ..."

"I am Arthur Nelstone, and this ..."

"Elsie Forrest! Yes, I know! I have seen you at the Opera House! Please, take a seat!"

Arthur and Elsie looked around, but there were no chairs.

"Oh, sorry, I sold them last week," he said, picking up a pile of papers and dumping them on the floor. "Please, sit here on the desk."

Arthur looked at Elsie and she motioned him to sit on the desk. Dix quickly moved his own seat around for Elsie to sit on.

"I thought you were all off to the States next week?" a puzzled Dix asked, nervously playing with his ring finger as he sensed a business opportunity.

"I certainly will be, unless you can offer us at least three weeks as part of your Gaiety Show," Arthur responded.

"Three weeks? I'll offer you both three months! You can headline our shows and perform at each of the permanent venues!" He paused for a moment, then added with relish: "I'll even reopen the Alhambra in Dunedin for you!"

Over the next fifteen minutes they worked out the nuts and

bolts of the performance contract, which Dix said he would have typed that afternoon.

"I wasn't called P. R. Dix for nothing!" he cried excitedly, the lethargic, depressed-looking figure of mere minutes earlier, had been transformed.

Dix reached out and gave Arthur and Elsie each a giant bear hug.

"We must celebrate!" he cried, turning and opening a wooden cabinet behind his desk. He pulled out an old unwashed glass and a near empty bottle. "Oh, I guess we'll have plenty of time for that later!"

* * *

The lounge at the Central Hotel was the scene of much celebrating late into the evening of Saturday 12 July. World's Entertainers had just completed a hugely successful two-month tour of New Zealand and after weeks of discipline and dedication, some of the troupe, were letting their hair down.

Elsie watched goings-on with a forced but pained detachment, already feeling the hurt that impending separation from this family of talented performers would bring. As she looked around the room, she noticed James Rial sitting alone on a couch. Unfair, she thought, that the joint financier and leader of the enterprise should be ignored as all others celebrated its success.

As she wandered slowly over, Rial patted the couch seating next to him, indicating she should sit close. "Come and sit here, treasure! I always have room next to me for a young lady the New Zealand press label 'chic, sweet, slender and refined, as pretty as a picture and as graceful as a fawn!' Or, so I recall," Rial said, wrapping a protective arm around her.

"My mother will no doubt use different words to describe me when she receives the cable we will send tomorrow," Elsie suggested, as she laid her head on his shoulder. "It really is most kind of you to accept Arthur's request not to travel with the troupe to America."

"Think nothing of it! The truth is J.C. and I always thought he would opt out of World's Entertainers to stay with you." Rial held his breath for a moment, as he wondered whether he should speak his mind, then continued: "Elsie, I am saying this to you as someone who cares about you and has spent a long time in this industry. You and Arthur are a perfect combination on stage, but that is where your relationship should stop!"

"Mr Rial!" Elsie exclaimed, lifting her head. "I am still only eighteen and not nineteen for nearly three weeks! Arthur is more than thirteen years older! He treats me like a younger sister and I respect him greatly for it!"

Rial placed his left hand softly behind her head and gently pressed her back towards his shoulder. "Shhhh! Calm down! I just don't want you to underestimate a man's ability to confuse familiarity with acquiescence. Besides, I dare say there is not a man alive who would not secretly wish he could know you more intimately!"

Elsie was quiet for a minute as she pondered what he had said. In all her innocence, she had never viewed herself in that way. Nor had she thought too deeply about the impact of her burlesque attire and the lure she had become. These were uncomfortable thoughts, so she changed the subject. "When do you sail?"

"2 pm on Thursday on the RMS *Sierra*, via Honolulu and Pago Pago to San Francisco. I must say I am looking forward to getting back to the States! And you, young lady, should get back to the troupe and leave this ageing lothario to his improbable dreams!"

Elsie rose and kissed him on the cheek. He squeezed her hand and she was off to her performing colleagues.

On the Monday morning, before their first evening performance with Dix's Gaiety Company at Auckland's City Hall, Arthur and Elsie sent a cablegram to her parents:

Mr & Mrs Thompson & Emma. 52 Carrington St Sydney.

Arthur remaining in NZ. We signed 3 month contract with Dix Gaiety Co touring NZ cities. Will be staying in separate rooms! See you late Oct. Love to all. Arthur & Elsie.

As they paid for the cable at the post office, Elsie could sense her mother's reaction upon its receipt. "My mother IS going to kill me!"

Chapter 21

The Marvel of the Age

He can crush a thousand walnuts — or so often I've been told
Lift a horse but single-handed, tow a barge with tons of gold
Women faint who feel his muscles, his physique is all the rage
On a pedestal they place him, this great 'Marvel of the Age'.

On the morning of Saturday 4 October 1902—and with Elsie still performing in New Zealand—anticipation had reached fever pitch in Sydney. For some weeks now, the population had followed with fascination the progress of a phenomenon, a true marvel of the age.

Extensive newspaper reports had tracked his progress from his arrival in Fremantle by boat, to sell-out appearances in Perth, Adelaide and Melbourne under the Harry Rickards management banner. Promotional posters, equipment and a book had appeared around Australia's first city to fan the fascination.

Walter Thompson stood anxiously under a tree in Wynyard Park, turning his head down to study his watch every few seconds. George Bretnall had promised to meet him there at 11.30 am. It was now 11.35.

"Sorry, old boy!" cried Bretnall, as he whacked Walter on the back and they started up York Street towards Town Hall.

Normally, Sydney pedestrian traffic was a balance of progression in each and every direction, but not on this morning. A stream of mostly men in black, dark grey and brown suits and hats was flowing south down streets such as York towards its target.

The light rain that had fallen overnight had dampened the ground, but not the enthusiasm of the thickening flow as it approached its goal.

They had all come to catch sight of a man who could transform people's lives.

Prussian-born Eugen Sandow had stepped from obscurity some twelve years earlier at a most unlikely venue, the London Aquarium. It was there that Samson, the self-styled 'Strongest

Man In The World' had issued a challenge to all comers. "Match my feats of strength and you can win a hundred pounds!"

One after another, his challengers fell woefully short, till twenty-three year old Sandow stepped on to the stage, to the disbelief of the crowd and the derision of many. At first glance, Sandow appeared nothing but ordinary. He certainly had none of the size and bulk of Samson, yet he wore Samson down to the point of humiliation, when the giant repeatedly failed to lift a weight Sandow had held aloft.

Eugen Sandow had become an overnight sensation, and went on to tour cities across the world, packing theatres and promoting his system of physical culture and body development.

His exploits had become legendary: how in the United States he had wrestled a lion into submission; how he had lifted a pony above his head with a single hand; how he had raised a whole troupe and a horse on a platform balanced on his arched body; and how he was rumoured to have triggered mass orgies through regular invitations to society women to 'feel his muscles'.

Then, there was talk about the role of Martinus Sieveking, Sandow's near constant 'pretty boy' companion, who was just another reason why Sandow became a man for all reasons, preferences and sexes. All this added to the publicity and intense interest in the progress of his first Australian tour, in which his English wife, Blanche, formerly Blanche Brookes, became an increasingly frustrated observer.

As the Sydney Town Hall came into sight, the York Street sidewalks became choked, with people pressing on towards the Druitt Street police barrier opposite the hall's northern entrance. The police had also cordoned off York Street parallel to the Queen Victoria Building to allow the crowd to spill across the roadway, something it did within seconds.

"It's bloody useless!" Walter exclaimed in frustration, more than a little annoyed that his friend's tardiness had restricted their view.

"Ah, there is the QVB itself!" cried George, as he dragged his surprised friend left and up the curving stone steps of Sydney's latest architectural icon.

"Hang on!" Walter urged, stopping against an ironwork railing, thinking George was trying to take him up to the second floor's The Coffee Palace for a better view. "The Coffee Palace closed last year!"

"Exactly!" responded George. "And you know what replaced it? Offices! And you know what one of those offices is? J. A. Griffiths Lawyers! And you know who works for them? Remember Robert Ede from Fort Street School?"

"And?" Walter queried, as he leant back admiring momentarily the magnificent stained-glass array that soared within touching distance.

"I was late because I was contacting Ede to open it for us!"

"Oh, you bloody genius, Bretnall!" A minute later they were knocking on the lawyer's door.

Ushered in by Ede, they headed straight to the large open window that provided a panoramic and unobstructed view across Druitt Street to the Town Hall entrance. Looking left, they could see police lining George Street all the way south towards Redfern Railway Station.

"Sandow is supposed to arrive by express train from Melbourne and be greeted on the Town Hall steps by the mayor at midday," Ede said, checking his watch, "so he can't be far away."

"I managed to get Father to put aside a copy of Sandow's book *Strength and How to Obtain It* in the bookshop. Which is just as well, as it sold out!" Walter said, easing a small red book out of his inner coat pocket.

"You lucky bastard!" swore George, as he and Robert alternated glances at the open pages with visual checks of George Street.

"I was able to buy a Developer, but the Spring Grip Dumb-bells sold out too!" added Robert.

"That's him! Well, that is the escort!" George exclaimed, as a line of four mounted police followed by four veterans of the Boer War's Imperial Light Horse emerged from the distant crush of south George Street. Behind them was an open-top motor with two passengers in the back. As it drew closer, George added: "The younger one on the right must be Sandow! I thought he would be much bigger!"

George was not alone in being surprised—nearly everyone always was. The billposters of Sandow that had sprinkled Sydney's streets and buildings correctly portrayed a heavily muscled frame, though in reality, Sandow was only five feet, nine and a half inches tall. This was not what people expected—surely a man capable of gigantic feats had to be a giant.

When Sandow and his promoter, Harry Rickards, stepped from the landau, a murmur of disappointment and suspicion rippled through the thousands watching. Sandow was well used to and prepared for this scepticism. He had sent instructions ahead that a young man was to stand stiffly by the side of Lord Mayor, Thomas Hughes.

This had been arranged, but an enthusiastic member of the crowd burst into the official party and Sandow mistook the interloper, who had just wanted to shake his hand, for the stooge.

Within a trice, Sandow had tossed him into the air and caught and held him with one hand, as he hollered, arms and legs flaying. "Stiff, stiff!" exhorted Sandow, encouraging the young man to transform his body shape into something more compliant to the task. But the young man was having none of it, and the crowd roared with appreciation and laughter as Sandow flipped his 'victim' and caught him with his other hand. It ended up being as little 'staged' an act, as the crowd had believed.

"Wow! That is amazing!" Walter said, shaking his head. "We must get tickets for a show!"

"I tried this morning, but they are sold out well into next week!" Robert said, before adding: "And they cost a fortune!"

The lads made a commitment to try for the following Saturday evening, a night that they were sure would be an unforgettable experience.

'The Mighty Sandow' shows were always sold out to standing room and were preceded by a select group of vaudeville entertainers, though Elsie Forrest was not among them.

Well, not this time …

Chapter 22

The Man in the Black Cape

Count the cards that I will show you, watch as each will disappear:
Now you see them there before you—then you see they just aren't here,
Know that magic is our future, and that you cannot escape
For I am the man you long for—I'm the man in the black cape.

James Thompson had hoped this moment would not come, but accepted that it was his obligation, as household head, to make the determination.

For quite some time, he stood gazing out the lounge room window of his Carrington Street home towards the twisted and turned trees of Wynyard Park. As the late March lure of this 1903 autumn loosened leaves from their long-lived homes and sent them spiralling earthward towards death and decay, he wondered whether his pronouncement would trigger an equivalent outcome for those he loved.

Behind him, sat three people, each with a significant vested interest in his decision.

Arthur Nelstone, for all Mary Ann's wariness of men in relation to her daughter, had, James felt, proven to be a decent, honest and trustworthy soul—quite apart from his extraordinary talent and value as an onstage partner. He had respectfully sought the Thompson's permission to allow his partnership with Elsie to continue, but this time in Cape Colony, southern Africa.

Elsie, at nineteen, was seeing her stage persona blossom and wished only for a continuation and expansion of this exciting ride. Cape Colony promised much, in an exotic new setting.

Mary Ann, however, was adamant about one thing after Elsie's delayed departure from New Zealand the previous year: Elsie would not travel overseas again without her mother as chaperone.

This is exactly what Elsie did not want. Such an arrangement guaranteed a repeat of the restrictive environment she had experienced in the past. Once again, she would be the only performer to have her mother as a near constant companion, even though she did not feel, physically or emotionally, like a little girl anymore.

"Mr Nelstone, sir! Would you be so kind as to accompany my daughter on a stroll in Wynyard Park for a few minutes, for I must speak to my wife in private," James requested, though Arthur was already respectfully on his feet before Elsie's father had finished speaking.

James watched them exit into the park outside as dark thoughts crossed his mind, stabbing at him as they circulated: why would a wife seek to spend many weeks—more likely months—away from her husband, if she was truly happy in their relationship? Was their age difference of more than twelve years starting to tell, now that he was nearly fifty-four and engrossed in the bookshop and his returning officer tasks? Perhaps this absence might be indefinite, if he were not to insist on an end point.

"Cissie, if you feel you must go, then you may, but please don't make it longer than you have to! Elsie will be twenty in August and I would expect you should be away no longer than her birthday. Why, that is just over four months away!"

Mary Ann could see that her husband was in some anguish and wrapped her arms around him as they stood by the window.

"I promise you I will leave no later than the day after her birthday!" she said. "You must understand, James, that I believe Elsie still needs my guidance and support. But I promise you too, that this will be the last time I am away."

James sighed heavily, accepting that for each of the others to get much of what they wanted, he would be the one to suffer most.

"Cissie, you may call them back inside."

All three waited in silence for more than a minute before James spoke.

"Were I a man more focussed on self-comfort and indulgence, I would not countenance your proposition for one moment," he said turning around towards the others with a facial appearance that looked markedly aged from the one that had gazed upon them mere minutes before. "You may go, Elsie, but only if your mother accompanies you, though I have insisted that she returns no later than the day after your twentieth birthday on August 2nd!"

Elsie and Arthur looked at each other appreciating that this was as good as it was going to get.

"Thank you, sir!" Arthur respectfully acknowledged, then added: "I would really like to tour Africa with my own company after time in Cape Town ..." though his voice trailed off as Elsie squeezed his knee. James unsteadily found the comfort of his armchair, feeling that he was already experiencing the painful days that lay ahead.

"Thank you, Father!" Elsie responded, with as much enthusiasm as she could muster given the yoke of her mother's promised presence. She rose and kissed him, then almost as a reluctant afterthought added: "And thank you, Mother!"

As a man of his word, James Thompson reached out for that day's issue of *The Sydney Morning Herald* and searched its front page. "Well, the White Star Line have a ship, the *Runic*, departing for Cape Town on Thursday next week at 3 pm. Fares are from 16 pounds and 16 shillings to 23 pounds and 2 shillings, though it states that there is 'Only One Class Of Accommodation', so I suspect we should look elsewhere."

He scanned across the page. "Here is another one: The Aberdeen Line's *Moravian*. Departs at noon next Wednesday—saloon cabins are 31 pounds and 10 shillings. It says that 'saloon cabins large and elegantly appointed', so it seems," he said, folding the paper and placing it back on the table, "that *Moravian* it is! I will be paying for your mother to share a saloon cabin with you, Elsie, but with your earnings young lady, such an expense is well within your reach!"

"Thank you, Father! I am most able and happy to pay my way!"

* * *

In April 1903, the SS *Moravian*, under the command of Captain Simpson, crossed the Indian Ocean with less trouble than might have been expected, though Elsie, her mother and Arthur (who had been to Cape Town before), were still relieved and delighted to catch sight of Table Mountain looming spectacularly over their destination.

As she was helped aboard the tender boat for her journey to the shoreline of Table Bay, Elsie felt the same tingle of excitement that she had welcomed when she first stepped on foreign shore, in New Zealand.

Arthur had already cabled ahead, booking two rooms at Claridges Hotel on the corner of Plein and Roeland Streets for at least a month. He assured his travelling companions that it was one of Cape Town's finest.

Heading up Plein Street from the wharf in a dray, Elsie and her mother noticed for the first time the dark faces of native Africa, sprinkled subordinately amongst the white Anglo faces of the Cape.

Very soon, they would come to see a third complexion, the Indian, that predominated amongst the servants in the hotel's foyer, along with a fourth, the mixed-race Coloured people, a group that Elsie and her mother had initially presumed in their ignorance, was 'Black'.

After settling in to Claridges, Arthur made enquires about their Cape Town stage debut. He was delighted to discover that they were scheduled, as anticipated, to open at the Good Hope Hall the following Saturday, along with noted American comedians Mr and Mrs Sidney Drew and the strongman 'Ajax'.

Mary Ann rose early the next morning, their first full day in Cape Town. Elsie was still sleeping soundly from the exertions associated with rehearsing with Arthur the evening before, so her mother made sure not to open the curtains to their room lest her daughter be awoken unnecessarily by the morning light.

She dressed quietly and quickly, then tiptoed to the door. Reaching for her hat and parasol, she eased the door open, while studying her daughter's sleeping form. There was not a sign of stirring.

After the door closed with a barely perceptible click, she hastened along the corridor towards the grand staircase, the rustling of her long dress disturbing nothing but the occasional beetle that had eluded the dusky morning cleaning patrol.

"Would you mind pointing me in the direction of the closest fruit market stalls?" she asked the Indian man at the reception desk.

"Madam," he began, momentarily intending to query her on whether the hotel's food was not good enough. However, he changed tack and provided the answer she was seeking. "Head down Plein Street till you reach Longmarket Street, then turn left and head along to Greenmarket Square, where you will find all that you need!"

"Is it very far?" she asked, concerned.

"Oh, no, just a few minutes! It is just three, then two!" he responded, implying the minutes away by cab, with one turn.

As she headed out the hotel's revolving door, Mary Ann presumed that the square was just five minutes walk away. She ignored the hansom cabs lined up outside the entrance to Claridges Hotel, one of which her informant had presumed she would take.

An unusually icy wind gusted up Plein Street and pressed its claws right through the full length of the garment that clung desperately to her well-shaped forty-one year old body.

It felt far more than ten minutes before she reached Longmarket Street—and Greenmarket Square was surely as distant as France would have felt to Napoleon's forces retreating through a Russian winter.

By the time she entered the colourful expanse of the square, she was freezing and miserable. A return on foot was unthinkable.

She searched through the lines of stalls that flanked the square for the best fruit she could find. Almost all the stallholders were black, wearing knitted scarves and head covers on this cool morning.

She found one stall where the fruit looked fresher than elsewhere and asked about the price.

"Two pence oranges, one pence apples," said an older black woman in a croaky voice, before she broke into a fit of coughing and spluttering right in front of Mary Ann, who thought little of it, beyond mild annoyance. Though she had no inkling of it at the time, the woman's actions were to have a profound and shortening impact on her customer's life.

* * *

A couple of weeks later, Elsie was down early to breakfast in Claridges, when a familiar-sounding voice in an American accent shattered the library-like peace of the dining room. "Well, I'll be! If it ain't Forrest Baby!"

Elsie twisted around in pleasurable surprise, as only one person had ever used that nickname. "Alf! … Alf Lawton! What are you doing here?"

"Making as much money in as little time and with as little effort as possible, you can be sure!" came the reply from a comedian who had long been a stalwart on the Australian and New Zealand circuit.

"The last time I saw you, we were on the same bill with Dix's in Wellington!" Elsie recalled.

"Yeah, you were the beautiful script and I was the promissory note! I'm still paying for it!" he quipped.

"So is Clara with you?" Elsie asked of Alf's singing and dancing thirty-nine year old Australian wife, Clara Spencer.

"Are you kidding? I only arrived here a minute ago, and it takes at least half an hour to transform the average dragon into something presentable of a morning!"

Eventually, Clara, along with Arthur, joined them. All seemed most cheered by the reunion.

Alf explained that they were opening at the Old Drill Hall the following Monday, but Arthur warned them that it was tougher here than in Australasia. That is when he put forward his proposal. "I plan to form my own small, performing troupe and head north from here towards Cairo, stopping in Port Elizabeth, Basutoland, Southern and Northern Rhodesia, Nyasaland, Bechuanaland and other places. What do you think? Would you like to join Elsie and me?"

Alf looked at Clara, but he could see by the glint in her eye that the prospect was enticing.

"Well, it sounds like one hell of an adventure, for I can't say I have heard of half those places! So, if you are the manager," queried Alf, "what is your cut?"

"We split the takings from each show equally, then I take twenty per cent of each person's cut to cover venue hire and travel costs. You only pay for hotel accommodation."

Alf and Clara looked at each other once more, as Arthur kept going, hoping not to lose the momentum he thought he had gained. "With your talent as a comedian, Alf, Clara, who, if I recall correctly, was once called 'Australia's premiere ballerina', Elsie's singing and dancing with me, and my efforts in the latter, we have a great range of talent. We probably just need one more performer with a different skill and we would be a great team!"

"Have anyone in mind, Arthur?" Clara asked.

"Not at the moment, but I am looking!"

Alf was still frowning, just a little. "So this enterprise, when do you reckon it could tee off?"

"Early June. We should have completed our commitments by then, and bled this place dry!"

Alf looked at Clara again and she nodded. "Very well! Count us in, Arthur! Only one question, what will the company be called, Nelstone's Nutties?"

"I was thinking more along the lines of King Arthur's Jokers and Other Cards!"

"Oh, I am sure you were!"

Arthur, however, was true to his word on another matter, for it was little more than two weeks before he confronted Elsie at dinner with the words: "I've found him!"

"Found who?" she asked.

"Him! The one I have been searching for! I bumped in to an old colleague from the London stage on Adderley Street this afternoon, and I think he is the piece missing from our new troupe's performing jigsaw!"

"Not a dancer, nor comedian, nor singer?"

"No, not any of these, but a real talent! In fact we are all going to see him perform on Sunday night!"

"We are?"

"Well, it is our night off and I have already asked Alf and Clara to join us. Of course your mother can come along too!"

Arthur was still being secretive as Sunday's daylight disappeared into night.

"We shall all be taking the electric tram down Somerset Road to Green Point! I shall pay!" was all Arthur was prepared to reveal.

None of the other four had a clue about the type of

performance they would soon witness, nor the venue that would play host, until the tram approached Green Point. All of a sudden, everyone could see a gigantic, glowing light-fringed tent looming ever larger before them on Green Point Common, near the Green and Sea Point Golf Club.

"A circus!" Elsie squealed with childish delight. "You know, I have never ever been to a circus!"

* * *

As the ringmaster welcomed the crowd, the performers and many of their animals were lined up behind him.

"Which one is HIM?" Elsie asked, as she scanned the colourfully attired assortment of acrobats, clowns and animal tamers.

Arthur just turned to Elsie with a smile on his face and tightly pursed lips.

"Oh, come on, Arthur! That is unfair!" she complained.

"Very well," he said, relenting. "It is the man in the black cape!"

Arthur had barely finished identifying him when the caped figure leapt into action, grabbing two large sticks, lighting their ends from a flaming torch and then juggling them as the crowd cheered.

"He is a juggler!" exclaimed Elsie.

"No, not really," Arthur cautioned.

The man in the black cape stopped, stretched both arms out sideways so he formed a cross shape with the flaming torches held vertically. Slowly, he moved each torch in turn to his mouth, putting out their flame. The crowd roared.

"He is a fire eater!"

"No, not really."

The man in the black cape spun around and when he stopped, he showed a pair of empty hands—the torches had disappeared in a swirl of his cape.

"Ladies and gentleman!" bellowed the ringmaster. "I give you the conjurer and illusionist, the one and only, George Stillwell!"

As the crowd cheered, Stillwell's black cape swirled around

and around, then slowly subsided to the ground as the crowd gasped.

"He's disappeared!" Elsie cried in astonishment.

"No, not really," said Arthur. "I am sure we will see him again!"

And reappear Stillwell did, after the lion tamer and the trapeze artists.

Elsie laughed and cheered as he produced brightly coloured handkerchief after brightly coloured handkerchief, seemingly from out of thin air.

As much as she watched his acts, Elsie was studying him. He appeared to be in his mid to late twenties, tall and of athletic build, had dark hair and a moustache, and was, from what she could discern from her somewhat distant location, most striking in appearance. The more she saw of him, the more attracted she felt.

"Mr Stillwell is very clever, don't you think, Mother?"

"Most clever and entertaining!" her mother replied.

Stillwell, however, was not done yet. Near the conclusion of the show, he wheeled out a glass tank, filled it with water and then covered it completely with a large silk cloth. As dramatic music played, he reached out and grabbed the edge of the cloth, revealing a woman lying in the bottom of the tank. The crowd gasped and cheered, once more.

The woman slowly rose from the water and was helped out by Stillwell to much applause. Stillwell then raised both hands to the sky and rotated his wrists repeatedly, with each twist and turn revealing more and more material in his hands.

After a final swirl of his cape, the material fell from his hands to reveal the Stars and Stripes flag of the United States of America.

"American? I thought Stillwell would be English!" Elsie said to Arthur.

"Oh, no, he is too much of a showman to be English!"

As they clambered aboard the tram for the trip back through the Cape Town night to Claridges, there was unanimous agreement that the proposed troupe of adventurers had a much-valued new recruit.

Elsie particularly, was buzzing with excitement. There was

something about that man she found magnetic. She was feeling considerable attraction.

When it was announced that Cape Town's Lord Mayor, William Thorne, would be holding the annual Performers Welcome at the Old Town House, Elsie realised this might be an opportunity to get closer to Stillwell.

For once, Mary Ann could not be included, but she was quick to let Elsie know that she was familiar with the Old Town House, as Cape Town's de facto city hall stood imposingly on Greenmarket Square. Just the previous year, it had been the site of the farewell to Australian, New Zealand and Canadian forces that had fought alongside the British in the Boer War.

Waiting to be introduced to His Excellency, Elsie toyed with the idea of expressing her disgust with the British decision of the year before, to execute Lieutenants Harry 'The Breaker' Morant and Peter Handcock of the Australian-led Bushveldt Carbineers.

However, when she stood before the seemingly amiable and bearded Englishman Thorne, she defaulted to platitudes about the colourful nature and population of Cape Town.

"Well, Miss …?"

"Miss Forrest, Your Excellency!"

"Miss Forrest, we are doing our very best to clean up the city. For nearly two years we've been moving the blacks to Ndabeni township, outside the city boundary, for everybody's benefit!" the mayor said, then turned to greet the next performer.

Elsie was just about to question the justice of this 'township' arrangement, when Arthur whispered that Stillwell had agreed to move to Claridges: "Come over and I will introduce you!"

Elsie quickly forgot about the mayor and his prejudice and followed Arthur through the throng of thespians.

"George, I would like you to meet Miss Elsie Forrest, my onstage partner!"

Elsie looked up and into George's dark eyes and George stared back in amazement at hers. "What a honey pie!" he exclaimed, in what to Elsie was a surprising southern American accent.

Their gaze locked in for so long that Arthur felt an interloper and awkwardly opted to fetch both of them a drink. On his return, he could see that both were still standing there. Elsie was having trouble breathing, while George could not take his eyes off her. Both seemed oblivious to the goings on around them. Then, just as Arthur was unsure they had spoken any further since his brief departure, George initiated the conversation. "Miss Forrest, will you join me on the balcony?"

"Most surely, serr!" Elsie responded with a smile, as she attempted to imitate his southern drawl.

Arthur was left standing alone and holding two glasses. For the first time he began to question the wisdom of his approach to Stillwell.

As they intermittently gazed over the hustle and bustle of a Greenmarket Square afternoon, George desperately wanted to find out more about the girl with violet eyes.

"So, Miss Forrest, you are Australian?"

"I trust my accent has not betrayed me beyond reasonable tolerance, Mr Stillwell."

"Oh, please, call me George!"

"And me, Elsie! Well, George, you are right! I am Australian and was born in Sydney."

"From a performing family?"

"Most certainly not! My mother might wish she had been on the stage, but never was, while my father is a bookseller and stationer," Elsie said laughing, though at the same time turning to look for Arthur. "Arthur sometimes gets lost without me, George, so I had better go. Sometime soon, I want to hear about you!"

She had started to leave, but George grabbed her arm and spoke to her with great earnestness: "Tell me one thing. Is there a relationship between the two of you?"

"No!" said Elsie, laughing again. "We are just stage partners and good friends. There would never, ever be anything beyond that!" She patted his hand reassuringly with her free one, and disappeared into the cackle of the hall proper.

George stood on the Old Town House's balcony, staring out past Table Bay towards the Southern Ocean for quite some time. A feeling that seemed a mix of longing, excitement and dread had captured his spirit, but left his feet riveted to the spot. Eventually, he had the courage to turn and look over his shoulder, expecting to see nothing of the crowd—yet they were still there.

This was no dream. Right there and then, George resolved that he would have to make a move on the young Miss Forrest, before what must surely be a host of potential suitors.

Chapter 23

The Indecent Proposal

When I saw her I did want her, from her smooth unblemished skin
Classic ears to hear seduction, curving lips suggested sin
As my fingers trace her outline, feel her hair fall from her head
Warm and sighing, she's in heaven, as she writhes within my bed.

The Claridges waiter had just taken the lunch order and departed, when a figure suddenly appeared in his place. "Would anyone care for a napkin?" the figure asked, before rotating his wrist, to reveal napkins for each of the three persons seated at the square table.

"George! Oh, how very clever!" Elsie said with some delight, as she had hoped they would meet again soon.

As George placed a napkin in front of Elsie, he said: "For the beautiful princess!" Then he added: "For the princess' sister!" as he carefully placed one in front of her mother.

"Sister! George, this is my mother!" Elsie said indignantly—though Mary Ann felt pleasingly flattered—just as George had intended.

"And here is one for the future manager of our troupe!" George said, trying to butter up Arthur, who was as receptive as stale toast.

"George! Come and take a seat! You have yet to tell us about your background!" Elsie demanded, though Arthur was not about to tolerate this courting charade.

"Excuse me, I have to get some fresh air!" he exclaimed as he stood up, then firmly placed his chair against the table, and stormed off. Elsie turned and watched him leave the room with some considerable concern, but it was Mary Ann who resuscitated the courting process.

"You were born where, Mr Stillwell?"

"Paris ma'am, twenty-nine years ago!" George responded, then after a smile and a pause during which Elsie and her mother looked at him with puzzlement, he added: "Paris, Kentucky!"

Elsie giggled, encouraging George to continue. "My parents

both died when I was quite young, so I was raised by an aunt," he said, while easing himself possessively into the fourth seat at the square table. "I was always bewitched by magic and the ability to seem to make things appear and disappear. I even tried to make my parents reappear—though sadly to date I have had no success!"

"Oh, that is so sad!" Elsie said, subconsciously reaching for the security of her mother's hand.

"You appear none the worse for your childhood deprivation, Mr Stillwell," Mary Ann chimed in, as she was beginning to find this young man even more interesting than she had suspected.

Sensing that he had his audience captive (with the exclusion of the departed Arthur) and at least partly enthralled, George thought it might well be time to play his trump card.

He showed open and empty palms and the backs of his hands. A twist and a turn later and three purple silk handkerchiefs were laid on the table.

"So, how many handkerchiefs are there, and what colour are they?"

"There are three and they are most definitely purple, Mr Stillwell!" said Mary Ann.

Stillwell picked each up in turn and fed them into his clenched left fist.

"What colour did you say they were?" he pointedly asked, once more.

"Purple!" replied Elsie, who was watching very carefully, as Stillwell pulled a yellow and then a white one out of his left hand.

"That is remarkable!" gushed Elsie.

"And how many handkerchiefs were there originally on the table, ma'am?" Stillwell asked Mary Ann.

"Why, there were three!"

"Three, four, five ..." Stillwell counted, as he pulled silk handkerchieves of different colours from his left hand.

"But none of them are purple!" exclaimed Elsie in protest.

"Ah, you want the one that most nearly matches your beautiful eyes? Very well then!" A twist and a turn, and lo and behold, a purple silk handkerchief was produced on command.

"Amazing! How did you do that?" Elsie's question was just what George Stillwell had wanted.

"I originated the Handkerchief Manipulation Act seven years ago at Kornig's Casino in Philadelphia. So many performers have tried to copy it since, that I had to take out a patent. Last year I had a booklet explaining how it worked, published in London." He reached into the left inner breast pocket of his coat and produced a cream and brown-coloured booklet which he placed before his audience of two.

"Mr Stillwell … George … I really must check on Arthur. Please excuse me," Elsie said rising and leaving her mother to read Stillwell's publication, for she had never seen her onstage partner so upset.

Elsie headed to the hotel's foyer and not seeing Arthur anywhere, stepped outside. He was sitting disconsolately on the hotel steps.

Elsie sensed his mood, so sat quietly but closely to him. Neither spoke for a while. Eventually, she tilted her head till it rested on his right shoulder.

"We are going to stay together on stage, Arthur, our combination is too good to break."

"There are some days—many days—when I wish we were more than that!"

As much as she cared about Arthur, this was not a path she wanted their relationship to take. *Perhaps, once a man gets an idea in his mind, it is impossible to shake,* Elsie thought.

She put an arm around him and gave him a squeeze—and a passing hobo witnessed what he had long forsaken.

That evening, George went to watch Elsie perform. He marvelled at the smoothness and elegance of her gait, the charm and attractiveness of her presence, her exquisite timing and her humour. By the show's end, he knew he had to have her in his life.

The next morning, as she headed into the dining area for breakfast, George dragged her behind a pillar and kissed her on the lips. Elsie was shocked but delighted and responded with breathless enthusiasm, reciprocating his advance until she looked nervously around for her mother, before apologising that she had to leave.

The encounter had left Elsie emotionally charged and wanting more—much more.

That lunchtime, Stillwell arranged a table for two where he had placed a red rose. It was obvious to Elsie that Stillwell meant to take their relationship further—and she was thrilled at the prospect.

It was now mere days before the new troupe's planned departure for Port Elizabeth.

As they sat together, Elsie waited for George to speak … and waited. He seemed to be struggling to find the right words to say, so Elsie spoke instead:

> There was a Door to which I found no Key;
> There was the Veil through which I might not see:
>   Some little talk awhile of ME and THEE
> There was—and then no more of THEE and ME.

Before he could ask, Elsie told him it was Quatrain 32 from the *Rubáiyát of Omar Khayyám.*

Confidence, even brashness, could have described the George she had seen to date, but the man before her now bore no relation to his previous incarnation. He hesitatingly told her that one day he would like her to work with him on his show—and that he felt they would be a great partnership.

By the end of the lunch, George had eaten little, but said enough to make Elsie sure that he wanted their future to be together.

Before heading back to her room, Elsie bought a postcard of Cape Town from the Claridges Hotel reception desk and wrote to Emma:

Dearest Em,

I think I might have met the man I am going to marry! He is quite tall and dark and handsome. He is a conjurer and illusionist by profession. Mother seems to like him.

Hope all is well. Cape Town is a city in a

That Sunday night, Elsie was sitting in the hotel lounge after dinner with her mother and the rest of the proposed troupe, when George stood up to leave. As he passed Elsie, he pressed a piece of paper into her palm.

Elsie pretended as though nothing had happened and waited till he had left the lounge before sneaking a peak:

Elsie waited far longer than she wanted, before whispering to her mother that she was just going to the ladies' room.

Mary Ann saw nothing unusual in this, though unbeknown to Elsie, Mary Ann had noticed that her daughter was earlier peering at something in her hand.

Elsie's heart was pounding in anticipation and excitement and she was soon in the corridor outside George's room. She knocked quietly on the door of 217. It was opened far quicker than she thought. George pulled her inside and they started kissing, passionately.

Soon their hands were exploring each other's bodies—caressing and squeezing, each seeking to get closer and closer to the other, as their fervour increased.

"I must have you!" George urged breathlessly—and Elsie could feel his erection pressing against her. "Dammit Elsie—I want you so much! I swear I will marry you if you let me make love to you!"

"I want you too, George," she sighed, "but I have never done this before!"

At that moment, Mary Ann rose from her seat and walked straight to the reception desk. Not only had Elsie been gone a while, but she had doubted that her daughter had headed in the direction of the ground floor ladies' room. She suspected that Elsie had gone to see George.

"Could you please tell me Mr Stillwell's room number? I was meant to meet him there, but have forgotten it."

The large Indian gentleman did a quick scan of his room listing and replied that it was 217.

As she approached the room, Mary Ann could hear sounds from inside, but was still unprepared for what she saw when she slowly and quietly opened the door: two figures on the bed, entangled in the throes of passion.

"Elsie, how could you!" she cried.

* * *

Exactly how news of their tryst leaked was unknown, however, when Arthur heard of their naked dalliance, he was incensed.

By quite some misfortune of timing, Arthur encountered George near the top of the main staircase as they headed down to breakfast the following day. The Englishman grabbed the taller and younger American in a physical contest he was never going to win.

As they fell wrestling to the floor, then rolling over and down the steps of the staircase, it would have been obvious to both— if they had time and opportunity to think—that the dream of Nelstone's troupe and a dash to Cairo, was well and truly dead.

Elsie desperately tried to persuade Arthur to stay, but he had been humiliated—and within two hours, the finest comic dancer of the age had packed his bags and left for Port Elizabeth, from where he appealed to relatives for the funds to return to England.

George apologised for his ungentlemanly behaviour, but pleaded with Mary Ann for understanding and the hand of her daughter, which she provisionally gave, pending James' approval.

Elsie's reputation had been compromised, and Mary Ann felt she had little option. In any case, George had promised that he would eventually head to Sydney and run the Thompson bookshop. For now, Elsie could join George as his assistant in his magic show, so her employment was guaranteed.

Mary Ann hastily sent a cablegram to James in Sydney:

> Elsie and George Stillwell, an American illusionist of note, wish to marry. Both smitten. He seems of good character and prospects. Says he will in time run the bookshop. Please advise.

To suggest that James was surprised would have been an understatement. Nor did he feel that the cable was sufficient for all the questions he wanted to ask. Nevertheless, he appreciated the limitations of their separation and replied the next day:

> If Mr Stillwell is a good man and my dear Elsie will be truly happy then I give my permission. I look forward to seeing them both. Cissie, please come home!

On Thursday 11 June 1903, Cape Town's acting resident magistrate officiated at the marriage (under special licence) of George Edwin Stillwell, aged twenty-nine, born in Paris, Kentucky, USA, and Elsie Caroline Thompson, aged nineteen, born Sydney, Australia—though Mary Ann had insisted that Elsie's age be recorded as twenty-one.

Three days later, a physically unwell Mary Ann, suffering bouts of coughing, sailed back to Sydney.

Chapter 24

Encounter with The Great One

Women melt who stroke my muscles, for their men are weak and stoop
Men, they dream they had my physique, and could pose within my troupe
You should take the chance to dabble with The Great One, here today
And experience the excitement, of my muscular array.

After three more months in Cape Town, the Stillwell Magic Show moved to Port Elizabeth and later into the Boer cities of Bloemfontein in the Orange Free State and then Johannesburg and Pretoria in Transvaal.

Despite speaking no Afrikaans, the magic needed no translation, and George and Elsie earned enough through the summer months to delay their progress east and south.

Yet, turn back to the English-speaking areas they did, first to the coastal city of Durban in Natal, then, a year after their marriage, they returned to Cape Town.

Elsie was now twenty, and was growing up quickly. For at least the initial months of married life, she had basked in the pleasure and companionship that a regular intimate relationship provided, as well as the freedom it allowed from the restrictions of being a chaperoned single girl.

At first, being George's assistant had been an exciting experience, though Elsie was smart and flexible enough to master what was asked of her quickly. Soon, the repetitive nature of the acts began to grate on her. She could only squeeze herself into a ball shape or rise from a flooded tank a limited number of times before the novelty and her enthusiasm disappeared.

Then there was the outfit George insisted she wear: brief and publicly appealing it may have been, but it attracted much unwelcome attention from men, and more especially, from drunks. In every city, Elsie had required protection or rescuing at some time.

She had come in to this profession as a thespian and performer under her 'own name', and now she longed once more to be a star in her own right.

Mindful that she was a decade younger than her husband and a minor part of his enterprise, she had kept her desires secret for a year. On the evening of their first wedding anniversary, she was determined to raise the matter, even if it was obliquely, after a bout of passionate lovemaking.

As they lay in bed in their room at Claridges Hotel—an expense both knew they could not easily afford, given their moderate takings—Elsie made her first tentative step towards what she hoped would be a new life:

> We are no other than a moving row
> Of Magic Shadow-shapes that come and go
>   Round with the Sun-illuminated Lantern held
> In Midnight by the Master of the Show;

"Is that the Khayyám fellow again?"

"Yes, Quatrain 68."

Then there was silence, during which Elsie wondered: *Why are men and women so different? Why don't they seem to understand each other? Can't George see what I am hinting at? Perhaps, I am being far too subtle!*

"Darling," she started carefully, "I really would like to perform in my own right and name. It has been a year now ..."

"What? How dare you!" he yelled. "I organised a lovely dinner and atmosphere to celebrate our wedding anniversary and all you can be is damn ungrateful!"

Clearly, he had no intention of changing the status quo. She was to be his assistant—and that was that. On their first wedding anniversary, they had the worst row of their marriage.

Due to their limited variety of performance acts, rehearsals were few and far between, so Elsie kept occupied with reading. Her favourite place in Claridges was the bay window seat on the edge of the lounge that afforded a reasonable view of the comings and goings on the street outside. Occasionally, when the sun deigned to spread its warmth from the west in winter, it was a spot any cat would love and one that any sun-loving winter bookworm would adore.

She was in that window seat on the afternoon of 18 July 1904, reading a book, while George had headed out for his daily walk around Cape Town's city centre.

As she tried to concentrate on the printed words, she repeatedly felt someone was staring at her. Eventually, she looked to her right, but could only see an elderly lady counting her money. She resumed reading, but the feeling returned, stabbing her like a dagger in the back of her neck. She twisted right and back—and that is when she saw him—looking straight at her from a couch on the other side of the lounge.

It is best not to hold his gaze! She went back to reading her book. She had not progressed far when she was interrupted.

A nervous hotel attendant said: "Madam, the gentleman on the far side of the lounge … he … he requests the pleasure of your … of your company."

"Really? Please tell the gentleman that if he believes he has the courage, he can come over personally and introduce himself!"

Soon the attendant was back. "The gentleman would like you to know that he is … he is the 'Great Sandow' … and that he is waiting for you!"

Elsie wheeled around in shock to see Eugen Sandow leaning back and smiling at her, his arms behind his head, hinting at the massive power in his biceps and sculptured body. Initially, she thought of rejecting his advance, but then decided to wander over.

"You are even more beautiful than from afar!" he said in a distinctly German accent that had been softened and anglicised through years of exposure to the English-speaking world.

"My name is Mrs George Stillwell," Elsie said, reaching out her hand and hoping that her martial status might just afford her a form of protection.

"The wife of Stillwell, the magician?"

"The very same!"

"I am most pleased to meet your beautiful self!" he said standing and then bending to kiss her hand. Then he added: "And you are welcome to personally feel my power in a private session, in my room!"

What! Elsie thought. *This is even worse—he knows of my husband, but doesn't care!* "But I am a married woman, sir!"

"And I am a married man, madam—but life is short and another thing is too big and too good to be wasted!" he said somewhat euphemistically.

Elsie was lost for words. Like all other performers, she had heard rumours about his regular infidelity—even orgies—often despite his beautiful wife being around. Yet, Elsie had not expected Sandow to be so brazen.

He reached in to the pocket of his coat and produced a card, handing it with great pleasure (in anticipation of the presumed upcoming experience) to Elsie:

Eugen Sandow
Strongman
Room: Presidental Svite

Elsie stared at the card for a few seconds and realised that everything on it was pre-printed, bar the misspelling of 'Presidential Suite'. If he had only arrived today, then he had probably just written out a pocketful of these invitations for distribution.

"I shall see you there at 3 o'clock—it is on the fifth floor!" he said with a smile, then pivoted with military precision and headed off.

Elsie did not respond as he strode away, but was wondering just how she might survive such an ordeal. She checked the grandfather clock swinging mournfully in the corner, indicting seven minutes to three.

At that moment, she could have settled back down with her book, but there was now an opportunity that she found too tantalising to ignore.

She could have chosen the lift, but opted for the stairs, as she needed time to think. After dropping her book in her room, she walked slowly on, mulling over her approach as she went. *He is the world's strongest man. It will be difficult to escape his grasp. Even if I do, he is likely to have locked the door. I can only escape if I have the key ... so the key is ... the key! If he is to lock the door, the key will almost certainly be in the key hole.*

She removed a white handkerchief from her right dress pocket, keeping it in her right hand. Taking a deep breath in full knowledge that this was a huge gamble, she knocked on the door of Claridges' Presidential Suite. Sandow was quick to open it.

As she entered, she slid around the frame of the door like a train track clinging to a steep mountainside, dislodging his hand from the doorknob and sending the door backwards.

"Oh!" she sighed in mock ecstasy, sinking back till she felt the door close behind her. "I can already feel your muscled member thrusting repeatedly inside me!"

As she said those words, her right hand went behind her back and felt down below the doorknob—and found the key. A quick jiggle, and the key was out, and a year of magic shows began to pay off. A twist of the right hand had tucked it safely inside the white handkerchief. She then passed it quickly to her left hand, which deposited it deftly into her left dress pocket.

Meanwhile, Sandow was still recovering from the shock and ease of his potential conquest's acquiescence. Fired by those words and seeing her head leaning back, with her eyes partly closed but her mouth open, he found her impossible to resist. He grabbed her right arm and flung her like a doll behind him and onto the large bed.

As he went to dive on top of her, she rolled sideways to the edge of the bed, leapt to her feet and then dived on to his back, pinning him to the bed before he had a chance to readjust his position.

She quickly sat on the small of his back, the warmth between her legs radiating into his body, as her dress flowed around him like a modesty blanket. He squirmed uncomfortably as he reached in, through the frills, to adjust the lie of his erect penis that had been bent by the mattress.

"Firstly," she said, "I will give you a massage!" She placed her hands on the upper part of his back, but all she could feel were bulging, hard muscles. In frustration, she used a karate-chop action, which only made Sandow laugh.

"Oh, shut up!" she demanded mockingly and slapped him across the back of the head, which only made him laugh more.

"Relax!" she commanded, as she pressed on his muscles, though she could tell they were not quite as tense as when she started. As she worked her hands around his back, she sang an Australian lullaby that she had written with Emma:

Into the rainforest
On flowing stream
Babble and bubble
And flow with your dream

Here in the grasslands
With joey by side
You and the kangas
Together can hide

Dive in the ocean
The fish are your friends
Twisting and turning
Past coral bank bends

Fly with the cockatoos
Yellow and black
Echo their magic call
Rise and sink back

Child of this dreamtime
The South Land's your home
Love and respect it
Wherever you roam

Yours is the future
So sleep on, and know
All creatures are with you ...
Wherever you go!

As she was singing this, she noticed his muscles relaxing, allowing her to work them more easily with her hands—something he clearly enjoyed.

"I didn't realise you could sing so beautifully, young lady!"

"Then you obviously didn't know that I was a singer, dancer, actress and comedienne with World's Entertainers!"

"Really? World's Entertainers? Gott im Himmel! You must join my troupe!"

This is exactly what she wanted to hear. Delighted that she seemed to have a chance of achieving what she had set out to do, Elsie still worried he might refocus on more intimate matters.

"Do you know any lullabies?" she asked, causing him to think carefully.

"I know 'O Tannenbaum', but it is a song about a Christmas tree."

"Then sing it to me!"

"O Tannenbaum, O Tannenbaum, Wie true sind deine ..." he started, before being interrupted.

"Why don't you write the words down so that we can sing it, together! Go on!" she said moving off his back and playfully pushing him towards the room's presidential desk. *Hopefully, this should keep his mind off seducing me!*

As he struggled to his feet, she noticed that the intense ardour of a few minutes before was barely discernable in his groin.

Sandow sat at the desk and pulled a letterhead pad towards him, flipped the cover from the inkwell and dabbed the nib of the pen into the depths of its dark contents.

It took quite some time for him to finish writing, particularly as he halted frequently to sing parts to jog his memory.

Elsie meanwhile, had taken up a position at the bedhead and urged him when he had finished, to sit beside her. This he did, and she looked with wonderment at the beautiful, disciplined and obviously educated handwriting on the Claridges' letterhead page before her. "I have never spoken German before, so you will have to help me with the pronunciation, Mr Sandow!"

"Es ist nicht difficult!" he reassured. "Just listen and copy— we will go slowly!"

After nearly half an hour of practising, and with Sandow's guidance, Elsie was able to sing the song without stopping.

"Now, we will try it as a round," Elsie said. "You start, then I will start from the beginning when you have finished the first line."

Quite quickly they were mixing up their tunes and words amid much laughter. Each found it difficult to concentrate on their part while the other was singing.

"Oh dear! It must be way after four and my husband will be wondering where I am!" Elsie cried, leaping off the bed and stealing a glance at the watch that lay on the bedside table.

"I think I just might have preferred something else, but it has been great fun!" Sandow admitted. "You will join us when we travel to the north and east in September?"

"I would really love to, as I have missed performing on my own. However, I cannot, unless my husband comes as well."

Sandow thought for a moment about his troupe and the format. "Well … we do not have a magician … so … very well, you can both join us! You can attend a planning meeting next month. You are staying at this hotel all that time?"

"Oh yes, Mr Sandow!" Elsie replied, though she was unsure they would have made enough money to remain. "You are so wonderful! Thank you so much!" She kissed him and started for the door, then stopped while reaching in to her left dress pocket. "I think you might need this for your next visitor!" she said with a wink, taking his door key out of her white handkerchief and tossing it to him.

Chapter 25

The Magical Easterly Tour

Darkened skin and Arab headdress, carved canoe and sailing dhow
Stately lion to cranky camel, crocodile to village cow
In its colour—more than rainbow, in its food, it's more than feast
It's a world that's worth embracing—welcome, to the magic East.

At the end of the second week of August 1904, George and Elsie received an invitation from Eugen Sandow to attend a planning meeting at 10 am on Thursday 18 August in Claridges' meeting room.

The opportunity to join Sandow's Company, the highest profile and most popular touring company on the planet, was simply too good to turn down–even if the two of them had no idea where the company would be going.

The Stillwell Magic Show was still pulling audiences in Cape Town, though nothing like the year before, so the prospect of guaranteed regular income was a godsend.

Elsie had not explained fully to George the circumstances associated with Sandow's original offer, nor did she have any intention of doing so. All he knew was that they had encountered each other and he was made aware of her talents.

As they entered the meeting room on that Thursday, Elsie realised there were four people there she had never met.

"Good morning, Mr Sandow!" Elsie said confidently. "I would like you to meet my husband, George Stillwell."

"A great pleasure to meet you, sir!" said Stillwell. "I have seen you from afar in the lounge and lobby!"

"Welcome, Mr Stillwell! Any gentleman with the skill and ability to tie down a young lady like Elsie is most welcome in our company!" Sandow was being gracious, perhaps, though the twinkle in his eye indicated he really meant what he said. "Elsie and George—please call me Eugen!" he added.

The others were seated around a large walnut table and Sandow had no intention that they should sit there unannounced. "Let me introduce you to your fellow cast members: Mr Burt Fentress, who is a tenor," Sandow motioned

214

with a wave of the hand, "and Mr John W World and Miss Mindell Kingston!"

"Ah, the singers and dancers!" cried Elsie. "You are performing at the Tivoli at the moment, are you not?"

"You are right on!" John W said in an American accent that Elsie recognised as different to George's, but that George suspected was from the north-east.

"Now, one vital person you have not met is our touring manager, Mr Robert McGreer," Sandow said, introducing a serious-looking gentleman at one end of the table. "I have always thought that the combination of German and Scottish heritage in this company's management is an excellent one. The German ensures that all boxes are ticked and the Scot makes sure that those boxes are cheap!"

McGreer had heard that joke before and urged that they get down to business as he had much to do.

Sandow scanned the list he had made in his diary. "First, let me assure each of you five, the performers, that a contract will be offered to you for signing at the conclusion of this session."

"I believe you will be offered very good rates," McGreer interrupted, "but you must appreciate that this is Eugen's show and the people will not have come to see you. Your performances must be of high quality and relatively short compared with your usual shows."

"From five to ten minutes, absolute maximum!" added Sandow. "Elsie, I want you to open the show on your own. Singing is fine, but I want you to include comedy as well!"

Elsie was shocked, as this was more independence and responsibility than she had expected.

"And how should you be referred to in the program, Mrs Stillwell?" asked McGreer.

"Elsie Forrest—by my stage name! Forrest with two 'r's!" she said without a moment's hesitation, though she noted George's sharp intake of breath and clear surprise. "Definitely Elsie Forrest!" she repeated, just in case anybody was wavering, given George's reaction.

"Burt, I want you to appear second, followed by your magic, George. If you still choose to use Elsie as your assistant, she will have time to change. John and Mindell, this makes you last, just before me. Any questions? Well then, I am sure you have all wondered where we will be going … it is a three-month tour to … 'The East'!"

Elsie felt her heart miss a beat as she wondered what 'The East' meant. She was not alone, so McGreer enlightened the performers: "The plan is that you leave Cape Town on 20 September and sail to Delagoa Bay in Mozambique. After around a week there, you sail to Aden in Yemen, then a fortnight later to Calcutta in India. Your time in India should see out your contract, though there is a chance you may join us when we move on to China, Japan and the Philippines."

Elsie was so excited she wanted to leave straightaway.

"Do you have enough billposters to cover till the end of the Indian leg?" asked Sandow, marking another point on his list.

"Currently, over a thousand, so we are right for now."

"Let me explain to the rest of you that Robert arrives up to two weeks ahead of the company at each destination, setting up a fortnight's worth of publicity articles and photographs in each of the area's papers …"

"And arranges the distribution of billposters; the appearance of key public figures at Sandow private sessions, including doctors and military leaders, so they can examine Eugen and endorse the Sandow System …" added McGreer.

"And we pay him well for all his great efforts!" said Sandow with a laugh. "By the way, do you have enough copies of *Strength and How to Obtain It?*"

"I will certainly have to order another reprint from Gale & Polden in London and have boxes sent to Calcutta. Do you think we should increase the price?"

"What is it selling for at the moment?"

"Two shillings and nine pence."

Sandow thought for a while as the others waited. "No, I think not. We need to get people to buy into the System and the key is to get the literature first. How are we with the Spring Grip Dumb-bells and the Developers?"

"Developers, we are fine, but we need to order many more Dumb-bells from America. I will have the crates sent to Calcutta as well. Perhaps we could increase the price of the Dumb-bells. The adult version is twelve shillings and sixpence, the same price as the Developer, but we sell many more Dumb-bells."

There was silence once more as Sandow studied the palm of his hand, as if the answer was etched within. "No, once again, I think not. I want people to start the System, and the Dumb-bell is the easiest way. Any more issues?"

"None, apart from the contracts!"

"Ah, yes, could each of you please take your contract from Robert and read it. Ask me if you have any questions, then, if you are happy, sign it and return it to me. I will be here till … 11 am," he said, looking at his watch. "I trust I can welcome you aboard for the Sandow Company's magical Easterly Tour!"

George and Elsie did not need any more encouragement than a quick glance at their promised remuneration—and signed on the spot.

* * *

On Tuesday 20 September 1904, the Sandow Company sailed from Cape Town on what Elsie fully expected would be her most spectacular tour yet. It would be new places, new audiences and new experiences. Elsie was as excited as a child just before the dawn of a birthday.

The troupe lined the deck's port side as they headed north into Mozambique's Delagoa Bay, which for mile after mile was fringed with palms. As they pressed on towards their mooring, they passed steamers and square-riggers from all parts of the world.

"I've seen a German ship!" said Eugen with pride, then adding that there were also British and Portuguese vessels.

Disembarking at the quay, it was plain to everyone that the port was the key to the area's survival. On dockside to welcome them was Robert McGreer, who was quick to provide a geography lesson. "Over here to your left you can see ships being unloaded, with many of their goods bound for Transvaal. President Paul Kruger originally had the rail link with the Portuguese territory of Delagoa Bay completed because it was vital for his landlocked Boer territory. The nearest other ports were British-controlled."

He then turned to Eugen. "I arranged for publicity in the

English papers along with translations in Afrikaans and Portuguese. You don't open till tomorrow night, so I have organised for a dray to collect us tomorrow at 10 am, for a ride through Lourenco Marques. I will stay with you for the morning, but sail in the afternoon for Aden."

The dray was waiting outside Lourenco Marques' The Bay Hotel on time the next morning.

McGreer, already quite familiar with the surroundings, guided the troupe along the acacia-lined main streets, the two-mile long Avenida Aguiar and Avenida Central.

No sealed surfaces here—and thankfully no cobblestones! Elsie noted.

"The city has a population of around 10,000 and about half of that is European, mostly Portuguese. Around a quarter are Indian and the rest are native servants," McGreer explained.

There was a symmetry and planned orderliness to the city, but both Elsie and George agreed it was no Cape Town, Melbourne, or even Dunedin.

That night, Elsie opened the Sandow Company's season in Delagoa Bay before a large and appreciative audience sprinkled with English, Afrikaans, German and Portuguese accents.

Two days later, the atmosphere changed markedly with a tragic event on the bay's outskirts. A young native worker at one of the storehouses had gone to relieve himself in the nearby grasslands, when he was mauled to death by a lion.

While not rare, such ambushes were less frequent than crocodile attacks for those who strayed near the rivers. It was a reminder to everyone that Africa was a wild continent and that humans were often intruding in other creatures' territory. Eugen had already warned the troupe not to venture near the rivers that emptied into Delagoa Bay, but after the lion attack, he insisted that a guard armed with a rifle accompany them whenever they left the hotel.

Elsie thought this somewhat ironic, as Eugen had, in part, built his status to legendary level by out-wrestling a lion in America.

* * *

After ten days on the doorstep of Portuguese south-east Africa, the Sandow Company set off on the lengthy sea voyage up the continent's east coast and rounded the Horn of Africa, sailing in to the British Protectorate of Aden, on the southern edge of the Arabian Peninsula.

For Sandow, the protectorate's garrison of three and a half thousand British and Indian troops, offered an excellent opportunity to inculcate a relatively isolated but important section of the Imperial Army with his system and methods.

As the ship pulled in to the Prince of Wales Pier, they all must have wondered if they had not arrived on another planet: the part of Aden before them was ringed by brown hills of lava—and nowhere was there even the slightest touch of green grass or vegetation.

They disembarked and grouped gratefully under the large steel canopy on the pier, sheltering in its shade from the glare of the midday sun. It may not have been summer, but the ground seemed to radiate the heat rather than absorb it.

While they waited for their luggage and company equipment to be unloaded, a British officer on horseback rode to the edge of the canopy and scanned the group of arrivals. For nearly a minute, he meandered backwards and forwards around the canopy, searching for something or someone.

Finally, in frustration, he asked one of the crew to point out Sandow, which the man duly did. The officer studied Eugen momentarily, then raced off at considerable speed, both his scarlet and buff uniform and his dark horse contrasting with the drab hills and the white-washed buildings in the background.

Eugen had seemed to be in deep conversation with McGreer, now a near two-week veteran of Aden. Yet, all the while he had kept a wary eye on the officer.

Eventually, the troupe and its equipment boarded a line of gharries—the horse-drawn coaches that constituted Aden's transportation service, if one did not want to travel by donkey.

It was just a short ride to the two-storey and French-run Grand Hotel de l'Univers in The Crescent. This was Aden's equivalent of Bath or Nice, it would seem, though the reality on arrival, was quite a few rungs down the social and architectural ladder.

A 2 pm reception at the regimental headquarters in the

area know as Crater, lured the troupe out of the hotel to the expectant line of Indian gharry-wallahs, who dusted their coaches like Cinderellas hoping for glittering transformations of their rotting pumpkins.

Elsie noticed that Eugen seemed quite on edge, insisting that she and George not travel in his gharry, the first in the line. Robert McGreer, alone, was to accompany him.

Burt, John and Mindell joined Elsie and George in the second gharry.

"The regimental headquarters in Crater!" Robert called, now quite familiar with Aden's layout.

After a few minutes on dusty roads, they reached Crater Pass, a narrow and remarkably high gap in the lava walls that was crowned by a fortified bridge-gate. Motioned on by the guard, they worked their way up Crater township to the regimental barracks that currently housed the 1st Battalion of Buffs—the East Kent Regiment.

At the sentry gates they paused to confirm their identity and purpose.

The sentry took a quick look in the lead gharry and then, with a smirk on his face, turned and yelled up the hill to the barracks behind: "Lads! Our 'strongman' is here!"

His insulting tone of voice sent a shiver through Elsie—and confirmed Eugen's worst fear when he had spotted the officer wheeling away at the pier.

"To the headquarters—quick!" Eugen yelled at his gharry-wallah, as men poured out of barracks on either side, yelling abuse at the lead gharry and its smallest occupant.

Meanwhile, Eugen tore off his coat top and shirt, just as a stone struck the top of his head and another smashed into the side of the gharry.

There were now mobs of soldiers either side of the road chasing Eugen's gharry and hurling abuse. "Imposter!" "Stone the fake!" and even "Kill the rat!" rang across the parade ground in front of the headquarters.

The five in the second gharry were terrified and its wallah just froze, leaving them helplessly watching the attack unfold before them.

Eugen told Robert to duck as he desperately scanned the area in front of the headquarters. He needed a circuit breaker, very quickly.

Then he noticed there were lead cannons either side of the entrance steps. They looked permanent and heavy, but this seemed his only hope.

As the stones rained down, Eugen leapt out of the gharry and raced to the cannon on the entrance's right side. Meanwhile, Robert had rushed up the headquarters' steps just as Major Ravenhill emerged, pistol in hand.

Eugen crouched and pivoted under the cannon, his hands feeling for what might be a balancing point. It was then that he noticed a chain running through the cannon's wheels and large pins locking the chain to the ground.

It would be difficult to say what came first: the pistol shot from the officer, or the gigantic roar from Eugen, as, from a squatting position, he pushed upward with all his might, wrenching the pins out of the ground, just as a stone struck him in the right shin and another thudded into his groin.

Eugen's roar that seemed part anger, part exertion and part pain echoed around the parade ground. The area fell still and silent as everyone watched in awe as Eugen, wobbling but determined, raised the mighty cannon high above his head.

The soldiers froze in collective guilt and embarrassment, until Ravenhill yelled for the battalion bugler to play the 'Warning for Parade', as Eugen lowered the cannon.

The second gharry wove its way through the assembling soldiers to the headquarters steps, where Elsie and Mindell rushed to Eugen's aid. Elsie used a handkerchief to stem the bleeding from his shin, while Mindell mopped his brow.

"You all move inside, while I get to the bottom of this!" the major ordered, motioning the company up the headquarters' steps.

It was to be nearly forty minutes of painful standing for the battalion, as the Shamal—the hot and sandy north wind— swept in to add its assistance to the interrogation. Eventually, and with much reluctance, the battalion gave up its guilty. The officer who had circled Sandow at the pier, was dragged off to solitary confinement, pending further action.

Major Ravenhill was most apologetic when he spoke to

the company inside the headquarters: "You must realise that nobody wants to be here and that their pay is close to a pittance. Some men thought that they had wasted good money in buying tickets for your show, erroneously, as they now appreciate."

"How long are they here, sir?" asked Burt.

"Aden is their last deployment after years in India and they cannot wait to return home to England!" Ravenhill paused for a moment, then added: "I am no different to my men! Aden is normally a one-year posting, but since the establishment of the Anglo-Turkish Boundary Commission last year, our departure will be delayed by six months."

"Will there only be Buffs in our audience?" asked George.

"Initially, yes, they will be there, though we also have four Indian battalions of the Imperial Army—the 101st and 102nd Bombay Grenadiers, the 94th Russell's Infantry and the 123rd Outrim's Rifles—serving in the hills and at the borders around the protectorate. The plan is that they will be rotated over the next fortnight to give them an opportunity to see the show."

Two mornings later, the company, minus McGreer who had left for Calcutta the day before, sat in the waiting room outside the Office of The Resident, overlooking the waterfront.

"I have heard that the show was good and much appreciated last night!" the resident's aide-de-camp commented politely as they sat in silence.

"We are just glad we can cheer people up," acknowledged Eugen.

"Most people view the Arabs as untrustworthy, their children as beggars or petty thieves and this place as a pathetic hellhole from which they can't wait to depart!" The door behind him opened as The Resident, Major-General Harry Mason, Britain's most senior official in Aden, appeared in welcome. "And," the aide-de-camp added, leaning forward and whispering: "I agree with them!"

For their first Sunday in Aden, Elsie arranged for a sightseeing tour of the hinterland. George was far less enthusiastic. He had been hesitant when the possibility was raised with Major Ravenhill the evening before, and the major had insisted that an armed escort from the Buffs accompany any foray.

"We do our best to woo the tribes of the interior, but their cooperation can never be guaranteed. Kidnapping for ransom is an established part of their cultural experience and given your transitory timetable, they may well view you as quick and easy money!"

A compromise was reached where a shorter than originally intented excursion was agreed.

Thankfully, the day dawned cooler than they had yet experienced. An armed officer sat with George and Elsie in the gharry while two followed on horseback.

They wound their way along the sandy track from Hotel l'Univers, through Crater Pass, then on up through Crater's townscape of largely flat-roofed and whitewashed buildings. Mostly sheltering within from the heat, were long-robed residents and shopkeepers. Their goods spilt like keepsakes from a long-lost and colourful treasure chest, spreading out to tempt the unwary.

Elsie called to the gharry-wallah to halt outside one such abode. She then alighted and headed towards a stand of colourful garments, guarded by a woman whose attire said more about her desire for anonymity than any possibility of confirming beautiful natural features.

"Madam! Careful!" warned the officer from inside the gharry, as children materialised from every direction.

The mounted soldiers wheeled their horses to block either side of the avenue, turning nervously with their rifles raised.

As she moved closer, Elsie noticed that the woman had large, dark pupils that were highlighted by the most beautiful white surrounds. The woman seemed fascinated by Elsie's eyes and for quite a few seconds—a time that felt far longer—they basked in the warmth of mutual admiration.

"Elsie! It is time we left!" George called, as children pulled at her dress and pressed cheap trinkets towards her for conscious approval.

Elsie was enjoying the interaction, but the appearance of a number of men in kaftans, keen on finding out more about their exotic female 'European' visitor, had the military escort worried.

"Madam! We must leave now!" demanded the officer from the gharry.

Elsie stroked the hair of a couple of the children, embraced the woman with the beautiful eyes with a final visual 'kiss', then reluctantly sidled back to the gharry.

They wove their way through the increasingly narrow streets of Crater until Elsie insisted they stop again. George wondered what the hell for, as he could not see anything of note in the area around.

"Look at the donkey! Isn't he beautiful!" Elsie cried, as she approached a dark grey donkey standing mournfully by the roadside.

She stroked his forehead softly, down from between his ears. The donkey leaned forward and nuzzled her dress around her stomach. "Oh, yes, you are so beautiful!" Elsie whispered in his large and furry right ear, her warm breath tickling his ear so much that it twitched, slapping her across the nose—and causing her to giggle with delight.

"Dammit! She has found her twin!" George exclaimed.

"Don't you listen to that nasty man! He is from Kentucky, and people from there are always talking about 'kicking ass'!" she quipped, looking back at George with a smile, prompting her husband to lean back and roll his eyes heavenward.

There were times when their ten-year age difference really showed, he thought, before registering his impatience with a beckoning wave.

"Goodbye, darling, I hope to see you on the way back!" she whispered, planting a farewell kiss on the donkey's forehead.

"Remind me not to be next in line!" George called, then, as Elsie clambered back into the gharry, George could not resist a parting shot. "See the way he is looking at you? He thinks you are the dumbest bitch he has ever encountered!"

"He does not!" replied Elsie. "He is just trying to discern whether my accent is from Sydney's northern or southern shores—and his opinion of you and yours has headed well and truly south!"

The gharry and its escort pressed onward and upward, eventually leaving the buildings of Crater behind. Before them, lay a series of dam-like structures that straddled the gap between mountains of lava.

"These are the Tawila Tanks," explained the officer, "and to take a closer look we need to leave the gharry at this point."

Sandwiched between the mounted escorts, they walked a narrow and winding path up the left-hand mountain. Eventually, they arrived at a spot where the remarkable perspective encouraged explanation.

"They were originally constructed between one and two thousand years ago to catch the rainwater flowing off the hills. I can tell you that it does not rain often here, but when it does, it pours!"

Elsie studied the maze of high brick walls that fringed deep pits running back towards Crater. "Some of the walls don't look very old!" she observed.

"Thirteen of the tanks have been rebuilt over the last fifty years. The one closest to Crater is owned by the Parsee merchants of Aden, who charge considerably for the water extracted," the officer elaborated.

Just then, one of the soldiers on horseback caught sight of something on top of a sand hill behind the tanks. "Arabs, sir!" he called, pointing to three men on camels who had just surfaced from the desert beyond. "They are armed, too!"

Each of the British soldiers scanned the hills around them, fearful of being trapped. Sure enough, two more armed locals surfaced menacingly from behind the lava hill on the other side.

"Quick! Back to the gharry!" Elsie and George needed no encouragement to join the scamper back down the rocky path and the return journey to the hotel.

After a two-week sojourn in Aden, that most in the company termed as 'different', they were not sad to embark on the long steamer journey to India.

* * *

On the morning of Saturday 29 October 1904, they grouped together on the starboard side as the steamer headed to the docks at Diamond Harbour, inside the mouth of the Hooghly River.

Navigation further up the river that led into Calcutta, the capital of British India, was inadvisable for a steamer of this size. Instead, they would have a train ride of about two hours, according to the captain.

First, he had said, there would be an unfortunate but necessary delay. All disembarking passenger luggage would be 'steamed' in the dockside sheds, due to the threat of bubonic plague. To emphasise the danger, he added that an average of 100,000 Indians a month had died of the plague during the year.

Even to someone familiar with the plague threat, like Elsie, this figure was astounding. In Sydney, a plague death warranted a dedicated newspaper article and biography. Here, one was 'fortunate' to be just another digit in a weekly body count total.

It was a scary though tantalising window into this land of extremes, and as Elsie stood on the threshold of entry, her adrenalin was pumping. While she leaned against the ship's railing with the others, she was looking here and there, trying to take it all in and decipher the lay of the land.

"Who are those men?" she asked, pointing at a group dressed only in white loincloths, that had fanned out across the dock. They carried long bamboo poles with nets atop in one hand, and wire cages in the other.

"Rat-catchers!" responded John W with certainty.

Just then, a bright blue and white motor with white-wall tyres glided into view from their left, stopping presumptuously on the empty area of dock adjacent to the gangway.

"Now that is one nice vehicle!" said George.

"Possibly English, though probably American!" suggested Eugen. "I cannot say that I recognise the make, and I cannot see a marque from this distance." Then, noting the looks of surprise from his fellow travellers, with regards to his knowledge and interest in the subject, he added: "Well, I do have a De Dion at home in London and am waiting on the delivery of another!"

Moments later, a stylishly dressed young man stepped out from the driver's seat side, closed the door behind him and gazed up at the ship.

"Oh, he is a bit of a dandy!" exclaimed Mindell, with more than a hint of admiration.

Elsie studied him as closely as she felt she could, noting his well-built frame and tanned complexion.

Within half an hour, she was able to confirm Mindell's assessment, as they walked down the gangway towards their first steps on Indian soil.

As they milled on the dock, the 'dandy' approached George asking after Eugen. George enlightened him and received the now usual reaction.

However, the 'dandy' moved forward and offered a hand to Eugen. "My name is Sonnie Paul, sir. Welcome to India!"

"Ah, thank you, Mr Paul! We are all happy to be here!"

"For me, sir, this is indeed a great honour to meet you. I help sponsor Jack McAnflinn's Boxing School in Park Street and we religiously copy everything you do!"

"Have you perfected the German accent yet, Mr Paul?" chimed in Elsie, as Mindell laughed.

Paul twisted around to face his questioner and was met by a smile and glinting eyes. He was lost for words.

"Please excuse Elsie, she is the comedienne in the company! She usually cannot help herself!" explained Eugen, as George gave Elsie a rebuking shove in the ribs.

"We must collect our luggage from the shed, Mr Paul, though do you know where the train is?"

"Just beyond the shed you will find the platform. It is fifty-eight miles to Sealdah Station in central Calcutta. I shall look forward to seeing you all on stage tonight at the Theatre Royal. I can tell you that all Calcutta is excited!" With that he nodded deferentially and headed off to his motor and the drive back to the metropolis.

It took nearly a further hour for the luggage, performance equipment and stage sets to be loaded aboard the Sealdah-bound train for the rickety-rackety ride north through fields and farm hovels and into the urban environment of Calcutta.

As they pulled into the multiple track Sealdah Station, people seemed everywhere, though most especially on their arrival platform, held back by lines of police with canes.

One figure was instantly recognisable, Robert McGreer.

"I thought you had been delayed by a dalliance with a dusky Indian princess!" McGreer joked as he welcomed Sandow.

"Nothing anywhere near as enjoyable my friend! Have you sorted our accommodation?"

"You know how we talked about the palatial Grand Hotel on Chowringhee Road? Undoubtedly it is the best, but it is right in the heart of the theatre world. I have opted for the Great Eastern Hotel on Old Court House Street, near Dalhousie Square. It is still good quality but has the European stores nearby and is only a fraction of the cost!"

"Speaking out of your kilt again, McGreer, but I like it! The Great Eastern it is!"

Just then, a familiar figure pushed his way through the heaving and curious masses and headed straight for Elsie.

"Miss Elsie!" he called, as George gripped Elsie's arm protectively.

"Why, Mr Paul, how nice to see you again, so soon!"

Somewhat unnerved by the close presence of George, Sonnie dropped his voice and looked straight into her eyes as he passed her a card. "Please join me for afternoon tea on Tuesday at my mansion."

"We would love to do that, wouldn't we, George? Oh, you haven't met George Stillwell, Mr Paul, he is my husband!"

It would be difficult to describe the dramatic transformation in Mr Paul's facial appearance at that moment, beyond stating that it went from hopeful optimism to severe distress.

"Of course ... of course," he verbally staggered like a drunk reeling out from last drinks. "Yes, of course ... you can both come! ... 2 pm? ... And where are you staying? I shall ... I shall pick up both of you!"

"The Great Eastern Hotel, I believe!"

As Elsie exited into the Sealdah Station area sunshine, the colours and smells of India exploded before her. It was a kaleidoscope that was part chaos, part poverty, part sewage, part curry, but, as with all novelty, it was wholly exciting.

Chapter 26

The Man with the Emerald Ring

Packed out theatres, raucous soldiers, smoke-filled air, Calcutta heat
Many focussed more on Sandow, orchestras that miss a beat
Spinning out into the spotlight, silly skits not hard to sing
For the heaving mass of patrons — and the man with emerald ring.

The evening of Saturday 29 October 1904, at Calcutta's Theatre Royal, arrived too early for the cast and support crew of the Sandow Company.

A late afternoon rehearsal with the local orchestra, confirmed for everyone that the musicians were as yet, not up to the standard and familiarity required. This was a concern, particularly for Elsie, as she would be first to perform.

She decided that the best way to mask their deficiencies was to exaggerate their impact in her act.

The Calcutta rainy season had theoretically taken its final bow, though there was still humidity in the air, if not the devastating heat of summer.

Elsie, dressed in the outfit of a maid, wiped away sweat from her forehead as she counted down to her involvement.

McGreer had hung around to play the 'ringmaster' on opening night, introducing the acts. It was a role he really enjoyed, though one he rarely had the opportunity to perform.

He waited with Elsie backstage until the orchestra played a sequence of bars and the audience had quietened.

McGreer parted the thick red velvet curtain and strode onto the front of the stage.

"Ladies and gentleman of Calcutta! The Sandow Company welcomes you to their first night on the Indian Subcontinent! First up, I give you, Elsie Forrest, Our Little Maid!"

McGreer slipped back between the curtains and whispered to Elsie in his Scottish accent: "It is bloody packed to the rafters out there! Must be ten to twelve deep in the standing areas! Go get them kid!"

Elsie waited till her orchestral introduction was complete, then slowly placed her arm through the join in the red curtains.

In her hand was a feather duster, which she used to 'dust' one half of the curtains that she could reach.

Soon, she had swapped to the other half, then the duster and its controlling arm seemed to pounce from one part and side of the curtain to the other, like a cat chasing a mouse.

As laughter consumed the theatre, Elsie made sure her arm disappeared—and waited … this was when the orchestra was supposed to play the first of two bars, after which Elsie's bottom, alone, was to emerge from between the curtains.

Elsie waited, but there was no sound from the orchestra, so she briefly pushed her bottom through the curtains, to great applause. The conductor noticed, but too late. Elsie went back inside and tried again … once more, the orchestral reaction was too late, so she disappeared again. Then the third time, they got it right, and as the audience roared their approval, Elsie stayed with her bottom swaying from side to side as if she was sweeping something.

Slowly, she moved backwards towards the edge of the stage, dusting as she went, until she had completely emerged. She now stood up straight, though still had her back to the audience.

As she dusted on high, she slowly turned and saw the audience and screamed, collapsing with shock to the stage floor. As she lay there, she realised two things: just how warm all the packed bodies had made the theatre, and the foulness of the tobacco smoke that battered her senses and seemed to seep in to every part of her being. She could not wait to get out of there, but she first had to perform.

From lying prostrate on the floor, she rolled till she could reach her duster out towards the conductor. She pretended to tap his head for his attention, encouraging the introduction to her song. When it started, belatedly, she rose to her feet and, behind his back, conducted the orchestra with her duster, much to the audience's amusement.

As Elsie swayed backwards and forwards across the stage singing 'Three Little Maids', two young men in the royal box watched on, entranced.

"She is so beautiful!" said the one to the right, Raj Rajendra, Prince of Cooch Behar, in wonderment. "And, it seems she can do everything—singing, dancing, comedy, the lot! What is her name again?" he asked of his friend to his left, but his friend was so spellbound, he did not hear the request.

Reaching across, Raj opened his still frozen friend's copy of the program. "MISS Elsie Forrest, it says here! My dear friend, I am going to send her the biggest bouquet of flowers!"

This time there was a reaction, but nothing that Raj could see: his friend's left hand tightly gripped the knob on his throne seat, ensuring the large emerald ring contrasted with his whitened knuckles. Meanwhile, the punkhawallahs behind the men, repeatedly pulled on the cords that moved the large ceiling fans, providing them with a degree of comfort that no other patrons enjoyed.

Elsie completed her song to thunderous applause, wolf-whistles from many of the British soldiers present, and cries of "Encore!"

She duly obliged, singing 'The Miller's Daughter', but could not wait to finish, rushing through the curtains and heading, coughing and spluttering, as quickly as possible for the fresh and cooler air of the theatre's verandah.

Her respite was to be brief, as she still had to head back and change for George's session.

* * *

When masses of flowers arrived at the hotel on the Monday morning, together with a card for 'Miss Elsie Forrest' from the Prince of Cooch Behar, George was livid. He grabbed the card and pocketed it before it could be seen by Elsie, and headed straight for McGreer.

Just minutes earlier, he had seen how *The Indian Daily News* had referred to Elsie as 'Miss', in stating that she was a 'fascinating young lady who understands the art of being graceful'.

"What the bloody hell are you doing, McGreer!" he yelled, as he cornered the manager in the dining room. "She is my wife, not a 'Miss' Elsie Forrest!"

Initially taken aback, McGreer struggled to respond, before insisting that he had not written that in the draft for the program.

"Don't you proofread the damn thing? That is your job! I may as well place her on a bed outside on the street corner, so the whole of Calcutta can line up for their turn!"

"Well maybe you should have thought about that before marrying her!" was the repost.

That was too much for George and he lunged at McGreer, grabbing him by the throat. The commotion had attracted the attention of others and Eugen was quick to separate the two.

But it was too late for McGreer. "That is it!" he cried. "He does not travel with the company to Bombay in a fortnight!"

As he headed off, George thumped the wall in frustration, realising that his reaction had drawn a bottom line on their involvement with the Sandow Company. Soon, they would be on their own again.

George was equivocal about the Tuesday afternoon tea invitation, though once Sonnie Paul arrived with his motor, he allowed a spark of interest, admiring the dark blue leather seat. There was only one, in bench-style upholstered leather, so the three of them squeezed in, together.

As they glided past a series of grand buildings on Chowringhee Road, Sonnie explained that the car was an Auburn—an American model—and proudly asserted that it was surely the only one in India.

"Look to your left here and you will see the Bengal Club at No. 33. If you want to be anyone in British Calcutta, you have to be seen there!"

Elsie found this comment interesting, as although he spoke perfect English, it did not seem to be of the snobbish variety. In fact, with his tanned skin, he did not even look British. As they drove into 3 Park Street via a curved driveway, Elsie began to wonder if he might be part Indian. Whether he was or not, he certainly was determined to have enough manners to open her door and help her out.

Sonnie ushered them through an entrance framed by classical columns into a sizeable foyer, as a woman scurried forward in greeting. "Adelyne, can you please get my guests a cold orange juice each and bring them into the lounge."

"Yes, sir!" she responded with an easy smile, making Elsie feel straightaway that she liked her, though she was quite puzzled about her ethnic background.

Sonnie seemed to read her mind and as they settled in to the lounge, he gave an explanation: "Adelyne D'Sonza is her name and she has been the housekeeper here since my birth."

"D'Sonza, that is … ?" Elsie began.

"Portuguese. There are quite a few people of mixed Portuguese and Indian descent in India, though they are more often found to the south-west and the south-east."

"And you, Mr Paul, what background do you have?" Elsie asked, as Adelyne arrived with drinks and biscuits.

"Please call me Sonnie, Mrs Stillwell!" he pleaded, causing Elsie to laugh.

"Then you must call me Elsie, and my husband George!" Elsie insisted, though George was already feeling left out. He had the very distinct impression that Sonnie was not the least bit interested in him.

"My background is in fact Armenian. Calcutta has a sizeable Armenian population, many of whom are in business."

"So what, Mr Paul—I mean Sonnie—as a young man in Calcutta, do you do?"

"I do as little as possible in the heat! I sponsor the Boxing Academy where I train daily and assist various causes, though have nothing in the way of a job. You see my father was the Advocate General of the Calcutta High Court, but he died four years ago, leaving me this wonderful home and an inheritance." As Sonnie said this, George could swear that he was looking even more closely at Elsie.

The conversation drifted from one subject to another faster than biscuits were consumed, till it inevitably arrived at their status with the Sandow Company. Elsie explained how in less than a fortnight they would part ways and not continue to Bombay. They would be on their own with Stillwell's Black Magic Show.

Sonnie thought for a few moments, but all the while he seemed to maintain his focus on Elsie. "I think I can help you a bit there. Yes, I think I can help finance your stay in Calcutta!"

"Oh, that would be wonderful, wouldn't it George!" Elsie said, turning to see her husband who looked like prey dazzled by headlights. For George now, there seemed no way out.

They said goodbye graciously to Adelyne and headed back to the Great Eastern in Sonnie's Auburn. Before alighting, Sonnie suggested they come for a drive around Calcutta the following Tuesday, at the same time.

"Oh, that would be lovely, wouldn't it darling!" exclaimed Elsie, though George could not even give a grunt of approval.

When they reached their room, George slammed the door behind them and started shouting that Sonnie should have just paid Elsie for sex, and got things over with. What subsequently transpired, was definitely the worst row of their married life, and for Elsie a watershed in her relationship with George. The next morning, she bought a postcard of the Great Eastern from reception, and wrote as tears ran down her face:

> Dear, dear Em,
>
> I miss you so so much and wish you were here!
>
> Calcutta is a surprising and colourful city with much poverty but many grand buildings and monuments. We are here for a while, though we finish with the Sandow Company next week.
>
> George is well, but at times we argue and I would much rather have you to hold and comfort me. I am not sure that he understands. Pass my love to Mother and Father.
>
> Lots of Love,
> El XXXOOO

As Elsie was writing, she failed to notice Eugen enter the lounge behind her. He was frowning, having just been handed a sealed envelope by the hotel's manager. Taking a seat in a comfortable armchair, he noticed a crest on the envelope's front, so he made sure to open it carefully:

Eugen looked at Elsie briefly, but concluded that it was best not to disturb her. He headed back to the manager. "Yes, thank you, tell the Maharaja that will be fine!"

However, by Thursday morning, Elsie was not at all well. The regular evening race to the Theatre Royal's verandah—in and out of the heat and tobacco smoke—had given her a chill, with a cold setting in. By Saturday morning, she had a full-blown cold and there was concern that she would not complete that evening's performance.

As a precaution, John W was asked to open, with Elsie to follow if she felt able. Buoyed by sympathy from the audience, as *The Indian Daily News* reported, she completed a cake walk followed by a coon song and even bravely responded to an encore despite the heavy strain.

By the next morning, she was feeling totally miserable.

Eugen emerged from the Great Eastern at the appointed time on Sunday morning, to find a well-dressed young man and another who was surely a servant, standing beside a gleaming red car with fawn-coloured leather bench seats.

Eugen had heard of maharajas, but never met one, and presumed that, if he was to meet one soon, it was not to be at this moment.

The finer dressed of the two, who Eugen noticed had dark skin, stepped forward and offered his hand. "Mr Sandow, it is a very great pleasure to meet you, sir!" he said in very good English.

As they shook hands, the gentleman could see that Eugen had not recognised him. "I am the Maharaja of Tikari—though

I give you permission to call me Raji!" he said with a smile.

Eugen was mortified. He had met royalty before and was well used to formalities. "I do apologise, Your Highness!" In truth, his mental picture of a maharaja was of someone much older.

"Raji! Remember!" the Maharaja said laughing. Then, as if he had read Eugen's mind he added: "Yes, I may only be twenty-one, but I am certainly the Maharaja of Tikari!" He looked behind Eugen at the Great Eastern's entrance and asked: "Is Miss Forrest fetching her hat?"

"No, Miss Forrest will not be joining us today as she has a very bad cold." Eugen thought, as most superstars do, that people's interest in others would surely not match their own appeal, but the Maharaja looked absolutely devastated at this news.

Eugen did not want to inform him that he had not even invited her, but knew he had to do something to cheer up His Highness. He quickly removed his coat and lay at the side of the car, before sliding underneath and settling on his back; then feeling carefully for its stronger parts, he made sure to avoid anything hot. Moments later, with a roar that would have surely out-snarled any Bengal tiger, he slowly raised the vehicle with his feet and hands.

He then called out for the Maharaja and his servant to sit inside, and repeated the feat. His efforts greatly impressed the mixed crowd of Calcuttans who had stumbled across this impromptu performance, but the Maharaja still appeared distressed.

To Eugen's surprise, Tikari had sat in the driver's seat, and directed the servant into the back. As they headed off south, turning into Chowringhee Road, Eugen felt he had to try to make conversation from the front passenger seat—and explain things.

"I don't think that Elsie's husband would have been happy if …" he started.

"Husband? … Miss Elsie is married?" the Maharaja asked, turning to Eugen as the car suddenly accelerated.

"Yes! … Oh! … Watch out!" Eugen screamed, as they headed straight towards a wagon of jute pulled by two buffaloes that had dared to cross its accelerating path, while attempting a turn right into Kyd Street.

Eugen buried his head in his arms anticipating the impact, but Tikari slung the car right ensuring that he only just clipped the back of the cart—which then sent the car's tail spinning in an anticlockwise direction. The Maharaja then furiously slung the wheel the other way—leading the car to mount the footpath and sideswipe a fruit stand. Just when Eugen thought they would crush a pair of beggars, sitting cross-legged on the stonework, Tikari swerved left again and back on to the dirt of Chowringhee Road.

"Sorry, Mr Sandow!" Tikari said, as he eventually managed to stop by the roadside, with men running from a car that had pulled up behind.

"Are you all right, Your Highness?" one called.

"Yes … fine … I am fine! Just make sure that those people are compensated!" he ordered, to what was clearly a car full of his servants.

There was silence for a while, until Eugen said what he felt: "You know, that was a pretty good piece of driving—in the end!"

"I have raced in Europe and beaten some of the best, so this should not have happened!"

Tikari restarted the engine and they glided slowly on down Calcutta's main street, the giant green Maidan rolling out to their right, punctuated only by monuments and large ponds known as tanks.

"Who is Elsie's husband?" Tikari asked, surprising Eugen with what seemed a one-track mind, just as St Paul's Cathedral loomed large on their right.

"George Stillwell."

"Stillwell! That old magician?" The Maharaja's eyes grew wide as they stared into the distance. Light reflecting off a large emerald ring, danced across the front of the dash on Eugen's side, as Tikari's left hand gripped and ungripped the steering wheel.

Chapter 27

The Trojan Horse

On the morning of Monday 7 November 1904, a young man of mixed descent and olive complexion, reached to open the black and gold pedestrian gateway to a mansion in Ballygunge Store Road, till he noticed the darkly clad armed guard on the other side.

"Mr Manolescu," he announced apologetically, and the gate creaked open.

"Sir," the guard gesticulated with a sweep of his right hand, indicating the long path towards the mansion's front door, as he held the rifle tightly in his left.

Passing the ornate ponds and hedges, young Manolescu wondered how long it had been since he was last here—perhaps a year, perhaps longer. As for his first visit, well, that must have been all of five years ago, when he was only just fourteen.

Entering the large, white, flat-roofed mansion, he followed a servant along a marble floor and after passing a flight of plush double stairs, he was told to wait in an anteroom.

His hands repeatedly brushed through his hair, betraying a subconscious acknowledgement of his Bombay-based father's occupation as barber, more than any particular nervousness with this occasion.

"You may see the Maharaja now! Please follow me!" the turbaned servant instructed, as they walked into a luxurious lounge area.

At the far side of the room, a figure relaxed on an ornate throne, a bowl of fruit and cool drink on a coffee table by his side. With a flick of his left hand, he signalled to all his servants to leave—an action that caused a beam of light to reflect from his large emerald ring, and dance from floor to ceiling, then back again.

238

"Eugene, my dear friend, please take a seat!" the Maharaja motioned for his young guest to sit on cushions on the floor.

"Thank you, Your Highness, it has been some time since we last spoke."

"How is your sister, Olive?"

"Mother and I have not heard from her in a while, though I suspect she is anxious over one matter or another."

"No doubt about that! I told her she should have married me and not Jind! Never mind, I have a very important role I want you to perform." With that, the Maharaja rang a bell and a servant entered.

"The money and ticket!"

The servant bowed, headed outside and was soon back with a handful of notes and a ticket.

"These are for you, Eugene: 100 rupees as initial payment and a ticket to tonight's performance of the Sandow Company. I want you to watch Mr George Stillwell, the magician, very closely. His young wife, who calls herself Elsie Forrest, will also be performing. Your task will be to get to know them very well! So well in fact, that they will ultimately share with you, their inner secrets!"

Eugene was quite surprised, though having known the Maharaja for several years, he should not have been.

"I suggest that after watching tonight's performance, you visit them tomorrow at the Great Eastern Hotel where they are staying. You tell Stillwell you greatly admire him and want to learn his tricks, and that you want to offer your free services as an assistant. Within a week, I want you to report back to me on their plans and their relationship!"

* * *

Young Manolescu entered the Great Eastern's foyer the next day at an opportune time.

Raised voices were passionately debating an issue in the lounge, as he asked after Mr and Mrs Stillwell at reception.

"That would be them!" the receptionist said, with more than a hint of resignation.

Eugene turned into the lounge, nervously fingering the

theatre program from the previous evening.

"So why should I be a party to this charade?" a man with a dark moustache and an American accent, who Eugene immediately recognised as George Stillwell, retorted.

"Because George, we have nowhere else to turn now, and he is prepared to help!" a young woman who Eugene realised was Elsie, tried to argue. She was even prettier up close than he had expected.

Elsie was about to say something more, when she caught sight of Eugene. "Yes? Can we help?"

"I was … I was hoping that you might … would you be kind enough to autograph my theatre program from last night … please!"

"Of course, sweetheart!" Elsie said reaching for the program, though rejecting the pencil that Eugene offered. "George, do you have your ink pen?"

George opened his coat pocket and passed over a silver pen, which Elsie used to sign the program. "Now, your turn, George!"

George seemed more reluctant, until Eugene said: "I really loved your magic tricks, Mr Stillwell! It would be a dream to be able to do even one as well as you!"

As George signed, Eugene added: "Would you be able to teach me a trick or two, sir?"

"I am busy …" George began.

Elsie interrupted: "Come on George!" as a car horn sounded outside.

"That will be your friend, Mr Sonnie Paul!" George muttered in a contemptuous tone.

"Yes. And you are coming too, George!"

"If I must, I will be sitting in the middle of that damn seat—between you!"

As they headed towards the hotel's front door, Elsie squeezed Eugene's arm in passing. "Come back at this time tomorrow and he will teach you a few things!"

On Saturday 12 November, the Sandow Company gave their final performance at Calcutta's Theatre Royal. Elsie wore a kimono and sang Japanese lullabies to much acclaim.

The next day was always going to be difficult. While George

had not endeared himself to everyone, Elsie had proved a popular member of the troupe.

George kept a respectful distance as they said goodbye, but Eugen wrapped his muscular arms around Elsie. "Mein Schatz! You will always be dear to me!" he whispered into her ear.

While she could not translate everything he had said, she was sure of its general sentiment.

As the company disappeared down the road, the Stillwells knew there were tough times ahead. For now, Sonnie Paul's assistance was helping with their accommodation at the Great Eastern, but with no chance of theatre bookings, the Stillwell Black Magic Show and their very existence in Calcutta was under threat. A week later, and change was in the air …

* * *

Eugene Manolescu was ushered into the lounge where Tikari was pacing up and down.

"I told you to report back to me in a week and it has been two since we last met!"

"Your Highness, I am so sorry, but there has been a lot going on!"

"Well?" Tikari questioned, as he motioned for Eugene to sit on the floor.

"My mother has offered her services," Eugene said a little hesitantly.

"Your mother?" said Tikari with a raised voice. "Your mother extorted 50,000 rupees from the Raja of Jind in exchange for Olive!" he yelled, as his left fist thumped the table with such force that the ring's emerald scratched the table's surface. "And, she has been trying to be an agent for European women ever since!"

"So, Your Highness does not wish my mother to assist?"

"Ah!" Tikari cried in clear frustration. "My arrangement is with you Eugene, not your mother! If she wishes to help, that is her business! Now, tell me, where do things lie?"

"As you requested, Your Highness, I have made friends with the Stillwells. Mr Stillwell has accepted me as an assistant!"

"Excellent, Eugene, excellent!" said Tikari, cheering up. "And the Stillwells—how is their relationship?"

"From all that I have seen and heard it is not the best. Mrs Stillwell is a most attractive young lady and Mr Stillwell is a decade older and seems quite frustrated at her popularity. Sonnie Paul is certainly very fond of her!"

"Who is this Sonnie Paul?" Tikari asked, as he signalled for a servant.

"Mr Paul is around his mid-twenties, quite wealthy and lives at 3 Park Street. It is a nice home and I have already been there with the Stillwells. Mr Paul's late father was the High Court's Advocate General."

"Yes … I think I had heard of his father. Can you write Mr Paul's name down on this piece of paper? I am not the best speller!" Eugene complied and Tikari passed the note to the servant. "I want you to make enquiries about Sonnie Paul of 3 Park Street. Anything good or bad that you can find, though particularly bad, would be helpful!"

As the servant departed, Eugene added: "They cannot stay in the Great Eastern for long, it is too expensive, and my mother says …"

"Not your mother again!"

"Your Highness, I was going to say that she has found that the room next to us in the Humayun Place boarding house, will be vacated by Mr Everleigh next week."

"Vacated? Next week? Really?" At this point Tikari sat down, as he needed to think clearly. "If … your mother arranged with the landlord for me to pay for the lease … then she could charge the Stillwells a nominal sum … which she could pocket. This would put the Stillwells right at your door and under your surveillance!"

"Brilliant!" said Eugene. "I think my mother would like that too!"

"So tell me—what do you think of Elsie?"

Eugene thought for a moment, unsure of the response the Maharaja might like to hear. Then he decided to opt for the truth from his subjective perspective. "She is funny, intelligent and has a great personality. Personally, I like her a lot, though she is a couple of years older than me. Oh, she is quite adventurous too—Sonnie Paul has taught her to drive his motor, and she takes him down to his boxing sessions, and then she heads off on her own around Calcutta!"

"She drives—and on her own!" Tikari said, partly in shock, partly in wonderment. He signalled for a servant and asked him to ensure Eugene was given 500 rupees, as he departed. "Make sure the next time you report to me, is within a week!"

As they parted, both had reason to believe that their meeting had advanced their causes.

* * *

Sonnie Paul's Auburn motor waited outside 4 Humayun Place for only a few moments as Elsie was ready. She had passed the Bengal Club on Chowringhee Road on many an occasion, and heard much about how it was THE place to be seen. As one of Armenian descent, Sonnie had long felt like an outsider in this most Anglo of establishments, though the opportunity to glide across its floors and strut within its walls with 'the prettiest girl in Calcutta' on his arm, was too tempting a piece of 'revenge' to resist.

After placing Elsie on a sofa in a quiet corner, he headed off to get her an orange juice, and himself, something considerably stronger.

He had been gone but a few seconds, when a man who Elsie immediately recognised as a shark of the human variety, circled once and then struck.

"Pray tell me, who is this gorgeous creature?" he said in an English accent so posh, Elsie wondered whether it was fake.

"A young woman from the Antipodes, most unused to these shark-infested waters!"

"Ah! Just the sort I like, though your accent gives little hint that you are a 'bloody Australian'!"

"We are a broad-based but relatively egalitarian society, Mr ...?"

"Colonel Fitzwilliam, though you may call me Rupert!"

"Rupert the Redcoat!" she quipped instantly, noting his formal military outfit.

"Do you perchance ride a horse, young lady?"

"Well I can, to a degree ... Rupert!"

243

"Then," he said, removing a card from his coat pocket, followed by a pen that he used to inscribe details on its surface, "you must join us for our monthly Paperchase rides around the length of Bally and Tollygunge. It includes a number of jumps and is great fun. We always have spare horses—and you will get to know many in the expatriate communities!"

Elsie took the card, but as she did, noticed that Sonnie had been waiting patiently, drinks in hand, in the background.

"Rupert, you must meet my husband, Sonnie. Sonnie darling, Rupert was just inviting me to go on long monthly rides with him." Hearing this and noticing Sonnie's size and physical strength, Rupert started to go red and back away.

Yet Elsie had not finished, for she added with a wicked glint in her eyes: "Rupert says that he and I should do a lot of up and down and moving around together!"

"I really must go!" Rupert winced, as he turned and fled, without even a backward glance.

Elsie sat back with Sonnie on the sofa and took a celebratory sip of her orange juice. "Sorry, sweetheart! I just had to do that to get rid of him!"

She had barely finished speaking, when a violent stabbing pain shot through her lower right abdomen. "Ohhhhhh!" she gasped as quietly as she could, then gritted her teeth and closed her eyes. It was to be the first of many such attacks.

* * *

The dawning of 1905 brought no real improvement to George and Elsie's prospects. Despite physical assistance from Eugene and some financial help from Sonnie, the recently renamed Black Arts & Magic Show, now only operated from passing trade, garnered mostly from the terrace of Humayun Place.

The relationship between George and Elsie swung between cordiality and confrontation. All parties could see that the marriage had no realistic future. It was therefore a relief to Elsie, when, towards the end of January, Sonnie offered George 10,000 rupees to take his props and show to Singapore and beyond—and leave Elsie behind.

George figured that being a cashed-up 'bachelor' with young

Chinese female assistants in the virgin territory of Singapore, was a far more tantalising prospect than remaining in British India's capital with Elsie. So he took the money and ran.

When Eugene relayed this news to Tikari, he was delighted, especially as Elsie was to remain at Humayun Place, under his protégé's watchful eye.

Elsie advertised her singing, dancing and comedy skills in the local papers, to try to ensure an income, independent of Sonnie.

In early March, Eugene raced to the Tikari mansion in Ballygunge Store Road with terrible news: Elsie was soon to leave India with Sonnie.

Sonnie had promised to arrange opportunities for her to perform in London, and had bought steamer tickets, departing in a fortnight.

Tikari was furious, for he could see months of planning (and some considerable cost) amount to nothing. Most of all, the young woman of his dreams would disappear.

"Abu! Get me Abu!" he screamed.

Appreciating that things could now get a little nasty, Eugene warned Tikari that Sonnie was strong and a boxer.

"Really?" said Tikari, with the sadistic smile of a chess player about to checkmate an opponent. "But then you haven't met Abu, have you?"

Chapter 28

The Trap

Some are born and some are built on, some are large and some are huge
In the pantheon of great men, some are leaders, some are stooge
Recognise your limitations, just as you should know your strength
For a fool creates his own rope, when he stretches out its length.

The 'blind' man, who had sat crossed-legged on the other side of Park Street for nearly two days, studying the comings and goings at No. 3, suddenly vanished into the fabric of Old Calcutta.

The trap was set.

Sonnie Paul rounded the corner from Chowringhee Road and nuzzled the Auburn up to the garage entrance of his mansion. He had just dropped Elsie off at Humayun Place after she had picked him up from boxing training.

Adelyne was sure to have a nice meal ready, followed by a refreshing bath, once he had eaten as much as was sensible.

What light the moon and a streetlamp had collectively chosen to disclose, shone over his left shoulder as he went to open the garage doors. He had barely put a hand on the large brass knob, when he was startled by what sounded like the cry of a young girl from the side passage.

"Mr Paul! Mr Paul, help me!"

He turned around the side of the building and started down the passage, his shadow spreading out like a protective blanket ahead of him. "Yes, I am here. What is it? Where are you?"

As he scanned through the dappled light towards the dead end, a large and ominous darkness spread across the passage. At first, Sonnie thought it was his own shadow, though he quickly realised that he had stopped, and that this shadow was still moving—and was far, far bigger.

"Good evening, Mr Paul!" a man with a deep Indian voice said from behind.

Sonnie wheeled around to face his addressor, but all he could see as he looked towards the light was the dark outline of a giant, a man who was surely around seven foot tall.

The menace was obvious and Sonnie figured that his only chance was to strike first, so he swung a right hook as hard as he could into the stomach of the giant—but the man did not buckle, he did not even flinch.

Instead, a giant right hand grabbed Sonnie's arm and twisted it back over his head, causing him to turn around. As he did, the giant hurled him sideways into the brick wall of his mansion. He struck the wall with a thud, and winded, started to sink to the ground.

Another giant hand reached in and picked him up. He was turned around and pinned to the wall, his feet dangling well above the ground.

A hand was holding him by the throat, but thankfully, allowing him to breathe—for now.

"You are to leave the country next week for London, alone!" the giant warned. "Miss Forrest is to stay behind! Do you understand?"

Sonnie struggled to object, but it was useless.

"DO YOU UNDERSTAND?" the giant repeated firmly, as he tightened his grip around Sonnie's throat.

"Yes … Yes …" squeaked Sonnie, struggling to breathe.

"Because if you do not, we will make sure the Guthrie case is reopened!"

Sonnie caught what little breath he had, as this was not something he wanted to hear.

The giant released his grip and Sonnie fell into a crumpled heap in the passage.

"I trust we will not have to meet again, Mr Paul … have a safe journey!" the giant said, before turning and ambling calmly off into the night.

* * *

Elsie was as stunned by the late cancellation of her planned journey, as Sonnie was shattered by having to give her the news. They had dreamed of starting a new life together in London. Now, he would be departing for London on his own, and he had no idea if he would return. Things had come up beyond his control, he said, though he would not elaborate.

Clearly, their relationship and his ongoing patronage were now over.

Chapter 29

The Paperchase

Seize the horse and seize the bridle, seize the very chance to fly
Over jump and stile and creek bed, through the brambles with closed eye
Calcutta dust in every crease line—it's no world for frill and lace
Institution in this city—called by all: the Paperchase.

In the days after Sonnie had departed, Elsie languished in her lodgings, even staying away from Eugene. Sonnie had left her enough money to remain in Calcutta for a few months, but she kept on advertising her availability to perform.

It was while checking on her own advertisement one Wednesday morning, that she noticed another:

Paperchase
Saturday
Jodhpore Thannah 7 am
Horses Provided
Report to Colonel Fitzwilliam

She remembered meeting him at the Bengal Club and recalled his obnoxious nature, but the lure of horse riding after so long out of the saddle was too tempting.

While staying at the Great Eastern, Elsie had become familiar with the shops on Old Court House Street and she well recalled one called Phelps' Riding Breeches, at No. 15.

At the time, she had paid little heed to its purpose, as things equestrian would have seemed 'a far gallop', though now, stepping through its threshold seemed the least she could do, if she was to challenge the British buffoons of the gymkhana set.

Making sure not to alert Eugene, Elsie grabbed a handful of rupees, crept quietly down the boarding house stairs and signalled a gharry for a ride to Old Court House Street.

Andrew Phelps was pleased to greet a customer, particularly one that wished to purchase not only breeches, but also boots, a top and a pith rider's helmet—the latter being on Andrew's insistence, given the firmness of the Bengali ground.

"What week will you be needing the breeches, madam?" he asked innocently, after getting his wife to take detailed measurements.

"By lunchtime Friday, please, as I am due to tackle the Paperchase at 7 am on Saturday!" came the most unexpected response.

The couple looked at each other with a degree of distress. This was not the sort of deadline to which they normally worked. "Very well, I will sew through the night if need be," Mrs Phelps conceded, "though there will be an extra charge to have it ready for fitting by midday Friday!"

"That will be fine, Mrs Phelps. I am most grateful for your attention to this matter!"

"You do realise, madam, that very few women ever compete in a Paperchase?"

"Oh, no, I hadn't. And I must admit that I am very much in the dark as to the nature of the whole enterprise. I just thought it would be fun to be on horseback once more."

The Phelps' seemed shocked, though they were not about to knock back a multiple-purchasing customer.

At midday on Friday, Elsie was fitted by Mrs Phelps, and soon after emerged from No. 15 looking quite the epitome of equestrian elegance.

The next morning, a quick and early gharry ride down through Ballygunge to Jodhpore Thannah, brought her to the assembly point. She was most surprised to see so many people with horses near the start. Far more spread out as far as her eye could see in coaches, on foot and on blankets, preparing to watch the Paperchase.

A knot materialised in her stomach as, for the first time, she felt she had opted to swallow far more than she could chew.

She spotted Colonel Fitzwilliam quickly, his aloof, aristocratic bearing and turned up moustache helping him to stand out amidst the jacket, breeches and boots of the Paperchase 'proletariat'.

He studied Elsie for a moment, before reluctantly admitting he remembered her from the Bengal Club. "Madam, if you wish to ride today, you must first pay the annual membership fee of 20 rupees."

Elsie was relieved that she had cleared the first hurdle, but there were more to come.

"It will be a further 3 rupees for horse hire, as I believe you have not brought your own," he added.

A group of experienced participants had now gathered around, curious to find out more about this 'newun'.

"She should not be allowed to take part! There are no other women here today, and nor should there be!" cried one.

"Here, here! If she wants to, she should enter the Ladies' Paperchase, not get in our way here!"

"Miss Hemingway was a regular in 1901 and Miss King before that in '96, but I swear we have scarcely had any since," said another Englishman.

"Bloody well let her ride!" a voice called out in a broad Australian accent, the first she could recall hearing in Calcutta. "If she has bloody well paid her membership, she is damn well entitled to ride!"

"I must agree with our Australian friend. After all, are not all Australians born to ride? It is my decision—and mine is that she starts!" ruled the colonel, with Elsie thinking she had seriously misjudged him.

Then, before she knew it, a strong hand had grabbed her by the wrist and dragged her away to the side of the gathering. She found herself facing a rugged-looking man of close to George's age.

"Now you listen to me, young lady—this Paperchase is no bloody little girls' picnic!" the Australian warned. However, seeing the puzzlement on her face, he added: "Sorry, madam, I am Ernest Ivan Jones. 'Deadly Ernest' they used to call me at school, though today it would make me sound like an Oscar Wilde creation!"

"And I am Elsie Forrest. Are you always in deadly earnest, Mr Jones?"

"Just call me Ivan, Elsie. I actually can't bloody stand Ernest! Look, there are some good riders here: Evers, Captain Rennie, Dr Forsythe, Captain Courage, Pugh and the like, but for the most part these bastards would all be delighted to see you fucked, on horseback or off it! They treat it like an Empire game—and we Australians are not supposed to rate. Have you seen your horse yet?"

Elsie was shocked at the language but appreciative of the support.

"No, but Colonel Fitzwilliam has kindly offered to pick one for me!"

"Yeah, sure he has! Look, the course is nearly three miles and we will have around fifteen mud, fence or hedge walls to clear as well as jungle to ride through. Whatever you do, make sure you are not in the middle of the pack heading in to the jumps, as they will conspire to see you end up on your head or your arse! You still bloody sure you want to race?"

"Yes!" Elsie replied with more bluster than genuine faith, as all the talk was starting to scare her. "I am very bloody sure!" she added with a forced smile she hoped would hide the fear that was building inside.

"Well, I'll do my best to keep an eye on you, but it is a long ride, with many jumps. Remember, stay wide!" he urged, as he squeezed her hand as they parted.

Just then, a pair of riders headed out, carrying the finely trimmed paper they would leave on the ground as a trail for the competitors to follow.

"Fifteen minutes!" came the call from nearby, as Colonel Fitzwilliam guided Elsie to a nearby yard, where he singled out Primrose, the horse for Elsie to ride.

Initially, she was delighted that Primrose seemed quite docile, then worried once she mounted, that the chestnut mare might not have any real go at all.

She trotted Primrose around looking for an obstacle to jump, but there was nothing in the immediate vicinity.

"Two minutes, gentlemen! Oh, and lady!" came the call.

She followed the lead of the others and lined up between two fixed flags, making sure to stay on the extreme left edge. She could see the rough line of strewn paper leading to what looked like a jump in the distance—and she began to shake, thinking *why, oh why have I committed to this?*

"Primrose, you must be a good girl! I will do my best to look after you!" she reassured her horse, stroking it softly on the neck.

A man on horseback with a flag moved out ahead on Elsie's side, raising the standard.

Then, it dropped, and all twenty-six horses to her right surged forward with great gusto.

"Go, Primrose! Go!" Elsie cried, as she urged her mount forward.

After a matter of seconds, she was enveloped in a cloud of dust and could scarcely see. There was no concern about being caught in the middle of the pack, as she was being left in its wake.

Her world had gone hazy brown and she could not even see past the reigns. She tried to urge Primrose on, but dust flew into her open mouth and choked her words before they could be uttered.

In the confusion of the dust trail, she failed to see the first jump—a log fence—until it was too late. She pulled up on the reins, but her horse's front legs clipped the top rail and the hind ones collected much of what remained beneath.

The horse crashed through and over, sending Elsie into freefall, to land with a thump on the hard ground on the other side.

Everything seemed to go silent and still.

She must have blacked out for a while, for the next thing she remembered, was someone calling her name and asking if she was okay.

A strong arm slid under her and she was raised up to a sitting position.

"Is Primrose all right?" a stunned Elsie muttered, as she tried to see through the haze before her.

"Just stay there for a moment. I'll get your poor bloody horse!" insisted an Australian voice she recognised as that of her new friend, Ivan, who had dismounted.

"Why aren't you riding—has the race finished?" Elsie asked slowly.

"As soon as we neared the second jump I turned back as I couldn't see you anywhere! Bugger the race—people are more important—and horses!" he said reaching out for Primrose's bridle, as the horse hobbled around. "Come on girl ... easy ... it is all okay now," he said, trying to calm her. "I just hope she hasn't broken a leg!"

"Oh no! That would be terrible!" cried Elsie.

"That Pommie bastard, Fitzwilliam, has given you the children's riding horse. She can barely raise a gallop let alone jump a fence!"

With one careful hand on Primrose's bridle, he moved back and helped Elsie to her feet.

"There is no way you can ride Primrose, so you are sitting up on my horse with me." With that he leapt onto his horse and reached down and swept her up till she sat in front of him, with Primrose waiting by the side.

"Now, we are going to head back to Jodhpore Thannah, but very, very slowly."

Elsie closed her eyes and carefully lay back till she could feel herself against Ivan's muscular front.

"I am sorry to have ruined the race for you, Mr Jones!"

"Don't dwell on it Elsie. And for Christ's sake, just call me Ivan!"

"I owe you a great debt of thanks, Mr Ivan Jones!" she said, allowing herself to be cheeky as he dug her in the ribs in response.

"You should think little of it. It's at times like this I have to remind myself that I am a married man!"

Elsie smiled. "You and my best friend Emma would really get along," she began, then realised that with Mr Jones' taste in language, they probably would not. "She is the best young lady on a horse that I have ever seen!"

"You don't do a bad job of that yourself, Miss Forrest!"

"Stillwell is my married name. It may have been a still well, but a lot has flowed under the bridge since our marriage. He is in Singapore or on the Malay Peninsula at this moment."

"And my wife of three years is in Sydney, expecting our second child next month!"

"So what are you doing here in Calcutta?"

"Business, among other things. I supply horses to the British, mainly Walers."

"Walers, what are they?"

"Horses from New South Wales, though I import whatever is good. It is only for business reasons I ride with these bastards in the Paperchase. By the way, there were plenty of good horses of mine in that yard, and bloody Fitzwilliam knew it!"

They meandered slowly on for a while in silence, till Elsie commented after some reflection: "It was so stupid of me to try to ride today, without finding out more about the Paperchase. I have no desire, whatever, to be back!"

"Then I shall miss you, Miss Elsie!"

"And I you, Mr Ivan!"

Chapter 30

Woodlands

Mown lawns and well-raked gravel, grounds that spread both far and wide
From the front gates, to the mansion, hedges clipped from side to side
White and grand, Ionic columns, servants milling, you should know
If you're ever in Calcutta—Woodlands is the place to go.

Elsie gazed out from the terrace of Humayun Place, watching the sun rise over another dusty, amber morning in India's capital.

George's departure, while in part a relief, had left a hole in her young life—and like most who have experienced such separation, there were times she wondered if anyone would want to take his place.

She was immersed in this fog of self-doubt when she realised that a figure had joined her at the terrace railing. It was Eugene's English-born mother, Lizzie Coleman, and her presence, Elsie reasoned, signified something.

"You seem lost in thought there, luv," she said, her English accent still marked, even after years in the subcontinent.

"I was just thinking, Mrs Coleman, of my family and best friend back in Australia, and just how much I miss them."

"Families are wonderful, but marriages are better! There is nothing like having a partner in life!"

"As long as he is the right one! I am only twenty-one and already feel I'm a worn out shoe!"

"No, you are Cinderella, just waiting for the prince with the right slipper!"

"I've made one slip-up already—I'd be a shoe-in for another!" Elsie quipped, as Lizzie laughed.

"I've had two marriages myself, luv, so I know how low one can feel. But as a woman of the world, I can tell you there are many men who would die for your hand!"

"I don't want to marry a dead man, Mrs Coleman—and right now I am not even sure I could handle a relationship with a live one!"

"Well, let me tell you, that Eugene has his heart set on

escorting you to Woodlands next Saturday night. The Maharani of Cooch Behar is hosting a gathering. I have arranged for you and Eugene to receive a joint invitation!"

Elsie was doubtful that this was something she wanted to hear. To be in the presence of Indian royalty meant dressing up and an inevitable re-evaluation of her limited wardrobe.

"I have even heard that the odd maharaja will be there," Lizzie said in a hushed tone as she moved closer to Elsie.

"Well, he would have to be very odd to be interested in me! Besides, I am still married!"

"Oh, don't let such a trifling detail concern you, for they don't worry about such things! Most of them have multiple wives!"

"Really?"

"Oh, yes! When I arranged for my darling daughter Olive, to marry the Raja of Jind, I insisted on a written agreement covering wives, nacht girls, prostitutes and the like."

"Did they all have to sign it?" interrupted Elsie with a smile.

"I suspect, if they had, the paper would not have been long enough! So, tell me, have you been to Woodlands before?"

"No, nor have I even heard of it!"

"Ah, well then you will most certainly be in for a treat! It is reckoned to be Calcutta's number three residence, behind the Government and Viceroy Houses."

Most thoughtfully, Eugene had insisted on a full classical set of coach and horses rather than a humble native gharry for the journey south-west to Woodlands.

After sweeping south on Chowringhee Road, they swung right into Lower Circular Road, then left into Belvedere Road. Keeping the Viceroy's House to their left, they turned right into Sterndale Road, but eased to a crawl in a line of coaches and motors as they reached the left turn into Diamond Head Road, where the entrance to Woodlands beckoned.

As they passed slowly through magnificent pillared and crested gates, Elsie gazed in wonderment, for she had never seen anything like this. Turning up the curved red gravel driveway, they slowly climbed past spreading trees to their left and immaculately prepared flowerbeds to their right. On either side, the occasional glowing lamp signalled the direction to advance—not that the queue of motors and coaches allowed for any variation in progression.

With the turning of the coach in preparation for its parallel arrival, Woodlands the mansion came into view: its huge, white stucco form fringed with a wide verandah that was supported by Ionic columns. But it was the warmth of the heart of the structure that Elsie found so compelling: a golden glow emanating from every door and window, seeming to say 'You are welcome home!'

Two servants leapt to the coach's side as it halted—one opening the door and another offering a solid arm of support to Elsie as she stepped out.

As they waited in line to cross the verandah, Elsie caught sight of a woman bedecked in jewels and in a glittering sari, standing to the right of the entrance.

"That is Suniti Devi, the Maharani of Cooch Behar. Woodlands is her Calcutta home," explained Eugene.

"Oh, she is quite beautiful!" gasped Elsie, taken nearly as much by the glittering jewellery as the Maharani's natural appearance.

Eugene handed the attendant their invitation card and they both stepped forward: Elsie mimicking his bow to the Maharani as "Mr Eugene Manolescu and Miss Elsie Forrest!" rang out from the verandah.

The Maharani smiled pleasantly as they stepped up into a large entry foyer. Elsie looked around her, immediately noticing a tall young man standing on the landing of the staircase in the background—who seemed to be looking straight at her.

She turned with Eugene to their right, walked on a few paces and between a few people—and then looked up again—and he was still staring at her. *There must be some mistake,* she thought, so she was happy when Eugene suggested they move on further right.

"I have a good friend who wants to meet you, Elsie … and here he is! Elsie, this is the Maharaja of Tikari!"

A young man with dark skin and jewelled turban joined them, as Elsie bowed respectfully. "Your Highness!" In truth, this was the first maharaja she had ever met.

"It is entirely my pleasure to meet you, madam! I shall get you a drink!"

With that he turned and was off, returning with a glass of champagne in each hand, just as Elsie had noticed that the man on the staircase was still staring at her.

Tikari stretched out his left hand on which a large emerald ring sparkled, offering her a glass. However, Elsie's attention was elsewhere—and the Maharaja noticed.

"Is anything wrong?" he asked.

"There is a man, behind you, standing on the staircase, who has been staring at me ever since I entered."

The Maharaja wheeled around, took one look, then moved to position himself to block her view. "Ignore him! Now, here is your champagne!"

"Thank you, Your Highness, but I only rarely drink, and … please excuse me for a minute."

Elsie had moved sideways so she could see the figure on the staircase. From this distance, his very glance seemed to have formed an attachment to her, and now she could feel herself being drawn towards him, as if he were a fisherman, pulling in a prize catch.

As she slipped past Tikari, the Maharaja called out a warning: "He is cursed!"

It was too late, for Elsie had drifted on through the gathering to the base of the staircase.

She had not taken her eyes off him, nor he off her. As he made his way down the steps towards her, she noticed just how tall and handsome he was—his stylish damask silken outfit and very pale blue turban, studded with jewels, only accentuated his attractiveness.

He started speaking, which was probably a good thing, as Elsie was, at least temporarily, speechless.

"Did you get the flowers I sent you, Miss Forrest?" he asked, though the degree of nervousness in his voice both surprised and calmed Elsie. At least she was not the only one trembling.

"Flowers, sir?"

As she responded, she remained unaware of a commotion that had broken out on the floor behind her. A maharaja had crushed a champagne glass in his left hand, sending a mixture of blood and champagne rushing through his fingers, across his emerald ring and finishing with a series of splashes and tinkles onto Woodlands' marbled foyer floor.

Elsie's admirer too, was oblivious to the servants converging to clean up the bloodied mess. "Yes, I sent a large bouquet to you after seeing you on opening night last October, at the Theatre Royal."

"Oh, why yes, I do remember a very beautiful and large bouquet, but I did not know who it was from!"

"I did arrange for a card, though it matters not—the main thing is you are here now!"

For a few moments, they just gazed appreciatively at each other, he noticing her amazing violet eyes, pretty face and well-proportioned body, and she his tanned but not overly dark Indian complexion, handsome face, slim but elegant height and exquisite styling.

"Let's go somewhere else," he urged, steering her towards a door at the side of the foyer.

As he reached out to open the door, Elsie was concerned. "Are you sure we can go in there?"

He stopped, looked at her, then smiled, appreciating her naivety for the first time. "Yes, I am sure it will be fine!"

They walked through in to a study and he closed the door behind them. In such circumstances, most women might have felt trapped, but Elsie only felt excitement.

"You don't know who I am, do you?" he suggested.

"No, sir, but I do sense that you are a nice and kind person—and sometimes, that is all that one needs to know."

He motioned her to sit down on a sofa with him.

"My name is Raj Rajendra and I am the Prince of Cooch Behar. My mother is the Maharani who welcomed you at the entrance. Woodlands is our family home when we are in Calcutta."

Elsie did not know what to say at first, as all this was most unexpected. "My young friend, Eugene Manolescu, escorted me here tonight. I dare not be away from him too long, lest he thinks I have been kidnapped!"

"Ah yes, he is acquainted with my dear old friend, the Maharaja of Tikari. Don't worry, they will not be running away too soon. In any case, I loathe crowds and am much happier to just have your company."

Elsie was pretty sure that Tikari had said that Raj was

'cursed'—though this did not seem the time or occasion for her to question what seemed to have been a long-term friendship.

Raj explained how he was the eldest of four brothers and three sisters and the heir to the throne of Cooch Behar. He had been educated in England and even spent his holidays with the family of the Duke of Connaught, Queen Victoria's favourite son.

Elsie spoke of her relatively humble background, though Raj insisted that it was not a barrier to their friendship. She then felt obliged to admit that she was a married woman, though her husband had departed for realms to the east and they were now effectively separated. None of this seemed to faze Raj in the least.

Elsie leant back on the sofa and wondered if she was dreaming. She felt herself being swept off her feet by this prince and now desperately wanted to stay longer in his presence.

They must have talked for a considerable time, because, eventually, a servant knocked on the door, stating that the Maharani had wondered where her son had disappeared—and requested that he mix with the other guests.

Most reluctantly, he consented, though arranged with Elsie that his chauffer, a Mr Davidson, pick her up at 10 am the next morning so that they could spend more time together.

That night, Elsie had trouble sleeping. She thought she had loved in a childish sort of way Mr Williamson; she also thought she had loved George rather than the mere convenience of marriage—freeing her from the control of her mother; but now, she was pretty sure she already loved Raj, as much for his quiet and soft ways, as his station.

Neither Lizzie Coleman nor her son appeared the least bit happy or impressed with Elsie's date—something Elsie found quite strange, as Lizzie herself had assured her there could and should be interest from Indian royalty.

Mr Davidson arrived right on time at 4 Humayun Place, dressed in a chauffer's outfit and driving a shining Renault bearing the Cooch Behar crest.

Raj welcomed her back to Woodlands with a cool drink and a stroll through the grounds. They walked around the building, passing the cricket ground, the riding track and the tennis courts before ending up in the shade of trees alongside the front drive. Elsie put down her parasol as Raj reached up into the branches of a tree overhead, picking off a few white, star-shaped flowers, which he carefully placed in Elsie's hair.

"My mother has left for Cooch Behar, so we have Woodlands all to ourselves, for as long as we want!" Raj assured her.

As they lay on the lawn, Elsie placed her head on his chest, making sure not to crush the flowers. She could honestly say that she had never been more content in her life.

Just a few days later, Eugene and Lizzie left for Jind, stating that Olive was ill and needed them. Elsie's rent at the Humayun Place boarding house suddenly became more expensive, and it was only her insistence that, as a married woman she should remain there, that encouraged Raj to pay her keep.

Elsie and Raj spent most of the summer together, sheltering in the cooler and fanned rooms of Woodlands.

Mr Davidson appeared as usual outside Humayun Place on the morning of Wednesday 2 August 1905. Elsie well knew that it was not 'just another day', though she was not one to make a big fuss about any birthday of hers, let alone her twenty-second.

Lunch was pleasant enough, with seemingly nothing different to the normal fare, though Elsie noted that the peacocks did seem to linger longer on the lawn outside the dining room doors, even strutting along the verandah on occasion.

Their proximity was too much for Elsie, who loved animals. She raced outside, causing the peacocks to engage in an orgy of calls and extravagant displays, each trying to outdo the other.

Raj watched proceedings in his usual quiet, subdued way, though Elsie could tell by his more frequent than normal smiling, that he too, was most content.

By early evening, he had become more distant and thoughtful, as if he had something on his mind. It was normal practice for Mr Davidson to be summoned after dinner to drive Elsie back to Humayun Place—though not this night.

One of the female servants guided Elsie to a bath into which a bottle of the finest French perfume had been emptied. After luxuriating, Elsie was given the best massage of her life, the servant's strong, dark hands pressing, pounding and smoothing out every muscle, as the flickering candlelight added to the dreamlike nature of the experience.

Elsie was so relaxed that she was wobbly on her feet as she reached Raj's bedroom, clad only in a large towel.

He was sitting there in light pyjamas with his hands behind his back.

As she sat beside him, he kissed her on the cheek. "Happy birthday, darling!" he whispered, passing Elsie a long, burgundy-coloured box. "Oh, by the way," he added, almost matter-of-factly, "consider this our engagement gift!"

Elsie realised immediately that it was a jewellery box, but was shocked when she opened it: inside was the most beautiful custom-made diamond and ruby necklace with an R, then a heart, then an E, sparkling at its centre.

That night, for the first time, she slept over at Woodlands, revelling in Raj's arms and the luxury and intimacy of his bed.

At an early hour of the morning, she was awoken by Raj, who was crying out in panic, as if experiencing a nightmare.

"What is wrong, darling? I am here!" she urged, trying to calm him. As she reached over, she realised he was drenched in perspiration.

"Oh, it is nothing, just nothing," he muttered, sinking back into the bed sheets.

Elsie rose and summoned one of the servants to bring a face towel and cool water. As she dabbed it over his face and washed down his upper body, she assured him everything was all right, though soon his eyes widened as if a ghastly scene had unfolded before him.

"But the stars and the astrologers ... they have predicted I will not live beyond thirty-two!"

For a split second, Elsie thought she might joke that this could not be true, as Woodland's street number was already beyond that ... then thought better of it. "I wouldn't believe a single thing an astrologer says!" she cautioned.

Chapter 31

The World of Cooch Behar

Heading north aboard a royal train, on small gauge and winding track
You may think you're heading onward—there's a feel you're heading back
Past plantations in the foothills, Darjeeling's tea is not too far
Vermilion, white adorn the palace, in the world of Cooch Behar.

It was only after a letter arrived from Emma in early September 1905, stating that George Stillwell was now performing as an illusionist at Sydney's Opera House, that the issue of what to do about Elsie's existing marriage, became a matter for serious discussion.

Raj was of the opinion that an agreed divorce from Stillwell was the only viable long-term option; otherwise, there would be absolutely no prospect of Elsie marrying the heir to the throne of Cooch Behar.

He undertook to seek legal advice on the subject, but in the meantime, wanted her to accompany him on a visit to meet his parents in the ancestral home: Cooch Behar Palace, in the north-east Indian state of Cooch Behar.

The plan was to depart at the beginning of October, once most of the rainy period had passed, and to stay for around a month.

Raj assured her not to be too concerned about packing clothes, though she would need a very nice dress for the introduction to his parents. This, and Raj's insistence that Elsie was to be introduced as 'Miss Elsie Forrest', clearly indicated that Raj was most concerned that his choice of future wife—and eventual Maharani—might not meet with his parents' approval.

On the morning of Thursday 5 October 1905, Davidson and Raj arrived at Humayun Place just after 5 am, to ensure everyone's smooth progression to Sealdah Station. Elsie presumed and hoped they would be journeying in one of the better class of carriages, though she was to be in for a surprise.

Even at that early hour, servants were at hand at Sealdah, to usher them through the gathering station crowds to Platform 7, where a special train awaited: the royal train of Cooch Behar.

Fronted by its own engine were three gleaming dark purple carriages emblazoned with the growling tiger and trumpeting elephant crest of the princely state.

As she was escorted into the luxurious central carriage, the extent of the personal journey she was undertaking began to hit home.

Born into a middle-class Sydney family, married to a performer with whom she had shared stages, she was now being transported into a world and to a station beyond her imagination. Even months of visits to the expanse of Woodlands, had seemed relaxed and inconsequential by comparison.

"Darling, let me tell you something about Cooch Behar," Raj began, as the train commenced its near twelve-hour northward excursion, towards the foot of the Eastern Himalayas.

"My father, Maharaja Nripendra Narayan is from the line of K-O-C-H—pronounced 'Coach'—dynasty, rulers of the state of Cooch Behar. He was the first Indian prince to be educated in England …"

"Does that mean he is pro-British?" Elsie interrupted.

"If you have some anti-British sentiments, I would urge you not to express them in my parents' presence! My father has said should the British ever leave India, he would ensure he departed earlier, for there would undoubtedly only be chaos!"

"Oh!" Elsie mouthed as she slowly buckled, dropping her head near her knees.

Initially, Raj had thought this a reaction to his explanation, but he could now hear by Elsie's wincing that she was in some agony.

"It is that stabbing pain again—in this area," she said indicating the lower abdomen with her hand. "Sometimes, it is so painful!"

"When we get to Cooch Behar, I will have the family doctor examine you," he urged, placing his hand softly over Elsie's belly, in the hope of easing her discomfort.

A few minutes later, he pressed a buzzer on the window ledge and within moments a servant appeared from the carriage ahead.

"A bottle of champagne, please!"

"Most certainly, Your Highness!" the servant said, bowing

respectfully and backing towards the carriage's linking door that featured the Cooch Behar crest etched into its glass.

Within seconds, the servant had returned with a bottle of champagne in a bucket of ice and two champagne glasses on a silver tray.

He started filling both, but Elsie assured him she would only have a sip. Before the servant had even departed, Raj had drunk his and was reaching to finish hers.

"No!" said Elsie firmly, restraining the reach of his hand. "You can finish mine later!"

If there was one concern she had from her months of close friendship with Raj, it was his fondness for champagne.

"Tell me about your father, Raj," Elsie urged, trying to shift his focus away from alcohol.

"Well, my father has only one wife, but has had many affairs! It is just the way of their world!"

"And you—when you become Maharaja, will you be any different?"

Raj thought for a few moments, but did not directly answer the question. "In many ways, I am different." Then he added: "Elsie, please do not wear the engagement necklace I gave you, while in Cooch Behar. I really want them to grow to like you first before they know my intention."

"You don't think they will guess?"

"Well, yes, they may well do so, but I would like you to sort out matters with your husband first. The engagement is just between us, for now."

The heat of the day began to toast the world outside, but inside the royal train, conditions could scarcely be more comfortable. Elsie rose from her seat and strolled around the carriage: past the dining table that was shortly to serve lunch; by the wardrobe that stored clothes; beneath the portrait of Cooch Behar's Maharaja and Maharani—and here Elsie paused for a moment, as Raj intended that her image and his would next hang in this spot; turning back past the luxurious sofa and matching pair of armchairs, the last of which she grabbed and squeezed, as if to check this was not a dream; to the bed that lay beckoning with a toilet and bathroom beyond—all with servants a button-press away.

Oh, how I wish Emma could be here with me too, thought Elsie. *That would just make this time even more magical!* She made a mental note to send Emma a postcard from Cooch Behar Palace—though she would have to take care with its contents, as George Stillwell was currently residing in Sydney.

It was not long before two servants emerged carrying a white tablecloth and cutlery, and proceeded to lay the dining table for lunch.

A sequence of tiffin pans followed, each containing a range of freshly prepared contents, ensuring lunch was laid out and devoured in very English style.

Elsie drifted off to sleep on the sofa in the afternoon, her head cushioned and occasionally caressed on Raj's lap. It must have been quite some time, before she was awakened by the squealing of the train's brakes, as it glided to a halt.

Raj was quickly to his feet after ensuring that a cushion replaced his lap. "Gitaldaha!" he called out, after checking outside. "The town of Gitaldaha is the start of the state of Cooch Behar! It is here that we change to the narrow gauge, two foot six inch track!"

A few minutes after they had transitioned to the narrow gauge, and with the afternoon sun's curving fall towards the horizon well underway, Raj was on his feet again—but this time urgently pressing the buzzer three times.

On this occasion, the train's progress ground to a halt far quicker than at the border town, as servants rushed in to inquire as to the problem.

"Football!" Raj called out in a muffled voice, as he removed his top. "I am going to play football!"

With that, he clambered out of the carriage and down a slope to join in with a dozen or so children. They were kicking a ball made out of tied rags between goals of the same composition, spread across a dusty dirt field.

The halting of the royal train and the arrival of the distinguished player brought adults and other children out of the reed huts near the field.

Elsie moved out to sit on the carriage steps to catch a better view.

"Do not worry, madam," a servant with a deep voice said

from the background, "the next train is over two hours behind us!"

Raj displayed skills of a remarkably high level for such a tall player, dribbling with great dexterity in and out of the little legs that tried unsuccessfully to dislodge the ball from his control. The children's squeals of delight and laughter rang across the countryside, as Elsie pondered just what a great father Raj would be.

After about fifteen minutes of participation, that had seen the playing group swell to more than two-fold its original size, Raj signalled he had to leave. As he did so, he called out to a servant to bring down some rupees, which were gratefully received by players and spectators alike.

Stumbling up the steps and on board, Raj slumped exhausted onto the sofa as servants arrived to wipe away the sweat that covered his naturally tanned body, wash his feet and provide a cool drink.

"Did I tell you that I went to the 1898 English FA Cup Final?" Raj queried, still gasping. "Nottingham Forest beat Derby County 3-1 at Crystal Palace!"

"Oh, I am glad that a team called Forest won!" chimed in Elsie.

Raj took a moment to catch that one, then added: "My father is a great football fan too. He is a patron of Calcutta's Mohun Bagan club and has donated the Cooch Behar Cup, one of the most prized trophies in Bengal."

As the train jerked its way back onto its rattling run, Elsie was sitting away from Raj, but with a big smile on her face.

Raj looked across at her and noticed her big eyes shining like violet jewels. At that moment, neither could be happier or more proud of the other.

"Look at the river, Elsie! We are nearly there!" Raj exclaimed, as the train started passing the first of four steel frames that made up the bridge across the Torsa River.

"It is so wide!" she responded in surprise.

"At the height of the rains it can turn into a raging, roaring monster, though even on a day like this the current is deceptively powerful. The water comes all the way from Tibet and Bhutan, flowing through the Eastern Himalayas."

When the train pulled in to Cooch Behar Station, Elsie was quick to notice the shining motor, sporting the flag of Cooch Behar on its bonnet, as well as the mounted officers. A turbaned officer on foot saluted as Raj stepped from the train. "Welcome back to Cooch Behar, Your Highness!"

Elsie felt uncomfortable, as she was certainly not royalty, so held back. "Follow three paces behind me!" Raj instructed.

One, two, three … Elsie counted as she estimated the distance, but by the time she thought she had worked it out they were already at the motor.

"She is travelling with me!" Raj instructed the turbaned officer, who held the motor's back door open, while offering a steadying hand and "Madam!" as she stepped into the open-topped vehicle.

"Oh dear, it is a bit humid!" Elsie said, while fanning her face and neck.

"Yes, it can be humid here, though it is never as hot as Calcutta. Our proximity to the Himalayas makes it cooler."

With the mounted escort in the lead, the small procession headed west from the railway station through a patchwork of lush green fields, peasant houses and occasional stone buildings and monuments.

People stopped what they were doing and watched the royal procession pass, some waving and smiling. Raj waved in response. After just a couple of minutes on the road, Elsie had the strong impression that the inhabitants of Cooch Behar were very fond of their royal family.

Sitting next to Raj in the back seat, Elsie would have lied if she had said she had not felt a mixture of pride, excitement and, well, stardom. It was like being recognised and asked for an autograph on a theatre program, though Elsie understood it was purely through her association with Raj.

As to the nature of the Cooch Behar Palace, Elsie had not given it much thought. Her only reference had been Woodlands, which was sizeable and splendid enough, so it was with this in mind that she framed her expectation.

At a 'T' intersection, the car followed the mounted escort right, and as it did, Raj pointed to their left. "There it is! My father had it built in 1887, incorporating elements from Buckingham Palace!"

Across lush green grass that was dotted with a series of ponds, sat the palace of the Maharaja of Cooch Behar … and if Woodlands was grand, then this was close to indescribable.

Elsie stared in amazement at the huge structure with arcaded verandahs on two levels, topped by a silver central dome that loomed ever larger. The car turned left through a gateway with pillars displaying the crowned lion and trumpeting elephant animals from the Cooch Behar crest, then headed down a long, straight and paved drive.

For the first time, she wondered if this might be what it would feel like to be 'coming home' as the new Maharani of Cooch Behar, some time in the future.

As the procession drew closer, Elsie could discern the colour variation on the building: largely vermilion walls with white verandahs and columns topped with gold, and vermilion trim arching to the top of the silver dome. "Oh Raj, it is beautiful—and so big!"

Members of Cooch Behar's own turbaned Indian infantry guard, the sepoys, stood to attention outside the porte-cochère, as the car turned under its protective cover.

Raj led the way around the side of the building and into a vestibule off which sat a series of guest rooms. "We have less than half an hour before you have to formally meet my parents at 6.30 pm. Your room is this one here," he said, opening the door to a spacious expanse that must surely have been the best of any guest accommodation. "Dress neatly. I will arrange for a maid to be at your door at 6.25, but please, remember not to wear the engagement necklace, or talk about our engagement!"

With that, Raj kissed her and left.

Elsie barely had time to take in the room around her, when there was a polite knock at the door and two servants entered with her trunk of clothes. A maid followed, offering to hang its contents in the cupboards, but Elsie insisted that she could do this herself. The maid departed looking distressed.

Another maid appeared at the nominated time and led Elsie to where Raj was waiting outside the Durbar Hall's entry door.

"The servants seem to want to do everything, but don't

understand that I am quite capable," Elsie protested.

"No, it is you who do not understand!" Raj responded in a most unusually firm voice. "There are over four hundred servants here in the palace. Each has a particular role that is their identity. Deprive them of their role and you take their dignity!"

Elsie had never had cause or situation to think about such matters, until now. She reached out and held Raj's hand, acknowledging that she needed his guidance. She was surprised to find that his hand felt clammy.

"I hate this sort of occasion!" he whispered, as attendants opened the large black double entry doors that hung below a beautiful arched fan window. "Just make sure you stay two steps behind me, this time, and to one side!"

As they entered the hall, Elsie's eyes immediately opened wider in an attempt to take in the size and magnificence of the space before her. She barely heard an attendant announce: "Prince Raj Rajendra and Miss Elsie Forrest!" Her attention had drifted to the long white rectangular columns that supported curving arches fringed with blue and grey, upward, to the building's light-filled dome.

She was so transfixed by the space that she neglected to notice the inlaid marble of the coat of arms, jumping in shock when she realised she had trodden on the tiger part of the state's motto, only to emit a squeal when she landed with a right foot on the elephant.

Elsie looked up in embarrassment, noticing for the first time that the Maharaja and Maharani sat before them on thrones, positioned on a raised red platform. The Maharani had a smile on her face to such a degree that she must have been trying to suppress laughter.

Raj bowed and Elsie curtsied.

"Welcome back to Cooch Behar, my son! Welcome, Miss Forrest!' the dark moustachioed Maharaja Nripendra exclaimed.

"Thank you, Your Highnesses!" Elsie snuck in quickly as Raj uttered: "Thank you, Father!"

There was awkward silence for a few moments, till the Maharaja decided to focus on what he saw as important. "What does your father do, Miss Forrest?"

"He is a bookseller and stationer in Sydney, Your Highness."

Again there was silence, though this time for longer. Finally, Elsie could not bear it any more:

> After a momentary silence spake
> Some Vessel of a more ungainly Make ;
>> " They sneer at me for leaning all awry :
> What! did the Hand then of the Potter shake ? "

If it were at all possible to be any more silent, or stunned, Raj's parents now managed to be both.

"Is that from the pen of Omar Khayyám?" asked Raj.

"See what a well-educated son you have, Your Highnesses! Yet, does he know which quatrain?"

Raj thought for a few seconds until saying: "81?"

"Close! Quatrain 86!"

"I think we should move elsewhere," the Maharaja declared, frowning as he signalled for a servant. "Please arrange for tea for four in the drawing room."

As they spread informally across neighbouring sofas, Elsie felt that the more relaxed environment might hopefully be reflected in the conversation.

Raj's hand on hers seemed to be telling her to speak only when spoken to.

After a waiter passed around cups of tea, the Maharani assured Elsie that the tea was of the highest quality. "It is grown nearby in Darjeeling. The countryside is most beautiful. We have a house there. Perhaps Raj will be kind enough to take you there in a couple of weeks."

"Most certainly, Mother!"

The conversation progressed over the next few minutes to a stage where Elsie sensed everybody was a little more comfortable, though she noticed that the Maharaja was quieter than his wife. *Perhaps,* she thought, *if I talk about the things he likes, they will more readily accept me.* At a temporary lull in the discourse, she asked: "Your Highness, have you been happy with Mohun Bagan's performances in the Cooch Behar Cup?"

The Maharaja's look of surprise was directed more at his

eldest son, than his guest.

"Elsie does understand football, Father, though, yes, I did tell her you were a great fan of Mohun Bagan and that you donated the Cooch Behar Cup."

"Did you also mention that Mohun Bagan won the cup last year for the first time and then repeated the feat this year?"

"Father, in such matters I defer to your infinitely greater knowledge of the game, and your powers of storytelling. If you could excuse us, I wish to introduce Elsie to my brothers, before dinner."

They bade farewell, and hurried towards the billiard room set in the palace's basement. "If my brothers are likely to be anywhere, it is there!"

After they had left the drawing room behind, Elsie asked Raj how he thought she had been received. Raj stopped, looked around to make sure nobody could overhear, then moved even closer to Elsie. "You must understand that my parents want me to marry someone from a royal line, especially as I am the heir to the throne. You are not as quiet as me. I doubt they will forget you in a hurry!"

This was not quite what Elsie wanted to hear, though she now understood why Raj had insisted that their engagement be a secret, for now.

The sound of laughter emanating from the billiard room was a clear indication that Raj's suspicion about his brothers' location was correct. As Raj opened the door, he was greeted loudly, though there was silence when they saw Elsie.

"This is Jitendra, Victor and my youngest brother, Hitendra."

Elsie made a point of looking each in the eye and smiling. She could tell by the way each looked back at her that they were impressed.

For her part, Elsie thought that eighteen-year-old Jitendra—four and a half years younger than Raj—was handsome to the point of being beautiful. Even better looking than Raj himself, though she was certainly not going to tell her beloved.

"Raj! I'll challenge you to a game of snooker!" Jitendra said, moving over to the room's second billiard table that had all its balls waiting in readiness.

"Jit only challenges me because he knows he will win!"

complained Raj, who well understood that such a game was a rare opportunity for Jit to undermine 'the order of things'.

As Jit split the pack of reds, music could be heard from the hall above.

"It is 7 pm," explained Raj. "The forty-piece orchestra will play for the half hour till dinner."

While Raj struggled to make any impact on the snooker scoreboard, Elsie enquired about his three sisters.

"Oh, they are in the zenana," he replied.

"The zenana? What is that?" Elsie asked innocently.

As Jit smiled in the background, Raj explained that it was the 'women and girls only' area of the palace. "All the royal palaces have them—and they are invariably guarded by eunuchs!"

Elsie was not sure what a eunuch was, but made a mental note to ask Raj later, rather than publicly display her ignorance.

"You will be meeting our sisters at dinner," added Jit, "though I am sure you will soon wish you hadn't!" All the boys chuckled at this. No different to the way most Australian boys viewed their little sisters, thought Elsie.

There was an orchestral halt at 7.20 pm for a dinner gong to sound its ten-minute warning.

Without hesitation, both snooker games ceased and the boys started resetting the tables.

"Father expects us all to be standing behind our chairs in the dining hall by 7.30 pm," explained Victor, before racing off to the bathroom.

The dining hall was the grandest setup Elsie had ever glimpsed. Apart from the ornate setting with high ceiling, the table was covered in gleaming silverware. There seemed to be an impeccably dressed servant for every diner, while the rice and fish main course was delicious. And then there were the three sisters ...

Pratibha, who insisted she was fourteen, even though, as Hitendra pointed out, her birthday was still a month away; eleven-year-old Sudhira and four-year-old Sukriti. All carried the extra name Devi, meaning 'goddess' amongst Hindus.

The Maharani reminded everyone that the area's greatest annual festival, the Durga Puja, was about to start and that the royal family would participate in the sacred ceremony on Maha Navami, the second last day.

That night, as Elsie went to change for a bath, there was a soft tap at the door. The young maid whose assistance Elsie had rejected earlier had returned.

"Can I help you undress, madam?"

This time, Elsie nodded and smiled and she noticed a beautiful smile beam from the maid's pretty, dark face.

When she had finished, Elsie thanked the maid and noticed the same smile, like a burst of warm sunshine on a winter's day.

"You are very pretty!" Elsie said, as she stroked the maid's hair.

The young lady grabbed Elsie's wrist and pressed it to her lips and kissed it. Then with a twist of her body that made her long dark hair spin, she disappeared.

* * *

The calls of a peacock, strutting proudly around the grounds of its palace home, were not enough to waken Elsie and Raj from an after-lunch nap in the drawing room.

Elsie could not have been too soundly asleep, however, because at some stage she felt a very faint brushing of her hair … then felt it again. She stirred momentarily, half opened her eyes then closed them again, as she was sure it was just Raj, softly caressing her.

Moments later it happened once more, though this time there was a childish giggle.

Elsie sat up and looked around to see Pratibha, Sudhira and Sukriti trying to hide behind the sofa.

"Shhhh!" said Elsie, not wanting to wake Raj.

"Miss Elsie," Pratibha whispered, "please, come with us to the zenana!"

With that, they scuttled off quietly towards the zenana, the patter of their bare feet barely audible upon the wood, carpet and marble floors across which they journeyed.

Elsie had eased herself out of the sofa and followed, though still emerging from her sleepiness, she was well in their wake.

By the time she reached the beaded curtain of the zenana, the girls were waiting with that 'what took you so long' look.

"Come on!" ordered Sudhira, as Elsie ducked through the lines of glistening beads and between the pair of guards who stood either side of the gateway to this 'women's world'.

After no more than a couple of steps, Elsie halted to take it all in: elaborate and colourful carpets, adorned with bright mattresses and cushions, were spread about the zenana, giving it a relaxed but joyous feel.

One thing that differentiated this area from the rest of the palace was the reflections—from mirrors, glass and beads everywhere.

Then, there were the magnificent 'Eastern' arches, columns and ceiling domes that reminded Elsie of her much-loved Palace Theatre in Sydney.

"It is so beautiful here! If this were my home, I would never want to leave!" Elsie exclaimed, still gazing in wonderment around her.

"Most of the servant women in here have never been to other parts of the palace, nor ever will," cautioned Pratibha.

If there was such a thing as a gilded cage, thought Elsie, this was it.

"We want you to come with us tonight to the temple, but first …" said Pratibha.

"First you need darker skin …" interrupted Sukriti.

"And so you just have to sit here …" Sudhira said, indicating an ornate stool.

"And I will apply this dark cream!" Pratibha said, as she brushed Elsie's hair aside and dipped her fingers into a jar.

"Don't put too much on!" warned Sudhira. "Otherwise, she will look like Kali!"

The others giggled until Pratibha, seeing that Elsie did not understand, explained that Kali was, among other roles, the goddess of death for Hindus.

As the cream was spread across her face and neck, a servant arrived with a bejewelled mirror, so Elsie could study progress. At first, she found it disconcerting, but the larger the area of coverage, the more Elsie accepted her transformation.

Her feet, hands and arms were also eventually covered and finally Elsie was ready for the next stage.

"Mala!" yelled Pratibha, causing a nearby servant to come scurrying. "Could you please see that Miss Elsie is changed into a red and gold sari!"

A few minutes later and the transformation was almost complete. Elsie had never worn a sari before, but she had to admit that her new look was a head-turner.

"Now you need jewellery," Sukriti said, reaching into a box of treasures. Bangles were found for her arms and wrists, while others with bells were added to her ankles.

As the last strands of the band's pre-dinner performance boomed from the Durbar Hall and the family collected in the dining hall, Raj and both his parents did a double take on seeing Elsie.

The Maharaja just stared, speechless, while his wife said: "Well … !"

"I do prefer your natural paler look, darling," Raj whispered, before adding: "of course, you still look very beautiful!" lest she thought he meant she was unattractive, for, as he well knew from experience, most women were nearly as sensitive as he.

"Isn't it interesting how we invariably prefer a skin complexion other than our own," Elsie observed. The contemplative silence from the adults present, told the speaker her comment was perceptive.

"See! Miss Elsie can now be part of the family at the temple tonight!" Pratibha insisted. And so it transpired, though Elsie was nervous.

As the small convoy of motors approached the Baradebi Bari— the temple home of the icon of the Great Goddess in Cooch Behar—Elsie could hear the chanting of thousands, before she even caught sight of the building.

Flaming torches illuminated the night, creating a flickering kaleidoscope as their light bounced off the colourful clothing of the seething masses. All had come to witness one of the highlights of the annual Durga Puja.

The vehicles inched slowly forward through the pressing crowds, as Raj told Elsie how she should greet the chief priest: "Hold your hands together, as in prayer, nod and then bend down and touch his feet after saying 'Pranam Maharshi'. It is a salutation that means that you recognise the God that is in him and acknowledge his status as chief priest."

Elsie made sure she was the last in the royal family line to greet the chief priest. "Pranam Maharshi!" she said with conviction, but she noticed that he looked at her for longer than one aught. For all that he might know, she might have been a distant cousin visiting, though hopefully not a poorly made-up white woman trying to gatecrash a 'royal family only' occasion.

Once they were inside the temple, the glittering eleven-foot-high statue of the goddess was the focus of attention. The chanting from the many minor priests, the pandits, hummed along continuously, as the members of the royal family took it in turns to make an offering of burning incense sticks to the goddess.

Finally, the Maharaja stepped forward and the chief priest met him beneath the statue with a golden bowl and a sharp knife. Elsie winced as the ruler cut a finger and squeezed blood into the bowl.

"A few hundred years ago, it was a human sacrifice. These days it is just some drops of blood, with a buffalo sacrificed earlier in the day," Raj whispered.

The chief priest went to the temple door and signalled to the crowd that their maharaja had given blood to dispel evil and welcome prosperity for his people. The cry of "Maharajer jit hok!"—'Hail the king!' in the local Bengali dialect—was taken up by the thousands outside.

And so, the night of Maha Navami ended, and on the next and final day of the festival, the idol of the Great Goddess, accompanied by tens of thousands, was to be carried from the Baradebi Bari, to be symbolically immersed in the waters of the Torsa.

For Elsie, the night had been the first real insight into the responsibilities of a world into which she might soon tread, firstly as the wife of a prince, then later as the Maharani. It was certainly exciting, but also a little daunting, as she felt she had so much to learn and understand about this very different culture.

As they watched the goddess being bathed in the Torsa the next day, waves of pain wracked Elsie's body once more.

On return to the palace, Raj called for the resident doctor, who, with Elsie's permission, conducted an examination of her lower abdominal region. He concluded that the pain was either intestinal or reproductive organ related and that Elsie should see a specialist. Both Raj and Elsie agreed that this should be done in Sydney.

In the weeks that followed, Elsie spent many dream-like and intimate days with Raj, waited on by servants at every turn, shown every part of the princely state, and even journeying into the foothills of Darjeeling. She had, she felt, become even closer to Raj, holding him tightly during his quieter and more fearful times and rejoicing with him in his happier moments, while trying to limit his consumption of champagne, as much as she could.

There could scarcely be a more pleasurable existence, than this life of a budding princess, Elsie thought, *where one's every wish and whim is catered for so assiduously, by servants just determined to please.* For a twenty-two year old from Sydney, this was more than a dream come true.

However, there was one more activity that Raj felt Elsie should participate in before leaving Cooch Behar: a tiger hunt.

Elsie explained that she loved animals and was not sure she could cope with the experience, but Raj insisted, stating that the Cooch Behar rulers had always been great hunters.

In her time in Cooch Behar, Elsie had yet to visit the pilkhana, the stables where the elephants were kept. From a distance she could not see the elephants, but there was an undeniable taste and smell of dust and elephant dung in the air.

As she moved closer to the enclosure, she noticed there were far more elephants inside than she had expected. In fact there were scores.

"Their mahouts—their handlers—are their best friend and understand them very well," Raj stated, as his offer of a banana was gratefully accepted by the long, dark, twisting trunk of the nearest giant. "Elephants are far smarter than you think!"

Elsie held out her hand with a few biscuits in her palm. The tip of a trunk danced across her hand, vacuuming up each morsel in a way that made her laugh.

"Tomorrow, we head out on a tiger hunt. We have heard that a village to the north, near the forest, has been menaced, so we will try to track the animal down." As he said these words, Raj noticed that Elsie looked concerned, so he added: "Don't worry, we will not be heading out alone!"

Whatever image Elsie had of this tiger hunting expedition, was dwarfed by the reality of the next morning's gathering. Seemingly hundreds of servants busied themselves with their own task as more than thirty elephants were prepared by their mahouts for the journey.

Some were loaded with giant tents, camping equipment, food and even carpets, while the gun keepers cleaned and checked a whole range of hunting rifles and pistols.

"This is our elephant!" Raj said, reaching out and patting the head of a large creature that for now was sitting on the ground. "Her name is Ruby. She will be carrying us both in the howdah on her back. She has been my elephant since I was a young boy."

Elsie could see that her fate was inextricably linked to her relationship with the elephant, so wanted to get off to a good start. She walked around the front to where Ruby could see her and knelt down. "Hello, sweetheart! You have such beautiful eyes, Ruby!"

As she said these words, Ruby's trunk started to search around Elsie for pockets that might contain biscuits. "No, no, no! I am not a girl who can be won over that easily—and nor should you be!" Elsie said cuddling and patting Ruby's trunk, as it curled around the back of her neck.

"It is time you climbed on board!" Raj called from the front of Ruby's ornate wooden howdah. He leaned out to draw Elsie up. "Put your foot on the running rail!" he instructed. With the next foot on the howdah's sidestep, she was soon on board.

Elsie looked around at her travelling setup. There was a front and back bench seat, both of which doubled as storage compartments. "Look at this one!" Raj said, as he lifted up the back seat. There, underneath, were four bottles of champagne in ice, and thankfully, bottles of water. Underneath the forward seat, were sandwiches and fruit.

As Elsie settled onto the back seat, she noticed that the howdah looked like a man-of-war: hunting rifles were clipped into catches on either side, a pair of pistols was clipped to the front, while ammunition sat in the front corners.

On the booming sound of a conch shell, the expedition started to stir like a giant after a decade of sleep.

The cry of "Oot!" rang out from the mahouts, sitting on top of the elephants' necks, with their hands on the back of each elephant's head. With this, each animal swayed sideways, then backwards and forwards as they staggered to their feet.

"Father always rides on his big bull elephant, called Rajah. But I prefer Ruby as she does not have long tusks that can get in the way of gunshots."

As much as Elsie was excited about the occasion, she was not looking forward to seeing an animal slaughtered, though by the time the cavalcade had reached the Patlakhawa Reserve, there had been no sighting or news of the tiger.

The sun had started to sink towards sunset and the signal was given to make camp on a firm but open piece of ground.

A large central fire was constructed in the hope that it would keep wildlife away, while two giant tents and innumerable smaller ones were pitched around it. For safety, smaller fires and sentries were placed on the outer ring.

The elephants and their mahouts were kept in their own, ringed compound, well away from the tents. The biggest danger to the party was a panicked stampede by the elephants. In such a situation, even their beloved mahouts risked being trampled to death.

That night, closer to the Himalayas, Elsie cuddled up to Raj in front of the warmth of the large central fire, ignoring his father's censorious glare. *Hypocrite,* she thought to herself.

By morning, news had filtered through of a tiger menacing a village near the edge of the Terai, just the previous evening. The decision was made to maintain their tent village as the base camp, but to head with as much speed as possible towards the area of the sighting.

Even so, it took a couple of hours before the affected village was reached. The Maharaja split his party into three: sending the long line of drum-beating foot-soldiers out to the west, to sweep north and then east and finally south, while the pad elephants headed in a tight formation east then north and south. The aim of these two columns was to close in on any tiger, forcing it towards a central clearing in the grasslands and the approaching royal elephants. Well, that was the theory.

"Watch the grass tops!" advised Raj. "If they move independently of the advancing lines, we can be pretty sure it is our tiger!"

Elsie could only imagine just how dangerous it would be on foot. The grass was up to eight feet high and there would be little or no warning of a tiger attack. At least on top of an elephant, the patterns and grass movement could be observed in relative safety.

To the west and north, the rhythmic sound of beating drums could be heard in the distance—a distance confirmed by the wavering of the grass tops. To the east and north, Elsie could see the line of pad elephants moving, trampling the grass as they progressed.

Raj loaded the howdah's rifles and pistols in readiness. "There!" he yelled, pointing to a wavering of the grass tops forward and to their left, ahead of the line of beaters.

Raj instructed Ruby's mahout to move left and forward to cut off any south-western escape route and force the tiger to the clearing. Elsie watched with a mixture of great excitement and terror as they moved closer to the rippling grass tops.

And then the king of the Indian jungle was in the clearing, pacing and snarling, twisting and turning in all its tan, black and white Bengali magnificence. It was large and powerful and angry, but still very beautiful. Elsie was transfixed.

"Elsie, you shoot it, as you are our guest!" ordered Raj, as he thrust the loaded rifle into her hands.

"But … I have never fired a gun!" Elsie protested, expecting her inexperience would exclude her from involvement.

"Just aim, look down the barrel and squeeze the trigger!" Raj insisted, placing the gun in position against her right shoulder.

With the beaters, as well as the pad and royal elephants surrounding the clearing, the tiger could see it was trapped. Frantically, it searched for a weakness.

"Shoot, Elsie! Shoot!" yelled Raj, but she had seen its beautiful eyes, huge furry paws and proud and graceful bearing. She simply could not.

At that moment, the tiger lunged towards the beater line in

a desperate attempt to escape. Screams filled the air and shots rang out as both the Maharaja and his son fired at the leaping animal as the line of beaters scattered like ninepins before it.

Elsie cried out in anguish as bullets struck the tiger in the shoulder, back and side of the head, sending it twisting and growling across the terrified bodies of beaters. A final shot from the Maharaja and there was silence and stillness for a few seconds, before the beaters gathered around the carcass.

"Never, ever do that again! You put people's lives at risk!" Raj said firmly, as Elsie sobbed. Yet, even as he said those words, he surely knew she would never want to go hunting with him again—no matter how close their relationship.

In the days that followed, Elsie wrestled uncomfortably with the idea of marrying into such a culture. True, the British seemed to love hunting too, but there was so much about Indian society that was so different.

The pain in her abdominal area had returned with a vengeance, and all agreed that a return to Sydney had to be expedited.

As they headed back to Calcutta on the royal train, Raj was even quieter than his usual self, as if he too had much to think about. On reaching Humayun Place, Elsie discovered a short letter from Emma that must have sat in Calcutta for nearly a month:

Dearest El,

You may or may not be surprised to learn that your brother Walter is to marry Stella Hancock on November 17 in Sydney. They have asked me to extend an invitation to you in the hope that you will be able to attend.

If and when my turn comes, I do not know, but I have started teaching international dancing classes and may just meet a prince prepared to give me a 'royal salute'!

By the way George Stillwell is currently boarding with your parents!

Everyone here is well—see you soon.
Love, Em XOXO

Well! The epileptic girl from Fort Street School! Elsie knew they were friends, but had not expected this.

She realised that it was now far too late for her to reach Sydney by boat in time for the wedding, so went to the Central Telegraph Office and cabled her apologies and best wishes to Walter, to be passed on to Stella.

The day before her planned sailing, Raj handed her an envelope filled with high-value rupee notes. "You will need this for the trip back, the divorce proceedings and any medical procedure."

"And your parents, will they ever accept me?" Elsie asked, for it was a question that had haunted her hopes since she had first met the royal couple.

"I will have time to work on them. Surely they cannot deny their eldest son the woman and the happiness he desires!"

In truth, Elsie had other concerns, relating to Raj's developing alcoholism and his obsession with the prophesies of an early death. Yet the tantalising prospect of becoming a princess, overrode such doubt.

They both agreed that though it would be painful, it would be good for them to spend a year apart—and appreciate just how much they missed and needed each other. They could then marry on her return.

Chapter 32

The Tart at the Gresham Hotel

'Ere! I've seen you wandrin' lonely, in a cold an' friendless state
Companionship is worth some pennies — special friends are worth the wait
Spoil me with a fancy ribbon, ply me with a drink or two
And I'll prove a faithful plaything — while I'm spending time with you.

James Thompson climbed the steps to their recently acquired Roslyn Gardens, Darlinghurst home, far more wearily than when he had descended them nearly twelve hours before.

The redistribution of electorates and the creation of a Darling Harbour entity for which he was now the returning officer, had meant he had to familiarise himself with an area of residences and establishments beyond those of his previous Lang responsibility.

"I am sorry I am late, dear. Once again my tardiness has shown disrespect to the one I love!" he sighed, as he closed the front door of No. 37.

Mary Ann had stood there, not saying anything, which he had found unusual. After placing his case on the floor, James looked up at his wife, puzzled at her silence. She looked back at him, desperately trying to suppress a very big smile. However, her eyes told him she was very pleased.

"Our special visitor has only just arrived!" she exclaimed.

James' bookshop and returning officer work had made him look and feel older than his fifty-six years should have allowed. He was so preoccupied that he had totally forgotten what lay in store.

"Hello, Father!" Elsie cried, as she rushed towards him with her arms opened wide.

"Oh, my darling! It has been so long since I saw you last!"

"Over two and a half years, Father!" Elsie exclaimed, as she hugged him. "Not since I left for southern Africa!"

"Let me look at you! … Yes, you have changed, just a little!" James said, only temporarily keeping her at arms length.

"Well, Father, I am older, and I hope wiser than when I left."

"And even more beautiful! Though you shall always be my little princess!"

"A real princess she may yet be, James. It would be a far better situation than her current marriage, though much needs to be worked through. Elsie, George stayed with us for six weeks, until the end of October. He was pleasant, though it was clear to me that you have no future together, and I believe he accepts this."

As Mary Ann served dinner, James insisted that the honourable thing would be to meet George and talk things over. "When he left here, he said he would be staying at the Gresham Hotel."

"Where is that, Father?"

"On the corner of York and Druitt Streets. It is, most certainly, a lovely structure, just on the other side of the road from the Queen Victoria Building and with a view across to the Town Hall. Please excuse me for one moment."

James left the dining table, but soon returned with a box of business cards.

"James, dear, please leave that until we have finished dinner!" Mary Ann pleaded.

"I'm sorry," James muttered, suitably admonished.

After dinner, they gathered in the lounge room and looked out over the lamp post dotted darkness that was Rushcutters Bay Park, flanked by the warmth of the house lights of some of Sydney's better dwellings, that sprinkled the hills around the bay.

"I had nearly forgotten about the card. I must have it somewhere in here," James said, as he searched through a stack of business cards. "Ah, here it is! Elsie, you may need his services. He was of great help two years ago, when books I had paid for did not arrive."

Elsie looked down at the card in her hand:

Ernest Robert Abigail

Solicitor

67 Elizabeth Street, Sydney

"If you need to visit Mr Abigail, I will go with you, darling," Mary Ann assured her. "However, you must speak to George first."

* * *

The sun had well and truly risen on a warm Sydney December morning, as Elsie stood before the five-storey arched and balconied edifice that was the Gresham Hotel. She checked her watch, noting that it was 9.27 and surely not too early to wake her husband. She headed through the double front doors, straight for the reception desk.

"Yes, madam, can I help?" a tidy-looking gentleman inquired.

"I wish to speak to Mr Stillwell."

"Mr and Mrs Stillwell are in Room 42, madam. Would you like me to call the room? I do not believe they have been down to breakfast."

"Did you say 'Mrs Stillwell'?" Elsie queried, for she could not believe what she had heard.

"Why yes, they arrived here on … on 1st November," he said, after reviewing his booking register.

Elsie had to think quickly.

"I could give the room a quick call?" he persisted.

"No, please don't disturb him. I will have a chat with Mr Stillwell when he comes down to breakfast. I will wait in the lounge."

As she turned away, she looked for a seat in the lounge where she could just see the reception desk, and the stairs. It took a couple of minutes, but eventually the man at reception turned his back for a few moments—and Elsie bolted for the stairs.

She hoped she had made the first landing and turn without being spotted, but pushed on up, presuming that Room 42 was on the fourth floor. By the time she reached the top floor, she was out of breath.

She looked around to her left and saw Room 41, then 42 straight ahead. It was the corner room on the top floor.

As she gradually reclaimed her composure, she wondered what she should say. By the time she had traversed the short distance across the burgundy and green carpet, between the landing and 42's door, she had already changed her mind twice.

Elsie took a deep breath and knocked politely and not too firmly on the hardwood door … and waited … but there was no response.

She tried once more, this time more firmly … again, there was no response, but just as she was about to knock for a third time, the door swung partly open and a blonde-headed young lady peered around the frame.

"Yeah, what do ya want?" she asked in a course Australian accent.

"I wish to speak to Mr Stillwell, if I may."

"George! It's some sheila for you, luv!"

"Ok, just give me a minute!" Elsie heard George call from the background.

After a bit of shuffling, George replaced the blonde at the door. "Elsie! Goddammit! What are you doing here?" In normal circumstances, one would have expected these words to be spoken quite loudly, but George had no intention of broadcasting his surprise.

"I need to speak with you, George!"

"Well, fine, just not here and now! I'll meet you downstairs in the hotel lounge in fifteen minutes!" he whispered, with serious intent through near-clenched teeth.

"Very well," Elsie accepted, before turning for the stairs. On reaching the landing, she could hear the blonde quizzing George about his visitor as their door closed.

Elsie must have sat downstairs for more than five minutes before it dawned on her what was different about George—he had no moustache. *It's funny,* she reflected, *how you can be so close to someone for so long, that you don't readily notice changes. You know them so well through their voice and their touch that you take everything else for granted. No doubt an occasional acquaintance would have picked up the difference immediately!*

Even in her world of limited experience, Elsie realised that adultery was ground for divorce. She noticed that same man was still at the reception desk, so wandered over for a 'chat'.

"Excuse me, sir. Can I have your name, please?"

The gentleman seemed a little taken aback, but responded: "I am Benjamin Samuels, the proprietor of this establishment!

And your name is, madam?"

"Elsie Stillwell. I am the wife of George Stillwell who is staying in Room 42, with a tart who is masquerading as me!"

Samuels was stunned, went red in the face and could only offer an "Oh dear!"

"Don't worry. George and I will be sitting down in the lounge and talking most civilly about matters," Elsie assured Mr Samuels.

When George reached the lounge, they sat in neighbouring armchairs, so neither needed to speak much above a whisper. "Perhaps, we could get back together, Elsie, if you can support yourself."

"Support myself! That would be most difficult without regular engagements. I would rather live with my parents under such circumstances!"

There was silence for some time as each searched for what to say, wary of making the wrong step in this marital minefield. Elsie knew she now had the grounds, though she did not have his firm commitment to another course. So, she took a gamble, though chose her words carefully, far more carefully than he would have supposed. "Oh, George, why don't you leave that tart and come back to me?"

"Tart!" he cried, raising his voice. "How dare you describe Fanny in such a way!"

With that he rose, turned his back most determinedly, and headed off in a huff, to breakfast in the dining room.

* * *

Mary Ann opened the glass door at 67 Elizabeth Street— which seemed entirely appropriate, as it had 'E R Abigail, Solicitor', etched into its surface.

The two women entered a small anteroom where a young gentleman was attempting to allocate individual pages to the correct file, a process that seemed to have got the better of him. He failed to notice the presence of the newcomers, patient observers of his predicament. As was almost inevitable, Mary Ann wheezed and coughed unintentionally, causing the young man to lift his head in surprise.

"Oh, I am sorry! Can I help you?"

"We are here to see Mr Abigail," explained Mary Ann.

"Do you have an appointment?"

"I am afraid we do not, though I suspect we shall not delay him too long, at all," Mary Ann assured him, in almost certain knowledge that this would not be the case.

The young man stopped what he was doing and went to the door to Mr Abigail's room, tapping gently on the glass before leaning inward to whisper. Elsie noticed that his shoes looked scuffed and were in bad need of a clean. She wondered if this was reflective of the quality of service.

"Mr Abigail will see you in a few minutes," was the message, as the young man resumed his seat and his sorting task. Well, he may have tried, though Elsie noticed he kept looking at her every few seconds, and was sure that no page found its home by the time Mr Abigail, a portly, middle-aged man with metal-rimmed glasses, called from the doorway.

"Come in ladies!" As they settled in to comfortable captain's chairs in a much more orderly room, he added: "Now, how can I help you?"

"We are after a divorce," said Mary Ann.

"I didn't think you could have married in the first place!" quipped Mr Abigail, as he smiled at the two women, causing Elsie to giggle. Mary Ann did nothing of the sort.

"My daughter needs the divorce, Mr Abigail!"

"She scarcely seems old enough to be married!" he responded.

"I am twenty-two years old, Mr Abigail!" Elsie replied indignantly.

"I was assured by my husband that you were a fine and professional solicitor—evidently, he was misled!" Mary Ann said, standing up and starting to leave.

"No, please! Sit down, madam! Accept my humble apologies. The legal profession is as dry as a dustbowl most times, so I occasionally feel the need to break out. Once again, I apologise, and please sit down!"

Quite reluctantly, Mary Ann did. Ten minutes of explanation later and Mr Abigail went to the door. "William, could you bring in one of the divorce petition forms, please." A further twenty minutes later and with all paperwork complete, the women rose to leave.

"My assistant, Mr Whitfield, will appear for you in the case and will do a good job. He is a bright young man. I will follow up with Mr Samuels in the Gresham. If he agrees to be a witness, any attempt at defence against adultery is surely wasted!"

As they left the anteroom, Elsie whispered: "Goodbye, William!" in a teasing manner, her flashing smile and twinkling eyes distracting him further from the task he was so far from completing.

George Stillwell was given notice to appear before the New South Wales Supreme Court on Thursday 22nd March, in the matter of Stillwell v Stillwell. He did not attend or seek representation.

Benjamin Samuels, proprietor of the Gresham Hotel, gave evidence that Mr and a 'Mrs Stillwell'—who was certainly not Elsie—had occupied a single room at the hotel for some weeks.

His Honour said: "I find ... in favour of the petitioner, and grant a *decree nisi* for dissolution of the marriage returnable within three months. Respondent to pay petitioner's cost of suit."

The *decree nisi* was made absolute on 26 June 1906. Elsie was a single woman again, and quick to write to Raj with the good news.

Chapter 33

The Surprise 23rd

Birthdays are a mixed-up blessing—anticipated much when young
As you climb the golden ladder, gifts appear at every rung
Then the lines and grey hair greet you—that's what passing time conveys
The mirror does not lie or shield you, from the truth your age betrays.

The knock at the front door of 37 Roslyn Gardens on the evening of Monday 2 July 1906, took all but James Thompson by surprise, for he moved towards the entrance with considerable alacrity.

A muffled greeting, a shaking of hands and a shuffling of feet later, and a tall but familiar figure stood next to James at the lounge room entrance.

"Mr Williamson!" Elsie cried, as she shot to her feet with every intention of rushing across the room and into his arms.

"Elsie, please!" warned Mary Ann in a quiet but firm voice.

"You look even more beautiful than when I last saw you, some years ago!" J.C. ventured.

"Please, sit down, Mr Williamson and I will get us all a cup of tea," insisted Mary Ann, before scurrying off to the kitchen.

J.C. sat on one end of the sofa, but could not take his eyes off Elsie, who was slowly, stealthily and most deliberately inching her way towards him, as he spoke: "You have no doubt heard that I am directing a group of international artists under the leadership of that great comedian, William Collier, in preparation for a couple of plays at His Majesty's Theatre. Well, due to illness, we urgently need a new Pearl—one of the two chorus girls in the first play, the other being William's wife, Helena."

"Yes! I will do it!" Elsie interrupted enthusiastically, eager to have a positive distraction, as her visits to a specialist about her occasional abdominal pain had proved inconclusive.

"Elsie, darling, please hear Mr Williamson out!" warned James.

"Somehow I thought you might be interested, precious!" J.C. admitted, as he extended an arm around the shoulders of a young lady who was by now almost next to him.

"Precious Pearl, alliteration and all—so it seems a very appropriate role for me!" she said, her eyes shining and face beaming with happiness as she looked lovingly into his eyes.

"The play is called *On The Quiet*. I am just doubtful you can cope with the likely three-week season."

"Oh!" she exclaimed, as she playfully whacked him on the chest, before nestling against his body.

"At this point, I must stress that I had absolutely no idea that you were back in the country, until I read the colourful account of your successful divorce proceedings. I then dropped in to see your father at the bookshop earlier today."

After Mary Ann arrived with the tea, Elsie told J.C. about her experiences in southern Africa, Aden and India. That night, Elsie could hardly sleep, so excited was she at the prospect of 'treading the boards' once more.

* * *

The reality of being back on stage, after intense rehearsals, was much as she had expected, with one exception: the twenty-four year old American actor John Barrymore.

From polite conversation, they had deduced that she had performed with his uncle, Sidney Drew, in Cape Town. From then on she had to 'shake him off', as he repeatedly demonstrated an interest in her. This would not have been an unusual experience for Elsie, except that he was a chain-smoker and she could not stand his addiction.

It was therefore with mixed feelings, that Elsie finished her commitments on Saturday 21 July. When, a week later, she ventured out with Emma for an early twenty-third birthday dinner in town, she did not think she would be returning to His Majesty's Theatre anytime soon.

Elsie's impending elevation from stage performer to princess, was all her friends and family seemed to want to talk about, with her best friend proving no exception.

"Do you think you will be living at Woodlands or in the Cooch Behar Palace?" Emma asked, demonstrating an impressive familiarity with Indian locations, as they waited for dinner.

"While Raj is just the heir to the throne, we may well split our time between both."

"It will be so difficult to choose, as you will have servants wherever you go!" Emma suggested. "But when you have children, I am sure the grandparents will want to have them at the palace! I am certain your children will be beautiful, but I wonder whether they will look more like you, or Raj?"

"Most likely a mix of both, Em, though I am not really sure how such things work out," Elsie responded honestly. "I would just hope that any child does not inherit Raj's melancholic outlook, though as we love each other and spend more time together, I am sure this will change!"

"Oh, melancholic or not, I would not mind! If I could only find a handsome prince of my own, El ... perhaps one of Raj's younger brothers!" Emma responded dreamily.

She sighed as she reflected on her predicament: the world of the family transport business contained many solid and reliable types, though nobody to date of the intellect and potential affluence to interest her. Similarly, her dancing classes had not so far yielded any prospects.

Elsie felt the relative pain of her close friend. "Oh, dear Em! You are still only twenty-one and have plenty of time! I always believe that special things happen to special people, so you will be fine!"

After dinner, as they strolled down George Street, Elsie noticed that Emma was looking at her watch, repeatedly.

"You won't need to do much of that if we go to the opening of the new railway station at the end of Pitt Street, next Saturday!" Elsie advised. "I have heard they will have plenty of clocks around the platforms, and ..." She was about to add that it would be bigger than Redfern, when a sudden pain shot through her abdomen, causing her to stop and bend forward in agony.

"Are you all right?" Emma asked, holding her hand. "Is it that pain again?"

"Ah ... yes! ... Ah!" grimaced Elsie.

"El, there must be something wrong if you keep getting that pain!"

"I know ... I am sure you are right ... but the specialist could not find anything … anyway, I think I am okay now …"

They waited another minute or so as Elsie straightened herself and regained her composure.

"Now, to cheer you up, as the second part of your surprise birthday present, I have bought tickets for tonight's performance of *The Dictator* at His Majesty's. I know that means you will have to see that John Barrymore again, but the reviews of the show say that it is very funny and clever."

It was not long after 8 pm, when the dimming of the theatre lights signalled the play's beginning, that Elsie's pain returned. At first, she just gripped the armrest as tightly as she could, but soon she doubled over in real agony.

"Elsie! Elsie!" Emma whispered frantically, but she was buckling even more from the pain. Emma grabbed her arm and tried to move her towards the aisle. "Come on, El, we are going outside!"

Elsie bumbled into knees and trod on the feet of other patrons as she was steered, stumbling to the exit.

As they emerged into the light of the foyer, Emma looked at her best friend who was bent over and moaning. One of her hands was closed tightly, reflecting her severe pain, and Elsie suddenly collapsed to the floor, throwing up as she fell.

"Quick! Someone please call an ambulance!" Emma screamed, as she placed one hand under Elsie's head and stroked her hair with the other. "I'm here, darling, it's all right!" she said, though in truth, she was really scared.

By the time the motor ambulance arrived, Elsie seemed only semi-conscious. Still bent in a foetal position, she was placed on a stretcher and moved into the back of the vehicle. Emma knelt next to her, holding her hand as the ambulance sped to the nearby Sydney Hospital, in Macquarie Street.

The emergency ward was crowded with the usual victims of a Sydney Saturday night. As Emma gave Elsie's details, the duty nurse was apologetic. "Can't tell you how long it will be before you see a doctor, luv. Look, I am sorry, but you will just have to wait in the corridor."

Emma looked around at the flotsam and jetsam that had washed up on the hospital's shore: bleeding victims of pub brawls, domestic violence and misadventure, some moaning and groaning like Elsie, though all seemingly resigned to significant delay in their assessment and future salvation.

Then Emma saw him, standing at a distance, but looking straight at her: a good-looking young man in a long white coat.

He seemed transfixed by the image of the young woman with long golden hair, with her darker-haired friend's head nestled in her lap.

As he moved closer, he could plainly see that Emma was protectively nursing Elsie with great love and concern, to try to counter her pain.

"I'm Dr Samuel Harris," the young man said squatting beside Elsie. He reached out and placed his hands gently either side of her head and slowly turned her as he said: "I want you to look at me."

Even in her current state, Elsie marvelled at the softness of his hands, and when she tried to look at him, his beautiful dark brown eyes. At the same time, Emma was smitten.

The doctor could see straightaway by the lack of focus in Elsie's eyes that she was in considerable pain. "Can you tell me, please, exactly where it hurts?"

Elsie indicated her lower abdomen and Dr Harris headed off to get something to reduce the pain. Moments later, he was back with a small flat stick that had been dipped in a solution. "I want you to bite and suck on this," he said, placing it in her mouth. "It will help relieve the pain. I will see if I can get you into theatre so I can examine you."

Soon, a couple of hospital orderlies arrived with a hospital stretcher, placed Elsie upon it, and took her into an operating theatre. All the time, Emma stayed by her side.

As Dr Harris arrived, one of the orderlies told Emma that she could wait outside, but Emma protested and Elsie gripped her friend's hand tightly.

"It is not usual, but she can stay!" Dr Harris ordered, as he signalled for the male orderlies to leave the room.

Emma clung tightly on to Elsie's hand as Dr Harris asked that a couple of female nurses attend.

"Now, Elsie," he said, softly touching the side of her face and waiting till he had at least her partial attention. "My training has been in gynaecology, so there is nothing about the female body that is a mystery to me. The nurses and your friend will help you undress so I can examine you."

Soon, Elsie lay in just her undergarments on the table in the operating theatre.

"I am about to remove your undergarments, is that all right, Elsie?" Dr Harris asked.

Elsie had heard the question, but her mind had raced back to another time she was laid out on her back on a wooden piece of furniture in her undergarments … it was 1897, she was fourteen and in her father's office at the back of the bookshop …

She looked up at Dr Harris, but all she could see was the lecherous visage of him, Dr … whatever his name was …

"No!" she cried emphatically, suddenly sweating and breathing heavily.

"Elsie, it's ok! I'm with you, darling! Dr Harris is a good man!" Emma said, as she stroked her hand.

Elsie closed her eyes and slowly calmed down. She reopened them and this time she saw Dr Harris. "I am sorry, doctor," she mumbled, the soothing stick still in her mouth.

"That is quite all right. I don't think this will take too long, as I am pretty sure I know what is wrong. Now, I am going to press gently in certain places and I want you to tell me when it hurts."

Elsie tensed for the inevitable shooting pain as Dr Harris' hands worked their way around her abdomen and through her pubic area.

"Ow! Ow! Owwww!" Elsie screamed as he pressed on one place.

"Nurse Ronan, bring the chloroform. We are going to have to operate immediately! Young lady," he said turning to Emma, "if you wish to stay with your friend, then you must wear a theatre cap and gown."

Soon, all was in readiness. Dr Harris took the stick out of her mouth and placed a metal frame over Elsie's head. Then he spoke to her in a very calm and quiet voice as he stroked her right arm with his soft fingers.

"Elsie, I am a surgeon who is qualified to do this sort of operation. I believe you have a cyst that needs to be removed urgently. In a few days you will be feeling much better, as the cyst must have been a problem for you for a considerable time. You have your dear friend holding your hand, so everything is going to be all right!"

Dr Harris draped a cloth over the metal frame, sending Elsie's world into darkness, as Emma squeezed her hand again and whispered: "I'm here, darling!"

He then started pouring chloroform onto the cloth and waited a moment for the fumes to start to take effect. "Elsie, please count backwards from twenty."

Elsie tried to count, but panicked and became frantic as she felt the cloth closing in on her, suffocating her. Dr Harris had to remove it, then, apply more chloroform—twice, as Elsie kept panicking.

After much reassurance, and on the third attempt, she only made the count backward to seven, before she was rendered unconscious. A tall frame with a sheet for a screen was wheeled over Elsie to shield the lower half of her body from view. Emma was relieved. Elsie's hand had already gone limp, and had the screen not been introduced, she may have left the room, as she had no desire to watch her friend being dissected.

Nearly half an hour later, Dr Harris placed a tray with a bloodied, light brown mass on the table nearby. Emma glanced at it, first in horror and then periodically in fascination, as she was certain that it was shrinking in contact with the air.

Finally, Elsie was ready to be wheeled away to a ward. "She will need to be here for about a week, then take things easy for the next month or so. She will be in a bit of pain from the operation for a while, but I would like to think that cysts like that might not return."

"Thank you, Doctor!" Emma gushed, silently wishing Dr Harris would play around with her body at any time he liked.

Over the next week, Dr Harris dropped in to check on Elsie a number of times, but it was not until Elsie's parents and Emma happened to be present on one evening, and Elsie was close to being discharged, that he said he wanted to have an important talk with his patient.

"The operation, thankfully, has been very successful, but there is something significant that I feel I have to say about your future. Are you happy for your parents and Emma to stay in the room, Elsie?"

"Please, I want them all to stay!" Elsie said nervously, as everything had been so positive for quite a while.

"Elsie can walk around now, and she says that she is no longer in pain, which is great. However, she will have to rest for a while." Dr Harris seemed troubled as he reached out and gently touched Elsie's hand. "You certainly are a strong young lady, but I have to tell you that from what I saw during the operation, that it is quite unlikely that you will be able to fall pregnant at any stage."

An awkward silence enveloped the room, until Mary Ann said: "Oh, dear!"

Emma moved in close to her best friend, reaching out for Elsie's other hand and pressing it to her lips.

"You mean I may never be able to have children?" Elsie asked, stunned, and hoping that she had misconstrued what the doctor had said.

"Yes, I am sorry, but that is what I am saying," Dr Harris insisted, as a shattered James walked towards the window, seeking salvation. "Of course, it is not impossible, and I am sure you have overcome many hurdles before."

Elsie, like most young women, had been raised on the seemingly inevitable prospect of motherhood. It was, she had been told, the single most important role she could play in her lifetime. Now, she felt like she had been banned from the stage of life. Indeed, would anybody now find her desirable?

When she had completely recovered from the operation, somehow, Elsie summoned the courage to write to Raj. It would be unfair for him to expect children from their marriage when she had been advised there would be little prospect of this occurring. As to how he would react, she had no idea.

Chapter 34

The Deal

The Maharaja of Tikari moved down the steps of his mansion in Ballygunge Store Road, with an enthusiasm and adroitness that belied his recent return from weeks at sea.

"You must see my new baby, Raj!" he said, while signalling to servants to open the garage. "I escorted it all the way home from Europe!"

The Calcutta light soon splashed across a white masterpiece of German engineering, sitting impatiently within its new home.

"Oh, it is truly magnificent!" exclaimed Raj, the Prince of Cooch Behar, on glimpsing the 1906 Mercedes Racing Car. He circled it slowly, admiring its sleek body and tan-coloured leather bucket seats.

"The only change I have made is to have the wheel spokes painted gold."

"Tikari, can I sit inside?" came the inevitable question.

"Of course, my friend, but don't think for a moment that I will let you borrow it. There is no chance of that, as I have barely driven it myself!"

"I wouldn't think of doing such a thing, Tikari! Besides, Elsie arrives by steamer next Wednesday in Colombo. She recently got a divorce from Stillwell, and I have made a booking at the Galle Face Hotel."

"Really?" Tikari said, surprised, as his left hand gripped the doorframe, squeezing the base of his emerald ring against the car's glossy white body paint. For a few seconds, he gazed off into the distance in contemplation.

"What is its top speed?"

"Officially, it is 93.2 miles per hour, but I feel it could go much faster, very much faster!" Tikari responded, his mind whirring, as he leaned forward and placed a finger on the speedometer.

"What is that?" queried Raj.

"That, my friend, is the current world speed record for a motor—109.65 miles per hour. It was set by Victor Hemery in a 200-horsepower Darracq in December last year."

"And you think this Mercedes can beat that?"

"I feel sure it can! It will probably take quite a few runs on long and straight tracks, but I am sure over the next week or so I can do it!"

Tikari noticed that Raj's eyes had grown wider, so he continued: "The person who breaks that world record will become immortal! Of course, I could, as your friend, offer to pick up Elsie in Colombo myself and bring her back to you, but that would be giving you that first chance at immortality ..."

"Immortality!" Raj repeated, gripping the steering wheel tightly with both hands and leaning forward as if he was squeezing every last effort out of the accelerator, while keeping his head low against the wind.

"All I have to do is take the needle past this point and I will forever be in the history books!" Tikari said, as he marked the record point on the glass of the speedometer with a pencil line.

Raj was in such a daze that he took a few seconds to react. "No! ... No, Tikari, my dear friend ... perhaps we could make a deal!"

"I would only agree to do this for my best friend, Raj! ... Okay, if you insist! I will pick up Elsie in Colombo. You can borrow the Mercedes for a week and set the world record. Telephone or telegram me when you have done so, and I will bring Elsie back here so that we can all celebrate your ascendancy to immortality!" he said, stepping away from the car and heading back to the mansion's front door.

Raj hurried after him, but could not resist a look back at the beautiful white beast. "Tikari, you are the best friend that a man can have!"

Chapter 35

Colombo 1906

There's an island to the south, where Buddhists predominate
Forests ring an ancient kingdom — Kandy's king was potentate
There's a city, Colombo, where passengers off great ships pace
Before they seek to head up northward — after pause at Galle Face.

Even before the steamship *Orient* had moored by the dock in Colombo, British Ceylon, Elsie was on deck, scanning the waterfront for Raj.

In the ten days since leaving the Australian mainland's last port of Fremantle, she had tossed and turned over her future, vacillating between the promised magnificence of life as a princess of Cooch Behar and her possible rejection despite her newly acquired single status.

Captain Nicolson's announcement on the public address system, that passengers could view Colombo Harbour's newly constructed north-west breakwater, failed to distract Elsie.

As the ropes were tossed between liner and dock, she searched desperately for sight of Raj's unmistakable tall and stylish figure amongst those milling on the pier. He had written in his last letter that he would be there, but, had he abandoned her for another?

With each step down the gangway she mulled over possible reasons for an estrangement from Raj: *Is it because I am not English, not posh enough, not from one of the notable families, perhaps a little too smart to play the role of his lifetime consort — or is it because I may not be able to bear a royal heir?*

By the time she neared the gangway's end, what confidence and hope she once had, had all but vanished.

"Miss Elsie! Welcome back to the subcontinent!" a vaguely familiar voice called out, causing Elsie to look right of the gathered throng.

There, in a smart suit was a dark-faced young Indian who waved in greeting, a gesture that saw the emerald ring on his left hand flash in the late morning sunshine.

The Maharaja of Tikari, she thought, *what is he doing here?*

Shaking hands with and farewelling Captain Nicholson, she swung right towards Tikari—the only face she recognised.

Before she could react, he had kissed her on both cheeks. "Raj has asked me to escort you back to Calcutta," he explained, before adding: "Abu! Please carry Miss Elsie's bag!"

A giant bearded man, wearing a turban, stepped forward, and with the casual sweep of an arm, gathered up Elsie's bag like it was a plastic toy.

"Abu is my personal bodyguard and valuables carrier. You must also meet my valet, Mr Abid Hussain!" the Maharaja said, introducing a much smaller man in a dark suit, who grinned and nodded respectfully.

"How is Raj?" asked Elsie, in a voice she was sure was loud enough, though Tikari seemed to ignore her.

"We are staying at the Galle Face Hotel, on the waterfront. I am sure you will find it most acceptable."

"Will we be travelling there by motor or rickshaw, Your Highness?" she queried, more to check he was actually listening, than to elicit any particular information.

"Motor is now becoming an old-fashioned term, for there are so many of them around. I prefer 'car' or even, as the French would say, automobile," he said, as he signalled to a waiting vehicle.

As they sped off on the three-mile journey south from the harbour to the hotel, Elsie tried again to get a response relating to her fiancé. "How was Raj when you saw him last?"

To her surprise—although he definitely heard her—the Maharaja took some time to answer, preferring to feign interest in the passing cavalcade of coolies and rickshaws. When he eventually spoke, his speech was slow and deliberate. "When I last saw him … he was fine."

Elsie did not know what to think about his answer, other than it made her feel a little uneasy.

"We are in the original wing of the hotel. You may find this hard to believe," he said, as a massive hotel fronted by tall, waving palms, came into view, "but it was built in 1863!"

As they were passing the hotel's reception, the Maharaja stopped in his tracks, but signalled for the others to continue to the lift. "Take Miss Elsie up to the room. I shall join you shortly."

He hesitated, waiting to see the cedar lift door close behind Elsie and his staff, then turned to the reception desk. "Any telephone call or telegram for me?" he asked, in an earnest but hopeful voice.

"No, nothing, Your Highness."

"Damn! Remember to summon me in person—but not any of my staff—the moment any communication arrives!" he said, slapping a five-rupee note on the counter.

"Most certainly, Your Highness!" was the enthusiastic reply, as the money was pocketed.

Meanwhile, upstairs on the top floor, Elsie was ushered into the Royal Suite. Its size and luxury were breathtaking, but she could not quite shake the sense that it had a slightly 'lived in' feel.

Abu placed her bag inside the bedroom, suggesting ownership, but Elsie headed to the nearest cupboard and flung open the door, revealing a series of clothes. She lifted out a suit coat that had a crest with the wording 'Tikari'. "Just as I thought, this is the Maharaja's room, but where do I sleep?"

Abu and Abid looked at each other, neither wanting to answer.

"Leave that to me!" a voice said from behind, as Tikari strode to the bedside telephone. "This is the Maharaja of Tikari ... I need an extra suite ... what is available?"

"I really don't need anything fancy," Elsie protested.

"Nonsense! You are my guest! ... Which one is that? ... Oh, the Governor's Suite?" Cupping his hand over the receiver, he asked Elsie: "Will that do?"

"Look, really, I ..."

"Yes, the Governor's Suite will be fine ... thank you!" he said putting down the telephone. "An attendant will be up with the key in a minute."

* * *

As Elsie and Tikari sat in Galle Face's main dining room, looking out at the palms fringing Ceylon's western coastline, a waiter arrived with the lunch menu.

303

Tikari scanned it momentarily, then asked Elsie: "What would you say to a chicken curry?"

"Oh, I love curry!"

"Really? I find most English people don't!"

"That may be, but I am Australian!" she said proudly. "Raj made sure we had it quite regularly during the month we were in Cooch Behar. I cannot say that I love it very hot, for as my father is fond of urging, 'moderation in all things'!"

Moderation was not exactly a much-utilised sentiment in Tikari's behavioural lexicon. "Two chicken curries and a couple of glasses of Orange Blossom!"

"Yes, Your Highness!" the waiter acknowledged, bowing so low as he did, that his head nearly touched the table.

When the meal and drinks arrived, Elsie enquired what was in the latter.

"Gin, vermouth and orange juice."

"I am sure Raj would approve, Your Highness, though I will have just a sip of mine. I would never wish to be in a situation where I cannot control what I do!"

Tikari became reflective for a while. He had learnt more about Elsie in the last few minutes than he had thought he had previously known.

"I do so wish Raj was here. I really do miss his company! We have been apart for a year, but there has not been a single day when I have not thought about him!" Elsie exclaimed.

To Raji, the Maharaja of Tikari, the mentioning of the similar-sounding Raj's name, was intensely irritating, if understandable for now. It reminded him to look out for any attendant scurrying in his direction, though all he could see were Abu and Abid sitting patiently but alert at a distant table.

The next morning, all four of the group were packed and waiting outside the hotel entrance, when Tikari decided to head back inside.

"If any message comes for me, please notify the caller that I shall be at the Taj Mahal Hotel in Bombay, in two and a half days time. They should call me there. If it is a telegram, please have it forwarded care of 'The Manager, In Confidence'!"

With that he shook hands with the Galle Face manager as a wad of rupees simultaneously changed possession.

The journey by boat north to Bombay was notable only for Tikari's increasing irritability.

On docking in Bombay Harbour, the Maharaja was quick to leave the vessel, taking the first and only waiting motor to the nearby Taj Mahal Hotel, with instructions for the others to follow with the luggage.

To this stage, Elsie and Abu had exchanged nothing more than polite nodded greetings, but on this occasion, the giant Sikh signalled the nearest gharry and offered his right arm as support as she clambered aboard.

Elsie sensed his strength and solidity instantly, as if guided by a statue. As she settled into the back seat, she thanked him with a smile, and he responded with a brief bow of the head and: "A pleasure, Miss Elsie!"

"Where is this hotel, Abu?" she asked.

With a step backward and a sweep of his left hand, Abu indicated the massive and regal edifice across the harbour front to their left.

"Oh, my!" was all Elsie could say.

In the meantime, Tikari had vaulted up the hotel's front steps, raced through the palatial foyer and confronted the clerk at reception.

"Good afternoon, Your Highness! Welcome back to the Taj Mahal Hotel! Your usual Presidential Suite is ..."

"Yes, fine! But are there any messages for me?" Tikari demanded.

"Not that I am aware of," the clerk said, searching through a pigeonhole's contents.

"No telephone calls or telegrams?"

"No, nothing, Your Highness!"

"Are you sure? I want you to check with any other reception staff and the manager!" Tikari said, getting agitated. "Now!" he added, causing the clerk to hurry off.

A couple of minutes later, he was joined by another clerk and the hotel manager, none of whom had heard of anything. Tikari made sure they understood that if any contact was made, it was to be with him alone.

By the time his co-travellers had arrived at the Presidential Suite, Tikari was nowhere to be seen. This was not too surprising, said Abid, as the suite was 5,000 square feet in area and contained fifteen rooms.

"I think, however, I know where he is, Miss Elsie," he added with a smile. "Just excuse me for a moment."

Soon he was back, confirming his suspicion that, after completing a soothing bath, his stressed out master would shortly be massaged by two servant girls.

The next morning, Elsie made plain to Tikari her impatience to return to Raj and ultimately Cooch Behar, as speedily as possible. To her considerable frustration, Tikari said they would most likely be staying at the hotel for at least two more nights.

By that afternoon, Tikari was a real bundle of nerves, even lighting a cigarette after high tea. As Elsie got up and moved away with the book she was reading, he questioned what she was doing. When she said she could not stand cigarette smoke, he was dumbfounded.

He was still trying to reconcile the Elsie he thought he knew with the reality, when an attendant appeared at his side.

"Your Highness, there is a telephone call for you at the bar." Initially, Raji did not react because he was so focussed on the smoking issue. "What did you say?" he asked, in a delayed reaction.

"There is a telephone call for you at the bar, Your Highness!"

The attendant had barely mentioned the word 'telephone' a second time, before Tikari had shot to his feet, surging past (but also partially into) the attendant, who lost his balance.

The commotion made Elsie look up from her book. From where she sat, she could see Tikari grab the telephone receiver, then pound the bar surface twice with his fist—the lights of the bar glinting in the reflection of his emerald ring, in the bar's mirrored wall.

Just a few seconds later, Tikari hung up and slumped onto the bar itself. He stayed in that position for some time, as Elsie watched him, fascinated. Whatever could have caused such a reaction?

Eventually, he turned slowly, very slowly, but almost inevitably, to look in her direction.

The Maharaja started walking towards her, then hesitated to signal for Abu and Abid to join him momentarily. A few words to them, and they departed.

As Tikari moved closer, Elsie searched for a clue in his countenance, though it seemed to betray no great joy or pain.

"Miss Elsie, I need to speak to you—in the suite!"

As she followed behind him, clasping her book, her mind meandered through a mix of possibilities, none of which seemed particularly likely, nor pleasant.

While she sat on the lounge in the suite, she noticed Abu move to stand in front of the door. A shiver ran down her back, for clearly, there was something wrong.

"Elsie," Tikari started, standing a few yards away, though the large violet eyes that looked up at him convinced him to move closer. "Our dear friend Raj has had a car accident ..."

"Oh, no!" Elsie cried, leaping to her feet. "Please, tell me that he is all right?"

Tikari hesitated, well knowing that what he was about to say would be even more upsetting for her. "Unfortunately, he is not expected to live."

"I must go to him, now!" Elsie cried in anguish, as she raced towards the door, only to have her path blocked by the giant frame of Abu.

"That will not be possible, Elsie," Tikari said, as he caught up with her. "His family has asked that you stay away!"

Elsie clung to Abu's chest and started sobbing uncontrollably. Within just a few moments, the Sikh felt her body go limp. She had fainted.

Quickly, Abu's giant left hand moved in to support Elsie's back, as he tipped to his left, and swept his right arm behind her legs, scooping her up in his arms.

A few giant strides later and he had carefully placed her on her bed, as servant girls came in to remove her shoes and massage her.

* * *

The booming sunlight of a Bombay morning sneaked slowly but gradually more emphatically, through the quietly opening curtain of Elsie's luxury room. The maid must have smiled, but from where Elsie lay, she could only see her dark features as a single silhouette.

Elsie squeezed her eyelids tightly, and then reopened them, though nothing seemed to change. The feeling of loss and loneliness covered her like a weighty blanket, pinning her to her tear-stained pillow.

She and Raj had loved each other, of that she was certain, though his parents' tolerance of their relationship had always been in question. How silly she had been to even hope that their attitude would change. And then there was the matter of the 'curse': the prediction of a short life for Raj, that so stunted his communication and dominated his psyche to such a degree that alcohol became a crutch.

Elsie had never known alcoholism in her family, but had seen its devastating impact on others. She was not the first and would not be the last person to believe that love and devotion alone, could reverse such a debilitating condition. Yet, it was Raj himself, cognisant of the prophecy that so menacingly shadowed him, who had seemed hell-bent on ensuring it was ultimately self-fulfilling.

Taking a big breath, Elsie hauled herself out of bed to perch on the windowsill overlooking the waterfront. Rickshaw riders, coolies and the hoi polloi of Bombay's heaving metropolis, interwoven with a smattering of well-to-do Indians and inevitably arrogant Europeans, passed each other—none caring for, nor sharing in her circumstance.

She was devastated. She felt very alone, and India, suddenly, was like a most foreign country. It had all seemed so perfect, just a short time ago. Everyone had shared her joy and expectation of being a princess-in-waiting, but now there was nothing for her to do but return to work in her father's bookshop. It was utterly humiliating, and certainly not what she wanted, but now, it was inevitable.

She sighed in resignation, then washed, dressed and brushed herself, before sitting down to write a farewell and thank you note to the Maharaja of Tikari. There was no reason to remain in India, so she would be heading back home. Fortunately, she just had enough money for the return passage.

Placing the letter on the coffee table, she dragged her bag to the suite's large oak door, where she used both hands to turn the brass handle.

When she reached down to pick up her bag, it was not there. A giant hand had reached over her to push the door closed.

"Miss Elsie, the Maharaja would not like to see you leave. Please, let us sit on the couch," Abu said, guiding her back into the heart of the room.

Considerable time must have passed, because when Tikari emerged, he was surprised to see Elsie asleep with her head in Abu's lap, and he, with eyes closed, softly stroking her hair.

"Abu!" he snapped.

The Sikh opened his eyes slowly, though without any appearance of guilt, like an owner basking in the mutual comfort of stroking his favourite cat. He pointed to the letter on the coffee table.

Tikari grimaced as he read its content. Elsie stirred, causing Raji to think quickly but carefully about what he was going to say.

As she sat up, apologising for having drifted off to sleep, the Maharaja addressed her: "Elsie! After lunch, Abu will escort you on a visit to the finest European clothing shops, that only the Bombay wealthy from Malabar and Cumballa Hill frequent. There, you are to buy whatever your heart desires. Abu will ensure the goods are paid for and will also purchase a large oak travelling trunk."

"That is very kind of you, Your Highness, but really I see no need to remain in India."

Tikari became agitated. Clearly he was not getting his message across. In his frustration, he came and sat down on the couch next to Elsie and grasped her hand.

"We have an old tradition which I intend to uphold. Whenever a woman is permanently separated from her loved one, a family member or close friend steps in and takes his place. I undertake from now on to care for and protect you. There will be no returning to Australia. You are part of my family now!"

Elsie felt comforted by his words, though in her current emotional state, was unsure exactly what he meant. She realised now that she had nothing to lose, so appreciated that she could wait to find out his meaning.

Chapter 36

An Attraction at Agra

Its walls are of white marble, it's a monument to love
From Shah Jahan, the ruler, to wife Mumtaz, his dove
All beauty and all symmetry—the Mughal 'golden fleece'
The Taj Mahal at Agra, is where she lies, in peace.

Elsie was stunned when she saw the massive and ornate Gothic-revival building that soared before her. But then the breathtaking Victoria Terminus in Bombay always had that impact on anyone who saw India's most beautiful railway building for the first time. The towering central dome, alone, was enough to guarantee veneration, but the turrets, ornate sculpture-work and 'Indian palace' appearance combined to create an intoxicating and memorable farewell image of the western metropolis.

The twenty-hour train trip from the great port city to Agra provided plenty of opportunity for Elsie to reflect on her circumstance. She had thought of writing a letter to Emma, though she was still in significant doubt as to where she stood emotionally, as well as where she would reside. The Maharaja had said he would look after her, but what exactly did that mean?

The newly constructed magnificence of Agra's white-arched Imperial Hotel promised to be a comfortable stopover for two nights, though as to their purpose in the city, the Maharaja was being deliberately evasive. He had quickly ascertained that Elsie had never been there before, nor was aware of its greatest treasure—and he wanted to keep it that way.

As Abu was directed to take Elsie's trunk to the Princess' Suite, Tikari lingered at the reception desk to ensure that the most knowledgeable and English-speaking guide was available to them for the next day.

After heading up to the suite, Elsie soon realised that there were two peoples' sets of clothes being hung up by Abid in the room—and only one large bed.

Oh, no! What am I going to do? He tried this sort of arrangement on the first night in Colombo at Galle Face, and I told him I was not happy, she recalled, *but now … could I refuse to share his bed, given he has promised to be my sole carer? In any case, exactly what sort of relationship does he want?*

She was determined to confront him, and did so, as soon as he entered the room. Raji quickly worked out that it was inappropriate that Abid and Abu be present, sending them off to the lounge.

"You must understand," he began, "that I could have let you return to Australia, but gave my word that I would care for you, just as Raj would have wished to have done himself. Raj's parents would never, ever, have allowed you to become the Princess of Cooch Behar, but both my parents are deceased, and I am offering you the crown of Tikari, as my maharani, my queen!"

"But Raji, I barely know you, and you are already asking me to share your bed with you and be intimate! That would be improper of me, given that we are not married!"

"As for knowing me well," Raji responded in a frustrated tone, "many Indian marriages are arranged by the parents of the couple, with love developing over time. As for sleeping in the same bed, I promise to respect you and not be intimate until we are married."

Elsie spent most of dinner wondering whether she should still hold her ground and insist on separate sleeping arrangements. Certainly, this was the proper thing to do, but would she place her prospects of becoming Maharani in jeopardy if she persisted with her objection?

The alternative seemed a lonely return to the bookshop in Sydney, and right now, the mystery and wonder of her current situation, combined with the possible elevation to Maharani, seemed far preferable. Raji had been most kind and generous to date, and if all he asked was to lie in the same bed, should she refuse?

By the time both she and the Maharaja had changed discretely into their nightclothes that evening, the die had been cast, and, against her conservative upbringing, Elsie was going to do nothing beyond insist on the protection of her dignity.

As she stepped into bed, she turned away from his side, but politely wished him goodnight.

It was not long before his hands started softly stroking her body. She tolerated it for a couple of minutes and then rolled over to face him, drawing her knees up and then pushing her feet out against his chest.

Despite all his efforts, she was pushing him back across the bed, and giggling, till he toppled over the edge and fell with a crash and a cry onto the tiled floor.

Rather than be angry, to her significant surprise, he began laughing. *At least,* she thought, *he too has a sense of humour. How funny that it is a moment of shared humour that brings us closer.*

A mini version of breakfast was delivered to their room far earlier than Elsie had imagined it would. For some reason, the Maharaja had insisted they make a very early start.

Two motors waited outside the Imperial Hotel in the darkness, their drivers making final sweeps of cloth across the bodies of their 'babies'.

Tikari reached out a hand of welcome to the gentleman in his fifties in the hotel's foyer. "Dr Khan?"

"Yes, Your Highness, Dr Naim Khan. I am most honoured to be your guide on the tour of …"

"Ah!" interrupted Tikari. "What we are about to see will, I believe, be a complete surprise to Miss Forrest here! I wish it to remain that way for as long as possible."

"But you would like me to provide background information, Your Highness?"

"Oh, most certainly Dr Khan, but please do not unveil the jewel until it is necessary!"

Elsie listened with some amusement and pleasure, as it seemed that the day's activities were largely for her entertainment.

Tikari asked that he and Elsie sit behind Dr Khan in the lead vehicle, and signalled that Abu, Abid and the collection of tiffin containers filled with breakfast, follow in the second motor.

They crept off into the darkness, heading south, then east and then north on a three-mile drive, till the vehicle headlights illuminated a large gate in a walled complex.

"The West Gate!" Dr Khan declared, as they exited the

motors. A group of candle sellers immediately besieged the party, causing Dr Khan to lose his temper after purchasing five candles from fewer sellers than was wished.

Guided now by candlelight, they made their way through the large, arched and pointed entrance to stand on the edge of a broad forecourt. "This space is the Jilaukhana," Dr Khan stated, leading the group on a walk of a couple of hundred yards, before turning left. They climbed a set of steps as their candlelight revealed a huge and ornate structure clad in red sandstone and white marble.

"The Great Gate!" Dr Khan proclaimed, as he led them on through the large edifice. He paused where a pair of massive and open iron doors framed an archway entrance. "You cannot appreciate it from here, just yet, but we will return to this spot later, as the view in daylight is special."

He led them forward to the edge of a paved terrace. "Be careful of the drop and the water just in front of us!" Dr Khan warned, as Elsie noticed a body of water disappearing into the darkness.

"Let me start at the beginning—and I will ask that you all face down this channel of water, in a northerly direction." Dr Khan began. "The Mughals were a people of Central Asia, with their capital in Samarqand ..."

"Samarqand! That is such a wonderful name!" interrupted Elsie.

"In the early 1500s, Barbur was their leader, and he was descended on his father's side from Timur—who Westerners call Tamerlane—and on his mother's side, from Genghis Khan. In 1526 he led an army from Kabul through the Kyber Pass, to establish a Mughal Empire with Agra as its capital. Look across the water now ..."

As they peered through the gloom, large dark shapes seemed to emerge as the first faint rays of sunrise lightened the background sky.

"Barbur's grandson, Akbar, became known as Akbar the Great. Despite being born Muslim, he was tolerant of all religions and can be said to have been a 'humanist'."

"Religious fanaticism is such stupidity. So many fighting and dying for their own version of God!" Elsie stated emphatically.

"That is a very interesting thing to say," responded Tikari, surprised.

"Akbar, his son Jahangir and grandson Shah Jahan, were all great builders. In their courts, art and literature flourished. Notice now how distinct shapes are being defined in the distance by the rising sun."

"Minarets!" Elsie cried out. "The tall shadows on the sides are minarets!" Then she continued:

WAKE ! For the Sun, who scatter'd into flight
The Stars before him from the Field of Night,
    Drives Night along with them from Heav'n, and strikes
The Sultán's Turret with a Shaft of Light.

"Ah, Miss Forrest, an English version of the first quatrain of Persian poet Omar Khayyám's classic work!" Dr Khan noted. "Well, that is quite appropriate here, because there was significant Persian influence in court—and the court language was Persian. Note now, how more detail is becoming clear on the structure in the distance."

As they stared at the evolving panorama, a golden light splashed across four minarets set around a large, central domed structure.

"So let me tell you about what is before us—and it is now fine for us to blow out our candles. Shah Jahan's favourite wife was his third, who he called Mumtaz Mahal Begam, meaning the Chosen One of the Palace. She was a Shi'a Muslim. He was utterly devoted to her, having been engaged to her when she was only fourteen, three years before his first marriage. Let us now walk down the side of the channel of water and move closer to the structure."

Walking onward, and down alongside the water channel, they could see the structure in a clearer and slightly less golden light.

"Mumtaz Mahal was said to be so beautiful in appearance and character that they soon became inseparable. They were married in 1612 and she bore him thirteen children! Shah Jahan became the Mughal Emperor in 1627, but Mumtaz died when giving birth, four years later, at the age of thirty-eight. Perhaps, we could just walk to our left here, and climb the stairs to stand on the platform."

Soon, they were looking across a second channel of water, one that was closer to the structure, whose image they could now see reflected in the water ahead. The stonework, that at first had appeared golden-brown, could now clearly be seen as white marble.

"Shah Jahan was absolutely heartbroken and he was determined that his wife be buried in the most beautiful of monuments. And here it is before us, the Taj Mahal—the greatest jewel of Mughal symmetrical architecture!"

Tears welled in Elsie's eyes as she beheld the astonishing sight before her. "It is just so beautiful, so beautiful!" She was overcome nearly as much by the story behind the structure as the Taj Mahal itself. *It reminds me a bit of the decoration inside Sydney's Palace Theatre,* she thought.

"It took seventeen years to build and was completed in 1648. Now, if we just walk to our right here, down the side of the channel, we will start to get a good close-up view of the mausoleum."

As they neared the Taj Mahal, what had seemed from a distance as just a large white marble edifice, was transformed into a creation of most intricate beauty, bathing in the highlighting of the early morning sunshine.

"You can now see that the sides of the structure are adorned with intricate calligraphy. These are quotes from the Muslim holy book, the Quran. The structure is made from white marble from Markana in Rajasthan, though the calligraphy is carved in relief and inlaid with dark stones."

Elsie could not resist running her hands across the carved and inlaid marble, her fingers falling and rising as they reached across the centuries, embracing this most beautiful symbol of eternal love.

"You will notice," said Dr Khan, "that higher up there is the most exquisite inlay work in polished marble and semi-precious stones."

As she looked up, Elsie marvelled at the beauty of the workmanship, with the dark lines of lily stems curving and flowing through the polished white marble over the arches and doorways, before periodically exploding into colour with the flower itself.

A lower section over a central door beckoned, so Elsie stretched up towards it, though in vain—until a strong pair of hands settled around her waist, and Abu's voice said: "Tighten your body, Miss Elsie!" Then, with one sweep, he lifted her up in the air, high above his head, where her fingers softly and lovingly traced parts of the structure that had previously been out of reach.

"Let us proceed inside," said Dr Khan, leading the enthralled group into the only slightly dimmer inner sanctum.

"You can now see how the Mughal Taj is a fusion of Persian, Indian and Islamic architectural styles, though I doubt you will see anything more beautiful in this world!"

As they headed in and around, passing walls and an octagonal marble screen, each person let their fingertips dance across the relief of the exquisitely carved pots, flowers and palms, then glide across the glossed smoothness of the inlaid representations of the natural world.

Finally, the small group stood before two cenotaphs, the central one of Mumtaz Mahal and just to the side, that of Shah Jahan.

"I must tell you," said Dr Khan, "that the ornate sarcophagi you see before you are not the real ones. The Mughal Emperor and his beloved wife were actually buried below, on a level that we cannot access. However," he added, first checking that there was nobody else in the Taj's interior, "do not move, but just listen, after I call."

While they were soaking up the magnificence in the heart of the mausoleum, Dr Khan cried out: "Allahu Akbar!"

To everyone else's astonishment, his words echoed back, again and again—and again.

"It might seem hard to believe, if you had not just heard the echoes, but sound has been known to echo for up to twenty-eight seconds from a central point!"

The group exited the mausoleum and headed for a neighbouring garden. There, Abid and Abu laid out rugs and set up a breakfasting opportunity that seemed scarcely necessary, given they had all just feasted on the finest Mughal architecture ever created.

Elsie rested gently against Abu, as they snacked on bread, dips and fruit from the tiffin containers.

"There is something else that I have not explained to you," Dr Khan teased, waiting for everyone's attention. "One of Shah Jahan's younger sons, Aurangzeb, led an orthodox Islamist revolt when his father became ill in 1657. The younger brother had his older brother, Dara Shikoh, who was the Emperor's designated successor, publicly executed for heresy, then saw that his father was thrown into prison in the Agra Fort till he died, away from his much-loved Taj."

"But he is buried here, that is what you told us earlier!" interrupted Elsie.

"That is true. That is a concession that Aurangzeb made, though it was not Shah Jahan's wish. He had dreamed of an identically shaped and sized black marble Taj as his mausoleum."

"Oh, that would have been magnificent!" cried Tikari. "Imagine it sitting there on the other side of the Yamuna River—or even in the area of the South Gate on this side—the black and the white together for eternity!"

Most would not have complained if their stay within the wondrous warmth of the Taj had dragged out for a similar distance, but one had other important matters in mind. Once back at the Imperial Hotel, Tikari had seemed distant. After what Elsie had told him the night before, he had arranged for two Hindu priests to accompany them back out to the Taj Mahal in the late afternoon.

As they stood in front of the final water channel that led up to the monument, changing colour as the sun set, Raji put his arm around her and spoke with what she interpreted as great sincerity: "Elsie, I have loved you from the first moment that I saw you on that opening night in Calcutta's Theatre Royal! I have asked these Hindu priests to conduct a short, symbolic marriage ceremony, so that you will be my maharani."

Chanting and the burning of sandalwood ensued, followed by the wrapping of a gold cloth around Raji and Elsie's joined hands.

Then, reaching into the pocket of his coat, Raji pulled out a white silk handkerchief and slowly opened it, to reveal four magnificent bracelets: two ringed with diamonds and the other two with emeralds.

He then held Elsie's left hand. She noted that his hands were trembling. She waited for him to say something, but for a moment he seemed lost for words.

"They are very beautiful bracelets, Your Highness!" she said most honestly, while hoping her comment would encourage conversation.

"Oh, Elsie, please call me Raji. You are now the Maharani of Tikari—Tikari's queen!" he proclaimed, as he threaded the bracelets up her left arm, till they nestled in a glittering and alternating pile above her elbow.

Now it was Elsie's turn to be lost for words. Only days earlier she had been permanently separated from the prince she had thought she might marry. Here she was, wedded to the ruler of a state she had never visited, nor even knew of its locality. He was darker and not as good-looking as Raj. And, there was the matter of that large emerald ring on his left hand.

"The emerald ring?" she asked tentatively.

"Ah, that is from my first wife ... I was only nineteen when we married."

"First wife? But you are not very old now, Raji!"

"I am only twenty-three."

"So am I. And I was married at nineteen too, though since divorced."

"Maharajas can have multiple wives—and usually do," he said, searching in vain for a sign that his words were having a positive effect.

"You mean she is still your wife?" Elsie cried, as her mind sped through the implications. "The poor woman. How could she live in the same building with me," Elsie agonised out aloud as she started to remove the bracelets.

"No! They are a gift for you!" Raji said firmly. "In any case, she no longer lives in the main palace. We rarely see each other," he added, making a mental note to telegram ahead the next morning, to ensure this would be seen to be the case. "Besides, I want you to be my Mumtaz Mahal!"

The sights and emotion of the day had made a significant

impact on Elsie. Now this maharaja was promising to make her the most beloved of all wives. There was also the not too small matter of her likely infertility. As all rulers would surely want an heir, how could she object to there being another wife, if she were to remain childless?

She closed her eyes momentarily, knowing that he had to be made aware of this complication, now. It might mean the end of their relationship, but it was only fair.

"You must know," she whispered, "that just a few months ago I had a cyst removed, and the specialist told me that I might never be able to bear children."

He paused, scanning the sky in the distance, as if seeking out an interpretive sign. He seemed to be mulling things over in silence for some time, before responding: "I have no children by my first wife either," a comment that made Elsie's heart sink with the pressure it implied. Then he looked at her with a smile on his face, before adding: "but that does not matter at all, my queen, because we are going to have great fun trying!"

* * *

That night, the Princess' Suite glowed with the light of candles, as burning incense wafted, creating an atmosphere of sensuality.

Elsie was asked to lie on the bed naked, and Raji stood for some time, transfixed by the beauty of her pale form. For so long he had dreamt of this moment. Elsie could see desire in his eyes. He knelt beside her, his fingertips caressing and revelling in the feel of her silken skin. Soon, his strong hands were massaging fragrant oil into and across her body.

"Have you heard of the Kama Sutra?" he asked.

"No," she muttered, barely audibly, as her mouth was pressed into the sheets.

"It is a Hindu epic that was written over 1,500 years ago. Kama means sensual pleasure, and the book is about how men and women can share this pleasure with each other. Tonight, we will start our journey through the Kama Sutra, together!"

He turned Elsie over on her back, pausing momentarily to marvel at her breasts before spreading his fingertips over her erect nipples then across the hills and valleys of what to him was virgin territory.

She caught sight of his erect penis for the first time, and was convinced he was considerably larger than George. Her excitement was building, but he seemed content to take his time.

He bent down to softly kiss her breasts. Elsie moaned with pleasure as he slowly progressed upwards to her lips.

For some minutes they playfully toyed with each other, kissing and softly biting, before Raji, his voice quivering with excitement and anticipation said: "The Frog—I shall teach you the Kama Sutra position we call The Frog!"

He squatted on the bed with knees wide apart and pulled her over till she sat astride him, her legs either side of him and her arms around his shoulders.

As they kissed and embraced, she could feel his firm penis entering the warmth of her vagina. He started rocking back and forth, penetrating further and further inside.

Their kissing became more and more passionate and frantic as each built towards an inevitable, rocking climax.

Over the next few hours, they got to know each other more and more intimately, he bending and twisting her into further sexual positions she had never experienced before, nor ever thought possible. It was an exhilarating and incomparable ride that permanently changed Elsie's appreciation of the sensual world, and bound her quickly and closely to Raji.

Chapter 37

Through the Night, Easterly

Pretend that you are kidnapped, being taken on a ride
'Cross the Indian subcontinent, maharaja by your side
New food, new smells, new languages — in short you've travelled far
On this journey through the night-time, to the region called Bihar.

The next morning, Abu was quick to greet Elsie cheerily in the Imperial's dining area.

"Good morning, Your Highness!" he said knowingly, with a big smile on his face.

Elsie reached out and grabbed his right arm, dragging him (with a fair degree of cooperation) into the corner of the room, behind a pillar. "You must tell me what Raji's first wife is like. I would feel awful if I were to hurt her in any way."

Abu glanced around the pillar to check that neither Raji nor Abid were within earshot. "She is the sister of a maharaja — and yes, she is beautiful. His Highness only courts beautiful women."

"Oh, Abu, nothing you have said has made me feel better!"

"Just remember, Your Highness," he whispered, "nobody should marry a maharaja and expect to be the only wife."

"But I still must see her and apologise. That is the very least I should do."

Abu checked around the pillar again, then spoke in an even softer voice: "She will not be living in the palace in Tikari Raj, but I promise I will arrange for you to meet her. We have to be patient and very careful as I do not think His Highness will be happy."

"Thank you, Abu," Elsie said, stretching her arms out in a vain attempt to encircle his giant frame with a hug.

As she sat down for breakfast, she was sure of one thing: though it was in quite a different way, she could honestly say that she was at least as fond of Abu as she was of her maharaja.

When Raji arrived, he was bubbling with excitement. "This afternoon we start the journey to Tikari Raj!" he exclaimed, placing a hand affectionately on Elsie's. "Ah, there is nothing quite like heading home!"

Elsie wondered exactly where Tikari Raj was and how they were going to get there. Later that day, the 5 pm overnight express steam train from Agra Fort Station, materialised as the answer to the latter.

The giant figure of Abu was standing in front of the entrance to one of the few first class carriages.

"I have reserved the whole carriage, just for the four of us," Raji explained.

As they clambered on board, Abu and Abid ensured all luggage was carefully stored, and then took up positions at the far end of the carriage, where they could watch and wait for their master's instructions, from a respectful distance.

Raji and Elsie settled next to each other on comfortable armchair-like seats, at a table.

A blast from the guard's whistle echoed down the gloom of the now relatively empty platform and the train lurched forward in a sequence of moves that soon transformed into a slow-paced rattling glide.

Elsie witnessed the buildings of Agra slinking towards the slowly setting sun, as the train inched its way eastward.

"We only have fifteen and a half hours to go till we reach Gaya," Raji declared, as he looked impatiently at his watch.

"I thought we were going to Tikari Raj?" Elsie queried, as she was now quite confused.

Raji looked around the table and picked up a serviette, then after feeling its texture, put it down in frustration. "Abid, pencil and paper, please!"

The speediness with which Abid responded indicated this was not the very first time such a request had been made.

"Now," said Raji, pushing a piece of paper so that it sat between them on the table. "If I put a 'C' here," indicating a spot near midway, not far from the paper's right edge, "this is Calcutta, which is part of the Bengal Presidency. It extends all the way up here, then around to the west and down here to the south," he added, as he completed a full circumnavigation of the sheet with his pencil.

Raji was going to mention that Cooch Behar was up in the top right-hand corner—then thought it better to let sleeping dogs lie, lest Elsie discovered a bone to pick with him.

"The compound where the Tikari Raj palace—called the White House—is located, is in the city of Gaya, which is here," he said, marking with a 'G' a spot roughly north-west of Calcutta, but nearer the left edge of the page. "But I also have a palace—the Sultanganj—on the banks of the Ganges River in Patna, and a mansion in Calcutta."

"So, how many miles is Gaya from Calcutta?"

"Over 250 miles, but we have a rail link and we even have a Tikari Raj carriage that can be joined to an existing train, or pulled by its own locomotive!"

There was silence for a few moments as Elsie thought about what she should say, if anything at all, for she did not want to appear too eager or greedy for a lifestyle so different to her upbringing.

"One thing you must understand," Raji stated, with surprising firmness, "is that Gaya is part of the region known as Bihar. And in Bihar, things often happen differently."

Exactly what he meant by this, Elsie was not sure, and Raji seemed reluctant to elaborate. Once again, silence prevailed, until Raji felt compelled to offer another morsel. "Nearly two hundred years ago, Bihar was a dangerous place. The Mughals needed support and safe passage through the area and one of my ancestors fought hard to supply it. He was rewarded with the title of Raja, which the Mughal emperor later raised to Maharaja, or 'great king'. My ancestors established a fort at Tekari, near Gaya. The ruins of a very large complex are still there, today."

Once more, he then became quiet and was thinking earnestly about what to say next. Elsie looked out the train window into the gathering darkness. She could only just make out lush green fields interrupted by the occasional smattering of thatched dwellings.

The lights in the carriage came on just as Raji tried to throw light on the nature of Biharis. "Biharis find it difficult, difficult to trust. Your next enemy could come from anywhere. I do not employ bodyguards from Bihar. Abu, my personal bodyguard, is a Sikh from the north-west, while a troop of Nepalese Gurkhas guard the Tikari Raj Compound and the White House."

He then drew a rough square around the letter 'G', though his creation seemed to lean a little to the right. "This is the Tikari Raj Compound. It is just over 100 acres in size."

Next, he drew a much larger shape, one that made the Tikari Raj Compound that lay at its heart, quite insignificant. "This is my Tikari Raj Estate. It has an area of 1,628 square miles, so I am told … though I think I have not quite got things right …" he said, as he added sections down the lower right and made pencil adjustments elsewhere. "I have not quite got the—what is the English word for it?"

"Proportion, Raji dear."

"I was educated at St George's School at Mussoorie, so I was brought up with English boys around me. However, I must say that Mr Keith, who was my private tutor, but is now the Tikari estate manager, deserves much credit. I still do not feel I speak too well and my English spelling is not good."

"Oh Raji, I think you do wonderfully well," Elsie said, giving him a squeeze.

"Of course, you know Raji is not my real name. In fact, Abu and I have the same surname."

"You mean you and Abu are brothers?" Elsie asked mischievously in a voice loud enough that Abu looked over in puzzlement. Elsie just smiled and winked back.

"No! Abu is only my nickname for him! His real name is Parminder Singh and, as I said, he is a Sikh. I also have Singh—which means lion—as a surname, but I am a Hindu."

"So what is your real name, Mr Lion?" Elsie questioned, looking at him with her big and twinkling violet eyes, that had a smile of their own.

Raji hesitated, more because her gaze reminded him of just one reason why he had pursued her so fervently.

"Gopal Saran Narayan Singh. My mother was Queen of Tikari, but I was only four years old when she died." He then hesitated, looked down at the table and then out at the darkness before adding: "I suspect one reason I love having women around is that I still miss her very much."

"Oh dear! Don't worry, Raji. I will be around to tuck you in at night!" Elsie said, with a reassuring hug.

As the train clattered on eastward, each spoke about their upbringing. Soon, it was just after 6 pm and the incessant rattling on the rails was overwhelmed by a squeaking of brakes, as the express reached its first stop: Tundla.

"Abid! Get us a snack, please," Raji ordered, causing Abid to hurriedly retrieve a plate from a trunk on a neighbouring seat.

Elsie watched as Abid disappeared outside the train and into a sea of food stalls that dotted the platform. Soon, he was back with a big grin on his face.

"Samosas!" he said, handing the plate over to Raji, before taking one himself after Raji gestured.

"What is in them?" Elsie asked cautiously of the baked pastries lying before her.

"Usually potato, onion … cheese, peas, spices … and … some meat," explained Abid between mouthfuls.

"He should know," Raji insisted, "as he is a very good cook."

Elsie took a bite from a pastry, then, quickly, another. "Oh! These are delicious!"

"Quick, Abid, another plateful … we have over three hours till our next stop and dinner!"

Five minutes later, the train was off again, though, this time, it at least tried to live up to its name of 'express'.

Elsie put her head against Raji's shoulder and must have drifted off to sleep, for it was after 7 pm when she stirred, as she felt him move. Gradually, she opened her eyes to see that he was gesturing to Abu.

After reaching in to a pocket and taking a few giant steps, the Sikh placed the contents of a huge hand in front of Elsie.

"Now you can have a matching emerald," Raji proclaimed as he opened a small green box to reveal a ring with a large rectangular emerald.

"Oh, it is so lovely! Do you want me to wear this?"

"Of course! I know mine is a bigger emerald, but …"

"Oh, please don't apologise, Raji. I really don't think I deserve something like this."

"Of course you do! You know, there was something you said yesterday that really interested me. You talked about religion and how it could be evil. I have similar feelings. I am a Hindu.

My caste is Bhumihar Brahmin—that is the uppermost, priestly caste—but I must say I am not very religious. I do not follow a strict Hindu diet and those around me are of different religions. Abu is Sikh, Abid is Muslim and you are Christian, are you not?"

"Well, yes, born in Sydney but baptised in the Church of England."

"So you see, I do not discriminate against any religion."

As the train pressed on at far greater speed than on the earlier leg, their talk turned to their passions, with Elsie asking Raji what he really liked to do.

"Motoring—driving and collecting cars and everything to do with them—is my greatest passion! I have won races in France and England!"

"I love driving, too."

"You do? You can drive?" he asked, incredulous, before remembering that Eugene Manolescu had informed him that she could.

"Oh yes! I was taught by Mr Sonnie Paul in Calcutta. Do you know him? His father was once the Advocate General of the Calcutta High Court."

"Sonnie Paul … no, I can't say I know him …" he said slowly as he gazed out into the darkness. "How many cars do I have, Abid?" he asked in a raised voice, quickly changing the subject.

"Currently five in Gaya, two in Patna and three in Calcutta, with another, the Locomobile Type E from America, here in around a month, Your Highness."

"I actually think there are now only two in Calcutta," Raji muttered quietly to nobody in particular.

"So you like motoring. Anything else?"

"Big game hunting! I have done it in Africa and of course many times in India. Going out on a tiger shoot and coming back with a trophy is something I always enjoy!"

"Oh," was all Elsie could say.

"You must come out with me next time," he suggested, trying to be helpful.

"Oh no! I would feel too sorry for the animal!"

"So, what do you like to do?"

"Apart from motoring, I like to read, sing, dance, act. Just the sort of things I have been doing for much of my life."

There was silence for a while as each pondered just how little they seemed to have in common. "They do say that opposites attract," Elsie suggested, though, as she said this, she realised the saying had more to do with personality than interests. "Well, another couple of 'likes' we have in common are Abu and Abid!" she added loudly, bringing embarrassed smiles and nods from across the carriage.

Raji leaned in to Elsie and whispered: "You must not forget that they are servants. They are just doing their job—as they should."

"It never hurts to acknowledge good work, Raji," she whispered back.

The train rattled on through the mid-December darkness of the state of Uttar Pradesh. Elsie placed her head against Raji's shoulder and he tilted his head against hers in an attempt to make two minds, feel as one.

Just before 9.30 pm, the train's brakes signalled another stop: Kanpur Junction.

"We will check out the food with Abid, then we can use the toilets in the first class lounge, if you wish."

Elsie had been looking forward to the opportunity of dinner and a toilet break for quite some time.

As they alighted the train, Elsie realised that Kanpur was Tundla magnified many times.

The platform was a mass of food stalls, with fires and colours and smells and sounds that could tempt an introverted hunger striker towards communal gluttony.

"What are they?" Elsie asked, pointing to large round balls in a sauce.

"Kofta—lamb meatballs with spices and onions," explained Abid. "The food in Uttar Pradesh has a strong Mughal influence—that is Persian/Ottoman/Central Asian. So you will also find kebabs. We are better off having the kofta with some naan bread, rice and vegetables."

"Arrange for four plates," Raji instructed. "Elsie and I will see you back at the carriage after going to the first class lounge."

Elsie was more than relieved with the state of the flushing

toilets in the lounge and felt sorry for the queues of passengers waiting to access the relatively primitive facilities outside.

On returning to the train, Elsie told Abu and Abid to use the lounge while they could.

After twenty minutes, the whistle sounded and the train surged into the north Indian darkness, bound south-eastward, for Allahabad.

Elsie was most certain already of one thing: *if this is the sort of food I will be served in Tikari Raj, dining will never be a concern!*

At 10 pm there was a polite knocking at the carriage door and two attendants arrived to convert the carriage into sleeping compartments. Seating and tables were moved until Elsie and Raji had a reasonably flat bed on which to lie. Before retiring for the night, Elsie leaned out of her drawn curtains to check on Abu and Abid. "Thank you for all you have done today, gentlemen."

"It was an honour, Your Highness," replied Abu.

"And a pleasure, Your Highness," echoed Abid.

Elsie giggled as she settled back in next to Raji—who promptly gave her a smack on the thigh. She reciprocated with a laugh, then ensured she hit him just a little bit harder.

Chapter 38

Tikari Raj

And when the morning greets you, your whole damn world has changed:
Servants at your beck and call, a line of cars arranged
Tikari Raj is at your service, and the White House can be seen
'Cause you went to sleep as 'commoner'—and woken up as 'queen'.

Raji had woken not long after the train had departed Mughal Sarai, on the last leg of the journey. Unable to sleep any further, he had joined Abu and Abid. The rise and fall in the intonation of their conversation—in a language that Elsie would soon recognise as Hindustani—provided her with a comforting but decidedly novel lullaby to accompany the rocking and rolling on the rails.

As daylight shone through the carriage's windows, Elsie allowed it to caress her face as she wondered about what lay in store. She thought of Emma and about her parents. She wondered what they would be thinking, if only they knew.

Attendants moved in to convert the carriage back into daytime travelling mode, as Raji pointed to the passing parade of green fields, palms and village huts. "We have now entered Tikari Raj territory," he stated with pride.

At 8.20 am the train eased into Gaya Junction Railway Station, and Elsie took a deep breath as she straightened out her crumpled dress. "Don't worry, you can have a long bath when we are home in the White House," Raji assured her, jostling hair that Elsie felt needed a long overdue wash.

Elsie noticed a dapper-looking young man in what looked like British military uniform, standing on the platform. As they alighted, she noted he brushed a tidying hand across his blonde hair and stood to attention. *Tidiness, order and formality must be important to him,* she thought.

"Elsie, I want you to meet my Aide-de-Camp, Cecil Kempster," Raji said.

Elsie instinctively reached out a hand, then withdrew it. "Oh, dear! I really don't know what I should be doing! Please excuse me!"

"Your Highness, it will be an honour to instruct you," the young man said with a bow and a smile.

"As ADC, it is Kempster's job to know all these things, Elsie. I am sure you will be a quick learner."

Abu and Abid, with assistance from other Raj staff, conveyed the luggage through the Gaya terminal building and out the back to a vehicle parking area.

A line of four cars stood waiting, each with a driver who came quickly to attention and saluted as they approached. There was something else Elsie noticed: four men in navy blue uniforms, armed with rifles. They looked different to the others, perhaps smaller but stronger. They came to attention in a well-coordinated fashion.

Raji could see where Elsie's attention had drifted. "They are part of Tikari Raj's Gurkha Guard. Kempster is their commanding officer. Now, Elsie, which car would you like to travel in?"

Elsie looked down the line of vehicles, each with their tonneau down, gleaming in their convertible elegance. "Oh dear … I … I really don't mind …"

"The first one is a De Dion Bouton; then a Panhard et Levassor Touring; then a Studebaker Touring; and finally, a Ford Model K Touring."

It is just so hard, thought Elsie, *when you have to choose between a number of beautiful things … sometimes it might be far easier to have no choice at all!* "I like the red one … particularly!" she said, appreciating that Raji was trying his best to impress and make things just the way she wanted.

"Ah, the Studebaker! Good choice!"

The luggage was loaded into the others and the sequence of vehicles changed so that two guards were in the front and rear vehicles, with the Studebaker second.

"I really much prefer to drive myself, and often do," Raji explained, whispering into Elsie's ear as they settled into the Studebaker's back seat. "But everyone has their role in the Raj and are proud to perform it. Take over their role and you rob them of their worthiness."

Elsie immediately realised she had heard this sort of comment before, in Cooch Behar.

The small convoy headed south on Railway Station Road, for about a mile, passing through areas sprinkled with small dwellings, on a patchwork of mainly rich green fields. People stopped and stared at the royal cavalcade, making Elsie wonder momentarily whether she should in fact wave—a thought that was quickly lost in a pit of embarrassment as she reminded herself that she would have to work hard for their respect, let alone admiration.

A turn to the right was quickly followed by one to the left, after which a high stone wall loomed beyond an intersection. "The Tikari Raj Compound walls—they encircle the whole 100 acres!" Raji exclaimed.

As the car swept to the left, Elsie noticed a pair of large iron gates with the words 'Tikari Raj' and the coat of arms emblazoned in colour at their respective centres.

Even before the car had taken a final right turn, the gates parted and clearly well-drilled and saluting Gurkha guards, stood as sentinels by the driveway entrance.

Elsie bit her lip, just to check she was not dreaming this, while reminding herself not to take anything for granted. *Expect little and rejoice in more, as my father often says.*

The four cars glided on, with Elsie gazing around her: the large lake to the left of the entrance; the neatly trimmed hedges that lined the blue metal stone drive; and the occasional tall palm tree proclaiming its presence and dominance on high.

Orchards and fields for vegetables spread out on either side, till after a slight curve to the right, a large colonnaded white building came into view. Elsie was just about to ask Raji, when he read her mind. "Our palace: the White House!"

It looks a bit like a large Roman temple, she thought. The realisation that it was certainly large, though nowhere near as big as the palace at Cooch Behar, saw Elsie berate herself for her comparative selfishness. She was just going to have to adjust to a new reality, though one far grander than any other Australian girl could realistically dream.

A line of tall white columns ran the length of the building, curving around a pair of wings that extended out and around an ornate garden area with a large fountain. The structure certainly trumpeted its grandeur in a landscape more characterised by fields of mud-brick or thatch houses.

The cars slowed to a stop under a porte-cochère on the building's east side. Attendants scampered backwards and forwards and Elsie noticed that there were more Gurkha guards either side of large double doors that featured panes of glass with the Tikari Coat of Arms.

Cecil Kempster quickly moved to open the door on Elsie's side of the car. "Thank you very much, Mr Kempster," Elsie said with a smile and a wink, as she was determined to have fun with what would invariably be, much formality ahead. To her delight, she noticed young Mr Kempster blush.

As she joined Raji to stride up the steps to enter the White House, the Gurkha Guard saluted with their right hand, leaving their left to hold their rifle just below its muzzle.

Raji saluted back, while Elsie just nodded and smiled.

On entering the grand foyer, lines of bowing servants fringed a red carpet that guided them on and over polished marble floors, first forward, then left, then right and finally right again, till they stood, facing a pair of large and ornate thrones, the largest and most ornate of which was to their left. "Elsie, you may sit there," Raji said, indicating the right throne in a tone that was at least half order.

Quickly but quietly, the giant figure of Abu moved in to Elsie's left side as she took her seat in this real-life fairytale. The little girl born in Millers Point, Sydney, had come a very, very long way.

While Raji greeted the court in Hindustani, Abu whispered a paraphrased translation of his words: "His Highness has ordered that there be a meeting on the parade ground at 2 pm."

Raji dismissed the court with a wave of the hand and they responded with a bow followed by a shuffle of dispersing feet, leaving Abu, Kempster, Raji and Elsie at least momentarily 'alone'.

"Come, I will show you around our palace," Raji suggested with great enthusiasm, a mood that was reciprocated by his new wife. "We are here in the grand foyer, or throne room, but I think I will ... yes, show you this way first," as he turned right and headed for the foyer's south-west corner.

There, a servant stood by a door to a south room. He bowed and produced an ornate key from his pocket, unlocking the large oak door.

"Follow me," encouraged Raji, as they stepped into a room flooded with light and warmth. "This is the pool room ..."

Elsie gasped in surprise as she took in the large tiled pool centred in the room, but spreading over more than half its width. Morning sunlight from the south, angled through the verandah, dancing on the water and bouncing reflections onto the Mughal-style tiled walls and ceilings. "There are benches for sitting and massage," Raji added.

They turned back through the grand foyer and into the dining room, where a long table sat below a magnificent chandelier. "The table is normally set for twelve, though it can accommodate many more."

As she walked around the table, Elsie noted that the white plates, already laid out in anticipation of lunch, featured a Tikari crest that she had not seen before.

"Through this door to our left are some of the key male servants' bedrooms, where Abu, our head chef Sayeef Ghosh, Abid and Mr Kempster, sleep."

Elsie meanwhile had been flippantly distracted by the chef's name and could most definitely see herself congratulating him on his latest culinary creation with the words: "Oh Ghosh, that was good!"

"I am sure Cecil will not mind us viewing his room and curved verandah," Raji suggested, causing the young man to visibly stiffen, as he had not left his private domain in the tidy state that an ADC should.

Elsie noticed his awkwardness, and came to his rescue, somewhat. "That is not necessary at this time, darling, though I very much look forward to providing Mr Kempster with my company in his bedroom on another occasion," she said with a wicked smile, accurately anticipating the embarrassment she would cause the young man.

The party turned around and headed back to one of the two marble staircases that flanked the thrones. "Time to head up to the first floor," declared Raji.

They entered a very large room with views across a verandah

to the south. Raji did not say anything, but just beamed with pride.

Elsie tried to take it all in: a full-sized and ornate billiard table sat in the middle of the room, while leather couches, small tables, a piano and the odd writing desk and chair spread out like planets orbiting the sun. Around the periphery of this universe were occasional bookcases, interspersed with gun and trophy cabinets, while above them all, on the walls, dozens of pairs of eyes from animals of all kinds, peered down on the party, courtesy of a skilled taxidermist. An array of ceiling fans added to the 'men's club' atmosphere.

Elsie glanced down at a creature spread-eagled at her feet, its glorious coat providing a luxurious carpet behind a raised and snarling head—then shuffled her feet back when she realised how close they were to its teeth.

"That is the first Bengal tiger I ever shot. I was only four years old at the time! And over there is my first bear! Aren't they wonderful!"

"They would be even more beautiful alive, darling," she retorted, though, fearing she may have offended him, she added: "still, the room does have a wonderful ambience."

Raji turned around and led them back through an arched doorway. "These are our private quarters … have you seen JG since we returned, Abu?"

"No, Your Highness. Perhaps he has gone for one of his drives. I suspect he will be back for lunch."

"Elsie, JG is John Guerney Wakefield, my dear friend and private secretary. His bedroom is just here to our left and his office backs on to my room. I am sure that you and JG are going to get along just fine."

The fact that Raji had to mention the 'get along' bit, made Elsie feel a little edgy.

"Of course," said Raji, leading them across a lounge lined with bookshelves, "you will have your own private secretary, who will have the bedroom here on the east side and the office next door."

"I really don't need a private secretary, darling. I am well able to write and organise myself."

"I will not have the only maharani in India to be without a

private secretary!" he said, in a most firm and decisive voice. "Besides, I do have someone in mind, and I believe she will be just perfect. I expect to appoint her very soon."

It was clear to Elsie that Raji was determined on this matter, so she consoled herself with the knowledge that the position would be taken by a woman.

Raji barked out an instruction in Hindustani, and two young women raced to stand to attention outside the door nearest the verandah. In common with most Indians she had seen in this area so far, they were dark-skinned, though they seemed a trifle bigger-breasted than most.

"Elsie, I would like you to meet your maids: Siri and Lala. They speak quite good English. They will make up your room, help you wash and dress and be at your service whenever you desire."

Elsie looked at the two pretty young women with beaming smiles and beautiful white eyes contrasting with their dark skin. She quickly realised that they looked identical. "How am I going to tell them apart?"

"It is really quite easy," explained Raji. "You see, Lala has a small jewel …"

The young women giggled and looked at each other before Lala admitted she had a jewel in her belly button. "It will be our honour to serve you, Your Highness," they added and bowed in unison.

"Your rooms are this way," Raji called, as he opened the furthest door on the right to enter a corridor.

Another door was opened and Raji urged Elsie to follow him. She looked around and noticed that Abu and Abid had respectfully not come through the first door, but waited in the lounge.

"Your bathroom, my dearest Elsie," Raji proclaimed with a flourish of the hand, the space inside easily allowing his arm to fully extend an invitation.

Elsie stepped into a world of Mughal-Moorish marble fantasy. Arches framed the entry to a large rectangular bath. "You have a dressing bench and a massage table, and around here, you have your own flushing toilet. All the toilets in the White House and in the estate manager's Red House are the latest flushing toilets! Generators make sure that there is hot water and electric light in both buildings."

By the time Elsie made it into her bedroom proper, she was close to speechless. It was everything that she could have dreamed: a large and ornate room decorated like a Mughal harem.

A huge and soft bed was the room's main feature, while a golden crown gleamed down from its canopy railing. A large and cushioned window seat framed ornate shutters studded with stained glass, while there was a dressing table with mirror as well as a large writing desk and bookshelf in one corner and a golden 'European' harp in the other.

"I ordered the harp specially for you!" Raji blurted with great satisfaction.

"Thank you, Raji. You are most kind, but I have never tried to play one." Momentarily, she pondered just how he could have acquired the harp in such a short period of time, though she put that thought aside to continue to rejoice in her magnificent new surroundings.

"I believe Siri has some experience—at least I know she plays the swarmandal. Come out on your own private verandah!" Raji opened glass doors and they walked out on to a large semi-circular area. "This is the northern corner of the east wing. Across there to the left you can see my matching verandah at the end of the west wing."

Elsie walked to the railing and looked down on manicured gardens that filled the area between the two wings. The main feature was a large and ornate fountain, determined to proclaim its presence in the relative silence of its surrounds. She turned to look north, the splash, splash, splash still dominating her audio sense.

She could see the compound gates to the north; in the distance, the large lake, orchards and the hedge lines obediently fringed the road south towards the White House. She closed her eyes and leant on the rail, for what to Raji must have seemed a very long time.

"It is all so beautiful, so very beautiful," she whispered, wrapping her arms around Raji.

"As Tikari's queen, this is your world now," he said,

protectively and affirmatively placing his arms around her. They just stood there, locked in an embrace.

It was only Lala's voice that separated them. "Would Your Highness like me to start the bath?"

"Oh yes, of course! Elsie, you must have a bath before lunch to freshen up after the long train journey. Go with the girls now and I will see you down in the dining room at 12.30 pm."

Elsie followed Lala into her bathroom. Both the girls helped her remove her European clothes as the water filled the bath.

No sooner had Elsie climbed in the water, than the girls started to remove their clothes and join her. One sat in front and washed Elsie's face with a facecloth and then let her soapy hands caress the curves of the front of her body.

Meantime, the one behind was scrubbing Elsie's back with a soapy brush. Elsie closed her eyes and wondered if she was dreaming.

When she opened them, she watched water run down the dark body in front of her and trickle over the even darker nipples, to splash into the sea below. Elsie looked down, hoping to see if there was a jewel in the belly button, but the soapy water hid that and other secrets for a while. She closed her eyes, wishing to increase the enjoyment of every touch.

One hand that was washing her front, slid down between her legs, causing Elsie to open her eyes wide in surprise. She was greeted by a bright-eyed smile and a giggle, so closed her eyes again, as fingers moved rhythmically from side to side, below.

Perhaps this is just the way things are done, here in Bihar, she thought. By the time the one behind said: "Keep your eyes closed, Your Highness, I am going to wash your hair," Elsie had already drifted off in a state nearing sensual ecstasy.

Ten minutes later, she was lying on her front, though still naked, on the massage table, with a pair of naked masseuse on either side.

She glanced sideways as the one to her left leant the lower half of her body against the table, the top of her pubic hair brushing over the surface. Elsie glanced up towards her navel—and there it was: the unmistakable green glint of an emerald. "Lala!" she exclaimed, twisting her index finger around to point in her direction.

Both girls laughed, as they continued rubbing fragrant oils into the length of her body. Nearly an hour later, Elsie was finally dressed in fresh European clothes after what she was sure was one of the most enjoyable and relaxing sessions of her life.

She thanked Siri and Lala profusely and delighted them by giving each a farewell kiss. Wandering back into her bedroom, she opened the writing desk and found writing paper, postcards of the White House and envelopes with a Tikari Raj crest in peacock blue on the back. It was then she remembered that she had seen the crowned 'T' crest on the plates on the dining table.

"So, you are the Australian!" a pompous voice, that just had to emanate from a figure in English trousers with braces, exclaimed from behind in a derisive tone.

Elsie spun around in her seat to see a man a little older than her, leaning against the wall of her room in a possessive manner.

"If you think so little of us then I suspect you are ill-informed!" Elsie retorted.

"Oh, quite to the contrary! I am John Guerney Wakefield and my ancestors had much to do with the settlement of South Australia and New Zealand!" he said with considerable arrogance.

Elsie thought for a moment. There was something about Edward Gibbon Wakefield that she had learnt at school. "Are you into kidnapping like your forebear, Edward Gibbon, Mr Wakefield?"

JG hesitated and his eyes narrowed, then said: "Not if you are the proposed victim. I came with a book for you to read. It is a Hindustani dictionary." He moved forward and placed it on the writing desk in front of her. "You can read, can't you?"

A Book of Verses underneath the Bough,
A Jug of Wine, a Loaf of Bread—and Thou
   Beside me singing in the Wilderness—
Oh, Wilderness were Paradise enow !

"You recognise the quatrain, Mr Wakefield?"

JG shuffled nervously. He felt he was being toyed with, and he was not at all used to such a circumstance.

"It is Quatrain 12 of the *Rubáiyát of Omar Khayyám*. Thank you for the dictionary. I must remember to test you at a later stage."

JG looked across the desk and noticed Elsie had started writing a postcard. "When you have finished your correspondence, make sure you pass it to Suraj Lal. It is his responsibility to handle all postage."

Elsie reached for a piece of paper and wrote down the name. JG looked over to check the spelling was correct, then added: "In fact, I shall send him to you after lunch."

"That would be very kind of you, Mr Wakefield. Thank you." She was trying very hard to be pleasant, but was most relieved when JG turned and departed.

For his part, JG felt he disliked this impudent interloper even more than he thought he would. Nobody could be allowed to threaten his place and standing in Tikari Raj.

Elsie rose and walked slowly to the window seat and opened the shutters so that she could look down on the gardens. She sat there for some minutes as she tried to put the last encounter in perspective. *Though it is most disconcerting to seem to be disliked, even before first meeting,* she thought, *I am now the Maharani, and this Wakefield is just a private secretary.*

She returned to the desk and completed writing the postcard to Emma, though she had to write in a small hand to fit it on the card. She then read through it again:

Dearest Em,

So much has changed, so quickly! I am sending this card from the palace in the picture on the front–the White House of Tikari Raj (not Cooch Behar). This is my new home as Raji (the Maharaja of Tikari) has asked me to be his wife–and I have accepted! Please tell Mother and Father. There is much more I want to tell you at another time, and will do so in a letter.

She picked up an envelope with the Tikari crest on the flap and addressed the front to Emma. Placing the card inside, she licked the flap and pressed firmly to seal. She then repeated this process, in writing a postcard to May Maxwell.

Shortly after a sumptuous lunch, a knock at her bedroom door roused Elsie from an early afternoon nap. She rose to find an Indian servant of about forty years of age standing at the door.

"Your Highness, I am Suraj Lal. Mr Wakefield told me you have some mail to be posted."

"Yes, of course," Elsie responded, reaching for the envelopes on the writing desk and passing them over. As the servant turned to leave, she called after him: "Oh, Mr Lal, where do you work?"

"In Mr Wakefield's office, Your Highness, just across the lounge. Ask for me whenever you have postal matters."

"I see," she said, taking a deep breath. "Thank you, Mr Lal."

She had barely uttered these words, when the booming sound of a conch shell echoed around the compound, signalling all to assemble on the parade ground in fifteen minutes.

By 2 pm, over two hundred Tikari Raj staff waited in the open space for their ruler. Raji mounted the podium and spoke to the crowd in Hindustani, as Abu translated for Elsie.

The Maharaja welcomed his new wife to Tikari Raj and stated that her wishes and her commands were to be treated as though they were his. As he was concluding, Elsie asked that she be allowed to speak. This was not what Raji was expecting, though he could hardly refuse, given the authority he had just invested in her.

Elsie stepped up and onto the podium next to Raji. Once again she felt the sort of buzz that years of performing on stage had provided. She hesitated, and looked left and then right across the assembly, ensuring each person's eyes were on her. Then she began, only to pause after each sentence to allow Raji to translate into Hindustani: "I would first like to thank my dear friend, our Maharaja, for having the courage and foresight to ask me to be his and Tikari's Maharani ... I would like to ask all of you to be patient, for, as an Australian, I have a lot to learn about your culture and language ... However, I am keen to learn as much about both as I can, and keen to meet and greet each of you personally ..."

At this point Raji stopped and looked at Elsie, before providing a translation that Elsie sensed was not quite verbatim. She then continued: "I thank you all for your welcome and hope that I will become a valued and helpful part of your Tikari Raj family."

As the crowd dispersed, Raji told Elsie that he wanted to talk to her upstairs, in his room. He did not say anything as they walked up the stairs and Elsie could sense that he was not happy about something.

For the first time, she entered his bedroom, but her solemnity disappeared when she saw his bed: she laughed when she noticed it had a 'running board' and 'wheels' just like a motor vehicle.

Raji commanded that she close the door, then walked to the entrance to the curved verandah and looked out, struggling to find the appropriate words. "Elsie, you must understand that our society is based on the caste system. It has helped to make me maharaja and others simple workers. Each should be happy in their role and not wish more than their caste dictates."

"So, are you saying there are people I cannot even greet?"

"We have people we call 'Dalits'. The British call them 'Untouchables'—and that is how they should remain!"

"And what crime have these people committed that they should be ostracised?"

"They remove sewage, slaughter animals and are comfortable in their status—and should be left by us to perform their role. That is all I wish to say on the subject!"

That night, when Raji came to Elsie's room on a welcome conjugal visit, both still carried the burden of their afternoon discussion. Elsie, for her part, as an Australian raised in a relatively egalitarian environment, was determined not to allow traditional Indian hierarchies to affect her interaction.

So, the next morning, when she headed out with Abu on a walking tour of the compound, she specifically instructed him to point out any Dalits.

They walked through formal gardens where she interrupted gardeners trimming hedges and pathways and tending flowerbeds. Each bowed and seemed to appreciate Abu's translation of her questions and interest.

Next, she moved to vegetable gardens, where she asked about the range of produce and growing seasons, while at the pilkhana, she discussed the ages and natures of the elephants with their mahouts.

It was while walking along a line of date palms, that Abu spotted something to his left. "Your Highness, Dalits, carrying buckets! They are emptying the latrines."

Elsie could see there were a number of women and girls carrying buckets from a building to a pit. "Stay with me, Abu!" she ordered, as Abu fell back and held his ground at a comfortable distance.

As she got closer to a young girl struggling with a bucket of raw faeces, the stench became overwhelming. Elsie grabbed the handle of the bucket and followed the path to the pit as the Dalits stopped in astonishment.

While tipping the contents into the foul-smelling morass, she realised she had excrement over her hands from the handle. "There you are, darling!" she said, as she placed the empty bucket at the girl's feet. She was now feeling nauseous and angry. As she turned back to Abu, tears ran down her face. "Tell them I love them, Abu! Tell them!" she yelled, as she staggered off to find the nearest tap to wash her hands.

It was quite some time before Elsie regained her composure and Abu had the courage to suggest there was still one place they had to visit. "The Red House, Your Highness. You have not met Mr Keith, the manager of Tikari Raj, yet."

They walked away from the White House, to the south-west, passing through a grove of mango trees before emerging in front of a very sizeable red stone and tile building.

"I can see now why it is called the Red House," Elsie said, as she knocked on its front door. A servant appeared, bowed and then quickly disappeared.

Elsie could hear an English voice speaking in Hindustani moving ever nearer the front door. Then, a middle-aged, cheery gentleman materialised and offered his hand, which Elsie instinctively shook—then quickly withdrew to check she had washed it properly.

"William Keith, Your Highness. I am sorry, for I should have bowed instead. Please, follow me inside."

"Oh Mr Keith, it is so refreshing to meet a happy soul."

"You have met some unhappy souls, Your Highness?"

"The poor Dalits, Mr Keith, and then there is Mr Wakefield!"

"Is there a connection between the Dalits and Mr Wakefield?"

At this point Elsie was very tempted to say that it would be appropriate if Wakefield was deposited by the Dalits in their pit, but she just succeeded in 'holding her tongue'.

"It is just that he seems very terse and even aggressive towards me, even upon our first meeting."

Mr Keith looked over his shoulder to confirm that Abu was indeed waiting outside.

"Please, sit down for a moment, Your Highness," he urged, indicating a comfortable chair. "Can I get you a drink? I shall have my housemaid bring one for you."

"Thank you, but I shall be fine, Mr Keith. I think I might find your understanding of the situation more refreshing."

"Well," Mr Keith said, easing back into his own chair, "as you may know I was Raji's private tutor for some years."

"Was he a good pupil?"

"Reasonable in his dedication, when hunting, motoring and women were not interfering. Quite good in his speaking, but a little wretched in his spelling, I am afraid to say. Still, the point is that Wakefield is an old friend of his from his days at St George's School at Mussoorie. In fact the two are very close."

"You mean that he might find me a threat?"

"An Indian woman is rarely a threat to her husband's friendships—and certainly his first wife was not—though I can see how you, as a European woman ..."

"Technically, Australian, Mr Keith."

"Australian woman, of course. You with your obvious intelligence, education and personality, may well be 'a different kettle of fish', so to speak."

"Oh, I hope I am not that slippery. So, you think it may be insecurity on his part? Interesting ..." Elsie said as she rose from her chair.

"I hope on your next visit you will have time to look over the accounts with me. We pay 0.9 million rupees annually to the British."

"What for, Mr Keith?"

"Well, because that is what we have to do, Your Highness, as an Indian princely state. We collect that value in crop, cash and kind from nearly 600 villages in Tikari Raj."

"So, are we struggling financially?"

"Oh, heavens no, there is plenty of money for the Maharaja to spend—and he is particularly good at doing just that!"

"Thank you, Mr Keith, for your insight and wisdom. I do look forward to returning soon."

With that, Elsie and Abu left the grounds of the Red House, the former more enlightened than when she had arrived.

After dinner that night, Elsie luxuriated in the bath, with assistance from Siri and Lala. A massage followed, which put her in a more relaxed mood for Raji's night-time visit. She opted to enjoy the sexual interaction, rather than spoil the atmosphere by daring to raise the issue of Wakefield.

After Raji had left, she lay awake, thinking of the Dalit girl and the others of her caste, condemned to a life nobody else would want.

The clock in her room chimed past another hour. Realising that she could not sleep, she rose and put on her dressing gown and headed out through the lounge enroute to the library area, to choose a book to read.

It was then she heard noises coming from Raji's room. She crept closer. It sounded like women's voices.

Placing her hand on the door handle, she pulled it firmly towards her before slowly and careful turning it open.

The sighing and giggling from two now familiar young female voices, interspersed with Raji's own ecstatic exhortations, made it very clear who was in the room and what they were doing.

Even in the near darkness, Elsie could see two darker shapes take turns to rise and fall repeatedly over Raji's erect penis. *Those girls must be nymphomaniacs,* thought Elsie, *and as for Raji, is any woman safe in his presence?*

Chapter 39

The Guardian Angel

In my dreams an angel comes, and watches over me
She checks upon my judgment, and she counsels generously
As champion and confidant, my secrets she won't share
She is my guardian angel, when I need her, she'll be there.

The opening of her curtains was enough to awaken Elsie, briefly, after a mostly sleepless night.

"Good morning, Your Highness!" Siri and Lala called in unison, as the reflected light from the north spread through the room.

It had only been Elsie's second night in her bed, but already she was feeling comfortable enough to call it home. She cuddled tightly into her pillow, as if to squeeze away the last drop of memory of what they were doing to Raji last night.

"I think she might be dead," said Lala in a whisper intentionally loud enough to hear.

"Well, we should check," urged Siri, as she reached across the bed and under the bed sheets to cheekily find Elsie's armpit with a tickle. Elsie did her best not to react but after another couple of tickles in different places, it was impossible.

"She is alive!" yelled Siri as she moved to straddle Elsie, pushing her left hip down so that she sat softly on Elsie's tummy. Meanwhile, Lala had moved in to run her fingers through Elsie's hair.

They are just like a couple of children, Elsie thought. *I should never have allowed them into the bath with me, or to give me massages. It can't be their fault what they did with Raji. He must have ordered them to perform.*

"Now that you are awake, we can get you breakfast," suggested Siri.

"Girls, girls, please! I am really tired and don't feel like breakfast now. I just want to sleep!" Then, almost apologetically, she added as they clambered away: "I do love you both very much …"

"Thank you, Your Highness," followed by giggles in unison,

let Elsie know there were no hard feelings, as she tucked into her pillow once more and fell asleep.

It seemed to be hours until Raji's voice said: "Elsie, darling, are you all right?"

Before she could answer, the bedroom clock started chiming. They both counted the chimes.

"Nine o'clock!" Raji exclaimed in surprise. "Darling, I have an appointment. I must rush—Kempster should have reminded me!"

"I am here, Your Highness, outside the door, waiting ..." came the response from the aide-de-camp.

Both men hurried downstairs with as much decorum as circumstance allowed, with Raji moving to sit on his throne and Kempster heading to the front entrance. After a short conversation, JG and a young woman moved up the red carpet towards the Maharaja.

"Your Highness, may I present Miss Grace Knighton," the private secretary said, allowing the young lady to step forward.

"Ah, Miss Knighton, it is lovely to see you again!" Raji cooed, for indeed she was one of his favourites. "Mr Wakefield, you may go now."

JG started to head up the stairs but slowed and then stopped to listen to the conversation.

Raji waited and listened, then rose from his throne and headed out to his right. "JG! I shall talk to you about this later!" he called out, receiving a grumbled response as his private secretary stomped up to his office.

"There are some things I wish to keep private at this stage. Now, Miss Knighton, I believe you have been told that I am looking for a private secretary for my second wife, Elsie?"

"Yes, Your Highness. It would be an honour to work for Tikari Raj, though I feel I must meet her first, as I believe it is important that we are compatible."

"Let me assure you that the job is yours if you wish to have it. The two of you must feel you can get on. She was in her room, last I saw her, but come upstairs and I will show you your room and your office."

Heading to the right through the lounge, he first guided

Grace to her proposed bedroom, then office, backing on to Elsie's bedroom suite.

"So, what do you think?" asked the Maharaja.

"I just hope I am worthy of such accommodation, Your Highness. It is not something with which I have been familiar."

"This is Elsie's door here. Just knock and open it. Last time I saw her she was in bed."

Grace was not at all comfortable with such an arrangement, but the Maharaja insisted. "Go on … I will wait out here."

She knocked, then, opened the door slowly and carefully, soon realising she was in a corridor outside the bedroom proper. "Your Highness? … Excuse me, Your Highness …" but there was no answer.

Grace inched her way carefully into the room, till she noticed Elsie lying on her side, and facing the far wall. She tiptoed around the bed end and stopped. "Your Highness?" she asked quietly, though still there was no response.

Grace eased up the side of the bed, stood there momentarily, but felt she should kneel in her presence. As she settled on the rug by the bedside, she looked at the woman before her and whispered softly: "Your Highness, my name is Grace Knighton."

Elsie slowly opened her eyes and Grace was amazed at their violet colour, the porcelain-like smoothness and seeming softness of her skin, as well as her long hair. "Oh, you are so beautiful, Your Highness!"

Elsie frowned and blinked a couple of times, to check if she was dreaming. "That is a lovely thing I think you just said," she whispered back, then studied the young lady kneeling in front of her carefully for quite a few seconds. "You are of American Negro background? You are really very lovely, yourself," she whispered and smiled.

A big smile broke across Grace's face. "Yes, my parents are Negroes from Chicago. I am twenty-four years old and Raji brought me out from London where we met a few years ago. I now speak Hindustani and can read and write most scripts. It would be a great honour if you would accept me as your private secretary."

"Grace, isn't it?" asked Elsie, a little unsure she had heard correctly. "When I first saw you I was so sleepy that I thought you might be my guardian angel."

"Yes, Your Highness, Grace Knighton … and if you wish me to be your guardian angel, I shall try my very best."

"Well, Grace, considering you seem to have the youth, elegance and joyfulness of the Three Graces, how can I reject three Graces for the price of one!"

"Oh, that is very clever of you, Your Highness!"

Elsie reached out a hand so that Grace could shake it, but she instinctively held and kissed it instead, then backed off in embarrassment.

"I shall tell the Maharaja," she whispered, bowed and headed outside.

Raji was sitting in the lounge, waiting.

"How did you find her?"

"She is very beautiful and I think very kind—and funny. I told her I would like the position and she agreed!"

"That is all very good, Grace, but there is something I want you to do," he said, waving his hand to indicate that she should sit on the sofa next to him. As she did, he put his arm around her and whispered: "I want you to be my eyes and ears. I want you to let me know everything—what she feels and what she thinks—about everything and everyone. Agreed?"

Grace was not at all sure. She had just felt as though she had found a new 'best friend' but was now being asked to betray that friendly confidence. "I am happy to accept the position," she responded tentatively.

"So you agree?" Raji persisted.

"Yes, I agree to be her private secretary."

"Good! Then you can move your things in immediately!" In fact, Raji was not at all convinced she had agreed to his suggestion to be an informant, but the prospect of having yet another attractive conquest, domiciled close to his bedroom, was just too tempting to refuse.

Chapter 40

A Jewel from the Past

A jewel reflects a permanence, and if its understood
Its shine projects a prominence — that promises much good
Some jewels are more than polished stones, they're human beings too
Whose beauty's etched in timelessness, with facets fine and true.

The arrival of Grace cheered Elsie considerably. At last, she had someone of her age and approximate intellectual ability with whom to spend worthwhile time.

Raji too, seemed enlivened by her presence, though Elsie by now had well noted that the proximity of attractive young women always appeared to improve his mood.

The Christmas morning of 25 December 1906 drifted towards midday with nothing to differentiate it from the increasing number of slow-paced mornings she had experienced to date, till there was a knock at her door.

Raji entered without waiting for a response, one hand stationed firmly behind his back.

"Elsie, I need you to sit at the dressing table, facing the mirror."

She had spent some time during the morning hours, thinking about what her family and dear friend Emma were doing on this special Christian day. She had not anticipated that Tikari Raj, in largely Hindu India, would attribute anything significant to this late-year Tuesday.

Raji's excitable manner and twisted posture suggested otherwise.

"Now close your eyes," he ordered, as he removed something from behind his back and struggled to fix it on her head.

She could feel him pressing a curve-shaped object into her hairline, and, eyes closed, tried to picture what it might be.

"Now open your eyes, darling. What do you think?"

It certainly was not what she had expected, for a huge emerald shone forth from the centre of a curved and jewelled band, studded with other emeralds, diamonds and pearls.

"Oh, it is beautiful!" she gushed, still examining the reflected image of the glittering banded tiara that adorned her head. "Is

350

this really mine to wear and keep?"

"Of course! Now, when you join me on our thrones downstairs, you will have something that comes close to matching the jewels on my turban."

"Oh darling, thank you!" she said as she stood and gave him a kiss. She then pivoted back to the mirror, turning this way and that. "You know, dearest, I think it would look much better if I wore saris rather than European clothes. After all, I am supposed to be an Indian, not a European queen."

"Oh!" was all Raji could say, for this was not a change he had ever anticipated. While she wore European clothes he could proudly show her off as his European trophy. In the Indian native sari, his 'exotic' catch would be far less obvious—if not invisible. "Perhaps we could ask Grace's opinion," he added, seeking a way out.

Grace was called in, though she quickly realised that she needed to tread carefully between two polarised views. "I myself keep both styles in my cupboard," she stated.

Elsie was insistent, for it was as if she had opted for a stage role, and wearing the associated costume was not a matter of choice, but necessity. "I am the Maharani of Tikari. As an Indian queen, I shall wear Indian clothing from now on! Grace and I shall go shopping for saris in Gaya tomorrow!"

"I was hoping that you would join JG and me on a two-day shoot in the southern jungle tomorrow," Raji said forlornly.

Elsie could see how much the atmosphere in the room had changed from one of love and giving, to disagreement and disappointment. So she tried to explain: "Darling, I love animals too much to ever go hunting. In any case, JG might accidently shoot me."

"JG is far too good a shot to accidently shoot anything," Raji explained. "He is nearly as good a shot as me!"

"Perhaps that is what I am worried about. I would really feel far happier and more comfortable strolling through Gaya with Grace and Abu, than in scrambling through jungles, darling."

"Abu? You are taking Abu too? He was going to join us as well …"

"Oh Raji, we need Abu as our driver. You love to drive yourself and you can take any number of the Gurkha guards."

It was only after Raji's shooting party had departed the following day that Elsie swung in to action. Grace had been surprised at Elsie's forceful stance, but she had not realised that Her Highness had something specific in mind.

The Ford Model K—the only vehicle left after Raji had taken the other four—crunched its way up the blue metal driveway and through the manned gates to be farewelled by salute.

Grace guided Abu to where she knew there were a number of shops dedicated to the making and selling of saris. For some time, while Abu waited patiently outside, the two young women strolled around the silk weaving looms, admiring the skill and obvious dedication required to make these colourful traditional outfits.

"You will find better and more luxurious examples in Calcutta," Grace whispered. "Red and gold are the traditional royal colours."

"These are my people, Grace, so I must buy from them, even if I also buy later elsewhere," Elsie responded, fingering a pretty light blue and dark blue piece. "Personally, I have always liked blue."

"That is because it goes with your violet eyes. You may as well try that one on."

A weaver indicated a side room with an ageing mirror of moderate length, hung in hope of a well-healed customer. It was to be her lucky day.

As Abu fought desperately to stop himself falling asleep in the Ford, Grace introduced Elsie to the secret world of sari draping.

"First," she said, shutting the door to the room, "you need to take all your clothes off and change into these. They are my own top and bottom, but they should fit you. You cannot wear your European underclothes with the sari, as they will be seen. The sari will go over most but not all of them."

After a series of tucks, pleats, tosses over the shoulder, more tucks and pleats and a final draping over head, Elsie could at last look and feel like a maharani. She was so delighted that she decided to keep wearing the sari.

Grace stepped outside the door and called out in Hindustani, dragging Elsie out behind her.

Suddenly, the click-clacking of the looms ceased and the workers rose, and cried out "Namaskar!" as they bowed and pressed their palms together, with their eyes closed.

"What did you say to them, Grace?"

"I just told them that you were Tikari's new maharani."

"Well then, I must pay accordingly!" Elsie said, emptying rupees from her purse onto a table after selecting four more saris in addition to the one she was wearing.

"But that is far more rupees than the saris are worth," protested Grace.

"Well, I thought I should leave a little 'bakhshish'," Elsie said with a wink, demonstrating she was studying her Hindustani.

As they left the building, they could hear Abu snoring. To Grace's great surprise, Elsie kissed him on the cheek to wake him.

"Well, what do you think of my new look, Abu?" she said, twisting and turning in a way no man could resist.

"Ah, yes, yes, very beautiful, Your Highness!" he stuttered, embarrassed at being found sleeping on the job, and determined to quickly open the car's back door for his passengers.

Before he could start the engine, Elsie reminded Abu of his promise to one day take her to see Raji's first wife—and that the time to deliver on that promise was now.

After travelling down what seemed to be a maze of dusty side streets, Abu eased the Ford to a halt behind a wall.

"Here?" Elsie questioned, looking in vain around her for the sign of anything befitting a maharani.

"Your Highness, I dare not take you further. There are so few cars ever in Gaya, that you surely would be recognised, were I to stop outside. The House of the Whistling Wind is not far from here: just go around this wall and down about 100 yards to your left. It is the large one by the riverbank, with a doorknocker of the Goddess Shashthi. I shall wait for you here."

Grace and Elsie turned around the wall and walked left, their sandals kicking up the dirt of the street as they headed towards the largest house within view: clearly the House of the Whistling Wind.

They had not gone more than a few yards, when Elsie

grabbed Grace's wrist and pulled her up to the left. "This way!" she ordered.

Soon, they were zigzagging up through a sequence of laneways, past surprised residents, and even through the middle of what Elsie thought might be a cooking lesson: the aroma of the curries soaking into their saris and staying with them long after Elsie had muttered her apology in English.

"It is this way I think," Elsie said heading left and only just avoiding a young child playing in the dirt.

"Your Highness," protested Grace, "I just don't understand!"

"I want to check on Abu, and see whether he is snoring … shhhh! I think the car is just down around this corner …" she said, peeking slowly and carefully around a broken wall.

Sure enough, Abu was sitting in the car, though Elsie could not tell whether he was asleep already.

She looked around her and found a stone. Turning it over in her hand, she tried to get a feel for its weight and potential. "Watch this, I will see if I can hit the back tyre!"

Elsie reached back and hurled the stone underarm down the slope towards the car's back left tyre—but it took a kick and bounced up, slamming into the side of the vehicle just behind the back seat passenger's door. The thud caused Elsie to wince and Abu to leap out of his seat, ready to take on the world.

"Oh dear! What have I done?" At that moment, Elsie was torn between alerting Abu to the reality of the situation, and fleeing—and instinctively chose the latter.

As Abu headed around the side of the wall, to check for Elsie and Grace's safety on the road to the House of the Whistling Wind, the young women raced back the way they had come, bowling over the child playing in the dirt; darting from laneway to laneway—then through the cooking class again— where this time Elsie called out "Pashemán! Pashemán!" as she recalled how to say she was sorry in Hindustani.

By the time they reached the main road, Abu was nowhere to be seen, having returned to the car. This time they headed for the large house and did not stop until they reached the grand door with the unusual goddess doorknocker. She was fixed with a steel pin through her head. A pair of large breasts that appeared to have been regularly polished, protruded, though the idea was clearly to grab the figure around the crossed legs, then bang her bottom against the door.

"The Goddess Shashthi is a fertility symbol. It is hoped that someone living within this dwelling falls pregnant," Grace explained. "Raji's first wife has been childless."

Elsie hesitated to grip the doorknocker, while she once more thought of the implications of such a situation for a few moments. Then she grasped the figure around the knees and banged it three times, causing a much louder than anticipated sound to echo through the rooms inside.

After an explanation from Grace to a servant in Hindustani, they were ushered inside, but not before they had left their sandals at the door, as was the accepted custom.

For some minutes they waited outside a beaded screen, sitting on cushions on the marble floor. Elsie looked around her at the furnishings. *Sparse but comfortable,* she thought.

A soft voice began talking from behind the screen in Hindustani, and Grace translated.

Elsie could see nobody but imagined she could and metaphorically reached out to the young woman behind the screen.

"I am here to beg your forgiveness and understanding, and hopefully seek your friendship. Raji has asked me to be his second wife and though I have accepted, I feel much sorrow for you."

A pause followed Grace's translation, then to the shock of both of them, she responded quietly and with a sad voice, in English: "You are very pretty, and Raji always has an eye for such women. He will not change. My brother was the Maharaja of Tamkuhi, so I should not have been surprised."

"Is there anything I can do for you?" Elsie asked.

"No. Raji visits me when he wants, and pays for this house and the servants, so I should not complain. You are most kind and brave to visit!"

Then there was a clinking of the beads as a hand reached out along the floor. Elsie noticed beautiful green and red jewelled bracelets, but most stunning of all were a sequence of attached Indian animals. She instantly recognised an elephant and a tiger among them—carved in ivory.

Elsie reached out her hand and softly touched the much darker-skinned one extended towards her. In silence her fingers ran over others and then traced a path inside the palm as it opened to greet her. Their hands were soon clasped in an embrace, leading Elsie to lean forward and place her forehead on top of them.

It was not long before the first wife felt Elsie's tears track over her knuckles and run towards the marble floor. "I'm sorry!" exclaimed Elsie in embarrassment. As she breathed deeply to regain her composure, she could sense sobbing on the other side of the screen.

"Do you have the chance to leave this house?" Elsie asked, hoping that the crying she had triggered could be stopped by talk.

"Sometimes. Sometimes I go to Calcutta."

Elsie wondered what she could say next, as she continued to stroke the hand before her. Then she thought to ask about something that had puzzled her: "Why is this house called The House of the Whistling Wind?"

"Ah!" the first wife said, almost laughing. "On the few days when the breeze rolls up the Falgu River bed, it makes a whistling sound as it passes through the blinds on the verandah."

"Abu is waiting for us, so we must leave," Elsie mentioned apologetically. After squeezing the first wife's hand and kissing it goodbye, then insisting they must meet again soon, she departed with Grace.

Abu was very much awake and still seemed agitated when they reached the Ford.

"Oh, dear Abu!" Elsie said, attempting to wrap her arms around him. "I must tell you something—and apologise!"

Chapter 41

Bodh Gaya and the Hermit

There is a wizened hermit who lives out among the hills
He'll see into your future and he'll diagnose your ills
Till Bodh Gaya lures you southward, with its temples and to see
Where Buddha found enlightenment, beneath the Bodhi tree.

The knock at Elsie's door had to be repeated a few times before the occupant heard it, for she had been relaxing on her verandah, enjoying the February morning air and view across Tikari Raj Compound's landscaped gardens.

"Come in!" she called.

Elsie turned to see a familiar dark figure scuttle across the floor towards her, with a letter on a silver tray, as had been his training.

"Ah, Mr Lal! You bring news of some sort, so you are always welcome!" Elsie looked down at the handwriting of the address—and instantly recognised the sender. She picked up the letter and was just about to open it, when she noticed that Suraj Lal was still standing there. "Thank you, Mr Lal, you may go now!"

She waited till the door clicked to a close behind him, then turned her attention back to the envelope, which she opened.

"Emma's first letter to Tikari Raj!" she said to herself in significant anticipation:

7 Jan 1907

Dearest El,

The news of your union with the Maharaja of Tikari has of course surprised but delighted us all. Naturally, I am extremely jealous! There are very few maharajas attending my international dancing classes, or active in the local transport business!

That, will of course be no surprise to you, but my next news probably will:

Elsie rushed next door to share her news with Grace.

"Perhaps you could buy a gift for her on the trip I have planned for this afternoon!" suggested Grace thoughtfully.

"An afternoon trip? It can't be too far then! So, what has my private secretary planned?"

Grace opened up her diary to the page for Tuesday 5 February 1907. "Travel to the hermit in the Dungeshwari Caves."

"A hermit in a cave, Grace—why?" Elsie queried.

"Your Highness, pilgrims flock from far and wide to hear his wisdom."

"Can he foretell the future?"

"Perhaps he can. I hear that he certainly has a big following and his supporters hang off every word he says!"

"In that case, Grace, you must take a pencil and paper and record our conversation for posterity!"

"I can do that Your Highness, but ..."

"You have done shorthand training, have you not?"

"Oh yes, Your Highness, Pitman Shorthand, though I have very rarely used it!" Grace admitted, while wincing at the thought of needing to revive the skill.

"And after our visit to this wise hermit, what then?"

"We should have time to see the Buddhist holy site of Bodh Gaya, as it is only ten miles due south."

"And these Dingisheri Caves. How far are they?"

"The Dungeshwari Caves are about nine miles, though across the river to the south-east, Your Highness."

"Excellent! Then we can take the P & L—and I can drive!"

"Your Highness, please remember that the Panhard & Levassor is Mr Wakefield's favourite motor!"

"Oh, I know that, Grace!" Elsie said with a smile. "I really do know that!"

Down in the dining hall, lunch had barely started when conversation turned to the afternoon trip.

"I have decided that I shall be driving!" Elsie said determinedly.

"Women should never drive!"

"Oh, please enlighten us, Mr Wakefield, as to why you think that should be the case."

JG looked at Elsie, surprised that she should even ask. "They are simply not strong enough to start or steer a vehicle. Besides, some of the judgmental decisions required are, I believe, way beyond what the female brain can handle!"

"Really, Mr Wakefield? And what do you think, Raji darling?"

Raji could see that he was being made to choose sides in the ongoing battle between his wife and best friend. So, he hesitated.

"Raji!" Elsie urged.

The Maharaja could see no way safely out of this bind. "JG, I must say, my dear friend, that I believe that Elsie can cope. Last week, when I drove Elsie to Patna in the P & L, I gave her the chance to drive ..."

"What? In the P & L?"

"Oh, I didn't think you English liked the French so much!" Elsie teased.

JG slammed his knife and fork down on the table in anger, rose and stormed off, up the stairs to his room.

"Abu and Grace shall be accompanying me this afternoon," Elsie announced, after watching JG carefully, until she had seen the last of him.

"Excuse me, Your Highness, but I cannot guard both you and

the vehicle at the same time if you are to leave it at the caves or Bodh Gaya," Abu cautioned. "We must take a Gurkha with us."

"Then I shall ask Sergeant Prabal Ghale to accompany you," Cecil Kempster offered.

"Oh, Mr Kempster! It is so nice to know that there is the odd Englishman with good sense here," Elsie exclaimed.

After lunch, the mechanics wheeled out the P & L. Drink and sandwiches were loaded on board. "Prabal, you sit in the back with Miss Knighton, please!" Elsie instructed.

Elsie reached down and turned the crank until it started the engine. Then, before climbing into the driver's seat, she waved up towards JG's room in the White House, from where, she reasoned, he would not have been able to resist watching.

"Bitch!" JG swore, as he slammed his fist onto the windowsill.

With Abu as navigator, the P & L weaved its way north through Gaya, then across the bridge over the Falgu and southeast towards the Dungeshwari Caves.

As they drove higher, the vegetation disappeared, until all around them was dirt, rocks and pilgrims. Elsie applied the handbrake, bringing the P & L to a halt in a small cloud of dust near the foot of a long series of steps.

"Prabal, stay and guard the motor!" Abu ordered. "We should not be too long!"

As the others approached the base of the steps, Elsie noticed that at least two of the three men guarding the entrance were armed.

Abu said something in Hindustani and the men bowed in Elsie's direction.

"They are toll collectors for Tikari Raj," explained Grace. "We don't have to pay!"

"But we must!' insisted Elsie, as she signalled Abu to hand over money. "We must be like everyone else!"

They then joined a small crowd climbing a sequence of sizeable stone steps towards a large rocky mountaintop, within which nestled three caves.

Soon they neared a large group who had congregated near a cave entrance.

"Shall I order them to stand aside, Your Highness?"

"Oh no, Abu! We have no more right than them, so we shall wait!"

"This is where, around two and a half thousand years ago, Siddhartha Gautama, the man known today as Buddha, was supposed to have meditated for six years before heading to Bodh Gaya and enlightenment," Grace whispered in Elsie's ear.

Elsie looked at those around her, clothed in the colours of the rainbow, though the saffron-coloured cloaks of the Buddhist monks made them really stand out.

"These caves are holy places to many," continued Grace. "There are Buddhist and Hindu shrines. The Wise Hermit is inside this one. That is why I think there is such a crowd!"

Time dragged on and on, yet the Tikari group only crept slowly forward towards the cave entrance.

In her boredom, Elsie looked around the hillside and noticed a man heading further up the hill, occasionally brushing a palm frond on the path in front. "Whatever is he doing?" she asked.

"He is brushing the ants out of his path so he does not kill them—he is a Jain," explained Abu. "To Jains, all creatures are sacred and must not be killed. They believe in non-violence towards all living things."

"How wonderful! I think I could truly be a Jain … though perhaps I would have to make an exception with regard to Mr Wakefield!"

"Oh, Your Highness!" reacted Grace with a chuckle.

The line that was once long was now short and suddenly tolerable. Within minutes, they stepped inside a cave where burning incense signalled over a thousand years of meditatory occupation.

Elsie noticed a bearded and aged man sitting cross-legged on a mat, with his eyes closed.

An assistant waved them forward after Abu made another payment, and Grace indicated that Elsie should sit on a long mat in front of the hermit, while she sat to Elsie's right and readied her pencil. Abu squatted respectfully to the left.

Elsie studied the hermit in silence, though she sensed that from the moment she sat down, that he too, had been studying her. His eyes were closed, that was true, but he seemed to be listening very, very carefully—even assessing her breathing.

Slowly and carefully his left hand reached out—though its less than immediate path to her hair made her realise that indeed the hermit was blind.

His fingertips felt gently and softly through her hair and then traced their way around her facial features. *He must be creating his own mental picture of me,* she thought.

"You have come a long way!" he said in a quiet but dignified voice.

"How do you know?" Elsie asked.

A smile broke across the hermit's face as he added: "Though not as far as many!"

Grace had already started scribbling down their conversation, which she would later transcribe to longhand, for Elsie. The hermit briefly transferred his attention to the scribe, his fingertips tracing her hand and the pencil it held, as she wrote:

ELSIE: I may be far from home, but those around me make the transition painless.

HERMIT: A journey can be physically completed, yet never emotionally or intellectually so.

ELSIE: I am trying to learn.

HERMIT: You must be eager—yet patient with others … I sense you are not without wealth nor the power that can accompany it.

ELSIE: My present situation is most recent in its manifestation. I doubt I have had the time to abuse it, sir!

HERMIT: Such temptations are invariably irresistible—and you shall do so just as all before you have done, and those after you will.

ELSIE: I trust that hurting others is not in my nature!

HERMIT: Your nature is for others to judge. If you need to explain, then you have already transgressed. The rich should listen carefully to the poor and learn from their more common existence. One's situation can too easily be reversed, even in this lifetime!

ELSIE: So, do you believe in an afterlife?

HERMIT: If I were poor, I would wish it were so, to give me hope. If I were rich, I might fear its possible variance.

ELSIE: So are you poor or rich?

HERMIT: I am rich, though not in the way most would perceive that state. Besides, beautiful young women from lands far away, travel long distances to be in my presence—what more can an old man wish for?

ELSIE: How is it that one who is blind can see so clearly?

HERMIT: I have none of many colourful distractions to deal with—just the certainty of my contemplation … every leader who looks behind himself will see that he has more than followers. Even followers just need a moment to metamorphose into something less supportive.

ELSIE: Do you mean I should be fearful?

HERMIT: Fearful, no, but careful, yes. For even a tiger cannot stay in the treetops indefinitely. Eventually, she will come down to earth … I think your friend is urging you to leave.

ELSIE: Thank you, oh wise sir!

HERMIT: Take care … Your Highness!

Abu had already risen, the top of his turban brushing against the cave ceiling. "We must leave now, Your Highness! We cannot afford to be out in the countryside at nightfall!"

"I am sure we will be fine, Abu!" Elsie responded. "Besides, I believe Bodh Gaya is not far from Gaya!"

"It is ten miles south, Your Highness!" interrupted Grace. "Though we have to drive back to Gaya first!"

After Elsie had started the car—having refused Abu's assistance—and Prabal had moved into the back, she noticed Abu had checked that his revolver was tucked in his belt. He was clearly on edge. Time, she guessed, was no doubt the key, so she flattened the accelerator, causing the P & L to fly faster than it should have along the winding dirt road.

Turning back into Gaya, then south, the P & L had a good run for a few miles, until it encountered increasingly large numbers of pilgrims. Eventually, they halted at a wall of coloured robes, that much later fractured to reveal another Tikari Raj toll party.

Elsie noted Abu's frequent frustration and patted him soothingly on the thigh.

When they reached Bodh Gaya proper, they were greeted by

a sea of stalls and people—and a sun well and truly into its descent.

Abu guided Elsie to park as close to the monuments as possible and signalled Prabal to stay with the vehicle.

"I will try to find a Buddhist monk who speaks English to be our guide," Grace advised, as she headed off into the throng.

"And I will just see if I can get something for my new niece!" Elsie called out in response, causing Abu to follow her, as was his duty.

By the time the two met up again, Abu was carrying a scarf full of objects, as they all followed a saffron-robed monk to the soaring stone monument called the Mahabodhi Temple.

"It built more two thousand year ago," the monk explained in hesitant English. "Is 180 feet high ... falling down twenty year ago ... British help rebuild."

Elsie pointed to the carvings on the wall around the temple's base.

"Hindu goddess bathed by elephant ... lotus leave ... not just Buddhist come here ... Hindu too!"

They joined the crowd heading in to the temple and slowed just as Elsie caught sight of flickering candlelight and a golden statue of Buddha. It took them a full fifteen minutes to exit and head for a spreading green tree.

"Bodhi tree! ... Most sacred site for Buddhist ... here Gautama meditate for week ... find Enlightenment."

"Under this very tree?" asked Elsie.

"Cutting from tree ... replant ... maybe four time ... same tree."

The sun was beginning to slip very close to the horizon and torches were being lit around the grounds. Abu was becoming more anxious.

"There are plenty of people here Abu, we should be safe!" Elsie assured him.

"Your Highness, many of these people are camping here—they will not be on the road back to Gaya!"

By the time they reached Prabal and the P & L, the sun had dipped behind the horizon and the car moved away from the world's most sacred Buddhist site, with lights on, passing a sea of flickering candles into a darkening countryside.

About four miles out of Bodh Gaya, Elsie noticed something leap out from her left into the range of the car headlights as they passed through a grove of palms. She swerved the car to the right to try to avoid hitting a pair of swamp deer, heading towards the river, but the back of the car slipped to the left on the pebbly bend. Desperately trying to straighten the P & L, she slung the wheel back to the left, though this only set the car on line for a palm tree.

Grace screamed: "Watch out!" Elsie tried to pull the handbrake as Abu threw himself in front of her to cushion the inevitable impact.

The front of the P & L slammed into the palm, and for a few moments there was silence, until the four occupants emerged from the vehicle to check the damage.

Elsie noticed that Abu was reaching for his back, which had been thrown against the steering wheel. Otherwise, everybody seemed uninjured, though the vehicle was most certainly worse for the encounter.

The impact had smashed in the front bar, starter mechanism and the front of the radiator.

Abu tried with his bare hands to bring the radiator back in to shape, but it was obvious that the damage was fatal to any hope of the car progressing under its own power.

By now, darkness had descended and only the light of a half moon rendered them cognisant of their surroundings.

Abu realised they could not shift the vehicle without assistance, but nor could they leave it to the ravages of the Bihari night. And, they were less than halfway back to Gaya. It would be a long and dangerous walk.

"Prabal! Here, take my revolver!" Abu said, after checking its chambers were fully loaded. "Give me your rifle. I will stay with Her Highness, Miss Knighton and the motor, while you run back to the Tikari compound for help."

The sight and sound of the Gurkha guard racing up the road to the north was soon swallowed by the night.

As time drifted on, Abu paced nervously back and forward, rifle in hand, till he heard voices from up the bank and back a bit. "Lay down on the seats! Quickly!" he ordered, as he opened the back and front doors of the vehicle.

Elsie spread herself across the back, while Grace lay across the floor in the front.

"Quiet!" Abu urged as they listened. The voices—and there were a number—came closer. "Bandits!" he said, cursing. "They have spotted the motor! Stay down!"

With that, Abu sprinted back down the road a few yards and tucked himself behind a palm tree. To draw attention away from the vehicle, he started yelling and threatening to shoot. Within seconds, bullets whistled towards him, one shattering the edge of the palm against which he was leaning. Then, he heard orders being yelled out to take the vehicle. Now, he had very little option …

Abu raced towards the P & L, firing as he ran, then took a giant leap, to land in the back, making sure the back of the front seat took most of his weight. Reaching down, he pulled a box of bullets out from under the passenger seat, as a couple of bullets slammed into the side of the vehicle.

"I am sorry, Your Highness—but stay down!" It was an order she could not disobey, as he had placed his body wholly but softly and protectively over hers. Reaching forward, he fired back in the direction of the shooters.

He expected fire to be returned immediately, but instead there were a series of warning calls as the bandits began to retreat.

Abu twisted around and looked north: closing fast on the dirt road were four pairs of headlights—just in time.

Raji, who well knew the danger of the Bihari night, was quickly out of the lead vehicle, elephant gun in hand. "Are you all right, Elsie!" he called, as he joined her briefly.

"Yes, fine, thanks to the bravery of my hero, Abu!" she replied, giving Raji a hug. "Thank you for arriving so quickly, darling!"

Armed Gurkhas and mechanics poured out of the vehicles, with the former joining Raji in pursuit of the bandits.

The mechanics, aided by oil lamps, quickly determined that the P & L's radiator was too damaged and that the vehicle would have to be towed back.

Over an hour later, the five-vehicle convoy, with armed guards at the front and end, limped slowly into the Tikari Raj compound.

"Abu, come upstairs please, as I want to have a look at your back. I think it will need some nursing," Elsie said, as she guided her much-loved bodyguard through the grand foyer.

Something made her look up, just as a shiver ran through her body.

Above her, standing on the landing of the staircase, was Wakefield. His arms were crossed and he had a contemptuous look on his face. He had warned them about her driving and now he had seen his favoured P & L dragged back, a disabled wreck—and he was not going to let anyone forget who was responsible.

Chapter 42

The Prostitutes of Calcutta

A wink, a word, or sideward glance, and company is yours
Escorted to a backroom and the charms of Bengal whores
With lips well laced with syphilis, they'll service every vice
Then offer up their children too, for barely half the price.

By the beginning of May 1907, Elsie had felt the turning of a cycle she had become familiar with in Calcutta: the transition from cooler and pleasant New Year temperatures, through the tolerable months, and towards the warmth and unpleasantness of mid-year.

The mango trees had noted change too. One of Elsie's greatest pleasures was to wander the gardens—both ornamental and productive—in the morning and early evening, chatting to the gardeners about their creations and the progress of their plantings.

It was then, during these visits, that she noted the maturation of the mangoes and was well prepared for the first crop.

Very early one morning, before sunrise, she and Grace had slipped downstairs and met up with Sahil, the 'master of the mangoes' as he enjoyed being called.

Together, they had walked to a mango grove and watched as garden staff climbed ladders to cut down the ripest mangoes of the new season. With more than two hundred in baskets, they headed for the formal gardens on the north side of the White House.

After ensuring that Sahil had quarantined the biggest mango, Elsie and Grace set about creating their own 'mango message'.

Then it was upstairs to pass 'the golden one', as prearranged, to Raji's valet Abid, who deposited it as the sole content of breakfast, under a silver dome atop a silver platter, with a card on which Elsie had written:

Look out the window
darling! XO

When Abid opened the curtains, the words HAPPY MANGO DAY! spelt out in yellow mangoes with a smiley face underneath, beamed back. Raji laughed, for he knew that only his second wife could have created such a thing, though he quickly ordered Abid to bring him a proper breakfast.

Raji had warned Elsie that a Gaya summer was more than even a Calcuttan would dare contemplate, so the need to get back to Calcutta soon was pressing. He had not been there for six months, a length of absence unprecedented in his memory.

JG arranged for two Tikari Raj carriages that were normally stored under tarpaulin at Gaya Junction, to be linked to the eastbound train.

Leaving the compound in the charge of Raj Manager, William Keith, the senior members of Tikari Raj and their key personal staff, as well as three crates of Tikari mangoes, headed to the capital of British India.

For Elsie, this was a return to somewhat familiar territory, though it was her first look at Raji's Ballygunge Store Road home. Sweeping up the drive through the landscaped gardens, she quickly recognised it for what it was: a quiet oasis in a city quilt pockmarked with pockets of chaos and poverty, alongside great elegance and affluence.

There was an air and amenity about Calcutta that Gaya could never provide, and for now the whole party was eager to sample its fruits once more.

"After lunch we have a bit of shopping to do, darling!" Raji exclaimed. Elsie could not help notice the raised eyebrows and smile exchanged by Grace and Cecil, respectively. Clearly, the latter's longer service with Tikari Raj had exposed him to habits that others would deem familiar, in time.

The Tikari entourage alighted from their motors on Chowringhee Road outside No. 22. The signage on the establishment stated 'Rai Budree Das Bahadoor & Sons, Jewellers—Since 1869'.

"We could have gone to Cooke & Kelvey or Hamilton & Co., but the pieces in here are unique, and in any case, it is an Indian, not a British establishment," said Raji. "We are going to The Bengal Club tonight, so I want you to be glistening! Certainly, some nice earrings, but also anything else you might fancy!"

This was not an opportunity Elsie had ever experienced before. Initially, she was hesitant and embarrassed. There were glass cases around the walls containing many beautiful pieces, all of which she would have been happy to own, but she had never felt comfortable just reaching out and taking things.

"That string of pearls—I want my wife to try them on!" Raji said, indicating a line of silver-white polished but natural balls glistening in a glass case. The shop assistant retrieved a key from his pocket and soon passed the string to Raji.

"Elsie, let's see how this looks," Raji said, as he placed the pearls around her neck. "Ah, just beautiful! What do you think, darling?"

The assistant held a mirror so Elsie could check if they looked as good as they felt. The smile in her eyes was all Raji needed to see. "We will take those! Now, Elsie, earrings!"

There was a large range, but one set caught Elsie's eye. It had five parallel strands of diamonds with ten diamonds in each strand. Raji had absolutely no doubt. The earrings were soon settled in their box within Raji's grasp.

"Next, I want you to go sari shopping with Grace!"

"Oh, Raji dear, I already have a number of saris!" Elsie protested.

"You don't have any of the quality you can find here at the best stores in Calcutta. Miss Knighton!"

"Yes, Your Highness! I know exactly where to go!" she said, grabbing Elsie's hand.

That same evening, the great lounge at The Bengal Club was a haven of hubbub until the moment the doormen opened the large double doors. Then, within seconds, a silence had spread throughout the room as all eyes, both men's and ladies', became transfixed by the couple walking into their midst.

It was not just that it was the unusual sight of a white woman on an Indian man's arm, but the sheer dazzling radiance of the former. Gold thread glistened from her red and gold sari. The fifty diamonds in each of her earrings flashed independent responses to the room's chandeliers. Her violet eyes sparkled and her smile spread warmth and welcome everywhere.

Raji was ecstatic. He was certain he had the most beautiful

woman in British India for a wife, and soon all Bengal and beyond would know about it.

As the days passed, Elsie slipped comfortably into the pampering and profile of high class Calcutta life.

Then one Saturday evening, after dinner, Grace pulled her aside. "Your Highness, I have arranged for Siri and Lala to pamper Raji, while we go on a special journey!" she said, grabbing Elsie's hand. "You should not dress up—just one of the older saris—and don't worry, we are taking Abu with us as driver, and a Gurkha to guard the motor!"

They drove north on roads Elsie knew well: turning left into Lower Circular Road, then right into the grand old lady Chowringhee, passing the Gothic revival style St Paul's Cathedral to the left, with the grand Victoria Memorial's access via Queen's Way in its background, and the many statues and tombs that littered Calcutta's vast Maidan. On they pressed, past the clubs, hotels and shops of northern Chowringhee, past the Ochterlony Road turnoff left to Government House, before taking a forty-five degree right turn east into the lengthy Central Avenue—north-central Calcutta's main north-south road.

Just after the road straightened out and they had passed Lal Bazar Street on the left, Grace called to Abu to stop: "Pull up outside the Chinese Temple!"

It was there they waited, under the lamplight for some minutes, Grace checking her pendant watch repeatedly. "She said she would be here at 8 o'clock ..."

It was not long before a motor drew up behind and an Indian woman emerged from the darkness, with a man who looked liked a bodyguard, by her side.

"Namaskar!" the woman said and gestured, pressing her palms together and bowing her head in greeting. As they responded in kind, Elsie noticed green and red jewelled bangles glisten in the lamplight, their lustre only temporarily interrupted by the jangling of attached ivory animals.

For a moment, Elsie wondered where she had seen that specific jewellery before, then realised it was on the hand of Raji's first wife. Now, even in the semi-exposure of the street lamp, Elsie could see that it was true: Raji only pursued the most beautiful of women.

"Elsie, dear! Grace and I have a surprise for you. We have decided that you should learn more about the real Calcutta and what goes on here. I have a very good friend who is just the person who can help! My bodyguard will stay with my vehicle, so Abu, you will have to come with us!"

As they navigated their way through the traffic and across to the east side of Central Avenue, Elsie tugged on Grace's arm and whispered a question, the answer to which she had wanted to know for some time: the name of Raji's first wife.

"Bibi!" Grace whispered back. "She is just happy to be called Bibi!"

Elsie was surprised, as she knew that 'bibi' was the Hindustani appellation for a lady or wife.

This area was not a part of Calcutta with which Elsie was familiar—and certainly not at night—for it had an unsettling feel. As they rounded the corner into Bow Bazar Street, the crowds grew—and they were nearly all men. Abu moved in closer to Elsie as they pushed their way through the boisterous throng, till they halted outside a solid-looking establishment.

There was large lettering on the front: The Golden Hind, Elsie thought it spelt out, though she wondered why a building had taken the name of Sir Francis Drake's flagship—until she realised there was an apostrophe before the 'H'.

"It is a high class brothel!" Bibi said excitedly. "An old friend of mine is the madam and has agreed to show us around!"

Elsie was inquisitive but unsure of what she might see, though reasoned that this was likely to be an opportunity she could never repeat.

The group headed to the front door that was guarded by a swarthy Indian who greeted Abu warmly, like a long-lost friend.

As they moved inside, they were ushered into a room to the left, where Bibi was embraced affectionately by a tall and large-breasted Indian woman, who Elsie thought might well have been quite beautiful at an earlier stage of her life. Right now though, she merely seemed intimidating.

As if reading Elsie's thoughts, the madam switched on a

welcoming smile. "Please call me Mama—all the girls and clients do!"

"Mama, this is Elsie, Tikari's second maharani!" Bibi said without a hint of jealousy.

"Your Highness, welcome to Calcutta's finest brothel!"

"I am fascinated to be here," Elsie responded. "Though, I must say I am glad I am just an observer!"

"You were on the stage were you not, Your Highness?" Mama asked, though the question had a rhetorical feel.

"Yes, that is right. I had always wanted to be on the stage and have been performing since I was seventeen."

Mama laughed. "You know, in India, there is a long cultural tradition of singers and dancers being prostitutes. No young lady seeking 'respectability' would dare venture onto the stage. There is not a man who would not believe he could lie with one of our dancing nautch girls, as easily as he could watch her perform!"

"Oh dear!" Elsie said, for this was in truth the first time she had contemplated the reality of her past performances through Indian cultural eyes.

"Beautiful girls are always welcome here! It is just sad that in this profession, they don't keep their beauty for very long! With the exception of the young men in St Joseph's College over the street, everyone is only interested in the young girls—the younger, the better!"

"What happens, Mama, when they age and become less attractive to men?" asked Grace.

"There is always a customer for them, but they will not work here or in the better establishments. The money will be harder to get and the work and clients more dangerous."

"Mama, what sort of people are your clients?" Elsie asked innocently.

"We have clients from every part of upper and professional Calcutta society. Some are what we call *bandha babu*, or regular clients and some of these are *timer babu*—clients who come here regularly on a particular day or particular time. They sometimes demand the same girl, but if they are regulars, they usually arrive through the back entrance."

"As their madam, how much of their earnings do you keep?" asked Grace.

"We provide the rooms for them to use with their clients, and often meals. For that they hand over half of their earnings. They must log their earnings in a book in each room. I review the book at the end of their shift and they hand over my share."

"Mama will explain how the system works with the rooms, later," Bibi added.

"Mama, how many prostitutes are there in Calcutta?" Elsie asked, finding this glimpse into a previously unknown world fascinating.

"There are many prostitutes here in Bow Bazar Street and in Harkata Lane, but there are many more to the north-west in the city's Sonagachi area. How many altogether? Perhaps ten thousand or more, I don't know. I only know that we keep our clients happy here near the heart of the city. They trust us and we trust them. But we don't take any chances."

"And your girls, Mama, are they all Indian?" Elsie continued.

"Oh no, not all. Apart from Indians, we have a Jewish girl, two Chinese, a Filipina and five Europeans on our books, so there is variety for those who want it!"

Mama hesitated, before adopting a more serious tone. "We will now go into the viewing room, but I must warn you of a few things that are very important. The room has one of the latest American inventions—a large two-way mirror—so I can check on what is going on in the lounge. This means our room must be kept in the dark otherwise we will be seen by the clients. Also, whisper only in that room, and please, if you recognise one of my girls or one of the clients, you must never speak of their presence here to anyone. Do you understand and agree?"

"Yes, Mama!" they all said in unison, as they followed her out the left door of that room to stop in front of a closed curtain. Mama waited till they were all inside before closing the door behind them and carefully opening the curtain.

There was just enough light filtering through from the brightly lit lounge, to outline the frame of an armchair in the middle-back of the viewing room.

"From here I can check on the actions of my girls and the

clients as they choose the girl, or girls, that they want." Mama said in a hushed voice.

Each of them looked into the lounge and wondered if they could recognise any of the clients who were currently sitting on sofas, or the girls who sat or stood nearby. One of the Indian girls was dancing suggestively and appeared to be singing, though it was not she that Grace reacted to. "Oh!" she exclaimed in surprise, as she squeezed Elsie's hand.

"Remember what Mama said!" Elsie whispered firmly, not wanting to know.

There were five clients in total and seven girls vying for their attention and money. The viewers watched for a couple of minutes in fascinated silence, as the clients selected their girls. First, an Indian man (who Elsie guessed may have been a lawyer or doctor), walked out of the lounge and towards the rooms with a blonde, English-looking girl; then a European— possibly Scottish, thought Elsie, as he had red hair—left the room with the all dancing and singing Indian girl in one hand and a tiny Chinese girl in the other.

At this point, Elsie just had to comment, in a hushed voice: "It is interesting how people seem to prefer those of a different race!"

"So often opposites attract, particularly in this business!" Mama confirmed. "Now, quietly follow me into the light board room, but wait at the door here until I have closed the curtain."

Within moments they stood in a small room, with a door to the right, stairs ahead and a panel of lights to the left—beside which stood a strapping Indian male whose role could only have been security.

"This is the panel control room," explained Mama quietly. "Through that door to the right is the corridor with our twelve working rooms, six on each side. When a girl enters a room with her client, she flicks a switch next to the doorframe that turns on a green light above her door on the outside, as well as a green light on the control panel next to her room number. If the girl has a problem with the client, she flicks a switch next to the bed, which turns on a red light outside the room and on the control panel. Ranjev here, who monitors the panel, will then race through this door and into the room to sort things out. Pretty clever, do you not think?"

"It is very good, Mama," said Elsie, "but what happens if the girl cannot reach the switch by the bed?"

"Quite possible, Your Highness, and I will give you a solution to this problem shortly. Any other questions?"

"Mama, when is the price and the service decided?" asked Grace.

"Before they enter the room, often in the corridor and sometimes in the lounge. Of course, no credit is offered—it must be all in cash rupees. When the client undresses, the girl must check him for syphilis. If she thinks there is a problem, he is given his money back and must leave, or Ranjev will be called."

Abu had been so quiet and contemplative; nobody had been reminded of his presence. So his question, when it came, surprised everybody. "Alcohol, Mama, is that a problem?"

"Exactly why we have no bar in our lounge, though some other so-called high class brothels do. Alcohol, sex and safety do not mix well! Are there any final questions before we move on?"

Grace shuffled her feet and wondered whether she should mention it ... then jumped straight in. "Can women visit this brothel as clients, Mama?"

Elsie and Abu were shocked, but Bibi looked at Mama with a pursed smile, keen to hear her response.

"It has been known to happen, though it is most unusual. In such circumstances we will generally arrange for our girls to make private visits to her residence, rather than arouse public suspicion."

Mama walked to the door that led to the client room corridor, and carefully and quietly partly opened it, poking her head around the door. Noticing that the corridor was empty, she opened the door fully but briefly, as she said: "Notice the relatively low height of the ceiling in this corridor? There is a very good reason for it!"

She then closed the door and continued: "The ceilings in both the lounge and the client rooms are much higher ... and this is why ... follow me very quietly up the stairs."

They partly ascended the spiral stairs that led behind and then above the panel. Mama stopped before they could complete the short spiralling climb. "This is a secret part of the building, so you must be very quiet as you move along the corridor. You will notice it is carpeted—that is intentional. I will whisper quietly as we go!"

They followed her, most of them curious and excited, wondering just what they might uncover …

"One girl is on shift in this corridor at all times," Mama whispered. "She is the room watch. You know how below, I said that the corridor had a low ceiling. Well, we are walking on top of the corridor ceiling now. The corner cornice in each of the client rooms features a plaster face, but it has eyes we can look through from here!"

They looked ahead and could see a number of green lights around shoulder height, glowing in the dark.

"You asked earlier, Your Highness, about what would happen if a girl in trouble could not flick the bedside switch. It is Karlina's role to be on duty this evening, and monitor each of the rooms. She will alert Ranjev to any problem. But you should take a look for yourselves!"

This was not something that Elsie or Grace had ever done before, but they could not resist the opportunity, taking turns to ogle at each viewing spot adjacent to a green light.

"I didn't know you could do that!" whispered Grace, pausing far longer at one station than she should.

"The man in here is being spanked repeatedly and seems to be sort of enjoying it! He must be English!' Elsie added.

"Sirhi!" Mama called, reverting to Hindustani in her minor panic and ordering everyone to the stairs. Karlina was first there, calling out to Ranjev to go to Room 9. Abu, who had refused to be party to the voyeurism, raced past the room watch and launched himself down the stairs in four strides.

Somehow, the prostitute in Room 9 had managed to flick the bedside switch and the red light had already alerted Ranjev. Abu was not far behind and together they dragged an Indian man out the back entrance.

"Mard-ne larki ko mára!" Ranjev explained in Hindustani, stating that the man had struck the girl. He then reached over and grasped Abu's hand warmly. "Bháí!" he said, indicating that they were like brothers.

"He will not be back!" assured Abu.

As they got their breath back beside the control panel, Mama asked if there were any more questions.

Elsie was keen to know if the girls were overworked, but Mama explained that they worked seven-hour shifts starting at various times, so there were always plenty of girls available to clients. Each room was cleaned and the sheets replaced with fresh ones over the hour after each shift, so that three full shifts made up each twenty-four hours. "The working conditions in The Golden 'Hind are probably the best in Calcutta—you will see this when we walk the street outside!"

True to her word, Mama soon led them out onto Bow Bazar, though she made sure Abu was close behind.

There were men, often in groups, wandering up and down the street, canvassing each building, shop and house front, searching for the telltale sighting of an object of desire, some of whom were kind enough to flaunt their availability from verandahs, or solicit on the street verge.

Mama and her new friends had not been on the sidewalk for long, when Elsie noticed a group of fairly small young men, walking towards them and studying them intently. As they met, one of them threw out an invitation in an unmistakable Australian accent: "How 'bout you sheilas and us guys have a good time, eh?"

Elsie could not stop herself from blurting out in her coarsest Australian accent: "Oh piss off back to Sydney you silly bastard!" causing Grace to giggle and the others to gasp.

"'Eh, 'ang on, I'm from bloody Brisbane I'll have ya know!" came the indignant reply, though they were soon panicked as Abu stepped in to monster them away.

"All right, 'old your horses! We woz only bein' friendly!"

As the Aussies drifted off into the Bow Bazar milieu, Elsie told the others that the young men were probably jockeys from the stables around the Tollygunge track.

"Yes, some Australians are here, but the largest number of foreigners are British army," Mama explained, as they passed a couple of young Englishmen in civilian clothes ushering away two young Indian women. "You won't see many uniforms around here!"

The further they moved on, the more depressing and potentially dangerous the encounters became. Young boys roamed the sidewalks pimping for their breadwinner. Around here, the women seemed less attractive, mostly older than usual, though some were even far younger.

By one door stood a prostitute, with a young girl of barely ten by her side. As Elsie watched, a scruffy man approached them both, but quickly took the girl by the arm and they disappeared inside.

Mama waved it away like it was an every minute occurrence. "This is nowhere near as bad as in Kerani Bagan Lane, nearby. There you will find the lowest classes of prostitutes and some of the worst treatment and violence."

Another thing Elsie had just realised, was that this end of Bow Bazar had young men and boys offering their services. It was something she had not seen before and she was shocked, especially as there seemed no shortage of interested male customers.

"Time we headed back!" decreed Mama. Then she added, as if she was a religious preacher, not a woman who financially gained from the sexual servitude of others: "There is only greater depravity ahead!"

As they turned, Elsie noticed a man drop a bundle of rupees as he eagerly grasped the arms of a couple of young rent-boys. Instinctively, she rushed over, picked it up and called after him: "Excuse me, sir, your money!"

The man stopped and turned, said thank you with an English accent, then for a moment made eye contact—a moment that was just long enough for both to realise, in great embarrassment, that they had met before.

"Colonel Fitzwilliam!" Elsie exclaimed in disbelief.

Chapter 43

Just the Way Things Are

In wanting more than what I had, I merely had to think
For mundane is most common, and can drive a man to drink
New car, new drug, new highlight — or gold piled by the bar
Surrender to this lifestyle, for it's just the way things are.

As the calendar slithered into the sweatiness of a Calcutta June, Raji ordered the abandonment of the great eastern capital of the British Raj for the more pleasant northern climes.

"We usually spend summer in Mussoorie or Simla, though this year we are going to Kapurthala in the Punjab, first. It is a tradition that the maharajas and their wives meet to kick off the northern summer, so we will be guests of Jagatjit Singh."

Elsie had only ever heard of Mussoorie, and had no precise idea of where it was, let alone the other places. As for Maharaja Jagatjit Singh, Raji would only say that he was 'a big man of great passion'.

Four Tikari Raj vehicles were loaded on to flat-topped wagons at Gaya Junction, tied down and then covered with tarpaulins for the journey north-west to Delhi. Elsie, Raji and key staff travelled in two wagons, with the balance of servants needed during their summer sojourn, to follow later by rail.

After an overnight stay in Delhi, the party set out in the four vehicles for Kapurthala, a 260-mile journey further north-west. Raji insisted that the drive could be completed comfortably by the latest arrival time of 4.30 pm, though when the De Dion had a flat tyre near the city of Sangrur, Raji's breakneck speed driving schedule went out the window.

It was nearly 4.50 pm when they arrived at Kapurthala's white Elysee Palace, and Raji was beside himself, as being late for official functions, particularly the very first of the summer, was seen as very poor form among the maharajas.

As was the custom, all Tikari staff and servants were ushered to quarters at the back of the building, while Raji and Elsie were taken to their own quarters to refresh themselves.

By the time they entered the main dining hall for the mixed

greeting ceremony, proceedings were already underway. A cheer had gone up and much laughter followed as the rather large gentleman at the end of the table, who Elsie later realised was the Maharaja of Kapurthala, drew firstly a maharaja's name from one bowl, then a maharani's name from another.

The two selected had stood up and walked off together guided by a servant.

As Elsie and Raji took their places next to each other, Elsie glanced around the room. All she could see were Indian faces looking back at her amid a hum of comments. Though there was one exception, Elsie realised, the woman with tanned skin in the far corner, was definitely European—both in appearance and clothing.

Raji had also scanned the room—and was now gravely disappointed. He was expecting Jagatjit Singh's sixth wife, the beautiful seventeen-year-old Spanish dancer, Anita Delgado, to be present. But alas, she was still being schooled on etiquette in Europe.

Everyone's focus soon returned to the bowls and the next couple drawn. After four drawings and four pairings and departures, the true meaning of the mixed greeting ceremony began to dawn on Elsie—and she was shocked and horrified.

When the fifth maharaja's name was drawn and a relatively aged and bearded gentleman rose, Elsie hoped it was not her name next.

"Elsie Tikari!" came the loud call from Kapurthala, as sighs of disappointment and curses rose from the seated maharajas who had missed out.

Elsie looked at Raji in vain for help. Surely he would not allow this to happen.

"No, go on and enjoy it!" he said, waving away her protestations.

A servant led them down a flight of stairs, which is when the maharaja started to grope her breasts. By the time they had passed through a couple of rooms, he was getting breathlessly excited. The servant pulled aside a curtain to reveal a pile of soft cushions, triggering a feverish attempt by the maharaja to unwrap her sari.

I cannot believe this is happening! Elsie thought, *though the longer I live in this world of maharajas, the less I should be surprised!* There was no prospect of opting out now, so she just had to make the most of the 'opportunity' presented to her, to enhance her reputation, and indirectly Raji's.

As she fell naked onto the cushioning, she noticed the significant bulge in his robes that soon revealed itself to be the largest example of that part of the male anatomy she had ever encountered.

She closed her eyes, leant back and opened her legs to the impatient interloper …

The sound of a gong echoing around the Elysee Palace, signalled a halt to all amorous encounters and a return to rooms for a wash before dinner.

After the formality of a six-course meal, the guests had just started to mingle for after-dinner drinks, when Raji pulled Elsie aside. "You need to go with the servant, darling!"

"I do? Where?"

"Don't argue! You will have a great time!"

Elsie was led downstairs and into a large bathroom where a wash and rubbing with scented oils awaited. She enjoyed this very much, though something told her there was more in store.

Once she was dried down and had fragrances applied, a robe was placed around her and she was led through a series of corridors. With each step she could hear orchestral music getting louder, till she stood on the edge of a large indoor but open area lit only by flaming lamps.

There, sprawled naked across a luxurious bed was the tanned figure of the European woman she had seen upon arriving, the only other non-Indian in the royal gathering.

As Elsie inched forward her robe was removed, though she did not notice, so transfixed by the combination of flickering light, music and the alluring image before her.

"Elsie, darling! You are even more beautiful than everyone has suggested. Come over and lie with me!"

As Elsie moved onto the bed, the dark-eyed beauty whispered: "I am Olive of Jind, and we are going on an adventure together! You can start by kissing me all over—but you are welcome to use your tongue if you want."

"But I have never done this with a woman before!" protested Elsie, as she moved her porcelain-white body over Olive, her long hair falling onto Olive's naked and welcoming frame.

"You can start with my breasts, if you like," suggested Olive, as Elsie's open mouth and tongue traversed Olive's right breast till it found her erect nipple.

"Ah!" Olive gasped. "Oh, yes!" she cried loudly, as she pushed her head back, opened her mouth and arched her chest, causing her nipple to be pressed further into Elsie's mouth.

As Olive's hands ran through Elsie's hair, she pressed her down onto her breast and added in a whisper: "Do whatever you like, darling! Even if you fake it, they won't be able to tell the difference!"

Elsie froze … what did Olive mean? Her dusky companion seemed to read her mind. "Oh, they are all watching us intently, while leering over the railing from above! The maharajas will probably be thrusting their members through the ironwork and the maharanis playing with themselves! That is just the way things are!"

That evening, Elsie expressed her frustration to Raji, but he waved away her complaints. "You will get used to it, you know! I hear that you are very popular already!" he added with considerable pride.

A fractured night's sleep was followed by a comforting hug from Olive the next morning at breakfast.

"Elsie, I want you to meet my husband, Raja Ranbir Singh of Jind!"

"I was told you were very good yesterday, Elsie!" the bearded and turbaned ruler said, as he reached out a hand. Elsie was a little unsure of exactly what he meant, though they chatted politely for a few minutes, before Olive drew her away for a stroll through the formal gardens.

"Have I got any food around my mouth?" Elsie asked, before they had gone more than a few paces. "He seemed to be staring at that part of me most intently!"

"Don't worry, he will find a use for your mouth quickly enough! No, in fact he is largely deaf and lip-reads to get by."

"Oh, dear! I am sorry to hear that. It must be difficult for you both."

"You adjust. You adjust to every moment of awkwardness and embarrassment or you decide to step off the royal gravy train—and right now such a proposition would be unthinkable! As for Ranbir, let me assure you that he may seem quiet and innocent enough, but he will have it up between your legs, dear Elsie, before you realise it is out of his trousers!"

Elsie did not know what to say, so thought that under the circumstances, she would just keep her mouth closed.

At 9.45 am, a trumpeter sounded a reminder to meet in the palace for a tour of the Gallery of Timepieces. The Maharaja of Kapurthala was renowned for his love of all things that whirred and ticked, especially if they were French.

For Elsie, this was a real treat: intricate pieces of great beauty, featuring legendary figures of warriors, maidens, kings, queens, gods, bears, tigers, deer and elephants in bronze, silver, gold and precious metals adorned the bodies of clocks made of marble and semi-precious stone in a kaleidoscope of colours.

"Your Highnesses!" cried the chief horologist. "Please shift your attention over here to this automaton, though as you do, please listen for the different sounds as the clocks strike 10 o'clock!"

Elsie had heard some of the clocks whir in anticipation of the hour and soon the air was filled with a cacophony of chiming tones, while the guests gathered around the remarkable sight of a maid raising water from a well, then emptying the bucket into a trough, that attracted cows; a masterpiece of a skilled automaton engineer's craft.

The royal guests cheered as one. The Maharaja of Kapurthala displayed a degree of pleasure that matched his sizeable girth, then reminded everyone that there would be a ceremonial welcome at 10.30 am, then later, after lunch, he would take everyone on a guided tour of his new palace.

As they gathered in the forecourt for the gun salute, Raji told Elsie to count the number of firings.

With the cannon fire booming simultaneously from either side of the grounds of the Elysee Palace, Elsie did as she was told, quietly. "One … two … three …"

"Are you counting?" snapped Raji.

"Yes! … Five … six …" responded Elsie, who could not understand why she was asked.

Finally there was silence and applause from the royal gathering.

"So how many were there?" whispered Raji intently.

"Fifteen … I counted fifteen … is that significant?"

"Yes!" said Raji, dragging Elsie to one side so nobody else would hear. "Every princely state that the bloody British favour is allocated a salute status up to twenty-one guns. Kapurthala has thirteen, but is allowed fifteen on personal occasions such as these."

"So how many does Tikari have?"

Raji looked away, so Elsie would not see his anguished face.

"Darling, how many do we have?" she tried again.

"The bastards," he began, for he had started to adopt some of the Australian vernacular, "have not given us even a single one!"

"Oh God! And Jind, does it have any?"

"Bloody eleven!"

"So how can we get some?" Elsie asked innocently.

"The more you grovel to the British, the more you pay, the more likely you are to get the guns!"

"That is disgusting! Who cares about silly guns in any case!"

Raji looked at her in way that needed no interpretation.

"Well then, what if I was to sleep with the Viceroy, would that help?"

Raji had not considered this option, but before he could give it serious thought, Elsie interjected: "I was only joking darling, although the way things are going, I will have probably slept with nearly everyone else soon!"

After lunch, they all boarded a line of gleaming cars for the short journey to the new palace.

Upon entering its grounds, they passed a magnificent sculpture of a prowling Bengal tiger, to which workmen seemed to be adding the finishing touches, then glided to a halt in front of a massive and unmistakably French, chateaux-style building, far larger than the Elysee Palace.

"Welcome to Jagatjit Palace!" Maharaja Jagatjit Singh of Kapurthala exclaimed with great pride. "It was designed by the French architects Boyer and Marcel. Building commenced five years ago, so it is nearly about time it was finished. My French construction manager assures me it will be another year or two as they have barely commenced the Versailles-like grounds. Externally, the structure of the palace is almost complete, but inside there is still a great deal to do!"

"You can see that he is a real Francophile, he simply adores everything French!" noted Olive.

"It is a wonder he has not got a French wife or mistress!"

"Oh, Elsie dear, just give him time. He is still only thirty-five!"

They proceeded in a conga line, threading their way past workers laying marble flooring; by others applying gold leaf to cherubim and other heavenly wooden relief objects; carpenters shaving a door to fit perfectly; electrical wizards laying their latest magic cabling to link with ornate light fittings; an artist mimicking Michelangelo with his pencil draft on a ceiling; a glazier fitting the second of a number of tall, curve-topped mirrors in a state apartment; a stonemason smoothing the curve of a blue-grey marble column in the dining room; and finally, stained-glass master craftsmen fitting the final pieces in the translucent ceiling of what all agreed was probably their favourite space: the magnificent representation of intricate Mughal splendour, that was the Durbar Hall.

"Oh, c'est magnifique!" Elsie said, congratulating the Maharaja in her schoolgirl French.

"Merci, merci ma chérie!" came the royal and pleasantly surprised reply.

"I hear that Ranbir has invited you and Raji to be our guests for the next two weeks on our houseboat on Dal Lake," Olive said with a knowing smile, as she grabbed Elsie's hand. "Of course, Raji has accepted. Naturally, the invitation is pretty obvious Ranbir code."

"It is?" questioned Elsie.

"Why of course, you poor, innocent thing! It means he simply can't wait to make you intimately familiar with a certain part of his anatomy. And for my part, I must make a re-acquaintance with Raji's."

Elsie wondered what Olive meant about that last bit, but did not dare ask. So she opted for a phrase that had stuck in her mind from the evening before. "Well, I suppose as you say, 'that's just the way things are'!"

"Yes, that's just the way things are!"

Chapter 44

The Lake Near the Roof of the World

Its shores are edged by mountains, and its air is crystal clear
Its peacefulness is legendary, and not just a veneer
Its houseboats are just fabulous — yet all of local make
You haven't sampled solitude, till drifting on Dal Lake.

The convoy of cars wound its way north on the 300-mile journey from Kapurthala in Punjab, to Srinagar in Kashmir.

Elsie lay across the back seat of the De Dion, contemplating the eternally blue sky occasionally, but more often the bearded and trusted countenance of Abu, that hovered protectively above. With her head on a cushion on his lap, Elsie felt comfortable and protected, as they journeyed towards a lakeside fortnight with her new friend Olive.

When Abu was not fanning her face to cool her with one of his giant hands, she was as conscious of his other hand nestled protectively and gently against her hair.

The sun was more than halfway into its descent from its midday apex, when the convoy snaked its way past more mosques than Hindu temples in the predominantly Muslim city of Srinagar. It then crossed one of the seven bridges fording the Jhelum River to arrive at a hotel not far from Dal Lake.

Raji headed inside the hotel to book the Tikari entourage's servants in for a two-week stay, only to emerge to a large and inquisitive crowd of locals gathered around the resting motorcade.

From there, Ranbir, Olive, Raji and Elsie drove to the shores of Dal Lake, where a couple of shikaras—small covered boats that resembled gondolas—waited to ferry them to the Raja of Jind's houseboat.

"Most houseboats here just stay tied to the shore, but we like to stay out on the lake," explained Olive.

Elsie had no idea what a houseboat might look like, though the large rectangular creations by the shoreline seemed far bigger than anticipated. As the shikara boatmen paddled them outward across the crystal clear and smooth waters, Elsie noticed a sizeable object in the distance.

With heart-shaped oars pushing them closer, what was surely Dal Lake's largest houseboat loomed. "Hello, darling!" Olive called out, waving enthusiastically to a small figure standing against the railing at the boat's stern.

"Mama! Papa!" the figure called and waved back.

"Bibiji! Bibiji!" Ranbir cried.

It was only at this moment that Elsie realised this must be their child. Olive had not mentioned this before, and Elsie watched on with considerable envy at the affectionate interplay that ensued.

"Dorothy!" Olive cried, as she swept the girl up in her arms. "Now I want you to meet someone special, darling!"

"Servant!" Dorothy stated quickly, her eyes firmly on Elsie.

"Oh, the mind of a four year old! She thinks because you are wearing a sari and not European clothes like me, that you must be a servant! No, Dorothy, this is my friend, Maharani Elsie!"

Elsie reached out one hand and tickled Dorothy, then ducked behind Olive before attacking from the other side. In no time, Dorothy was squealing with delight.

Knowing she now had Dorothy's attention, Elsie pretended to ignore her, while pulling her along as if she were on a string, though her own attention was more focussed on the magnificence around her.

First, a large lounge area with intricately woven carpets and chandelier; then a dining area and kitchen through which access could be gained to a couple of luxurious bedrooms, each with their own bathroom. Further on were Dorothy's room and quarters for the staff.

"This is truly wonderful, Olive!" Elsie exclaimed, as they headed back towards the lounge for a drink.

With Ranbir and Olive preoccupied with Dorothy momentarily, Raji seized his chance. "It is nice, but I could do better!" he whispered competitively.

Olive returned with a drink for Elsie, passing her a glass with contents that looked a bit like a strawberry milkshake. "As you are not much into alcohol, you should try this! It is called Rooh Afza, and is the latest craze from Delhi!"

Gingerly, Elsie took a sip, quickly followed by more. "Oh, I do like this! It is really nice and refreshing! What is in it?"

"It has fruit, herbs and vegetable extracts. You just add the concentrate to milk and ice and shake it a bit!"

As the sun slipped, to cast its splash of light across the snow-capped mountains that fringed the lake to the east and north, Olive and Elsie sat at the side of the stern, dipping their bare legs into the mirror-like lake, with glasses of Rooh Afza at hand.

"You know that around our palace in Sangrur right now, it would be over 100 degrees, while here it will not even have reached 80!" Olive observed. "And, the roof of the world is just over those mountains!"

Dorothy, who had very quickly warmed to Elsie, had fallen asleep in her new acquaintance's lap, her head resting against her breasts. As Elsie softly stroked Dorothy's hair, the odd tear trickled down her face. "It is just so beautiful here ... just so beautiful!"

Olive could hear the choking in Elsie's voice and looked at her in surprise. "Are you all right?"

"I am fine, just fine," she said reaching down to kiss Dorothy on the top of the head. By now, the alluring aroma of north Indian cooking had wafted through from the kitchen, merely adding to the assault on Elsie's senses. "In fact, I don't think I have ever been more content!"

Olive earnestly tried to make sense of it all, for something was not quite right. Then, she took a 'stab in the dark'. "You are only young Elsie, and have many years to have children."

"I have a newborn niece called Marjorie in Sydney, but as yet, no children. Yes, I am still only twenty-three, but ..." she began, followed by a deep sigh.

"But what, darling?"

"But I just don't know that I can ever have children—at least a specialist in Australia thinks it is most unlikely."

"Oh, darling!" Olive said, as she moved in tight to Elsie and put her arm around her. "Does Raji know?" she asked quietly.

"Oh yes! I told him when he proposed, as it would not have been fair. He was very good about it and said we would keep trying. I guess I cannot complain about other women in his life, if I cannot do the job for which I was designed!"

There was silence for some time as Olive hugged Elsie while Elsie stroked Dorothy.

That evening, when a servant came to take Dorothy off to bed, the child was delighted when Elsie volunteered to tell her a bedtime story.

As the royal Jind houseboat rested on its sea of glass the next morning, Olive took advantage of a gathering of the four royals in the lounge, to reveal the plan that she had developed overnight.

"I think Elsie needs a dog or two as a companion!"

"I do?"

"Darling, at Sangrur, we have the largest series of dog kennels in the princely states! If Ranbir were not so deaf, even he would have been driven crazy by the barking! But, dogs are his passion—well one of his passions, anyway. There is bound to be one dog that desperately wants to go to Gaya with Elsie!"

"I think I might prefer cats."

"Nonsense, darling! Dogs are such faithful companions. You do love animals, don't you?"

"Oh yes, generally. However ..."

"Well that is it then! You and Raji drop in to Sangrur on your way back to Gaya and select a dog."

Elsie could see that arguing was futile and that Olive, with Ranbir's agreement and Raji's more tentative consent, had determined that she needed a barking child-substitute.

There was a degree of passion and determination in Olive that Elsie found fascinating and when they sat alone that afternoon at the stern, dabbling once more in Dal's dreamlike waters, she dug deeper. "Olive, your tanned complexion, where does it come from?"

"Ah, my mother is English, but my father was an Italian barber of Romanian background based in Bombay."

Elsie knew enough about ancestry to suggest that he may have been at least part gypsy.

"I don't know about that. His name was Manolescu."

Elsie was silent for a few moments, but her mind and memory were whirring frantically. *That name and other details seem so familiar!* "You are not by any chance related to a young man we lived with in Calcutta, called Eugene Manolescu?"

Olive laughed at the coincidence. "Eugene is my younger brother!"

"So, Lizzie Coleman is your mother?"

"Raji ..." Olive said with lowered voice, turning to check that he was not in the background, listening, "wanted to marry me when he was just seventeen! Ranbir was a bit older and already had a wife, but he offered mother 50,000 rupees in compensation which she couldn't resist—so you could say I married for money!"

Elsie thought momentarily, before deciding to add to this confessional session: "I was married at nineteen, to a magician, and was friends with Raj, the Prince of Cooch Behar, before his car accident."

"I hear he survived the crash, but that he had earlier turned to drink after his parents refused to allow him to marry an English actress," Olive responded, innocently.

Elsie dared not say anything. *This 'English actress' is obviously me*, she thought. *It is best that I not mention that Raj and I had been secretly engaged. Better to let 'sleeping dogs' lie, and move on.*

* * *

After three more idyllic days becalmed in the centre of the lake, a pair of boatmen, using long poles that they pushed into the shallow lakebed, steered the houseboat towards the eastern shore.

There, spread out before them was Nishat Bagh, which translated from Hindustani meant Garden of Joy. Built from 1633 by the Mughals, it was a joy to behold.

Strolling through its formal terraces and by its water channels, hand in hand with little Dorothy and Olive, with the rugged Zabarwan Mountains looming in the background, Elsie thought she was surely close to paradise.

A few days later, the houseboat had eased further north and the party disembarked for the short walk to Shalimar Bagh. It was the bigger of the two great Mughal gardens, and the older one.

"Emperor Jahangir had it built for his wife, Nur Jahan. Just what every ruler should do for his beloved wife!" Olive declared, turning pointedly to Ranbir and Raji.

The statement may have made an impact, because after Elsie had restated her love for the area and the houseboat lifestyle that evening, Raji rose with much determination in his voice: "I will build for my dear Elsie, the largest and grandest houseboat ever to glide on Dal Lake! What is more, I shall ensure that it is steam turbine powered!"

He was going to add that it would be 'unlike the silly pole-pushed versions', though wisely realised this would be not be viewed too kindly by his generous hosts.

Before departing to meet up with the servants at their hotel in Srinagar, Raji stopped by Dal Lake's southern shore to meet with boatbuilders, ensuring that his word would be kept and construction of his Dal Lake dream could begin.

Chapter 45

The Golden Moment

I shed my shoes and shuffled, 'cross the greatest of Sikh sites
With crowds of pilgrims 'round me, I did witness sacred rites
Within the Golden Temple, midst chanting from a nook
I marvelled at their reverence, for their most holy book.

Abu was as happy as Elsie had ever witnessed. They had left their summer home in the hill town of Mussoorie in late August, heading for Sangrur in Jind, but Raji had agreed that the motorcade should split.

While three of the vehicles continued to Jind, Raji, Elsie, Grace and Abu would sidetrack north-west to Amritsar in the De Dion, to visit the holiest of all Sikh sites, the Harmandir Sahib, or House of God—better known in broader society by its English name: the Golden Temple.

"I have been there once, Your Highness," reminisced Abu. "It was many years ago, though I have walked its marble pathways and stood within its walls many times since, in my dreams."

Elsie imagined that a structure so named would be a large golden building on a hill. Her only other experience of a major religious holy site structure was the Buddhist Mahabodhi Temple at Bodh Gaya, which, while towering and spectacular, was quite different to the breathtaking architectural beauty of the Taj Mahal at Agra.

Here was a third iconic site, this one granted by the Mughal emperor Akbar to the Sikhs, then built on from the 16th century. It was one she soon realised was quite different to any she had seen or imagined before.

A large complex of buildings connected by laneways surrounded a central area that was not wholly visible until they stepped past the Sikh Museum and onto a marble pathway, called the Parikrama, that framed a rectangular lake.

"And here it is!" said Abu, though in truth no eye could have missed the gleaming, golden edifice that shone within the heart of the waterway. It was a golden moment for them all, and they paused to take in the scene, barefoot and with their heads covered in respect for the local rules.

They followed Abu to the north, and though the crowd of pilgrims increased as they walked on, Abu's height made him the ideal travel guide for a popular destination.

He paused to explain in front of a large stone multi-storey building topped with golden domes. "This is the Akal Takht, the seat of the supreme governing body of Sikhs. It is from here, at sunrise every morning ... every morning ... every ..." There was a long pause as Abu was clearly struggling to speak, then he turned away.

Elsie reached out and grasped his giant right hand, causing him to turn back towards her. She could see tears streaming down his face and into his beard. Soon she and Grace too were struggling to hold back theirs. Raji, who Elsie had never yet seen cry, was the only one unmoved.

With some difficulty, Abu regained some composure and continued: "The holiest Sikh book ... the Guru Granth Sahib ... it is carried into the Golden Temple ... for readings ... then returns on nightfall."

They followed Abu as he walked slowly along the lamp-lined causeway to the golden structure, to pause in front of an open door.

"There is a door on each side of the temple," he said, taking a deep breath. "This shows that this house of God is open to all, no matter what faith you are or your background."

They entered through a series of arches and, true to accepted custom, were soon seated on the ground, listening to a recital from the holy book. Elsie could understand some words and phrases, but she was most captivated by the beauty and intricate detail on the walls around her.

After respectfully touring the three levels of the temple, the group headed for the meal hall, to dine for free with thousands of others, on lentil soup served with flat bread.

Having eaten, Elsie made sure to purchase a postcard to send to Emma.

Little was said on the drive from Amritsar to Sangrur, though minds scarcely needed topping up with mere 'empty words'.

Elsie reflected on the richness, beauty and complexity of the Indian religious and cultural experience—something so foreign to her Anglo-Australian upbringing. How limited by comparison were the lives of her old school colleagues and even her much-loved best friend.

* * *

On arrival in Sangrur, Olive, with Dorothy in tow, gave Elsie a tour of the cream and white Sangrur Palace and their overnight accommodation.

Morning brought an eager Ranbir, who could not wait to show off his extensive collection of dogs. "Which one would you like?"

The question was not one Elsie had ever had to contemplate before. She, Raji and the Jind royal party toured the enormous kennel complex to a cacophony of excitedly barking canines. Any of the many dogs that approached her could have been the one, but they just needed to have something special.

"You are better off with a bigger dog, especially if we build the hunting lodge," Raji advised.

Elsie had almost exhausted her search when she noticed a young, brown-grey dog, studying her from a distance. As she leaned against the meshing of his pen, she expected him to rush forward to try to greet and lick her, but this dog was doing nothing of the sort. It was watching intently.

"Hello, sweetheart!" Elsie said, not taking her eyes off him for a moment. His tail began to wag, but he was not moving towards her. "Either he is scared, or too proud!" Elsie speculated—and she liked to think it was the latter.

"He is a Great Dane with a brindle colour mix," explained Ranbir, opening the gate to the pen. "You can see the tiger-like stripes though he is only a very young puppy!"

As Elsie entered, the dog's tail wagged even faster, though he still held his ground. He had cute floppy ears and beautiful brown eyes.

"Darling, how would you like to come with me to Tikari Raj?" she asked, as she slid along the ground towards him. He responded by mimicking her movement until the two met; at which point the dog rolled, leading Elsie to enthusiastically pat his outstretched paws and rub his chest and tummy area.

"He is the one!" she cried with delight.

"He will certainly grow big enough!" Raji noted.

"Of course, he must have a companion, so you should take his older sister," Ranbir stated, indicating a similar-looking Great Dane nearby.

And so it was that Larka (Hindustani for boy) and Larki (girl) became part of the Tikari Raj household.

"Well, I shall have to become an expert on dogs very quickly. There will be a lot of reading for me, and a lot of hard work and obedience from you!" Elsie said firmly, wagging her finger at the two animals.

She was to be true to her word, for though she could not have anticipated it at that time, she would go on to write a regular column on dogs, their care, behaviour and dog shows, in the Calcutta press.

Chapter 46

The Secret Meeting

The visitor to their Ballygunge Store Road mansion had not stayed very long, though this was not what had piqued Elsie's interest in the last days of March 1908. It was more the nature of his conversation—only whispered, and only with Raji.

The next day, the Maharaja appeared in what could only be described as 'gardening clothes', an occurrence unique in Elsie's memory, for he was invariably a snappy dresser.

"Raji! What are you doing?" she asked.

"I need you to change into the oldest and poorest sari you have—and please don't wear any jewellery!"

Elsie just stood there, stunned, but Raji was becoming irritated. "We have an important meeting at 10 am, I will explain later! Now go and get changed!"

Why, thought Elsie, *am I being told to dress down for an important meeting?*

As Elsie emerged to join Raji at the front door, he handed his and Elsie's emerald rings to Abu, grabbed Elsie's hand and headed off, down the steps, through the gardens, out the gates and turned west up Ballygunge Store Road, before soon crossing the road to the other side.

"I don't understand, darling! Why are we walking to an important meeting? Is it nearby? And, why is your hair so messy?"

"Stop asking questions and just do as I say!" he insisted.

After a considerable walk, they turned right into Chowringhee, where Raji checked a watch he had stuffed into a pocket. "We should be right to take a gharry now!" he said, signalling to the nearest attendant and their animal waiting by the Maidan verge.

"Harrison Road, Howrah Bridge end!" he ordered, as they

climbed on board. The gharry headed north to the relative disorganisation of one of Calcutta's less salubrious shopping streets.

"Here, stop here!" Raji ordered, as they clambered out and he paid the driver.

Raji took a deep breath and looked around the vicinity. Elsie did too, and she noticed something a little odd: spread out through the normal pedestrian traffic, there seemed to be some well-built Indian men, watching warily the waves of walkers.

"Cover your face as much as possible!" Raji whispered, as they approached two burly figures in front of a doorway. Raji first checked a piece of paper in his pocket, then uttered: "Varanasi!"

The name of India's most holy city for Hindus must have been a password, for the two men urged them to walk through the door, but still looked at Elsie with suspicion.

At the top of the stairs, they were directed around a corner and through a room away from the street, where they were stopped.

An argument ensued between a guard and Raji, the gist of which Elsie well understood.

"No, I am not English!" she said in her best Hindustani. "I am Australian!"

The hubbub had caused a figure to emerge from the back room, peering around the frame of the door. "Tikari?" he queried. Then for a few seconds he studied Elsie carefully, his dark brown eyes carving a path around her figure like a sculptor admiring his latest masterpiece. "Of course, she may come in too!"

"Namaskar!" came the mutual greeting, before the trio lapsed into more anglicised speech.

Raji and the gentleman shook hands before Raji introduced Elsie. "This is my wife Elsie. Elsie, this is Mohandas Gandhi!"

Elsie had reached out a hand in respect and was met with a soft, almost effeminate response, just as it dawned on her she was face to face with the great Indian nationalist lawyer and leader.

"I thought you were in jail in South Africa! I am sure I read that in the papers!"

"I was released about a month ago and arrived yesterday morning, secretly, at Armenian Ghat. If the British find out I will no doubt be jailed again—and if the public find out there are likely to be nationalist riots. I am supposed to be convalescing at the Phoenix settlement outside of Durban, and plan to be back there in just over a week. I only have time to catch up with key people in the nationalist cause, such as your husband. Please, sit down, Your Highnesses!"

"I apologise for our outfits, but I thought it best we come in disguise!" said Raji.

"Ah, Tikari, you can change your clothes, but you should never change your heart!" came the smiling reply. Gandhi then spent some more moments studying Elsie, before saying: "I knew I should have postponed my vow of Brahmacharya!"

Both he and Raji laughed, as Elsie looked at her husband quizzically. "I shall explain it later, darling!" he said, patting her hand.

"So Elsie, tell me, how do Australians view the English?" Gandhi asked.

"I dare say with far more tolerance and less real understanding than myself, Mr Gandhi. Undoubtedly, the English have given the world much in terms of organisation, order and civility, but there is a degree of arrogance and self-centredness that nearly outweighs the value of the positive contributions!"

"Fascinating!" Gandhi responded. "I am glad your husband insisted you come. Now, Tikari, tell me about the conference next month in Patna. I hear you are one of the biggest landholders in Bihar, so it is important that you will be there."

"The Bihar Provincial Congress Committee will hold its first meeting in Patna, as you obviously have been informed. The meeting will be chaired by a Muslim, Ali Imam."

"That is very good! What are relations like now between Hindus and Muslims in Bihar?"

"Excellent, in fact as good as or most probably better than anywhere in the country!"

"Just be very careful!" Gandhi warned. "The British will seek to divide us, to weaken our movement. They are already trying to turn Muslim against Hindu."

"We are also hoping to have a greater degree of independence for Bihar from Bengal. There are far too many Bengalis involved in Bihari administration!"

"Please, Tikari, independence for our nation and freedom from British rule should be the priority, with sectional interests secondary!"

As conversation continued, Elsie focussed on this man with the short dark hair and close-trimmed moustache, who looked in his late thirties. He was certainly not a big man, but his ideas were powerful enough to stir fear in some and fanatical devotion in others.

Eventually, Gandhi and Raji rose and shook hands. "Take care, sir!" urged the Maharaja.

"Remember, *Satyagraha*—non-violent non-cooperation—in all potential conflict situations, and we will win the day!" Gandhi emphasised.

Elsie offered her hand to Gandhi, but he bent down and kissed it. When he looked up, she could see that he had a twinkle in his eye.

As they headed back south in another gharry, Elsie turned to Raji. "What did he mean?"

"No! We will talk later!" Raji snapped, indicating the proximity of the driver.

Stepping out by the Maidan, they strolled back towards Ballygunge Store Road and the mansion.

"So, can I ask now what he meant by postponing his Brahma-something?"

"Brahmacharya. Gandhi took a vow of chastity two years ago!"

Briefly, Elsie pondered whether it would not have been fun tempting him to break that vow. Outwardly, she was just happy to echo that well-worn line: "You men are all the same—you only ever think of one thing!"

Chapter 47

The Birth of Bhalwa

A hunter needs a hideout, where his trophies are displayed
Best if nestled near the jungle where his victims will parade
A place where no man's startled when the shotguns do explode
Ah, Bhalwa by Mahane, it is off the Grand Trunk Road.

The Studebaker turned sharply off the Grand Trunk Road and swung through a clump of trees that curtained off the area from the ancient Calcutta to Delhi trade route, before straightening up in a grassland clearing area punctuated by palmyra palms. Around them, particularly to the south, massed what looked like thick forest.

Raji checked the car's odometer and did a quick calculation. "It is forty-two miles from Gaya!" Then, turning to Elsie in the passenger seat, he asked: "What do you think?"

Elsie was not sure what he expected or wanted her to say, so she opted for her usual frankness and honesty. "There is nothing around. It is a bit isolated and pretty, but I don't know where we are nor why we are here!"

Raji had armed himself with his elephant and tiger guns and insisted Abu carry a shotgun as well as his usual revolver. With the Great Danes, Larka and Larki, under Abu's care in the back, they had driven south from Gaya on a 'surprise journey'; bypassed Bodh Gaya keeping the Falgu River to their left, turned left on to the Grand Trunk Road, crossed the Falgu River, then east past the village of Barachatti, and lastly crossed the Mahane River and entered this private oasis.

"I call this area Bhalwa, and have hunted in the jungle on the edge of here for years! You can find tiger, wild elephant, sambar and black buck in the forest and even crocodile in the Mahane!"

This is all fine for Raji, thought Elsie, *though as I abhor hunting, why have I been brought here?*

Making sure shotguns were loaded and in hand, Raji and Abu stepped out of the Studebaker and urged Elsie to follow. She did, but made sure she had a tight grip on the dogs' leads.

They walked for a couple of minutes through the grass, until Raji stopped. "What about here?" he asked Elsie.

"Here, what, darling?"

"A hunting lodge, of course! It is all Tikari Raj property and the Mahane River is only a couple of hundred yards away on the boundary, so we can have water and irrigation for gardens. We could have more than one hundred acres here, sealed off as our own compound on the edge of the jungle."

"Aren't we having a houseboat built, Raji? Surely we cannot afford two things at once?"

Before answering, Raji mentioned that he thought it would be fine to unleash the dogs, as they would be quick to return if they noticed anything potentially dangerous, so Elsie unclipped the leashes from their studded collars.

"The houseboat should be finished next year, so it will be time for another project. We should turn our attention to this after our London trip is out of the way."

"Our London trip? Are we going to London?"

"Didn't you know?" Raji said, both surprised and a little embarrassed. "We sail in June. JG has been making all the arrangements and told me he has been keeping you updated!"

"Well, he is a liar, because he has not mentioned a single thing to me!"

All the way back to Gaya, Elsie was tormented by conflicting emotions: delight and excitement that she would be visiting London for the first time, but considerable anger that she had not been informed or consulted by JG. There was also the not so small matter of Raji not mentioning such a significant event to her. For the very first time since her arrival in Gaya, she wondered if she was not already 'on the outer'.

By the time she strode up the staircase in the White House, it was clear from the pace and determination in her walk, what emotion had come to the fore.

"Wakefield!" she yelled, as she reached the top of the landing, "I want to see you in the lounge room, NOW!"

It was more than a minute before JG surfaced and his words indicated that he well knew the crime for which he had been summoned and convicted by his judge, jury and executioner. "I was unaware that you had been to London," he responded with sarcasm. "I therefore presumed that you had nothing of value to contribute!"

With that, he turned with a dismissive look on his face and headed back to his office.

Chapter 48

Salad Days at The Waldorf

"Well, I'll be damned, no chocolate ones!" The guest did cry distraught
As he scrutinised the high tea cakes, laid out within Palm Court
'Twas sure to send staff scrambling – just one of many ways
For this was hotel Waldorf, and these were its 'salad days'.

The waves of heat even reflected off the black hull of the RMS *Orotava*, washing over the Tikari boarding party and flowing out and over the port of Colombo. It was just that sort of day.

Elsie scanned the breadth of the ship, noting the odd front and rear masts that seemed to contrast aesthetically and technologically with the central pairing of funnels.

"It won't be this warm when we arrive in London, will it, darling?" Elsie inquired.

Raji showed their tickets at the start of the gangway and did not reply until they were halfway across.

"June-July is a great time for weather in Britain, but the British think that 70 degrees is an intolerable heatwave," Raji said as he turned back and hesitated, causing the line of boarding passengers to bottleneck behind. "That is, until they come to India! Then they learn what hot really is!" he added, as Elsie prodded him to move forward.

They shuffled on and were soon ushered to their first class cabin amidships. Raji always insisted on the best cabin available, but was not particularly impressed with his travel quarters. "Is this the best JG could arrange?" he exclaimed. "He should have booked us on a better vessel!"

Raji was very rarely critical of his great friend, but Elsie could not let the moment pass unremarked. "Oh, don't tell me, Wakefield has made an error!" she sighed in feigned shock.

The eight-person Tikari party was spread around five near-neighbouring cabins, with JG and Grace occupying two of the few 126 cabins that were singles. Abu and Abid shared a twin room, as did twins Siri and Lala.

The first few days passed with card games and, for Elsie, reading. For the first time, she was introduced to and fascinated by the writings of the Bengali, Rabindranath Tagore, and amused by Raji's stumbling attempts to read his poetry.

"He is a Brahmin and an Indian nationalist!" exclaimed Raji, and she encouraged him to read on, though he was clearly more comfortable with a steering wheel or gun in hand, than a text.

By the time the *Orotava*, under the command of Captain Jenks, had glided into the Suez Canal, all on board were well used to the repetitive nature of on-board life.

It was on that very evening, as the sands spread into the distance, both to starboard and port, that Elsie noticed the musicians who normally accompanied diners in the first class dining room, were absent.

It started as a daring thought that quickly grew to an unstoppable urge.

"Waiter!" she called, signalling to the young man and making eye contact.

"Yes, Your Highness?" he asked, bowing reverently to her as he approached.

"The musicians, are they not playing tonight?"

"Your Highness," he whispered, leaning in as close as he dared. "A few have come down with a stomach bug, and they will not be making an appearance."

"Thank you!" Elsie said, as she pressed her knife down firmly on the table and rose to her feet.

"Where are you going, Elsie?" asked Raji. It was a wonder that she responded, as she was almost in a trace-like state.

"I shall be back shortly," was all she said, as she drifted away to the open floor space normally occupied by the musicians and their instruments.

She took a deep breath and turned to face her 'audience', who were almost all focussed on their food. "Ladies and gentlemen! Can I please have your attention! Unfortunately, our musicians cannot play tonight, so my husband has suggested I should sing a song instead. Being a woman who cannot resist the urgings of any man, I will therefore perform 'The Animated Toy'.

With that she twirled a couple of times, just to ensure that everyone was watching, then began.

A few minutes later, she bowed as all her audience rose to their feet applauding. Everybody, that is except one gentleman, who had strode to the exit door. It was Wakefield, and he had seen and heard enough.

Having ignored him, Elsie basked in the adulation. She had missed the stage and the spotlight, but now, if only momentarily, she was back.

* * *

The London summer shone with all its subdued brilliance as the group was driven to their accommodation at The Waldorf Hotel at Aldwych.

Elsie was like an inquisitive child, looking left and right excitedly and catching glimpses of places she had only heard about, or at best seen in photographs in the newspapers.

The multi-storey and impressive Waldorf towered above them as they alighted, but Elsie was most delighted to see that there were theatres, The Waldorf Theatre and The Aldwych Theatre, flanking the hotel.

"That is why I told JG we should be booked in here!" Raji admitted proudly. "This area of the West End is the heart of theatre land!"

From that moment, Elsie felt certain that she was going to love her salad days at The Waldorf.

After settling in to their luxury suite, that included a balcony and floor area for occasional orchestral performances, Elsie headed down to the concierge in a bid to have a look around the empire's capital.

Lala and Siri had been expected to join Elsie, as it was their first time in London too, but Raji made it clear that he was looking forward to enjoying a session of 'sensual manipulation'.

Her desire to see more of iconic London could only be satiated by a guided tour, and, according to the concierge, the senior driver of The Waldorf, Charles, was just the man for the job.

And so it was, burdened only by the comforting presence of Abu in the back seat (who was separated from the pair in the front by a glass window), that Charles and Elsie set off on a short tour of London in a dark green Talbot Landaulette, with 'The Waldorf Hotel' emblazoned on its side.

Heading first west, they passed the grand and curving façade of the Gaiety Theatre, which somehow Elsie had not recognised as they had arrived. Realising that she could see the famed Gaiety Girls almost on her doorstep, Elsie was nearly beside herself with delight—though this would have been impossible given the Talbot's bucket front seats.

They drove on down the Strand and Elsie watched the wonder of Trafalgar Square open up before them. "You can see here above us is Lord Nelson on his column, with lions at the base, the pair of fountains and then in the background, The National Gallery and the church of St Martin's in the Fields!"

On down The Mall they pressed, overtaking horsedrawn vehicles of every description, including trolleybuses. They swept along St James' Park and soon the dominating presence of Buckingham Palace was in sight.

"Been the home of the Royal Family since the start of Queen Victoria's reign in 1837," Charles remarked, before adding: "Wonder if as royalty yourself, Your Highness, you will get to look inside?"

Elsie did not answer as she was fascinated by the scale and grandeur of it all. Calcutta's great buildings, monuments and maidans certainly whispered empire, but London shouted it.

They curved around and past the Palace of Westminster, with its Houses of Parliament, before Charles unnecessarily startled a couple of boys pushing carts with a series of horn blasts as they sailed over Westminster Bridge and turned left into South London.

Here, the traffic banked up around Waterloo Train Station and Abu sat up straight and tense as the atmosphere changed significantly. Gone was the business and toffee-nosed air north of the Thames, replaced by the gritty reality of factory life, fumes and the sight and sound of the working class.

When a malevolent miscreant thumped a panel of the Talbot, Charles knew it was time for drastic action. He forced the vehicle across traffic and through a series of zigzagging streets lined more by streetwalkers and their brothels, than anything more sophisticated. He apologised for even steering to the South Bank, but Elsie would hear none of it.

"There are two sides to the coin of life," she said, before

adding in a cockney accent: "I would be flippin' daft to ignore the underside, Charlie me boy, for it be far more interestin'!"

As the Talbot turned north on to Tower Bridge, leaving South London behind, Abu's loud sigh of relief could be heard from the front seats.

"If you look ahead, Your Highness, you will shortly see the Tower of London, which is around 800 years old. It has seen a lot of history!"

"As well as a few beheadings, if I recall my history correctly," Elsie added.

"That too, but it is well worth a walk around, if you have the time later."

Swinging left and eventually back to the Strand and then Aldwych, Elsie was returned to The Waldorf, much appreciative of the guided tour.

As she passed reception, she was told the rest of the Tikari party was having drinks in the hotel's already famous Palm Court.

Raji had an orange juice ready, though Elsie teased him that she would have preferred a Rooh Afza.

"No chance of that! We are probably the only things Indian in London!" Raji said. "Did you enjoy the tour?"

"I now realise," said Elsie, "why the English consider themselves superior to all others! I cannot accept it, but I can understand how they might think so, given the grandeur of the north bank of the Thames."

"This place, Palm Court, was pretty grand in January this year, according to the waiter," Raji mumbled, as he devoured yet another cucumber sandwich. "They had a champagne reception for the hotel's opening."

Elsie took a few moments to soak in the atmosphere around her: green walls and white-framed arched windows with palms placed at every opportunity, to add a relaxed feel. "It is very, very nice! I must send Emma a postcard of the court, if they have one!" she added, rising and gliding so gracefully to the reception desk, that its attendant was momentarily entranced.

A minute later, she was back with a postcard of Palm Court, and writing to Emma:

Dearest Em,

London is so much bigger, dirtier, grander and full of possibility than I could ever have imagined. Raji says that the 8 of us will be based here at this establishment till near December, so please write to me care of The Waldorf Hotel. I am sitting in this beautiful Palm Court as I write!

Lots of Love,
El XOXOXO

"Before I forget to mention it, darling, tonight we are going to see a musical called *Havana* at the Gaiety Theatre," said Raji, as his fourth cucumber sandwich headed inexorably for his stomach.

"Oh, dearest! That is so kind of you to think of me!"

"Naturally, I always do, but I cannot claim credit. Blame Miss Knighton! She has a way of knowing just what everybody likes …" Raji's voice trailed off as he reminisced about their most recent sexual tryst.

"Grace, that is so thoughtful of you!"

"I have been working on a packed series of theatrical experiences starting with tonight," Grace announced, checking her notes. "Tomorrow there is the Theatrical Garden Party in the Botanic Gardens at Regent's Park—it raises money for the Actors' Orphanage Fund. Then on Wednesday, there is the final vocal performance of the Swedish Svadstrom Sisters at the Aeolian Hall at 3.15 pm. Raji will love that too, followed by something we must not miss …"

Grace's voice drifted into a distant hum as Elsie gazed around Palm Court, lost in the magic and convenience of it all, and the hope that one day, she too might be starring on the London stage.

Chapter 49

Of Ghostly Rolling Royces

I closed my eyes in Derby, and I dreamt that I was in
The swishest style of motor, made of silver, not of tin
Yet open eyes did find that, my deceitful Midlands host
Had stitched me up within a wreck, and not a Silver Ghost.

Raji's old friend and publisher of *Car Illustrated*, Lord Montagu
of Beaulieu, was going to open the new Rolls-Royce factory in
the Midlands city of Derby, on Thursday 9 July 1908. He most
kindly organised a late invitation.

The problem was arranging accommodation and train travel.
JG had huddled over information passed on by the reception
desk, including the railway timetable, in The Waldorf Hotel's
lounge. It was Tuesday afternoon, but he had struggled to put
together their last-minute itinerary.

The best hotels were already booked out, so he had no option
but to settle for something more modest.

Wednesday the 8th dawned to a cloudy and grey sky, with
the portent of changing scenery.

By the time the motor cabs filled with Tikari travellers, armed
with three days worth of clothing, had arrived outside the
grand St Pancras Station, the showers had made their presence
felt.

Just as everywhere else they had gone in London, people
stopped and stared at this bevy of sari-wearing, jewellery
bedecked, exotic beauties, accompanied by dark-skinned
gentlemen in exquisitely tailored suits. JG may have felt
ordinary by comparison, but Elsie simply loved the attention.

Scurrying deep under the station's protective cover, they
joined the milieu searching the boards for the right platform
that would send them north into the very centre of the realm.
The 10.06 am for Derby was impatient to depart.

The first class carriage of the red Midland Railway train soon
had them clickety-clacking through a mix of patchwork quilt
countryside and quaint villages, as well as the brick buildings,
steel structures, smoke stacks and rail yards that were a less

than attractive testament to the industrial age.

Elsie made sure she had a window seat, soaking it all in like an excited child on her first visit to a sideshow. After their timetabled 11.41 am departure from the train's Kettering stop, Raji signalled to all that they should soon head to the dining carriage for an early lunch.

Shortly after, the group was luxuriating in its high-backed wooden seats with plush green upholstery. Needless to say, the food provided did not match the quality of the surroundings, but this was something, Elsie thought, she was going to have to get used to when travelling.

Alighting at Derby, they waited under cover, for the showers had travelled north too. They had been assured that motor cabs would be there soon, but after the second passing of the circuit tram, which attracted every other waiting visitor, Raji was becoming incredibly irritated. He was used to buying his way out of a fix, but there seemed no opportunity here.

Naturally, when one motor cab finally appeared, it was Raji who spotted it first, focussing on it like he would a prize Bengal tiger after an otherwise fruitless day's hunting. Ordering Abid Hussain and JG to wait with the remaining girls for subsequent motor cabs, he besieged the approaching vehicle before it had even stopped. This failed to impress the driver, who still had to be paid by the passengers he was delivering.

A few choice words were exchanged between the two, with the driver even demanding that Raji show him that he had enough money to pay for the journey.

At this point, Elsie stepped in, complimenting the driver on his (ordinary) vehicle and (questionable) attire. Then, when she moved in to sit beside him in the front seat, after firmly directing Raji into the back, the drive across the River Derwent and through the cathedral precinct of Derby proceeded in mutual silence.

When the motor cab pulled up in front of The Old Bell Hotel in Sadler Gate, Elsie asked if they could be picked up promptly at 9.30 am on Friday, in time to meet the 9.57 am train back south to London.

The driver looked fleetingly at Elsie before turning around to address his comment slowly and deliberately at Raji: "You may not need to be picked up—didn't you know The Old Bell is haunted?"

"Rubbish! What utter rubbish!" cried Raji, hurling more money than necessary at the driver. Abu unloaded the luggage and they stood on the roadside looking up at The Old Bell, as the motor cab disappeared, no doubt back to the station to get the others.

"What has JG done?" Raji sighed, as they studied the multi-storey but aged Tudor-style edifice before them.

The clanking bell on the back of the doorframe announced their entrance into a world little changed from its construction in the 1600s. After the size and opulence of The Waldorf, the facilities here were coffin-like by comparison.

The three of them waited downstairs in the bar, a room with heavy wooden furniture, old beams crisscrossing the ceiling and a pair of circular light-holders that looked as though they had not been modified since the Middle Ages.

That night, none of the group slept well, but Elsie and Raji even less so, as Grace fled her room for theirs in fright, after repeated shuffling sounds across her floorboards. A little reluctantly, they had taken her in to their own cramped bed.

By the time Elsie and Raji made it to the site of the new Rolls-Royce factory in Nightingale Road the next morning, each was feeling and looking the worse for wear.

A large and a small tent had been set up together, next to the factory wall, and a couple had just walked in through a gateway, so Raji followed with Elsie in tow.

"Eh! You! Darkie!" yelled an attendant. "No entry wivout an invitation!" he said as he pushed Raji back.

"Take your hands off me, you fool!" Raji retorted, as the commotion brought men running from inside.

"Tikari!" one stylish man in his forties called out. "He is fine! He is my guest! Oh, and so is the lady with him!" he said, obviously taken by Elsie, despite her sleepless night.

"Monty! Thank goodness! That oaf was about to have me thrown out! Elsie, this is my great old friend and publisher of *Car Illustrated*, Lord Montagu! Monty, this is my wife!"

Lord Montagu smiled, dipped his head and reached out for Elsie's hand and kissed it with such style and care that she barely felt his moustache brush her skin.

"Come through! I want you to meet Claude Johnson, the Commercial Managing Director of Rolls-Royce … Claude! I have a couple you just must meet!"

Elsie was fascinated as yet another suited and distinguished-looking gentleman in his forties with a moustache, approached.

"Claude! This is the Maharaja of Tikari, and his beautiful wife, Elsie!" The way Monty described her, not just the words themselves but the flow and intonation of his expressive voice, showed Elsie he really meant it.

I like this man, she thought. *He has great style and manners! Yes, I really like this man!*

"I am most honoured to have Your Highnesses with us. Do you have a Rolls-Royce yet, Your Highness?"

"Not as yet, Mr Johnson, but …" Raji started, before Monty interrupted: "Tikari has one of the largest collections of motorised vehicles, perhaps only Andrew Carnegie has more!"

"Well then, Your Highness, you must have a Rolls-Royce Silver Ghost. We are justifiably calling it 'The Best Car in The World!' Please help yourself to champagne from the table in the small tent, then take a look at the beauty over there!"

Raji glanced only momentarily at the table covered with champagne bottles, cakes and sandwiches, for his eyes had glimpsed something he had never seen beyond the odd newspaper photograph.

For a while he was speechless as he walked around the giant, glistening silver machine with emerald green leather seats: the special display Silver Ghost. Elsie could tell what he was thinking, so hugged him. "Oh, it is just magnificent … simply magnificent!' he sighed. Elsie too was enraptured.

However, there was another car in the room that caught Raji's eye. It had fewer admirers but a signboard that said *Silver Rogue 70 hp*.

"70 horsepower!" exclaimed Raji. "The Silver Ghost is only 40/50, is it not, Mr Johnson?"

"Yes, Your Highness, the *Silver Rogue* is a special car that Eric Platford, our chief tester, drove to victory in this year's International Touring Car Trial over 2,000 miles."

Raji looked from one car to the other, then back again. Elsie much preferred the Silver Ghost. While they both carried the red, interlocked capital 'R' of Rolls-Royce on the top of the front of the radiator, she could tell that Raji's love of speed and power was swaying him the other way.

Eventually, they drifted into the factory proper, where chairs had been set up for the seventy guests in front of a table of dignitaries. A large silver trophy sat on the table.

"It is the Dewar Trophy," whispered Raji. "It is awarded annually by the Royal Automobile Club for meritorious performance by a motor vehicle. Rolls-Royce won it last year for the 40/50 …"

Raji was going to say more, but went silent as Lord Montagu stood for a few moments, waiting for the chatter to die, then spoke:

> Welcome to you all, Your Highnesses, the Honourable Lord Mayor of Derby, the builder Andrew Handyside, dear friends, fellow drivers, journalists and purveyors of all that is great in our motoring world! … Those categories were not mutually exclusive, by the way!

A ripple of laughter flowed through the audience.

> Thanks to the mechanical genius of Henry Royce, that most skilled of drivers, Charles Rolls, and that most astute man of business, Claude Johnson, we now have the greatest of all British cars, the Rolls-Royce Silver Ghost! In fact I am proud to call it the very finest car in the world—and equally proud to tell you that I have just ordered one myself!

This was greeted by acclaim.

> This magnificent modern factory will be constructing and assembling the chassis for this masterpiece for years to come. I am told that what we see today is but a small part of what will be in evidence in the years ahead, as neighbouring land has been made available for expansion. It is with great pleasure, that I now declare this, the very first stage of Rolls-Royce's Derby Motor Works, open! Drive safely and drive often!

After much applause, Johnson invited everyone to go on a tour of the factory, starting with the foundry where the engine parts were cast. Then it was back into the main building, to see how the car parts moved along lengthy lines, sometimes via pulleys along steel beams, with each specialised location adding towards the finished product.

The large, single-storey building had significant glass roofing, allowing plenty of light—even on an overcast day—to splash down on a shining line of Rolls-Royce Silver Ghost chassis.

"As you can see, these are finished chassis with the Rolls-Royce radiators and our mark, all ready for the coachbuilder to add the body, according to each customer's desire," Johnson explained. "If, for example, Your Highness wished to have a raised shooting seat for a tiger hunt, Barker in London, who does most of our bodywork jobs, could oblige. However, every customer knows he gets a genuine Rolls-Royce engine and chassis."

The party moved on to the repair garage, before ending back at the refreshment table, where Johnson introduced Raji and Elsie to Charles Rolls and Henry Royce, once he could prise them away from the journalists.

Raji soon excused himself, as he wished to talk to Lord Montagu, for he had a burning desire to know more about Andrew Carnegie's fleet of vehicles.

"I was up at Skibo Castle just over two months ago, Tikari. Carnegie let me drive as many of his cars as I liked. It was truly, great fun!"

"This Skibo Castle, Monty, where is it?"

"In the Highlands of Scotland. Why, do you want to go there?" Monty asked, though just looking at the dreamy-eyed young maharaja, he knew the answer. He thought for a few moments, then added: "Look, I'll telegram Carnegie and say you are a great friend of mine. He is an affable chap who loves his cars and his golf, so I am sure you will get along famously— and I am certain he will love to meet Elsie! I will let you know the result via a message to The Waldorf."

"Monty, that is very kind of you, but I have never played golf and we have no transportation!"

"The golf, well you can practise at St Andrews on the way

up, but the transportation ..." Monty immediately signalled for Johnson's attention, which was difficult as he was focussed on explaining to Elsie the differences between the Silver Ghost and the previous models. "Claude! When you have a moment, please!"

Johnson wandered over with Elsie in tow. "You got another sale for me, Lord Montagu?" he asked, only marginally in jest.

"Perhaps I might, though maybe not immediately ... Tikari wishes to borrow a car ..."

"Two cars," corrected Raji. "We have a travelling party of eight."

"Yes, two cars for a return trip to see Andrew Carnegie in Scotland!"

"Two Silver Ghosts please, Mr Johnson!" Elsie added, with an irresistible smile.

"Well I ..." started Johnson.

"If you do, I will guarantee I will buy a Rolls-Royce by year's end," promised Raji. "The long drive north and back will give me a good idea of just what I should purchase."

"I suppose you can, though when will you need them?"

"Probably in a few weeks," Monty cut in. "I must first make contact with Carnegie and check things at his end are okay, then I can let you know, Claude, when they need be delivered to Tikari at The Waldorf Hotel in London."

Johnson pulled a notepad from his pocket and started scribbling. "They would probably be test cars used by Barker in London, is that all right?"

"Fine! Absolutely no problem! I am used to driving fast over the roughest of terrain and in bad conditions. After a short while, the newest of vehicles will be well used!"

And so it was that the deal was done, though Elsie had her doubts about whether the next car in the Tikari stable was to be a Rolls-Royce Silver Ghost. For, as they were about to leave, Elsie had to drag Raji away from the side of the unique and name-plated *Silver Rogue*.

Claude Johnson had offered to drive them back to their hotel in the Silver Ghost display car. As they nestled into the luxurious green leather back seats, Johnson asked what Derby hotel they were staying at.

"The Old Bell Hotel. Do you know it?"

"Know The Old Bell?" he replied, most surprised as he was expecting something much more salubrious. "Everyone in Derby knows The Old Bell. It is the most haunted building in the Midlands! Room 6, or so I am told, is the worst!"

Elsie reached slowly into her purse to check her key, but she was all but certain what was written upon it.

"So, what did happen in Room 6, Mr Johnson?" Elsie asked hesitatingly.

The Rolls rolled on, taking corner after corner smoothly before its driver replied: "A pregnant maid hung herself from the beam in the room, so I am told, after hearing of the child's father's death in battle … mind you, it happened a few hundred years ago … though some say, her ghost is still around!"

The Silver Ghost glided down Sadler Gate and eased to a halt in front of The Old Bell. Mr Johnson was congratulated once again on the magnificence of the new works, thanked for the lift back, and reminded of the promised purchase by year's end.

As the Silver Ghost drifted off, Raji and Elsie looked at each other, wary of what the night might have in store …

Siri and Lala gripped each other tightly like Siamese twins as the floorboards creaked around their bed; Abid Hussain fled to the seeming safety of the communal toilet after an eerie light had drifted around his room; JG and Abu had separately fled downstairs to the old dining room, but soon headed back up as plates rattled and cupboard doors opened and shut; Grace was quick to join Raji and Elsie in their bed, but the beam straddling the ceiling above in Room 6 soon creaked and groaned as if it was under the weight of a hanging corpse.

The 9.57 am train from Derby to St Pancras, London on the morning of Friday 10 July 1908, was greeted like a long-missed friend.

They would absolutely, definitely, never stay at The Old Bell again.

Chapter 50

To the Games of the Fourth Olympiad

If ever you have wanted, to see the very best
Race faster than a leopard — well, overtake the rest
The Olympiad is the event and Shepherd's Bush the place
With Franco-British Exhib spread 'round the Stadium space.

The Sunday high tea of 12 July 1908, in Palm Court, was making its delightfully lavish progression from mini cream buns to chocolate macaroons, when a doorman ushered in a young lad carrying a sealed envelope.

"For the Maharaja of Tikari, special delivery!" he had said at The Waldorf's reception, before being directed to his target in Palm Court. During a low and lengthy bow, befitting of greeting the highest of rulers, the youngster raised his right arm that held the envelope, knocking a macaroon out of Raji's grasp.

Elsie's spluttered laugh, halfway into the devouring of a cream bun, sent its contents spraying across the round table.

When decorum was restored, Raji read the contents of the envelope as Elsie fussed over the young lad, even brushing his hair with her hand and embarrassing him further.

"Monty has confirmed that we are all welcome at Skibo Castle for three nights from Tuesday 21 July. And, he assures us that Andrew Carnegie and his cars will make us most welcome! Wonderful!"

But there was more in the envelope: a card and a note. "As he is a member of the Council of British Olympic Associations, Monty has sent me an invitation to visit the royal box as part of the official party and attend festivities at the opening of the Fourth Olympiad, on Monday 13 July. Oh, that is tomorrow!"

The young lad was given a handful of shillings by Elsie and told to pass their sincere gratitude to Lord Montagu.

As he departed, Elsie was wondering what she should wear to meet royalty. "Should I wear the emerald necklace, or even the banded tiara?" she mused out loud.

"Elsie!" Raji said, standing and grabbing her by the hand.

"There is something I must tell you!" As they wandered out of Palm Court and into the lounge, Elsie wondered what on earth it could be.

"We have not faced this situation before, but on formal and public royal and vice-regal occasions, the English do not allow us to be seen together."

"What?" was all Elsie could initially say.

"They do not agree with marriage across racial lines, dark with white for example, so we cannot be together on such occasions!"

"Oh, the bastards!"

"I agree, but if we were together on such formal occasions, that might signal approval on their part."

"In that case, I do not desire to meet the King or Queen, though you may do whatever you feel is right! If I go, I am happy to stand with the common folk!"

After an in-depth discussion and advice from The Waldorf Hotel's concierge, it was decided that the journey to the stadium at Shepherd's Bush for the Fourth Olympiad's opening ceremony, should incorporate a stroll through what they were assured was the highlight of modern-day London: the 1908 Franco-British Exhibition.

As they were located side by side, there would be no need to take anything but the same underground train.

Even while lying in bed on the morning of Monday 13 July, the rain sounded heavy and most determined to hang around till well after breakfast.

By 10.30 am, the downpour had eased to the occasional shower as the group of eight made its way into the Strand's underground train station. This was a new and exciting experience for Elsie and the other three young ladies, though the men had all ventured in to this Orphean world before.

An exhilarating rush of air foretold an imminent arrival, though they were only to be on this line till the next stop, at Holborn. Then it was a hundred yard scurry up and across and then down to the British Museum Station, a stop on the Central London Railway Line.

Racing through the tunnels of brick and stone, Elsie could now understand why the service was nicknamed the 'Tube'.

Nine stops later, they reached Shepherd's Bush, but they had been told the closest to their destination was in fact Wood Lane, the last on the Central Line.

It was no surprise when the carriages emptied in unison and they journeyed in a sea of straw-boatered men and parasol-carrying women to the exhibition entrance gates. Entry was one shilling, which gave access from 11 am to 11 pm.

Raji purchased four copies of the exhibition map and guide. It was only while looking at the map that they began to get a feel for the size and complexity of the Franco-British Exhibition. One hundred and twenty buildings, and twenty pavilions, did sound a lot, but the scale of what greeted them when they passed through the ornate two-towered entrance gate was mind-blowing.

The huge and majestic Court of Honour spread out before them: a large complex of white buildings and domed towers in Indian style, that would have looked quite at home in Rajasthan, in India's north-west.

In the centre of it all was a bridge that crossed a large pond, upon which boats cruised, up and down. Some even ventured up canals that flowed onward, out of the Court of Honour and in to the broader world of the exhibition.

Siri was quick to suggest they take a boat, and given that the dirt paths were muddy from the morning rain, the others quickly concurred. All eight fitted in a motored boat that was steered by a driver seated on a chair at the back, meandering them north and east towards the Fine Art Palace.

As they left the Indian-inspired Court of Honour, the sheer scale of the exhibition grounds became apparent: spectacular structures spread side by side, classical creation after domed oriental edifice, and all in a wedding-cake whiteness that sprouted from alongside symmetrical and intricate garden surrounds, as far as the eye could see—and much further.

The Fine Art Palace was just south of the stadium where they would watch the Olympic Games in the afternoon. The palace's symmetrical design and grand central entrance hinted at traditional art in a formal layout. They were not to be disappointed.

Elsie was happy to pay for the 220-page art catalogue, as

it numbered every piece, giving also its name, creator and current owner. French art was displayed to the left and British to the right half of the building. As they had entered through the left entry arch, they found themselves at the start of French sculpture.

Elsie took some pleasure explaining to the others what the labels on the pieces meant, though this was severely stretching her schoolgirl French. "Here is a marble piece by Henri Levasseur called *L'aube* which means 'Dawn'. Then over here is a plaster statue by Mathurin Moreau called *Le Sommeil*, 'Sleep', which is very lovely, don't you think?"

It quickly became obvious that for the others to maintain any interest, refuge had to be taken in the British half. They headed right and into the first of three linked galleries titled 'Oil Paintings by Deceased Artists'.

Here Gainsboroughs, Turners, Constables and Reynolds draped the walls and Elsie clothed herself in their inspiration and familiarity much as one welcomes a favourite dressing gown on a chilly evening.

"Now there is a fine picture!" Raji exhorted, as he spotted Sir Edwin Landseer's 1851 masterpiece *The Monarch of the Glen*. A large stag with a fine array of antlers stood proudly with the craggy and clouded peaks of Scotland as a backdrop. "How I would love to shoot one of those at Skibo Castle!"

"Turner's paintings always have this moody, depressing feel. I cannot say I like them," Elsie said, quickly changing the subject as she moved him on.

Siri and Lala were studying the exhibition map and paying so little attention to the art around them that Elsie had everyone group around a map. "Siri and Lala, where would you like to go? Perhaps we can all meet up at number 37 on your map, the Grand Restaurant, at 12.30 pm for lunch. It is just north of the Elite Gardens."

"We would love to try The Canadian Tobbogan, The Spiral …" started Lala.

"And the The Spider's Web and of course the Flip Flap," added Siri.

"Well, then go with Abid Hussain and JG, and we shall meet you for lunch at 12.30!"

"Thank you, Your Highness!" the girls cried in unison as they scurried out with the two gentlemen in hot pursuit.

"Thank God JG has gone!" Elsie sighed, after the departing foursome had left the gallery. "I just find him and fine art a most inappropriate combination!"

Grace tried to hide her smirk and made a mental note to concentrate on each and every artistic work in her path.

"*The Blue Boy!* Gainsborough's famous *Blue Boy!*" Elsie exclaimed in delight, as an image she had only seen in books materialised as exhibit number 69.

Eventually, they moved north into the 'Oil Paintings by Living Artists' area. Elsie noted that Raji was starting to look at the map as well. Then she gasped in admiration as she came to a halt in front of a life-size painting she had never seen before.

"Isn't it beautiful, darling! Look at the intricate inlay in the furniture; the detail of the oriental carpet; the magnificent column in the background; the delicate folds in her nightdress; and her lovely feet on that exquisite, ornamental marble floor! ... number 161 ..." she said scanning the catalogue.

"And, she is beautiful!" Raji conceded.

"It is by William Holman Hunt and called *Isabella and the Pot of Basil,* painted in 1868 ... oh dear, I just remembered Keats' poem was Isabella, or the Pot of Basil ... so that means inside the pot Isabella is caressing, is the head of her murdered lover Lorenzo!" This certainly added an extra dimension to what was before them, but did not make the painting any less arresting, Elsie concluded.

When Raji began studying his exhibition map for a second time, Elsie had to stop. "I can see, Raji, that you want to be elsewhere!"

"I have noticed there is the Bisley Rifle Range. Perhaps Abu and I could ..."

"Go on! We will meet you for lunch! Grace will stay with me and we shall be fine, won't we dear? We will pretend we are lovers, just as the British aristocracy women have their female lovers, as you have told us, Raji. Now, come on Grace darling! Those philistines must leave us, but we have more beautiful art to view!"

After a three-shilling-a-head lunch at the Grand Restaurant,

Elsie hauled Grace, Raji and Abu off to number 91, the Australian pavilion, just as the band of His Majesty's Irish Guards began playing from the bandstand in the Elite Gardens.

The plan was for the Tikari group to meet at the main entrance to the stadium on the west side at 2.45 pm, to watch the official opening of the Games of the Fourth Olympiad.

Everyone was still buzzing with excitement from what they had seen and done: the food, wood, gold, fine art, sheep and a sleepy koala at the Australian pavilion; the Irish and Senegalese villages; but most of all the Flip Flap, which Siri and Lala had experienced together and could not stop talking about.

As they filed in to sit under the left edge of the stadium's western grandstand, Elsie could see the royal box area filling with royalty from around Europe. She had also spotted Raji, who was seated two rows behind the royal enclosure, in animated conversation with Monty.

Just before 3.30 pm, the Royal Standard was raised, everyone stood, and King Edward VII and Queen Alexandra, accompanied by Baron Pierre de Coubertin entered the royal box. The national anthem God Save The King was sung to the music of the Grenadier Guards Band.

Athletes arranged in their national teams, emerged from the tunnels at both ends of the stadium, marching behind their country's flag bearer. They then massed behind the swimming and diving pool, which ran parallel to the western grandstand, and just inside the concrete track.

Then in words that Raji could hear, but Elsie could only guess at, the King declared the Games of the Fourth Olympiad, open. The athletes marched around the pool and in front of the royal box, as their flag bearer dipped their flag to British royalty—all expect the Americans.

A murmur of shock and dismay ran through the crowd, though Elsie giggled. Raji distinctly heard the King react in anger, with the words: "American barbarians!"

As gymnastics by Norwegian, Danish and Swedish athletes and a high diving display gave the crowd alternative attractions, tandem cycling and 1,500 metre running races were held.

Just before the Tikari group departed to take in more of the Exhibition, they witnessed Tom Tartakover, representing

Australasia, win his 400-metre heat in the pool in a walkover, though he still had to swim the distance to the ironic cheers of the crowd.

Re-entering the Franco-British Exhibition, the group found some of the last empty seats among the 3,000 in the open-air Indian Arena, with only minutes to spare, before the 5 pm performance of Our Indian Empire.

Acrobats, snake charmers, jugglers, wrestlers, dancers, singers and musicians appeared in an Indian extravaganza that was topped off by a tiger hunt, in which a dozen live elephants slid down slides into a pool. The audience loved it.

With five more hours of the exhibition's day still to be enjoyed, the party moved out into what was supposed to be a slowly gathering gloom that was transformed with the flick of a switch into an illuminated fairyland.

Every boat, every building, every bandstand, every ride, every walkway and every corner glowed with coloured lights that only added to the excitement of the enveloping evening.

The plan had been to have the four-shilling-a-head dinner at the Grand Restaurant at 7 pm, but the party had queued at the most popular attraction of all, the fabulous Flip Flap.

At the appointed hour, they were just nearing the front of the queue. They had watched in awe as fifty persons had clambered into a caged platform, to be lifted in an arc up 200 feet in the air. There they had halted for a while within shouting distance of another platform performing a mirrored passage, before completing a semi-circular arc back to earth on the other side.

When it came to Elsie's turn, she clung tightly to Raji, who was far more excited than scared. When they returned to earth, Raji was emphatic: "I now know what it might be like to fly and how the Wright Brothers felt! One day, I want to fly like the Wright Brothers!" Elsie should have known Raji better, than to dismiss the possibility.

The delayed dinner was wolfed down with great speed, as everyone could not wait to get back out into the magic of the night. There was a whole range of experiences yet to be had, such as the Mountain Scenic Railway (in which the tram cars reached speeds of up to fifty miles an hour), a walk through a model of Old London Town, the latest animated cinematographic displays, and opportunity for Raji to ogle the topless beauties in the Senegalese village.

At 9 pm, fireworks exploded across the skyline, though the party was still enthralled by the time the 11 pm closing was announced.

For a day that had started out with rain and cool showers, Elsie could not have wished for a more fantastic transformation—and she had postcards of the Franco-British Exhibition, to post to Emma and May Maxwell to prove it.

Chapter 51

The Royal & the Ancient

The ball did look up mournfully, as clubface it did turn
To shank the gutta-percha into Swilcan's watery burn
With the Royal & Ancient Golf Club, St Andrews has it all
Stroll in history on the Old Course—you'll feel proud to lose a ball.

The pair of Rolls-Royce Silver Ghosts made a spectacular and welcoming sight at the steps of The Waldorf Hotel.

Their initial target was St Andrews and its Old Course, next to the clubhouse known as the Royal & Ancient Golf Club of St Andrews. Here, Monty had said, they could gain the very best golf coaching available, from one of the greatest golfers of all time, Old Tom Morris.

However, that was all yet to come and a fair drive away. First, Raji had to pick between the two structurally identical Silver Ghosts from Barker, the coachbuilder. They were the same in every respect but for their paintwork and their leather seating.

The one with green upholstery had silver and dark green panels, while the other had burgundy seating with a silver and cream body. Elsie preferred the latter, but Raji, perhaps with memories of Derby, or with his fondness for emeralds, chose the green gem. In truth, both were marginally disappointed, as they had envisaged a wholly silver Silver Ghost, just like the one on display in Derby.

The cars had been custom-fitted with extra-long luggage trays at the back, ideal for the large trunks that a maharaja and his entourage inevitably transported. With help from hotel porters, they were strapped on tightly.

The eight members of the Tikari party were teamed up in Elsie's preferred combination: Raji driving with Elsie beside him, and Grace and Abu in the back; JG driving the second vehicle, with Abid Hussain as front-seat passenger and Siri and Lala in the back.

Armed with Monty's advice to buy extra petrol cans at signposted chemists if need be, they headed up the Great North Road in what felt like royal procession. It seemed that on every street and at every corner, people stopped to gawk in admiration at this pair of shining, and partly silver stallions.

They surged on, achieving their aim of reaching the old city of York before 3 pm. Having washed and had some afternoon tea inside the five-storey yellow-brick Royal York Hotel, they stretched their legs with a walk to the nearby York Minster, one of Europe's greatest and largest Gothic cathedrals.

The magnificent stone and arched pillars that had stood for over 600 years were a testament to the skill of craftsmen whose bones had long crumbled to dust. The space around, when standing in the nave, was awe-inspiring, while the stained-glass windows were as intricate and beautiful as any Elsie had seen.

The first stage of their journey north was only half done, for the next day's destination was Edinburgh in Scotland.

In England, the fields were most universally green, certainly greener than Australia's, though was it just Elsie's imagination, or were Scottish fields a richer green again?

As they drove in to the heart of the metropolis of Edinburgh, they all could see a darker, perhaps less washed stone than that common in their southern neighbour. It gave the city an initially cold, even depressing air, though it was not one shared by the nature and welcome of the Scots.

After settling in to the baronial splendour of their large North British Hotel suite, the Tikari party went for a stroll around the town centre and the Royal Mile. While they had to admit that understanding what everybody said in Scotland was not easy, Elsie was delighted at how welcome she was made to feel when stating she was Australian.

"They just hate the bloody English!" Raji whispered, but only after making sure JG was out of earshot first. He too had felt more comfortable here, as if the locals were quick to appreciate that at least, he was not one of 'them'.

With two nights in town, they took the advice of hotel reception and had a picnic lunch made to take with them on the walk along Princes Street, through the beautiful Princes Street Gardens (where they laid out a couple of picnic rugs and dined, on what locals assured them was an unusually fine day) and then meandered around and up and through the forbidding-looking Edinburgh Castle.

They then initially drove west, then turned north to the old city of Perth. There they visited the nearby Scone Abbey, the site of the crowning of Scottish kings for millennia, then turned south and east as they headed to St Andrews.

"Now this is an ancient town!" Raji exclaimed, as the Silver Ghost rattled over the cobblestones and past the fountain of St Andrews' Market Street.

Turning back south through the town, they found their way to Rusacks Hotel, near the Old Course. The hotel had been booked for the night, as both Raji and Elsie were keen to learn more about that great Scottish pastime of golf.

Their porter bade them step out on the balcony of their expansive suite. Spread out before them, like a crinkled rich green blanket, lay the most famous golfing links on the whole planet: St Andrews' Old Course.

"Over to your right, that large brown building with the clock face, is the Royal & Ancient Golf Club of St Andrews, an exclusive establishment, while away to our left and in front of us is the twisting Swilcan Burn, crossed by the old stone Swilcan Bridge. You'd do best to avoid the burn when you play!"

Raji and Elsie stood there for a few minutes taking in the beautiful scene, with golfers and their caddies moving about it like figures on a diorama.

"We had better go and try this game before lunch," Raji urged. "Mr Carnegie will expect us to be experts by the time we reach Skibo!"

Elsie immediately realised that she could not play golf in a sari, so borrowed European clothes from Grace.

With only Abu to accompany them, they headed, as suggested, to the starter's box.

Raji reached in to his pocket and pulled out a piece of paper upon which Monty had written a name. "My wife and I must have lessons from … Old Tom Morris!" he said, after reading the note.

"Nae, ye cannot!" came the definitive accented reply from the Scotsman seated inside the box.

"Now look here, I am the Maharaja of Tikari, and I will pay

well for the best coaching! Where is Old Tom?"

The starter stared silently at him for a few seconds, then turned and pointed to the south-east. "He is in yonder cathedral!"

Raji studied his watch, seeing that it was now 11.07 am. "When will he be back?"

The starter looked Raji up and down, then did the same to Elsie. "I expect ye won't be seein' 'im any time soon!"

"But he will be back for lunch, won't he?"

At this point, the starter stood solemnly and explained: "Old Tom Morris died a wee two months ago!"

"Oh, I am sorry, that makes things awkward!" Raji apologised.

"Perhaps Young Tom Morris could coach us then?" Elsie asked hopefully.

The starter had not resumed his seat, but continued in his mournful tone: "Ye can find Young Tom Morris in the cathedral too—he died in 1875! I will get Jock Richardson to give ye some lessons!" With that he opened a door at the back of the box and urged them to follow him.

Minutes later, they were on the practise ground being introduced to a game neither had ever tried before.

"We will start with the niblick as ye want to swing easy from the start. The longer hitting clubs ye can try later," Richardson advised, though Raji was confident, as he had always excelled at sport.

Raji grabbed the hickory-shafted, iron-headed club and jumped in next to the gutta-percha ball lying nearby and took an almighty swing, missing it completely, losing his balance and falling over, as Elsie laughed.

"Perhaps Ya Highness might like to try?" Richardson said, handing Elsie another niblick. "Make sure ya feet are steady on the ground, slowly take the club back while watching the ball, then smoothly through!"

Elsie had a few practise swings, trying to make sure she kept her balance. Then she settled in next to a ball, concentrating on it most seriously, then swung—back and through … with the ball travelling about forty yards, but as Richardson explained, the niblick was only for shorter iron shots.

Determined not to be outdone by a mere woman, wife or not,

Raji addressed a nearby ball with more concentration and less brute force than his first attempt, though it barely made more distance than Elsie's.

Over the next hour of tuition, they tried all the clubs, including the mashie iron and the wooden-headed bulger for driving. It was only near the end of the session that Elsie suggested Abu, who had been watching with more amusement than real interest, be given a swing.

The giant took hold of the longest hitting club, the bulger, then swung it with the ease and smoothness of a professional, sending the ball sailing into the distance. Everyone, even Richardson was astounded, but Abu said that was enough for him today, as he must have been lucky.

As it was nearly 12.30 pm and lunchtime, they finished with some putting practise on the practise green, before Richardson confirmed a 2 pm tee time with caddies on the Old Course.

Raji paid Richardson handsomely, so much so that he insisted he would caddie for Raji in the afternoon—for an extra fee, of course.

While strolling back to Rusacks Hotel, Raji admitted that the game was harder than it looked.

* * *

"Next on the teeing ground, the Maharaja and Maharani of Tikari!" the announcer called at 2 pm from the starter's box.

Raji was nervous, very nervous. A sizeable crowd had gathered to watch them tee off on the world's most famous golf course. This was certainly not the time to miss the ball completely. Raji stared down the fairway of the first hole, then focussed down on the ball. The bulger went back and then through with a firm 'thwacking' sound and the ball sailed forward a very good distance.

"Done it!" cried Raji triumphantly.

"Oh, bad luck Ya Highness, it has just gone a wee bit too far and rolled into the burn!" Richardson commented.

Elsie was certain she could not hit that far, but wanted to stay on the fairway. She still had a great deal to learn about the game, but already appreciated that being on the fairway was far safer than any other option. She swung conservatively but cleanly, getting a round of applause from the gallery. They were off, with the best available young caddie, Duncan Mackenzie, carrying Elsie's clubs.

Richardson fished Raji's tee shot out of the burn and told him he had to drop it. "Stand facing the hole and drop the ball back over your shoulder. That is the rule in the official Royal & Ancient Golf Club Rules of Golf!"

As Raji selected the niblick for his next shot, Richardson reminded him that it would be his third, as there was a one-shot penalty for having to fish it out of the burn.

Raji hit his third with some anger, but it sailed to the right and short of the green. "Ye should have used a mashie, Ya Highness!" Richardson counselled after the event.

"Why didn't you tell me that before I hit, Mr Richardson!" said an irritated Raji. So, from then on, Richardson made all the club selections, though this did little to assist Raji extricate himself from the five pot bunkers he visited in the round, only one of which he managed to escape in a single shot.

Then, there were the gorse bushes, which he encountered on the 2nd hole and impetuously tried to retrieve his ball. Scarred by the savage thorns, he vowed to let Richardson, who had donned a purpose-made arm-length leather glove, the honour of performing such a task, should the need arise again.

Elsie meanwhile, followed the advice of young Mr Mackenzie to the letter. She could not hit anywhere near as far as Raji, but used the grass driver, mashie and, when closer to the green, the spoon, with considerable skill for a beginner. However, putting on the large curving greens, proved a great challenge for the two novices.

As they stood on the teeing ground of the final hole, just recently renamed Tom Morris in honour of the late four-time Open Championship winner, course designer and St Andrews icon, Raji knew that barring a debacle, he should just finish ahead of Elsie.

While placing his ball on the tee, he heard some distant cheering from the direction of Rusacks Hotel. Elsie noticed the other five members of the Tikari party, standing on balconies and waving. Elsie waved back, but Raji was too focussed to reciprocate.

It was with much relief that he put his tee shot over the burn and up towards Granny Clark's Wynd, the public walking track that crossed the 18th and 1st.

Elsie was never going to hit that far, but at least managed to clear the burn and lie safely. They strolled across the ancient and small stone Swilcan Bridge and onto a stage setting befitting any play or opera finale. Swept up in the history and emotion of it all, Elsie reached the green in four and two-putted for a double-bogey.

Raji hit his second into the Valley of Sin just short of the green, chipped on and putted in for his very first par of the day. He was elated, especially when scores were added up and he found that his 117 had beaten Elsie by four strokes.

Before they carried away the clubs and balls, Richardson and Mackenzie were thanked profusely and paid accordingly. It is doubtful they had caddied a better rewarded round.

Raji, Elsie and Abu headed to the Royal & Ancient Golf Club itself for a drink, though the doorman refused them entry, insisting that it was 'members only'.

That night at dinner, they both reflected on their golfing experience, Raji freely acknowledging that the game was the most complex sport he had ever tried. Elsie admitted that she now understood, to a small degree, why her brother Walter found the game so addictive.

As it was still summer and light until late, Elsie suggested they take a short drive to the cathedral.

It was old, mostly in ruins and certainly not what they were expecting, but Elsie found what she was looking for, by a wall. At lunch she had asked Grace to go out and purchase four bunches of flowers. Together, they each placed one on the graves of first, Young Tom Morris and then his much-venerated father.

Raji and Elsie had encountered Old Tom Morris—though not quite as Lord Montagu had envisaged.

Chapter 52

Towards the Highlands

If you wander north you'll realise, that this world is what they say
From Edzell out to Dunnottar, Slains Castle, Cruden Bay
It is old, wild and historic — so it's easy to forget
You've bathed in Scottish beauty — though not in the Highlands yet.

The manager of Rusacks scratched his head as he scanned the map of Scotland.

"Nae, there is no short way across the Tay. Ye must go to Perth and then east. I recommend Edzell Castle, here, will take you about two hours in your fine motors, maybe forty minutes more to Dunnottar Castle, aye, ye must see that! Then Cruden Bay is up to an hour and a half further north. Has anyone read *Dracula*?"

"Oh yes!" said Elsie eagerly. "I read it on the boat from India!"

"Well, Bram Stoker, the author, stayed in Cruden Bay and his inspiration for Dracula's Castle was Slains Castle on that coastline."

"Raji! We must go there!"

Raji was doing the maths. "Two hours, plus half an hour in Edzell plus an hour to and in Dunnottar, then how far to Cruden Bay did you say?"

"Up to an hour and a half."

"That is five hours to Cruden Bay. To be there by lunchtime, we must leave at 7 am! How long would it take to get to Skibo Castle from Cruden Bay?"

"Do ye wanna go via the coast road? I think it is prettier!"

"Oh, yes please!" pleaded Elsie.

The manager measured out the distance using his fingers from the scale as he twisted them back and forwards along Scotland's north-east coast and into the Highlands. "I reckon 160 to 170 miles. Five, maybe six hours …"

"So we could be there by 8 pm if we left Cruden Bay by two!" noted Elsie, as Raji was still doing the mathematics.

"JG, telephone Skibo Castle. I have the number here. Say they can expect us by 9 pm tomorrow, though not for dinner!"

* * *

Driving through an old stone and pointed archway entrance to the small town of Edzell, Elsie began to wonder where this Edzell Castle was and just why they should be bothered.

After enquiring in the village, they took a left turn and shortly after, pulled up outside a caretaker's house, close to a small walled area with a red sandstone tower.

There was nobody in the caretaker's cottage, so they all walked towards the castle. As they did, the loud call of a peacock carried clearly across the site.

"Look! There he is!" cried Elsie, pointing to the large and beautiful creature resplendent in peacock blue that was strutting towards them. Within seconds, it had fanned its feathers out in a magnificent display of self-confidence and pride.

The Tikari party walked through what would once have been a gated entrance in a long wall. Ahead of them stood a four-storey high red sandstone tower in reasonable condition, though its neighbouring two-storey small palace was but a ruin.

"Is anybody there?' Elsie called a couple of times, before a man holding a trowel appeared in the small arched entry to the walled garden to their left.

"I am working in the garden, but you are all most welcome," he said, with little trace of any Scottish accent. "You may climb the tower if you wish, but apart from that, everything to see is down here in the walled garden."

They joined him and headed south, not knowing what to expect. To their great surprise, a beautiful and classically hedged layout presented itself in the middle, but what lay within the outlying walls was amazing.

"It is the only one of its type in Britain," the caretaker confirmed. "Earl Lindsay created the walled garden from 1604. He was a scholar and intellectual and wanted to display something of his knowledge in the walls."

The caretaker went on to explain that the east wall contained

434

stone panels featuring intricate reliefs of the seven planetary deities, including Venus and Jupiter; the south wall, seven liberal arts, such as geometry and astronomy; while the west wall displayed seven cardinal virtues, which included justice and charity.

Each of the carvings, the caretaker continued, was believed to have been done by highly skilled German stonemasons, however the money to complete the garden ran out and Earl Lindsay had to sell, becoming a broken man and dying six years after he started.

Elsie was particularly taken with the beauty and intelligence of the walled garden, so cornered Raji when they were at the top of the tower a short time later. They could see the caretaker on his knees, lovingly tending the garden. "Raji, we must give him something to help its upkeep, something significant!"

While the others headed towards the Silver Ghosts, Elsie quietly walked back into the garden and squatted by the caretaker. "Mind you don't get dirt on your beautiful Indian dress, my lady!" he cautioned, while continuing to work the flowerbed with his trowel.

"Sir, my husband and I would like to help you with the cost of maintaining this remarkable place."

"Ah, when you love something, money is not so important!" he retorted.

"Perhaps Earl Lindsay would not have agreed, sir. Here, take this," she said, handing over thirty pounds. He was speechless. "A man with a mind and heart like his should never be forgotten!" she said, as she rose and walked slowly out of the most beautiful and symbolic walled garden she had ever seen.

Soon, they were driving onward to Dunnottar Castle, near Stonehaven.

It would be hard to imagine a more spectacular sight than Dunnottar's setting, with the castle battlements and buildings crowding the peak of a small, almost island-like outcrop on the edge of the North Sea.

The manager of Rusacks had said that Cromwell had besieged the now ruined medieval fortress for eight long months, but the Crown Jewels of Scotland were kept from English hands.

As they walked towards the structure, they passed embedded

iron bases from Cromwell's cannons, still pointing at their target. Walking down a hill, they had to turn up a steep and thin ramp to reach the massive wooden doors and gatehouse that no Englishman was meant to breach.

The Tikari party spread out once inside, admiring the view north in particular, from the ramparts, and noting the date 1648 carved into the stone above the fireplace of the main residence.

As they aimed to be at Cruden Bay by lunch, they pressed on, merely stopping at a chemist in the grand city of Aberdeen to buy out its stock of two-gallon petrol cans for refilling the vehicles.

They made good progress, pulling up outside The Kilmarnock Arms Hotel in Cruden Bay at 12.21 pm, just in time for lunch. Elsie and Abu went inside to enquire about eating, but soon called the others in and they settled down to a hearty meal.

Discussion with the proprietor quickly turned to Bram Stoker and his novel *Dracula* and the nearby Slains Castle. The gentleman disappeared for a couple of minutes, before returning with a green visitors' book. There, in an entry dated '2 to 29 August 1894', Bram Stoker had written:

Mr and Mrs Bram Stoker
Noel Stoker
G Vaughan Hart, London

Second visit to Port Erroll. Delighted with everything and everybody and hope to come again to the Kilmarnock Arms.

"I remember them well!" said the proprietor proudly. "Mr Stoker was a nice man and Slains Castle was an inspiration in the writing of his book, which was published three years later."

After lunch they took the proprietor's advice and headed to the Cruden Bay Golf Course, which he had said was one of Old Tom Morris' very best designs. In the distance, beyond the snaking burns and fairways, they could see the ruins of Slains Castle. After each had taken turns to look through Raji's binoculars, they hit the coast road again, heading north and then west, through the spectacular seaside town of Cullen, with its seafarer's cottages hugging the harbour and the railway viaduct crossing the town and framing its western edge; then inland through the elegant stonework of Elgin, past the city of Inverness and deep into the Scottish Highlands near Dornoch.

Just after 8 pm on Tuesday 21 July 1908, they drew up in front of a sequence of four turretted and curved columns that were linked by black and gold steel gates: the entrance gates of Skibo Castle, home of the richest man in the world.

Chapter 53

Carnegie and Skibo

If near to ancient Dornoch, there's a knock upon your door
And a servant guides you downstairs, to a setting you adore
You're in grand Skibo Castle, and can hear the bagpipes play
Just relax and let the millionaire, Carnegie host your day.

The large central gates opened and a guard in tartan approached Raji and saluted.

"The Maharaja of Tikari," Raji said, introducing himself quickly to avoid any embarrassment.

"Of course, Your Highness, Mr Carnegie is expecting you. Please follow me."

With this, the guard stepped into a red 14/16 hp Argyll with 'Skibo Castle' emblazoned on its sides, and drove slowly up the drive, lined by tall and ancient trees.

The Rolls-Royces inched forward, their occupants marvelling at the estate's grounds. Soon the magnificent light honey-coloured stone of Skibo Castle was in sight. Curving up and around the back, the Argyll passed through a large open door and within moments the Tikari party vehicles were in a well-lit and enormous basement area under the castle.

A group of porters and valets stood waiting as the cars came to a halt.

Before one could spell Scottish Highlands backwards, they had all luggage removed and placed inside an open luggage lift.

Meantime, Raji had been distracted and awed by the glistening and seductive lines of mainly American-make automobiles parked away to his right, near what looked like a mechanic's workshop.

"The latest Otis Passenger Lift, Your Highness. It is perfectly safe!" the guard gestured, indicating that all the party could enter with him, though Raji could not resist a last, parting glimpse.

A press of a button and a slight rise later in the large wood-panelled lift, and the door opened on the verge of the hall, a cavernous and richly decorated masterpiece in wood and luxurious carpets and fabrics.

"Mr Carnegie, sir, may I present the Maharaja and Maharani of Tikari!"

Raji and Elsie could not quite believe what they saw in front of them. They had seen photographs of the white-bearded Carnegie in the press, but the images had never effectively conveyed his size.

"Yes, just five foot two but eyes a blue!" Carnegie quipped self-deprecatingly in the softest of Scottish accents, well used to such reactions. "Your Highnesses are most welcome at Skibo. Especially so, as we have had prime ministers and presidents here, but never a maharaja—and his beautiful wife!" he added, after little more than a momentary glance at Elsie.

They were introduced to his American wife, Louise, who curtsied to both Raji and Elsie. *Ah, Americans,* Elsie thought, *they do love royalty, not being encumbered by any of their own!*

"Our daughter, Margaret, cannot wait to meet you, but Andrew has insisted she gets an early night, so she will greet you in the morning," Louise explained.

Carnegie then insisted on personally welcoming each member of the Tikari Party—something Elsie thought was most unusual, but admirable—then motioned everyone to join him in the lounge close by.

"I have had sandwiches and biscuits prepared as I doubt you have had a good dinner! Anyone for a drop of the finest Scottish whisky?"

There was a general indication of 'yes please', though Elsie declined.

"As a friend of Lord Montagu, Your Highness, I had mistakenly assumed you would most likely be of his age, though you are considerably younger!"

"I trust such an occurrence is not a severe disappointment, Mr Carnegie!" Elsie said.

"Most certainly not—my wife is twenty years my junior! Youth is something to be admired, but so quickly lost!"

"Elsie and I are both twenty-four years old," Raji volunteered.

"Remarkable! Well, I am exactly three times your age, though I dare say I might still provide a challenge for you on the golf links!"

"As any outing on your course would be just our second golfing experience, I am sure you will have a great deal to teach us both, sir," Elsie suggested.

The butler moved close within view and Carnegie asked who in the Tikari party could assist with room allocations. All the best of the twenty visitor suites would be made available, he insisted.

Raji signalled to JG to go with the butler and sort things out.

"No!" Elsie said firmly, as she heard Siri and Lala asking the waiter for a second glass of whisky. She well knew that if their consumption of alcohol continued, no living creature was safe from sexual molestation.

At the close of the evening, Carnegie told everyone that breakfast would be taken at 8.30 am in the hall. What he did not say, was what would happen at 7.45 am.

Everyone chose to walk up the grand staircase and admire the five huge stained-glass windows from the landing. Then it was up to the first floor and their palatial rooms, all with large claw-footed baths.

* * *

The shrill call of the bagpipes rang out from the terrace of Skibo, flowed across the loch and even penetrated the forests where deer twitched their ears as if irritated by this regular 7.45 am wake-up call.

As an habitual early riser, the former great industrialist, now philanthropist, had a fearsome reputation for hard work during his working life. Retirement had proven no different, for each morning was spent with his secretary reviewing possible donations and correspondence well before most guests had stirred.

Margaret whispered into her mother's ear and Louise soon relayed the question to Elsie. "Margaret thinks you are very pretty, but does not know whether you are a queen or princess, Your Highness."

Elsie smiled and looked at Margaret for much longer than she needed to, then said: "Queen of Tikari would be more accurate—as maharani in Hindustani means 'queen' and I am married to a maharaja, or 'great king'—but I am happy for you

440

to call me a princess, if that is what you wish. And, if I was ever as pretty as you Margaret, I would be even more proud!"

The eleven-year-old tossed her light brown hair in embarrassed delight, but it was the sparkling of her blue eyes, that gave away what she was really thinking.

Unsurprisingly, when all the ladies decided to spend the day strolling through the gardens and grounds of Skibo, Elsie soon held Margaret's hand within hers.

The day was unusually fine and mild for a Scottish summer, and as they meandered under parasols through the formal gardens towards the loch, the roar of four car engines could be heard as each of the 'boys' pushed their temporary toy up, down and around the pebbled and dirt drives of the 20,000 acre estate.

Every now and again, there would be the unmistakable slithering sound of the back end of a vehicle flying around and almost out of control on a pebbled corner. Each time Elsie would close her eyes and await a crashing sound that miraculously did not occur.

She well knew who the 'child' responsible was, though knowing that he enjoyed 'living life on the edge' was little comfort.

As they wandered into the forest and further away from the recklessness, Elsie relaxed, particularly as deer appeared and Margaret began to coax a small group in for a pat. There was no way, Elsie decided, that she was going to allow Raji to go stag hunting.

After having a picnic lunch in a clearing, they were driven by Carnegie's personal chauffer to the far edge of the estate, before walking near Lake Louise.

At dinner that evening, in the magnificent dining room with its extravagant wood-panelled ceiling, Carnegie, on Raji and Elsie's insistence, spoke about his life, how he left Dunfermline as a twelve-year-old for the American states, where he worked as a bobbin boy. It was only through much hard labour while always 'dreaming big', that he eventually ended up selling Carnegie Steel to J.P. Morgan for $480 million in 1901.

At this point, Carnegie paused and looked firmly at Raji. "A man can only become rich when he enriches others. I believe that were I to die rich, I would die disgraced! I have given away many millions to fund libraries, the arts and the like, to enrich others' lives—and I will continue to give!"

Elsie interrupted:

The Worldly Hope men set their Hearts upon
Turns Ashes—or it prospers ; and anon,
   Like Snow upon the Desert's dusty Face,
Lighting a little hour or two—is gone.

"Sounds like Omar Khayyám," Carnegie suggested.

"You are right, well-read sir, Quatrain 16."

"That is very good! I like that you read so much … Princess Elsie!" he said smiling. "You know that I have funded the establishment of over two thousand libraries. Reading and education are key markers of the progress of man! Now, I trust you gentlemen enjoyed the automobiles today?"

"They were just wonderful, sir, and so many different ones for us to drive. Thank you very much!" Raji stated, as JG, Abu and Abid nodded in agreement.

"Well, they are nothing compared to what I believe the Tsar of Russia has, but I am glad they were all returned in one piece!"

"The Tsar of Russia!" Raji could be heard to murmur as his gaze and thought drifted … though Elsie still caught his drift.

"Tomorrow morning you must join me for a round of golf before lunch. Then, after lunch, what would you like to do?"

Elsie knew that Raji and JG wanted to go stag shooting, so quickly suggested trout fishing.

"Excellent!" Carnegie exclaimed. "We shall have the gear down to Loch Ospisdale after lunch!"

The way JG looked at Elsie did not need decoding. This was their last day at Skibo and their last chance to shoot.

Thankfully, Carnegie quickly changed the subject and asked everyone to move into the library. As they stood back from the desks, Carnegie told them about his one million pound gift to found the Peace Palace in The Hague.

"That was only the first step. Today, I got news that they have accepted my recommendation as to who should design the gardens around the Peace Palace. We held a competition and I selected Englishman, Thomas H. Mawson." He opened a wide draw and laid some large papers out across the desk. "Look at his designs!"

As Carnegie laid out the plans, he admitted to just a bit of bias: Mawson had previously designed most of the gardens at Skibo.

"We are after a top garden designer for our hunting lodge grounds at Bhalwa!" Raji exclaimed enthusiastically. "Do you have his business card?"

Carnegie rustled around in a draw and came up with Mawson's card. "You must understand, he is a busy man!" he warned.

That night, Raji had little sleep as his thoughts scurried between the potential gardens of Bhalwa and the possible line-ups in the Tsar's garages.

After breakfast on their last morning at Skibo, Carnegie told Raji and Elsie that there were a few places they must visit on their way back to London. He spread a map out in front of them and explained each location.

"The first one you must see is very close, only about six miles away. It is the village of Dornoch, which has some very old and interesting buildings. Then I suggest you head north about ten miles to catch a glimpse of Dunrobin Castle, near Golspie. It is the biggest castle in the Highlands, with 189 rooms, but the best part is the beautiful gardens. It is owned by the Dukes of Sutherland."

Grace was desperately trying to take notes, as Carnegie continued: "You can then head south, and may I suggest you stop down here, at the spa town of Strathpeffer. A very pretty place with sulphur springs. From the spa town it is about a twenty-mile drive to the battlefield of Culloden. It was here that the Jacobites under Bonnie Prince Charlie were massacred by the Duke of Cumberland's mainly English troops in 1746."

"Is there anything to see?" asked Elsie.

"You will feel far more than you will see when you walk across that ground, for there are a number of large stones with clan names to show where the mass graves of Highlanders lie."

"And where do you recommend we stay the night, sir?" queried JG.

Carnegie thought for a moment and then did a bit of a calculation with his fingers on the map. "You should be able to head a fair way south by this evening, so I would suggest a nice little hotel, the Loch Lomond Arms at Luss, on the lake's shore. But, before you go there, promise me you will take in the view at Glenfinnan, which is here. Promise me!"

"We promise ..." came the straggled responses, for in truth they had no idea what they were buying into.

"It was at Glenfinnan that Bonnie Prince Charlie rallied the Highlanders in 1745, raising his standard. That is where the Jacobite Rising effectively began. On that spot today is the stone monument of a Highlander. With Loch Shiel lying between hills in the foreground and the Glenfinnan Viaduct sweeping around behind, there is no more beautiful spot in Scotland! Promise me you will go there!"

"We promise!" came the coordinated and this time emphatic response.

As they passed through the Skibo Castle gates on their retreat from the Scottish Highlands, Raji could not resist a comparative jibe. "You know we have five times as many servants in the Tikari compound as he has!"

"Oh, how uncharitable you are!" Elsie cried, giving him a smack. "Well, I am sure theirs work at least five times as hard— and they have a more generous boss!"

* * *

The following afternoon, Raji was double-checking the business card he had pulled out of his coat, as the two Rolls-Royces sat in a street of old Georgian stone houses in the city of Lancaster, just south of the Lake District in England's north-west.

"Highmount House, 2 High Street," he said, reading the card, then the brass plate on the door. "This is it, Thomas Mawson's office! Elsie and I will go in. We shouldn't be long!"

After what Carnegie had said about Mawson being very busy, Elsie had insisted on wearing Grace's best European clothes, for she had a plan ... just in case ...

Nearly an hour later, Raji was fed up. Mawson's secretary had said that he would be available shortly, but Raji could still see

444

the figure of Mawson bent over a desk in the room behind the secretary. There seemed no prospect of change.

Raji stood up and marched past the surprised secretary and straight into Mawson's room. "I am the Maharaja of Tikari, and I cannot wait any longer!"

Mawson slammed down his pencil and stood up to his full height. "How dare you interrupt my work! I don't care who you are! You can leave right now!"

With that, he pushed Raji out into the waiting room and past the secretary.

"Vat a rude young man!" Elsie cried in a Central European accent, as Raji was ejected through the front door.

Mawson turned to face Elsie. He was, Elsie thought, in his late forties, but with his thick and dark moustache and height, quite handsome.

"And you, madam?"

"Princess Katerina of Moravia, darlink," she said offering her hand. As soon as he held it and looked in to her eyes, she knew she had him hooked. But she sighed, withdrew her hand and turned away, saying: "I had just vanted a couple of minutes of your presus time, but I can zee zat you are zo busy … zo I vait …" With that, she sat down.

"Well … well a couple of minutes … yes, a couple of minutes would be fine. I should be … I should be able to fit you in, right now!" he said, surprised at his own breathlessness.

Elsie pulled her chair uncomfortably close to Mawson as they sat at his drafting table. "Ze Prince and I ver zinking about ze unting loj ve ope to have build. You are ze only genius who can make ze grounds like a dream, darlink!"

Mawson swallowed and pulled out a sheet of drafting paper as Elsie's right leg rubbed against his left.

Elsie drew the outline of the estate at Bhalwa and fifteen minutes later, she walked out of Highmount House with a draft plan for the gardens that included 1,500 rose bushes as well as a driveway and path network—all created by the Edwardian period's finest garden designer, for nothing.

Chapter 54

The Palace of Crystal

When they dreamed of crystal, they could scarcely dream of it:
So much Fuller than expected, it delivered every bit.
And when they wanted justice, the green, white, purple set
Had Dora in their vanguard—the 'Aussie' suffragette.

Their arrival back in London after their journey to Scotland, provided an opportunity to relax after the days of travelling. However, Elsie had only just sat back on a lounge in their Waldorf suite, when there was a knock at the door. An envelope had been waiting for their return, and it took just a momentary glance at the writing on its front, for Elsie to know the sender.

"Father!" she cried with delight, as she grabbed a letter opener from the writing desk, then settled back down:

My Dearest Child,

Miss Emma has kept us well abreast of your progress, including your ensconcement in The Waldorf Hotel. You are truly blessed to have such a good and devoted friend.

The Waldorf was not in existence when I was last in London, though so much would have changed in over 30 years.

You might recall that your grandmother, my mother, was born Susannah Fuller. Her cousin was Francis Fuller who in time became a surveyor and railway entrepreneur.

He was the driving force behind the successful persuasion of Prince Albert to back the Great Exhibition of 1851 and did the surveying work for its home, which became known as the Crystal Palace. He was offered a knighthood, but declined.

"Well, I admire him for that! " Elsie said. "It would have been easier to accept!"

> A few years later he led a group to purchase the huge glass structure and had it recreated on a hill in Sydenham. For many years he was the Crystal Palace Company's Managing Director.
>
> It would therefore be most appropriate that you visit the site. Were you to remark that you were related, you would inevitably be received most cordially by its entire staff, and certainly any and all of your Fuller relations.
>
> There is however one member of the extended family, about whom I must advise that you should not volunteer connection.
>
> Dorothy Fuller is a daughter of Francis and became Dora Montefiore after her marriage to a Sydney merchant. She has become a prominent member of the Women's Suffrage Movement in England and from what I read in the papers, an anarchist.

"How shocking that women might want to vote!" Elsie said sarcastically, though she continued reading:

> Any familiarity with such a person cannot be positive for your acceptance in higher society ...

"Yes, Father, I can just see myself being a silly filly and diving under the hooves of the King's horse ... though he would probably like it if I were under his table at dinner!"

> given the difficulties you already face with a mixed-race association.

"Association!" Elsie muttered, annoyed at her father's use of the word. She mulled over this point for a minute. Perhaps, just perhaps, she and Raji needed to be formally wed, beyond the symbolic linking at Agra. Somewhat distracted, she read on:

> Walter and Stella send their love. Little Marjorie is now more than one and a half years old and destined I feel to be quite an attractive young lady, though hardly on a level with her aunt!
>
> Your mother still struggles with her breathing and frequent coughing and hopes the day when we can welcome both you and Raji to Sydney is not far off.
>
> With fondest love from us both,
>
> Your Father

Two days later, with Raji's approval, the Tikari party gathered in The Waldorf's foyer preparing to catch a train to Sydneham.

On seeing the reception clerk smile at her, Elsie remembered there was something she should ask: "Have you heard or read anything about a Dora Montefiore?"

"Oh, now that name sounds a little familiar, Your Highness … ah, Mrs Jenkins!" he called out, attracting the attention of the housekeeper who was scuttling past. "Can you recall a person called Dora Montefiore?"

"Montefiore, would that be the suffragette?"

"Quite possibly," Elsie responded, trying to be non-committal.

"Yes, she was the one who barricaded her house last year for six weeks and refused to pay taxes, because she couldn't vote!"

"Oh, good on her!" Elsie enthused, though she noticed that the others did not seem to share her sentiment.

After taking the train to the Crystal Palace High Level Railway Station, they eventually emerged from the underground at the semi-circular arched front entrance of the massive glass building.

Whatever preconceptions they had about its size, they were dwarfed by reality.

"Welcome to the Crystal Palace!" said a doorman. "Our palace of crystal is over 1,800 feet long and nearly 130 feet high!

Step inside and feel the light and space."

For nearly an hour and a half, they wandered the light-filled galleries, past fountains, ferns, trees, fine art and even dinosaur skeletons.

On departing, Elsie placed her forehead and hands softly against the entrance glass. "Francis Fuller, wherever you are now," she whispered, "know that I think you are a true genius!"

As if reading her thoughts, Raji warned: "Darling, we could not possibly construct this in India, for it would cook anyone who came inside!"

Outside, the party headed down steps that flowed into a huge formal garden, spreading out in a mostly symmetrical fashion.

As they were strolling past one of the central fountains, Elsie checked to see that JG was not watching, then pulled Raji sideways behind a line of sculpted bushes.

"Raji, my father wrote about our 'association' in his letter, as if it were something, well, almost improper! Is there any way we can be formally married?"

"It is something, darling, that I have been thinking about too! Look, we meet Ranbir and Olive at Christmas time near Mussoorie. They were formally married, and ..."

Elsie placed her fingers over Raji's lips, for JG had poked his head around a bush having discovered their whereabouts.

"How many times do I have to tell you to wipe your mouth and chin after you eat!" she berated Raji, wiping his face with her fingers.

That evening, Elsie noted that JG had a number of whispered conversations with Raji. It was easy to become paranoid, but she was learning that when it came to JG Wakefield and her relationship with Raji, nothing was impossible.

During the night, Elsie sensed that Raji's breathing indicated that he was not sleeping, but thinking. "Darling, we should talk about what is on your mind," she urged, switching on the bedside light, and anticipating discussion related to a proposed formal marriage.

"Oh, I was just thinking about how wonderful it would be to see the Tsar's car collection!" Raji responded, before turning away. Elsie groaned.

Chapter 55

The Challenge at Olympia

Raji settled back in their suite in The Waldorf as Abid Hussain removed his boss' shoes. For the last couple of days, Raji had been fixated by *Motor* magazine's 3 November 1908 issue, previewing the 7th Annual International Motor Exhibition at Olympia, in London's West Kensington.

While the exhibition was to open the next day, Friday 13th, and run for a week, there was just no way he was going to delay his arrival. Raji believed in two key principles: firstly, always buy the best, and secondly, buy it before anybody else.

To achieve his aims, every purchasing opportunity was scoped and planned with the thoroughness of a hunting expedition. Initially, Olympia 1908 was to have been no different to most, but it had been simplified by his July agreement to purchase a Rolls-Royce.

Now, all he could do was look through the *Motor* magazine and wonder what he was missing out on. But then, there was always the option of a second purchase.

On the morning of Friday 13th—an interesting occurrence, as Elsie had reminded everyone—the whole party breakfasted early. Raji was determined that they be first in line at Olympia for when the doors opened.

To ensure this happened, JG had studied the underground train map and determined that it should be possible to take the train from the Temple stop on the Victoria Embankment, all the way to West Kensington. As all the stops were on the District Railway Line, there would be no need to change trains.

However, nobody had used the Temple Station before, and though it was relatively close to The Waldorf Hotel, the party took the wrong turn at Temple Place and missed the next train. Despite racing like a regiment of rats when they emerged in

West Kensington, nine stations later, they ended up with seventeen persons ahead of them in the motor exhibition queue.

"What happens if each of these people want one of the display Rolls-Royces?" Raji whispered to Elsie as he seethed. "Perhaps I should try to bribe them so I can get to the front!"

Elsie insisted he should stay and be patient, so it was a relief to the whole party when they arrived unchallenged in front of the Rolls-Royce stand, to be greeted warmly by Claude Johnson.

"I can see Your Highness is a man of his word!" Johnson said immediately, just in case Raji wanted to change his mind.

"The 40/50 is a wonderful car, Mr Johnson. We had no problem with it on the drive to Scotland and back!"

"I also think it is wonderful, Mr Johnson," Elsie could not resist adding, for she knew its purchase was as good as done.

At that moment, Raji's eyes wandered left and he noticed a familiar-looking vehicle with its front end facing the walkway. "Is that …?" he began to ask.

"The car that won the 2,000 Mile Time Trial with its 70 hp engine. We call it the *Silver Rogue!*" Johnson confirmed.

Raji was soon scrutinising the racing car with the same degree of admiration he had exhibited in July, when he saw it at the opening of the Derby Works.

"Of course, as a one-off, it is much more expensive than the 40/50," Johnson cautioned in a very calibrated way, for he well knew the type of person with whom he was dealing—someone who would invariably choose unique or rare over common and not worry about the price.

The challenge for Raji was this: he knew that Elsie and the others loved the 40/50 car, the so called Silver Ghost model, and that he could have it shipped back to India; but the *Silver Rogue*, as a race car, would most likely stay in England.

"Put a sold sign on the *Silver Rogue!*" Raji demanded. "Mr Wakefield will sort out the payment with you."

Raji turned and headed out to look at the nearly 300 other cars on exhibition, including Mercedes, Panhard, Hotchkiss (about which the publicity swore there were virtually no complaints), Sunbeam, Iris, a light runabout with a 2-cylinder 9 hp engine called Pilgrims Way, White Steam Cars and even a car from

America making its show debut called the Ford Model T.

"It looks a bit common!" Raji snapped at the sight of the latter, before moving on to admire the Brown Brothers 6-cylinder monster on stand 86.

By now, the whole hall was jammed full of people milling around the latest gleaming automobiles. A man and his money could quite quickly be parted in such an intoxicating atmosphere.

* * *

It was not long before Raji's purchase was making the news. *Motor* magazine, in its 19 November issue, just six days after the show started, featured three separate pieces of commentary in its Showscripts section that delighted Raji, as he never shied from publicity:

> The 'Silver Rogue', erstwhile the 'Silver Silence' and sister to the 'Silver Ghost' was purchased on the first day of the show by H.H. the Maharajah Tikari ...

> Ah! Silver Rogue, you'll cross the seas,
> The latest vogue in Hinduese
> Your cylinders will there be classed
> As Brahmins of the highest caste.

"What they don't know," Raji smugly stated, "is that it is not leaving Europe!" Keeping it there, enabled him to have the option of racing it in England or in the classic races in France and elsewhere on the Continent, something that he had already done for years, with some success. He read on, as he sipped on a cup of tea provided by Abid:

> 'The Purchasing Rajah' is surely as deserving of immortalisation
> as 'The Galloping Major'. Thus the parodist:

> When he is at Olympia, the man at the Stand, you know,
> Is never a bit afraid

That purchases won't be made

By visitors who are catalogue-keen, for he is a moderate charger

But his heart beats quick

When the turnstyles click

And there enters an Indian Rajah

Everyone declares

He's a moderate charger,

And his heart goes bumpety-bumpety, bump –

Here comes the purchasing Rajah!

Elsie was a little less euphoric, for she was sure that his reception would have been far different, even hostile, if he had not the title, nor the money. She was also disappointed that the opportunity to buy the equivalent of the more practical 40/50 Silver Ghost had been missed, in favour of a 'toy'.

In the three weeks before the Tikari party left England on the maiden voyage of the P&O's RMS *Morea*, bound for Colombo via Marseille and Suez, Raji took every opportunity he could to race the *Silver Rogue*, driving it on a number of occasions around the steeply banked Brooklands motor circuit, south-west of London.

Chapter 56

The Linking at Lucknow

Midst a drifting screen of sandalwood, for conversion to Hindu
Take a splash or three of water, add a mantra chant or two
For a linking in Lucknow, now becomes formality
Once she ventures in as Elsie — and emerges Sita D.

The Daimler and the Renault pressed on and up the winding dirt road into the hill town of Rajpur in India's north.

It was midafternoon when they stopped in front of the low, classical arches of the luxury Prince of Wales Hotel. Elsie had never been here before, but the prospect of meeting Olive again was foremost in her mind.

They had barely settled in to the lounge when Ranbir and Olive arrived from their room, explaining that young Dorothy was staying with servants in Jind. While disappointed, Elsie was very pleased to see Olive again. She felt that Olive was the only one who could appreciate the challenges she faced as a white wife in this darker and different, Indian world.

A few minutes after their conversation began, a slim young man in a suit glided past the lounge. It was not just his smile in her direction that made Elsie stop mid-sentence in her conversation, it was his familiarity.

"Eugene?" Elsie mouthed quietly, unsure, as she had still not made the connection.

"Didn't I tell you that Lizzie Coleman had bought the Prince of Wales Hotel and that Eugene Manolescu was its new manager!" Raji exclaimed. "Why did you think we were here?"

Elsie felt embarrassed, for in truth Raji had not mentioned this at all. About Olive and Ranbir, yes, but not about Eugene.

Olive gestured to her younger brother to come over and he warmly greeted both Raji and Elsie, before returning to his office.

Raji soon turned the conversation to formal marriage, though any conversion to Sikhism and subsequent marriage, as Olive had done, was quickly ruled out. It was not till that evening, when guests returned for Christmas Eve drinks, that a breakthrough was made.

Raji had spotted an old friend and eagerly brought him over to meet Elsie. "Vijay, meet my wife, Elsie. Elsie, meet Vijay, the Maharaja of Vizianagaram!"

Elsie could tell he was about Raji's age, though a considerable degree lighter in complexion. "Where is Viziana ...?" Elsie queried.

"Vizianagaram is near the eastern coast, around 500 miles south-west of Calcutta. You can call me Viz—Tikari usually does!" he said with a laugh.

A pleasant enough chap, Elsie thought, though as the evening drifted on he was to prove most helpful. He was familiar with the Hindu sect Arya Samaj, which welcomed Muslim and Christian converts. There was a sizeable grouping of the sect near his holiday bungalow in Lucknow. He undertook to consult them and get back to Raji.

* * *

On the morning of 2 May 1909, Elsie embraced Hinduism as practised by Arya Samajists, at a ceremony at the Phool Wala Bungalow of the Maharaja of Vizianagaram, in Lucknow. Over the next month, accounts of the goings-on were published in newspapers around the English-speaking world:

A CONVERT TO HINDUISM

... Miss Thompson is an Australian lady who came here purposely to renounce Christianity and embrace Hinduism ...

The ceremony was performed in the small courtyard at the back of the house, which began to fill from an early hour, and became packed by 7 am. An awning was thrown across the walls of the courtyard, and under the arch of the north-east gate leading to the Gumti, a small pit was dug, and sandalwood placed in a pit for burning ...

At about 8 am the young convert passed down the courtyard and took her seat on a mat near the pit, and by her side sat the

Manager of the People's Bank of India. The young lady, who was dressed in an Eastern costume, wore a beautiful pale blue sari, bespangled with gold, and a veil fell from the back of her head over her shoulders. Her arms, save for gold bangles, were bare to the elbows.

She did not appear nervous, but she smiled pleasantly, and nodded to those around her. During the water ceremony she was asked questions, and responded in Urdu. Her responses, however, could not be heard by the spectators. Three separate times she took a little water in her hand, and after each question put the water to her lips. Then she washed her hands, and, dipping her fingers into the bowl, touched her eyes, her forehead, her ears, her waist, and threw a little water over her body.

Next she held a spoon filled with burning oil, stood over the pit, and threw the fire on to the sandalwood therein. The fire blazed up, and she fed it with more oil. Some reading of Hindu scripture followed, and it was now seen that Sita Devi, the new name that the convert had received, was looking faint from the intense heat. The ceremony took over an hour ...

A week later, Raji and Elsie were formally married at the same venue, as Perth's *Sunday Times* and many other newspapers reported:

BREAKING THE COLOR LINE

Sydney Girl Marries A Maharajah

Miss Elsie Caroline Thompson, the only daughter of Mr James Thompson of Fern Street, Randwick, was on May 9 at Lucknow married, according to Hindu rites to the Maharajah of Tikari, after the reports state, embracing the Hindu faith ...

The Raja and the new Raaj, with their guests, adjourned to the dining hall, where 25 people partook of a sumptuous wedding dinner, consisting of various rich Indian dishes, in true Oriental style. Though the wedding was a quiet one, everything went off with much eclat.

Elsie was quick to cable Emma, her own parents and May Maxwell with the news. A notice appeared in the marriages section of *The Sydney Morning Herald* with some incorrect spelling:

TIKARI – THOMPSON. On May 9, 1909, at Vizyanagram House, Lucknow, India, Gopal Saran Singh, Maharajah of Tikari, to Elsie Caroline (Elsie Forreste), only daughter of James Thompson, JP., Taunton, Fern Street, Randwick.

Elsie Caroline Thompson of Sydney had formally become Sita Devi, Maharani of Tikari.

Raji had a surprise in store, so they headed north-west to Dal Lake, where he presented Elsie with the lake's first luxury houseboat powered by a steam turbine: *The Elsey*. Of course, it was a spelling error on Raji's part, but Elsie was not concerned, as the vessel was magnificent.

They spent an idyllic couple of weeks drinking Rooh Afza and drifting on Dal Lake, Elsie's very favourite location.

Chapter 57

A Public Crowning

To anticipate is welcome, though it isn't always wise
To count your chicks before they're hatched, you might get a surprise
A rose is surely beautiful, yet often there's a thorn
Though a queen may rule a chessboard, just beware the vengeful pawn.

The balance of the year 1909, then 1910 and much of the first part of 1911, were spent either on Dal Lake or training and exhibiting the dogs, Larka and Larki, for dog shows. Elsie's demonstrated expertise with her animals saw her take up the writing of a regular column in the Calcutta daily *The Statesman*, called 'Dog World'.

Towards the end of that period, she spent considerable time supervising the construction work on the hunting lodge and grounds at Bhalwa. Selecting and locating 1,500 rose bushes, as recommended by Thomas Mawson in his design, took a great deal of research and planning.

The rather inconvenient death of Edward VII on 6 May 1911, threw a spanner into the Bhalwa work as Raji thought it would be a great idea to attend the coronation of George V in London. If they had not been in Calcutta at the time, such an enterprise would not even have been contemplated.

Frantic cables to London resulted in Raji receiving an invitation for the 22 June 1911 coronation, though this left precious little time to arrange boat passage to the imperial capital.

Elsie had put her foot down, insisting that Wakefield was not to join them on the trip—either that or she would stay in India. Cecil Kempster would go in his place. Elsie was quite fond of Kempster so such an arrangement augured well for a far more pleasant stay abroad.

Not surprisingly, Wakefield was shattered, all the more so because he had made all the last-minute arrangements. If there had been hope for a thawing of the relationship between JG and Elsie, such a prospect had been put on ice by his 'freezing out'.

Elsie was not entirely without charity when it came to

Wakefield, for she allowed him to attend their farewell dinner and drinks at the Tollygunge Club on Friday 12 May.

Kempster might well have driven the recently acquired Rolls-Royce 40/50 back to the Tikari mansion in Ballygunge Store Road, but he had to leave early to meet up with a young female friend. Taking the other Tikari car, he dropped off Abid, Grace and Abu at the mansion, for the Sikh, especially, never enjoyed late nights.

Raji wisely rejected the option of driving as he had drunk far too much, so Elsie, who had already driven the Rolls on a number of occasions, wanted to step in. Wakefield was not having any of it. She had deprived him of the opportunity to travel, so he was going to drive the Rolls, on a circuit of central Calcutta, no matter how much he had drunk. It was to prove to be a fateful decision.

Around 1.15 am, the Rolls left the Tollygunge Club, driven by Wakefield, with Raji in the passenger seat and Elsie, along with three members of the Tikari Ballygunge Store Road mansion staff: Mrs Ada Robertson, her daughter Rachel and the young Beatrice Mumstedt—who Raji had determined was exhibiting significant potential—crammed in the back.

The Straits Times (Singapore) of 17 May 1911 reported what happened next:

A serious motor-car accident has occurred near Wellington Square, Calcutta, the victims being the Maharajah and Maharanee of Tikari and three European ladies. The party was driving down to Dharamtollah Street, when the car was suddenly precipitated into an excavation of a depth of 20 ft. The occupants of the car were thrown to the bottom of the pit, from which they were eventually rescued by the cries of the injured ladies. The Maharajah, as well as all the ladies and the European chauffeur, are said to have sustained serious injuries, besides severe shocks to their nervous systems. Wellington Square was being excavated by the Water Works Department in order to link up the whole of the city system.

Miraculously, Elsie suffered only severe bruising, though all the others had that and multiple broken bones.

As they were ferried off to hospital, it was obvious that any attempt to reach England for the coronation had to be abandoned. Instead, Raji had to look forward to many weeks of recuperation at his Calcutta mansion.

Some minor compensation for Elsie was that she would still be in Calcutta when the June 1911 issue of *The Empress*, a 60-page illustrated society magazine, was published. It carried a full-page photographic portrait by Bourne and Shepherd of Elsie, 'The Maharani of Tikari' in a sari on its cover, while the inside article mentioned:

> ... She has a charming personality and is much liked in the particular circles in which she shines ...

A still sore Raji was delighted with the assessment and coverage, while Elsie enthusiastically paid one rupee for an extra copy, signing across the bottom right-hand corner of her cover photograph with the words:

> With fondest love
> to Wal

She then posted the issue to her brother Walter's Holt Avenue, Mosman home in Sydney.

Chapter 58

"Mohun Bagan!"

They play the game of football, in bare feet, maroon and green
Are their colours, sported proudly by their fans—as can be seen
And if you ask, all innocent, just where it all began
A patriotic Indian, will cry: "Mohun Bagan!"

The heat of a Calcutta summer was never something Raji or Elsie enjoyed, but his injuries necessitated his stay at Ballygunge Store Road, far longer than he would have liked.

Just when it seemed that a move to Mussoorie or Dal Lake looked possible, something very unusual happened—and Raji just had to be part of it.

While purchasing a second Rolls-Royce Silver Ghost, as the first underwent significant repairs from the crash, Raji fell into conversation with an ardent fan of Calcutta's most popular Indian football team, Mohun Bagan.

They had made the semi-final of the Indian Football Association (IFA) Shield, a competition that had always been dominated by British teams, invariably based around military units.

Playing in bare feet, Mohun Bagan's progress to the IFA Shield Final was a most unlikely prospect, so it was with much delight that Raji read of their 3-0 semi-final replay victory over the 1st Middlesex Regiment, before a record crowd that had packed the ground at Dalhousie.

"Mohun Bagan!" he cried, leaping to his feet and punching the air with his fist in celebration.

Elsie was delighted to see his excitement, for she had feared he was sliding into depression after more than two months of minimal activity.

"Mohun Bagan!" she responded in kind—and the servants copied. It was then that Elsie had an idea.

What if she would add something to the chant of 'Mohun Bagan!' like short and sharp cries of 'one, two, three', but in Hindustani, that is: 'ek, do, teen'?

So she started: "Mohun Bagan! Ek, do, teen! Mohun Bagan!

Ek, do, teen!" punching her clenched fist high in the air on 'Mohun Bagan!', then raising it halfway up with each number of 'Ek, do, teen!'

Her rhythmic swaying, almost dancing from side to side soon drew Abu, Siri and Lala to join in, at which point Raji could not help but link with that crazy wife of his. This brought Abid, Grace, Rachel, Beatrice and even Cecil in too.

For a couple of minutes they danced and chanted from side to side, until Raji got his feet tangled trying to add a fancy element, bringing the line down like a group of capitulating ten pins, amidst the odd scream, but overwhelmingly, laughter.

There was absolutely no way that Raji and Elsie were going to miss the final, after all that, though he was lucky enough to get two tickets to the Calcutta Football Club's small and only grandstand. As fortune would have it, the ground was just across Ballygunge Store Road.

In the days leading up to the Saturday 29 July 1911 final against the East Yorkshire Regiment, a special feeling spread throughout Calcutta, the state of Bengal—even India. No Indian team had ever won the IFA Shield nor even come close to doing so. Now, at last, the natives were rising, and the British had better watch out.

Raji walked up to the roof terrace of the Tikari mansion and spread his arms up to embrace the morning, as if it was what he secretly hoped it would be: the dawning of a new age of Indian nationalism. He could feel it coming and desperately wanted to be there when it arrived.

Elsie joined Raji and hugged him, for though she was often frustrated with his repeated 'playing of the game' in bending to the British, she too sensed this might just be a turning point.

The newspapers were full of talk on the game, while extra steamers, trains and tramcars were put on to bring the expected crowd of between 80,000 and 100,000 who could enter the ground and the many thousands of others who could not get in, to the Calcutta Football Club venue.

The Mohun Bagan players went to the Kalighat Temple to pray before a statue of Kali, the goddess of power and the destruction of evil, as well as death.

As the afternoon progressed towards the 5.30 pm kickoff,

Raji returned to the rooftop terrace time and again to soak in the atmosphere as the crowd gathered.

The servants had left long before, trying to get the two-rupee tickets that had now risen to fifteen or more for general admittance.

Raji and Elsie watched in fascination from their terrace as the crowd swelled across the road, getting more colourful and boisterous by the minute.

By 5 pm, they dared not leave it any longer, as it was just half an hour before kickoff. Even so, they struggled to get into the grandstand packed with white English supporters of the Yorkshire lads.

Elsie wore a maroon sari, but had her hair and wrists ribboned in Mohun Bagan's maroon and green colours. Raji sported a green jacket to add to his usual dark countenance that even sunglasses could not hide. It was not difficult to spot their variance from the Caucasian crowd around them.

A terrific roar greeted the arrival of the players, led out by the referee, Mr Pooler. Elsie was quick to note that the Mohun Bagan players were again barefoot. Their crunching tackles with the big-booted boys in black uniforms from Yorkshire, produced gasps from supporters of both sides during an even first half that delivered no goals.

"Do you think Mohun can win it from here?" Elsie asked a tense Raji at half time.

"They have done really well so far, but I dare not think that they might win, but they could, though who knows?" he replied, between nervous bites of his nails.

Elsie smiled as she remembered something:

> The Ball no question makes of Ayes and Noes,
> But Here or There as strikes the Player goes ;
>   And He that toss'd you down into the Field,
> *He* knows about it all—HE knows—HE knows !

"Quatrain 70, my friend Omar!" she added with a smile.

It was fifteen minutes into the second half when Yorkshire took the lead. Rajendranath Sen Gupta fouled Yorkshire captain Sergeant Jackson in breaking up a dangerous attack. Jackson himself, scored from the free kick. The grandstand, save for two isolated Mohun Bagan supporters, rose as one to celebrate what now seemed an inevitable triumph.

Black kites, with the number one upon them, became airborne around the ground to inform the many who could not see, that the team in black, the favourites, were one goal up.

English men and women even started setting fire to maroon and green effigies, something that enraged Raji. "Curse them!" he cried. "Curse them all!"

Elsie could hold back no longer. As relative calm and quietness returned after the Yorkshire goal, she took a deep breath, leapt to her feet and yelled out: "Mohun Bagan! Ek, do, teen!" She then kept going in her loudest soprano voice, while punching the air. Raji, after initial surprise, joined her.

The crowd in the grandstand could not believe what they were seeing and hearing, but in the massed throng in front of the grandstand, one giant figure did.

Abu, his huge frame and turbaned head soaring above all others, launched his right fist towards the heavens as his voice rang out in matching defiance: "Mohun Bagan! Ek, do, teen!" Immediately, the Tikari servants around Abu joined in as fists rose in a tsunami of support that sent waves of rising arms surging to the left and right.

What had started merely as a cry from the grandstand, and had been transformed into a roar from the terrace, evolved into thunderous support right around the stadium for the men in maroon and green.

On the field, the natives responded, with their captain, Shibdas Bhaduri, slamming the ball into the Yorkshire net after a mazy dribble, with just ten minutes to go.

Urged on by the tens of thousands, even clinging in treetops and crowding rooftop vantage points, Mohun Bagan surged on. With just two minutes left, a great left-footed through ball by Bhaduri put centre forward Abhilash Ghosh free and he rounded the Yorkshire goalkeeper to score the winner.

Pandemonium erupted. Referee Pooler's final whistle could barely be heard but everyone could see the Mohun Bagan players sink to the ground, as, for the first time ever, the British

Raj had been brought to its knees. It had been defeated by Indians at the game that they, the British, had invented.

Raji was on his feet, jumping and yelling in jubilation. Elsie was ecstatic too, but crying tears of joy, which were halted temporarily by a whack across the back of her head from a match program swung by an ungracious Englishman.

Maroon and green kites carrying Mohun's final total, soared proudly into the early evening sky, as fireworks whizzed and exploded around them. This was indeed an occasion that all Indians could celebrate. Perhaps, just perhaps, it was a portent of things to come.

As the official party moved to make the presentation of the IFA Shield, Elsie noticed a figure in their midst she had not seen since the days of their engagement, five and a half years earlier: Raj Rajendra of Cooch Behar. He looked stooped and worn out from years of injury and alcoholism, though he was only twenty-nine years old.

Chapter 59

The Delhi Durbar

Come sway with the elephants, through throng at Red Fort
Who gawk at the glitter and cheer more than ought
No splendour's sufficient, as it's all great PR
For the Emperor and Empress, attending Durbar.

Two events occurred that would have, under normal circumstances, been deemed of particular note. Firstly, there was the sale of The Prince of Wales Hotel in Rajpur by Eugene Manolescu, after the death of his mother, triggering his departure to Jind as private secretary to Ranbir. Secondly, the death in September 1911 of Cooch Behar's Maharaja Nipendra Narayan, elevating the ailing Raj Rajendra to ruling status.

Neither of these, however, caused more than passing interest in Gaya, as India became consumed with what was to come—the Delhi Durbar.

Raji and Elsie had been unable to visit London for the coronation of George V, though they were not to be entirely out of 'luck'. The King and Queen had kindly determined that their Indian subjects should not miss out on making a fuss of them. They decided a crowning in Delhi as Emperor and Empress of India, in the cooler weather of 12 December 1911, would be simply smashing.

Sadly, it seemed to Elsie, most of India, including her husband, appeared to agree. She wondered if Raji was schizophrenic: one day holding secret talks with Gandhi and boisterously celebrating Mohun Bagan's victory, then the next, joining the queue of maharajas kneeling before the foreign sovereign.

All the British had to do was suggest the prospect of a medal—in this case a golden Delhi Durbar one for attending maharajas—or an increase in gun salutes, and the maharajas would transform into lapdogs, competing amongst each other to show who was the best pet.

Of course, when it came to a grand occasion, there was no grander than a durbar, when all the maharajas gathered to pay homage to their British sovereign.

The Viceroy, Lord Hardinge of Penshurst, oversaw arrangements for the occasion, and appointed Sir John Hewett to preside over the organising committee. They held meetings at which the schedule and protocol surrounding the Delhi Durbar were detailed.

Raji had naively hoped to be on this committee, after it was made known that four Indian princes were to be included in its number at 'the King's own initiative'. When Gwalior, Idar, Bikaner and Rampur were announced, he was disappointed.

In fact, although he could be part of the public parade of maharajas at Delhi, he would not be amongst the select group of ruling chiefs presented to the King and Queen on December 7 or 8. Only minor consolation occurred when Raji was informed that he could be part of the formal welcoming party when the King moved east to Calcutta. He would be introduced to His Majesty as the 'Representative of Bihar Landowners'.

This was fine, Raji assured, but the most spectacular event would be the Delhi Durbar and its single greatest display would be the parade of maharajas, on their elephants.

Formally, Elsie could not take part, being a 'European' wife, though she was determined to flout the ban. So, when Raji stated that he would have a golden howdah built for the parade, Elsie insisted it have two thrones, with one behind the other, and not just one.

"Just pretend that the back one is for Siri or Lala, or even Bibi," she told him, though when JG emerged, ready to measure the selected elephant for the howdah, she made no comment at all.

As all three stood in front of the Tikari Raj pilkhana, Raji outlined the requirements for a durbar elephant: "It must be strong, but have a calm nature and not be panicked by large crowds. It must have long, symmetrical tusks that do not curve in. Only male Indian elephants have long tusks so it must be male! Which one do you think it will be?"

Elsie scanned the twenty-three elephants in the pilkhana and saw one to the left that seemed to fit the bill. "That one?" she ventured, pointing.

"Diranda? No, can be a bit moody. Try again!"

Elsie tried again, this time noticing an elephant that had previously had its backside pointed in her direction. "How about that one?"

"Yes! Tika! He is our best choice for the big occasion!"

Raji signalled for Tika's mahout, his elephant handler, Rasheed, to bring the animal forward for measurement.

JG walked up and down its side with a stick. "Plenty of room for a single throne!" he declared, as he wrote down the measurement.

Elsie squeezed Raji's hand and he quickly got the message. "No JG, I want a double throne, one behind the other!"

"But you know the rules, Raji! SHE must not make an appearance at events such as this. It would bring disgrace to Tikari!" JG protested.

Elsie squeezed Raji's hand again until he countered: "The second throne is for Maharani Bibi or Lala or Siri. I cannot have tens of thousands in Delhi think that the Maharaja of Tikari cannot attract a wife!"

JG was clearly unhappy with the result and slunk off to complain to Willie Hathaway, the newly appointed replacement for Mr Keith as manager of Tikari Raj. Elsie had already spent some time with Willie, finding him pleasant and approachable, but made a mental note to chat with him after JG's visit.

From that time on, till they departed for Delhi, Elsie made sure that Tika got to know her in the pilkhana. At first, this was quite scary, for moving in an enclosure with so many elephants, any one of which could easily kill her with a misstep, was terrifying.

Her only previous experience of elephants had been with Ruby, in Cooch Behar, and Elsie knew already to trust the mahouts, and to rely implicitly on their understanding of their animals.

Rasheed told Elsie to greet Tika and the others clearly and in a friendly tone, but to never surprise them with loud noises or sudden movements, lest they panic.

After only a few days, Tika would spot Elsie before she reached the enclosure, and would move slowly towards its entrance. After a week, she was reaching up to stroke towards his forehead, though the first time she did this she was scared he would suddenly lift his head and strike her with a tusk. But she called him a 'beautiful boy' and he seemed to understand, looking at her with a caring softness, she thought, from those lovely big eyes.

Soon she was whispering in the end of his trunk, her breath tickling him. He retaliated by reaching in and tossing the ends of her long hair—though she held her breath and watched those tusks each time he did.

In the early morning of the day of the parade, Elsie lay naked upon a bed inside the huge Tikari tent, within a sea of tents that stretched as far as the eye could see, and further, to near Delhi.

Siri and Lala had specially prepared dark cream that they rubbed into every visible part of her body, causing Elsie to laugh and cry out: "You don't have to put it there!" when Lala's fingertips worked their way deep in to her groin. Siri gave Elsie a playful smack and the girls giggled, as they continued work on their masterpiece.

After rolling over, the same was repeated as she lay on her newly darkened stomach, Elsie revelling in the feeling the 'creaming' elicited, while at the same time hoping it would be effective.

When she finally stood for detailed inspection by Raji and self-examination via a large mirror held by Siri and Lala, everyone was impressed, as the normal white marble Elsie had been transformed into a dark beauty.

"My baby is magnificent!" Raji exclaimed.

"No, your Bibi is magnificent, remember, I am going to be Maharani Bibi of Tikari!" Elsie reminded everyone.

The elephants, maharajas and maharanis representing the princely states assembled in an area away from the massive encampment, for fear of the chaos a charge of 'rogue' elephants could reek on the tented plain.

Every elephant was cloaked in a large colourful cloth that glistened with rich inlaid decoration. The decoration flowed down the elephant's forehead and sometimes around their tusks. Every ruler was trying to make their elephant more spectacular than everyone else's, a feat they no doubt achieved in their own eyes.

Tika was no exception. He seemed to understand the importance of the occasion and Rasheed ensured he was on his best behaviour.

Tika knelt so that Rasheed and Abu could help Raji and Elsie climb up into the new golden-roofed howdah, where they each had cushioned thrones, one behind the other.

Elsie thanked Raji and squeezed his jewelled hand, for she knew the risk he was taking were she to be discovered.

Raji looked resplendent in his turban, long cream coat and ornate boots, every piece sparkling with the aid of diamonds, emeralds, rubies and sapphires. Elsie wore a spearmint sari that glinted with golden flecks. The emerald and diamond banded tiara sat upon her head and many more of the same jewels hung around her neck, clung to her wrists and dangled around her ankles.

They looked like a poor person's dream of ultimate wealth and style, but they were just one pair in a long line of rulers sitting in gilded cages on prized elephants, and Tikari was not going to be anywhere near the front. Just so the maharajas remembered 'the order of things', they would parade in gun-salute sequence. The British controlled and limited everything, even aspirations.

Abu paced himself carefully in front of Tika, bearing the standard of Tikari, while a uniformed Gurkha walked by either side. The long procession wound its way towards Delhi, swaying gently as huge crowds gathered to gape in awe at the splendour, for the people revered their Indian royalty as virtual living gods.

As they passed the Red Fort, they bowed in respect to the King-Emperor and Queen-Empress who were seated on a temporary throne on the fort's wall.

They circled the fort and eventually headed, elephant-less but elated, for the main camp—that huge tented city erected on the plains north-west of Delhi, that was capable of hosting 200,000. At its heart, were a bazaar and free kitchens, paid for by the Maharajas of Jind, Faridkot, Nabha and Patiala, while Olive (who had waited in the Jind tent), was quick to remind Elsie that Ranbir had also provided a free hospital.

Elsie knew that Ranbir was just trying to make up for his sin of marrying a European woman, but who was she to be critical of his choice.

Having survived the parade of maharajas, Elsie was determined to take things a step further. On the afternoon of

Saturday 9 December, a hand-picked selection of forty Indian maharanis, that excluded Tikari's, was due to be presented to the Queen-Empress in the throne room tent of the imperial camp.

Olive was adamant. "Oh no! Elsie you cannot! If you get caught—and you almost certainly will—there could be big trouble for Raji! Remember what happened with the Gaekwar of Baroda yesterday. He broke the rules by not wearing his jewels and turning his back quickly after the slightest of bows to the King-Emperor. His name will be as mud for quite some time!"

"The Maharani of Patiala is leading the group I hear. I know her, so everything should be fine!" replied Elsie, with a degree of confidence Olive refused to share.

"In any case, if you go with your full set of jewels, the Queen-Empress will probably take some. I have heard she is a kleptomaniac!"

"A what?" asked Elsie, incredulous.

"An habitual thief!"

"Yes, I know what it means! Does she really steal things?"

"So I hear! If she likes something shown to her, she lays her hands on it, and it is as good as hers!"

"Well, she won't be stealing anything of mine!" Elsie declared defiantly.

"Your Highness, please, the Maharani of Jind is right. If you try to go in there without an invitation, all of us could be in big trouble, not just you!" Grace insisted. "How can I be your guardian angel if you do not listen to me!" she added, close to tears.

* * *

That afternoon, in the throne room tent, a glittering gallery of forty maharanis bedecked in a kaleidoscope of colourful saris, spread themselves reverently before the far less attractive Queen-Empress, Mary of Teck.

The Maharani of Patiala stepped forward carrying a black velvet cushion, upon which sat a large and glittering necklace, within which sparkled nine large emeralds surrounded by two concentric rings of diamonds. As the Queen-Empress' eyes narrowed with avaricious delight, Lady Hardinge announced that it was a gift 'in love and admiration from the women of India'. The Indian queens all bowed in deference, though Sita Devi of Tikari, was not among their number.

Being on the elephant in the parade of maharajas was one thing, but being in that throne room when not on the invitation list, was quite another.

She had listened to her 'guardian angel'.

Chapter 60

Just Flying!

If I could drive much faster, I'd be taking off the ground
And soaring with the birdies, looking down on all around
Racing 'round at Brooklands, is a buzz on which to bet
But just flying in an aircraft is another level yet.

The frost of a 1912 March morning in Surrey, England, had only just started to dissipate, when the slow but inevitable crunching of car tyres eased its way up to the Brooklands motor track start line.

Lord Vernon brought the 1908 GP Mercedes to a halt, as its owner, the tall and confident car dealer and occasional racer, Gordon Watney, baited Raji once again.

"Do you want to lose another 100 pounds, Tikari? Or do you want to make it 200?" he asked, as he leaned on the back of the Merc.

Raji had lost 100 pounds when Watney's Mercedes had gone up against his 60-hp Renault. He was not going to make the same mistake twice. This time he had a more powerful De Dietrich and he was sure that he could win.

"200 pounds it is, Mr Watney! The fastest time for one lap!"

"You can pay me now, if you wish!" came the ever-cocky reply, as Lord Vernon started to rev the Mercedes' engine.

Starter and timekeeper, John Lea, checked the positioning of the car, gave the thumbs up and moved to the inside of the track. "Three, two, one, go!" he cried as, with the spinning of tyres and the roar of the Mercedes' racing engine, the car took off, leaving smoke and a group of impressed observers in its wake.

As it headed towards the first bend of the 3.25-mile track, it was obvious the 200 pounds was sitting lightly in Raji's pocket.

"Jesus! It's just flying!" Lea exclaimed, double-checking his watch in disbelief as the German automobile passed the halfway mark on the far side of the track. "It has to be doing over 100 miles an hour!"

Raji turned to watch the Mercedes curve up and around the

steep final banking and then rocket out of it as if propelled by a slingshot. As he did so, he noticed a biplane clear the banking and dip to land on the long airstrip that had had been built inside the motor track.

Raji started his engine, swung the De Dietrich right and forward, and headed off towards the biplane, just as the Mercedes shot past Lea and the finish line.

"Hey! Where is my 200 pounds?" Watney yelled, as he spluttered on a mouthful of De Dietrich tyre dust. Thankfully, Raji was too far away to hear Watney add: "You black bastard!"

Raji pulled up alongside the biplane and waited for the pilot to clamber out. "I hear you do flying lessons," he called out, but as the man came within reach, he exclaimed: "Oh, you are young!"

"And you, sir, seem to be Indian, so I guess we are square!" the young man quipped. "Thomas Sopwith," he added, extending a hand.

"The Maharaja of Tikari, but I guess you can call me Raji. I didn't think you would be younger than me!"

"Flying is not about age, Your Highness, it is about ability and experience. I have both, though yes, I am only twenty-four! And, it is dangerous—there are no bad pilots alive!"

"Well, Mr Sopwith, how long will it take to get a pilot's licence?"

"That depends on aptitude. The record is nine hours flying over three days." Then he stopped, for he could see Raji calculating. "Forget about any records, Your Highness. Have you flown before?" Raji's shake of the head gave the answer he expected.

"Well, with respect, can I suggest that you come on a one-pound joy-flight with me and see if you like it, before you join the Sopwith School of Flying. You might never want to fly again!"

"One pound? I think I can manage that!' Raji said, removing his wallet from his coat pocket and opening it.

Just then, the screeching of brakes followed by the pounding of feet, signalled the arrival of an insistent Watney, right on time. Raji counted out 200 pounds and thrust it into Watney's outstretched hand. "I will be winning that back soon!" he warned.

That afternoon, with a leather cap stretched over his head and goggles helping keep the cap in place, Raji took to the air for the very first time.

He was partly frightened, partly amazed, partly exhilarated, and wholly cold and windblown. From on high, he saw the patchwork quilt of the English countryside: cottages and farmhouses that looked like toys, and villages that looked like models.

When they landed, Sopwith asked him the obvious question and received, what to Raji was the obvious answer. "I want to be the first Indian ever to get a pilot's licence!"

Chapter 61

La Belle Époque

Welcome to the Continent, and time La Belle Époque
Where the flow and style of Art Nouveau, presents a culture shock
For Paris is its heartland, from Élysée to the Seine
Your conscience says you'll count the days till you are back again.

The Tikari party crowded around a table in The Waldorf Hotel's Palm Court, as Cecil opened their copy of *Bradshaw's Continental Railway Guide.*

The decision to escape London by basing themselves in Paris for a few weeks, had excited everyone, even Raji, who had been assured he could continue flying lessons on Farman aircraft close to the fabled city, before returning for final assessment at Brooklands.

For Elsie, visiting Paris would be achieving a childhood dream. She had learnt French at Fort Street School, though speaking and interpreting it years later would, she understood, be a far tougher challenge.

Cecil turned to the back of *Bradshaw's* where cities were listed alphabetically, finding Paris. He then flicked backwards and forwards through the listing of hotels, as Raji commented on the merits of those he knew from previous visits: the Élysée Palace Hotel, Hotel Continental and Hotel Majestic.

When Cecil returned to the start of the Paris listing, Elsie noticed that the advertisement for 'Grand Hotel', Paris, at 2 rue Scribe, stated it was 'Close to the Grand Opera'. Given that it had been 'Entirely Renovated' and had a telephone in every room, private bathrooms and hot and cold running water, Raji agreed: Le Grand Hotel it was to be.

Elsie was very excited to take her first steps towards the Continent. Now, the sequence of a train on the South Eastern and Chatham Railway, departing from London's Charing Cross Station, followed by a boat from Dover, then the train from Calais, were going to deliver her to the capital of France.

* * *

After being driven in a Darracq motor cab from Gare du Nord through the streets of Paris to Le Grand Hotel, Elsie could see that Palais Garnier, Paris' main opera house, was just around the hotel's corner. "C'est tellement beau!" she exclaimed, extending her French a little closer to its limit than she dared admit.

Le Grand itself was at least as good as the advertisement, with marble public floors and the most beautiful formal dining and ballroom, called the Salon Opera. There, large, arched and mirrored 'windows' ringed a circular room on two levels, while a massive chandelier hung from an ornate ceiling. It was truly breathtaking. Then there was its famous restaurant, Café de la Paix, on the corner overlooking the Place de l'Opéra and the Boulevard des Capucines.

Nearly as good, was reception's decision to assign Madame Lemaire as special maid to the Imperial Suite. Though of mature age, madame spoke perfect English and French, having been born in Kent and married to a Parisian. Her pasty, but not unattractive face, thought Elsie, gave a clue to her ancestry.

"It was in this very suite, Your Highnesses, that in 1869, the publisher of the *International Herald Tribune* met with Henry Morton Stanley, to convince him to search for David Livingstone in Africa!"

Elsie digested momentarily the utter contrast between the lavish state of the suite and 'the wilds of Africa', before madame added: "Paris has a way of seducing you that perhaps Stanley did not understand! You can even see la tour Eiffel if you step out on the balcony!"

She departed, after stating that they need only ask and she would be most happy to assist them in finding whatever they wished in Paris.

Elsie and the other young women in the Tikari party could not wait to get started. Meanwhile, Cecil and Abid Hussain agreed to accompany Raji on his biweekly journeys east to the Farman Flying School at Châlons-sur-Marne. This meant rising early on a Monday and a Thursday and catching a train from Gare de l'Est, having personalised tuition from Henri Farman in his Farman III aircraft, then returning in time for dinner in Café de la Paix.

It was on their first such Thursday evening, that Raji found Elsie bursting with excitement about what she had seen that afternoon. Naturally, she was not going to tell him what it was, she was going to show him the next morning.

With Grace, Siri, Lala and Abu happily in tow, the other three joined them in a walk along rue Royale, until they stood in front of a distinctive-looking shop. 'G. Fouquet' the sign said in a flowing style, and the remarkable decoration and colours inside seemed to melt from the walls.

"Welcome to Boutique Fouquet! I am Georges Fouquet, at your service, Your Highnesses!" a smartly dressed man inside said, well remembering, as every good businessman did, any esteemed client from a previous visit.

"Ah, a jeweller's!" Raji exclaimed. "You want some jewellery, darling?"

"No, Raji! Look at the beautiful shop: the tiles on the floor, the counters and the magnificent peacocks and the beautiful ceiling!" she said, quite frustrated.

"It is what we French call Art Nouveau style, with everything designed specifically for me by that master of Art Nouveau, the Moravian, Alfons Mucha," Mr Fouquet elaborated. "You may have seen his posters down by the Seine."

"The way the peacock drapes from the cornice, and the display stands seem to come to life, yet melt into the floor! Oh, it is so gorgeous!" Elsie gasped. "I have never seen a more beautiful shop, have you, darling?"

It was obvious what Raji had to answer, but in truth his eyes had now opened to the beauty and novelty around him. "No … I have not. It is remarkable, just remarkable!"

"Thank you, Your Highnesses! I am so proud to work in this environment. It is, I believe, a high point in a time I call 'La Belle Époque', 'The Beautiful Age'. We are so fortunate that people value beauty today over ugliness!"

Raji carefully studied the full range of jewellery pieces in the various display stands, then bought butterfly earrings, a dragonfly brooch and another exquisite one that featured a woman with flowing hair, for Elsie. He then added a diamond and ruby snake brooch that he thought would go well on his turban.

"This man who designed the shop, what was his name again?" Raji asked.

"Alfons Mucha, Your Highness."

"So, he created those posters of beautiful women too, did he?"

"Yes, Sarah Bernhardt and other famous ones."

"He is still in Paris?"

"Oh no, Your Highness. He now lives and works in Western Bohemia. He is a busy man, for he is painting a major sequence called The Slav Epic, which he expects will take him years. We write to each other every now and then."

Raji thought for a moment, while looking at Elsie. "If he can draw Sarah Bernhardt, he can do the Maharani of Tikari! Do you have his address?"

Mr Fouquet disappeared briefly into the back of the shop and returned with a card, upon which was printed:

Alfons Mucha

c/- Castle Zbiroh

Western Bohemia

"Alfons does not welcome visitors, but if you permit me to say so, Your Highness, he may make an exception for your wife. He does like his women!"

As they walked back along rue Royale, past the Place de la Madeleine and into the Boulevard des Capucines, they all agreed to keep an eye out for any Art Nouveau they could find. Before entering Le Grand, Raji noticed a shop called Louis Vuitton at No. 1 rue Scribe, just opposite the hotel. Half an hour later, they emerged with a series of versatile travel bags, of a type none had seen before.

The next morning, Elsie spotted Raji seemingly transfixed by a photograph in the Saturday newspaper's supplement on European royalty. Shortly after, he called her over to look at the image. "Which do you think is the most beautiful?" he asked.

Elsie studied the four young girls, who she instantly recognised as the daughters of Tsar Nicholas II. "Oh, you men are so one-dimensional! I would just as rather know who was the nicest, the kindest and the most caring—and I wouldn't know that unless I met them!"

For a few moments, their suite was then so silent that Elsie could hear the clock ticking … or was that Raji's brain ticking over?

"Well, why don't we!" he suddenly cried, thrusting the paper on to the coffee table and rising to his feet.

"Why don't we what, darling?"

"Why don't we meet the Romanovs? Remember, Carnegie told us the Tsar has a huge car collection!" he exclaimed, revealing the real reason behind his desire to head east.

Before a surprised Elsie could say anything more, Raji had picked up the telephone and asked for Madame Lemaire to be sent to their suite. She confirmed what he had expected: that the Tsar and Tsarina had stayed in their suite, and that the Russian Embassy in Paris had been responsible for handling their visit.

"I will go to the embassy on Tuesday!" he announced.

By Tuesday afternoon, Raji was less confident. The embassy could not guarantee how long a response would take. And, if it were at all possible, there were likely to be some conditions, though what these might be was not made clear. The Tikari party simply was not in Paris often and long enough to just sit around and wait.

The next morning, 17 April 1912, in part to escape the ongoing and depressing newspaper coverage of the *Titanic* disaster, the whole Tikari party visited the Eiffel Tower, hoping that, as it was a Wednesday, the queues would be short. They were disappointed. After a wait of nearly an hour and a half, they reached the platform on the first level.

This was as high as anyone but Raji wanted to go, while Lala was feeling particularly queasy. They spread out to take in the view, when Elsie heard crying nearby. Lala had thrown up over the first floor railing, spraying the crowd queuing far below.

Elsie managed to get her cleaned up and calmed down in the first level shop, before she held Lala softly as they descended.

They had planned on doing some walking, but Lala's fragile condition led Raji to hire two motor cabs. Madame Lemaire had kindly listed some Art Nouveau sites for them to see, with the first, architect Jules Lavirotte's 29 avenue Rapp, 1901 apartment creation, only a short distance from the tower.

They gazed in wonderment at the curving and sculptured surround to its front entrance: a large wooden and glass door that defied instant interpretation. Then there were the curved walls, balconies and windows that gave the building an almost living form.

Nearby were the courtyard buildings of 3 square Rapp, after which they headed south to Octave Racquin's 33 rue du Champ de Mars building with its cast-iron railings and floral motifs.

Then it was north across the Seine to Lavirotte's 1904 Hotel Ceramic, followed by a drive east to see the ornate gold and floral lettering of the La Samaritaine store, near the Pont Neuf.

Here they were dropped off, for Madame Lemaire had said that the hundreds of riverside green wooden stalls, known as bouquinistes, sold books, postcards and posters. As the others rested on benches, Raji and Elsie went from one dealer to another looking for Art Nouveau cards.

They ended up with three by Mucha and two by Belgian artist Gisbert Combaz, one of which was called *La Mer*, which Elsie really liked, even more than the Muchas.

At one stage, Elsie had trouble prising Raji away from a stall. When she went to investigate, she found him eagerly sorting through a pile of postcards of nude women. Some were even pornographic to a degree Elsie had scarcely even thought possible.

She told him that the pornographic ones were not to be purchased, but would allow him a couple of the other, more classically beautiful images. After considerable deliberation, as if he were choosing another wife, he selected *Rêverie*, along with *Heure de Nuit*, a photograph of a young lady who seemed to be floating, naked of course, on clouds.

As the group walked back to Le Grand, passing the green cast-iron Art Nouveau entrance to the Louvre Metropolitain underground station, Elsie noticed that Raji kept glancing at his two favourite cards.

Early that evening, as they sat in the lounge before dinner, a young bellboy waited patiently for Raji's attention, but he was in deep conversation with Cecil.

"Yes, sweetheart, what is it?" Elsie called, waving him over.

In the boy's hand was an envelope addressed to Raji. "Raji! The young man has something for you!"

Raji broke off his conversation and took the envelope, which he noticed had the double-headed eagle of Russia upon it. He then nodded to the boy to depart. Opening the envelope, he read the contents silently, before repeating part of it aloud: "... In view of complex nature and significant work to process, payment of sum is requested to see work completed with great speed and success. Audience with Tsar are rare. Special gift to show bond between people of Tikari and Russia may make meeting possible ..."

"In other words they want to be bribed!" chimed in Cecil.

Elsie turned to Raji. "It depends how much you want to go there, darling."

"Well, I do really want to see his cars!"

"Not to mention the family and the palaces!" Elsie added, feeling that Raji's priorities were askew.

"Very well! On Friday, Abu and Kempster will join me in a visit to the embassy. Abu, you must bring the jewels with you."

Two days later, they arrived at the Russian Embassy, prepared to do a deal. A significant payment in francs was made to expedite their request, though the gift part was more complicated.

Raji was prepared to offer a valuable gem in return for an agreed meeting with the Romanovs, but started with a small emerald. This was rejected, politely, as 'disrespectful'. A larger sapphire was proposed, and was inspected by an 'approved' jeweller.

A conversation then took place in Russian between the embassy secretary and the jeweller, where it was suggested that Abu may well have something more 'up his sleeve'. He did indeed, though Raji was reluctant to play his final card, so protested when he sensed that the sapphire might be rejected.

In this battle of brinkmanship, the sapphire was, as expected, rejected, and Raji was forced to anticipate a final offering, but not before feigning to leave, so disillusioned did he pretend to be with developments.

The secretary and jeweller departed the meeting room for consultation with the ambassador, only to return shortly, and in a most apologetic tone, insist that just one, small final step higher was likely to bring progress towards what Raji wanted.

The final card, a large ruby, was then produced, was checked by the jeweller and the ambassador was summoned. All agreed that the promised gift of the ruby would give the best chance of a meeting, so the gem and Raji were photographed and details of the Tikari entourage, their requests and requirements taken. The photographs and information were passed to a courier, who left immediately for St Petersburg. All Raji had to do now, was wait as patiently as he rarely did.

It was a full week before the embassy passed on the news, that they had received a telegram from the Romanov court confirming that the visit and meeting could go ahead on the Gregorian calendar date of Wednesday 5 June 1912.

As per the agreement, Raji had to deposit the ruby with the Russian ambassador to confirm acceptance, which he did.

For Elsie, Paris was Europe's shop window to elegance, though it guaranteed her one great regret: she could not, in deference to her new sari-wearing lifestyle, purchase any of the beautiful European dresses that filled the couturier's Parisian boutiques.

There were now four and half weeks left, till their St Petersburg appointment. While everyone loved being in the French capital, the whole Tikari party agreed that, as they had to head east eventually, this was an excellent opportunity to take a whirlwind grand tour of the Continent.

So it was, that Raji, Elsie, Cecil and Grace spent two days of deliberation at the suite's dining table, leafing through atlases, Le Grand's English-language European guidebooks and *Bradshaw's Continental Railway Guide*, before determining the tour content.

When they had finished, Elsie bought a postcard of the Eiffel Tower and wrote to Emma:

Dearest Em,

Paris is so much more than the Eiffel Tower: beautiful fashions, smart cafes with sumptuous cakes, elegant avenues, Art Nouveau, magnificent monuments! Oh

Even Madame Lemaire was hauled in for her advice, though she gave it on one condition. "My son Jean, works as a hairdresser in Passage Choiseul, not far from here. He is struggling financially, but is only young, and I feel, very talented at his craft. It would be a great honour if both Your Highnesses would allow him to cut and shape your hair, before your departure!"

Madame Lemaire had been such a help, that refusal was not an option, though Raji wondered whether he might not have to get his hair redone prior to their arrival in Russia.

On the morning of Friday 3 May, they strolled from Le Grand towards Passage Choiseul with some degree of apprehension. What if this Jean was not the master-craftsman his mother believed?

Following Madame Lemaire's instructions, they headed down Avenue de l'Opéra until they reached rue des Petits Champs, where they turned left. Soon, they were outside the entrance to Passage Choiseul, a tiled and glass-covered walkway flanked by mid-range shops.

As they strolled north, the clock above the classical marble balcony at the passage's end, made the first of ten chimes ring through the near deserted corridor. Before the tenth chime had echoed, they found 'Salon de Coiffure-Choiseul'.

Although, it is perhaps more appropriate to state that the shop found them, for a handsome and dark-haired young man stood outside, beaming in their direction. Elsie offered her hand, as this had to be Jean, but he held her fingers only lightly and bowed deeply.

"Who would like to be first, Your Highnesses?" he asked with what sounded to Elsie as very stylish and sweet, French-accented English.

Elsie reasoned that she would take longer, so offered herself as the first guinea pig, while Raji wandered off to look at the shops nearby.

It was over an hour before Elsie's appointment had ended. Raji was amazed with the result. In India, most women, including Elsie, kept their hair straight, but Jean had added waves and curls, turning Elsie into an Art Nouveau masterpiece.

Elsie's response, like most women's, was as much determined by the reaction of others, so she too was delighted. As Raji moved in to the seat to replace her, he passed her a bottle of just-released perfume he had bought from 'Parfumerie de Choiseul', a couple of shops along.

Though normally directive in how Raji's hair should be cut, Elsie let Jean do what he wished, and headed into the passage, to try the perfume. The flowery, oriental fragrance, with a dusky scent that seemed like sweet almond cake was something she had not experienced before, so she checked with Raji again. He confirmed he loved it too, so she marched straight into the perfume shop and asked that every single bottle of Guerlain Paris' L'Heure Bleue in the store be packaged and sent to The Waldorf Hotel in London.

While Jean was finishing with Raji, he noticed that Elsie was watching intently—watching everything. Jean checked and double-checked with Raji that he was happy, and with Elsie, that she was too. Raji was so delighted with the result he paid Jean's boss four times the charge. Then Elsie pulled Raji into the passage, telling Jean that they would be back in a minute …

Chapter 62

The Grand Tour Begins

When I was young, a walrus spoke of cabbages and kings
Of medieval castles and the settings for such things:
"For fabled art and history, the Continent's the lure
You can be the architect—design your own Grand Tour!"

Tears ran down Madame Lemaire's face, but they were mostly tears of joy and gratefulness. Elsie had convinced Raji that young Jean should become the official hairdresser at Tikari Raj, on a significantly boosted salary. Unsurprisingly, the young Frenchman had accepted on the spot.

It was agreed that he would be at The Waldorf Hotel in London by 1st July, then later accompany them on the steamer back to India.

Madame, Jean and the hotel manager waved goodbye as the vehicles carrying the Tikari party and their Louis Vuitton luggage headed for Gare de l'Est station to begin the grand tour.

They only had one month before they had to be in St Petersburg, so all appreciated they would only be seeing some highlights of the Continent. Nevertheless, everyone was most enthusiastic, even Raji, who had not ventured beyond France, Belgium and Switzerland before.

To begin, there was a long first-day journey to Munich in southern Germany via Nancy and Stuttgart, but Elsie made sure that she had a window seat as the express train eased out of Paris at 9 am on Saturday 4 May 1912, heading east.

After a few hours of looking at the countryside and occasional towns, came lunch in the dining car just before Nancy, afternoon tea before Strasbourg, and then tea after Karlsruhe in Germany. The repetitive clickety-clack on the rails sent Elsie off to sleep not long after leaving Stuttgart and heading south.

It was Grace who gently whispered into her ear to awaken the sleeping beauty: "Your Highness! We are in Munich!" Elsie awoke from what had been a deep sleep. It was 11.23 pm as the train slipped into platform 14, one of twenty-two at Munich

486

Hauptbahnhof.

By the time the group shuffled in to the grand Bayerischer Hof in Promenadeplaz, it was close to midnight. Even at that late hour, Manager, Hermann Volkhardt, alerted by Cecil's telegram detailing their late arrival, was waiting in the lobby.

This was to be Elsie and Raji's first but certainly not last experience of typical German discipline and efficiency.

After a lengthy sleep in, the group emerged for lunch, and, after a suggestion from Herr Volkhardt, an afternoon tour of the sights of Munich.

Three cars and knowledgeable drivers were soon made available—for a fee—and for two and a half hours they slowly wended their way past the most historical buildings of the Bavarian capital. As it was a Sunday, the streets were somewhat quieter than usual.

Following a hearty German meal that included bratwurst, sauerkraut and dumplings, then apple strudel for dessert, the group settled in for another comfortable night in their suites.

Monday brought much promise, which it certainly delivered. Herr Volkhardt had organised three vehicles for 9 am, and they were there, waiting with a few minutes to spare.

They headed north-west, what in decades past would have been a two-hour carriage ride out from the Residenz, the main royal palace in the heart of Munich. Before them on the city's outskirts, spread a ravishing beauty in all her finery: the summer home of the kings of Bavaria, Nymphenburg Palace.

A guide first took them through key parts of the Baroque-style palace buildings, highlighting the magnificently frescoed ceilings and the carriage collection. They then entered the remarkable Gallery of Beauties, featuring thirty-six beautiful young women, all selected by King Ludwig I and painted by the court painter.

Raji and Cecil spent some time with the beauties, critiquing an elite group, but concluded that Elsie would have been a sure and favourite selection, had she stepped back over seventy years.

They shared a picnic lunch that was kindly provided by the hotel, then set off on a meander around the extensive 500-acre estate that was first turned into gardens in the 1600s.

It was bisected by a canal, and sprinkled with small but ornate buildings, including a hunting lodge, a bathhouse, a temple and even a folly that was a monastery ruin.

They eventually wandered back, up the broad, statue-lined avenue to the front of the elongated palace buildings, where at 4 pm, their transport back to the hotel arrived.

That evening, Elsie told the group that if all tours were as beautiful and historically interesting as this one had been, she could happily be on a grand tour for the rest of her life.

The next day, a short train journey south from Munich brought them to the town of Fussen by midmorning. The weather that had held out for so long, threatened showers, though these dared not spoil a visit to one of the icons of tourism, the extravagant Neuschwanstein Castle.

Gasps of awe and wonder spread through the omnibus, as Ludwig II's first creation came into sight. Situated on a rocky outcrop above a valley floor, Neuschwanstein looked everything a dream castle should be. From that moment, Elsie decided she was joining Ludwig's team, no matter the criticism or cost. She was metaphorically standing by him—and she had not yet ventured inside.

Raji had bought an Eastman Kodak Brownie 'box' camera in Paris and wanted Abu to take a photograph of him and Elsie with Neuschwanstein in the background. This they did from the swaying Marie Bridge, perched high over the gorge, as Lala kept her distance.

If the castle was impressive from outside, it was nothing like Elsie had expected within: magnificent murals depicting scenes from a heroic Middle Ages, long past. The guide said that many were from Wagner operas, of which Ludwig II was a huge fan. The Throne Hall, with its majestic size and sheer beauty—just like a richly decorated Byzantine church—and the Hall of Singers with its sequence of ornate chandeliers and arch-decorated stage, were Elsie's favourites.

Everywhere Elsie looked, the decoration was colourful and perfect. *This Ludwig had great taste!*

"Ludwig and his doctor drowned in Lake Starnberg on 13 June 1886. He was only forty years old and never married, so he may have liked men more than women. He had spent a lot of money, so there were rumours he was murdered," informed the guide.

"Raji doesn't!" Siri exclaimed, before adding, due to quizzical looks: "I mean he doesn't like men more than women! Anyway, how sad about him dying young! Imagine what he could have created if he had lived to an old age!"

After lunch in a restaurant in the adjacent village of Hohenschwangau, they toured the nearby Hohenschwangau Castle, where Ludwig was born and raised. "I can see where he got his ideas from!" Elsie commented, upon seeing scenes of knights and fair damsels festooning the walls, along with the ubiquitous white swan, the family and castle symbol.

Before leaving, the guide tossed a departing thought hand grenade into the group. "You English," she said—and here, Elsie thought she could have only been talking to Cecil—"may be interested to know that Ludwig's family, the House of Wittelsbach, are the rightful heirs to the British throne through the Stuart line!"

Elsie could not resist saying: "Oh, imagine how much more creatively Buckingham Palace might have been designed!"

Everyone was still buzzing with excitement when they sat down for dinner in the Bayerischer Hof. Herr Volkhardt was delighted to hear they enjoyed their excursion, but a little concerned that their next planned journey was a day trip to Lindau.

"Lindau is old and its harbour and Lake Constance are beautiful, but it will take over four hours in the train just to get there. May I suggest an alternative, Your Highnesses?"

"Please, by all means, Herr Volkhardt!" Raji insisted. "After all, we do not have the local knowledge!"

"Then, if you don't mind, as you really enjoyed Neuschwanstein, can I suggest that tomorrow you go instead to Ludwig's favourite creation, Linderhof. It is so rarely visited, but well worth the smaller journey of about two hours. I can arrange a driver and an omnibus along with a packed lunch. What do you say?"

"I say, that sounds just smashing! The more of the so-called 'mad' king's creations the better!" cried Cecil, accentuating his Englishness.

So it was, that at 9 am on Wednesday 8 May, they set out for Linderhof—and found out that Herr Volkhardt was right.

Set across rolling hills and surrounded by craggy peaks, the Rococo-style Linderhof Palace, was surrounded by a beautiful mix of English and French-style gardens, urns, statues and a central pond. Elsewhere in the grounds were other gems such as the Moorish Kiosk, the Moroccan House and the Venus Grotto.

Herr Volkhardt was elated to hear his suggestion had been so well received, throwing in a free bottle of wine for their last night in Munich.

"Where do you head tomorrow?" he asked, sensing another opportunity to impart his knowledge.

"Salzburg!" responded Cecil. "We will use it as a base."

"Excellent! It is a beautiful city, but can I suggest that you take a day trip back to Berchtesgaden, its salt mines, which you can and should go in, and also the nearby Lake Königssee."

Grace noted these down with the best spelling she could manage, then, the manager made one final suggestion. "Please, also take a day trip by train south from Salzburg to the lakeside town of Hallstatt. You will not regret it!"

On the Thursday, they travelled by train east through the spectacular Bavarian countryside, stopping at Prien am Chiemsee to detour to Ludwig's third famous creation, Herrenchiemsee, a large Baroque-style palace and grounds that Ludwig modelled on Versailles. Not having been to the latter, all were impressed by its positioning on an island in a lake, but not as entranced as they had been at Neuschwanstein and Linderhof.

On the next stage, the train travelled east through the finest scenery yet: steep hills dotted with quaint houses, bypassed by blue-green flowing rivers.

Leaving Germany, they arrived in Salzburg, Austria, the birthplace of Mozart, where they perused their accommodation at Hotel Zum Goldenen Hirschen, an inn with a few rooms above, on the Old Town's most famous street, Getreidegasse. It was certainly not the luxury they were used to elsewhere, but it was at least central.

As they wandered the streets of the Old Town, passing the

building on Getreidegasse where Mozart was born, as well as the many little shops and taverns hidden down covered passageways, they wondered if there could be a prettier old city heart in the whole of Europe.

After stopping to buy chocolates and some ice cream, they found themselves in Residence Square facing a line of horse-drawn carriages.

"Raji! Please can we go for a ride?" pleaded Siri, knowing her request was never likely to be refused. Soon, the clippety-clop of horse hooves echoed through the alleyways and squares of the Old Town, as four carriages snaked their way around this European jewel—their first experience of the Austro-Hungarian Empire.

The next morning, they had an early breakfast and took motor cabs to the Salzburg Railway Station, where Cecil made sure they caught the 8.23 to Berchtesgaden. An hour and forty-five minutes later, they stepped out into a pretty German town nestled below the snow-capped and shark-toothed Watzmann.

After inquiring at the station, they paid for a short ride west to the Berchtesgaden salt mine, where, to their surprise, they were told that the women had to change from their saris into white trousers and a belted coat, to enter the mine, astride a small train.

Following a safety lecture in German and English about staying together and with the guide, the train took off through the narrow arched but lit tunnel, on a claustrophobic ride, with Abu keeping his head down to ensure it and his turban stayed attached. Two slides and a drift across Mirror Lake later, they emerged from a truly unique experience.

They were advised that a hearty lunch could be had at Königssee, so they headed there next, before taking a magical boat ride across Lake Königssee, fringed by towering peaks, to the iconic pilgrimage Church of St Bartholomew, isolated on the lakeside.

The group comfortably made the 4.22 pm train from Berchtesgaden back to Salzburg, but Raji—not for the first time—expressed concern about the quality of their Salzburg accommodation. It was not anywhere near their usual standard, and Cecil was grilled as to why it was chosen.

He admitted that he had found it in a travel book, not in *Bradshaw's*, but said that none of those that were in the latter, happened to be situated in the Old Town. Elsie was keen that Cecil be seen of value rather than criticised, as this would only make Raji pine for his friend Wakefield, so she said that he had asked her opinion, and that their current accommodation had been her decision.

One night trying to sleep in a substandard room above a noisy inn was enough for Raji, and he was not going to countenance another. Before dinner, Elsie found him, deep in *Bradshaw's*, discovering that the Hotel Bristol, at the entrance to the Mirabell Gardens, just across the Salzach River from the Old Town, would have been a far more appropriate choice.

The Bristol's proprietor, Herr Fleischmann, was most accommodating, but warned them that in order to travel by train to Hallstatt and arrive by lunchtime, they would have to leave Salzburg Station at 7.15 am the next morning.

Creeping out of a sleepy Salzburg, and initially heading north-east, they were fortified by cold meat slices with cheese on crusty bread, followed by fresh fruit. Soon, the train turned south, gliding by beautiful lakes fringed by tall mountains, then passing Kaiservilla, the summer home of Emperor Franz Josef, at Bad Ischl.

The train slowed considerably, till, forty minutes after leaving Bad Ischl, it creaked to a halt in what initially seemed the middle of nowhere, as there were no buildings, just a platform.

"Hallstatt!" the attendant called out and then waved to the Tikari party to follow him. He stepped out on to the platform then offered an arm to assist each of the ladies.

"Oh, what a lovely gentleman!" cried Siri. "Thank you, sweetheart!"

The attendant seemed most pleased as he climbed back on board. He did not hear Siri say to a giggling Lala: "He is probably messing up his trousers right now!" Elsie gave Siri a rebuking whack on the backside, as the train slid away before they all turned to face west.

A short walk brought them to a jetty on the edge of Hallstattersee, a long and deep lake surrounded by high peaks.

Chugging towards them was a ferry on its regular trip to meet train passengers.

In the distance, dwarfed by the mountains, Raji could see Hallstatt, desperately clinging like a non-swimmer to the lower hull of an ocean liner. "I will go up front so I can get some photographs!" he announced.

As the ferry headed back, the captain caught Elsie's eye. "You lucky! Very lucky!" he said with a smile, as the boat sliced its way across the blue-glass water that reflected the sky. "Many time cloud! Nicht heute!"

After a filling schnitzel lunch in the centre of the small town, Raji was recommended an English-speaking guide, Rosa, the wife of the restaurant owner. She started by taking them up a series of steps towards a church, explaining that Hallstatt had been populated for around 4,500 years, and that, traditionally, the men worked in the salt mines.

The more they climbed, the more spectacular the view became, till they stood by the side of the 12th century Catholic Church of Ascension of Our Lady, and on the edge of a small but very pretty graveyard that overlooked the town and lake. "You could say that the dead have the best view in town!" Rosa quipped. "But not for long, as after ten years, yes, they are dug up, their bones are cleaned, and then they are brought over here! Please follow me!"

They turned and walked into the lower level of St Michael's Chapel—the Beinhaus.

"There is no space in the graveyard, so their bones are stored in this bone house."

The Tikari party looked around the room in astonishment. There were levels of skulls with names, dates of birth and death and even artwork upon them. Though they were familiar with the Hindu practice of burning bodies on the ghats, this still came as a shock. Elsie noticed that the skulls seemed to be in family groups, going back generations. Rosa said that some were over 800 years old.

She also pointed out to Raji the best point, down to their left, where a photograph could be taken that highlighted the Evangelical Church of Christ with its clock tower, and the many beautiful old houses in Hallstatt, clinging to the mountainside.

After a full cruise of the lake, they met the train, eventually arriving back in Salzburg after 9 pm. It had been a long but memorable day. Tomorrow, they were off in search of the master of Art Nouveau.

Chapter 63

The Man of Mucha Do

The man with the greying circle beard, walked back into the studio and ordered the three models posing for a part of the third panel of his Slav Epic, to leave and return in a couple of days.

"Please, see Petr on your way out," he called in Czech. "He will pay you now for the days lost!"

Alfons Mucha was not suited or used to interruptions. The world-acclaimed master of Art Nouveau had carved out international fame for his drawings and designs. Now he wanted to focus solely on what he hoped would be his greatest work: a series of monumental canvases telling the story of the Slavic peoples.

So why was it, that when a very mixed and unusual group of visitors arrived at Zbiroh Castle unannounced, he had chosen to stop? Mucha paused for a few moments, running his thumb and forefinger through his beard. He gazed through the skylight wall of his studio, as if searching for his rational reasoning.

Was it the sight of the giant Sikh wearing a turban? Certainly, he was a most marvellous physical specimen, of the type never seen before in these parts. Was it the money of the obviously rich maharaja? Was it the trio of dark-skinned young women whose appearance suggested mystery and erotic excitement?

Or, was it that woman of pale skin yet great beauty, standing behind him in a sari with jewels accentuating her attractiveness? Yes, he knew exactly what it was.

Mucha turned slowly around to face Elsie. He moved closer to her, reaching out his right hand towards her chin. "Those eyes of yours are amazing, for they are so rare. As an artist who knows his colours, I could swear they are violet!"

As he said those words, Elsie smiled and her eyes shone. Alfons could feel his whole body glow in response. As an aesthete—a lover of beautiful things—he had always sought to portray his passion. Now, as his career had turned to the depiction of the struggle and occasional triumphs of his people, he still longed for those days when pure, idealistic and unadulterated beauty ruled.

"Please, Mr Maharaja, leave her with me for the rest of the day and I shall hand you a completed poster tomorrow afternoon!"

"That is all fine and good, Mr Mucha, but I insist that our bodyguard, Abu, stays with you throughout the whole process!" Raji well knew that the painters of women had a reputation for ravishing their subjects, and he had no wish to have Elsie spreading her knowledge of the Kama Sutra in this Bohemian realm.

It was only after the others had left, that Elsie asked Mucha something she had thought about, since the moment they had arrived: "Can you please show us what you have painted of The Slav Epic, sir?"

No creative person could realistically be expected to ignore such a request, and Mucha was no different, ushering Elsie and Abu into a large and dark inner room, where they stood very still until he switched on a light. There were two giant curtains, one on each side of the room. Mucha went towards the one on the far wall and pulled on a cord, until a giant work of art was fully revealed. "This is Panel 1: *The Slavs in their Original Homeland."*

Elsie and Abu gazed in amazement at the work, for it was truly huge.

"Perhaps it will be my biggest," admitted Mucha.

In the painting's foreground, a shaft of light illuminated a young man and woman in white, while, above them, warriors on horseback seemed to be pillaging the countryside, which appeared to be burning against a starry night sky. Elsie thought that it was wonderful, but nothing like the Mucha posters she had seen.

"I did a lot of reading and travelling to try to unravel the history of the Slavic peoples. This is the first in the series. I finished it in January."

"So how many paintings will be in the series?" Elsie asked, genuinely fascinated.

"I have already drafted twenty titles, though their exact content is uncertain. As long as my Chicago benefactor, Mr Charles Crane, continues to pay, I will continue to paint!"

He closed the curtain, while explaining that he wanted to preserve them, by keeping them away from the light. He then drew across the second curtain. "This one, I only finished at the beginning of last week. It is the second in the series and called *The Celebration of Svantovit*."

Elsie looked at the picture for a short while and then asked what 'Svantovit' was.

"He was a Slav pagan god."

Elsie studied the second canvas carefully. It looked nearly as large as the first, though she thought not quite as appealing. There seemed to be too much going on. "I have to say, Mr Mucha, that I prefer your first work, but there is so much I do not understand about the Slavs, that perhaps if I did, I would appreciate this more. In any case, both are remarkable!"

No artist enjoys criticism, though Mucha could tell that Elsie was a bit more intelligent and analytical than his usual female model. He waved them out of the storage area and back into his studio, a room flooded with light. There, he pulled out an easel and attached a long sheet of paper, while Abu took a seat on a chair in the background as Elsie leaned against a table.

"Tell me about the things you like, Your Highness."

"Beautiful things, performing, kindness ..." she began.

"No, no! What sort of objects, creatures?"

"Roses, we have a large collection at our hunting lodge at Bhalwa; we have peacocks there too ..." though she hesitated because she saw he was making notes. "There are palmyra palms—I quite like those, and of course Bengal tigers. They are so beautiful, but my husband and his best friend do their darnedest to kill them!"

Mucha picked up his piece of paper and moved to a bookshelf on the other side of the room, where he pulled out a few books and spent around five minutes leafing through their contents. Elsie could see that they contained detailed drawings.

Bringing them back to his table, he asked Elsie to stand so

that she faced the light of the skylight window, while he turned his easel so that he had the table with the reference books to his right and his back to the light.

"What is the name of the place you rule?" he asked.

"Well, it is called Tikari, and formally my name is Sita Devi, and I am the Maharani of Tikari."

"Could you spell that out for me, please?" She did, and could see him recording it on a piece of paper, though he also seemed to be drawing a large, vertical rectangle.

"Now, I want you to stand for a while, but hold this small stick as if it were a bunch of roses." 'A while' turned in to nearly an hour, during which he frequently walked up to look closely at her earrings and even handle her sari, as if he could translate its feel onto paper. And all the time, she noticed he was still working in pencil.

Then, quite suddenly, he took the sheet of paper off the easel and placed it upside down on the table, so Elsie could not see what was upon it, even though she tried.

He then asked her to turn at an angle, and replaced the stick in her hand with a lead, which he wrapped around the back of her hand, before adding a second sheet to the easel. By midday, he said he was finished with her and she could go. He would do the ink work and add the colour—and have a completed work for her by 4 pm the next afternoon.

* * *

As Mucha's studio filled with the Tikari visitors the next day, Elsie looked around the room for the sign of a finished product, but there was none. However, she did not see sheets hanging over the back of the long easel.

Mucha seemed in a grumpy mood, explaining that the work had kept him up during much of the night, whereas he far preferred to only work in the daylight. As he said this, he turned a sheet back over to the front of the easel, stunning everyone else in the room, for the image could have come out of the best of his poster era.

A palmyra palm framed the left side and the words Sita Devi flowed from their edge along the top to the right. In the middle, standing, and gazing with a beautiful smile was Elsie, holding a bunch of roses. A magnificent peacock curled around her feet and to the right, and the title Maharani of Tikari ran along the bottom of the image.

"It is just beautiful! Fantastic! It looks so like her too—and the colours are wonderful!" cried Raji, and everyone agreed. Elsie was overcome with emotion.

"I had another idea, too, so I created a second one!" Mucha explained, turning a second sheet to the front of the easel, to reveal a second poster. This one had Elsie partly side on at the left, with the edge of a domed Indian palace to the right. In one hand was a gold chain that hung loosely, finishing around the neck of a magnificent Bengal tiger, that seemed to be looking imperiously at the viewer. There again, at the top and bottom were the words:

Sita Devi and Maharani of Tikari

though this time Elsie noticed the Mucha signature.

Raji immediately paid Mucha double and Elsie moved forward and gave him a long hug and a kiss. "You are a genius!" she whispered.

"She is a charming, beautiful and intelligent woman, Mr Maharaja," he responded. "You are a very lucky man!"

As they headed out of Zbiroh Castle with the posters in a tube, Elsie turned to Raji and informed him that she would be giving the 'Tiger' poster to her dear friend Emma.

Chapter 64

Through the Heart of the Empire

You can taste it in their cafes, hear it when they speak a bit
You can sense it from their manner, these two cities don't quite fit
Vienna and Budapest — no twins were more apart
The Austro-Hungarian Empire had a fracture in its heart.

Late on Friday 17 May 1912, the train delivered the Tikari party
into the very heart of eastern Austria, its capital Vienna.

From Wien Hauptbahnhof, motor cabs transported them the
two and a half kilometres to Grand Hotel Wien.

"You must take a trip on the tram around the Ringstrasse," the
gentleman at reception said, indicating it on the city map. "The
Opera House is magnificent and also St Stephan's Cathedral,
which we call Stephansdom; then, there is the Hofburg Palace
from where you can take a carriage ride, and the many great
cafes. But let me tell you about a place that you really must see,
and hardly any tourists seem to go!"

They leaned forward, for the receptionist whispered this
part: "It is the Imperial Crypt beneath the Capuchin Church,
and it is here." He marked a spot on Neuer Markt Square with
a cross. "If you love your history, you should go there!"

"Is there any Art Nouveau to see?" Elsie asked innocently.

"Any Art Nouveau? This is what in German we call Jugendstil,
and here in Vienna you are in the capital of Jugendstil! The
Secession building, here, is a classic example. Then, there are
the buildings designed by Otto Wagner and Josef Hoffman.
Jugendstil buildings, you will see them on nearly every street
in the city! Then, there are the paintings of Gustav Klimt ..."

"Unfortunately, we only have a day, as we leave on Sunday
morning for Budapest," Cecil interrupted.

The gentleman leaned forward and spoke in an even quieter
but no less earnest voice: "You know I really should be telling
you to eat here, as our dining room is just magnificent, but the
weather now is good, so you should take a walk tomorrow
evening through the Naschmarkt, which is over here." He
pointed again to the map. "It has food and items of interest

from everywhere!"

Before they headed off to their rooms, Elsie pulled Cecil Kempster aside, telling him that she feared for their schedule given the amount of sightseeing they were doing and their St Petersburg deadline. "Please, Cecil, show Raji that you are in control of things, otherwise he will wish he had Wakefield here, instead!"

The next morning, while at breakfast in Grand Hotel Wien, Cecil impressed on everyone the need to be in St Petersburg on Monday the 3rd of June at the latest. "We have a meeting with the Tsar and his family two days later, so we have to ensure our schedule gets us there on time. We either stay in fewer places than planned, or we make shorter stays."

"We just do not know when we will be back. We must admit that we cannot see everything, even if we were to stay for longer," Grace contributed.

Raji was in no doubt. "It would be an absolute disaster to be late into St Petersburg! Cecil, make whatever changes are needed!"

"Yes, Your Highness!" responded Cecil, though his concerned look in Elsie's direction, clearly indicated he would need her assistance.

* * *

The friar in the black robe with a white cord, who opened the door to the Capuchin Church in Neuer Markt Square the next morning, spoke only enough English to appreciate that Friar Robert was needed as a guide.

The balding Friar Robert could have literally journeyed from Sherwood Forest, thought Elsie, though his English was augmented with an excellent knowledge of the contents of the Imperial Crypt.

As Friar Robert lit the pair of large candles that he and Raji would carry, it was the sharp-eyed Siri, who noticed it ... "The matchbox, Your Highness, look at the matchbox!"

Instantly, everyone, including Friar Robert, did, and realised to their amazement that on the lid of the matchbox was a printed colour drawing of Elsie, with 'THE MAHARANI OF TIKARI' above and 'MADE IN AUSTRIA' below.

"It looks like it was drawn from *The Empress* cover photo!"

observed Cecil.

"That's funny!" said Friar Robert. "I never noticed this one before, though I do recall we have a current Austrian matchbox series featuring Indian rulers! If you would be kind enough to autograph the matchbox, Your Highness, before you leave, I would feel most blessed!"

They passed down the stairs, Elsie wondering what and whom they might see, but it was only as they stepped through the gateway and into an area with a low stone and vaulted ceiling, that the scale and type of what they would encounter became evident, even in the candlelight.

"We have 147 members of the ruling Habsburg family interred here," the friar said, pointing down rows of gleaming metal sarcophagi, before adding: "The earliest dates from 1633, when Emperor Mathias and Empress Anna were brought here. Please take your time to walk around, and I shall meet you down the end of the isle, before we go around the corner and into the modern section."

Following like moths clinging by a flame, they noticed ornate and gilded caskets. Some had long inscriptions, but most just relief ornamentation. Lala let out a squeal, only to quickly apologise, when she saw the grinning and crowned death's head on Emperor Charles VI's sarcophagus.

Ahead in a much higher domed area lay a clearly important paired casket. Far grander than any other, with excessive ornamentation and great size, its occupants must have chosen the spot and their ultimate resting surrounds well before they died.

"Empress Maria Theresa and her husband," explained Friar Robert. "Turn right from here and pass through a sequence of other vaults, until you reach the last one. I will meet you there."

The centrepiece of the final vault where Friar Robert was waiting, was a pair of gilded and raised tombs, with a space between them.

"The one here on our left is our late Empress Elisabeth, commonly known as Sissi. She married Emperor Franz Joseph at just fifteen and lived a generally unhappy life, before she was stabbed through the heart by a file-wielding Italian anarchist. She was the first cousin of Ludwig II of Bavaria. You may have heard of him."

"Oh yes!" responded Elsie eagerly. "We visited his palace creations and loved them!"

"So, Friar Robert," asked Grace, "what is the space for, next to Sissi?"

"Ah, that is where our current emperor, Franz Josef will lie. Over to our right is their son, Crown Prince Rudolf. Another tragic story, for he killed himself and his mistress in a murder-suicide."

"Are their bodies really inside?" asked Lala, still feeling a bit uneasy about the whole experience.

"Yes, but a few of the rulers have their organs elsewhere. Even though she was from the Bavarian ruling house of Wittelsbach, Sissi's heart is buried in Hungary, for she learnt their language and had them incorporated in the dual monarchy."

"None of this sort of thing will be for us, Friar Robert," Raji chimed in. "As Hindus, we will be cremated on the banks of the Ganges or its tributaries!"

Elsie was still digesting the thought of that ultimate scenario, as they wound their way back through Habsburgs of the past, then up and out into the light and movement of modern-day Vienna. From there, they walked along to St Stephan's, admiring in particular its roof tiles.

After lunch in the beautiful Café Central—an occasion that Elsie found more painful than enjoyable due to the number of smokers—they strolled through the caramel marble magnificence of the Opera House. They then took an open carriage ride to the Secession building, delighting in the sight of the stone lizard climbing its façade and its golden dome of laurel leaves.

From late afternoon to the early evening, they meandered up and down the rows of stalls in the Naschmarkt, marvelling at the range of goods and sampling the food.

* * *

It was after midday the next day, when the train pulled in to Budapest's Keleti Station, and a further half hour before they stood at the large windows of the best suite of rooms in the Grand Hotel Hungaria, on Belgrád Rakpart, overlooking the Danube.

They might well have headed out to look at the city nicknamed 'The Paris of the East', but Cecil had been nervous and irritable all morning and Elsie wanted to get to the bottom of it.

Leaving Raji in their salon, she went to Cecil's room, staying for over an hour. When she emerged, she was wiping away tears, for there was simply no way around it: the tour had to be reduced in content to ensure they made St Petersburg in just over two weeks time.

At a meeting of all eight travellers, she apologised for pushing Cecil to include a cruise from Venice to Constantinople, with planned stops at Ragusa and Cattaro on the Dalmatian coast, the site of Olympia and the Parthenon in Athens, as well as the historic city of Constantinople itself. This was entirely impractical given their deadline.

"What grand tour does not include Florence, Rome and Venice and while these were always to be part of our schedule, it is now these that we must concentrate on. Cecil has been most correct, in alerting me to the impossibility of the schedule!"

* * *

That evening, as they dined in the Hungaria's Winter Garden room, under its glass ceiling and with the fountain babbling away nearby, Raji backed out of his seat to get a better look at the beautiful mother at the table behind—and straight into a waiter about to place a bowl of goulash soup in front of the man at her table.

"Isten!" the man cried in Hungarian, as the bowl's contents emptied down his cream suit.

It took a while for calm and order to be restored, by which time it was obvious that the paprika in the goulash had ruined the outfit. Raji was most apologetic and insisted that he would pay for a new suit and more, though he still took the opportunity to again appreciate the attractiveness of the man's wife.

The elegant gentleman in his forties with a moustache, took a business card out of his soiled coat and handed it to Raji:

Öszi Kornél
Editor, Magyar Turf
Budapest IV, Szép utca 3

"Mr Kornél, let me emphasise …" Raji started.

"No, no! Hungarians are the only Europeans who write their surname first. In English, my name would be Kornél Öszi!" he said, in good but accented English.

"Well, Mr Öszi, I am the Maharaja of Tikari, and I insist that I get you a replacement suit tomorrow!"

"Your English is very good, Mr Öszi," Elsie noted.

"I travel a bit as the editor of the *Hungarian Turf* newspaper. In fact, I was in England in 1907 to see Orby win the Epsom Derby."

"My wife, Sita," Raji interrupted, appreciating she had not been introduced.

"And my wife, Jolán, and my daughters, Kató and Joli. Are you in Budapest for long, Your Highness?"

"No, we just have a full day in Budapest tomorrow before heading towards Florence."

"Well, then, Your Highness, I offer you a deal. Tomorrow, we will go together and order a new suit. In return, I will have the great pleasure of showing you around this beautiful city!"

This was an offer too good to refuse and Mr Öszi suggested they meet at Café Gerbeaud in Gizella Square, at 10 am. "It is easy to find. Just walk up Váci Street until you reach the square and it will be the big white building facing you."

The Hungaria's receptionist gave them directions as they stood in the hotel's high, arched vestibule. "Walk two blocks back from the hotel and the Danube, then turn left onto Váci utca, the main shopping street. Gizella tér will be just ahead."

The Tikari party found Váci utca with ease. As they walked up the street, their initial impressions of yesterday were confirmed: Budapest was most civilised and ornate in its appearance. It was not quite what they had expected.

Café Gerbeaud too was a shock, with its large four-storey building, ornate interior, rococo ceiling and chandeliers.

As they relaxed at tables, surrounded by carved wood, smoothed marble and fashioned bronze, Mr Öszi pointed out the myriad of cakes on offer behind the glass counter.

"Hungarian food is so good that Hungarians live rich and short lives!" he joked. "You must try one of our national favourites: the Dobos torta. It is a layered chocolate sponge cake topped with caramel."

"Please, everyone! Take whatever you wish with your tea or coffee—I will pay!" Raji insisted.

As Abu, Abid and the others checked out their sweet options, Elsie asked Mr Öszi if he had a horse as he wrote about horses.

"Only a few hundred!" he replied, with a smile.

Upon leaving the café, their host insisted they drop in to the Budapest Tourism Office, which happened to be just on the corner of Gizella tér, at Deák Ferenc utca 2. There they bought city maps and Elsie purchased postcards for Emma and May Maxwell.

"That suit, Mr Öszi, we must buy that!" Raji insisted.

"Just a few steps up Deák Ferenc, Your Highness, at No. 10!"

After walking up the street just less than a block, they reached a large and ornate seven-storey department store with polished black marble framing its huge display windows. On show were bridle dresses and clothing of all kinds.

Standing on the corner of Deák Ferenc and Becsi utcas, they all looked up at the elaborate store entrance: above and to the sides of an Art Nouveau entrance cover, large lamps hung from the mouths of bearded mythological creatures, while the Austro-Hungarian Coat of Arms—signifying royal appointment—sat in relief on a curved pressed steel sign over the words: Kunz József és Társa.

"Does that mean it is the business of József Kunz?" asked Elsie.

"Very good, Your Highness! 'És Társa' means 'and Company'. We nickname this place the 'Kunz Palace'."

They walked inside and were very surprised with the space and modern layout. There was an atrium and oriental carpets could be seen hanging from the railings on the first floor, with specialty areas off to each side, featuring everything from bed sheets, tablecloths, stylish clothes and underwear, to walking canes and hats.

A distinguished-looking and impeccably tailored older man with a neatly trimmed white beard approached and greeted Mr Öszi warmly: "Szervusz Kornél!"

"This is the owner, Ferenc Kunz," Öszi said. "Ferenc, meet

my new friend, the Maharaja of Tikari and his party!"

Ferenc looked around the group, but his eyes lit up when he spotted Elsie—and their host noticed too. "Ferenc's English is not good, but every Hungarian appreciates that beauty is universal!"

While Mr Öszi was measured up for a new suit, the others ventured up the lift and around the three public levels of the store. By the time they were ready to leave, they had selected a number of items, the cost of which needed to be tallied on the firm's counting slip that totalled purchases. Raji was delighted to find a walking stick topped by a silver motor car handle, Elsie chose a parasol fringed with Hungarian peasant embroidery, while Raji added a selection of silk cravats and ties for the male members of the Tikari party. He had the purchases packaged together and couriered back to the Hungaria.

The suit for Mr Öszi, Ferenc insisted, would be made by the women working on the top floor and ready by 5 pm that afternoon.

They all walked down to the end of Váci utca and through the massive Great Market Hall, that was filled with wares and food, before turning back to have lunch at Mátyás Pince Restaurant. There, as a gypsy band played, they noted that Mr Öszi was checking his watch.

Just before 1.30 pm, he rose and excused himself momentarily. He climbed the steps and headed outside, before returning. "It is here. Time to go!"

Mr Öszi had hired an omnibus, and for the next three hours, their host guided the whole Tikari party on a zigzagging tour of the Hungarian capital. First, on the Pest side, looking at the grand statues, woodwork and stained glass of the monumental parliament, then the opulent opera house, which Elsie thought was even prettier than Vienna's. They then ventured on to the sculptured parklands of Margaret Island in the middle of the Danube, before turning back to pass the Art Nouveau façade of the Gresham Palace building.

Crossing the Elisabeth Bridge to the older, Buda side of the Danube, they parked in the Castle District and went inside the Gothic and centuries old Mátyás Church and marvelled at the view from the seven-towered Fisherman's Bastion before walking around the royal palace.

They had paprikás csirke followed by pancakes for dinner at Gundel Restaurant, back on the Pest side in the XIVth District, where Mr Öszi explained that the restaurant's twin elephant logo had nothing to do with India, rather its proximity to the Budapest Zoo.

That night, Raji hugged Elsie as they stood on Gellért Hill on the Buda side, looking down on the lights of Budapest, twinkling from a thousand lamp posts and outlining the cross-Danube bridges. With the curving river bathed in the glow of moonlight, Elsie wondered if there were many prettier sights on earth.

There may not have been, but, as their grand tour turned south to Italy, she would be searching for them.

Chapter 65

The Angels of St Petersburg

Each face it is well known, from the papers in the West
But a picture tells a story, only on the surface best
Of the Angels of St Petersburg, who shines most like a star?
Who is the greatest jewel within the family of the Tsar?

Raji and Elsie collapsed, exhausted, onto their large bed in the multi-roomed Presidential Suite in the Grand Hotel D'Europe, on Nevsky Prospekt in St Petersburg.

It was the afternoon of Monday 3 June 1912. They had kept to their prearranged schedule to be in Russia's imperial capital before their meeting with the ruling Romanov family on the Wednesday.

The sheer intensity and excitement of seeing some of the world's great buildings and works of art, day after day, was always going to eventually take its toll.

In Florence, they had wandered through its medieval streetscape, crossed the iconic Ponte Vecchio, before strolling through the gardens of the Pitti Palace. They then viewed the works of Botticelli, da Vinci, Raphael and others in the Uffizi Gallery, prior to seeing the tombs of Galileo, Dante, Michelangelo and other greats in the Basilica of Santa Croce.

In Rome, they had visited St Peter's Basilica, picked their way through the ruins of the Roman Forum, clambered through the Colosseum and stood within the near 2,000-year-old magnificence of the Pantheon.

Meandering across Italy to Venice, they had ventured into St Mark's Basilica, then, stepped on the Bridge of Sighs and the Rialto, before spending hours on a motor launch traversing the Grand Canal and many of the city's minor waterways.

Having read so much in the past about Italy, for Elsie it was almost like visiting an old friend. Raji's eyes all too often became glazed, when forced to look at ever more works of classical beauty, but to Elsie, they were more like oxygen. *Everything has been marvellous,* she reflected. *Yet, after the frantic pace of the past few weeks, I wouldn't mind a return to my normal Indian palace routine.*

Even more tiring had been the multi-day train journey to Russia. Now, the soft, luxurious pillows and sheets of their St Petersburg hotel bed offered many hours of sanctuary.

* * *

The knocking at the door of their suite may well have started long before Elsie had heard it. As she wrapped her gown around her and exited the bedroom, she glanced at the French clock on the mantelpiece in the formal dining room—and then a second time, just to make sure, for it said 9.47. All she knew was that it looked like daytime and that the knocking was continuing. She opened the door to a smartly dressed butler.

"Your Highness, so sorry to wake you. Would you and His Highness like breakfast in your suite?"

Such an offer was not to be refused, and within minutes an assortment of breads, fillings, fruits and juices were spread across part of their French Empire dining table.

Before the butler departed, another, though more familiar figure, appeared at the door. The hotel's Swiss General Manager, Josef Wolflisberg-Giger, stood still and silently in the doorway—and it looked as though he had something behind his back.

Elsie wondered if he should come in, but he seemed to be determined to wait until the butler departed. She also wondered if she could call him 'Joe' given his impossibly complicated hyphenated name, which she had already forgotten.

Joe, the manager, smiled at the butler as he slipped out, then asked if he might come in, saying that he felt he should also close the door. Once inside, he drew his right hand out from behind his back and handed an envelope to Raji, telling him the message was very important and that none of it should be communicated to anyone outside of the room.

The first thing Raji noticed was that the envelope carried the double-headed eagle crest of royal Russia on both the front upper left and above the seal on the back. He sensed that it must have something to do with their visit to the Tsar, but still

510

opened it with some trepidation. Elsie moved in next to him to read it:

—In Confidence—

Your Highnesses
The Maharaja and Maharani of Tikari,

As the Imperial Guest Liaison Officer, I will be meeting you in Grand Hotel D'Europe's lobby at 2 pm on Tuesday 22 May.

The General Manager will point you out to me. We will have some time to see St Petersburg, but for security reasons, you must wear ordinary clothes and no details relating to Wednesday are to be discussed with anyone.

Natalia Bazhenova
Office of the Tsar
Ministry of the Imperial Court

"There must be a mistake!" cried Raji, fearful his chance to meet the Tsar had been lost. "Today is Tuesday 4th of June and the 22nd of May was nearly two weeks ago!"

"Please, Your Highness, do not panic, it is a common error," explained Joe. "Dates in Russia work on the Julian calendar, thirteen days behind the Gregorian. If you were due to meet the Tsar tomorrow in European date, then it is the 23rd here. All will be fine!"

"I do remember, darling, that the note from the Russian Embassy did state 5 June on the Gregorian calendar, though I must admit I did not understand its significance," Elsie said.

As 2 pm approached, Elsie stood in the lobby studying the street outside. There seemed to be more people: a newspaper seller, a beggar and gardener had all appeared in the last few minutes. She was just going to tell Raji it seemed a little odd, when an attractive Russian woman in her forties, partly disguised beneath a peasant headscarf, moved very close and whispered in excellent English: "Don't worry, Your Highness, they are our people! I am Natalia. How many are in your travelling party?"

511

"Eight, including my husband and I."

"And the others?"

Elsie pointed to the other six, waiting in the lobby. Natalia took one look at the giant Abu and said: "No! His turban must come off. He will be recognised as a foreigner too easily and our safety will be compromised!"

Raji stepped in—and he was angry. "He is a Sikh and a turban covering his hair is part of his religion! I will never ask him to remove it!"

Natalia, rather than backing off, moved close to Raji. "I have my job to do, Your Highness, and I know this city and its people. It is bad enough … well, the fact that you are dark makes you stand out as a foreigner. There are people who might kidnap or kill you. There are revolutionaries and anarchists out there. We can never be too careful, you must understand, it is part of my job!"

The last thing Raji wanted to do was compromise their visit to the Tsar, so he knew he could not take the matter further. Instead, he went over to the other six, telling them they had his permission to go out into St Petersburg, but to do so separately from him and Elsie—and to take great care.

How ironic, thought Elsie, *that our own bodyguard is viewed as a security risk!*

Natalia turned and made a hand signal to a man near the front door, who promptly disappeared. "What would you like to see in St Petersburg?"

"Oh, everything would be great, but do you have any Art Nouveau?"

"Yes, we call it Style Moderne … you will see … follow me!" she ordered, as she headed further in to the hotel, then took a right turn down a corridor. Before opening a door that was a side entrance, she turned and double-checked Raji's and Elsie's appearance. Both were wearing regular European clothes.

"Good, we go!" Natalia said, pushing open the door to reveal a carriage drawn by a pair of horses with two scruffy-looking men in the driver's seat. "Interior Ministry Security," she said quietly, indicating in their direction with the barest lifting of a finger.

They stepped inside, with Natalia making sure she sat

between both Raji and Elsie on the bench seat. Elsie could not help looking around, as much to try to spot members of the security detail as the novel scenery.

On the first bend, Elsie slid sideways into Natalia and felt something hard against her side: Natalia had a pistol concealed under her clothes.

Their carriage turned east on to the long and broad main thoroughfare, Nevsky Prospekt, before dodging a couple of electric trams rattling along their pair of rails, that were attempting to service the transport needs of the people who choked St Petersburg's main artery.

Soon they paused outside the Art Nouveau masterpiece of the Elisseeff Brothers Emporium, with its statues and stained glass. They then continued down Nevsky until reaching Fontanka Canal, where they swung around to the other side before heading back west to marvel at the massive Gostiny Dvor shopping complex.

After glimpsing Grand Hotel D'Europe on the other side of the Prospekt, they stopped on the verge of the grounds of the huge Cathedral of Our Lady of Kazan. Natalia pointed across the avenue to the remarkable grey and red granite House of Singer, the headquarters of the sewing machine company's Russian operations. With its ornate arched windows, gold ornamentation, and unique glass tower and globe, Natalia seemed quite correct in declaring it was "Surely the finest Style Moderne building in St Petersburg!"

Next, they swung past the Singer building and down the side of Griboyedov Canal, Natalia commenting that St Petersburg was often referred to as 'The Venice of the North' given the kilometres of canals that threaded through the city.

"We were just in Venice, which was beautiful," said Elsie. "Before that we were in Budapest, which we were told was 'The Paris of the East'. There may be some similarities in these cities, but really, they are so different, too!"

Soon a remarkably colourful, onion-domed building came into full sight. "It is the Church of Our Saviour on Spilled Blood, built over the spot where Tsar Alexander II, Tsar Nicholas' grandfather, was assassinated in 1881," said Natalia. "I will take you inside."

The closer they got, the more magical the structure appeared, with colourful mosaic icons decorating the outside. Inside, the space and colour were simply breathtaking—and the first time Elsie and Raji had ventured into a Russian Orthodox church.

As they walked around, amazed at the beauty of the tiling and rich mosaics on the ceiling, Elsie noticed a number of men wandering the site who seemed more interested in watching them than the treasures all around. "Our security!" whispered Natalia, ever watchful herself.

They stopped in front of a covered and sealed-off area that had a religious feel. "It was on these very cobblestones that the Tsar fell. He had stepped out of his carriage after a bomb had been thrown, only to be struck by another on this spot."

For two hours more, they crisscrossed St Petersburg, trying to take in as much as they could of this northern marvel, before Natalia had them back at the hotel. "11 am tomorrow you will leave for the Winter Palace. Captain Rek, the Tsar's personal bodyguard and I will be at the door of your suite at 10.15 am. You should each have only one attendant present at that time, ready to dress you. No peasant clothes this time!"

That night, just like the previous one, was warm, though this was not what kept Elsie awake. It must have been after midnight when she rose, lured by the sound of traffic on Nevsky Prospekt.

Peering through the curtains, she was stunned to see nearly as many people out on the streets as during the daytime.

Yet it was not the street noise, but the prospect of meeting one of the greatest and most powerful rulers on earth that had her mind racing …

* * *

The promised 10.15 am thump on their door, signalled that their escort was on time. As Elsie opened it to Natalia and a powerfully built officer, she noticed a group of armed soldiers in the background.

Captain Rek introduced himself and immediately ordered Raji and Abid Hussain into the bedroom of the suite. Elsie was told to go into the bathroom with Siri, where Natalia joined them. Both Raji and Elsie had already been dressed in their finest Indian outfits complete with jewellery, but both were ordered to strip, naked.

Piece by piece, as their Russian minders watched carefully, they were dressed again until the jewels were applied and the 'all clear' was given. *Obviously,* Elsie thought, *this was a security check.*

Abid and Siri were then ordered back to their own rooms. Captain Rek checked his watch and signalled it was time to leave. Cocooned in a wall of security, they took the lift to the ground floor where a line of soldiers indicated they were not heading out the front.

At the back door, a sequence of three cars waited and they were ushered into the centre one. Raji realised it was custom-made as the seat they sat on faced backward, while Captain Rek and Natalia had the forward view, sitting facing them.

As soon as the cars swung into Italyanskaya Ulitsa, Elsie could see things were different. Soldiers lined the street—and continued to do so as they turned left alongside the Griboyedov Canal. When they curved into Nevsky Prospekt, Elsie was shocked to see the normally thronged main avenue had been sealed off.

It was only then that Captain Rek provided an explanation—and almost an apology: "Last month we uncovered a plot in Paris by anarchists to assassinate the Tsar. Even under torture they would not reveal their accomplices. You came from Paris?"

"Yes," said Raji. "But ..."

"We could not take any chances. You do not get a second chance in this game. I was the Tsar's personal bodyguard at the coronation of his cousin George V last year in London. You had an invitation, but did not attend!"

"Yes ..." Raji said again, "... but ..."

"And what, dear Captain Rek, do your intelligence services tell you about me?" inquired Elsie.

"Nothing that would discourage me from having the pleasure of meeting you in person, or hearing you sing, Your Highness!" he said, with a reciprocated smile.

The cars took a final turn right before eventually coming to a halt in front of the Winter Palace, on the Neva River side.

Captain Rek stepped out, then helped Natalia, before saluting, as Raji and Elsie exited onto a red carpet flanked by soldiers. Two lines of Interior Ministry troops were brought to attention, as the captain motioned them on for the climb up the stairs.

Once inside, the red carpet flowed around and upward across a long flight of marble steps. The white walls with gold ornamentation, high ceiling and huge grey marble columns at the top of the stairs caused Elsie to stop momentarily with wonder.

"The Jordan Staircase," Natalia whispered, as Elsie decided to push on, embarrassed that she might be holding up things, given the armed soldiers lining both sides of the red carpet.

"The Great Ante-room," Natalia stated, as they entered a large hall with beautiful flooring. By now the red carpet and lines of soldiers had been left behind, but Elsie could see that there were a pair of different-looking soldiers guarding the door ahead. They sported black wool caps and had long light blue tunics over red shirts, and slightly curved sabres, as well as daggers and pistols, tucked in their belts. They did not look like the type of people to mess with. She was about to ask Natalia, when she received the answer. "Cossacks. They are the Emperor's personal palace guard. Here in the palace they wear soft boots so they don't make a noise—and help polish the floors!"

The Cossacks opened the doors to reveal a huge hall with many large curve-bottomed chandeliers hanging from an ornate ceiling. "The Nicholas Hall," Natalia said—and it took some time to reach its other side—but still they went on, Elsie and Raji wondering whether they would ever get to meet their hosts.

"The Concert Hall!" Natalia proclaimed, as Cossacks opened more doors to another hall. "Nearly there now," she added with a chuckle, no doubt borne out of much experience.

The Cossacks ahead did not open the next door, but waited for Captain Rek to check. He disappeared for a moment, before waving them on. "The Arabian Room!" Natalia announced, as they stepped into a barrel-vaulted room that was smaller than the previous ones, though had another important difference. At the room's end stood four exotically dressed black men, one standing either side of two separate pairs of doors.

"Moorish?" Elsie whispered to Raji, for their white turbans, gold jackets, scarlet trousers, curved shoes and swords suggested elements of Arabic North Africa.

Captain Rek halted their progress in the middle of the room, and they waited, Elsie soaking in the atmosphere in anticipation and silence.

The Moors on the right were the first to move, opening their pair of doors in response to a faint knock.

The man who strode through the door in a military-style black uniform with a bright blue sash was instantly recognisable from newspaper photographs. As he looked in their direction, Elsie could have sworn he smiled. The fact that the Emperor of all Russia had just smiled at her, made her relax, just a little.

Tsar Nicholas was followed into the room by Tsarina Alexandra. She was wearing a glittering tiara with many gemstones, shading her own just slightly, Elsie thought.

The imperial couple halted in the middle of the end of the Arabian Room, some eight paces ahead of their visitors.

"Your Imperial Majesties!" Captain Rek proclaimed. "May I present the Maharaja and Maharani of Tikari!"

Elsie waited for Raji, as what they should do now was new territory for her. "Come on, they are not like the English!" Raji whispered, and she followed him halfway forward. As he stopped and started to bow, she did too, even holding her bow as long as he did.

To their surprise, the Tsar smiled again and moved forward, offering his hand. The Tsarina then did the same.

"Please, let us go this way!" the Tsar said, pointing right towards a door.

They stepped into an elaborately furnished drawing room. "You will understand why this is called the Malachite Room," the Tsar said, focussing their attention on the many rich, deep green but smooth stone columns that spread around the walls.

"Oh, they are so magnificent!" Elsie uttered in wonder, for in truth she had never seen a more beautiful stone.

For about ten minutes, they sat on plush, bright red sofas, talking about St Petersburg and their amazement at its grandeur—with the Tsar saying that the city now had about two million residents—and about India and Australia, neither of which the Tsar had visited. Elsie was a little surprised, but relieved, that both of their hosts spoke such excellent English.

Then they paused, as the Tsar made a signal to Captain Rek, who disappeared into the next room, momentarily, before emerging with a line of children.

"Your Highnesses, let me introduce you to the angels of St Petersburg!" the Tsarina announced, rising and moving towards her brood.

As Elsie followed Raji, she whispered to him to remember to choose the prettiest.

The children, dressed all in white, formed a line from eldest to youngest, as their mother introduced them.

Olga: *strong and confident,* Elsie thought; Tatiana: *perhaps classically beautiful;* Maria: *certainly a little pudgier than the others;* Anastasia: *seems determined not to be ignored, though she is the youngest of the grand duchesses.*

"I will be eleven in two weeks!" Anastasia said in Russian-accented English.

Finally, there was the only boy, the seven-year-old Tsarevich, Alexei. "And I will be the next Tsar of all Russia!" he declared. He was wearing a sailor suit, and as Raji reached to shake his hand, the man standing next to Alexei and wearing a matching sailor's outfit barked "Nyet!" motioning Raji away.

A little embarrassed, the Tsarina explained that Alexei had a cold and that Derevenko, his attendant, was only trying to protect their guests.

The children all joined them on the sofas and it was not long before the Tsar greatly surprised both Raji and Elsie, with the words: "We are not very fond of formality among royalty, and would be happy if you called us Nicky and Alix!"

"If you wish ... Nicky ... then you must call us Raji and Sita."

"You can call me Empress Anastasia!" chimed in one young lady who was soon rebuked by her mother: "Anastasia Nikolaevna!"

With a wave, the Tsar dismissed Captain Rek and Natalia, who had till then remained in the background, as everybody rose to head to lunch in the adjoining private dining room.

After lunch, the girls were determined to show 'Uncle Raji and Auntie Sita' as much of the Winter Palace as they could.

They started at the most secretive part of the palace, the Treasury, where the crown jewels were stored.

Maria explained one particular piece: "You can see here the huge diamond in the Imperial Sceptre. It was given to Empress Catherine the Great by Alexander Orlov ..."

"No, Fatty!" cried Olga. "It was given by Grigory Orlov!"

At this rebuke, Elsie could see Maria blush with hurt and slink to the outside of the group. Elsie moved in behind her and started stroking her cheek and running her hands through her long hair.

"They always call me Fatty!" the twelve-year-old protested in a pained whisper.

"Darling, you are not fat, you are just beautiful!" Elsie said, her breath tickling Maria's ear so much that she giggled away her pain and turned and gave Elsie a hug. From that moment on, Elsie knew who was really the most beautiful of the girls.

On the chime of 3 o'clock, Tatiana exhorted: "The Hermitage!" and the girls, with Maria holding Elsie's hand, Raji in tow and Alexei following a little behind with Derevenko, headed east.

As they reached a door guarded by Cossacks, Tatiana explained that the Hermitage Museum closed to the public at 3 pm, so it was now all theirs, but a firm word in Russian from one of the Cossacks indicated that they should wait until a sweep of the Hermitage declared it empty and safe.

For nearly twenty minutes, they sat on sofas and waited, until they were waved in, but with guards close at hand.

Neither Raji nor Elsie had ever seen anything like the Hermitage before. It was huge, with beautiful ceilings, paintings, sculptures, colourful marbles and inlaid floors. In every single room the patterns and styles were different.

Elsie was particularly taken by some of the breathtaking marble statues, which seemed to have been carved from frozen milk.

Olga spotted a man standing on a stool and adjusting the hands of a magnificent gold and black French clock.

"Mikhail Kirsanov!" she called out, then when he turned, she gave an instruction in Russian. His hand gestures suggested an element of frustration, but the party followed him into a large room that on one side featured beautiful mosaics while intricate white and gold railings fringed an upstairs area filled with Moorish arches.

Mikhail moved towards a large golden display in a glass case and headed around the back. "He is the Master of the Clocks, and this is the Peacock Clock automaton," Olga explained. "Watch it move on the striking!"

Multiple chimes rang out and the bird lifted its array of feathers and turned, then looked down as a dragonfly alighted from a mushroom. "This has happened every evening at 7 pm since the late 1700s!" Olga added. As the group rushed off, Elsie thanked Mikhail, and he seemed to understand, acknowledging her with a nod and smile.

It was near 5 o'clock when the order came for the group to return immediately to the Malachite Room.

There, the Tsar announced that they would, as planned, be taking the royal train back to the Alexander Palace at Tsarskoe Selo, but would like Raji and Sita to join them there for two nights, if they could.

Raji looked at Elsie, just as the Tsar said: "Raji can test my car collection!"

"We would be delighted!" Raji said, as the children cheered— and Maria hugged Elsie.

Chapter 66

"Our Friend"

He sees what others cannot, and he blesses open-palm
He ravishes the female folk, who seek his holy charm
To him alone, the Romanovs are faithful to the end
This 'starets'—mortal saviour of Alexei—is "Our Friend".

The half-hour train ride south to the village of Tsarskoe Selo, did not begin till after 7 pm, as it was agreed that two days of clothing for Raji and Elsie, along with some personal items, had to be transferred from the Grand Hotel D'Europe.

His Majesty's Own Railway Battalion, a specialist security group that fanned out along the length of the twenty-four kilometre track, had easily enough daylight to check for those who might try to derail the royal train, so everyone made it to the village safely.

The Alexander Palace was by far the smaller of the two palaces at Tsarskoe Selo, but was much the preferred home of this generation of Romanovs.

Even its yellow and white paintwork hinted at a more homely environment, a retreat from the gross extravagance and multitudes of St Petersburg.

As they grouped at the white arrow-topped palace gates, waiting for the palace police to complete the recording of all visitors, Elsie could see the end of the east wing just ahead of her and the west wing in the distance.

At this stage, neither gave a clear indication of the embracing warmth of the neoclassical structure until they had strolled up towards its centre. To the children, it had been home since 1905—for two of them, the only home they could reasonably remember.

The two wings reached forward like embracing arms, while a Corinthian colonnade ran across the centre.

"There is my room!" Olga called out, pointing to the upper level.

"Are you all on the top floor?" asked Elsie.

"Yes, and Mama has a lift to get up to us from her suite on the ground floor," Tatiana answered.

"So, how many rooms are there?" asked Elsie, persisting in her questioning as she felt the communication was a good way for the girls to become comfortable with her.

"There are 100 rooms, but there will only be 99 after I burn down Maria's room!" exclaimed Anastasia, for she had noticed that Maria was once again holding Elsie's hand.

Elsie gave Maria's hand a reassuring squeeze, while she made another mental note in her quest to understand the girls' personalities.

Maria leaned in to Elsie and whispered: "We share a bedroom so she would be burning down her own, too!"

Raji and Elsie were delighted to find that dinner was served at 8 pm in the less than formal Maple Drawing Room, a sizeable space with a decided Style Moderne appearance. They complimented their hosts on the design but the Tsar said the blame lay, in part, elsewhere: "Alix, and her brother who visits occasionally from Hesse, are primarily responsible. I just hope I can find my things in all the clutter!"

After exactly forty minutes of dinner comprising soup, fish, some meat, as well as fruit and cake for dessert, the formalities concluded with military precision when the Tsar put his cutlery across his plate on the final course. Immediately, the children were ordered upstairs for a warm bath.

"Do you think you can cope with a game of Dominoes?" the Tsar asked, as he rose from the table.

Elsie, who had not played the game since childhood, was enthusiastic, while Raji professed his ignorance, surprising everyone. "Follow me, then!" the Tsar ordered, as he climbed the stairs in the Maple Drawing Room and crossed above the passageway, before stopping. "Welcome to my favourite room: the New Study!"

As they descended on the other side, Elsie noticed that the line of stairs turned at right angles, sealing in a lovely alcove with a fireplace and bench seating of the flowing Style Moderne type. Ahead of them there was a curved bench seat in a corner that could have accommodated the whole family, while nearby there was a billiard table, with what clearly was the Tsar's desk in the far corner to their left.

Between the billiard table and the desk sat a round table flanked by four chairs. Upon its green felt cover nestled a box of dominoes with the Russian royal crest. As the Tikari visitors sat with Russian royalty either side, Alix insisted on one thing: "Nicky, please explain the rules to Raji!"

The dominoes tumbled in a clatter of ebony and ivory onto the felt, as the Tsar began a brief outline of the game. "It is really simple, darling!" Elsie insisted, delighted at the informal and homely feel that the evening had adopted.

Around half an hour later, there was a knock at the door and one of the children's maids entered. "Excuse me, Your Imperial Majesty, but Maria Nikolaevna requests that … 'Auntie Sita', visits her in her bedroom."

"Well, that is an honour!" said the Tsarina. "You must have made an impression!"

"I trust it is a good one, Your Imperial Majesty—I mean Alix!" Elsie added, with a smile and an apologetic hand softly placed across the right hand of the Empress. "If you could excuse me for a few minutes."

Elsie followed the children's maid out into the corridor and after they took a few turns they climbed a flight of stairs. A walk along a darkened corridor was lightened by the glow of a light in a room ahead. The maid stopped at the door and waved Elsie into a large, predominantly pink and white bedroom. The light was a bedside lamp, and Elsie could make out Maria lying on a surprisingly basic camp bed, with only a thin cover and pillow. She had expected a plush bed, but this was nothing of the sort.

"Maria?" Elsie said, as she drew closer.

"Yes, Miss Fatty Smelly is there!" came Anastasia's voice from the other side of the partition.

Elsie moved and sat on the side of Maria's bed, but Maria pulled back the cover, clearly indicating what Elsie should do. "Okay!" whispered Elsie, as she slipped her shoes off and squeezed in next to the grand duchess.

Maria lifted her head and looked at the light, causing Elsie to truly appreciate her deep blue, saucer eyes. Elsie reached over, switched off the light and then nestled into the pillow until Maria's head was next to hers.

"Auntie Sita," Maria said quietly.

"Yes, darling?" Elsie asked.

Then, they were quiet for a moment, for they could both hear the sound of footsteps behind the partition, as Anastasia crept closer to catch their conversation.

"If you were in love with one of the guards, what would you do?" Maria whispered quietly.

"How old is he?"

"I don't know, I think maybe twenty."

"And how old are you, darling?"

"Twelve, but I am nearly thirteen—I will be on June 26th!"

"Does he know?"

"I don't know, I don't think so, but I do smile at him as much as I can."

"You know that if I were a young man—palace guard or even a prince—I would be in love with any girl with a golden heart like yours!" Elsie said, as she softly stroked Maria's hair.

For a short while Maria was quiet, and obviously thinking, before she asked: "Was it love at first sight when you met Uncle Raji?"

"Oh, definitely not—well, not on my part! Darling, sometimes it can take many months, even years, to get to know and love someone!"

Just then, the grandfather clock in the room chimed once to signal 9.30 pm.

"Oh, Auntie Sita! You had better go because our friend will be here soon!" Maria exclaimed. Elsie wondered who 'our friend' might be, though it did not seem polite to ask.

"Very well, but you have a good sleep and I will see you in the morning, darling!" she said, giving Maria a sequence of three farewell kisses on the cheeks in the Russian style, after she slipped on her shoes.

"Goodnight, Anastasia ... darling!" she called to the youngest grand duchess who was just slipping back into bed, on the other side of the partition.

The room was now dark and the corridor barely lighter, though Elsie did notice a slight glow on a staircase further along. She headed towards it, but only realised as she was heading down its narrow steps, that this was not the one that had led her to the upper floor when she arrived.

There was however, a light in a room just past the base of the stairs and some sound. No doubt this would be a quicker way back.

As she reached the last step, the sound transformed into a young woman's sighs—a mix of agony and ecstasy.

She turned into the doorway and into the light, where she saw that a very large man with a long straggly beard, wearing a peasant gown, was standing by the end of a kitchen table, thrusting rhythmically into the spread-eagled figure of a young serving maid.

He paused, momentarily, as he caught sight of Elsie, and a lecherous smile spread across his face which seemed to energise his whole being, for he launched back into his young prey with even more ferocity than before.

Shocked, Elsie turned and fled back up the stairs and eventually found her way to the New Study.

* * *

The next morning after breakfast, the Tsar insisted it was time that he and Raji dedicate the day to their joint passion—motor vehicles. "Have you ever driven a Delaunay-Belleville before, Raji?"

"I have seen the odd one, but no, never driven one, Nicky!"

"Well, high time you did! They are fantastic cars, and my favourite! I just recently received a 45-horsepower 6-cylinder Phaeton. Oh, you can drive, can't you?"

Raji gave Nicky a most surprised look, but the Tsar just grinned back, before adding: "Don't worry, I have been told about your driving exploits. I doubt the cars could be in safer hands. Anyway, I have a garage full of thirty here that we can test!"

Armed with a picnic lunch, they were off, only to be subsequently spied dashing through the distance as they crisscrossed the Tsarskoe Selo estate.

Elsie and the children spent some of the morning in the Tsarina's favourite room, her Mauve Boudoir. Nearly everything—and there were a lot of things in this cluttered room—except perhaps the freshly cut flowers, was either mauve or white.

For the first time, Elsie noticed that the Tsarina was suffering from a back complaint of some kind, for she stayed in bed well towards midday and kept a walking cane nearby.

The children were determined to get out and about before lunch, on another beautiful summer day. Olga suggested they take Elsie on a tour of the Catherine Palace, and with their mother's approval, they were soon under way, and on foot, because it really was not far.

A protective line of palace police secured the few hundred metres from the Alexander Palace gates to those of its big sister.

As they stepped into the deserted Catherine Palace forecourt, Elsie realised that there really was no comparison with what they had just left. This one was a blue, white and gold palace with grounds on a monumental scale, though apart from gardeners and the building's caretakers, there was nobody around.

"You just must see the most beautiful room in this palace, Auntie Sita," insisted Tatiana, before turning around a corner, then leaning back and adding: "You will understand why it is called the Amber Room!"

Magnificent panels of amber covered the walls, surrounding exquisite inlaid pictures, with long, thin, vertical mirrors and masses of gold leaf ornamentation. It was nothing like anything that Elsie had ever seen before. *Craftsmen must have worked on this for years,* she thought to herself.

As they explored the rest of the opulent but empty palace, Elsie's most memorable moment was when the children, with Derevenko in tow looking after Alexei, raced back towards her screaming with laughter as they scampered down the length of the upstairs grand enfilade. Catherine the Great would not have appreciated their exuberance, but Elsie found it delightful.

Later, Derevenko carried a tiring Alexei during a stroll around its grounds, which were, Tatiana said, designed like the palace by the Italian architect Rastrelli in 1756. "Peterhof Palace is much nicer! It is on the edge of the Gulf of Finland."

As they headed back home for lunch, Elsie noticed that a

crowd from the village had gathered to catch a glimpse of the children.

The afternoon was spent with the girls, playing around the house on Children's Island, an area linked by a bridge across the pond in front of the Alexander Palace.

The evening game of Dominoes was well under way, when a large—and to Elsie, familiar—bearded figure strode confidently into the room and straight up to the Tsarina.

Kissing her three times on the cheeks, he stopped and looked admiringly at Elsie.

"This is our friend, Father Grigori Yefimovich! He is a holy man, what we call a 'starets'. He does not speak English, but I will tell him who you are in Russian."

As she did so, Elsie remembered that she had read about a man called Rasputin, who reportedly had the Romanovs in the palm of his hand.

Grigori looked at Elsie with a smile and nodded, his intense gaze making Elsie feel as if he were stripping away her clothes and even exposing her soul.

Chapter 67

The Fabulous Fabergé

In diamonds and in platinum, lapis lazuli and gold
Small intricate creations, all a wonder to behold
From eggs to pure exotics, all perfect in display
Each timeless piece of workmanship was stamped with 'Fabergé'.

It was while sitting in the Empress' boudoir on their final morning in Alexander Palace, that Elsie asked Olga if there was a postcard of the Alexander Palace she could send to her friend Emma in Australia.

Olga thought not, but a quick search, directed by a pointing Alix from her chaise longue, uncovered a recent photo card of the Romanov family from the year before. Alix kindly insisted that Elsie could use it, so her guest wrote on the back:

> *Dearest Em,*
>
> *Raji and I have just had the most amazing time as personal guests of the Tsar and Tsarina of Russia and their beautiful children. The palaces in and around St Petersburg are remarkable, while the Hermitage museum is the finest I have ever seen.*
>
> *Lots of Love,*
> *El XOXOXO*

When she explained that the card was to her very best friend, who lived in Australia, to her great surprise the children all insisted on signing their names in full (and not just the girls' collective abbreviation of OTMA) on the card as well, so she squeezed in:

> *The royal children have signed too!*

Maria then found an official palace envelope to place the

528

card in, while Elsie imagined just how delighted Emma would be upon its arrival on the other side of the world. "How long would it take for the card to reach Australia from St Petersburg, Nicky?"

Before the Tsar could reply that he did not know because he had never sent anything there, Anastasia interrupted: "A very long time as it has to go to Ouagadougou first!"

"Anastasia Nikolaevna!" her mother said in a very stern voice.

"At least she studies her atlas," Elsie suggested, as she tried to recall just where Ouagadougou was.

"It is further away than the Gulf of Finland, which is where we will be from next week," said the Tsar. "All of us love the two weeks we spend on the royal yacht *Standart*."

"The *Standart*! Of course, the Fabergé Eggs!" Tatiana cried, as the children all rushed out of their seats and headed two rooms up the corridor, to the Maple Drawing Room.

By the time Raji, Elsie and the Tsar arrived, Tatiana was standing on a sofa and already had the glass door of a cabinet open. "Careful! Be very careful!" the Tsar warned. "Only one at a time!"

"Only one each of these has ever been made ..." started Olga.

"And they are made by the Jeweller to the Imperial Family, Peter Carl Fabergé!" continued Tatiana.

"Every Easter, Papa or Mama have an Easter egg made," said Alexei.

"And this one is of the royal yacht *Standart*, from 1909!" Tatiana said, as she very carefully wrestled a large glass egg-shaped piece with an ornamental dark blue, white and gold base to the table in the room.

Raji and Elsie peered in amazement at the intricate golden scale model of the ship inside the egg.

"The real ship is nearly 130 metres long and weighs 5,000 tonnes, but this is the next best thing!" the Tsar said proudly.

"Then there is the ... Coronation Egg, made by Fabergé in 1897," said Olga, placing an unbelievably brilliant yellow-gold egg, crisscrossed with a black double-headed eagle, on the table.

"Children, please stand back!" warned the Tsar, as he opened the top of the egg and brought out a golden model of the Coronation Coach.

Then there was the Lilies of The Valley Egg with its Art Nouveau styling and portraits of the Tsar, Olga and Tatiana; the brilliant blue Chanticleer Egg from 1903, that had a rooster pop out of the top, flap its wings, move its beak and crow on the hour; the iridescent green Fifteenth Anniversary Egg from Easter 1911, featuring miniature paintings from highlights of the Tsar's reign … and so it went on …

Just when their guests thought there was no more Fabergé magic to unveil, the Tsar told everyone to stay where they were for a minute. He returned with a large egg on a base, initially hidden under a silk scarf.

"Alexei, come on! You open it up and show Uncle Raji and Auntie Sita what is inside!"

The Tsarevich opened the egg and started to remove pieces of a golden railway carriage, which he carefully and proudly assembled on the floor, until he had all five carriages and the locomotive together in a line. "It is the Trans-Siberian Railway Egg!" Then, after Alexei turned a key in the locomotive, the train started to move—and everyone cheered.

"We have many beautiful things in India, but nothing like these!" exclaimed Raji.

"You know, Raji, you should visit Fabergé yourself in St Petersburg," the Tsar insisted. "I will arrange for him to be called, and told you are my guest and friend and are to be made welcome. He has a four-storey building with a shop at its base and craftsmen working above. It is near the Winter Palace. Please, take this card and pay him a visit. He has many remarkable items!"

Peter Carl Fabergé
Jeweller
24 Bolshaya Morskaya
Saint Petersburg

Raji and Elsie could not resist this opportunity. The Tsar said that he would make one of his French cars and its driver available, along with a four-vehicle security escort, for their journey back to Grand Hotel D'Europe.

As they walked out under the western porte-cochere of

Alexander Palace and bade their farewells, Raji invited the Romanovs to Tikari—if they were ever down that way. The Tsar said that would be unlikely, but he hoped they could all meet up in England some time, when they were visiting his cousin, George V.

Kisses were exchanged with everyone, even soft ones with Alexei, and they were about to step into the car when Maria pressed a blue, padded jewellery box into Elsie's hand.

Elsie gave her a hug and another kiss. "Remember, you are the most beautiful princess in the whole world—I will always know that is true!" she whispered, and they were off, speeding in a line out of the secluded world of the Russian royal family and back towards its imperial metropolis.

* * *

That afternoon, taking the liberty of having the other six members of the Tikari party in tow, they visited the headquarters of Fabergé. From the outside, its elegance was obvious: the name engraved in large gold letters on brown marble pillars.

On the ground floor, was a spacious and elegant display room with stylish glass cabinets showing the latest in up-market Fabergé accessories.

Once Raji had purchased a silver and gold cigarette case and Elsie a diamond cat brooch, Fabergé himself was kind enough to take them upstairs and show the workshop, where many men sat at tables under the supervision of workmasters.

Fabergé strode up and down the tables until he spotted something he did not like, wrenching a piece of intricate work from an employee, swearing in Russian, then taking the piece to a table where he smashed it with a hammer as the aghast man looked on.

"Perfection! That is what I demand! Perfection!" he cried in English, ensuring his visitors appreciated the Fabergé 'perfection without compromise' de facto motto. Given the reaction of the employee, Raji and Elsie hoped that this was just for show and not a regular occurrence.

On the drive back to the hotel, Elsie remembered she had yet to discover the contents of the blue box that Maria had gifted to her as they parted. She opened it, revealing a beautiful gold, white and blue angel brooch, with the Fabergé signature in Cyrillic on the base of the angel's feet and on the inside of the box lid.

"And who did you think was the most beautiful of the Romanov girls, Raji?" Elsie was reminded to inquire.

Raji thought only momentarily. "Definitely Tatiana! Yes, definitely Tatiana!"

"Oh, you men are so attracted by the superficial!"

Chapter 68

The Twist of the Knife

In retrospect, I wish I had, but did not wish intrude
I was not being calculating, obsequious or rude.
Oh no, of course I understand, such matters are mere froth,
Let's concentrate on consequence—and pass the local broth.

In mid 1912, the Tikari party sailed back to the relative mundaneness of London aboard the SS *Imperator Nikolai II*, named after their Russian host.

Tucked inside their luxurious cabin, Raji and Elsie reflected on an unforgettable few weeks and wondered if and when they would ever be back to the many grand places they had visited.

The group spent four weeks based in London, during which time Raji completed and gained his pilot's licence with Thomas Sopwith—this time in Sopwith's new Hybrid training aircraft. Subsequently, the Tikari party, now numbering nine, as hairdresser Jean Lemaire had joined, sailed back to India.

There was much for Elsie to supervise in the development of the hunting lodge, but she found herself occasionally back in the White House at Gaya.

It was on one such day in late 1912, that she noticed something move out of the corner of her eye, while she sat on her verandah, reading.

She quickly turned—then as quickly looked back to her book. "Mr Wakefield, if you must decide to enter my room, please have the courtesy to knock, first!"

"I would have thought that it was I, doing you a courtesy by passing on some information, Your Highness," he said, though his final two words were not said with anywhere near the reverence their titling would suggest.

"Scuttlebutt is not my stock in trade, Mr Wakefield, though no doubt you are more familiar with the like."

"Well, if you would rather not know the truth, then I shall leave," he said, starting to back out of the room, though pausing, as if he might miss an opportunity.

Elsie returned to her reading, but after a couple of paragraphs noticed that he had still not departed, so closed the book and put it down. "Yes, Mr Wakefield, what is it?"

Wakefield moved closer, though only just enough so he could see her face, as, like a pyromaniac, he had to see first-hand the impact of the fire he was about to light. When he spoke, it was slowly and deliberately: "I just thought you would like to know that Raji has decided to take a third wife!"

There was silence for a few moments as Elsie battled with her emotions and desperately tried not to show any weakness or hurt to a man who clearly wanted to see both. "Do you not think, Mr Wakefield, that, if this were true, Raji would have informed me, before you?"

Again, there was silence, though only long enough to hear her words again in her head, appreciating that her questioning was entirely rhetorical, for she knew the answer.

She felt a stabbing pain that was as much metaphorical as it was physical, and reached down and reopened her book to try to disguise her true feelings. She went back to reading, though could not recall a single word before her, as all she could sense was the smirking figure behind her shoulder.

"If that were so," she said, as nonchalantly as possible, "then I could well understand it, as he wants an heir, and I have yet to produce one. Now, could you please leave, as I am up to a most interesting part of this book!"

But Wakefield had no intention of leaving—well, not just yet. In fact, he took a step closer, poising like a matador about to deliver the coup de grâce. "Let me tell you, Your Highness, that he already has a son born in 1910 by the woman he will make his third wife!"

Elsie could feel a knife twisting inside her, but knew that at this moment she needed to call on all her strength and acting skills. "Mr Wakefield, if you read as much as I do, you would appreciate that there are times in most works when a reader wishes to be left alone to enjoy their impact in an intimate environment. This is one such time, so please leave!"

He turned, wiping the blood from his knife as he departed the bullring. Elsie was not a person prone to hate, in fact it was an emotion she very rarely felt, though right now she truly hated John Guerney Wakefield.

It took a great amount of control to not raise the matter at all with Raji, until he was about to have a session with Siri and Lala in his bedroom after dinner. Elsie blocked the young ladies' path as they headed to his door.

"Girls, I just need to spend some time with Raji. We will both probably need you afterwards!"

Entering his bedroom, she noted that the light was off, but that the last rays of sunlight had allowed her to feel her way in. Raji was lying naked on the bed and clearly was not expecting her.

"Raji, we need to talk!" she said, causing him to move to turn on the light. "No, leave the light off. You have kept me in the dark for so long that you can hold me there a little longer!"

Raji lay back on the bed and seemed to be staring out the window. Elsie could not be sure that he knew what she might ask.

"JG mentioned something to me today that I would have hoped to hear from you first," she said, as she sat on the side of the bed.

Raji shifted uncomfortably, but still chose to remain quiet.

"He said that you were planning to take a third wife. Do you not think that, as your second wife, I should have been the first to have known?"

Raji stirred and sat up, then moved off the bed and stood looking out the window. "JG has to make the arrangements, and after all he is my best friend."

"And my feelings do not come in to the equation?"

"Look, Elsie, you will always be my favourite wife, believe me! That will never change!" He paused, then added: "You have not asked who she is. She is the mother of my only son. As I am Maharaja and ruler of Tikari, it is essential for the family line to continue!"

Elsie could not argue with the logic of such a decision, so she sought to find out more on how she would be affected. "Will she live here in the White House?"

"No, she will be installed in the Sultanganj Palace near Patna. Obviously, I will make regular visits." He moved back to sit beside her on the bed, before continuing: "She is a Muslim, so I will have wives born into three different religions."

Elsie thought: *He makes it sound like he is acquiring a stamp or car collection, or nearing a full house in a card game. But he is toying with the closest of relationships and threatening our future.* There may have been a question Elsie could have asked, but she suddenly felt quite alone, despite the presence of her husband next to her. Inevitably, her thoughts turned homeward. "My mother is not well. I feel I should spend some time with her in Australia."

"Sure, why don't you take a few months next year to visit her." He put his arm around Elsie, and she put her head on his shoulder, and they sat there in silence for a few minutes. They may have been physically together, but for the first time, she felt them growing apart.

"It would also mean that I could at last see Emma again," said Elsie, trying to find as much light and positivity as she could on a dark day.

* * *

On 16 April 1913, the day before Elsie sailed from Calcutta for Australia, Raji arranged for the signing of a deed of annuity. It read:

> I am Maharaj Kumar Gopal Saran Narayan Singh, son of Babau Ambika Prasad Singh and grandson and heir of Maharaj Ram Kishun Singh Bahadur, deceased, by caste Brahmin Bhumihar, by profession Zamindar, resident of Tikari, Pargana Sanaut, district Gaya.

> WHEREAS Sita Devi formerly Elsie Caroline Thompson embraced the Hindu Faith and thereupon contracted a legal and binding Hindu marriage with me in the Vedic Form and is and has been living with me openly and to the knowledge of my relatives, friends and dependants as my wife since May second one thousand nine hundred and nine the date on which the said marriage was solemnized by Araya Samaj at Lucknow and whereas it is incumbent for me to provide for the said Sita Devi, during her life so that she may pass her days in ease and comfort, I of my own free will and consent without any undue pressure or false representation on the part of my said wife or anybody else settle a life annuity of thirty-six thousand rupees

on the said Sita Devi to be paid to her in twelve equal monthly instalments of three thousand rupees to be paid to her or her nominee on the first of every calendar month the first payment of which shall be made on the first day of May one thousand nine hundred and thirteen.

And I herewith charge my properties stated and fully set out and described below with the payment of such annuity which properties after paying the Government Revenue and Rood-cess and Public Work Cesses yields me a clear annual income of more than thirty-six thousand rupees.

Neither I nor after me my heirs executors or administrators shall have any right to sell mortgage or in any other way alienate the said properties during lifetime of my said wife the security holder. If I or any of my heirs executors or administrators do so, it shall be null and void. The said annuity shall cease at the death of my wife the said annuity holder.

In witness hereof I the said Maharaj Kumar Gopal Saran Narayan Singh have hereunto set and subscribed my hand and seal this sixteenth day of April one thousand nine hundred and thirteen.

Signed (Solicitor)   Signed (Maharaja)

Chapter 69

The First Australian Princess

Debuted on stage in teenage years, as only Aussie star
Then married maharaja, in a land both strange and far
Her jewellery, it's fabulous—and looks, I must confess
No wonder that we call her: first Australian princess.

"I've done it!" called Grace excitedly, as she opened the door of Elsie's first class suite on their liner, the P&O's RMS *Morea*. "We will just have to wait and see if anyone turns up!"

Grace had the crew cable the newspapers around the Fremantle area about Elsie's imminent arrival.

Elsie had wanted Siri and Lala to join Abu and Grace in her entourage for the Australian sojourn, but Raji had emphatically ruled it out. At least five months without those girls was more than he could bear.

As the boat steamed in to the port of Fremantle, Western Australia, on the morning of Tuesday 6 May 1913, Elsie caught sight of her homeland for the first time in six years. It may not have changed hugely, though she certainly had. She had left as a just-divorced singer, dancer, actress and comedienne, and returned a maharani.

The captain personally alerted Elsie that two members of the press had boarded and were currently in the dining room. Elsie insisted that they be brought up to her suite, while Grace and Abu were instructed to remain behind the cabin door curtain—and to do their best not to laugh, no matter what she said.

* * *

James Thompson put down the newspaper in surprise as he sat in the morning sun on the porch of his Macpherson Street, Mosman home. He and Mary Ann had recently moved there to be closer to Walter, Stella and their six-year-old granddaughter, Marjorie.

"Cissie! Cissie! Come and look at what is in the paper!" James called out, and they were soon reading it together. They knew Elsie was returning, but the large newspaper article was a shock:

HER HIGHNESS MAHARANEE OF TIKARI
THE FIRST AUSTRALIAN PRINCESS
HAS SHOT TIGERS AND RED BEARS

Her Highness the Maharanee of Tikari looked up at the pressmen on board the R.M.S. Morea this morning.

Perhaps it would have been more gallant to say that in a stately, regal manner she gazed coldly down upon them: but this would have hardly been correct ...

So Her Highness continued to be her natural self, and looked up and laughed and talked with the pressmen for fully a quarter of an hour ...

* * *

The Australia Hotel, on the corner of Castlereagh and Rowe Streets in the heart of Sydney, had not seen anything like it. It had opened in 1891 as the city's grandest hotel, with Sarah Bernhardt, its first guest. Mark Twain, Nellie Melba and other luminaries had followed, but the sight that greeted porters and bellboys was a first: two women dressed in saris and a huge man wearing a turban stood amidst a large pile of luggage crates outside the entrance.

After Elsie sailed past the polished granite columns and across the mosaic-tiled floor of the vestibule to the reception desk, she discovered that she had been listed erroneously as 'Rita Thompson' in the register. Given that she was staying in the hotel's finest suite, on the second floor, and the servants in rooms beside, for at least five months, she thought they could have done better.

It took more than an hour for all parties and their luggage to be allocated properly. For Elsie, everything had to be right. Her relatives were going to be transported to the hotel in a Rolls-Royce driven by Abu, for their audience with 'Her Highness'.

There was a personal and emotional aspect to her return that was important to Elsie, but theatre had played a big part in her development and success, so the occasion was always going to be a show.

James and Mary Ann had never been in a Rolls-Royce before, let alone been chauffeured. As they emerged from the lift on the second floor, Mary Ann held a handkerchief close at hand.

Abu knocked three times on the door of the suite, then followed up by uttering the prearranged words on entering: "The Maharani of Tikari, will see you now!"

It had seemed so simple in the planning, but when it came to the big moment, Elsie 'fluffed her lines' and raced crying into her father's arms.

"Oh, Father, I have missed you!" she sobbed, as he eventually held her at arms length to look at his beloved daughter.

Elsie turned to her mother and realised that she, much more than Father, had aged. Her mother looked far older than the fifty-one year old woman she was supposed to be. "Mumsie! Mumsie!" she said, as she hugged her tightly, but she quickly loosened her grip as her mother coughed, and was clearly in pain.

Soon, they were gathered around a series of crates that Abu had opened. They contained hand-worked Indian curtains and cushions, beautiful carpets and inlaid furniture of all kinds, including a hand-carved lady's writing desk. James and Mary Ann were quite overwhelmed, but Elsie insisted that they take what they could, as she was not going to take anything back to India.

After they had made their selection, Elsie said: "Mumsie, I have a surprise for you!" She handed her mother a sterling silver dressing table tray, complete with silver mirror and brushes.

"Oh, darling! They are beautiful! Thank you very much!"

"You can thank Raji too! As you can see it is engraved to 'Mumsie' and carries engraving on the top 'Rajie' and the bottom 'Elsie', on each piece."

"Now, Father, this is for you—and for Mother. I think you heard that Raji and I played Dominoes with the Tsar and Tsarina of Russia last year … well, here is a set of ebony and ivory dominoes!" she said handing him a wooden box.

James opened it and took out two of the pieces. He tossed them in his hand and they made a lovely clicking sound. "Did you hear that? Oh, they are just terrific! You should know Elsie, my dear, that we have named our new home in Macpherson Street, *Sita,* after you!" James stated, still entranced by his latest gift. "I just don't know how we will get all this back to Mosman."

"Father, don't worry about any of that. I will arrange for its delivery. Right now, you are my guests for dinner. After that, Abu will take you on the drive west and across the bridges to get back home. He said that the journey from Milson's Point to Bennelong Point on the steam ferry across the harbour, involved too much waiting time."

Elsie's guests the next evening, were her brother Walter, sister-in-law Stella—and a special delivery, which Abu carried in his arms.

The knock at the suite door was far softer than Abu's usual—and when the door opened, Elsie saw her six-year-old niece for the first time.

"Oh, my! Look at you! You must be Marjorie!" said Elsie, taking her from Abu's arms, though coping less well with the child's weight. "And you have lovely ribbons in your hair!"

"Hello, Your Highness!" Walter said, with a cheeky grin. "Does this mean I have to obey you now?"

"Now and always, Walter! In fact I think you owe me nearly a lifetime's worth!"

Elsie gave Stella a big hug and kiss. It had been many years since she had helped that shy, epileptic girl, at Fort Street School, and so strange they should be linked in a way Elsie would have never dreamt.

After they had chosen items from the crates, Elsie advised she had a few special 'somethings'. "Walter, I bought this one when in England last year—you might have heard of the golf club," she said, handing over a flat-based putter with a D-shaped head.

Walter turned the putter upside down and noted the writing and crown on the base of the head. "Oh, made at Royal St George's in Kent! The Open Championship was held there just two years ago—won by Harry Vardon from Jersey, if I recall correctly! Oh, this is some putter, El—I mean, Your Highness!

My putting has been somewhat off recently, so this is bound to help!"

"Stella, this is something I am going to give to you, but it is a gift that I hope you will all share," she said, as she handed over a heavy, flat object, wrapped in velvet.

Stella threw back the cover to reveal a marble square inlaid with beautifully coloured precious and semi-precious stones that formed a multi-squared pattern. "It is very, very lovely, but what is it, Elsie?"

"You cannot guess? Well, perhaps these might give you the clue you need," she said, passing Stella a wooden box from behind her back.

Stella opened the box and immediately knew. "Oh, a chess set! How extraordinary!"

"The pieces are all carved out of ivory. You can see that the kings are really maharajas!"

"And there are camels!" interrupted Marjorie.

"Yes, there are, darling! The set was made in Rajasthan, in north-west India. How about you help me put all the pieces on their squares? You can see that one ivory set has a red base, so they go on the other side of the board," she advised, as she and Marjorie squatted on the floor.

After they had finished, Elsie had a request. "Walter, can I borrow Marjorie tomorrow? She will be my guest for the day, and we will go shopping with Abu."

"Well, she does have school."

"Daddy, can I go with Auntie Elsie?"

Walter looked at Stella and she nodded.

"Great! We will pick her up from your house in Mosman at 10 am."

At the appointed time, Elsie was on the doorstep, wearing a sari and with diamond and emerald earrings and glittering bracelets. Marjorie was ushered into the back seat next to Elsie, while Grace and Abu were in the front. They took the slow way in to the city, waiting for the steam ferry at Milson's Point.

The sight of a large open-top luxury vehicle driven by a giant man with a turban, accompanied by two sari-wearing beauties, pulling up outside the David Jones store on the corner of George and Barrack Streets, had drawn an inquisitive crowd.

Many had already heard of the arrival of the first Australian princess in town. Now, they just had to catch a glimpse.

By the time Elsie, Marjorie and Grace emerged from the store—the latter struggling to carry the largest doll anybody had ever seen—such a crowd had gathered that police had to be called. It was a piece of pure theatre played out before a packed house, when they drove off with the giant doll sandwiched between Elsie and little Marjorie on the back seat.

Meeting family again was one thing, but catching up with her best friend in the whole wide world, was quite another. Somehow, Elsie had managed to delay the occasion until her third evening in Sydney.

As twenty-eight year old Emma Bellamy reached the lift area of the Australia Hotel, she noticed the light indicated it was on the seventh floor, but she was too impatient to wait. Not caring about any decorum, she ran as fast as she could up the stairs to the second floor and stood puffing and already crying in anticipation outside the door to Elsie's suite.

Inside, Elsie had made sure that she and Grace were in the background, in a side room. When Emma knocked, it was Abu who answered the door. "The Maharani of Tikari has been expecting you, madam. Please come in!" the giant Sikh said, as he stepped aside and gestured for Emma to enter.

Elsie had planned to slowly emerge, but the sight of her dear friend after so many years apart, brought both women rushing into each other's arms. Soon, there was not a dry eye in the suite.

Eventually, Elsie regained her composure and introduced Emma to her servants: "And this is my private secretary, Miss Grace Knighton!"

"Oh, El, Grace is so pretty!" Emma whispered to Elsie a few minutes later.

"I am glad you like her, because I want the two of you to work closely together on something!"

Chapter 70

The Social Event of the Season

When Elsie handed Emma a long tube, her friend was not sure what to expect, but on pulling out its contents, she was delighted. "This is just beautiful!" Emma exclaimed.

"Do you recognise the artist? It is an original, of course!"

"The Art Nouveau style is familiar, but …"

"Alfons Mucha, the world's very best Art Nouveau artist. You can see his signature on the bottom, underneath the Bengal tiger. We visited Mucha in Bohemia last year."

"I shall have to get it framed and hang it in my room!"

"Em, I will give you five pounds to cover any framing, but, now, just take your pick of whatever else you would like from what is here in these crates!"

Before Emma left, Elsie informed her that she wanted to host an afternoon tea at the Australia Hotel for the cream of Sydney society. With Emma's local knowledge, she could suggest to Grace who to invite.

"Well, there are Sir Gerald and Lady Strickland, and …"

"Who is he?" Elsie asked innocently.

"The Governor of New South Wales, of course, although he was only recently appointed. Then there is the Lord Mayor …"

"Em, you work out the guest list, but make sure there are no more than one hundred. Grace will arrange for the printing of the invitations. It must be an 'invitation only' event, with only the great and the good attending!"

That very evening, Elsie, Emma and Grace toured the ground floor of the hotel, seeing what room might be best to hold the event. One stood out: the smoking room. It had Moorish styling and arches, just the sort of thing Elsie loved.

"The Lord Mayor, Sir Arthur Cocks, will like that!" Emma was quick to state. "I hear he has a very strong cigar habit!"

Elsie was not having any of it. "I am not going to have myself and my mother choking in that atmosphere. This is my function, and I will decide how it will be held. If they don't like it, they don't turn up!"

After discussing the matter with John Ure Smith, the Manager of Australia Hotel, it was agreed that the room could be set aside for the function on Saturday 14 June. As part of her role, Grace arranged for the printing of the invitations:

You are invited to
Afternoon Tea
with Her Highness the
Maharani of Tikari
- The First Australian Princess -

in the
Smoking Room, Australia Hotel
3 pm Saturday 14 June 1913

Dress is Formal

RSVP to Miss Grace Knighton c/- Australia Hotel
by 7 June.

Note: Due to the special nature of this function
and to preserve the health of the Maharani and her mother,
no smoking will be permitted in the venue.

By the week before the afternoon tea, it was obvious that the 100-person limit would be exceeded, with people clamouring to be added to the guest list.

In no small part, the popularity of the afternoon tea had been enhanced by newspaper accounts of the appearance of Elsie in a gold-tissue sari and covered in jewels, and Grace in a black sari embroidered in gold, at the May 22nd Shakespearian Ball, at the Sydney Town Hall.

In preparation for the afternoon tea, Grace arranged for incense to burn for all the previous day in the smoking room, in an attempt to rid the room of the cigarette and cigar smell. Some were left to burn during the afternoon itself, to add to the oriental and mystical atmosphere.

As the 112 invitees arrived, Emma announced them from the door. They then stepped forward to greet Elsie, who was a stunning sight wearing her emerald, pearl and diamond banded tiara, long diamond-studded earrings, a large sparkling necklace that seemed to spread out rays like the sun, and a mass of glittering bracelets. Sydney had never seen the like of it.

"Sir Henry and Lady Stephen …"

The couple stepped forward and bowed as Elsie offered her hand for a light and brief touch.

"Captain and Mrs Hollander," and so it went on …

"Dr and Mrs Devorin …"

An elderly gentleman and his wife stepped forward and they bowed. As he and Elsie's eyes met, she realised she had seen him before … and she had a momentary flashback … to the back room of her father's bookstore in Erskine Street … she was fourteen and had been laid out on the table and he was leaning over her …

He suddenly recognised Elsie too and a look of horror crossed his face, just as Elsie's open hand slapped it firmly. There was a gasp from all those who witnessed it.

"Outrageous!" cried Mrs Devorin, but her husband was already beating a quick retreat, pulling her away and back through the door, as whispering spread through the room.

Emma stepped quickly to Elsie's side and asked what that was all about. "Just something between the good doctor and me, which I might tell you about some day," she said, waving Emma on to continue the introductions.

"Mr and Mrs Hamilton …"

Soon the room was nearly full and the governor and his wife were the last to arrive. As was usual, God Save the King was sung to welcome them, with Elsie's voice leading the way, to much approval.

On conclusion of the national anthem, Elsie addressed the room:

It is an honour for both me and my Indian staff to welcome you all here this afternoon. For me, personally, it is a great pleasure to be back in the city of my birth after six long years away.

Let me tell you a bit about Tikari Raj. It is one of India's hundreds of princely states, and while it is lesser known than others such as Hyderabad, Patiala, Kapurthala and even Cooch Behar, I am told by others who assure me they know such things, that it is India's third richest.

Our Tikari Raj Compound is in the city of Gaya, in Bihar state, about one day's drive north-west of Calcutta. There we have our own palace, known as the White House, about 200 servants and currently, when I last counted, eleven motor vehicles. I even managed to crash one a few years ago!

The territory of the broader part of Tikari Raj is extensive and incorporates thousands of villages and land around the Buddhist holy site of Bodh Gaya. In our part, which is the majority and royal section of Tikari Raj—and legally known as '9 Annas'—income from production is important, but my husband, the Maharaja of Tikari and I are most proud of what we give back.

We pay for hospitals and schools in Tikari Raj and schooling for girls is a very important focus for me. I grew up with books, as my father was a bookseller and stationer in Erskine Street and I gained a terrific education at Fort Street School. I know that such education gives you power, because it gives you options.

My husband is a member of the Viceroy's Council, and since the shift of the capital of India from Calcutta to Delhi, spends increasing time in the latter. On at least three occasions recently, he has raised the need for universal education—that is education for absolutely everyone, irrespective of caste, religion or sex.

We have both been pushing for a university to be established in the state capital of Patna, to the north. There is real hope that this will happen soon.

Omar Khayyám once wrote in Quatrain 9 of his *Rubáiyát:*

Each Morn a thousand Roses brings, you say ;
Yes, but where leaves the Rose of Yesterday ?
    And this first Summer month that brings the Rose
Shall take Jamshyd and Kaikobád away.

There are a great many million potential roses in India, many million in Bihar state and a very large number in Tikari Raj territory. I want to see all potential roses bloom and then maximise their opportunities throughout a long lifetime!

There are four girl schools full of potential roses in Gaya and as the president of these schools I have had the great honour of presenting their prizes.

Prior to the most recent occasion that I did so, I let it be known that I would prefer to see them at the award ceremony 'out of purdah'—that is without the veil that so often hides the natural beauty of Hindu and Muslim girls and I feel is symbolic of their limited opportunity and freedom.

I am proud to say that of the 300 or so girls who attended the prizegivings, only three still wore the veil on that occasion.

I am also proud to say that I speak Hindustani fluently and am becoming familiar with Urdu in its Persian script. I am more than delighted to have adjusted to eating Indian curries and actually miss them when we travel—a reason why we frequently travel with staff who are good cooks!

Thank you for attending today. My staff and I would be delighted to talk to you about Tikari and life in India.

I look forward to an ongoing and warm relationship between the people of Tikari Raj and those of New South Wales.

Thank you for listening, and now I believe the governor has a few words to say.

The Governor of New South Wales, Sir Gerald Strickland, then spoke, welcoming Her Highness back to Australia as the first Australian princess and as a link between peoples separated by both distance and culture, who were now far closer as a result of her visit.

The Lord Mayor, Sir Arthur Cocks, then asked that everyone charge their glasses and toast the relationship: "To the people of Tikari Raj and New South Wales!"

It was not long before Elsie was asked a question she felt surely was inevitable. Lady Barton wondered just how many tigers she had shot.

"I could lie and tell you a very large number, but it is only my husband who could respond in such a way and be honest. Quite frankly," Elsie said, whispering and smiling in a semi-agonised way at the same time, "I cannot stand seeing any sort of animal killed! You should not believe everything you read in the press!"

Emma had joined Elsie, as Lieutenant McKell asked her about servants and exactly how it was possible to have so many efficiently employed.

"Two hundred does sound a fair number, though their roles tend to be quite specialized ..." Elsie was explaining when Emma interrupted: "Her Highness even has someone who addresses her envelopes!"

Elsie looked at Emma strangely. "No, I always write my own envelopes!" she exclaimed. At the next available opportunity she pulled Emma aside and asked her what she meant. "Em! I always seal my postcards in envelopes I have addressed!"

"Not the ones from Tikari, El! I know your handwriting and those are in somebody else's hand! I keep all your postcards and envelopes, so I will bring some in tomorrow to prove it!"

Chapter 71

The Good, the Bad and the Ugly

"A husband should be perfect, yes, in each and every way
He will lavish me with presents and he always will obey!"
"Good luck I say, to find such one – I'll watch from the whorehouse
As you gossip with your spinster set, more poor than a church mouse!"

The day after the afternoon tea, Emma was at the Australia Hotel before Sunday lunch, with a box full of postcards.

"I cannot believe you keep them, Em!"

"Oh, I would never throw them out—and this one is my favourite!" she said, producing the one from St Petersburg. "How many people would have a photo card signed by the four grand duchesses?"

Emma had only to show one example of an envelope for a postcard sent from Tikari, for Elsie to sense what was going on. "When I first arrived there, I was told to give all my mail to one of the servants, Suraj Lal, who would arrange its posting …"

"So, it is Suraj's writing?" asked Emma.

"Oh no! It is definitely not his hand! I recognised that handwriting straightaway. Suraj is the assistant to Raji's private secretary, John Guerney Wakefield—and this is Wakefield's writing! This can only mean one thing: that he opens the envelopes to spy on my correspondence before it is posted!" said Elsie, fuming.

"At least he finds them interesting!" Emma said, trying to make light of a serious matter that had clearly upset her best friend. "I know Joe enjoys reading them!"

Elsie was so caught up in thinking of alternative methods to torture then murder Wakefield, that she took some time to ask the obvious question. Eventually, she did. "Em, who is Joe?"

Emma rose from the edge of the bed and walked to the window of the suite. Her blonde hair shone in the morning sun as she looked out at the world of central Sydney, though her mind was not even lingering upon the streetscape at all. "Joseph Binstead … El, I think I might have met the man I want to marry!"

"Em! That is wonderful!" Elsie cried, rushing to embrace her best friend. "How long have you known each other?"

"We have only been seeing each other for a couple of months, but I think he might be the one!"

"Is he tall, dark and handsome?"

"Oh, well, yes, sort of …"

"What prospects does he have?"

"He is currently the youngest inspector in the telephone department of the Postmaster-General!"

"Really? Well, that all sounds good, Em, but importantly, is he a nice person?"

"Yes, I think so, but I would welcome your opinion, El."

"In that case, why don't you both come for afternoon tea with me here at the hotel, next Saturday?"

* * *

The man who joined Emma and Elsie at the Australia Hotel was something like Emma had described. *Well, he is dark-haired and quite good-looking,* Elsie thought, *and from his easy smile, he seems to have a sense of humour.* She just hoped he was the man Emma had always wanted.

"It is an honour to meet you, Your Highness! Emma always talks about you!" Joe said, as Elsie could swear his eyes were twinkling.

"Mr Binstead, I give you formal permission to call me Elsie, though strictly speaking, I am now known as Sita. It would be too confusing, as Em always calls me El!"

After a pleasant afternoon, Emma hung behind to find out just what Elsie thought.

"He certainly seems nice enough, but you have only been together a short while. Give it a few more months at least, and if you still feel strongly about each other and truly think you will love and care for each other, well, the rest is up to you. I am twenty-nine and on to my second husband—I am not sure I am the best judge!"

Over the next few months, the Tikari party spent most of their time in Sydney, though Elsie and Grace did travel to Brisbane where they stayed at the Hotel Daniell and went to the theatre.

The Brisbane Courier newspaper reported they attended *Get Rich Quick Wallingford* at His Majesty's. It was while in Brisbane in July, that Elsie was greatly saddened to hear of the death of J. C. Williamson, in Paris. He had been such help and inspiration to her during the fledgling stages of her career—and from a distance, her unrequited first love.

Barely two months later, on 1 September 1913, Raj Rajendra, Maharaja of Cooch Behar and Elsie's former fiancé, died in London at the age of thirty-one. The astrologers, who had predicted he would not live beyond his 32nd birthday, had been proved correct.

Though sad about Raj, Elsie was now more philosophical: *Given the demands of his parents and the prediction of the astrologers, our relationship was probably doomed from the start.*

* * *

Elsie had always intended to return to India in November, but the strengthening of the relationship between Emma and Joe and a deterioration in Elsie's mother's health, caused her to linger.

On Wednesday 4 February 1914, Emma Mabel Bellamy married Joseph Robert Binstead at St Barnabas' Church, Broadway, in Sydney. They promised to hang the framed Mucha poster of Elsie in the lounge room of the new house they would buy together.

* * *

As she gazed out of her suite in the Australia Hotel, on her final morning in Sydney, wondering just when she might next be back, Elsie noted something a little unusual: a man was pacing up and down the line of street sellers, whose tables fringed Castlereagh Street.

He was short and stocky, but she could see from the sellers' reaction to him that they were terrified. For every now and again, as she watched, he would use a silver walking stick that he was carrying, to strike them.

It was only when he reached the end of the line and had turned to come back, that Elsie noticed exactly what he was wearing:

a faded Union Jack waistcoat. That build, that waistcoat, that stick and that sort of behaviour, in combination were, even years on, familiar.

She shuddered as she remembered the skull on the top of the stick, then watched as he slammed it into the raised arms of a fearful stallholder. She had seen enough.

"Abu! Please come here to the window!" she called. For a short time they stood together, watching the troublemaker's progression along the line. "I have a plan, Abu. Follow me downstairs!"

Elsie crossed Castlereagh Street to the other side, though all the time keeping an eye on the man in the Union Jack waistcoat. As she approached, she heard a stallholder appeal for mercy: "I gave ya a pound last week, Billy, and I need to feed me kids!"

Billy! thought Elsie to herself. *Yes, that is his name: Billy from The Lord Nelson!* He was in his late forties, but undeniably the same cockney scum who had threatened Walter and Elsie in their teenage years.

Elsie opened her purse and took out a pound, placing it on the man's stall just as Billy was about to swing his stick. "There is more where that came from," she said to Billy, "if you have the courage to take it!"

With that, she turned and scurried off in the direction of a laneway, hoping he was not too close behind her, though following … and following he was, for there was no better combination than a nice young lady and money.

She could hear his footsteps getting closer and closer, so she hurried up, but he was starting to run.

She turned the corner into the laneway and there was nobody in sight, just brick walls and bins. She raced a little further but was stopped in her tracks by a powerful arm holding a skull-topped walking stick.

"Perfect!" cried Billy, puffing a little. "Just perfect! 'Ow 'bout ya 'and it all over, me beauty!"

Just then, a giant hand slammed down on the back of Billy's neck while another grabbed his trousers and he was lifted up high. He hung there momentarily, squirming like a beetle on its back, before being hurled through the air with great force into a brick wall.

The last bit of air oozed out of his near lifeless frame. He sank like a rag doll into the bins below, just as the walking stick rattled on the cobblestones, beating a final farewell.

Elsie hugged Abu, then stooped down and picked up the walking stick and noticed the skull seemed to be grinning. She headed back to the last stallholder Billy had threatened.

"He won't be needing this anymore!" she said. "I am sure it would raise at least a pound!"

That afternoon, Elsie and her Tikari party sailed for London, to meet up with Raji.

Chapter 72

Pictures for the Ages

The camera shutter clicked just as Elsie was about to say something. "You might need to take that one again!" she suggested.

"Oh no, Your Highness, I think that will be a picture for the ages!"

She had come to the 25 Old Bond Street studios of Bassano Limited, Royal Photographers, complete with banded tiara and her other favourite jewellery, as Raji had said that this was the place all high society had to be photographed.

Once the series of twenty photographs were processed, Elsie was offered a set of photo cards—postcard-sized copies. She immediately started writing on the back of one to Emma, before remembering, just in time, that her best friend was now a married woman:

Dearest Em (and Joe),

You may well think I am about to swallow a fly on the front of this card, but Bassano think it is a good one. I hope you are having a great time and really enjoying the start of a long and happy life together.

Lots of love to you both,
El XOXOXO

* * *

On the morning of 29 June 1914, Abid Hussain delivered the paper to Raji at their dining table in their Waldorf Hotel suite.

He lingered for a few minutes, reading over Raji's shoulder.

It cannot have been great news, Elsie reasoned, because they both looked quite serious.

"Surely, it is now only a question of time!" Raji exclaimed.

"What is 'only a question of time', darling?" Elsie asked.

Raji did not respond immediately, but kept reading for a few moments, before uttering: "War!"

"War?" Elsie queried, shocked. "War between whom, and why?"

"Archduke Franz Ferdinand of Austria and his wife have been shot dead in Sarajevo … by a … nineteen-year-old Bosnian Serb nationalist, called … Gavrilo Princip, who is believed to be linked with a group called the Black Hand … There are alliances everywhere now in Europe. Too many toes to tread on!"

After Germany had assured Austria-Hungary, on 5 July, of its support in any action against Serbia, Raji was convinced there was no turning back. "The Serbs are allied with the Russians, and so is Britain. Elsie, I want you and Grace to spend a few months in New York, away from this developing chaos. The *Lusitania* sails in late July for New York—I want you to be on board!"

Elsie was not about to refuse. She had never known war, though presumed it could not be much fun, despite the jingoistic and mostly anti-German sentiment that seemed to be running rampant in the press.

A theatre friend ensured she was invited to the Tuesday 7 July Vaudeville Artists' Day at Hendon Aerodrome. Though Raji had his pilot's licence, Elsie had never flown in, let alone sat inside an aircraft. This was a great opportunity to do both, if she had the courage. She realised a sari would be impractical attire for the occasion, so donned European clothes.

She had wanted Raji to take her to Hendon but he said that he had 'very important' meetings to attend, so instead, she just went with Abu as driver.

Being a vaudeville event, it did not take her long to recognise familiar faces, after Abu had parked the Rolls in a line of vehicles near the even longer line of aircraft hangers.

Nor was it long before others recognised her. While she was watching the four-wheeler carriage race—which resulted in a dead heat between two of the contestants and had to be rerun—a gentleman in a brown suit approached.

"Your Highness, I am Alfred Cooke, the Royal Aero Club's official photographer. I was wondering if you could pose for a photograph inside the cockpit of one of the planes after the races have finished?"

"That would be fine, Mr Cooke, but I hear there are donkey races next and being photographed on one of those dear creatures might be more appropriate, as in an aircraft I would only make an ass of myself!"

Cooke blushed, then noticed her smile, which was so beautiful, he thought, that he simply had to capture it. "The aircraft will be brought back to their hangers in a few minutes. I will find one that will suit!"

True to his word, it was not long before Elsie was helped up into the pilot's seat of a Bleriot biplane. "Okay, Your Highness. Look down at me, but smile! … Great! I will just take another … Thank you, that should be fine!"

Cooke helped her down and was just about to take his leave when he noticed another aircraft nearby. "Oh, Your Highness! Can I impose and ask that you have one taken with French pilot Louis Noel," he urged, before adding in a quieter voice: "If war is declared—and it could be at any time—this may be the last we ever see of him!"

Elsie was introduced to Noel, who told her that his aircraft was a Maurice Farman M7. She was helped up into the passenger seat and then told to stand up, to be clearly seen in the photograph behind the pilot.

Cooke took a few shots, but complained about the Frenchman. "Louis only smiles when he is flying!"

Louis became more friendly after Elsie started talking in French, though she occasionally had to lapse into English to complete a sentence.

He told her that he had gained his Royal Aero Club pilot's licence in August 1911, but had been a flying instructor for two years. He then asked if Elsie would like a joy-flight. She thought that if Raji had summoned the courage to fly, then she should too.

Louis told her to take off her turned-up hat and don a pilot's cap and goggles. He also passed her a leather coat that was many sizes too big, but wrapped her in a cloak of professionalism.

Elsie waved and blew kisses to Abu, as a man started the big propeller spinning a few yards behind Elsie's seat, and the craft set off down the runway.

Elsie forgot about how uncomfortable the cane seat beneath her felt, as she clung to the top edge of the plane's fuselage on either side.

Soon, the nose and front rose off the ground and the craft began to soar, making the huge hangers, cars and people seem like little boxes, miniature toys and ants, respectively.

It was cold and it was windy—and Elsie could not tell if she was more terrified or ecstatic.

After a couple of circuits of the area, Louis eased the biplane down to the runway. Elsie was relieved to be back down to earth safely, but was mindful of what the photographer, Mr Cooke, had said about Louis.

She leaned forward and kissed him on the cheek, while saying: "Merci mon ami! Que Dieu te protège!"

Chapter 73

Lusitania: Ship of Doom

Its hull was black and massive and its body crisp and white
Its funnels signalled power and pace, its rooms were clean and bright
Forget all recent accidents, Titanic tales of tomb
How could this great behemoth, ever be a ship of doom?

On Saturday 25 July 1914, Elsie and Grace gazed up in awe at the sight before them. Towering above the Liverpool dock was the vessel once proudly proclaimed as 'the largest ship in the world'.

Lusitania, with its four huge and angled funnels, gigantic black hull and crisp white body, seemed every bit as permanent and safe as a ship could be. Yet, nobody on board, barely two years after the sinking of the 'unsinkable' *Titanic,* could deny that the odd deep dark fear could be lurking near the surface of their subconscious.

The masses of vehicles and crowds lining the dock area and the chatter of excited passengers soon had the Tikari pair focussed on the majesty of the experience.

After all, they were going to travel in true luxury, as Raji had booked one of the two Regal Suites on board. As they toured their two-bedroom, dining room, parlour and bathroom suite, both agreed it would be a memorable experience.

However, determined not to be isolated in their 'ivory tower', they spent the first three of six trans-Atlantic nights dining with the other passengers in the French neoclassically decorated and domed two-storey first class dining room.

On the fourth night, Tuesday 28th, they opted to have dinner served in their own dining room. To their surprise, but also delight, Captain Daniel Dow, a slightly rotund man in his mid-fifties with a walrus-like moustache, asked if he could join them.

They talked for some time about ships and the sea, obviously a great passion for the captain, until they were interrupted by a knock at the cabin door. The First Officer entered with a piece of paper, which he handed over after whispering something in the captain's ear, then disappearing.

Captain Dow's face turned ashen grey as he stared briefly at the note in front of him. He then turned it over and put his hand on top of it, as if he hoped it would go away.

"Is everything all right, captain?" inquired Elsie, but the captain did not answer—he just stared into space.

Elsie got out of her seat, came around the table and sat next to him, placing an arm softly and affectionately around him. Clearly something had upset him and she wanted to show she cared.

"That is very kind of you, Your Highness ... ah, I shouldn't be so worried about things, but I feel a great responsibility for everyone on board."

"And the note, captain?"

Captain Dow looked at Elsie and she could have sworn that the dark circles around his eyes had not been present a mere minute before. "Austria-Hungary declared war on Serbia today. We can expect that it is the first of many declarations!"

"Oh dear!" Elsie muttered, though in truth, given what Raji had told her, she was not surprised.

* * *

New York, when it came, was something of a relief after days at sea, though the city was bigger and more bustling than she could have imagined.

For her thirty-first birthday, Elsie took the opportunity to pose in the New York studios of Kadel & Herbert Photographers. Her favourite resulting photograph, had her looking straight at the camera, but with arms outstretched to her right and fingers interlocked. She was wearing an ever-present sari, with her usual pearl necklace, five-stream diamond earrings, along with her four-piece diamond and emerald bracelet set, just above the elbow.

She was so delighted with the image, that she sent copies to Emma and May Maxwell. Another, more demure version, she posted to her parents.

Accommodated in the Waldorf Astoria for a few months, and with only a side trip to Chicago to meet Grace's parents, Elsie and Grace had their pick of Broadway and theatre productions to take their minds off other things. This was just as well, as on 6 August, Britain declared war on Germany.

Although the United States was not formally part of the conflict, the progress of the war and its inevitable successes and setbacks, were covered in detail in the local press.

* * *

When Elsie and Grace went to board the *Lusitania* at Pier 54 for the return journey to England, they received a great shock, for the black and white ship with brown and black funnels had been transformed into a uniform grey.

"Oh no! It looks like a ghost!" exclaimed Grace. They both agreed that it looked 'creepy'.

Elsie had obviously made an impression, as Captain Dow paid a visit to their suite on that first night at sea. He joined them at their table, and she offered him a glass of water, understanding that he should not drink alcohol while on duty.

As he took the glass in his hand, Elsie noticed the water sloshing around as the glass shook. Just as a few months before, she moved over to his side of the table to comfort him. "We are a passenger ship, captain. The Germans would not try to sink a passenger ship!"

Captain Dow took another drink of water, as if it were a fortifying brew. "Maybe, when you are older, you will realise that almost everything that governments tell you is a lie. It is propaganda, designed to make you believe just what they want."

"So we are not a passenger ship?" asked Grace.

He said nothing for many seconds, then spoke, though they sensed, reluctantly: "If ... absolutely hypothetically ... we secretly carried arms and munitions ... and the Germans found out ... we would be a ship of doom!"

Chapter 74

Hi Ho! Hi Ho! It's Off to War We Go!

With Timmy, Dan and Johnny, and my other mates I'll go
There is far too much excitement, to ever think of "No!"
We'll bash the Hun so badly, that from Flanders they will flee
Then leave the next day's morning and be back home here for tea.

By the time Elsie and Grace had returned to London and The Waldorf Hotel in October 1914, the streets of the capital had been transformed in content and sentiment.

A person could not travel any moderate distance, without seeing a requisitioned omnibus full of men. They were heading to a recruiting station, transferring to a training ground or carrying uniformed and just-trained troops off on the first stage of the journey to France and the front line.

Given the cutthroat nature of war, Elsie found their universally exuberant expressions admirable though puzzling. *Is it because this is all one great adventure that contrasts starkly with their normally mundane lives? Is it because they are going with their mates? Is it because they think it will all be over soon, perhaps by Christmas? Are they scared of being branded a traitor if they choose to stay at home? Or is it because they love their King and country and hate the Germans so much?*

The truth, she thought, lay in part with all those possibilities, though she wondered just how long the prevailing mood might last.

The government had hoped for 100,000 volunteers, but had been inundated with many times that number. And not just from Britain, but eventually, also the dominions like India, New Zealand, Canada, South Africa and Australia.

Mostly, dominion troops formed their own battalions and rarely a day passed when a roaming Londoner did not encounter one group or the other, heading for training or preparing for a long-awaited departure.

It was in such an atmosphere on an October morning that Elsie went looking for Abu. Nobody had seen him—or so they claimed. Soon, Raji had cornered Elsie in their Waldorf suite, with earnestness in his eyes and a most unusual quivering around his mouth.

"Elsie, please, listen to me!" he implored. "Abu has gone to Flanders to join up with the 47th Sikhs!"

"No, Raji! No!" Elsie protested, hoping that somehow it was untrue. "He did not say goodbye!" But as she looked at Raji, she saw another unusual sight: tears welling in his eyes.

"He told me he loved you too much to tell you, for fear you might dissuade him."

Elsie just shook her head and cried. Abu had been the one person she could rely on at all times. Then she sat disconsolately on the couch for a while, sniffling occasionally and wiping back tears. Eventually, she said slowly: "I guess you will be telling me soon that you will be joining up too!"

Raji did not respond, but his drifting away from her to gaze upon the streetscape outside, unsettled her. What he could not tell her at that moment, was that the King-Emperor had just announced in the *London Gazette*, dated 15 October 1914, that Raji had been made an Honorary Lieutenant in the Expeditionary Force. That night she held him close, lest he be snaffled from their bed.

An announcement from Raji himself, she feared, was imminent, though when it came, it was proclaimed in his usual cheery fashion. He had promised to donate eight Rolls-Royces to the military cause, at least one of which he would keep for personal use. For his generosity, Raji had been given the special role of aide-de-camp, driver and dispatch rider to General Sir Locke Elliot.

Elsie was stunned. "But Raji, you might be killed!"

"Oh, I don't think so. The senior staff is not silly enough to put itself on the front line! I will be close to all the planning action but none of the dangerous stuff. It will be great!"

Elsie went to the bathroom and took out a pair of scissors. She then carefully cut two long sections out of her hair, one from each side of her head. She patiently braided them into a wristlet that he could wear during the war. "Now, I will always be with you, and not just in spirit!" she said, as she tied them around his right wrist.

From that day, he only returned to London sporadically,

spending much of his time in a liaison role between the War Office, on the corner of Horse Guards Avenue and Whitehall, and the General Headquarters at St Omer in France. Raji took Abid Hussain with him as his valet and assistant, but ordered the other servants back to Gaya. Elsie found Grace's departure for prospective marriage to a childhood sweetheart in Chicago—given the years they had spent as close confidants—the most painful.

Elsie wanted to stay in London, with its theatres and proximity to Raji in France. However, this meant she was left feeling like a lonely bird, in her elaborate Waldorf cage. On the afternoon of 16 February 1915, Raji delighted Elsie with a brief visit.

He had alerted her by cable that he would be coming, but she was reading, as usual, when he knocked on the door. "Daddy!" she screamed, thrilled that he had arrived.

"Why don't we go to Murray's for dinner and a dance?" he suggested.

"Fabulous, darling! I have been waiting for you to suggest just such a thing!"

"I can only stay for a couple of days, so we have to make the most of our time."

Murray's Night Club in Beak Street, had opened less than two years before, but already had the reputation of being the best dining and dancing club in the capital. With its large dance floor fringed by columns, high chandelier-riddled ceiling and huge spread of casual tables, it was a magnet, particularly in these bleak times.

The formal dining area was up a flight of stairs, but Raji and Elsie started by finding a place at the casual tables to the side of the dance floor. Many of the male patrons were in military uniform, making the best of their brief respite from the war zone.

As they sat down at a table, Raji became serious. "I can tell you from being around the high command, Elsie, that this war is not going to end next week, next month or even next year!" Just then the band, situated at one end of the dance floor, sprang to life.

"Come on, Daddy darling, let's have a dance!" Elsie suggested, dragging Raji to his feet and into the tango. They had only been dancing for a few steps when a commotion broke out behind them and nearer the band.

A man in an officer's uniform started yelling: "You are all a bloody disgrace!"

The orchestra's performance stuttered to a stop as he raised a pistol into the air, then fired, the bullet slamming into the ornate ceiling plaster, sending a rain of chips and powder that had been part of a putto, showering over the floor and some tables. Women screamed and Raji grabbed Elsie and they rushed for shelter behind the nearest table.

"Men are going through hell out there and all you can do … is bloody dance and party!" he yelled, firing a second shot which shattered part of a glass chandelier, before he started breaking down. "They are dying out there for you … and all you can do is celebrate!"

As he said those last words, the pianist managed to grab his pistol-holding arm as a man in military uniform put a restraining hold around him. "They are all dead!" he still managed to cry hysterically, sobbing as others came to disarm him. "It is hell … all my friends … they are all dead … yet you dance!" he protested, as he was dragged outside, his voice becoming fainter, as if drowning in the general sea of nationalism.

"Poor bastard!" Raji muttered, as they emerged from behind the table. "There are many men going mad with what they experience."

"I think he is right," commented Elsie. "He actually sounds quite rational, though obviously traumatised."

The patrons in Murray's seemed to adopt a more subdued and respectful edge for the rest of the evening.

To cheer Elsie up, Raji mentioned the real reason for his return: "I think I have found a place that we can call home in London. I want to show it to you, tomorrow!"

Chapter 75

The Gated Mansion

London can be loathsome, with its crowds and smog and grime
Dickensian-type characters, who live a life of crime
Yet inside my gated mansion, with my servants and my friends
I'll spend my life at leisure, tying up the odd loose ends.

The Rolls-Royce headed north-west of central London, with Raji remaining quiet about their destination. As the car turned up the side of Regent's Park—a place Elsie was familiar with and fond of, from previous visits—it slowed as it neared a large, modern, cream and red stone apartment complex.

"Portland stone, or so I am told," Raji said, as he turned into a driveway off Prince Albert Road and pulled up in front of a gentleman, sheltering in a long and thick grey coat against the winter chill.

"Good morning, Your Highnesses!" the man called from beneath his protective clothing.

"Darling, this is Mr Percy Johnson. He is the managing agent for North Gate Mansions!"

Mr Johnson bowed and opened the door for Elsie to step out. She looked around the width of the building, but Percy was quick to focus her on his pride. "Your flat, No. 82, is up there on the third floor, Your Highness. I consider it to be the very best in the whole complex! Please, follow me!"

The way Mr Johnson spoke, Elsie wondered whether Raji had already agreed to rent it.

They followed Mr Johnson through a columned entrance over which were stamped the words 'North Gate Nos 75 to 88ᴬ'.

Proceeding through the doors into a spacious foyer, they then walked up four marble steps to stand in front of a lift with wood-panelled sides.

"Only the finest and most up-to-date of lifts, of course!" Mr Johnson said, as he pressed the button. Elsie noted the option of the stairs to the right, though if 'their flat' was on the third floor, she was not very likely to use them.

The lift sailed smoothly upwards to the third floor, where

it eased to a stop. "This way to our left, please!" Mr Johnson indicated, as they turned out of the lift to face a large, white door with the black number 82 emblazoned upon it.

Percy took a key from his pocket, placed it in the lock—then stopped. "Before we go inside, let me say that although the building of this complex was started in 1913, this flat is still being completed, but should be available by mid-year."

"Is there any reason for that, Mr Johnson?" Elsie asked.

"Let me say that we want it to be our finest. Works of art do take time. When finished, it will be priced beyond what most people can afford!" For most potential renters, such a statement would have finished their interest, but Percy Johnson well knew the type of clientele he had before him.

He turned the key, then the handle and waved them inside into the entrance hall, which even had its own fireplace.

"You might have thought that on a day like this we could well have done with a raging fire, yet, as you can feel, it is quite a pleasant temperature in here!"

"How many rooms are there, Mr Johnson?" Elsie enquired.

"There are nine, Your Highness, excluding the two bathrooms. Perhaps we could look first at these three rooms at the front."

"Enough room for you to have a live-in maid and a live-in cook!" Raji whispered.

Mr Johnson led them forward and to the right. "I call this the drawing room. It has this beautiful balcony," he said, opening a door. As they stepped outside, they were greeted by cool air, but a sublime and extensive view over Prince Albert Road and across Regent's Park.

"It almost feels like a gated mansion up here on the third floor, with nothing but Regent's Park spreading out on this side!" Elsie whispered to Raji, not wanting to compromise any attempt on her husband's part to perhaps bargain for a better price.

Retreating inside, they turned to the other two rooms on the park side: the lounge with its magnificent bay window and the dining to its left.

"Of course, we have the kitchen backing on to the dining, then a pantry, followed by a bathroom, a bedroom, that could well be for a servant, and so on. Please, just take your time and enjoy contemplating the possibilities, as you wander through to the back of the flat. Just remember, all the best available fittings are yet to be added!"

They headed off down a long corridor of what began as herringbone-patterned wood, but which came to a quick and jagged halt. Stepping into unfinished areas that Mr Johnson had mentioned, they reached a storage room, a potential smaller bedroom and then three large rooms in line across the rear of the flat, in a mirror image of the ones at the front.

"Darling, this end one on the left would have to be the main bedroom, as it has what I am pretty sure will be the main bathroom set in front of it." Elsie could already see herself comfortably ensconced.

Raji had seen enough, but he still wanted to ask questions. "How many square feet is it altogether, Mr Johnson?"

"Exactly 3,400 Your Highness!" came the immediate reply, for Percy Johnson prided himself on remembering every small but important detail—except his own wedding anniversary.

"Just give me a few moments, Mr Johnson!" Raji said, as he pulled Elsie towards what might one day be their bedroom.

"What do you think?" she asked.

"I am happy with it, but do you think you could live here?"

She looked at him and smiled. "Of course. I think it will be beautiful when finished!"

"We will take it!" Raji blurted, as he returned to the entrance hall.

Percy was delighted but a little surprised, as a quarterly rental price had not yet been discussed. "Excellent! Please follow me a mere two hundred feet away to my office, and we can note down some details!"

The managing agent produced a large green book and opened it to the page stamped with the number 76. It had 82 under the column headed 'No.' on the left side. Then he wrote in the date '17th February 1915' and 'Maharaja of Tikari'.

"The rent will be 400 pounds inclusive of rates per quarter. What sort of lease period would you be after, Your Highness? Three years is the minimum."

"Twenty-one years!" came the response. Percy raised his eyebrows in shock, but he was happy to record it.

"Twenty-one years ... now I have on my calendar that the flat should be completed by the beginning of the week of 21 June, so would you be happy to start on Thursday 24 June?"

"I will check the flat in the company of my husband's lawyers—Douglas Grant & Doid—at the start of that week," Elsie responded, appreciating that everything needed to be verified as finished and appropriate.

As they drove away through light rain, Raji explained that he had been keen for her to move from The Waldorf Hotel after the first German zeppelin raid of 19 January.

"The area of Regent's Park is a bit removed from key public buildings and docks. The talk in the War Office is that we can expect many more air raids in the months ahead!"

Chapter 76

Return of the Heart

Sometimes, just sometimes, we delay or vacillate
And we baulk to share some words, all before it is too late
For oft'times, invariably, those persons do pass on
And the heart does soon regret, what the mind had just forgone.

Elsie was not to see Raji again till 19 March 1915. It was to be a day she would never forget. She had been sitting in an armchair with her feet up, reading, when there was a soft tap at the door of the suite.

"Come in!" she called, still engrossed in the novel.

She could hear a fiddling with the door handle and a slight creak of the door, but initially, no other sound.

"Who is it?" she asked, then, when a few seconds later there was still no response, she turned and looked towards the entrance. It was then she noticed Raji.

She leapt to her feet, tossed her book on to the couch and raced towards the door. "Daddy! It's so good to ..." she started exclaiming, slowing as she neared him, because she noticed something she had never seen before: tears were streaming down his face.

"Oh, darling! Come to mummy! I will look after you!" she urged, as she led him inside to sit on the couch.

They sat there, she cuddling him for a couple of minutes, before she dared say anything more. Finally, she asked him what was wrong. He did not respond verbally, but fumbled inside his coat and removed a white handkerchief, before passing it to Elsie.

Though it was folded, Elsie could see it had colouration inside, so she started opening it. It was only as she did so, that Raji said: "He made me promise to pass this on ... if anything happened."

Elsie opened the handkerchief out to reveal a hand-sewn red heart with the names Abu and Sita stitched inside.

"No! ... Oh no, no, no!" Elsie wailed, as she clutched the handkerchief to her breast.

"He said he had loved you … from the moment he first met you—and would have done anything for you!"

For a long time Elsie just sobbed as she nestled against Raji, until she eventually found the energy and courage to ask how Abu had died.

"The great offensive at Neuve-Chapelle … it began on March 10. The next day, so I was told, Abu … with the regiment under orders to attack, led … he led a group of the 47th Sikhs out of the trenches in a charge on the German positions … they were about 150 yards away. A survivor of the assault, claimed Abu was the only one to breach the barbed wire and make the open ground … the area in front of the German trenches … but he was cut down by machine gun fire …"

* * *

In the months ahead, nearly as much to distract from the impact of Abu's passing as any practical concern, Elsie launched herself into preparing for the move to North Gate. First, she made enquiries about improving her singing and acquiring the services of a professional musician and coach.

To this end, she had reconnected with sixty-year-old Benno Scherek, a talented pianist and conductor of grand opera, who had agreed to assist Elsie during the time he remained in London.

The two had met years before, when Scherek had worked for J. C. Williamson in Melbourne. They shared a love for performing, opera and, most importantly, given the times, a great sense of humour.

To facilitate Benno's involvement, Elsie had received Raji's approval to have a custom-made and extra large grand piano for their new flat, though the only problem was getting it inside. Access via the lift or stairway was not possible, by just a few inches, so the erstwhile building manager at North Gate, Mr Gregory Phillips, devised a somewhat unconventional plan, that he assured Elsie might just do the trick.

With Elsie determinedly in tow, Mr Phillips climbed up a series of narrow stairs towards the top of the complex, before tackling a final vertical ladder, above which was a metal manhole cover.

Elsie was helped up onto the rooftop to admire a spectacular view across the width and depth of Regent's Park and towards the heart of London. It was less scary than she had imagined, as there was a terrace-type setup with a low wall at the end and ornamental pots at either side.

"Over here we have anchor points that were utilised in bringing building materials up to different levels during the work on the flats. I could have a system of ropes and pulleys rigged to lift the piano to your balcony!" It all sounded simple, though the structure took two days to prepare, while the grand piano sat mournfully, downstairs in the entrance foyer.

Quite a crowd had gathered to watch, when on Tuesday 29 June, a long line of men hauled on a rope, and the piano made its grand progress skyward, before being eased onto the balcony of No. 82, then squeezed through the centre-opening pair of doors to reach its final resting place in the drawing room.

Elsie had already advertised for a cook and a maid, both of whom were to be live-in. Given the general location and the exclusive nature of the immediate surroundings, there was no shortage of young women keen to commit.

Somi, a cook of Japanese heritage and Violetta, a beautiful young Italian maid, were recruited. The latter was particularly valuable, as Elsie intended to add Italian to her string of languages, something she felt sure would assist her in progressing in the world of opera.

At the beginning of July, she sent a postcard of Regent's Park to Emma:

Dearest Em (and Joe),

Our new 9-room flat is on the north-western edge of this beautiful park. Being on the third floor I have a most magnificent view to inspire me each day—helping to forget the terrible events not so far away. Raji sends his love and is currently safe, thank goodness!

The address here is: 82 North Gate

Mansions, Prince Albert Road, St John's Wood NW8 London.

It would be great if you both could be living next door, but not many dreams can come true!

Lots of Love,
El XOXOXO

In early October, she received a short letter from Emma, with some important news:

Dearest El (and Raji—I think I had to write that)!

You are an auntie again! Stella gave birth to another girl on 27 August, who they have named after you: Elsie St Ledger Thompson! They are now living at 21 Boundary St in Roseville, in a house they have named Tikari! See, your influence is everywhere!

Joe and I are looking to buy a house some time next year, with the Ryde area the most likely location. He is well, but is often on the road—so I do know how you feel!

Your father is fine and your mother as good as can be expected, given her condition. They send their love and best wishes.
We all keep thinking of you and Raji and hoping you stay safe with the bombing in London and war on the Continent.

Lots of love,
Em XXOO

Elsie was delighted to have Raji home for the Christmas of 1915. Somi had made a lovely Christmas cake and Elsie had bought a Christmas tree and decorations to make No. 82 even more inviting.

The news he brought was quite surprising: The Commander-in-Chief of the British Expeditionary Force, General Sir Douglas Haig, had in the last week asked Raji to become his personal driver and dispatch officer. He could keep Abid Hussain as his valet and assistant. Naturally, Raji accepted. He was now going to be at the very heart of the war operation, though kept at a safe distance from the front, in the General Headquarters.

For her part, Elsie informed him that, guided by Benno Scherek, she had performed with 'pronounced success', as the papers had put it, at the London Palladium Theatre, where she had donated all takings to the War Fund.

She was very loathe to have Raji depart in the early New Year, and was not expecting to see him home again so soon …

The very instance that Elsie had opened the door of the flat on the morning of 29 January, Raji was quickly and earnestly urging her to be quiet. "Tell the servants to go into their rooms, close the doors and stay there until they are asked to come out!" he ordered.

As Violetta and Somi scurried away, Elsie noticed there was a man wrapped completely in a large trench coat with a cloth cap pulled over his face, standing at the entrance.

Raji checked that the corridor was clear of servants, then signalled for the man to enter, though the gentleman only did so after fastidiously wiping his shoes on the doormat.

They headed into the lounge where Raji indicated an armchair and said: "Sir, please be seated."

"Raji, your friend and I have not been introduced!" Elsie protested, for she had a suspicion just who this might be.

"General Sir Douglas Haig, Your Highness!" the gentleman himself said in a Scottish accent, removing his hat and coat, which Raji eagerly took from his grasp. "Tikari has told me a lot about you, though he never could quite convey just how charming you are!"

"In that case, I better charm you further with a cup of tea!" she said, exiting to the kitchen. She soon returned with tea and cakes, a welcome sight on a cool day.

Conversation was difficult, and Elsie sensed that they both had knowledge of impending matters that were top secret, which she felt could explain the reason for their appearance in

London. The general acknowledged little more than conceding that if God willed it so, the war might soon be won, though he was more forthcoming on the subject of Australian soldiers.

"Your countrymen," he said to Elsie, "are an enigma to most all of us. By reputation from Gallipoli and elsewhere, they are frequently ill-disciplined, almost always disrespectful of authority and seemingly casual at critical times. Despite these flaws, I doubt there will soon be a single soldier on the Western Front who would not want an Australian fighting by his side when the chips are down!"

"I sometimes wish my husband would engage with such sentiment more frequently!" Elsie said, with a wink at Raji.

What Elsie did not know and could not have been told, was that Haig and Raji were on their way just north of London to view a secret but well-organised demonstration of the army's potential new weapon—the tank. An area of land in the grounds of Hatfield House had been laid out to resemble a battlefield, complete with craters, barbed wire protected trenches and swampy ground, all to test the effectiveness of the contraption.

Its original drawings and containers had been labelled 'Water Carrier for Russia' to disguise their purpose, until it was pointed out that, abbreviated, this was W.C., so the word 'Tank' was substituted.

As they set off north, the general turned to Raji and joked: "If I had a wife like that, I think I would have deserted long ago!"

Chapter 77

To the Gates of Hell

I counted out the seconds, bang through whistle then to thud
As around me lay the wounded, both in agony and mud
And I thought about my family — by Christ I wished them well
And I prayed that they should never know, these putrid gates of hell.

Shortly before Haig's planned March 1916 shift of General Headquarters from Saint-Omer to a castle near Montreuil, thirty-seven miles south-west within the Pas-de-Calais region, Raji made his move.

For well over a year now, he had transported senior military figures and important documentation around the fringe of the Western Front, but had never gone to the front line itself. He was now determined that this should change.

On the pretext of having to be in London by a sick Elsie's side, he had taken leave for a week, allowing Abid Hussain to temporarily take over his role.

Borrowing another Rolls-Royce, Raji sat at the intersection outside Saint-Omer. Were he to turn right, he would soon be travelling up the coastal road to Calais, then by boat to England. Left, well that was another matter …

Raji flattened the accelerator to the floor and flung the steering wheel left, causing the back of the car to fly out in a shower of stones and mud as the front headed towards the city of Arras. Later, a turn south, saw him entering what would become the most infamous killing fields of the whole war: the Somme.

Raji knew, from being close to Haig, that a major Somme offensive was planned for the summer, but it was months from summer and what passed for roadways were becoming less navigable, the further he went.

Pulling up outside an officer's cottage, he arranged for the Rolls to be left alongside, and flagged down an omnibus packed with British soldiers, heading for the front line. Raji had only his favourite rifle concealed inside its cover, and a few tins of cartridges stuffed in his pockets.

As the vehicle crept on down the muddy track, he quickly

realised there was no mirth or merriment on board, for each seemed lost in their own thoughts. There was also a war-weariness in their eyes, as this was a journey they had made before.

"Welcome to the gates of hell, Darkie!" was all one private could utter.

The omnibus finally reached a point of no return, where the track had deteriorated into a muddy pathway that terminated its progression.

Raji stepped out into what seemed a dastardly diorama. From a field hospital on his left he could hear the cries of wounded, as others supported by mates and in stretchers queued for attention; the terrain was pock-marked by craters and any doubt on Raji's part as to their cause was dispelled after a whistling overhead and a cry of "Watch out!" was followed by an explosion nearby that sent bodies flying.

He swallowed, gripped his rifle firmly and pressed on, threading his way along a muddy, stinking path past dead horses and donkeys and what seemed like dead bodies that he had no intention of further examining.

There was now more whistling and more explosions nearby, but he kept going, for he knew from what he had been told that these pathways led, eventually, to the most forward positions.

Sure enough, he was soon inside a sand-banked area that was deepening into a trench and within a few paces he could see a wall of sandbags ahead. He had reached the front line.

Turning left, he headed along the trench to the nearest group of British soldiers, who seemed surprised to see him. "Where are the Germans?" Raji asked, in all innocence.

"I'll show ya!" said one, reaching for a can, placing it on the end of his rifle and holding it aloft. Within seconds, shots rang out and soon the can was spinning wildly from being hit by German bullets—to laughter and cheers from the German side.

"That's where they are! 'Bout 100 yards away!"

"You point them out and I will shoot them!" said Raji.

"Oh, forget about that! They have toughened glass shields protecting their trench lines. The bullets just bounce off!"

"We will see!" Raji said, removing the rifle from its cover, loading its two barrels and placing it inside a firing hole within the sandbags.

"What the devil is that gun?" one of the soldiers asked.

"A Westley Richards Dangerous Game Double Rifle. It fires 0.476 Nitro Express cartridges, so we'll see how the Germans like this!" Raji uttered confidently.

He pulled the trigger and almost instantly a glass shield exploded in front of the German trenches. "He's smashed a bloody shield!" a British soldier looking through a periscope yelled, to cheers from those around.

Raji reloaded quickly and fired again, with the same result. He continued for nearly fifteen minutes, but it became obvious from the yelling from the German trench lines that the foe was not at all happy.

Soon, a British captain rushed into their trench to ask what the hell was going on. The Germans had lodged a complaint about someone firing an illegal weapon, the use of which in war was a breach of the Hague Convention.

Raji's gun was checked and he was asked to follow the captain to see the colonel—and to bring the gun and bullets with him.

They had only taken a few steps back from the front line when there was a loud whistling sound and then a massive explosion that picked Raji up and threw him back against the trench wall.

The next few hours seemed a blur but when he woke up, he was lying on a stretcher in the field hospital, aching all over and covered in the captain's blood and body tissue.

Explosions continued throughout the night, making sleep impossible. Every time he heard that dreadful whistling sound of an imminent shell strike, he grimaced, waiting for the impact. After two sleepless nights, he sneaked out of the hospital and stumbled through the mud, eventually finding the Rolls next to the cottage.

Haig had already heard about the use of the elephant gun, so Raji had to apologise for misleading him. Aware that Raji was not too keen to stay on, Haig raised the possibility of him becoming an aide to Lord Chelmsford, India's soon-to-be Viceroy.

To seal the deal, Raji promised to pay for three of the new tanks for the front line (via a loan from the Maharaja of Darbhanga), in return for his departure back home. He could, he suggested, always join up with British forces in Mesopotamia, later.

Elsie now had a difficult choice to make: should she follow Raji back to the heat of India and the negative influence of Wakefield, or should she remain in London in her comfortable flat—with its long-term lease and regular access to the world's best theatres—and occasional visits from Raji? Unsurprisingly, she chose the latter.

Raji consented, as Elsie was in the latter part of her possible childbearing years, and he had access to women in India, whenever he wished.

After a London farewell at the Eccentric Club in Ryder Street—an event at which Elsie gave a humorous speech, as the newspapers reported—Raji sailed for India aboard the P&O *Kaisar-i-Hind* on Saturday 11 March 1916. Lord Chelmsford was also on board. The ship narrowly escaped being struck by German torpedoes in the Mediterranean.

Elsie was informed by cable from Bombay, that Raji had arrived back in the subcontinent and was initially heading to the peace and tranquillity of their houseboat on Dal Lake in Kashmir to recuperate.

On 4 May 1916, Elsie wrote to Raji, in part about what seemed to be a Tikari Raj power struggle between Wakefield and the incumbent, though temporarily absent manager, Willie Hathaway:

Daddy Darling,

I took the Hathaway boys to a Matinee yesterday and afterwards met Willie, who showed me your long cablegram from Bankipore. For your sake dear, I am glad that you are going to Mesopotamia, but for my own, I am sorry.

What has happened in India? You see, I have had no word from you since your cable announcing your arrival in Bombay and naturally I am anxious.

Why do you not want Willie out in India in November? He has let his house, booked his passage, and made all arrangements to leave early in June by the Kaisar-i-Hind, and your sudden change of plans upsets him. Surely, if you are going away it would be better to have Willie in charge, wouldn't it? Oh Dad Dear, please wake up and attend to your own interests!

I should so much have preferred that you had left Willie in charge before you went away. Why have you changed your ideas Dearest? Do tell me.

The flat people made a second application for their rent the other day. I sent their first application in to Cox & Co. on the 15th and doubtless you will settle things in a satisfactory manner before you go away. The lights keep on fusing and I seem to get no satisfaction whatsoever from the Estate agents about it.

I am well Dearest now, but have been suffering terribly with my head lately and had to call Dr Lewis Smith who soon put it right. He sends his very best wishes—so do Carlie and Mysie Boffie-King, Tommy Blackborn and Dr Piccoli.

Carlie and Mysie have been very sweet to me and take me motoring every Sunday whilst I am without a car. I had to break into my precious 100 pound today-bank informed me that I was overdrawn and so I had to send the money along. I was so glad that I had it.

My voice is doing splendid by these days. I am sure now that I will try things with it if I only keep my strength. Tommy thinks the same.

The Talbot Chassis is ready, her lighting set on and her self-starter operational and as soon as we hear from you work commences on the body. Did I tell you Dear that the duty on cars above 20 h.p. is treble what it used to be!

The zeppelin's give us an anxious time these days, with raids almost every night, or so. I keep the 'family jew holes' safe at hand always. The weather is gorgeous now and the Park opposite us looks beautiful.

Take care of yourself dear old Raji and do realise that to at least one person you are very precious. Whatever you do, wherever you are, God be with you. With my dearest love and a kiss.

I remain always,
Your devoted wife,
Sita Devi (little mother)

A short letter from Emma cheered Elsie up considerably:

Dearest El,

Joe and I are very excited. We have bought our first house together! The address is 'Rosemonde' Parramatta Rd, Ryde. It is between Adelaide Rd and Shepherd St and we have lovely neighbours, the Robinsons and the Grahams, so we are very happy.

Your mother and father have new neighbours too! The Middle Harbour Public School opened immediately across the road from them in July, so they now spend even more time on their verandah! They both send all their love and hope you have enjoyed the English summer.

The Taronga Park Zoo at Bradley's Head opens in a few weeks. We have agreed to take Marjorie, but Elsie is still a little young so she will stay with Stella.

As promised, we had the Mucha poster of you framed and it now hangs proudly in our new lounge room, so at least when I feel I miss you a lot (which is almost always) I can look at it for consolation.

Please tell me about any new dances in London when you next write.

Lots of love,
Em XXOO (and Joe)

On 23 November 1916, Elsie wrote to Raji again, though clearly in a more frustrated tone:

Daddy Darling,

It seems useless to expect many letters from you, and although cables are very nice, they don't tell one very much, do they? Anyhow, it is good of you to keep me posted of your whereabouts. I don't believe you will ever leave Kashmir-you have been 'going' for so long.

Thank you Dear. I know you will send me the money for my new fur coat (I ordered it ages ago) and I shall take it as my X'mas present, so please don't think of sending me anything else, for you know Dearest that I have heaps and heaps of jewellery, much more than I can ever possibly wear.

Of course the best present I could have would be your dear troublesome self, for I miss you horribly you dear gunny old Daddy. I shall look forward most eagerly to next summer and you will come then won't you?

I have an idea that I should like to have a house in the summer at Maidenhead for it seems that there, you would perhaps be content to stay with me, and I do so much want us to be 'real' next time. We have sown all our wild oats now dear Dad and we really must settle down.

When you do come, bring Abid Hussain as your valet, because he will be able to make us curries too—and I have not tested a curry for ages.

Dear old Bobbie was over from France for a week's leave last week, and we all did our best to give him a good time. He has been wounded, but is all right now. He sent all sorts of loving messages to you. For his last night I took him to the new rave at the Palace 'Vanity Fair'. It isn't very good and the fair Teddie scarcely gets a chance in it. In any case she has gone off very much, and even you I think would have to admit that she isn't clever. Nelson Keys practically runs the whole show—and although he is very funny one gets too much of him.

Ciro's was raided by the police a fortnight ago and will I think lose their licence. I haven't been there since you left nor to Murray's.

In this cold cheerless weather I love my flat and do not care to go out at all at night. My new cook is splendid, so is my little Italian maid and since I have got rid of Somi, there is a complete atmosphere of peace in the house.

Dear—I do hope that you sent the rent for the flat, and there will be another one due before Christmas don't forget. It would be better if you arranged this with Cox as you said you would.

My voice is doing really well now, Dear, but I still peg away at my old exercises, and shall continue to do so until next July (my second year) when I want to commence to learn the opelas with an Italian accompanist, Maestro Veroli. I still take my Italian lessons with Madame Fornaghi, but oh the Italian grammar is terribly difficult.

It's going to be a funny old Christmas this year for me Dear (without you) and I shall spend it very quietly. Just Carlie and Mysie and Dr Piccoli and myself—but I shall give the servants a little party if I can afford it. Prices of provisions in England still continue to rise alarmingly—all round in the last year a 98% rise. Eggs are now 4/6 per dozen and coal is 1 pound 17 per ton.

I only run my car on Sundays, but I do enjoy that run and it sets me up for the whole week. She is a beauty Dad and goes so fast. If you are good I will lend her to you when you come home. Provided I go too of course. I know lots of lovely places where we must go, and I can send the maid on always by train.

Do be a darling when you get back to Gaya and write me a nice long letter, all about everything you know. Dearest this one-sided correspondence is rather dull.

'Good bye' God bless you. I do hope that you are well and happy. With my dearest love and a big kiss.

Your ever-loving wife,
Sita Devi

PS: I forgot to mention that on 16 August I was on the cover of the English magazine 'Country Life', in the sari you most like me to wear!

If Elsie had hoped that her letters would encourage Raji to visit her in London or to even write soon, she was to be disappointed on both counts.

Chapter 78

The Perpetual Annuity

In thinking of forever, I've forever put in place
A deed, a bond, a promise, that shall cover every case
A perpetual annuity, on properties and more
For I'm thinking of my favourite wife, the woman I adore.

The need to regularly remind Raji to pay the rent on the North
Gate flat was tiresome and unsettling, so it was a blessing when
Elsie received a cable from Raji on 23 July 1917, alerting her to
a second annuity that had been signed, though this one would
replace part of the first.

A copy was passed on from his solicitors in London.
Significantly, while the first annuity of 1913 was to be paid to
Elsie for as long as she lived, this new one was to be perpetual,
that is, 'to her and her heirs in perpetuity for ever'. It read:

I, Maharaj Kumar Gopal Saran Narayan Singh, son of Abika
Prasad Singh and grandson and heir of Maharaja Ram Kishun
Singh Bahadur, deceased, by caste a Brahmin Bhumihar, by
profession a Zamindar residing at Tikari, Pargana Sanout,
district Gaya send greetings whereas by a deed under my
hand and the seal dated the sixteenth day of April, one
thousand nine hundred and thirteen and duly registered in
the Calcutta registry office in book 1, volume XIII, being
No. 1026 for 1913 I settled a life annuity of rupees thirty-
six thousand on my wife Sita Devi to be paid in the manner
therein mentioned and charged my properties in the said
deed set out and described (being the properties set out and
described in the schedule hereto and intended to be hereby
charged) with the payment of the said annuity and in the said
deed it was provided that the said annuity should cease at
the death of my said wife, whereas I am now desirous out of
the love and affection which I bear to my said wife the said
Sita Devi of granting to her and her heirs in perpetuity for
ever an annuity of rupees fifteen thousand per annum and of
charging the payment of the same upon the properties set out

in the schedule hereto but so that the said perpetual annuity shall be taken and accepted by the said Sita Devi in lieu or substitution of rupees fifteen thousand part of the said life annuity of rupees thirty-six thousand per annum and the said life annuity to that extent shall merge in the said perpetual annuity.

Now this Indenture witnesseth that for the consideration aforesaid and for the purpose of carrying the said desire into effect I the said Maharaj Kumar Gopal Saran Narayan Singh hereby grant unto the said Sita Devi her heirs executors administrators and assigns one perpetual annuity or clear yearly rent charge or sum of rupees fifteen thousand to be issuing and payable out of and charged and chargeable upon all and singular properties and villages lands hereditaments and premises set out and described in the schedule hereto which said perpetual annuity or rent charge is to be paid by equal monthly instalments on the first day of each and every month free from all taxes and deductions whatsoever except income-tax the first of such payments to be made on the first day of August next.

To hold the said annuity or annual rental charge unto the said Sita Devi her heirs executors administrators and assigns for ever to the extent that part of the said life annuity of thirty-six thousand per annum to the extent of rupees fifteen thousand per annum shall merge into and be extinguished in the said perpetual annuity of rupees fifteen thousand hereby granted provided always that if the grant of the said annuity hereby granted shall for any reason become ineffective or void in law the right of the said Sita Devi to the whole annuity secured by the herein before recited deed shall become valid and effectual capable of being enforced ...

[Signed] Arthur Hinds, Solicitor, Calcutta

[Signed] Gopal Saran Narayan Singh, Maharaja of Tikari

[Signed] W. Hathaway, Manager, Tikari Raj

[Signed] J. G. Wakefield, Private Secretary, Tikari Raj

18 July 1917

Elsie was surprised to see Wakefield as a signatory. She wondered what arm-twisting must have had to occur for him to sign.

On Tuesday 31 July 1917, Elsie wrote to Raji:

Daddy Darling,

Your cable of 23rd from Calcutta reached me yesterday and I am glad to know that you are well for I had been worrying about you a great deal-and not ever receiving any letters from you Dear causes me unhappiness. After all, you are my husband-the one person in the world whom I feel I can rely on-and when I see other women so happy with their husbands it causes a big lump in my throat, and I see what I have missed and am missing in life. Perhaps you feel like that sometimes too, do you Dearest?

Thank you for promising to send me the money for my birthday-you are always so good in these matters, dear Raji. The money will be much more useful to me than any jewellery-of which I already have too much-and I shall be able to pay up some pressing bills.

Dearest-I do hope that you will come to England soon, for I long to see you so much, and am so tired of living alone.

There is now another important reason why I want you to come-don't let it worry you though, Dear-it is nothing serious. I told you that I have not been feeling very well lately. So today I called the Doctor in. He finds something wrong with my inside again-says he is afraid there must be a small operation when I return from Devonshire.

Well, Dear, if this must be so I feel that I would like to have you near me, you see. I have already gone through so much suffering Dear and one never knows what might happen. I have such a dread of going under chloroform again—I don't know why—but if you were here, I should not mind.

Please, please write to me Dearest and give me your advice. My Doctor is a nice man Dr Murray Morris who lives quite close to me but of course, he would not perform the operation in any case.

In the meantime in Devonshire, I am to take certain medicine which he has given me—and am to rest as much as possible—and then when I return he will have a specialist examine me.

I am rather longing to get away from London. I think I have stayed here too long, and then, too, I miss so much the loss of motoring.

Bothie Robertson is still in England in a Sanitarium in Blackpool at present. He is going to try to get to Devonshire for a couple of weeks. I hope he will succeed—it will be nice to have a big strong brother to look after me. Men are very scarce these days Daddy Dear.

I hope that all is well with you over there and that you are happy. With my love and a big kiss.

Little Mother

Chapter 79

The Times They are a Changing

As Father Time walks onward, he will never miss a beat
He'll toy with all those ignorant, while strolling up their street
Leaves grow and curl in deference, his path is ever ranging
He ensures that for us mortal ones, our times are ever changing.

A cable from Emma in early January 1918 brought most upsetting though not totally unexpected news:

Dearest El,

Your mother died 2 Jan. She at last can rest in peace. Father will write soon. Joe and I send much love and condolences.

Em XXOO

A few weeks later, a letter from Elsie's father arrived:

My Dear Child,

Emma has told me she has passed on the news of your mother's death on 2 January. Naturally, this has been a time of great stress and sadness for me. At just 56 years of age, she was taken from our lives too soon.

You are well aware that your mother had been most unwell and suffered badly for many years. Deaths from consumption are sadly most prevalent these days, though this should not diminish the pain she and those around her felt. She is at last suffering no more, but in the hands of the Lord.

You should know that she was always very proud of you and took great delight in hearing the latest news relating to India, London and your performing.

I had my dear Cissie buried in the Field of Mars cemetery, not far from her father Charles Roffey. I asked that a double grave be prepared so that we may be together again soon.

My Macpherson St house is already too empty and I fear I am struggling to cope. It might be possible that I move to be near Walter, Stella and the grandchildren in Boundary St Roseville.

In these depressing times when war and death so dominate our lives, having Marjorie and little Elsie close at hand gives me strength to keep going.

Oh how often I have wished I could wear a pair of London-made shoes, but we walk in the shoes the Lord has made for us and should be grateful for whatever mercies he chooses to bestow.

With the greatest love and a wish that we might embrace again soon,

Your Father

Elsie sat for some time, before asking Violetta to join her on a sofa in the lounge in front of the warmth of the fire. There she lay, with her head in Violetta's lap, as her maid stroked her hair. Elsie cried quietly as she stared into the flames.

"Scusami!" Elsie whispered, apologetically.

"Non scusarti, Your Highness!" insisted the young maid, giving her hand a kiss.

* * *

Ever since March 1917, when Tsar Nicholas II of Russia had been forced after the revolution to abdicate and live with his family under house arrest in the Alexander Palace, Elsie had keenly followed developments.

While she was happy to give proceeds from her occasional performances to the War Fund, she was equally keen to show and state her support for the Romanov family, by wearing the Fabergé angel brooch that Grand Duchess Maria had given to her in 1912.

On the morning of Monday 22 July, Violetta headed out to pick up the morning paper as she usually did. Elsie had opted to lie in bed on this summer morning, warmed by the sunlight filtering through the large windows of her bedroom.

She could hear the lift rise and stop on the third floor, the doors open and close and Violetta open the locked door with her key, then close it ... then silence ...

"Violetta, darling! You can bring the paper in now!" Elsie called, but there was still no answer. "You can come into bed with me and we can read it together!" she added, hoping that this would trigger a reaction.

She could hear the shuffling of feet down the corridor and she prepared the right side of the bed—away from the window— for her maid.

Violetta paused at the door and seemed unwilling to enter.

"Darling, what is wrong?" Elsie asked, wondering how or when she could possibly have offended her.

"Il giornale, Your Highness, il giornale ..."

"What about the newspaper, darling?" Elsie asked, for she could clearly see that Violetta had it closed in her hand.

"Scusa ... mi dispiace molto ..." she said, gingerly handing over the paper.

As soon as Elsie opened the paper, the headline's words screamed at her:

EX-TSAR SHOT

Elsie read on for a bit, barely able to breathe. "Damn him! Damn King George V! He was Nicky's cousin, he could have saved him, but he let him die!"

What she did not know then, and what the Bolsheviks did not dare announce, was that Alexandra, son Alexei, and her daughters, including Maria, had been shot, bludgeoned to death or bayoneted by their captors, at the time of Nicky's killing. It was possible that one daughter, believed to have been Anastasia, might have survived and escaped.

The Fabergé angel gift from Maria suddenly became even more important to Elsie.

* * *

In November 1918, World War I, a conflict that had stripped so many countries of their young and not so young, came to an end.

On 12 September 1919, well after the war had finished, the *London Gazette* announced that Raji had been promoted to Honorary Captain.

Also in 1919, Raji contested elections as a member of the Indian National Congress, an organisation dedicated to freeing India from British rule.

In that same year, the thirty-six year old Raji formally married a fourth wife, fifteen-year-old Vidyavati Kuer.

Chapter 80

The Royal Imperative

I'll tell you just what you should know — though it may not all be true
You must only do as I tell you to — though it's not what I will do
My birth has brought me privilege, and royal prerogative
To satisfy the urgings, of a royal imperative.

The tall man with blonde hair and pallid features appeared to
Elsie to be an ex-military type — and now she was closer to him,
she realised that she had seen him at a few of her performances.

"Do you make a habit of following me, sir?" she asked, though
her smile indicated she was not overly concerned.

"Oh, Your Highness, I only follow those that I can learn from
and those that I can help," he replied, somewhat enigmatically.

"And pray tell me, which camp I fall into, Mr …?"

"Henry Culliford, Your Highness, and I think you fit a bit in
both."

"Really, Mr Culliford. And how to do you think you can help
me?"

"In singing. I have been classically trained and I have a good
knowledge of, and acquaintances in, the London music scene. I
think I might be able to train you."

"I am a married woman, Mr Culliford!"

"I certainly realise that and would respect it. After all, the
last thing I would want is a maharaja charging after me like
a wounded elephant! Why don't you join me on Saturday
afternoon at 3 pm for afternoon tea, at my mother's house?"

"Mr Culliford! We have only just met and you are already
asking me to meet your mother! Do you not think that is a little
premature?" Elsie said this with such a smile and twinkle in
her eyes that Culliford knew she was not trying to dissuade
him.

"My mother, Eliza, lives at 21 Oppidans Road, Regent's Park."

"Oh, I think I know where that is! She lives not far from me!"

"You live near Regent's Park?"

"Yes, in North Gate Mansions, so I shall walk there. Saturday
at 3, you said, Mr Culliford?"

"Yes, Your Highness," he responded, a little stunned that his suggestion had been so readily accepted. "Oh, and please call me Henry!"

"Only if you call me Sita or Elsie!" she said, with another smile.

"Oh, I don't think I could do either—we have only just met!" he said, and they both laughed.

"Well, there may be the odd thing I can help you with … Mr Culliford!"

"Great! Well, I shall see you there at 3 pm—21 Oppidans Road, remember, Your Highness—I mean … Elsie!"

"I shall be delighted … Henry!" she said, with a smile as they parted, leaving Culliford shaking his head and smiling too.

* * *

Over the next few months, Henry regularly visited North Gate, playing the piano and assisting Elsie with her vocal work, though they always ensured that at least Violetta was there as well.

Henry had targetted Armistice Day, 11 November 1920, for Elsie's big performance.

It was to be an auspicious day. That morning, huge and silent crowds had lined London's streets to watch the body of the Unknown Warrior, carried on a guncarriage, and followed by the royal family, wind its way to its final resting place of the western nave of Westminster Abbey.

That night, Elsie headlined a show at the Aeolian Hall at 135-137 New Bond Street. She sang 'Songs and Arias', had Italian Manilo di Veroli on piano, and was also supported by the English String Quartet.

After the show, a tall, dark-haired young man in a naval uniform approached Elsie and offered his congratulations. "Lord Mountbatten," he said confidently, offering his hand. "Why don't you join me for a celebratory drink at my flat? It has been one hell of a day for both of us!"

"Why thank you for the offer, Lord Louis," she responded, for she recognised him from the papers. "However, as you say, it has been one hell of a day and I am rather tired." She looked around the backstage area and spotted Henry, calling him over. "Henry, would you mind dropping me home please!"

As they drove towards North Gate, Elsie expressed her surprise at Mountbatten's offer.

"He may be the great grandson of Queen Victoria, but, from what I hear," said Henry, "he would be up any reasonable woman faster than a rat up a drainpipe!"

What they did not realise at that moment was that Henry's car was being followed.

Parking outside the entrance to North Gate, Henry escorted Elsie to the lift and they headed up to the third floor. As the lift set off, a figure raced through the foyer and up the stairs, keeping track of the lift's progress. When the lift slowed and then halted on the third floor, the figure dashed past and further up the stairs, hiding just out of sight.

Elsie unlocked the door and warned Henry in a whisper: "It is late and I don't want to wake the servants or the neighbours. Thank you for everything you have done for me, Henry. You deserve as much credit as me for the performance!"

"It was a pleasure, Elsie! I will see you on Tuesday!"

"Thanks again!" Elsie said as she kissed him on the cheek and he departed.

Elsie entered the flat, closed the door and locked it with the key, which she left in the latch, then put her purse down on a couch, just as there was a soft knocking at the door.

"Oh, Henry! What have you forgotten?" she whispered, as she opened the door, but it was not Henry.

"Hello, Your Highness!"

"Lord Mountbatten! ... I am sorry, but you must leave!" she said earnestly, as she tried to shut the door ... but he thrust his shoe in the gap to stop it closing.

"Really!" she called out much louder than she had wanted. "I am a married woman!"

"Just the sort I like!" he said, though he seemed to be toying with her as he had made no effort to open the door beyond the width of his right shoe.

Just then Violetta, awakened by the commotion, rushed down the corridor in her nightdress. "Your Highness! Che cosa c'è che non va?"

"Oh my!" Mountbatten said admiringly of Violetta, for his

limited view encompassed the full width of the corridor, and her approach, with long hair billowing.

"Bambina! Please, go back to your room and lock your door! I will be all right!" Violetta hesitated, but Elsie insisted: "Tesoro, vai via! Subito!" Reluctantly, Violetta headed back to her room.

Elsie realised that a young man of Mountbatten's strength could surely push the door open at any time he wished, so she just had to think of a way of getting him to pull his foot back.

"A beautiful woman like you deserves to be spoiled every now and again!" Mountbatten insisted.

"I am thirty-seven, you realise—nearly old enough to be your mother!" she responded.

"Age is irrelevant when a woman is as desirable as you!" he countered, correctly anticipating that such a statement would make Elsie feel flattered.

Just then, a voice called out from across the foyer. It was her neighbour, Mr Fowler, from No. 81: "For God's sake, tone it down! Some of us are trying to get some sleep!"

Elsie could sense Mountbatten turning back towards the voice—but it gave her a moment to reflect on her situation.

She had not had a visit from Raji for quite a while, and she missed the physical interaction this provided. The prospect of a liaison with the well-connected young Mountbatten, who might also open doors in high circles, suddenly appeared tempting. So, she capitulated.

"Shhh!" she urged in a whisper, as she fully opened the door. "Come in, but be quiet!"

* * *

In late January 1921, Elsie received unexpected though joyous news, in a note from Emma:

Dearest El,

I am delighted to inform you that I am pregnant and that both Joe and I are overjoyed. The doctor says that I can expect to give birth around June, by which time I will be 36 and Joe 38—quite late to be first-time parents!

We have decided that whether the child is a boy or a girl, we really want you to be its Godmother! Please let us know if you are willing to accept this onerous task!

Also, Walter and Stella had a third daughter on 9 December and have called her Stella!

Lots of love from us both,
Em and Joe XXOO

Elsie was quick to cable back her delight and acceptance, but there was something troubling her. She had managed to perform Indian songs in her soprano voice at the Aeolian Hall, including one titled 'Children's Rain Song' in Hindustani, but was being beset by abdominal pain.

For weeks, Elsie became less and less comfortable, till one day she called out from the toilet in great pain. "Violetta! Get Dr Morris, quickly!"

By the time he had arrived, the pain had subsided. Dr Morris talked to her about what had occurred, examined her briefly then made the pronouncement: "I would love to say, congratulations Your Highness, you are indeed pregnant—though sadly, I cannot! A pity, for it would have been remarkable for a lady who told me she would never be able to conceive—and I am sure the Maharaja would have been ecstatic!"

"Yes, I am sure he would have been over the moon!" said Elsie, frustrated that the ongoing saga of her abdominal pain would once again, remain unresolved.

Chapter 81

The Secret Return

If I could but always travel, incognito I would go
And would spy the world's great moments, as a patron does a show
I would ghost by old acquaintances, and glimpse them all off guard
As I catch them out in confidence, within their own backyard.

Wakefield leaned against the verandah railing of the White House and looked straight at Raji, for he had figured out a way to reduce financial pressure on Tikari Raj. "Do you honestly believe that she could go years without having a connection?"

"Well, I don't know, but perhaps not."

"A woman like that can't help herself. I bet that she has been fucking every prick in London for years and you have been paying her to do so!"

"That is a bit crude JG … but do you really think so?"

"Well, why don't you have her put under surveillance and followed—I know what you will find out!"

Raji thought for a while. "I guess you are right—I should do something about it. I could hire a private detective … ok!" he said leaping to his feet. "Then we will see what we find!"

* * *

On 8 June 1921, Elsie received a cable from Joe Binstead:

Sita Binstead born Mon 6 June. Mum and baby well.
All send love to Sita's Godmother. Joe XO

Elsie was delighted, for not only were Emma and the baby well, but they had honoured her by giving the little girl her Indian name.

Elsie cabled back that she would be sending a christening gift in the post, then went out and bought a spoon and a two-handled silver christening bowl upon which she had engraved:

* * *

In August 1921, Raji received his first report on the surveillance of Elsie. Wakefield was keen to read over his shoulder at the results.

"A Mr Henry Culliford … is a regular visitor to 82 North Gate … neighbours spoken to are concerned Elsie might be bringing the complex into disrepute …"

"See, I told you! And I bet he is the tip of the iceberg and was not the first!" Wakefield insisted.

"Here is a photograph of Mr Culliford in his motor."

"There is only one thing you can do now Raji—stop paying her the annuities! She's been playing you for a fool for too long! You have been paying for her to act like a prostitute! Money is tight at the moment in the Raj and not paying Elsie regularly will make things far easier."

"You are right my friend! Quite obviously you are right! I will have her kept under surveillance, and will stop the annuity payments—right now!"

From September 1921, Raji ceased all annuity payments. Initially, Elsie cabled him asking what was going on. Then she wrote letters, but he refused to reply.

At Christmas, a detective claimed to have tracked Elsie and Culliford to the Princes Hotel in Hove, Sussex. There, a Mr McCabe, the porter, said he was told by the hotel's manageress, a Mrs Musgrave, that Elsie was a princess and should be referred to as 'Your Highness'. McCabe himself, thought she must have been a Russian princess fallen on hard times, and Henry, an army officer.

From 10 December 1921 until 7 January 1922, Elsie made thirty-six appearances under the name Sita Devi, in the role of Yvonne Durosel in the London musical *The Little Girl In Red*, at the Gaiety Theatre. Sadly, the producers of the show ran into financial problems, and struggled to pay the cast.

With Elsie's costs mounting and no regular income, she

made the heartbreaking decision to dispense with the services of Violetta and the cook, intending to later sublet the flat to a Captain Hartman.

For more than three months in early 1922, Elsie rented a room at the Richmond Hill Hotel in Richmond, Surrey. Her application to request a licence to underlet the North Gate Mansions flat had meanwhile run into trouble, as Cox & Co. insisted they could only do so with the Maharaja's approval.

The money had now run out, so Elsie turned to pawning the one group of items she had of real value—her jewellery. At first, she chose to sacrifice the pieces she least liked and wore less frequently, but as time went on, the choice became harder and more painful.

* * *

In September 1922, a year after the annuity payments had ceased, Elsie made the momentous decision to secretly return to India and confront Raji. Initially, she took a room in Calcutta's Great Eastern Hotel, then in October, headed to Gaya.

It was very late on a warm afternoon when she arrived at Gaya Junction Railway Station. She had no doubt that she would be denied access to the Tikari Raj Compound if she asked at the gates, so she wandered into the town's market area looking for someone who would make a delivery there.

After questioning in Hindustani, she found a farmer who agreed to hide her under sacks of grain for three rupees.

The ride to the compound seemed to take forever—and she had severely underestimated the weight of the sacks. At the compound gates, she could hear the muffled voices of the Gurkha Guards … and held her breath, hoping that she would not be discovered.

The jerking forward of the cart indicated they were heading inside, and Elsie mentally tracked their progression along the road past the White House, and into the provisions shed.

It was now nearly dark as the farmer started unloading his produce and Elsie slipped off the cart's side after a couple of sacks were removed. She glanced around quickly to see that she had not been spotted, then scurried towards the servants' entrance to the White House, making sure her sari covered her face.

Elsie ducked inside the entrance corridor, and kept going. *Look strong and confident—as if you know what you are doing!* she tried to convince herself.

In the grand foyer, she paused momentarily as she looked up the marble staircase. She knew that the one person she did not want to meet was Wakefield—she just had to reach Raji first. *But what if he is not even here?* As it was now October, she had not really considered the possibility that he might be in the hunting lodge at Bhalwa.

At the top of the stairs she saw Abid Hussain exit Raji's room with an empty drinks tray. *If Abid is here,* she thought, *so is Raji!* She hid in the corner entrance to Wakefield's office, until Abid had passed.

She then moved out and forward, ever so quietly opening Raji's bedroom door and sliding inside. She could just see him sitting on the verandah with his back towards her, sipping a drink.

Elsie crept closer, though very quietly. Finally, a few steps from the verandah, she spoke: "Raji!" she said, in the most positive tone she could muster.

He went all stiff for a few moments then stood up and turned around, looking at her with mouth open, as if he had seen a ghost.

"Raji, darling, we need to talk!" she said as calmly as she could.

"You! How did you get in?" he asked incredulously, then moved quickly to the verandah edge, calling out: "Guards! Guards! To my room! Now!"

Instantly, Elsie realised that the situation was worse than she had anticipated and that she was in very real danger. She raced out of the room and headed down the main staircase, just as Gurkhas were heading up, unaware of their target.

Racing through the servants' entrance corridor, she reached the outside, but instead of heading right to the main gate, she headed forward and left towards a large clump of mango trees. Threading her way through them, she reached a point where she felt she could not be seen from the White House.

Just then, she heard the shuffling sound of feet nearby and heavy breathing … she clung to a tree expecting to be grabbed … but there was whimpering, nuzzling and a lot of excited licking … it was the Great Danes, Larka and Larki—they were very old but still alive. It had been more than six years since they had last seen her, but they had not forgotten.

"Oh, darlings, darlings!" she said, as she cuddled them as their tails wagged excitedly against each other's. "You must be quiet! Shhh … quiet!"

For a short time she lost herself in the fond embrace of her old friends, but the area around the White House and much of the road to the front gate had been illuminated and she could see guards fanning out with flaming torches to search the areas around.

"Look, darlings, I must go!" she said, holding back tears. "This does not mean that Mummy does not love you!"

Elsie looked through the trees and down towards the Red House, home of the manager of Tikari Raj. She could see lights on inside. If she could get there, her old friend Willie Hathaway would be sure to protect her, or at least negotiate a way out.

In the background, she could hear the guards and servants calling, their torches coming closer to the mango trees. If she was going to make a run for the Red House, now was the time.

She raced as fast as she could, picking the path of lighter shadows through the dark vertical trunks, until she broke through into the open ground. It was only a few more seconds to the welcoming light of the Red House front door, so she pushed on, only slowing when she reached its threshold, as the Great Danes followed with their aged, meandering gait.

"Rahná!" she said firmly to the dogs, telling them to stay in Hindustani. They both settled down and watched intently as she moved into the house.

"Willie! Willie! I need your help!" she called, as she raced towards the lounge where she could see a figure. Then she came to a grinding halt—for the man in front of her was none other than J.G. Wakefield. "You!" she uttered.

"Well, well! What a surprise—I suspect it is for you too! Most sadly you see, Willie Hathaway is no longer here. I am now the manager of Tikari Raj!" he said arrogantly.

Elsie was so shocked, she did not know what else to say, but Wakefield had already summed up the situation.

"Come and sit down and we can have a talk," he said, indicating a couch. "Please, take a seat, Elsie. I will get you a cup of tea and we can have a chat."

He moved out of the room to make tea as Elsie sat down. She could hear him talking from the other room, as, unknown to her, he watched the torches dance across the compound grounds as calls from their hunter-carriers echoed through the early evening.

"Elsie, how many sugars would you like with your tea?"

"One, just one thanks," she said, feeling there was something odd, for she had never been able to trust him. She stood up and turned around, then walked back to the lounge entrance. He was standing with his back to her and speaking into the telephone—a telephone connected to the White House.

"And Elsie, do you have milk with your tea, Elsie?"

Before he had even mentioned her name a second time in that sentence, she was off, rushing towards the back door and out into the darkness beyond.

She headed left, away from the direction of the front gates and towards the back of the compound and the pilkhana.

Inevitably, the dogs tried to follow her, so she slowed as she neared the elephant enclosure. "Darlings, you know I love you," she whispered as the big dogs stood up and placed their paws on her.

"She is down here! Elsie is down here!" she could hear Wakefield yell to the hunting pack.

"Rahná! Rahná!" Elsie said to the dogs, who dropped obediently on their haunches. "Mummy does love you, but wants you to stay!" she emphasised again, as she searched in the half-moon light for the bolted gate to the pilkhana.

The pursuers were closer now, their torches having reached the ground below the Red House. Then she saw it—and slid the bolt sideways while taking a deep breath, for anyone entering an elephant's territory was playing a dangerous and potentially deadly game.

The calling and torches were closer now and the mahouts,

who always slept within proximity of their elephants, were stirring.

Elsie glided as sensitively and lightly as she could through the towering black and grey shapes, quietly whispering an elephant lullaby, in the hope it might somehow protect her.

A large bull elephant swayed as she neared, its giant frame stepping back towards her. As she moved to step away from being crushed by its huge back right foot, she trod into a mound of dung—but this was no time for squeamish sentiment.

As the bull elephant's trunk reached out to her, she stretched to the back wall of the pilkhana, for she knew that, somewhere along its way, there was a small, bolted exit gate to the outside world.

She crept along the wall, feeling as she went, for the giant elephant bodies had blocked out the illuminating glow from the moon, hiding not only her gate to freedom, but also her presence.

Then, she felt it: some wire and a bolt in the pilkhana's rear wall. The mahouts were on their feet, moving through the pilkhana, as she quietly pulled the bolt back and eased herself into the outside world. As she closed the gate, she could hear mahouts calling that they had not seen her.

She picked up the bottom of her sari and ran, stepping in and out of gullies and fields, but making sure she stayed off the main road.

More than an hour later, she staggered into Gaya Junction Railway Station and sank down onto a bench, physically and emotionally exhausted.

That night, she took the last train to Calcutta, realising, that in all likelihood she would never set foot in Gaya again.

Chapter 82

The Congress at Gaya

In the spirit of jailed Gandhi, and of Das and of Nehru
They had gathered here in Gaya, in last days of '22
At the 37th Session—Indian National Congress
The delegates debated how to bring about—progress.

Elsie's brief appearance at Gaya could scarcely have occurred at a worse time for Raji. For months, he had been closely involved in the planning for one of the biggest and certainly most important Indian National Congress sessions to date: the 37th Session at the Tikari Raj Compound in Gaya, from 26-31 December 1922.

Tikari Raj was to host a gathering of Hindus and Muslims from across the country—all united in their dream of an independent India—though long divided on exactly how this outcome could be successfully achieved.

There were representatives from right across the political spectrum, from M.N. Roy and the Indian Communists to the most obviously bourgeois, Maharaja of Tikari.

The policy of *Satyagraha*—or non-violent resistance and non-cooperation—long-advocated by Mahatma Gandhi, had become Indian National Congress policy until the events of 4 February 1922.

On that day, thousands of Non-Cooperation protesters had rallied in Chauri Chaura in the United Provinces, in what was initially a protest against the high price of meat. Police arrests over a three-day period had inflamed the situation, to the degree that when thousands marched on the police station, the police opened fire. Three protesters died, enraging the crowd, who burnt down the police station with twenty-three Indian police officers inside.

Gandhi was horrified that his non-violence movement might be blamed and hijacked, so therefore disassociated himself from future Non-Cooperation activities. Despite going on a hunger strike to register his disapproval, he was arrested after the Chauri Chaura incident and sentenced to six years in prison. When the Gaya Congress took place, Gandhi was in a jail in Poona.

Many within the Indian National Congress felt that the Chauri Chaura incident should be viewed as a one-off occurrence and should not derail the drive towards independence from British rule. However, their jailed leader's wishes still had an immense influence on Congress members.

The 37th Session at Gaya, under the chairmanship of barrister Chittaranjan (C.R.) Das, was seen as critical to determining future direction.

In an attempt to gain some advantage before the relative mayhem of the Congress, Das had called on key figures to meet with him in the White House on 25 December.

As they sat around the large dining table, with preparation well underway outside and visible through the windows, Das outlined his vision: one where Congress members should contest the recently British-announced Government Reform Council elections and sabotage their functioning from within.

Gandhi was known to oppose Council participation, so the whole issue was fundamental to deciding future direction.

After speaking, Das asked for contributions on the subject from the cognoscenti present: "Starting with our host first, where do you stand on the matter, Tikari?"

As all heads turned towards Raji, their host only had eyes for something outside.

"Tikari? … Tikari, are you with us?"

"She's there! … I think she is there! … She has returned again to torment me!" Raji said in an anguished voice.

"Who, who is there?" Das asked, as those gathered around the table followed Raji's gaze out the window.

"My wife … my Australian wife … I thought I had seen the last of her!" Raji muttered, though nobody else could see any woman outside. Raji was now sweating profusely and Das asked that he be wiped down with a towel by one of the attendants.

"If this woman is a problem, we have the best lawyers in the country here. You will help Tikari, won't you Polak?" Das said, appealing to Gandhi's old friend and lawyer Henry SL Polak.

"Of course, and I expect my friend Syed Hasan Imam would as well, would you not?" Polak said, deferring to his Muslim colleague, who was reputedly India's finest barrister.

"Absolutely!" Hasan Imam responded.

"There you are, Tikari—that matter is settled—you have the very best legal minds at your service if you wish it!" concluded Das. "So we can now get back to the important issue—Council participation, or not!"

* * *

For just those few days, the Tikari Raj Compound was transformed with a gigantic tent covering more than the parade ground outside the White House. Officially, there were 3,248 delegates registered who had tickets to be inside, but more than 15,000 others sought to watch proceedings.

As no chairs were allowed, to maximise space, the Congress was sitting on the floor or standing only. The Gurkha Guards and police fought manfully to control access, trying to keep many thousands behind temporary fencing, though at times it was a losing battle.

The battle for Congress hearts and minds was fierce too, though its outcome was rarely in doubt. The publication in newspapers of the 'Programme of Social Democracy' from 21 December—a proposal originally outlined in the *Vanguard*, the official organ of the Communist Party of India—panicked delegates with the spectre of Bolshevism at their door, resulting in a flight from radicalism towards the conservative.

In the end, a resolution by Motilal Nehru (the father of the man who was to become India's first prime minister after independence) to support entry to Councils, failed by a two-thirds majority, resulting in the formation of the Swaraj (Independence) Party, led by dissenters of the likes of Nehru and Das. Jawaharal Nehru, however, refused to join his father, staying firmly in the Congress fold under Gandhi's guidance.

At Gaya, in late 1922, pilgrims on the rocky road to Indian independence, took another stumbling step.

Chapter 83

The First Skirmish

If you ever need a lawyer, then make sure he's of the kind
Who can justify his gross expense, and soothe your anxious mind
As for length of court proceedings, well, a piece of string or more
There's no such sell as last round bell, when dealing with the law.

William Jackson wiped the sweat from his brow, then looked up at his potential client seated across from his partners' desk in his solicitor's office in Calcutta.

"It all looks pretty straightforward to me, Your Highness. The only thing I must ask you, is how you are going to pay for the services of my assistants, Mr Mitter and Mr Bose, as well as myself?"

Since November 1922, Elsie had been appearing under her name 'Sita Devi, Maharani of Tikari' at The Conservatoire, 34 Park Street, just to help pay the cost of her accommodation at the Great Eastern Hotel.

On Sunday 26 November she had recited Kipling's poem 'If' and sung a lullaby; on 10 December she had sung a Hindu song and other pieces, while advertising her services as a private tutor; then in her latest performance on Sunday 7 January she had sung 'Un bel di Vedremo' from Puccini's *Madame Butterfly*.

The Statesman newspaper on 9 January 1923 proclaimed:

Her exquisite soprano voice was heard to full advantage in this effort, for which she was heartily applauded ...

Earlier, Elsie had even participated in a contest to select 'The Most Beautiful Woman in India'—and, to her amazement, at the age of thirty-nine, won.

Her image was splashed on the front pages of newspapers across the world. The Utah, USA daily, *The Ogden Standard Examiner*, of 24 December 1922, had her image on the centre of the front page, under the headline:

India's Most Beautiful Woman
Plans Visit to United States

American eyes, next year, may have the opportunity of feasting on the beauty of Her Royal Highness, the Maharanee of Takari, shown above, wife of the Maharaja of Takari. The Maharanee, who was selected recently as India's most beautiful woman, expects to visit this country.

Elsie wrote to Emma and May Maxwell with the news. May was at that time working as the editor of the women's section in the Melbourne newspaper, *The Herald*.

May arranged for the news to be on page one of the Wednesday 24 January 1923 edition of the *The Sun News Pictorial*, under a large copy of the 1914 Kadel & Herbert photograph of Elsie. With the exception of the misspelling of Tikari, and the claim that she was from Randwick (where her parents once temporarily lived), Elsie was delighted:

AUSTRALIAN GIRL TRIUMPHS

H.R.H. the Maharanee of Takani, who was selected recently as the most beautiful woman in India, was Elsie Forrest, a girl from Randwick (N.S.W.). She appeared first in Melbourne as a vaudville artist with the World's Entertainers at the Bijou.

Naturally, none of this was ever going to be enough to pay for a court case.

"If I have to, I will sell more of my jewellery, Mr Jackson," she said determinedly. "How long do you think the case will take?"

"I should not think very long, though I am unfamiliar with the courts in Gaya—in fact I have never been there! I just hope it is not as damn hot as Calcutta!" he added, wiping his brow again.

Given that this was a Calcutta winter and Gaya was invariably hotter, Elsie thought silence was better than a truthful response to the meteorological issue. She wondered too, if she had made

610

the right choice of solicitor, though truly, beggars could not be choosers.

"Mr Jackson, Gaya is what it is, but, for my part, I shall not be returning there, as I fear for my life!"

* * *

On 27 January 1923, Mr Jackson made the following petition to the Court of the Subordinate Judge, in Gaya, on Elsie's behalf:

Sita Devi… Plaintiff
Maharaj Kumar Gopal Saran Narayan Singh… Defendant

1. That she has instituted this suit to enforce two instruments of charge dated respectively the 16th of April 1913 and the 18th of July 1917.

2. That in order to avoid repetition the plaintiff craves reference to the plaint in this suit and she says that the statements made therein are true.

3. That since September 1921, the defendant has ceased to maintain the plaintiff or to pay her the monthly annuities secured by the said instruments. The defendant has further treated her in a cruel manner particulars whereof are not necessary to be stated here. Such cruel behaviour and the stoppage of the annuity have resulted in the plaintiff being reduced to a destitute condition and have driven her to institute this suit. She has been maintaining herself by pledging her jewellery. She has now little means left to maintain herself or to defray the costs of this suit.

4. That the defendant is a rich, powerful and influential Zemindar. During the last three months several offers were made to the plaintiff purporting to come from the defendant requesting the plaintiff to take a lump sum of money and to relinquish her interests under the said instruments. The plaintiff did not accept the said offers. The defendant has now threatened to wear out the plaintiff by protracting this litigation by raising all manner of objections to the plaintiff's claim. The plaintiff has no idea of the nature of such objections.

But the plaintiff apprehends that the defendant, having regard to his present feelings, may even go to the length of making deliberate default in the payment of Government revenue and thereby endanger the property charged and defeat the very object of the suit.

5. That even if the defendant does not make a deliberate default in the payment of the Government revenue the plaintiff apprehends that, inasmuch as the defendant is heavily involved in debts and is always in need of money, the payment of Government revenue may be neglected from sheer want of money.

6. That the arrears of annuity now due and owing to the plaintiff by virtue of the said instruments amount to Rs. 51,000 for the period September 1921 to January 1923. She is further entitled to get Rs. 3,000 a month as will appear on reference to the said instruments.

7. That the plaintiff states that she is urgently in need of money and unless some provision is made in that behalf it will be impossible for her to maintain herself or to prosecute this suit and her rights will be absolutely defeated.

8. That the defendant is in possession of the properties which are charged with the payment of the annuity to the plaintiff, and they are situate within jurisdiction of this court.

9. That the plaintiff has been reduced to a helpless condition and she submits that it is just and reasonable that a Receiver should be appointed to take charge of the said properties.

The plaintiff therefore prays:-

(1) That a Receiver may be appointed of the said properties which are fully described in the said instrument of the 16th of April, 1913 annexed to the plaint.

(2) That the said Receiver may be directed (a) to pay to the plaintiff Rs. 3,000 or such other sum per month as to this court may seem proper pending the final

determination of this suit and (b) to sell a sufficient portion of the said properties to pay to her the said arrears.

Or in the alternative an interim order may be made providing for the plaintiff's maintenance and her costs of this suit.

(3)   For the order of this application.

And for such further or other order in the premises as to this court may seem meet.

And for this act of kindness your petitioner, as in duty bound, shall ever pray.

"She is not getting a damn rupee!" Raji yelled, as he slammed a copy of the suit onto Sayed Hasan Imam's desk.

"Raji … Raji, please calm down!" Hasan urged. "There are ways we can ensure that this is just the first skirmish in what will be a long, drawn out war. But from what I see, she will not last that long because she does not have the assets."

"We must break her, Hasan! The longer it is dragged out the less likely she can continue and the sooner I will be rid of her!"

"Raji, there is something else I must tell you. I have already taken the liberty of speaking to Sir Ashutosh Chaudhuri. He has agreed to convene a meeting between you and Elsie at his home on 4 March, with a view to reaching a mutually agreeable settlement."

"What? Why would I agree to something like that?"

"Raji, please, listen to me! This is not about compromise. It is about delaying proceedings, assessing her legal team—and I must say I don't think there is much to them—and finding her weaknesses. We do not compromise at all!"

Raji paced up and down and thought for a while. "Actually, I have to agree with you. That is a good move! That is why I hired the best barrister in India! However, we must not underestimate Elsie. I will continue to have her under surveillance and have ensured that any mail she posts from the Great Eastern will first be opened and transcribed by hotel staff."

On the evening of Friday 4 March 1923, Elsie, Raji and their legal teams descended on Sir Ashutosh Chaudhuri's 6 Sunny Park home.

Elsie believed Chaudhuri—a judge of the Calcutta High Court—was probably a good choice as a mediator. She knew him as a great friend of her favourite Indian poet, Rabindranath Tagore, whose work *The Gardener* she had gifted on more than one occasion.

Chaudhuri's wife, Prativa Devi, was also known to Elsie through the latter's music and singing, so that evening's hosts promised to be more welcoming than her husband.

As things transpired, Chaudhuri was unable to broker any agreed settlement, with both parties unwilling to modify their 'all or nothing' positions.

Driving away in his Rolls-Royce, Raji made it plain to Hasan how things would now proceed. "We will draw the suit out Hasan, and break her!"

However, on 29 March, the Subordinate Judge of Gaya ordered that Raji pay Elsie 1,250 rupees per month until disposal of the suit. Raji appealed to the Patna High Court and the monthly payment proposal was set aside.

Raji signalled the broadening and extending of the case by hiring Gandhi's friend, Henry SL Polak, who had a legal practice in London, to manage the contributions of British-based witnesses prepared to support his position and undermine Elsie's. The following letter of 2 October 1923 was produced in court:

My dear Hasan,

I hope that you and Mrs Imam reached home safely, and that you had a pleasant voyage.

The Maharaj of Tikari has commissioned me to do certain professional work for him in the Sita Devi suit that you are conducting on his behalf. He has placed the papers in my hands. I am opening up investigations.

With best wishes to you all,
Yours affectionately,
[Signed] HSL Polak

Raji then sought a postponement from January to May 1924 as Hasan Imam had other legal matters to deal with. This was refused, and Hasan's barrister brother, Sir Ali Imam, joined Raji's elite team.

On 4 January 1924, Raji then sought to force Elsie to pay 50,000 rupees as security to cover his estimated costs, knowing that Elsie would find such a payment virtually impossible to make. However, on 29 January the judge refused it stating:

> ... the defendant appears to have been taking time more than what is reasonable under the circumstances of the case ...

The sourcing and inclusion of British witness statements extended the case further, forcing Elsie to sell her two large emerald and diamond armbands, though she held on to the banded tiara for now.

To make matters worse, her counsel, William Jackson, found the Gaya heat unbearable and was unable to continue, leaving the work in the case to Mitter and Bose.

Raji's expert legal team counterattacked on multiple fronts, trying to undermine her claim to and suitability for the annuities. These included:

1. Claiming that Elsie's 1906 divorce from Stillwell should have been rendered invalid, as he was not domiciled in New South Wales, so the subsequent annuities were obtained under false pretences. The suit had only been instituted to blackmail Raji.

2. Utilising expert testimony from prominent religious authorities to claim the Arya Samaj conversion was inappropriate and did not make her a proper Hindu wife.

3. Producing numerous witness testimonies and intercepted private mail to third parties, designed to cast doubt on Elsie's faithfulness and allow Raji to claim infidelity and misconduct.

4. Producing copies of newspaper advertisements, theatre programs and drama reviews to show that Elsie had utilised her title as Maharani of Tikari and performed in public as a singer, dancer, actress and comedienne—and thus disgraced Raji.

5. That Elsie could expect no relief unless she returned jewellery entrusted to her, for her use while a faithful wife.

Elsie's lawyers countered that even in an Indenture of Trust executed by Raji on 26 September 1917, he described Elsie as his wife, when identifying her as one of twelve trustees to oversee the creation and management of schools for Indian girls, a 'Tikari' trusteeship grouping that included Hasan and Sir Ali Imam.

From the lodgement of Elsie's petition on 27 January 1923—when it was thought that this was to be a relatively straightforward matter—there were 103 separate days of court-documented deliberation, until the Gaya court made its decision on Elsie's petition, on 26 August 1924.

Judge Narendra N. Chakravarty of the Court of the Subordinate Judge of Gaya decreed that Elsie's suit was dismissed with costs yet to be determined.

On 10 September 1924, the Gaya judge ordered Elsie to pay 4,879 rupees in court costs to Raji.

Raji and his team were jubilant. They had cornered and shot the beautiful tiger—however, she was not dead yet ...

Chapter 84

The Chalk and Cheese Alliance

In my mirror he would invert—he would be all upside down
He is nothing like me, really—not in presence or renown
Yet there is a strange concordance in the way that we have grown
For this chalk and cheese alliance has a future of its own.

It was July 1923, and Elsie was preoccupied with the then unresolved Gaya court case. She did not recognise the man who approached her in the dining room of the Tollygunge Club.

"Well, I'll be buggered!" he said, with a distinctly Australian accent. "It is Elsie, isn't it?"

"Yes, it is me," she said hesitantly.

"I have been following you in the papers over the years—you have made quite a splash!"

"Well, I trust I have only wet myself then, sir, not drenched others with my notoriety!" she responded, though in doing so he sensed a degree of reserve that indicated he still had not been recognised.

"You don't remember who the hell I am, do you, Elsie—although I should call you Your Highness nowadays!" he said, as he sat down at her table and offered his hand. "Ernest Ivan Jones. We met at that bloody Paperchase event in … when was it? … About 1905 or so, I think it was … Jeez! That's nearly twenty years ago!"

Elsie nodded and smiled as she remembered how he had helped her after she had come off her horse. "Ah yes, I seem to recall you liked the name Ernest!" she said, now cheered by the encounter.

"Don't you start calling me that! Ivan it is!"

"So, 'Ivan the Terrible', how has life been treating you since?"

Ivan paused to think for a few moments. "I reckon I had one son when we last met, but I had a second since … oh, and a divorce!"

"Oh, you have nearly had a full house—congratulations! By comparison my divorce and a remarriage scarcely rates!"

"So, do you come here often?"

"Curried prawns at the Tolly on a Sunday is now the only indulgence I allow myself. I have had to sell much of my jewellery to fund the court case and shall be moving out of the Great Eastern soon, I'd say. I am paying the price for fighting for what I believe to be right, but I am going to fight on!"

Ivan reached into his pocket and picked out a business card, then scribbled an address upon it. "If you ever get in a pickle, come and see me!"

Elsie studied the address and then looked around her, before leaning forward and whispering: "Do you have a place in your house where I can hide something?"

"Well, yes, I suppose so. But what is it and why are you whispering?"

"I don't feel my jewellery is safe. I am being followed, those I meet with are being identified and photographed and along with my private letters, that sort of information is being produced in court!"

"Really! The Maharaja is doing that? Oh, what a bastard!" he exclaimed, then leaning forward too, he said slowly and very certainly: "You can rely on me, sweetheart!" before adding with a smile: "I just hope they don't capture me in profile!"

As he departed, he left behind a warm glow that had been missing for a very long time. Ivan was as tough as teak and as rough as red gum, but she felt that with him, what you saw is what you got—and she liked that. In many other respects they were chalk and cheese, for he would never shine at a society ball, but right now, that was not the partner that she needed.

* * *

Over the next year, as the protracted court case progressed in Gaya, Elsie left the Great Eastern Hotel and took lodgings in the sublet rooms rented by Mrs Lillion Williams in Harrington Mansions for a month from 19 August 1923, before moving on to 20 Park Street, Calcutta.

Mrs Williams later gave evidence to the Gaya Court in May 1924 that letters to 'Ivan' had been found in her room and a young Muslim man who Elsie had called "darling" had made an appearance at her door. Raji's lawyers produced a posed photograph of a Muslim man, and Mrs Williams said it was identical to the man she saw.

Unhappy with the security of her accommodation and desperate to ensure the safety of her jewels, Elsie handed them to Ivan for storage, though she checked on them each time she visited.

She spent many late afternoons at her lawyers' Calcutta office, going through the latest court transcripts available from Gaya and often taking long calls from Mitter and Bose during which she would give them direction. Despite the difficulty in maintaining the case from a distance, she felt that returning to Gaya was never an option.

The decree by the Gaya Court came as a massive but not totally unexpected blow. Many, with equally few assets and as much hope, may well have thrown in the towel at that point, but Elsie was not having any of it.

She ordered a full transcript of the Gaya proceedings, then, over a series of weeks went through each part of it with Mitter and Bose, underlining points that should be contested and ensuring they noted key issues.

Ivan dropped in occasionally when his horse import and other businesses allowed, and he marvelled at her tenacity and intellectual capacity.

To pay for not just the Gaya court charges but also the ongoing ones for her lawyers, Elsie took the heart-wrenching decision to pawn the banded tiara. The emerald, diamond and pearl masterpiece was the single most valuable piece of jewellery she had left. It was also the most obvious manifestation of her status as an Indian queen.

Determined to demonstrate her independence, she refused to tell Ivan until the sale was complete, smuggling it out of his house and into the jewellers, Cooke & Kelvey, as she felt Raji's favourite jeweller, Rai Budree Das Bahadoor & Sons, were most likely to alert her husband.

Elsie reasoned that an appeal to the High Court in Patna, heard away from the Maharaja's immediate power base of Gaya, stood some chance of success.

Together with her lawyers, they drafted twenty-seven points, including that:

- The Gaya Court had misconceived the scope of the suit.

- It was wrong to dismiss the suit, whereas it should have been decreed with costs.

- Many issues the court had allowed the defendant to raise were irrelevant and many witness statements were mere hearsay.

- The court had been wrong in its view of the Australian Law of Divorce and wrong in concluding that the divorce was obtained by fraud.

- The court was wrong to conclude that there was no legal marriage between the plaintiff and defendant and should have held that the issue in regard to validity or otherwise of the marriage was wholly irrelevant to the enforceability of the two documents.

- The court was wrong in finding that at the time of the suit the plaintiff was leading an immoral life and by reason thereof was disentitled to enforce the said documents.

- That the learned Subordinate Judge's determination that the plaintiff was not entitled in any event to succeed unless she returned the family jewels was erroneous and irrelevant and his finding upon the existence or value of the jewels or their nature was erroneous and not based on legal evidence.

- The court had misinterpreted the texts of Hindu law, and failed to consider that various forms of marriage were recognised.

- That the finding that the plaintiff "relapsed to her former vocation and was leading an immoral life" was unsustainable on the face of the record and that the said finding could not be supported inasmuch as the witnesses were all interested in discrediting the fair name of the plaintiff.

With the submission of the appeal on 24 November 1924 to the High Court of Judicature in Patna, Elsie was happy to be free of the immediate concern of legal matters. From what she could discern, any appeal could take years, and she had day-to-day living issues to attend to.

It was a surprise, one evening, when Ivan invited her to dinner at the Bengal Club. All he had asked of her was that she 'dress up'—something she thought she did regularly in any case—and that she have an open mind.

He seemed quite nervous, though first chose to talk about someone irritatingly familiar. "I heard from one of my horse contacts today that your great friend at Tikari, Mr Wakefield, has been raving about the Rolls-Royce delivered to the Red House for his personal use a few weeks ago. He claims it is the best of the six Tikari Raj has had."

This was not a subject upon which Elsie wished to dwell before a special meal, so she responded sarcastically: "Well, I am thrilled that the non-payment of my annuity has contributed to his happiness!"

Soon after soup had been dispatched, and Ivan had fiddled for a few moments with the remaining cutlery, he mentioned that he had a proposal he hoped she would accept. "I have a ring here and I want to place it on your finger … Elsie, I have watched and admired you greatly over the last few months … and have grown to love you. I want you to be my wife and for us to be married. Then, we can leave this place and return to Australia."

Elsie closed her eyes for a few moments and tried to think quickly. She well knew what she was supposed to say, but what she wanted to say was a little different. It had nothing to do with the fact that he was eight years older, but everything to do with her situation. She just had to respond in a way that would minimise his hurt.

She rose from her chair, moved behind him and put her arms around him, kissing him softly on the cheek. Then she held his strong hand—the one holding the ring—and continued to do so while she sat down. She looked him straight in the eye and smiled reassuringly.

"Ivan, it would be a very great honour for me to be Mrs Jones. As you know, I have fought for a long time to be recognised as the Maharani of Tikari and I wish to forever be remembered as such, and do not want to risk even morally forfeiting my right to the perpetual annuity by remarrying! However, I would be very proud to live with you for the rest of my life, pretending to be Mrs Jones!"

She caressed his hand and watched his face carefully as it initially reddened in reaction to her statement. He was still quiet and thinking for some time, so Elsie said:

> Ah, make the most of what we yet may spend,
> Before we too into the Dust descend ;
>   Dust into Dust, and under Dust to lie,
> Sans Wine, sans Song, sans Singer, and—sans End !

"What the hell was that?" he asked, as Elsie was pretty sure he would.

"The *Rubáiyát of Omar Khayyám*, Quatrain 24, darling! … Oh, I should have added one more qualifier to my counteroffer: I am to fund the appeal through the sale of my jewellery!"

"No!" he said firmly, placing his left clenched fist on the table—and Elsie already knew that he was not a man to be challenged. "As I will take you on in the terms you earlier described, I insist on helping you financially as the appeal progresses!"

Just then, the main course was brought to their table, though Elsie had reservations about being able to devour it. "Oh dear, I have already made a meal of things!" she quipped with a wink.

In 1926, Elsie and Ivan departed India to settle permanently in Melbourne, while the appeal process in the High Court at Patna drifted on.

Chapter 85

The Long Way Round to Home

In my journeys very often, I have dillied and have dallied
Taken low way not the highway, oh far more than I have tallied
May be madness in my movement, on the roads I choose to roam
Yet there's something sentimental, 'bout the long way round to home.

As the black-hulled and twin-funnelled liner RMS *Maloja* sliced its way from Colombo, through the equator and south across the Indian Ocean, Ivan felt it necessary to make a minor apology. "It is a bit of a long way round to home, Elsie, but I feel it is the best way. You have to damn well meet my boys at some stage, in any case!"

The plan was to leave the ship briefly when it docked in Fremantle so that they could meet up with Ivan's sons Owen, twenty-three and Jack, twenty-one. Then, it would be on to Adelaide. From there, they would travel inland to a place Ivan called Mundrabilla Station, where he had significant business interests. After that, it would be across to Melbourne and their new house and home together.

Treading on Australian soil for the first time in twelve years should have made Elsie feel more elated than she did. *Will I find Australia too parochial, after London, or even Calcutta?*

As she and Ivan walked down Fremantle's South Terrace on Monday 10 May 1926, she spied her first bit of classic Australiana: the iconic two-storey pub, the Sail & Anchor, on the terrace's corner with Henderson Street.

"She's a bloody beauty, isn't she, Elsie?" Ivan exclaimed, and Elsie had to agree. "The boys should be waiting for us inside!"

With intricate ironwork railings fringing its large first-floor balcony, Elsie was relieved to see that it looked more than just the standard Aussie pub.

"Across Henderson Street, are the Fremantle Markets," Ivan added, as they were about to step inside. "Many of the stall holders and patrons drop over for lunch and a beer."

As they moved inside, Ivan soon spotted two young men sitting at a square table with four chairs.

"How the bloody hell are ya, boys?" Ivan yelled, as he reached out a big and gnarled hand to each son.

Elsie had been wondering how he would greet his sons. She had thought a kiss was most unlikely, though felt that a hug would surely have been warranted. But it was not to be, for this was Australia, and it was just not the way tough men behaved.

"I'm dyin' for a fish 'n' chips! You boys want one too?" Ivan asked. Their murmurs and nods indicated approval and Ivan headed off to the bar to make the order, forgetting to introduce Elsie.

"You must be Owen and Jack then! I am Elsie, Ivan's companion," she volunteered, offering her hand with a smile. She had very deliberately called John, 'Jack', as Ivan had said that he much preferred the latter. The Jones boys seemed pleasant enough, though she had to remind herself that, as the replacement figure for their birth mother, she was only going to be tolerated at best.

When Ivan returned, he realised his mistake. "Jesus! That was bloody rude of me! I suppose you've met my good friend Elsie by now? ... Drinks! What would you like—a pint of beer each, boys?"

Elsie was delighted that she could settle for an orange juice rather than beer with her fish and chips, as Rooh Afza would never, ever have been heard of, for this was Australia, after all.

As they downed their drinks while waiting for the fish and chips, Ivan insisted that Elsie try the beer, a Swan Stout. "Come on, El, it tastes just like chocolate!" Elsie took a sip, but left it at that.

"Four snappers with chips coming, sir!" the waitress said, as she started placing the battered fish and chips on the table. "Fresh from the sea this morning, madam!" she added, as she eased one down in front of Elsie.

After a delicious lunch, they said farewell, unsure how soon they would meet again. As the boys headed off, back to their jobs on the land, Ivan was predictably unsympathetic. Wrapping his boys in cotton wool was just not his way.

"I might see them when I am next in Perth on business, or I might not. I had to do my apprenticeship the hard way—and that is the best way for them. They can start spoiling themselves when they have bloody earnt it!"

Elsie asked what Ivan thought of their reaction to her. She had tried to be pleasant without being in any way 'gushing'.

"They are never going to give you a bloody star, because you are not Marie, their mother. This is my life and my choice—and that is all that bloody matters!"

Mundrabilla Station was already on Ivan's mind. Occupying a vast and timeless landscape just across the South Australian border in Western Australia, and sitting on the Nullarbor Plain, it said something about the size of the western state, that it was more easily approached from Adelaide than Perth.

Seeing Mundrabilla for the first time was to appreciate instantly its isolation. A farmhouse and a series of stables and sheds set in a sea of saltbush, occasional grasslands, and otherwise emptiness. *How can anything possibly survive out here?* Elsie wondered.

"It is more than a million acres!" Ivan exclaimed. "It's primarily a sheep station, but the sheep tend to congregate closer to the shearing sheds and waterhole near Emu Well. Looks dead, pretty barren, bloody hopeless, doesn't it!" he teased, with a grin on his face. "Most businessmen would run a mile! But they don't know this place. They don't know a good investment when they see one!"

They moved in through the homestead's open and creaking door—there were no locks here. Having left most of their luggage in Adelaide, choice was sparse when it came to changing into something more practical—which is what Ivan insisted Elsie do, as he tossed her a pair of trousers and a shirt from a cupboard. "Welcome to the outback, El!" he grinned, obviously taking great pleasure in bringing her 'down market'.

Minutes later, they were both in the saddle, heading out to look at 'the paddocks'. Ivan drew his horse next to Elsie's and traced the line of a fence with his index finger as it disappeared into the distance. "That one is the inner paddock," he said. "You may not be able to see them yet, but there are hundreds of Walers—horses born and bred in New South Wales—that we bring over here each July, within the inner paddock."

Ivan was right—Elsie could not see any yet, and she wondered why anybody would bring Walers over here to this arid landscape. Ivan had read her mind.

"I am in the import-export business. Walers are the best horses for the British Raj. We keep some here for breeding, but most only stay here for nine months before they are shipped off to India. A summer in these conditions toughens them up for anything the subcontinent might toss in their direction."

"But where is the water?" Elsie queried, for she knew that nothing could survive out here without it.

"You would be surprised. There are a number of artesian bores that tap into a vast reservoir of water under the ground. There are small dams and watering holes spread across this landscape."

As he spoke, he spotted a group of Walers away to their right. "Come on!" he yelled, as he pulled his reins to the right and dug his heels into his horse, sending it off after the group.

Elsie hesitated, for she knew she could not catch him, and wanted to take in the sight of him being swallowed up momentarily in the landscape he clearly loved.

By the time she reached Ivan, he had corralled a group of Walers, just by moving in ever decreasing circles, whistling and talking to them. He was using a language of love and affection that he would never waste on a human being.

"Elsie, draw your horse in slowly, but just keep it facing away from the group, as if you are just going to circle!" he ordered. "That's it! Well done! ... Now come in closer, tighten that circle!"

Soon Elsie was reaching out and patting the Walers, though Ivan warned her to do it slowly and without sudden movement. She knew they were not wild horses, but unsaddled as they were, she could always pretend.

"Okay, enough of that!" Ivan ordered. "We have to head off and find Bluey and the black boys."

"Bluey and the Black Boys!" Elsie parrotted. "Sounds like a jazz band!"

"Ha ha! You and your music! Come on, follow me to the outer paddock!" With that he wheeled his horse away from the Walers and headed off, with Elsie in pursuit. They soon reached a gateway in the fencing. Ivan carefully unwrapped the chain, opened the gate and ushered her through, while still on horseback. He then closed the gate and threaded the chain back, linking the gate and the fence once more. "We don't want to lose any Walers!"

A short ride and a climb brought them to an area called The Cliffs. They rode along a raised plateau for quite some time before Ivan stopped. "There they are!" he cried, as he pointed to a cloud of dust that seemed to be spinning like a reverse catherine-wheel in the valley below.

"Do we ride down there?" asked Elsie, for she wondered just how easy it was to work her way down.

"No! We stay right here! If they do their job right they will work the mob of wild horses up towards The Cliffs and then lasso one of them when they trap them beneath a ridge."

Fifteen minutes later, a young but captive wild stallion emerged from The Cliffs' track, surrounded closely by four riders.

"Ivan! Good to see ya, mate!" the lead one called. He had to be Bluey, Elsie reasoned, as the other three were young blacks—Aborigines.

"Bluey, I would like you to meet my friend, Elsie!"

As he manoeuvred his horse to greet her, Elsie realised how he got his name—those crystal-blue eyes. "Not many women get out this way, so you are welcome!"

The black boys seemed too shy to introduce themselves, so Elsie made a point of moving around to shake each by the hand. The most she could get out of them was a toothy grin, a nod and "Miss Elsie!"

After the young stallion was shut in a holding pen, where it would later be 'broken in', a fire was started in a pit in front of the homestead.

As the sun began to slide towards the horizon, kangaroos gathered to nibble on the clumps of grass nearby. They would look up and around, periodically, just to check they were safe, before scratching themselves.

"Look!" said one of the Aboriginal boys to Elsie. "See he play with her tail."

Elsie watched as a male kangaroo clawed at a female's tail, causing her to hop a few steps away.

"What does that mean?" Elsie asked innocently.

"It mean he interested!" the young man replied, laughing.

"You never did that to me, Ivan!" Elsie protested, as the fire took hold and the cooking of the dinner of scrambled eggs, followed by damper sprinkled with cut apple, got under way.

As the light waned, Ivan told Elsie to have a shower. "The water in the tank has been warmed by the sun, but it will be cold in the morning! It is on the other side of the homestead. Any of you bastards go around the back while Elsie is having a shower and I'll beat the bloody crap out of you and string you up before I leave!" he warned.

Just after Elsie left, one of the black boys pretended to follow, before quickly rushing back, as the others laughed.

As she stood naked before the last rays of a setting sun, rejoicing in the refreshing water that washed away the dust of the desert, Elsie could understand how some people, including no doubt Ivan, preferred the hard simplicity of this life.

* * *

Melbourne had never been a permanent home in the past for Elsie, though at least she was generally familiar with the grid pattern of its central business area.

Its suburbs were quite a different matter. Ivan had bought land in Hawthorn some years before, and had a three-bedroom home built on the second block down from the corner with Hawthorn Glen.

"Welcome to *De Montfort* and 30 Fordholm Road!" he said proudly. "Welcome to our new home!"

Chapter 86

Myrtle the Pearl

Not all of life's small pebbles, will end up like a jewel
And sparkle on a special stage, or be the dux at school
They'll never grab a title, be a duchess or an earl
Their worth's in common decency, like Myrtle, the pearl.

Elsie did not take long to settle in to Fordholm Road. She particularly loved the two sets of full-length French windows at the front that let in the morning sun and could be opened up on a day of light or no breeze.

Then, there was the delightful overhead Art Nouveau fretwork between the front foyer and the hallway. True, No. 30 was absolutely nothing like the White House or even the North Gate Mansions flat, but it had a very cosy feel.

Her first call, once the telephone had been installed, was to Emma, who had written recently to Elsie in Calcutta to inform her that they had moved to 63 Collingwood Street in Manly, on Sydney's northern beaches. They were living there while they had a bigger and better house built on the block next door, at No. 65.

Elsie had not seen her dear friend Emma since her marriage, nearly thirteen years before, so when Ivan very kindly gave his approval to Emma and little Sita joining their household in Hawthorn for three months from the New Year, Elsie could not wait to call Emma and make the invitation. After some discussion in the Binstead household, the go-ahead was given as long as Sita could attend school in the Hawthorn area.

As Joe was often away for business—and Ivan occasionally— the arrangement seemed to suit both parties. Emma and Sita arrived at Fordholm Road in late January 1927.

Elsie had stood at the French windows for some time, waiting for the taxi. When it pulled up outside, she raced through the front foyer, stepped only momentarily on the Federation tiles under their covered front entry, then hurdled the four steps before reaching the front gate in record time. There before her, standing on the nature strip was her very best friend in the

629

world … and a golden-haired look-a-like.

"Oh, Emma!" she gushed, as the two women embraced and held each other tightly. Five-year-old Sita looked up forlornly, wondering if she had been forgotten.

It was not long before it was Sita's turn. "Oh, aren't you gorgeous, sweetheart!" Elsie said, squatting down and giving her namesake a big squeeze and a kiss. "You are just like your mummy!"

But something was worrying Sita so much that despite the joyous reception, she was frowning. "You're not wearing your crown!" Sita said disapprovingly. She had heard so much about how 'Auntie Elsie' was Sita Devi, the Maharani of Tikari and the first Australian princess, that she thought a crown was the very least she could expect.

"Well, maybe I will have to put one on, just for you!" Elsie replied, before recalling that she had sold her banded tiara.

Prior to moving inside, Elsie had a stern warning for Sita. "Uncle Ivan will get very cross if you are not a good girl, so make sure you don't upset him!" It was a message little Sita took very much to heart, so much so that despite being a very well behaved and polite little girl, she never felt too relaxed in Ivan's presence.

Within a week, Sita had been enrolled in The Hawthorn School in Manningtree Road, Hawthorn, just three blocks up from Fordholm's intersection with Riversdale Road. The weekday walk up to and later back from school, hand-in-hand and either side of Sita, became a joyous highlight for Elsie. She could not admit it out loud, but at times like these she was envious of Emma, and pined for the child she could never have.

With Sita settled into school, Elsie and Emma had time to see the Melbourne city area together. Shortly after their return to Australia, Ivan had bought a Ford Model T made in the recently opened Ford factory in Geelong. Elsie was quick to demonstrate her prowess behind the wheel, though adjusting to the special rules relating to driving in and around Melbourne's tram network was initially both trial and error.

It was that tram network they utilised whenever Ivan used the car, for the tram into the city ran from near the intersection of Fordholm and Riversdale Roads.

On one such morning when they opted for the convenience of the tram, Elsie carried her special bag in which she secreted her jewellery, with her. It was something that she had been most careful to hide for years now, even if in Melbourne she felt it was safer.

It had been some time since her strings of pearls had been polished, a task that had previously been done by her servants. This time, she was seeking professional advice, so after a search of the telephone book, she discovered WM Drummond & Co., Jewellers, who advertised that they made the Melbourne Cup trophy for each year's big race.

During a telephone call, she organised a meeting with the company's owner, Andrew Drummond. Arriving at 344-46 Collins Street, Elsie was ushered into a back office, while Emma waited in the showroom. Mr Drummond, a middle-aged man with an English accent, surveyed the contents of the bag with significant surprise.

After a closer examination of the pearl pieces, he announced that they desperately needed polishing. He rose and went to the door. "Miss McLeod, could you please come into the office!"

Elsie looked up to see a small and well-built woman of about thirty with light brown hair.

"Miss McLeod, this is the Maharani of ... I'm sorry, where did you say it was?"

"Tikari, India, Mr Drummond."

"Ah yes, of course, Tikari. You are to address her as 'Your Highness'."

Myrtle was awestruck, because she had never previously met anyone even remotely connected with royalty. She made a bumbling attempt at a mix of a bow and curtsey, forcing Elsie to somehow contain a laugh. Instead, Elsie held out her hand.

"Your ... Highness!" Myrtle said, thinking that Elsie was also the most beautiful and stylish woman she had ever seen.

"Myrtle, the Maharani has a number of pearl pieces she needs to have polished. Can you have them ready for her on Friday, please!"

From first glance, Myrtle was transfixed by the pearls, some of which were straight strings of chokers, while others were mixed with diamonds and emeralds. "Yes ... Friday ... yes,

Mr Drummond! … Thank you, Your Highness, it will be an honour!"

"Will the pearls be safe here until then, Mr Drummond?" Elsie queried, for she was most reticent to have them away from her control.

"They will be most safe here, Your Highness," Mr Drummond assured her. "We have not had a robbery here since 1918 — and that was by a store employee. If only Arthur Seymour had seen more and taken less!" he joked. Then seriously: "No, let me assure you that Miss McLeod is ultra-reliable!"

And so it proved, for when Elsie returned on the Friday, she saw her pearls appeared to have taken on a new and glittering lustre. She was delighted—and Miss McLeod was too—delighted and honoured. That is when an idea occurred to Elsie. It was not just the younger woman's dedication to task, but also her respect, even adoration, that appealed.

After a word with Mr Drummond, it was agreed that Myrtle would make house calls to 30 Fordholm Road at 2 pm each first Thursday of the month. She would polish the pearls and check and maintain the other jewellery—and be regaled and fascinated by Elsie's tales of lands and cultures far beyond her experience. Neither Elsie nor Myrtle realised it at the time, but it was to be the beginning of a life-long friendship.

Ivan's practical approach to child rearing included the making of things, and it was not long before he had volunteered to make a cubbyhouse for little Sita. Much sawing, hammering and the occasional (but regretted swearing later, Sita had a little home of her own in a tree in their backyard. She was still very wary of him, but now knew he really did have a softer side.

When the time came for the Binsteads to return to Sydney, everyone was sad. Elsie had managed to have more time with Emma than they had shared since their early teenage years and Sita had settled in at The Hawthorn School.

"You must come up to Collingwood Street at some stage, El!" Emma insisted. "I am sure that Joe will be happy to see you too!"

*　*　*

In early 1928, Ivan announced that he had to go to India for a few months for business reasons, but that he also wanted to make contact with the legal team handling the appeal to the High Court in Patna.

Losing Ivan for that time was difficult for Elsie, for they had grown close despite their very different backgrounds and natures.

As compensation, Elsie reached out to Myrtle. She was delighted when Myrtle agreed to move into 30 Fordholm Road and be her companion while Ivan was away.

A cable from Ivan in April 1928 brought unexpected but fantastic news:

> Appeal won in Patna High Court.
> More detail later—we did it!

The court decreed that Raji had to pay Elsie 15,000 rupees a year in perpetuity, as well as monies unpaid since September 1921, plus interest.

Raji and his high-powered legal team were shocked by this 16 April 1928 decree by the judges in the High Court of Judicature in Patna. They immediately decided to apply for leave to appeal to His Majesty in Council, in London. This was the Privy Council, the highest court in the British-administered world. On 20 July 1928, they listed twenty-five grounds for appeal.

Chapter 87

Shelter from the Storm

I've heard it once, I've heard it thrice, I'm sick of being told
By each man with a treasure map, that guarantees him gold
I've heard your 'reasoned argument' on how this boom's the norm
You'll join a lengthy queue my friend – seek shelter from the storm.

"Lunatics! Bloody lunatics!" Ivan yelled, as he slammed down the newspaper on the coffee table. He paced up and down the lounge room getting more and more agitated.

"What is wrong, darling?" Elsie called from the kitchen.

"I go to the hairdresser and Lou tells me his best stock tips … I go to the grocer and Angelos tells me he made two months' pay in a week on a particular stock and is borrowing money to buy more … I go to the bootmaker and Dominic whispers his 'secret tip' to me, no doubt for a stock he has already bought. Every idiot is suddenly an expert and a potential millionaire from the share market!"

"Well, if they are making money darling, you can understand their enthusiasm."

"That is not the point! They are just gambling, and for now they are winning. But it cannot last! I have horses, I have land and I have houses. I can feel and touch what I own. All they have is a slip of paper that says they bought stock in a particular company on a particular day at a particular value—and I bet they have no idea what that company does, apart from the fact that it has risen in value recently!"

"The papers seem to be supportive of the rise in the share market too, darling."

"Of course the fucking papers …" Ivan began.

"Darling, I understand you are upset, but please don't swear like that!"

Ivan grabbed his personal telephone directory and flicked to the letter 'J'—though in truth he really should have known the work number of his friend and solicitor, Edgar Percival Johnson, principal of EP Johnson & Davies Solicitors. He made an appointment for 3 pm that afternoon.

He was welcomed in to Edgar's office at 430 Little Collins

Street and asked to sit in a familiar seat.

"So, what is the latest with the damn Indians and their appeal to London?" Edgar asked.

"I was hoping you might tell me—but really, I am not here about that," Ivan insisted.

"You are not? Well, how can I help then?"

"Perhaps I might be seen to be seeking shelter from the storm, in these uncertain times …"

"Uncertain times?" Edgar queried, leaning forward and whispering: "Do you know that at the rate my share portfolio is rising in value, I will be able to retire early!"

"Oh, Jesus! Not you too! And I thought you were an intelligent and rational man! This whole thing is going to end badly. My advice to you is to sell now while you're ahead!"

"Sell them? But I just bought more yesterday!"

"Edgar, this is all going to go very badly wrong very soon, and you are going to want to be one of the first out, otherwise you will be dying in your solicitor's chair! Anyhow, mate, I have more important things to talk about than your obstinate stupidity. I want to set up a will and have you as my executor."

After a couple of hours of discussion and note-taking, Edgar asked his secretary to draft up a will for Ivan. "Come back on Thursday 24th and you can check and sign the will."

On Thursday 24 October 1929, Ivan walked back into his solicitor's office.

"You sold those bloody shares yet?" was the first thing he asked Edgar, for the share market had wobbled ominously for the last few days.

"Yes. I did listen to your advice."

"Well, thank Christ for that! If you think the tremors of the last few days have been disconcerting, you just wait and see what is around the corner, mate! Now, let me review that will and hopefully I'll sign it!"

On that day, Black Thursday in New York, the Dow Jones lost eleven per cent on opening. On Black Monday, 28 October, it lost thirteen per cent and the following day twelve per cent, in a period forever remembered as the Wall Street Crash. It was a prelude to the Great Depression.

* * *

"I could lose all this!" Raji exclaimed, looking out on the manicured gardens around the White House.

"Well, perhaps you have to start thinking smart," Wakefield suggested.

"And how do I do that?"

"Well, maybe you have to start hiding your assets. Think of it as a game of chess. If I am under threat, but move, you cannot take me!"

"But we might yet win the appeal to the Privy Council!"

"Yeah, you might. But if you don't, you will be trapped. I am no legal expert, but Elsie cannot take what you don't have. And if you don't have the villages anymore …"

The Tikari Raj estate had been divided in two in the 19th century. An Anna was one-sixteenth of a rupee. It was this unit that was used to differentiate between the subsequent parts.

The elder of two brothers received the title 'Maharaja of Tikari' and the Nine Annas Estate being nine-sixteenths of the total. It contained large tracts of jungle. It was this Nine Annas Estate that Raji eventually inherited.

The Seven Annas Estate (seven-sixteenths), originally given to the younger of the two brothers, was smaller in size but had more fertile land. Eventually, Seven Annas became the property of Rani Bhuwaneshwari Kuer, who, in the 1920s, was reputed to be the second richest woman in all India, behind only the Begum of Bhopal.

On 12 March 1930, Raji married off his young daughter, Rani Umeshwari Kuer (a child of his fourth wife who he had married when she was fifteen), to the third son of Rani Bhuwaneshwari Kuer. Umeshwari was only eight years and seventy-seven days old.

On 29 March 1930, Raji had Nine Annas transferred to Rani Bhuwaneshwari Kuer in exchange for a lifetime annuity. She eventually converted the Tikari Raj Estates into trusts, creating the General Trusts of the Tikari Raj Estates.

On 15 May 1930, King George V granted Raji leave to appeal to the Privy Council, but only after the Maharaja had deposited 400 pounds as security for costs.

* * *

When the telephone rang in Fordholm Road on the morning of Sunday 26 October 1930, Elsie hesitated to pick it up—though at the time she did not know why.

It was Emma, and the news was not good. Elsie's father James had died late on Friday. As she tried to recover from the initial shock, she wondered why her brother Walter had not rung her earlier, himself.

Emma said the funeral was to be the next day, Monday, but Elsie, through tears, explained that she just could not get to Sydney in time, asking Emma to take a giant wreath of flowers and a card on her behalf.

The funeral, Emma said, would be at Wood Coffill's Mortuary Chapel in Chatswood, with the motor cortege moving on to the Church of England section of the Field of Mars Cemetery where he would be buried next to his dear late wife Mary Ann.

Emma later read out to Elsie the newspaper obituary, which stated that apart from being a well-known and liked bookseller and stationer, eighty-one year old James Thompson had been the Returning Officer for Lang, Darling Harbour and West Sydney, though to Elsie this could not fully describe just what a selfless and honourable gentleman and father he had been.

In a strange occurrence that would be matched by an eerie echo down the years, James' personal details were never chiselled on Mary Ann's headstone, nor was he given one of his own.

Chapter 88

The Privy Council Verdict

The Lords and mostly knighted, dressed in wig and wrapped in gown
Did deliver of their judgment: Privy Council, London Town
Then on 17 December, the King did add his seal
Giving order to their finding on Tikari Raj Appeal.

An ageing Abid Hussain shuffled silently through Raji's bedroom and towards the verandah where his master sat.

In Abid's right hand was a silver tray engraved with the Tikari Coat of Arms, upon which nestled a drink. Gripped in Abid's left were the latest 1931 issues of *Motor* and *The Autocar* magazines.

Their Art Deco covers alone, were a feast for the eyes, with *Motor* being Raji's favourite, as it highlighted his two great passions: motor vehicles and women. It frequently featured an image of a beautiful woman and a gleaming limousine on its cover.

Raji seized the magazines with the determination of a drug addict eager for his next hit, and it was not too long before he had paused on one particular page. His breathing pattern changed and he started to sweat.

He put the magazine down and walked away momentarily as if trying to steer clear of the sirens—but they urged him back, and he could not control his addiction.

He had the annuity case hanging over his head and claims for unpaid taxes from the State of Bihar, but the lure of a V16 Cadillac, the first V16 motor car ever and the most powerful road car in the world, was proving absolutely irresistible.

"Yes! … Oh, yes! … Oh, I have to get that one!" he said to himself, as he grabbed the magazine and headed off to arrange for the manufacturer to be cabled to create a right-hand drive version.

* * *

The Privy Council delivered its judgment on Raji's appeal on
19 November 1931:

Privy Council Appeal No. 39 of 1931
Maharaja Kumar Gopal Narain Singh – Appellant
v.
Sita Devi – Respondent

FROM

THE HIGH COURT OF JUDICATURE AT PATNA.

JUDGMENT OF THE LORDS OF THE JUDICIAL COMMITTEE
OF THE PRIVY COUNCIL, delivered the 19th November 1931.

Present at the Hearing:
Lord Thankerton.
Lord Salvesen.
Sir George Lowndes.
[Delivered by Sir George Lowndes.]

The question raised by this appeal is as to the right of the
respondent to enforce the terms of a deed dated the 18th July
1917, by which the appellant purported to grant to her, "her
heirs, executors, administrators and assigns," a perpetual
annuity of Rs. 15,000 charged upon specified immoveable
properties. The Subordinate Judge by whom the case was tried
held that the deed was unenforceable on various grounds. The
High Court came to the opposite conclusion.

The suit of which the appeal arises was instituted by the
respondent in the Court of the Subordinate Judge of Gaya.
It was founded upon two deeds, both admittedly executed
by the appellant ... Both Courts in India have rejected her
claim under the earlier deed. She has not appealed against the
decision, nor has she appeared upon the present appeal.

The material facts in the case are not in dispute. The plaintiff
was an Australian by birth, and apparently an actress by
profession ...

... The parties admittedly lived together openly as husband
and wife for a number of years, and seem to have been on

the best of terms in 1917 when the deed in question in this appeal was executed. The annuities under the deeds were paid till 1921, when payment was stopped in consequence of her infidelity, which has been affirmed by the judgments of both Courts in India …

… in their Lordships' opinion, the deed of the 18th July, 1917, was clearly not a contract at all. It was in form and substance a gift for which no consideration was necessary …

… there is no evidence of misrepresentation by the respondent, or of the mistake or ignorance of the appellant. He did not in fact go into the witness-box, and there is no indication that he was deceived.

There was a suggestion that the respondent had improperly retained certain "family jewels" of the appellant, and that her claim under the deed should only be affirmed upon the condition of their return. The High Court was of the opinion that there was "no evidence worth the name" to substantiate this allegation, and their Lordships are in complete agreement with their finding on this head.

For the reasons given their Lordships think that the decree passed by the High Court was right and that this appeal fails, and they will humbly advise His Majesty accordingly.

The Privy Council verdict to support the Patna High Court decision and reject Raji's appeal, was reported in newspapers across Australia from Saturday 21 November 1931. *The Sydney Morning Herald* had a piece on page thirteen:

MAHARAJAH OF TIKARI
Privy Council Appeal Dismissed

The Maharajah of Tikari's appeal to the Privy Council has been dismissed.

The chief point of the Maharajah of Tikari's appeal against the Maharanee's claim of an annual allowance of 15,000 rupees was that the wife's divorce in New South Wales in 1906 from an American actor, George Stillwell, whom she married in Capetown in 1903, was invalid because the latter was not domiciled there.

She was an Australian actress named Thompson, but after her divorce in Sydney professed Hinduism and adopted the name Sita Devi. She married the Maharajah of Tikari in Lucknow.

In 1917 he executed a deed granting Sita and her heirs an annuity in perpetuity. Payments were stopped in 1921 on account of her alleged infidelity.

The Maharajah pleaded at an Indian trial in 1923 that his wife's divorce was fraudulent and collusive. A Judge upheld the invalidity of the divorce, and, therefore, the marriage of the Maharajah was declared invalid. The Indian High Court, however, decided in favour of Sita.

The decision of the Privy Council was then formally presented to and approved by King George V, in Buckingham Palace on 17 December 1931:

> ... HIS MAJESTY having taken the said Report into consideration was pleased by and with the advice of His Privy Council to approve thereof and to order as it is hereby ordered that the same be punctually observed obeyed and carried into execution ...

Elsie and Ivan were naturally overjoyed. Elsie insisted she wanted to give some of the annuity to Raji's first wife, Bibi, who she felt had been shabbily treated. It had been ten years since Raji had stopped his payments. Now, finally, after drawn-out action in three courts, the case had been definitively won, as there could be no appeal against the result of an appeal to the Privy Council.

** * **

Inside the White House at Gaya, Raji was in discussion with his legal team and Wakefield.

"We just delay, delay and delay—perhaps say I am broke—but I just won't pay!" Raji insisted. "You people are good lawyers. You should be able to come up with tactics to drag this out!"

Just then, the telephone rang. It was Cecil calling from the compound gate: the 1931 V16 Cadillac Fleetwood Sports Phaeton, custom-made with right-hand drive, had arrived.

Raji was to his feet immediately and racing down the stairs like a child anticipating a long-promised present.

By the time Wakefield and the lawyers reached him, he was already ogling the emerald green and silver monster under the White House's porte-cochère.

"Isn't it fantastic!" Raji gushed, admiring its whitewall tyres, paintwork, style and sheer size. "Look! It has lower headlights that can swivel and see around corners as the front wheels turn," he demonstrated by just managing to turn the front wheels of the stationary vehicle, "and even has a supplementary speedometer and clock on the back of the front seat, so the back-seat passengers can follow progress! Come on! Climb in everyone—let's go for a drive and get this V16 roaring!"

* * *

The months rolled on and on, yet there was no payment or communication from Raji. Ivan had lawyers try to follow it up, but Elsie was indignant, reminding Ivan: "The highest court in the Commonwealth—and the King—have ruled that he must pay, but he refuses!"

"Elsie, just give it a break, for God's sake! I am working with my lawyers on it!"

Chapter 89

Gone West

In dreams I quickly escape—and am heading to the West
Where the sun sets on the ocean and Moana's coffee's best
The sands are rich in redness and the wildflowers bloom in spring
And Mundrabilla's vastness, overpowers most everything.

On Tuesday 1 November 1932, Elsie was outside the front of *De Montfort* in Fordholm Road, and had just finished emptying the household rubbish into the metal rubbish bin—when she first heard it …

Brringg, brringg … Brringg, brringg …

It took her a few seconds to react to what at closer quarters would have seemed obvious.

For a moment, she thought it might be the neighbour's telephone at No. 32, but its insistence caused her to race as fast as her forty-nine year old body could towards her front door.

Brringg, brringg … Brringg, brringg …

As she climbed the flight of four steps to the porch, she wondered how much patience the caller might have.

Brringg, brringg … Brringg, brringg …

Opening the front door and deliberately neglecting to close it to speed her approach, she passed under the fretwork and reached out and grabbed the telephone that sat on the hallway table—just after it gave a final brringg.

"Hello?" she said gasping, as she put the telephone to her ear— only to find that a dial tone was the depth of its reciprocation.

"Oh no!" she exclaimed aloud, as she slumped into the chair beside the device.

Five days earlier, Ivan had sailed on a steamer from Melbourne to Fremantle on one of his semi-regular business trips to the west. He should have already been in Perth and had promised to ring.

Several minutes passed, during which time Elsie reflected on how much she missed his company and commanding presence.

Brringg, brringg …

The ringing telephone startled Elsie so much during her

daydreaming, that she was as breathless as she had been when rushing in from the front nature strip.

"Yes ...?" she gasped. "Hello?"

"Elsie, where were you?"

"Oh, Ivy darling, it is so good to hear your voice! I was putting out the rubbish. It must have been you who called earlier ... how are things going?"

"Well, I managed to catch up with Jack today in Perth. You will not be surprised that he does not send his regards, but, bugger that, there are more important things in life than 'step sons'!"

"Ivan, don't you think that Jack, Owen and I should spend more time together one day and perhaps their attitude would be different?"

"Elsie! We have covered this ground before!" he stated in a firm and slightly annoyed tone. "As I said, there are more important things. Anyway, I had a very productive meeting today with a representative of a buyer seeking a dozen polo horses for Calcutta. I have undertaken to select them myself from Mundrabilla, so am heading there tomorrow by plane."

"By plane? To Mundrabilla?"

"Well, not directly. I bumped into an old acquaintance of yours today—a Charlie Snook."

"Charlie Snook? The name is odd but does not sound familiar. What does he do?"

"He is a pilot and flying instructor. When I told him that I lived with the Maharani of Tikari, he said that he knew you from Hendon Airfield near London, during the war."

"Ivan! A lot of those pilots knew of me, but I really only knew very few of them!"

"Anyway, he said he will fly me in his Air Taxis Moth from Maylands Airfield to Kalgoorlie. He will refuel there and then fly on to Mundrabilla. It gives me more time to round up and select the horses."

Elsie had listened as patiently as she could. "Ivy darling, I don't like you flying. I would much rather you went by train!"

There was a pause at the other end as Ivan struggled with his emotions—and frustrations. "I am going to fly! Yes, it is an open cockpit aircraft, but the blokes here reckon that Snook is the very best bloody pilot in the country, and an Aussie to boot! Anyhow, landing at Mundrabilla is no bloody problem. There's only about a million acres of flat land and bugger all trees!"

Elsie remained quiet, as she could see that he was absolutely determined to fly, while Ivan dwelt on the thrilling prospect of flying in an open cockpit aircraft—an experience he anticipated might be like riding his very fastest stallion at top speed.

After a pause, Ivan offered what he hoped would be comfort for his wife. "Look, Elsie, I will ring you from the Kalgoorlie Airfield. As Charlie has to refuel there, I will have a bit of time. We take off from Maylands at 11 am, and Charlie reckons we should be in Kalgoorlie by 1 pm. So, I will call you then."

"Do take care. Remember that I miss you and love you!"

"Same here, sweetheart. I will speak to you around 1 pm Western Standard Time, which is 3 pm in Melbourne."

With that he put down the telephone. Elsie just sat there in the chair for some minutes. An odd feeling came over her and she started to shiver.

* * *

Ernest Ivan Jones rose just after 7.30 am the next day, Wednesday 2 November 1932, and peered out through the curtains of his room on the top floor of Perth's Palace Hotel, discovering an overcast morning.

He showered and dressed, then headed down the stairs to gorge himself on the huge breakfast spread laid out in the magnificent dining room. A quick look at his watch hastened his departure back to his room. "A quarter to nine!" he muttered to himself. Minutes later he was downstairs with his suitcase and checking out.

"Would you like a taxi, sir?" the receptionist asked.

"What is the forecast?" Ivan shot back.

"Sixty-eight degrees and perhaps the odd shower around midday, though just cloudy till then, sir."

"In that case, I shall walk," he responded, without giving away his destination. He reached down and picked up that morning's complimentary edition of *The West Australian* newspaper and stepped out the William Street entrance. He then started up the hill towards Hay Street on his own 'secret mission', wincing with the effort it took to walk uphill on a very full stomach.

Reaching the corner with Hay Street, he turned right and headed east along part of its length. It was a stroll he had made in each of his previous journeys to Perth and like a pre-match ritual, he now dared not opt out.

He crossed Hay Street before he reached its junction with Barrack Street and the imposing edifice of the Perth Town Hall.

In front of him stood Moana Chambers, with Moana Café's terrace stretching out above him on its first floor. Its large and open terrace doors seemed to offer a warm welcome into the very bosom of the establishment.

Ivan walked down the entrance passage then turned past the Moana Chambers tenants sign, heading up the zigzag flight of stairs that led to the café's glass entry doors. He laboured up the sixteen steps on each stairway, suitcase in hand, but tried to focus on who might greet him on his arrival.

Pushing a door open, he scanned the width of the grand café. He admired once more the corner lounges, steel tables and chairs, and arched wall feature that ran the length of this fine, high-ceilinged establishment. Yet Ivan was not here just for the coffee.

Surely, he thought, *she must be here …*

He turned his attention to the terrace, where he noticed the bottom of a waitress who was serving customers outside the terrace doors.

It looks like … I think it is … oh I hope so … and then as the figure straightened and turned to come inside, he recognised the person he had come to see.

Almost at that same moment, she spotted him—and a broad smile spread across her pretty young face and her eyes shone. "Mr Jones!" she cried.

The feeling that surged through Ivan was one that he would find difficult to describe, but easy to embrace. "Anna!" he responded enthusiastically.

"Where are you going to sit, sir?" she asked, though, as he had already moved to his left, she added: "Ah, your usual corner couch!"

As he placed his suitcase on the floor and the newspaper on the table, she was now close by and he only had eyes for her. The brilliant virginal whites of her eyes were as yet unstained by that trio of tormentors: drink, debauchery and decay. The smile was still on her lips and in her eyes and it was intoxicating for a man in his late fifties to imagine he was being seduced by a young lady like Anna.

"So, sir, what can I do for you?" she said, moving well within touching distance, with her mouth still open and pencil poised at an erotic angle to her notepad.

Ivan noticed all this while trying desperately to focus on what must have been the real intent of her question.

"Ah … I'll have a white coffee with two sugars, please … Anna!" he said, still catching his breath from the dual exertion of stair climbing and fantasy creation.

"No problem, Mr Jones!" she said with a lovely smile, then pivoted with such a seductive twirl that saw her skirt swirl first one way, then back, that Ivan wondered whether she had not practised the movement repeatedly in front of a mirror.

He glanced at his watch, finding it was only 9.13 am. Still plenty of time, he thought, as he opened his copy of the newspaper.

Snook had told him that he should be at Maylands by 10.45 am for the 11 am takeoff, a journey of around half an hour by taxi from the taxi stand on the Hay and Barrack Streets corner, just outside. *A 10 am departure from Moana would give me more than enough time,* he reasoned, as he turned his attention back to the day's paper.

He scanned page one with its array of death notices and shipping information, smiling at the familiarity of the ship names as he read down the columns.

Opening out the paper, a raft of film and theatre advertisements caught his eye on page two, as Anna arrived at his side with his coffee.

"There you are, Mr Jones!" she said, with a smile that seemed to resonate from her words, enveloping him in a warm hug of happiness.

What a girl! he thought.

"Have you got meetings in town today, Mr Jones?" she asked, happy to linger by his side.

Ivan thought he recalled that on his previous visit he had mentioned to her he was from the east coast, but owned the station at Mundrabilla. At least he thought he had mentioned it … sometimes it was hard to recall what he had mentioned and to whom …

"No, today I fly in a specially chartered Moth to Kalgoorlie and then on to Mundrabilla. I have to select a dozen horses for shipping to India."

"Oh, how exciting!"

"The pilot is a flying ace from the war, so I will be in good hands!" he added for extra effect, now that she seemed to be hooked.

"Wow! I would love to fly one day!" she exclaimed, turning to look wistfully out through the terrace to the sky beyond.

"Then, I will have to take you!" he added quickly … then as quickly took a deep breath as he realised the import of what he had just said.

"Oh, would you? That would be just wonderful! I would have to ask my parents first …"

God! Why is that every time, as a middle-aged man away from home, my mind turns to fantasising about young women, he thought to himself, as he self-consciously turned the page of the paper to view pages four and five, as if seeking to change the subject, in his guilt.

"Oh, you are going to do the crossword?" Anna questioned in hope. "I do so admire a man with a brain!"

"Well, I …" was all he could mutter before she interrupted the start of his attempt at a feeble excuse.

"I will get you a pencil!" she said, pivoting tantalisingly once more.

Damn, Ivan thought. Elsie was forever trying to do crosswords with him, but to date that experience had rendered little improvement.

He had barely had enough time to glance at the paper and realise that his challenge on page five was labelled CROSSWORD PUZZLE—NO. 59, before she was back at his side again.

"There you are, Mr Jones, I always like them long and sharp!"

Ivan looked at her open-mouthed for a moment then realised that she was not conscious of any double entendre. She had a shocking level of innocence, that some lucky person would one day soon enjoy corrupting.

"I will be back later to see how you are going," she added with a smile, before spinning off to splash her sunlight across other fortunate customers.

Ivan closed his eyes briefly then focussed on the serious affront that NO. 59 presented to his manly reputation.

"1 Across," he whispered to himself. "This West Country town must be musical, it contains nearly all the band …" *Oh Christ, I hate this stuff!*

He looked up in frustration and in doing so caught sight of Anna serving a table about twelve yards away.

At that moment, Anna turned, looked at him from afar and smiled. *Oh hell, she might be back here soon—and I don't wish to be found wanting,* he thought. He smiled back somewhat sheepishly, then looked back down at his paper, sitting beside his long-emptied coffee cup.

His eyes caught sight once more of the words 'West Country' in the 1 Across clue, but it was only then that he realised that this may not mean Western Australia. "Bloody England!" he cursed, in full acknowledgment of the fact that he knew as much about English geography as most Englishmen knew about Australian rail gauges. His pitiful effort to show he was a crossword king had been well and truly derailed.

In his search for solace, he turned his attention to the myriad of articles to the left on page four, finding their content far more to his liking, for this was the sports page.

Time drifted on and on as Ivan ploughed his way slowly through article after article. He was just reading about another batting failure by the much-loved Don Bradman, when nearby footsteps woke him from his sporting fix.

"Mr Jones! You haven't completed any of the crossword yet!" Anna exclaimed with much disappointment.

Ivan, meanwhile, was desperately thinking of how he could salvage his reputation.

"Ah, well … you see, I prefer to mentally build the whole

crossword in my mind … checking all possibilities, before committing only those I have determined as absolutely correct, to paper. At that point, I complete the whole crossword in one go!"

"Oh … Mr Jones, you are so smart!" she gushed. "When I marry, I should be very lucky if it is to a man half as much like you!"

Ivan said nothing aloud, but his gaze followed her as she retreated back to the bar, moving to stand behind the counter and beneath a large clock. Ivan's eyes drifted momentarily skyward and then widened in shock at what he saw. In a panic, he checked his watch … it was 10.27 am.

"Oh shit!" he yelled out in a voice, so loud that everyone in the café looked in his direction.

He shot to his feet, grabbed his suitcase with his left hand and thrust his right hand into his inside coat pocket, from where he pulled out a ten-pound note.

"That is for you, Anna!" he called, throwing the note on top of the paper before rushing to the doors.

He opened the right-hand glass door with such force that had anyone been on the other side, they would have been bowled over. Speed was of the essence. He had to get to the taxi stand and then on to Maylands Airport … and then just hope that Snook and his Moth were still waiting for him.

He turned right at the top of the stairs and launched himself over the first couple of steps, but the suitcase in his left hand was trailing, and whacked into the curved metal railing at the head of the stairs, turning him over in midair …

In an instant, his years of experience in riding and falling from horses kicked in. Instinctively, he tucked his right shoulder under his body as he flew through the air, making sure that he would roll and hopefully protect his head from impact …

As his body crashed down the stairway and rolled onto the last few steps, he felt that the worst was over as he had saved his head from injury. Unfortunately, the landing floor had only been polished the night before. He skidded across its surface and slammed head first into the metal railing on its edge—the metalwork leaving an imprint in his temple.

For a moment everything went quiet—and Ivan realised that there was nobody around to acknowledge his stupidity. "Bloody fool!" he muttered to himself, as he struggled to his feet, picked up his suitcase and surged towards the second line of stairs.

The sure-footedness that had for so long marked his progression through life deserted him, as he stepped out over the top of the stair line. He misjudged the depth of the second step and his left ankle buckled. Still stunned from the previous tumble, his natural instincts failed to kick in.

He fell headfirst downward, striking his head with a great thwack into the hardwood staircase.

"Aargh!" he grimaced in pain. He swayed slowly to his feet, steadying himself against the railing as he eased past the Moana Chambers tenants sign at the foot of the stairs.

Staggering along the wooden-floored passageway that led to Hay Street, Ivan felt a strong pain in his chest. By the time he reached the footpath, passersby were dodging his erratic progress, though he only had eyes for the taxi stand just yards ahead.

Hopefully, I can get to the airport quickly enough, he thought—but the images in front of him started to swing from side to side, become blurred—and then all went black as he slumped forward, sinking onto the footpath on the corner of Hay and Barrack Streets.

A few valiant pedestrians came to his aid.

Upstairs, on the terrace of Moana Café, two young gentlemen who had ordered coffees, rose to watch a crowd gather below.

Moments later, Anna arrived with their order. "Here you are, sirs!" she said with a sweet and seductive smile, as they turned back to acknowledge her delivery.

"Someone has collapsed on the corner!" said one of the young men.

Anna, with the edge of Ivan's ten-pound note still sticking out of her breast pocket, moved to a position where she could glimpse people surrounding a prostrate figure. "Just another stupid drunk!" she said dismissively, pivoting and turning her back on Ivan's fight for life.

* * *

In Fordholm Road, Hawthorn, Elsie had sat for over an hour next to the telephone from before 3 pm, Melbourne time. The concern she had felt when Ivan had told her just a day earlier, that he would be flying, had not dissipated. Rather, as time progressed and with the telephone remaining depressingly silent, her fears grew.

She rose and headed into the kitchen to try to while away some time until he called … perhaps storms had delayed his takeoff … perhaps the telephone line at Kalgoorlie was down … perhaps he had just forgotten to call? There were surely many possible reasons.

As she chopped vegetables in the kitchen, she listened intently for the telephone—but all she could hear was the incessant tick-tock of the clock.

Around 7 o'clock, dinner was ready, but still no telephone call. Tick-tock, tick-tock, the clock echoed through the house.

Elsie served her dinner, then realised she had no appetite for eating. She pushed the plate away from her at the dining table and placed her head on her arms. Tick-tock, tick-tock …

She did not know how long it was that she had lain there, but finally she heard it … brringg, brringg …

She had been hoping and praying for so long and now finally, the telephone had rung. "Oh God … thank God!" she cried as she rushed and picked it up. "Oh darling! …" she said, then realised that there was only a dial tone. "Ivy! Darling? …"

As she held on to the receiver in hope, she heard it again … brringg, brringg … that is when she realised that it was somebody turning the front doorbell.

At least someone is communicating with me, was the only thought she had as she put down the telephone and walked the few yards to the door. As it was now getting dark, she turned on the porch light.

She could see two figures quite clearly as she opened the door. Her heart skipped a beat as she recognised the one to her left was a policeman.

"Yes? …" she asked, very tentatively.

"Mrs Elsie Jones?" the policeman queried in a slow, world-wearied voice.

"Yes … is there something … wrong?" As she said these

words, the possible significance of her visitors began to dawn on Elsie—and she started to shake.

"Mrs Jones, my name is Sergeant Albert Hampton of the Hawthorn Police," he said, taking off his hat. "And this is Major Margaret Jorgensen of the Salvation Army ..." he added, hesitating, as he always hated delivering this sought of news. "Your husband, Ernest Jones, collapsed in Perth this morning."

"No! No! Please, no!" Elsie cried, as she backed away from the door, gasping for air as panic took hold of her. "But ... he is ok now ... isn't he?" she asked forlornly.

"Mrs Jones, I think you should sit down," he said, moving forward as Elsie's legs began to buckle. "Marg! Quickly! Get on her other side!"

They manoeuvred Elsie into the lounge area and eased her onto the couch. "I think I shall wet this," Margaret said, removing a handkerchief from her pocket and looking for the bathroom.

"Please tell me he is all right now!" Elsie demanded between sobs.

Margaret returned with the damp handkerchief and sat next to Elsie, dabbing it on her face and pulling her close to her ample breasts.

"I am told ..." the sergeant started haltingly "... that it was fairly quick. He passed away in the St John ambulance on the way to hospital."

"Ahhhhh!" Elsie exclaimed, as she began sobbing uncontrollably.

"He's safe in the Lord's hands now!" Margaret said softly, as she stroked Elsie's hair.

Sergeant Hampton had been saddled with this task for years, and never got used to it. Dead bodies were one thing, but the pain witnessed when informing their living loved ones, was on quite another level. He stood, fingering his hat for a few moments, wondering if Elsie would even hear anything else he had to say. "Perth police have told me that Mr Jones' son Jack is taking care of arrangements."

The sergeant moved slowly towards the door. "Margaret, if you need any more support, just give the station a call."

Chapter 90

The Morning After

The morning after starts a phase, of wishing to forget
The nightmare that won't go away, the longing and regret
If only hands upon the clock, could wind back to his charms
And guarantee the one I love, was back within my arms.

Elsie reached out instinctively across the bed to caress the figure of Ivan that she was sure would be there—but there was only space and cold.

The morning light had started to dance its way through the drapes, in welcome to yet another day on its endless rotation.

Elsie sensed the light and woke up with a start, as she began to recall pieces of what surely must have been the worst of all nightmares.

She sat upright quickly, trying to shake off the memories and look for reassurance around her. She looked left and right, yet nothing indicated anything but a bad dream.

Pulling the sheets back, she stepped out of bed, but her slippers were not in their usual spot—*not a good sign*, she thought.

She headed into the kitchen and noticed that there was more than one cup near the sink—*invariably an indication that Ivan is around.* She sighed with relief, then recalled that he had not been in bed.

She turned to go back to the bedroom to double-check, but in doing so caught sight of a figure dozing in the lounge room.

"Oh! … Oh!" was all she could say, as the significance of seeing Major Jorgensen began to paint in the reality of her new circumstance.

The major struggled to her feet and wobbled towards Elsie with her arms open. "It is okay, Elsie, darling! Come and sit down with me!"

For about twenty minutes they sat together as Elsie cried. "I must call Emma!" she said, her eyes red and cheeks tear-tracked.

Major Jorgensen helped her to the telephone and stood by her with a hand on her shoulder, as Elsie dialled.

In Manly, it was just before 8 am on a Thursday, and Joe Binstead was eating breakfast, though when the telephone rang, as per family protocol, it was he who went to answer it. "Joe speaking …"

"Joe, it is Elsie," she said, taking a deep breath. "Could I please speak to Emma?"

Joe could sense the tension and urgency on the other end of the line. "You okay, sweetheart?" he asked, but there was no immediate reply.

"Could I please speak to Emma!" she said again, though this time it was no question.

"Em! It's Elsie!" he called, then, as he was about to hand over the telephone, he covered the mouthpiece and added: "I think something is wrong!"

Joe stayed by the telephone as Emma was given the news. "Oh no! … Oh, Elsie darling!" Joe looked with concern at Emma for more information.

Finally, Emma cupped her hand over the mouthpiece and said: "Ivan has died!"

"Jesus!" Joe exclaimed, as he tried to think of the implications, then looked up with concern as he realised that eleven-year-old Sita had just emerged from her bedroom, wanting to know what was going on.

"Elsie, just a moment darling, I want to ask Joe something." Cupping the mouthpiece, Emma asked Joe if Elsie could come and stay with them in Manly for a few weeks.

"Whatever … no problem … of course!" Joe stumbled over his response, as he was still coming to terms with what he had heard.

"Elsie, we would love you to come and stay. We can catch the ferry to the city and walk across the new Sydney Harbour Bridge together, go to the theatre … look, Elsie darling, who is handling the funeral arrangements? … So, will it be in Melbourne?" Emma asked. "Jack? He is in Western Australia, isn't he? … Yes, I think you should ring him, darling … just remember that they are two hours behind … yes, let me know the result … well, if it is in Melbourne, we will do our best to be there … just don't forget, that after the funeral you should come up and stay with us for a few weeks."

At this point, Emma cupped the mouthpiece again. "She can stay for Christmas, can't she?" Joe nodded his approval, but Sita still looked puzzled. "I will explain things in a minute, darling," Emma said as an aside to her daughter, though Joe was already pulling Sita away.

"Uncle Ivan has died!" he whispered to her.

"Elsie, everyone here sends you their love, hugs and kisses and we are with you darling … I will call you at 7 pm tonight … of course you can ring me at any time! … We love you very much too! … Okay darling, speak to you then!"

Emma put the telephone down with a heavy heart. "You just never know when something might happen. Sometimes I think we take each other for granted," she said wistfully, looking at her dear husband and daughter. The goodbye hug and kiss she gave each that morning was even more heart-felt than usual.

Back in Hawthorn, Elsie tried to focus on the love and support of her best friend and Emma's family. To keep herself occupied until 11 am—which she figured was the earliest possible time that she could call Jack in Perth—she went into the kitchen to make breakfast, though found Major Jorgensen already there, well progressed with breakfast preparation.

Just on 11 am (and with the major now departed) Elsie opened up the little alphabetic telephone book to the 'J' page. She knew Jones, Jack was at the top. As she studied the number, she took a deep breath, for she realised this would not be easy.

It took no more than a ring for the telephone to be picked up, as Jack had been waiting for a call (though not one from Elsie).

"Jack? … It is Elsie calling from Melbourne … Elsie Jones …"

There was silence for a moment as Jack struggled for the appropriate words.

"Jack … darling … I am told that you are making the funeral arrangements. Do you know when and where it will be?" Elsie asked.

"The funeral will be here in Perth!" he said firmly. "I am just waiting for a call to confirm that it will be tomorrow afternoon at Karrakatta Cemetery."

"Tomorrow? In Perth? … But Jack, he is my … partner!" Elsie pleaded, as tears ran down her face.

"Yes, and he is my father and has been so for far longer than you had been together!" Jack retorted. "You will be pleased to know that I have acknowledged you as 'wife' in the death notice that will appear in *The West Australian* tomorrow. Now, I am expecting that call from the funeral directors at any moment, so I am sorry to say that I must finish our conversation." And with that, Jack hung up.

Chapter 91

"Welcome to Collingwood Street!"

There is a place in Manly, where you'll feel 'mongst family
As comfortable as furniture, be it breakfast, lunch or tea
"Make the Binstead's, your new home, and the place to put up feet
El, you're always welcome, right here in Collingwood Street!"

Getting out of Melbourne and at least temporarily away from 30 Fordholm Road, certainly felt like the right thing for Elsie to do. The train trip to Sydney was long and uneventful. Thankfully, the constant rocking of the first class carriage seemed to evoke a comforting feeling of care and support akin to early childhood times in a cradle.

It had been more than eighteen years since Elsie had last been in Sydney, the city of her birth, and she was fascinated by the changes: some newer buildings, roads, more traffic—and of course the Sydney Harbour Bridge.

Her nieces had sent a letter to her, describing how the whole family—Walter, Stella, Marjorie, Elsie and young Stella—had walked along the centre of the structure on its day of opening earlier in the year, Saturday 19 March. The crowds had been huge, they said, but the experience just wonderful. Marjorie, the driver in the family, had since driven them across.

As Elsie approached the bridge pylons for the first time, passing Millers Point to her left where she had been born, she asked the taxi driver to slow down in the left lane so she could take in the view—forward, above and sideways. Soon the vehicle was drifting past bridge supports, intermittently and momentarily blocking out the late afternoon sun, with Elsie marvelling at the scale of the structure and the distance above the harbour water far below. *J.C. was right in his play prediction of decades ago—what a pity he did not live to see it!*

In what seemed just seconds they were on Sydney's North Shore and heading towards Manly and 65 Collingwood Street. The telephone had long allowed personal communication over long distances, but being able to hug Emma once more after nearly six long years and the recent bereavement, was always

658

going to be something special.

"Welcome to Collingwood Street!" said a beaming Joe Binstead, giving Elsie a hug and a kiss, after Elsie had opened the small iron gate and walked down the side of the house to the front door. Joe took Elsie's suitcase, but she watched it protectively, as Emma rushed towards her.

Oh! Emma definitely looks older and a little worn out, thought Elsie, *but, I suppose, nothing much beyond what standard parenting might inflict. As for Joe ... well! He's put on a bit of weight and is certainly looking older than the young man who charmed me at their wedding!*

Elsie and Emma embraced for a good minute, before her host ushered her into the lounge room, with the words: "Now, see how your goddaughter is growing up!"

There was Sita, smiling. Elsie was sure that Sita had to be the nicest and kindest eleven-year-old in the whole world, so gave her an affectionate squeeze and kiss—during which time young Sita recognised the same beautiful French perfume she had first sensed as a five-year-old visiting *De Montfort.*

"Oh, Emma, I miss Ivan so much! He was so strong and reliable!" Elsie sighed, as she sat down on the sofa in the lounge room, after glancing briefly at the framed Mucha poster of herself, hanging on the wall above.

"I know, darling!" Emma said, moving in beside her. "But you are here now and we will all support you. You are with people who love you! By the way, how are things now with Raji?"

"Oh, I don't trust Raji at all. I did once, but not any more. He has not paid any of the outstanding annuity. In fact, I would fear for my life if I returned to India. Even here, I am almost paranoid about my jewellery, and try to keep it near me as much as possible. I certainly couldn't leave it back in Fordholm Road," she said, rising and then removing the jewellery bag from her suitcase. "And I wouldn't mind if you could still be the address for any mail from Raji. I really don't want him having my Fordholm Road details!"

"That is fine, darling—we will continue to post anything on," said Emma, though she wondered whether perhaps Elsie was too sensitive about things.

Elsie's use of the term 'paranoid' seemed to be appropriate, for when Emma and Elsie prepared for a theatre trip into the heart of Sydney, both had to wear Elsie's full range of jewels, as Elsie would not allow them to be left in Collingwood Street, nor risk carrying them in her handbag lest it was snatched.

At least they were able to wear most of the jewellery out of sight and under clothes, but Emma felt the burden of wearing the two pairs of separate emerald and diamond bracelets and a ruby ring on a finger. At least young Sita was spared that psychological burden, though she did not enjoy coping with the rise and fall, and rocking and rolling on an unusually rough ride on the Saturday Manly Ferry to Circular Quay.

From there, they caught a bus to the Sydney Town Hall where they had agreed to meet Walter's three girls.

They had been wondering if the Thompson girls had forgotten, when there was a rushing of shoes towards them as they stood in the square alongside Town Hall.

"Oh, I thought you were the press!" exclaimed Elsie, as she greeted Marjorie, as well as young Elsie and even younger thirteen-year-old Stella, both of whom she met for the very first time.

The group of six then headed off to the 2 pm matinee debut performance of the comic opera *The Chocolate Soldier,* starring Gladys Moncrieff, at Her Majesty's Theatre. It was, after all, a J. C. Williamson Ltd production, as Elsie pointed out, and she felt she had to pay homage to her favourite theatre entrepreneur with her presence.

The ability to mingle with relatives and close friends regularly in Sydney, had Elsie thinking about shifting permanently north, especially after a wonderful Christmas Day when she presented Sita with her own personalised notepads, with her name written and underlined in gold in the top left-hand corner.

Emma had suggested that if Elsie remained in Melbourne, she should try to persuade Myrtle McLeod to move in with her, though, with no regular income, nor permanent residence, Sydney was looking a more likely option.

A few days later, Elsie was contemplating what she should do, as she leaned on the windowsill, watching Sita dancing with an imaginary partner in her backyard. A pinch of her bottom caused her to wheel around, expecting to see Emma—but it was Joe.

Elsie went to smack him in a similar location and they engaged in a 'tit for tat' laughter-filled battle that traversed various rooms of the house.

That night, at the Binstead's New Year's Eve dinner table, Elsie found a pair of feet wrapped around her ankles, playfully and gently moving her feet from side to side. She looked up to see Joe smiling at her. *Interesting,* she thought, *very interesting.*

Joe was utterly captivated by Elsie. *Amazing,* he thought, *that she is nearly as stylish, charming and disarmingly beautiful as the woman I first met nearly two decades ago!* She seemed like an exotic and luscious fruit that he desperately wanted to taste.

On New Year's Day 1933, Elsie stood on the platform at Sydney's Central Station. Warmed and comforted by the hugs and kisses from Emma, Joe and Sita, she was about to catch the train back to *De Montfort* and Melbourne and an uncertain future.

"I honestly do not know what will happen with Ivan's will and estate. Perhaps I will receive nothing. When that is added to the nothing that Raji has sent me to date, I could have nothing but a few pieces of jewellery to my name—and nowhere to go!"

"If that should ever happen, darling, you know you are always welcome here!" Emma assured her.

The guard's whistle blew and Elsie hurried inside the carriage and to her seat, where she leaned out the window to wave goodbye to the family group to which she was closest.

Chapter 92

The Reading of the Will

If I should die I'll leave you — p'rhaps — a bit of this or that
I can't be more specific now, my lawyers are 'flat chat'
My wishes will be bound by law, then wrapped in codicil
You'll find just what intent I have, at the reading of my will.

A telephone call from Ivan's solicitor and executor of his will, Edgar Percival Johnson, alerted Elsie to a meeting in Edgar's office the next day: Tuesday 3 January 1933. As Elsie suspected, this would be an effective reading of the will. She was just thankful she had arrived back in Melbourne in time.

Elsie entered the room at 430 Little Collins Street with no great expectation. She merely hoped that Ivan's word that she would be looked after would be kept.

Apart from Edgar, there were already three others in the room, all of whom she recognised: Ivan's Melbourne-based sister Marion had been pleasant enough on the handful of occasions that they had previously met; while the other two, Ivan's sons Owen and Jack, seemed bigger and stronger than at their last meeting.

"What are you doing here?" Owen asked pointedly.

Elsie, for once, was a little lost for words. She could not say that she was hoping she might get a slice of the estate, but on principle she could not disown any interest. Instead, she just looked at Owen and smiled.

Mr Johnson, who remained sitting imperiously behind his solicitor's desk, started by thanking each of them for finding the time to be present. At this moment, Elsie thought, three of the other four in the room would be very nervous, for she was sure that, like her, none knew just what the will held in store.

The solicitor then cleared his throat, looked sternly over the rim of his glasses at those gathered before him—and began reading the will:

I <u>ERNEST IVAN JONES</u> of "De Montfort" Fordholm Road Hawthorn in the State of Victoria, Commonwealth of Australia Gentleman formerly carrying on business at 12A Mission Row Calcutta India Merchant hereby revoke all former wills and codicils made by me and declare this to be my last will. And I further declare that my domicile is Victorian and that I desire my will and any codicil I may make to be construed and to take effect according to the law of the said State of Victoria.

1. I APPOINT Edgar Percival Johnson of 430 Little Collins Street Melbourne in the said State Solicitor and the Equity Trustees Executors and Agency Company Limited of Queen Street Melbourne aforesaid to be executors and trustees of this my will for the purpose of dealing with my property wheresoever situate.

2. I DECLARE that in the interpretation of this my will the expression "my trustees" shall (where the context permits) mean and include the trustees or trustee for the time being hereof whether original or substituted.

3. I DEVISE my dwelling house and land known as "De Montfort" Fordholm Road Hawthorn aforesaid and I BEQUEATH all plate articles furniture linen glasses china pictures prints musical instruments books and other articles of domestic or household use or ornament in or about the same premises unto my trustees UPON TRUST to permit Elsie Caroline Thompson of "De Montfort" Fordholm Road Hawthorn aforesaid personally to occupy the said dwelling house and land and to have the use and enjoyment of the said furniture and effects during her life free from all rent rates taxes and expenses of repairs and insurance and other outgoings in respect of the said dwelling house and land and the said furniture and effects which I direct to be paid and discharged by my trustees out of the annual income of my residuary estate And I direct that the said Elsie Caroline Thompson shall not be required to sign an inventory of the said furniture and effects and that neither she nor my trustees shall be in anywise responsible for any damage thereto or loss or destruction thereof PROVIDED ALWAYS and I declare that the said Elsie Caroline Thompson shall be at liberty

at her absolute discretion to sell any of the said furniture
and effects at any time during her lifetime the proceeds of
such sale being applied in the purchase of other furniture or
household or domestic effects And from and after the death
of the said Elsie Caroline Thompson the said dwelling house
and land and the said furniture and effects (including any
furniture and effects which may be purchased by the said
Elsie Caroline Thompson as aforesaid) shall sink into and
form part of the residuary estate.

Elsie had caught her breath when she heard her name
mentioned, then, as it was made clear she had been left
De Montfort to live in for the rest of her life, she heard sighs and
mutterings of disapproval from those seated to her right. Mr
Johnson continued:

4. I BEQUEATH to my sister Marion Jane Jones all my
watches jewellery clothing and other articles of personal use
or ornament …

Mr Johnson went on to read how Ivan had left small amounts
to his New Zealand-based brother and to Mr Johnson himself,
then:

6. I BEQUEATH to my trustees the sum of Twenty two
thousand five hundred pounds UPON TRUST that my trustees
shall invest the same in their names in any of the investments
hereafter authorised and shall stand possessed of such
sum of Twenty two thousand five hundred pounds and the
investments from time to time representing the same UPON
TRUST to pay the income thereof to the said Elsie Caroline
Thompson during her life and after her death I declare that
the said sum of Twenty two thousand five hundred pounds
and the investments for the time being representing the same
shall sink into and form part of my residuary estate …

Elsie now not only had the use of the house, but also an
income to help her live week to week. She could ask Myrtle to
move in with her, as companion and servant, rent-free.

Shocked but grateful with what Ivan had done, she could feel the antagonism from those seated to her right so much that she had to stand and move away.

After distributions to organisations of which he had been a member, the balance of Ivan's estate, including extensive business interests in Calcutta and in Australia, was held in trust for his two sons. Ivan also bequeathed the use of the house *Te Whare* in Barrington Avenue, Kew, to his sister, in the same way Elsie had been bequeathed *De Montfort*, while she lived.

When the reading had finished, Elsie thanked Mr Johnson, but did not want to say anything to Ivan's relatives, lest it be viewed as condescending. As she headed out the door, a male voice called from behind: "You got more than you deserved—you haven't heard the last of this!"

* * *

In mid January 1934, Elsie received an envelope from Emma, containing a registered letter from Raji that he had addressed to 'Madame Devi—c/- Mrs Binstead, 65 Collingwood St, Manly, New South Wales, Australia'. Raji had handwritten it on yellow Tikari letterhead paper in his typically poor but mostly phonetically spelt written English. The back of the envelope carried the Tikari Raj crowned 'T' in peacock blue. The letter read:

Gaya 14-12-33

My Dear Elsey,

I got your letter of 19 Oct on the 7th of this month, through Lesley and Hind's. I had been wondering what had happened to you and in what part of the World you were, do you realise that it is about 6 years that I last saw or heard of you, how long have you been in Australia, and how have you been doing?

You want to know if I can meat you and talk matters over I can and will meat you

any where you like but I suggest New
Zealand, as you will not have far to come
and I can fly from here to Java and thence
by boat, What do you think of this idea,
I have not consulted my lawyers as if I
do they will sugest ways that these will
increace my feas and I will have to spend
a lot more and you will get nothing out
of it, I think we should let by gowns be
bygowns and burry the hachet, and meat
as friends and fix up things, I am sorry
for what happened in the case but when
one fites all sorts of nasty things happen,
but both of us are much older and not
so stubun, any how what do you think of
our meeting in New Zealand let me know
and also how much I should send you and
please register your letter to me.

Yours as ever
Raji

In a burst of initial hope and enthusiasm, Elsie cabled Raji
and followed up by sending a copy of the cable in a registered
letter. She subsequently wrote in pencil on the back of Raji's
envelope:

Copy of cable sent to Rajie

… and further under, months later, she added:

Grieved and disappointed that my registered
letter sent Gaya remains unanswered

Elsie

* * *

Once again in January—though this time 1935—Emma
redirected a letter. This one was from Willie Hathaway. *Do*

they, Elsie wondered, *have an agreement to communicate with me in December each year, at the most!* The letter was handwritten on Tikari Raj letterhead paper. It read:

> Tikari White House,
> Gaya 9-12-1934

My dear Sita,

You will probably be surprised to hear that I am back in Gaya with Raji, I arrived last April from New Zealand. You will be pleased to hear that Raji is well, but he has been through a really ghastly time lately, as usual some of his so called friends here, let him down badly and things became desperately complicated, with law case after law case in the courts. However, matters are improving now, and I hope that soon he will be over his worst difficulties and successfully too.

You will I know be pleased to know that the Lees, Wakefields etc, are of the past, they are still in the Gaya District, but we never see anything of them.

Raji is a little stouter now, and of course like the rest of us a little older, but still outwardly his old self, philosophically smiling his way through life, in spite of all his worries and troubles, and believe me he has had some.

However he will win through all right, and I think that there is a special rod in pickle, for some of those he befriended here and who have done their utmost to do him down.

Raji has given me your address, and has

told me about your letters etc, he has written to you himself and he really intends to come over and see you to settle up matters, just as soon as he can get things fixed up here, to permit him to leave India.

I shall be glad too, as I think Raji needs a change and a holiday badly, away from all his worries and troubles here, so we are trying to get something fixed up here soon, which will enable him to get away.

I am sorry to say that Anne has not been at all well for some months past in New Zealand, she is now on her way with Peter, and I am hoping that the sea voyage will set her up in health again.

I find great changes in India after seven years, and not for the better, but the whole World is in trouble it seems.

With kindest regards and best of good wishes, hope you are well,

Yours sincerely,
Willie Hathaway

Elsie wrote on the top of the letter in pencil:

Sent to me by the English Manager of Rajie's Estate. He was formerly a draper in Mussourie. I replied telling him to leave my affairs to ourselves.

Sita Devi.

Chapter 93

The Betrayal

At times, yes, I have dreamt it, of her hair upon my face
Of her arms squeezed tight around me, of her lips and of her grace
Betrayal—it just means nothing, for her charms do so consume
As I drift my way to heaven, on a raft of her perfume.

On an early Wednesday evening in December 1936, there was an unexpected visitor to *De Montfort*.

Myrtle had responded to the knocking at the door, and Elsie, seated and reading in the lounge room, heard the muffled interchange of voices. "What is it, Myrtle?" she called out.

She looked up to see a red-faced Myrtle at the lounge room entrance. "It is Mr Binstead," she said breathlessly, "and, he has a bag!"

Elsie reached the hallway and saw Joe standing in the doorway with his travel bag by his side. She was not surprised at this, as she knew he flew regularly on company business—but why was he here?

"Don't worry," he said. "I flew under the name of Joe Barnett, so Emma won't see my name in the published passenger lists for flights to Melbourne. I got the name from the tyre company advertisement in the newspaper!"

* * *

For that Christmas, Elsie posted fifteen-year-old Sita a silver make-up compact, engraved with:

$$\mathcal{Sita}$$

Xmas 1936

* * *

In late January 1937, Elsie received a handwritten letter that Raji's attorney, Henry SL Polak, had sent to Collingwood Street, and that Emma had passed on. It read:

19 Albert Road
Allahabad
Dec 28 1936

Dear Madame Devi,

When he returned here, Mr CA Andrews spoke to me about the matter of your allowance from the Tikari Raj.

Upon my arrival in Patna, I spoke about it in confidence to Sir Sultan Ahmed, Tikari's legal advisor and also friend of mine, in whom I can trust completely as a man of honour.

He promised that, if you would write him a full statement of the facts, he would place the matter before Tikari and would do what was possible. Naturally, as Tikari's advisor, this would have to be done privately and without commitment.

Will you therefore write to him fully to Patna, marking the envelope private and personal, and ask for his friendly intervention. You can mention Mr Andrews' name and my own.

With kindest regards,
HSL Polak

Address:
HSL Polak
265 Strand
London WC2

Elsie was most annoyed by this letter, for Polak, who had been hired by Raji, had been privy to all the details of the case from near its inception. Now, he wanted her to write 'a full statement

670

of the facts' in the hope that Tikari's own legal advisor might persuade Raji to 'do what was possible', rather than what had been legally demanded.

Chapter 94

The Stinson

The clouds were looking ominous—but then they often do
You rise above their petulance—and all the sky is blue
I'd flown this route many times, however could I see
That me and this plane Stinson, would fly into history.

Joe Binstead looked at the skies over Brisbane's Archerfield Aerodrome—and did not particularly like what he saw. It was Friday 19 February 1937, and the forecast had been less than pleasant. The local newspaper, *The Courier-Mail* had stated on the right side of its front page:

Unsettled, with squally south-east, backing
southerly winds.

A company director who flew regularly between cities, Binstead was well used to the vagaries of flying, and, wanting to be back in Sydney for the weekend, had pushed on into the airport terminal and the Airlines of Australia check-in desk. However, he was running late and still had the seven-pound fee for the flight in his hand, when the 1 pm scheduled takeoff time was reached.

"Apologies!" he said panting.

"At least you made it, Mr Binstead!" said the young lady handling the passenger bookings. "Oh … I mean Mr Barnett!" she quickly added, correcting herself.

"That is better!" Joe said, smiling with relief and taking his ticket before heading for the exit door to the tarmac. The Brisbane to Sydney flight aboard the Stinson A had already been called over the public-address system.

The *City of Brisbane*, as it was called, was a thirty-six foot long, three-engined dark blue plane with orange trim and VH-UHH registration number on its side—and familiar to Joe. It was also the only one of the four Airlines of Australia Stinsons not to be equipped with radio communication.

As Joe clambered on board, he noticed that four of the eight seats were already occupied. He glanced at his ticket and realised that he had seat 3, the second of three seats going back against the left-hand window side.

He settled down, nodding in acknowledgement to the middle-aged man across the aisle from him in seat 5, as he was sure he had seen him before. Joe liked seat 3, for at least for now, it had a vacant seat 4 next to him, upon which he could rest items. The only other paired seats were the two immediately behind him—seats 6 and 7—with 6 occupied by a young man. The other occupied seats were single ones: 1, immediately in front of him, and 2, across the isle from 1.

No doubt seats 4, 7 and 8 will be taken when the plane stops at Lismore in New South Wales, presumed Joe, though that was around an hour away, on a three-hour flight.

The most important thing was that he would be home with Emma and Sita in Sydney that evening. It was something that he repeated over and over to himself during the next half hour, as the plane took off six minutes late and climbed into the wind and the buffeting of dark cloudbank after dark cloudbank as it headed south.

The stretching, creaking, jolting, rocking and rolling of the plane was most disconcerting, and Joe tried to bury himself into James Joyce's novel *Ulysses*, in an attempt to make the time pass.

Yet, time and again, he battled to focus on the words as he was drawn to the swirling mist of grey-black clouds and now rain, that had engulfed the plane.

It was on one such glance out to his left that he noticed to his alarm, treetops—far closer to the plane than he thought they ever should be. He twisted to his right and looked forward, wondering if he should press the ALERT button to notify the captain and co-pilot, but he could see that they seemed to be communicating calmly with each other.

He had just returned to his book when the plane tilted to the right and tried to climb, but only managed to dip alarmingly, for it had been caught in the down-draft from cyclonic winds that had surged over the Macpherson Range.

Moments later, it clipped treetops and headed down, with a huge tree limb tearing through the right side of the plane, just before the main fuselage slammed into a large tree about thirty feet above the ground—and sank to the rainforest floor.

Joe had instinctively put his arms up to protect his head, but he had blacked out … and he did not know whether it was seconds or minutes before he came to, as flames had taken hold of the front and rear of the plane.

The young man from seat 1 directly in front of him had smashed away the remnants of the large oblong window next to his seat, as smoke and flame started to fill the cabin.

As Joe clambered forward through the mess, he tried not to look where seat 5 had been, as he could see that the man he had greeted with a nod was well and truly dead.

The fellow from seat 1 was trying to ease himself through the broken window, so Joe tried to push him up by the legs. The man let out a scream of pain, indicating at least one of his legs was broken.

When out, he bravely hauled Joe through—an effort that must have taken great courage.

To the surprise of both of them, there was a third man alive— the young man from seat 6 behind Joe, though he had burns to his back and his right hand from the fire that had taken hold of the tail of the plane.

The three of them staggered to the base of a tree not far from the plane—though away far enough from the searing heat, just in case the plane exploded. It was obvious now that there were no other survivors, and soon the wreckage was consumed by flame, incinerating the bodies trapped inside.

As the rain started to pour down and some of the initial shock wore off, they introduced themselves. The man with the badly fractured right leg was John Proud, a thirty-year-old mining engineer from Sydney, who was a director of Prouds, the jewellers. "I shouldn't have been … on this bloody flight," he winced through the pain. "They didn't have a seat … once the Lismore bookings were considered but … but they figured that the weather was so bad down south … that the plane would fly straight to Sydney instead. So … so they gave me a seat, because … because I insisted. Bloody idiot, I was!"

The man with burns was a twenty-six year old Englishman, James Westray, an employee of Lloyds Insurance, who was in Australia on business. He was staying at the Australia Hotel in

Sydney. Joe quipped that they would all have a drink together there, when they were rescued.

At fifty-four, Joe was nearly twice their age. Miraculously, however, he had no major injuries, apart from general soreness, obvious shock and torn clothes.

That night, they made a fire with the few dry matches they had left, then the sight of a distant plane in the morning, initially raised hopes that soon dissipated.

Westray swore that he had seen a farmhouse in a not too distant valley, as the plane had approached, just before crashing. He said he was going to go for help. Though he was young and fit, both Proud (who Joe had started calling Jack, instead of his birth name John) and Joe, were against this, for they hoped the bit of burnt bush at the crash site would soon be found.

But Westray insisted—and he soon headed off.

Joe and Jack then tried to establish a routine, that, if nothing else, kept them focussed and motivated. Every half hour, one of them would call out "Coo-ee!" just in case there were searchers in the area.

Jack chose to call on the hour and Joe at the half-past, with both synchronising their watches.

Jack could not move and Joe made sure his right leg, which was not looking very healthy, was propped up on a log. The only problem then was to keep the flies away, so Joe found and bent a piece of steel over the leg, to protect it. He also gave another piece to Jack who wanted to start a diary using his penknife.

Water was now becoming a necessity. Joe Binstead reasoned that as they were at the top of a gorge, there was every chance of water at the bottom. After searching the wreckage of the plane—and trying to avoid looking at the charred bodies—he found a dented and darkened thermos.

He set off down the side of the vine-covered gorge on a 200-yard journey to the bottom. He was right—there was fresh water. Joe filled the thermos and started the journey back, but by the time he reached the top, his hands and feet were bleeding from the thorns and rocks—but at least they had a thermos full of water.

* * *

Meanwhile, that Saturday morning in Fordholm Road, Hawthorn, Elsie and Myrtle had heard the story of the missing Stinson plane on the radio. Such things were always sad but so rarely personal—until the telephone rang.

It was Emma. She had scarcely slept all night for Joe had not returned to Sydney. She had contacted Airlines of Australia, who confirmed that he was on board the missing plane. Elsie was shocked and heartbroken for her friend. They agreed that they would monitor things and hope that the plane had just landed at another airport in the bad weather.

When Myrtle returned with a copy of that evening's *The Herald*, the headline was:

12 PLANES SEARCH FOR MISSING STINSON AIR LINER

… while within the article, the missing passengers included:

Mr J Barnett

There was also a small profile of each of the other passengers and crew, though they had nothing to print about Mr Barnett. Yet, both Elsie, and now Emma, courtesy of the airline, knew exactly who Mr Barnett really was. In case anyone doubted, *The Sydney Morning Herald* of Monday 22 February—and many other newspapers—carried a photograph of Joe with the following minimal biography:

> Mr J. R. Binstead who was one of the passengers in the missing Stinson air liner. Mr Binstead is managing director of Telesports Ltd, and was making a business trip from Brisbane to Sydney. Mr Binstead was travelling under the name of Mr J Barnett …

Chapter 95

The Search and the Promise

"I'm just a damn wool broker!" I did cry out to the Lord
"You've trapped me in this cursed place, to die as a reward!
What pound of flesh you ask of me, what price must I repay?
To see me back to wife and child—to live another day!"

From the moment the Stinson was reported missing, its fate and those of its passengers dominated the nation's radio and newspapers. Everybody seemed to have their own theory on what had happened, with people coming up with recollections of having seen the plane pass overhead, though absolutely none of those publicly aired were even close to its real crash site—still within the state of Queensland.

Melbourne's *The Herald* reported on the Monday evening of February 22:

TWO CLUES TO LOST PLANE

CRASH HEARD IN FOREST AREA

Search Planes Comb Broken Bay District

SYDNEY, Monday. – From dawn today, 10 planes searched vainly for the Stinson air liner which vanished while flying with two pilots and five passengers from Brisbane to Sydney on Friday afternoon.

They covered a strip, 35 miles wide, between Sydney and Newcastle, and concentrated on the rough and heavily-timbered country around Broken Bay – about 30 miles from Sydney.

Much reliance is placed on two reports:

1. A fisherman heard a plane flying over about 5 p.m. on Friday, followed by an explosion, which he thinks was between the Hawkesbury River and French's Forest.

2. At the same time a resident heard a crash in Dead Man's
Gully in the same area.

Miss Jean Batten, the New Zealand flier, who is taking
part in the search, says it would be possible to fly within
100 yards of the dark blue Stinson and not see it in the
undergrowth ...

The Courier-Mail carried an article on that day by a searching
pilot:

PROBABLY STRUCK THE OCEAN

While Flying Low In Blinding Rain

By J. PERCIVIAL, jun., who took part in the search
with Captain P.S. Taylor.

SYDNEY, Sunday. It seems that the disappearance of the
Brisbane-Sydney Stinson airliner VH-UHH will provide
a mystery similar to that of the Southern Cloud, which
has never been seen since it left Sydney for Melbourne in
March, 1931.

It would appear that the machine, flying just above the
ocean in blinding rain, to avoid the low cloud and severe
atmospheric conditions on the land, struck the sea, filled
with water and sank ...

At the crash site, it was Tuesday morning and there was no
sign that Westray, who had left three days before—a fact they
knew because they marked each passing day with a scratch
on a piece of tin—had alerted residents in the valley. Joe was
struggling to cope with his evening climb down the gorge,
where he would spend the night, hoping to have the energy to
climb back up with water for Jack in the early morning.

As they had no food, Joe had started removing red berries
from palms near the creek. He just hoped that they were not
poisonous. Though not great to eat, there was no other option.

Joe's hands and feet were cut and raw with trying to cling to
the vines. Going back up, with each journey getting harder and

taking longer than the previous one, he had to hold the thermos and use the other hand to steady himself on the vines. There was no room for the berries, which he carried in his mouth. He would joke with Jack in a mumble as he approached: "Here comes Momma Bird with the eats!" then spit them out and wash them for Jack to consume.

That day, searchers around the country were starting to give up hope. *The Courier-Mail* indicated that the end to the search was nigh:

GROWING BELIEF THAT STINSON PLUNGED INTO SEA

Owners Give Up Search, but Stand By to Help

NO TRACE BY AIR OR LAND

SYDNEY, Monday. Airlines of Australia Ltd., owners of the missing Stinson, decided this afternoon not to continue to search, but to have two machines in readiness to act on any information received from the searching Air Force planes, land parties, or reports from reliable sources.

Further reports today were conflicting, but in general they tended to confirm the opinion that the Stinson, after passing Box Head, headed for the sea and disappeared.

Many pilots are being brought to the conclusion, as a result of the intensive search of the land, that the missing 'plane plunged into the sea within less than 20 minutes' flight of Sydney ...

After reading the latest *The Herald* article on the fruitless search, and talking to Emma over the telephone, Elsie felt she could no longer stay in Melbourne while her best friend and goddaughter battled to cope with the likely loss of their Joe. It was agreed that Elsie should catch the Thursday train from Melbourne to Sydney and keep them company at Collingwood Street.

The Courier-Mail of Thursday 25 February, summed up the feeling of authorities:

ALL HOPE NOW ABANDONED

No Sign of Missing Stinson

SYDNEY, Wednesday. Searchers by air, land, and water have now abandoned hope of finding the missing Stinson air liner.

Hundreds of miles of coast and hinterland were combed to-day by planes and by land parties in charge of police to investigate reports that the liner had been seen passing over various points. Nothing was found, however, to indicate its whereabouts.

The two liners making trips between Brisbane and Sydney diverted their course and flew low over certain areas which, it was thought, might have been on the route of the Stinson. Land parties under police from Lismore also combed the thickly timbered country round Nimbin where an Italian farmer said he heard a plane crash after it had passed over his property on Friday, but they found nothing ...

Late on that Thursday, Joe felt his strength had waned significantly. Jack asked him to go for help—a prospect that Joe could not bear to contemplate. Firstly, he was weak and did not know which way to go. Westray had left five days earlier and nobody had yet found them.

Secondly, he knew that Jack was too injured and weak to move and needed water. Without help from Joe's trips to the creek, he could not survive long. He turned to Jack and told him firmly: "I'm not leaving you to search for help, mate! You saved my life in getting me out of that plane, so I'll be staying with you to the end!"

That evening, Joe Binstead so doubted his ability to have the energy to get back up the gorge from the creek the next morning, that he etched with Jack's penknife the following message on a piece of the plane fuselage:

Elsie reached Sydney and Collingwood Street for a sad reunion with Emma and Sita. They hugged each other for quite some time, without saying anything. What could one say?

Eventually, Emma said that she would like a memorial service for Joe and the others to be held that Sunday, and would go to St Matthews Church at Manly the next morning to see if that was possible.

A desperate Mrs Proud, Jack's mother, had meanwhile offered 500 pounds for a continuation of the search, but Airlines of Australia refused the offer, replacing it with 200 pounds of their own, and saying they would concentrate on the area near Sydney.

* * *

By midday Saturday, Joe felt he had no more strength to continue his journeys down the gorge and back up the next morning. His latest journey back had just taken him nearly five hours, and he scarcely had any energy to coo-ee on the half hour.

As he sat next to Jack, trying not to look towards his mate's now maggot-infested and festering open leg wound, Joe figured they were almost done. It had now been a full week since Westray had left and there was still no sign of help. "It would take a bloody miracle now," he muttered.

Jack thought for a moment, then said through his pain: "Do you believe in God?"

"Well, I did go to church regularly—but that doesn't seem to matter any more—I think we have been abandoned."

There was silence for a while, before Jack said: "Maybe … maybe we have not given him cause to save us."

"What do you mean?"

"Perhaps we haven't given him a reason … you see, when I was younger, I sometimes took a penny from … from my father's coat pocket in the cupboard, when I found … found he had more than a couple there," said Jack before pausing. "I have always felt … felt guilty about that."

"Well, I forgive you, mate!" Joe said, putting his hand on his friend's shoulder.

"Thanks … but if we somehow ever get … get out of here, I promise … I will confess to my family," Jack confided.

There was silence for a while as it was clear to Joe that he had to make a contribution.

"And you mate?" Jack queried.

"Well, I guess it really doesn't matter anymore …" Joe began. "You probably don't know that I fly under the name of Barnett … Joe Barnett. It means when they published the passenger list, my wife couldn't see where I was flying—as I did last December when I flew to Melbourne—to spend the night with her best friend and the godmother of my daughter …"

"Oh Jesus!" was all a shocked and single Proud could say.

"Anyhow, when you are faced with dying, these things don't seem so important." Joe could see that Jack was still in shock, so he continued: "If I ever get out of here alive, I promise I will tell Emma."

"Oh Jesus, mate! … What was this friend … this friend like? … She must have been good!"

"She is the most beautiful and seductive woman I ever met. She was even married to a maharaja!"

"You're joking!" Proud said, turning his head just enough to see Binstead's serious face. "Jesus!" he exclaimed again.

"She even knew the Kama Sutra!"

"The Kama … Kama what?" queried Jack.

"Yeah, that is what I thought—until she used it!" Then Joe sighed. "But as I said, none of that matters any more …"

* * *

Bernard O'Reilly and his wife Viola ran the isolated O'Reilly's Guesthouse in the Lamington National Park. They had spent the week repairing damage to fences and their property from the cyclonic winds of the week before.

On Friday 26th they had visited Bernard's brother in the Kerry Valley, where Bernard finally got to read the papers. His

682

brother mentioned that a neighbour said he thought he had seen a plane pass overhead. Riding back home in the gloom, Bernard felt that the *City of Brisbane* might be lying 'in his own backyard'.

The next morning, Saturday, Bernard rang that neighbour to confirm the line the plane he had seen was taking, for Bernard felt sure it had come down in the Macpherson Range. After checking a map, he set off on his mare The Great Unknown with a billy can, a drinking cup, tea and sugar, a pound of butter, two loaves of bread and half a dozen onions.

In truth, he was searching for a wreck, for after eight days, there was surely nobody alive.

He released the mare a few miles in and she headed back home, for the terrain was becoming too rough. Progress was rarely possible in a straight line.

After camping in the bush on the Saturday night, he reached a mountaintop around 8 am on the Sunday morning. He scanned across the tree-covered ranges, and noticed a light brown treetop, standing out among the sea of greeny-blue on the Lamington Plateau, about eight miles away. *It could just be,* he thought.

At 1 pm he heard a coo-ee coming from the direction of that tree, but he pressed on through the rainforest, without answering. Finally, he heard it again at 4 pm—it sounded only about 200 yards away.

"Coo-ee!" he called out as loudly as he could and there was an exchange of coo-ees as he fought his way through the tangled undergrowth.

Bernard was excited, but he reckoned the callers could only be searchers—but then he saw the crash sight, the wreckage and charred bodies.

Finally, he was stunned to notice the bedraggled and battered Binstead and Proud and called out: "Oh, you poor bastards!"

Joe replied with delight: "Come down here, we want to shake hands with you!"

"Me too!" added an elated but exhausted Jack.

After shaking hands, they were all too excited to speak, until Joe said: "Well, we will be able to have that drink at the Australia Hotel after all!"

Bernard was shocked at their condition, for Jack Proud's leg was now going green. He started boiling a billy with water he was carrying, and they had tea and some bread, though wisely, the survivors did not eat too much.

They told O'Reilly about Westray and the direction he had left. Bernard left food with Jack and Joe and decided to head off at 4.30 pm for a small town in the valley, but he wanted to follow Westray's trail first.

It was easy to pick up, and after about a mile he saw where Westray had left a line of crushed lilies, as he had slipped through the undergrowth and fallen about twenty feet to the rocks below.

Eventually, Bernard made it down and followed the tracks made by what must have been a badly injured and crawling Westray. After passing four small rapids, Bernard saw a figure propped against a boulder with his feet in the stream. He called out, but the figure did not respond. As he got closer, he realised that Westray was most certainly dead, so he pressed on towards human habitation …

At that moment, Elsie was sitting with Emma and Sita at the packed memorial service in St Matthews Church at Manly. There too were Mrs Proud and relatives of the other victims …

* * *

O'Reilly battled on for hours until he came across a sixteen-year-old, shooting flying foxes near the hamlet of Christmas Creek. It was just before 9 pm on the Sunday night …

* * *

The police car skidded around the corner into Collingwood Street and headed up the wrong side of the road, to slide to a halt in front of No. 65. The superintendent knew the house well, as he had visited a number of times during the week, and attended the memorial service.

He slammed the car door, hurdled the gate and raced down the side path to the front door. Startled by the commotion, Elsie went to open the door as the officer blurted out: "They've found the crash site—they've found Joe! He is alive!"

Having just come through the emotional and seemingly definitive experience of the memorial service, Emma could only gasp: "Is it really true? … And he is alive! … Where is it?" before collapsing into Elsie's arms.

* * *

Immediately on reaching the settlement, O'Reilly had made a telephone call to Airlines of Australia and it was agreed that he could coordinate the rescue parties.

Families had settled down, preparing for a good night's sleep. Rain was falling when the call went out across the farms and small townships of the region for men to cut a track to get the survivors out. These were tough farmers, young and old, hardened to the challenges of the Australian bush and bound by that indefinable bond called 'mateship', that in part meant they would always help a fellow in trouble.

By midnight, more than 100 had gathered and formed three separate teams: two to reach Binstead and Proud, consisting mainly of experienced bushmen, and the third and largest one, to hack their way through the undergrowth and create an exit track. The news had also alerted journalists, photographers and movie cameramen, who were happy to follow in the wake of the more adventurous, on a cleared path.

Dr Lawler, from the regional centre of Beaudesert, was a key participant, as Proud clearly needed urgent medical aid. Armed with implements for cutting, and provisions, the race to get the survivors out was underway in the darkness.

Melbourne's *The Age* of Wednesday 3 March, carried a volunteer's account of part of the epic rescue attempt:

> In single file, with the aid of lanterns and torches, we began our perilous ascent of the gorge. Each man was heavily laden, for we carried canvas shelters and stretchers, medical sundries and food for three days. Apart from the rugged nature of the country with boulders, vines and heavy foliage, we had to cross and recross the stream often. Rain had caused further difficulties by making the ground and boulders so slippery that a fall was always

likely to bring serious injury. Every member of the party
was warned to use care because of the delay that an injury
to anyone would cause ...

It was an exhausting and dangerous mission, though, in the end, a packhorse that fell to its death over a cliff was the only major casualty.

On reaching the survivors, Dr Lawler gave Proud a general anaesthetic, but it was to be a great many hours on an eleven-mile journey, before they were brought out. They stopped every now and again to rest, giving the journalists tagging along, a chance to interview Binstead. Everyone had been warned not to mention Westray's fate, lest it have a deleterious effect on the survivors.

Binstead was, for the most part in a jovial mood, though he was wondering when someone might ask a particular question—for which he had already determined an answer.

Preferring that the truth not be publicly revealed, when asked why he flew under the name Barnett, Joe responded: "With passenger lists published in the papers, I used the name to relieve my wife's anxiety, as she has been opposed to my business trips by air."

Chapter 96

A Promise Kept

It happened in an instant — when my mind was most unclear
I just did what I felt was good, and not what I should fear
Might wound or betray a friend, I've had for many years
I didn't mean to hurt no one, nor cause so many tears.

If the loss of the Stinson plane had been big news, the remarkable discovery and tale of its two survivors was even bigger.

Binstead, Proud and O'Reilly became household names across the country. Bernard O'Reilly, in particular, became a national hero. He received a personal telephone call of congratulations from Prime Minister, Joseph Lyons, and was showered with public donations.

An advertisement in *The Courier-Mail* of Thursday 4 March 1937, under ENTERTAINMENTS, showed how big the story was, with film footage distributed across the country:

'PLANE CRASH SCOOP!!

Cinesound's exclusive pictorial record of the rescue of the sole survivors, Messers. Proud and Binstead, from the wrecked 'plane in the fastnesses of Lamington's lost world.

Highlights include a personal message from Mr Binstead; shots of the rescue parties, the wrecked plane itself, the jungle country, and aerial shots of the location.

ARRIVING BY 'PLANE and SHOWING AT
ALL SESSIONS TO-DAY

On the same day, Elsie opened *The Sydney Morning Herald* to see a large photograph on page twelve of Emma and Sita in the back of an ambulance with Joe, under the heading:

STINSON SURVIVOR AND FAMILY REUNITED

Emma and Sita had been flown north at the expense of Airlines of Australia, while Elsie stayed in Collingwood Street.

Joe and Jack were transferred to Beaudesert Hospital, where they stayed for quite some time.

When Joe eventually made it back to Collingwood Street, Elsie greeted him with open arms, a hug and a big kiss, but when he had looked at her, and when they embraced, she felt a distancing that she could not explain.

The next day, Joe and Emma farewelled Elsie at Central Railway Station. On arriving back home to Manly, and with Sita out with a friend, Joe thought it was a good time to tell Emma the truth—if there could ever be a 'good time' for such announcements.

"Emma, darling … when I was on that mountain, I promised Proud that I would tell you something if I ever got out alive …"

Emma had thought Joe's use of the name 'Barnett' to be odd and unnecessary—but had never suspected this … and she went absolutely 'ballistic'.

"How could you!" she yelled, though as her husband was at least being honest, her rage quickly turned in Elsie's direction, for she must, Emma felt, have been the instigator.

As Joe cowered with his hands over his head in the corner of the lounge room, Emma wrenched the framed Mucha poster of Elsie off the wall and marched it into the backyard, where she smashed it against the bricks of the outdoor fireplace.

She then strode back into the house and grabbed years of treasured postcards and mementoes from Elsie and took them into the backyard and incinerated them, along with the poster. When Elsie rang that evening to say she had arrived back safely to Fordholm Road, Emma unloaded on her.

"How dare you! After so many years of our friendship, to treat me like that!" Emma yelled down the telephone. "That is it! Our friendship is over!" she added furiously, then slammed down the receiver.

Elsie went into shock and could hardly breathe, as she realised what must have happened. She became distraught and physically ill as the impact of the emotional roller coaster of the past days since Joe's disappearance hit home.

The disintegration of her relationship with Emma, her

greatest ever friend, left Elsie traumatised and vulnerable. For many subsequent nights, she asked Myrtle to sleep with her, often cuddling up to her like a newborn sheltering within a mother's protective embrace.

During the waking hours, she tried to paper over the hurt by throwing herself even more enthusiastically into singing opportunities, theatre visits and social events—even catching up with old friend May Maxwell on occasions—but she had to admit, that in Emma, she had lost someone irreplaceable in her life.

At first Elsie thought, *if I move to Sydney, to be close to Emma, she will be reassured of my commitment to her and that everything can be sorted out between us.*

A 21 July 1937 newspaper article even suggested Elsie ('Madame Sita Devi') would change location:

> ... to continue her singing studies in Sydney under the guidance of Frederico Longas, the brilliant pianist, composer and accompanist who is accompanying Tito Schipa on his Australian tour. Madame can converse fluently in French, Italian and Persian, if opportunity offers. For some time she has been preparing a repertoire for a song recital, and she is taking these lessons with the idea of including some melodies of a Spanish character ...

There were also rumours of a relationship with Schipa, a renowned Italian tenor, but plans to move permanently interstate, and away from Melbourne, never eventuated.

"Oh, Elsie!" exclaimed Myrtle, as she read through the 22 September 1937 paper. "There is a piece here under 'Melbourne Chatter' that mentions you at the Town Hall the other night. Listen to this:

> Rubenstein packed the Town Hall and drew a crowd that put on its "pretties" in his honor. Velvet wraps in gay colours took the place of sombre furs, and many smart figures were gloved to the elbows in light-coloured kid. Madame Sita Devi, a chic personality, set off black velvet

and a Parisian toque with long suede gloves in shell-pink color. At the close of the concert, a steward had to be placed on duty at the outer door to regulate callers wanting to have a word with the artist ...

I must say that it is a little unclear whether the steward is for you or Mr Rubenstein, Elsie."

"Now don't be churlish, Myrtle—even Mr Rubenstein deserves the occasional moment of public adoration," she joked, though she wished the truth had been otherwise.

As the months dragged on into 1938, with no hint or prospect of reconciliation with Emma, and no sign of Raji obeying the Privy Council's direction, Elsie's mood dipped occasionally into depression—a state that neither colour nor humour could banish.

She was in such a mood, filled with frustration, twisted by torment, and with a heart riven to retribution, that she marched past Myrtle one day, carrying her will. "My friends don't see me anymore!" she declared, before incinerating their promised portions in her backyard fireplace.

* * *

Elsie read voraciously and occasionally wrote letters to the editor. One such letter was during the Second World War, and published in *The Argus* on 21 January 1941:

WOMEN IN CANTEENS

Sir – The Government should think seriously before sending Australian women canteen workers to the Middle East. The East is not the West. Through one false move our prestige might so easily be endangered and capital might be made out of it by our enemies. Let women with seasoned and thoughtful minds be consulted – and most certainly those with a knowledge of the East and its customs, its ideas, and its people.

Madame Sita Devi, Hawthorn

Increasingly, Elsie relied on Myrtle's strength, basic good sense and loyalty when issues real and imagined became too much. Myrtle had become indispensable, but only in fairytales does anything last forever—and this princess was not going to be quite that lucky.

Chapter 97

The Opera Thieves

"If I could but loan a diamond, ruby, amethyst or two
My social life might just explode — I'd be but one of few!"
"That string of pearls, divine dear, and that brooch would suit me best!"
"I can sense all men go weak at knee, that pendant near my breast!"

By 1947, the pressure put on Myrtle by her mother, to move back home and look after her rather than a non-family member, became too great. Most reluctantly, Myrtle departed *De Montfort*, though she promised to drop in each Friday on her way home from work. Elsie now felt as safe and comfortable as an exotic animal set loose on a firing range before trigger-happy hunters.

* * *

Crash! The glass smashed onto the marble floor of Raji's bedroom, shattering into pieces as he staggered through the dark, stepping onto the shards of glass and only increasing his agony.

"I will lose it—I will lose it all!" he cried, now nearly as much in pain from the pieces of glass piercing his feet as the nightmares that tormented him.

His rantings, as he headed down the staircase, had awakened his faithful valet, Abid Hussain, who rose and switched on lights to reveal a trail of bloodied footprints across the grand foyer.

He and other servants caught up with their master, slumped over the throne, sobbing: "She will not leave me alone—she is haunting me! We will all be destitute! She will take everything!"

"We will get the lawyers in the morning, Your Highness—they will sort things out!" assured Abid. "There must be something they can do!"

* * *

The rhythmic plod, plod of footsteps had at first seemed like many others, as Elsie walked around the Melbourne central business district. Yet, unlike others that came and went, these seemed to be following her.

She swung left off Little Collins Street, into Block Lane, but they were still there: their incessant and regular beat creating an air of bloody-minded determination that Elsie felt reached forward towards her. She darted right, across the mosaic magnificence of the Block Arcade floor beneath the dome, threading her way through the fashionable froth of a Melbourne Friday, past the stained glass and elegant shopfronts of the southern capital's Galleria—but still the beat of those shoes seemed to follow.

She ducked out into Elizabeth Street crowds and scurried onwards, towards the safety of a Hawthorn tram, where she rested against the window and closed her eyes as the vehicle lurched on its way, leaving the stress of the city behind.

They had been a man's shoes, most certainly, she reasoned, though their import lessened with each tram stop that passed. She alighted on Riversdale Road and began walking down Fordholm, hearing the tram rumble away behind her, before its sound was replaced by another—plod, plod. The footsteps following her were back.

In panic, she picked up pace to escape the insidious tread, but the footsteps were relentless. She rushed across Hawthorn Glen and to her gate, opening it quickly and making sure she closed it before racing up the steps to her porch. Her hand had already retrieved the key from her handbag and she unlocked the door before closing and locking it behind her.

For some moments she lay back against it, as if to keep out a powerful beast, before catching her breath and heading into the lounge and peering through the French doors—but she could not see anyone.

* * *

It had all started so innocently. At least that is what Elsie had thought.

She had been wearing some of her jewellery at the Christmas Eve Opera Event of 1948. It was something she always did when she occasionally performed or regularly attended the opera.

A couple of Melbourne society women had approached her at the opera intermission, inquiring as to where she had purchased her magnificent jewellery. She was free and honest with her description, stating that she was married to a maharaja—something that the women found amusing.

In sheer frustration, Elsie mentioned that she had more than what she was presently wearing, so could prove her unusual past.

She was immediately invited to a house in Toorak to meet 'the others' the following Tuesday evening. It was an offer that, as a lonely but sociable person, long used to the company and admiration of others, she could not refuse.

The taxi dropped her at the address she had been given, leaving her to admire the gated mansion in front of her. It was no White House, but for Melbourne, it was among the finest.

As she walked up the circular drive, she clung tightly to her handbag, which contained her bag of jewellery. The front door was opened by one of the two women she had met the previous Friday at the opera, and she was ushered inside.

"Okay everyone!" the woman called out. "This is our new friend … I am sorry, I didn't get your name, darl!"

"Sita. You can call me that because it is my married name as the Maharani of Tikari."

There was relative silence for a few moments, punctuated by a few giggles and one woman whispering to another: "I told you so!"

"Well, I am Mrs Smyth-Davis, and you just must have a drink—or two!" she said, as she ushered Elsie towards the drinks credenza, covered in an array of colourful bottles.

"Oh, I can take your handbag, Sita, and will put it in the bedroom."

"Thank you, but I am fine Mrs Smyth-Davis. I prefer to hold on to it!"

Soon, Elsie, who could never even have been described as a moderate drinker, had consumed far more than she should, so that when the group had encouraged her to expand on her background, she was a little unsteady on her feet and unsure of her reasoning.

They all seemed friendly and attentive, so Elsie started

removing pieces from her jewellery bag. One by one, she placed them in the centre of a round table that their hostess had very kindly covered in a red velvet tablecloth. Its colour and texture merely accentuated the majesty of each item.

As the rings, bracelets, necklaces, chokers, pendants and earrings, composed of and covered in diamonds, pearls, rubies, sapphires and emeralds, appeared, to gasps and sighs from the admiring circle, Elsie tried to explain how and why she received each, though the effect of the few glasses of alcohol was impairing her memory.

"This one is special to me," Elsie said, removing a box from the bag and opening it to reveal the gilded angel brooch. "It was given to me by Grand Duchess Maria of the Romanov family, in 19 …, oh … I think 1912 or was it 1913, … and was made by the jewellers to the Tsars … oh, I cannot remember their name …" Her vision was starting to be affected and she was becoming dizzy.

"It is probably all stolen goods!" whispered one woman to another.

And then it started: one vulture after the other … Mrs Smyth-Davis began the feeding frenzy by picking up the angel brooch and pinning it on her dress, before asking others what they thought. "I will borrow this for a few weeks, Sita!" she exclaimed, triggering Mrs Hansen to grab some diamond earrings, Mrs Webster a string of pearls, and so on, till all the pieces on the table had been claimed.

Elsie was quick to close the jewellery bag, holding her remaining jewellery to her chest in horror.

"What's wrong, Sita? We will all look after them!" insisted Mrs Smyth-Davis. "After all, Mabel's husband is the Deputy Police Commissioner, so they will all be safe!"

By now Elsie was feeling distinctly unwell and insisted she had to go home.

"Where do you live, Sita?" asked Mrs Smyth-Davis.

"Fordholm Road … Hawthorn …" Elsie muttered.

"Well, Frieda lives in Hawthorn, don't you, darl—you will take her home," she said, getting Mrs Hansen's nodded agreement.

* * *

Three days later, Myrtle arrived at No. 30 on New Years Eve, to find Elsie upset and fearful that her jewellery had been stolen.

"Oh Elsie darling, why did you need to show them the jewellery?" she asked, though it was a rhetorical question for she already knew the answer. *It is far better,* Myrtle thought, *to never have been the subject of admiration, adulation and fame, so the years of anonymity can be more easily borne!*

Elsie seemed to be depressed and Myrtle noticed a mostly empty bottle of alcohol in the lounge—something most unusual for a woman who rarely drank.

Myrtle picked up the bottle and asked if the remaining jewels were safe.

"They are in the jewellery bag, inside my handbag," Elsie replied, though she picked up the handbag and opened it, just to check.

Over the next few days, Elsie returned to Toorak and Mrs Smyth-Davis' mansion demanding to have her jewels back. She was told the first time that they would be returned soon, but on her second visit, she was told that she was imagining things and that the police would be called if she returned.

When Myrtle arrived at the Fordholm Road house on Friday 7 January, she carried a bag of her own in her pocket. She had never been a thief in her life, but she realised she now had to steal, to help her dear friend.

As she passed Elsie a cup of tea that she had just made, she ensured she sat between her dear friend and her handbag.

Rising, to go and get her own cup from the kitchen, she stealthily picked up the handbag and kept it out of sight. Within a minute she returned with her cup and deposited the handbag back on the sofa, behind her.

* * *

The next day, Fordholm Road had a surprise visitor. Mrs Hansen seemed most keen to look past Elsie and into the house, but she was not allowed in. However, her invitation to take Elsie with her to a city café on Monday morning and an assurance from her visitor that they would sort things out, together, was accepted.

Chapter 98

The Setup

We stay well within the shadows, till our time is judged as right
Our contacts are top secret, and should never come to light
Each man possesses genius, though fool does lurk within
So our setup's pure 'coincidence'—it's time it must begin ...

On the morning of Monday 10 January 1949, the sergeant, dressed in a waiter's outfit, pointed over his shoulder, back to the corner of the café. "Constable, see the lady in blue sitting on the bench by the table, clutching her handbag next to her?"

"Oh, yes, I see her," whispered the policewoman temporarily wearing a waitress's outfit.

"Well, that is her! When her coffee is ready, take it to her. As you place the coffee in front of her, she should release the handbag. Grab it, let her see you have taken it, and move away, but don't run! If we can get her to assault you, things will be even easier. Just make sure the bag gets to me!"

With the coffee ready, the waitress headed to Elsie's table and moments later had hold of the handbag. There was a commotion as Elsie called out and tried to retrieve it, but it was delivered into the safekeeping of the 'waiter', just as policemen who had been in hiding, raced in to grab Elsie.

"Take her to Prince Henry Hospital—they'll be expecting her there!" the sergeant ordered, as Elsie was dragged away, complaining bitterly.

With Elsie out of the way, the sergeant opened the handbag and quickly spotted the jewellery bag. "This is what we were after boys!" he said, pouring its contents onto a table in the café. However, what tumbled out were a series of clearly plastic children's jewellery. "Bugger!" he exclaimed.

"This means that the real ones must be in her house!" said a constable.

"Yeah ... we could always break in," said the sergeant, ferreting around in the handbag, "but when you have the key," he added, removing a large door key, "you don't have to! Let's go treasure hunting!"

Fifteen minutes later, two carloads of police pulled up outside *De Montfort*.

The sergeant hesitated at the front door with the key in the lock. "I want the place turned upside down! And when we find them, I want to know straightaway—no pocketing! Righto boys, off ya go!" he called, as the boys in blue tumbled inside in an enthusiastic rush.

Back in the city centre, inside the jewellers WM Drummond & Co., Myrtle had been waiting much of the morning to speak to her boss, Andrew Drummond, and it was not till after 11 am, that he became available.

"Miss McLeod, you wanted to see me?"

"Yes, sir. It is a private matter."

"Would you like any of the other girls present?" he asked, unsure of the nature of her concern.

"No, sir, just you will be fine!"

They both headed into his office and he motioned Myrtle to sit.

"Sir, you remember the Maharani and her jewels?"

"Ah yes, the lady whose pearls you clean and with whom you boarded."

"Yes sir. Well, just lately some people have been loaning and not returning them. I have been worried about what little remains, sir."

"Are they in a secure place?"

"Not really, sir," she said, removing a paper bag from her pocket and emptying its contents onto his desk.

"Oh my, Miss McLeod! I think these need to be put in our safe!"

* * *

A severely stressed and near hysterical Elsie was taken to Prince Henry Hospital and kept under guard. By late in the afternoon, two doctors—Kay and Maurer—had separately completed and signed *Mental Hygiene Acts—Schedule Fifteen* documents by inserting her name on the pro forma, to say she should be moved on:

... and that the said Elsie Caroline Thompson is apparently insane, but as the symptoms of insanity are not sufficiently marked to enable me to say that the said Elsie Caroline Thompson is insane, the said Elsie Caroline Thompson is, in my opinion, a proper person to be received into a Receiving House ...

After work, Myrtle caught the tram to Fordholm Road, to check how Elsie was and to break the news carefully to her that she had ensured the jewels were safely locked away. Myrtle had her own copy of the door key, but was shocked when she reached the porch: the front door was ajar and it was clear before entering that the place had been ransacked, as every piece of furniture had been moved. As she entered, she noticed that draws and cupboards had been opened and emptied as well.

She immediately rang the police, who did not promise how soon they could arrive. As Elsie was nowhere to be seen, she called her mother to say she would be late home.

Myrtle began the big job of tidying up and had nearly finished when a police sergeant arrived. He did not seem too interested in what had happened, merely in what might have been on the premises that might have led to the ransacking. Myrtle played 'dumb', more concerned now for where Elsie might be.

Before he left, the sergeant suggested she check Prince Henry Hospital for her friend.

It was 6 pm on that same day, Monday 10 January 1949, when Senior Constable McVicar signed Elsie into Royal Park Mental Hospital. If Elsie had looked behind her as she was taken inside, she might have noticed Frieda Hansen standing at the reception desk, and completing the patient information card on Elsie's behalf. In doing so, she stated that Elsie was 'Widowed' (though she had never married Ivan), born in 'England' (not Australia), was '60' years old (born 1889—not the actual 1883), and that her last occupation was 'Singer'. She also noted that she, Frieda, was a 'friend'.

Shortly after arriving, Elsie was assessed by the chief psychiatrist.

Later that Monday evening—the very day she was taken in

to custody—the director of Mental Hygiene, signed off on an *M.H. 20* form, that stated Elsie should:

> … be detained for a further period not exceeding two months.

Elsie was locked in a secure room with a bed for the night.

On the Tuesday morning, the chief psychiatrist greeted his colleagues: "We had a real nutcase admitted last night! She puts on a very educated voice and says she was married to a maharaja, had hundreds of servants and met Gandhi and Lord Mountbatten!"

It was not until the Wednesday morning, that Myrtle tracked Elsie down to Royal Park. She had kindly been given some time off by Mr Drummond, but reported back to her boss that she had not been allowed access to Elsie and that Elsie had been committed there for up to two months. Myrtle asked that a note be passed to Elsie, stating that Myrtle loved her and was going to do what she could.

Mr Drummond asked about *De Montfort* as it was now unoccupied. Myrtle responded that Elsie had been left it for life, along with a sum of money. Both the house and money were managed by Equity Trustees of 472 Bourke Street.

Mr Drummond thought for a moment, then started searching the telephone book, before saying to Myrtle: "I am going to call the Office of The Public Trustee. They should be able to help coordinate efforts to help Elsie. If I can get a contact, will you go and speak to them and tell them what you told me? Then I think you should go to Equity Trustees and discuss whether they can store the jewellery safely."

Myrtle took a deep breath, because she had never viewed herself as anybody of substance. However, she was tough and determined. "Yes, sir, I'll do whatever you say, as long as you can give me the time off."

Mr Drummond made the call and soon Myrtle had talked over the situation with Mr Witcombe from The Public Trustee at their office. She also passed on the telephone number for Walter, Elsie's brother in Sydney. Later, Myrtle met Mr McGrath at Equity Trustees, and was relieved that they agreed they could safely store the jewellery.

The next day, Thursday, Myrtle received a call from Mr Witcombe, to say that he had spoken to Walter, but Elsie's brother had felt he could not assist. Myrtle was furious about this. After all, Walter was Elsie's only sibling.

* * *

In a remarkable coincidence, Jack Jones, normally resident in Western Australia, happened to be in Melbourne at the time and paid a visit to Royal Park on that Thursday 13 January.

"My father's partner, Elsie Caroline Thompson, was recently brought in to Royal Park and I was wanting an update on her situation."

"And you are? ..." queried the serious-looking woman at reception.

"Jack Jones, madam."

The receptionist picked up the telephone and spoke briefly, then told Jack that he should take a seat, as the chief psychiatrist would not be long.

A smiling man with dark glasses and wearing a white coat soon ushered Jack in to a side room. A few minutes later they both emerged and shook hands. Jones departed, leaving the psychiatrist shaking his head in disbelief.

He returned to his room and picked out Elsie's record adding the following dated note on Jack Jones' visit, underlining a particular section in his black ink. It was later also underlined in red:

> 13-1-49 Mr Jones visited says patient <u>was actually married to a Raja</u> and is Madame Sita Devi. She was the mistress of Mr Jones' father and she was always a bit odd, but very charming. He knows of no psychotic episodes previously.

The chief psychiatrist was now concerned that Elsie may have in fact been telling the truth. He headed to the director's office, and knocked on the door.

"Excuse me, sir, I was wondering if you have a moment?"

"Yes, what is it?"

"I have a recently arrived client in my care who, although a little agitated, seems intelligent and lucid, and is really most charming, but says some amazing and most remarkable things. At first I thought she was totally barmy, but a visitor pointed out to me that at least one thing she said was true: she was married to an Indian maharaja!"

"This is the Thompson woman, isn't it?" the director said, taking off his glasses.

"Yes, sir, that's right. Elsie Caroline Thompson!"

"I am sorry," the director responded. "I cannot help you. She is to remain in the system. Use ECT so she forgets about such things—that is what the equipment is designed to do!"

* * *

Myrtle, in her desperation, turned to Elsie's former best friend, Emma Binstead, even though communication had been non-existent since the immediate aftermath of the Stinson crash of 1937.

Emma could never forgive Elsie, but was shocked to hear of her situation after Myrtle called. She suggested that Myrtle come up to Sydney briefly and that they see Walter, together. Emma said that Myrtle could stay at Collingwood Street and that she would reimburse all her travel costs.

Myrtle was given leave by Mr Drummond, while a friend kindly agreed to check on Myrtle's mother for a few days.

The train trip north was an eye-opener for Myrtle, who had never been outside the state of Victoria.

Walter was courteous though reluctant to become involved, when they met at his home, *Tikari*, at 21 Boundary Street in Roseville. Grudgingly, he agreed to travel to Melbourne in the next few days to see what he could do.

He visited Equity Trustees, where he discovered that the Jones' solicitor had been seeking to take possession of *De Montfort*.

Standing in front of the reception desk at Royal Park, many thoughts and emotions were sweeping through Walter. He could see in the background patients being escorted by the stereotypical 'men in white coats'. He could feel the burden

702

of the long-term illness of his epileptic wife Stella, the extra work relating to running his part-time philatelic business, the Atlas Stamp Company, and the unpredictability of the weight that any meeting with his less conservative little sister would invariably add.

"Can I help you, sir?" the Royal Park Mental Hospital receptionist asked.

"Ah … no … no, I think I am at the wrong institution!" he said, backing away, then turning and heading out the door.

Before returning to Sydney, he went to The Public Trustee at 412 Collins Street, telling Mr Witcombe: "We have very little in common and have scarcely seen each other in nearly fifty years. Our meeting again would upset her too much."

Once Walter had returned to Sydney, Myrtle was determined to see Elsie. She got leave from Mr Drummond to depart work early and arrived at Royal Park just before 4 pm. Perhaps it was chance, perhaps it was staff rotation, but she managed to have a few minutes with Elsie, though they were separated by glass and a wire grill.

Myrtle told Elsie that she still loved her and always would, and that she would keep fighting to get her out.

Elsie seemed upset but determined, saying she wanted to go home as soon as possible.

On the morning of Friday 21 January 1949, two male nurses came in to Elsie's ward and strapped her into a straightjacket. They placed her on a trolley bed and wheeled her out, and down a maze of corridors. Elsie could only gaze at the ceiling as the light fittings whizzed by.

She could feel the bed turning one way, then the other, until finally it passed between a pair of swinging doors. She was removed from the straightjacket, but then strapped to a bed.

The chief psychiatrist entered and smiled at Elsie, though not in a way she found comforting. "We are going to make you feel better now, Elsie. You won't have to worry about any of those silly thoughts."

Two assistants attached electrodes to Elsie's head, wrists and ankles. The Electroconvulsive Therapy (ECT) session was ready to commence. The theory was that the surge of electricity could deprive the patient of the memories or thoughts that plagued them—all the better if it was administered at the very moment they were accessing such thoughts.

"Now, Elsie," the chief psychiatrist said, with his finger poised on an on/off switch on a panel. "Tell me about your background ..."

"I am the Maharani of Tikari, and lived in India ..."

At that moment, the switch on the panel was moved to 'on' and an electrical charge surged through Elsie's body, causing the muscles to contract. Within seconds she had a seizure and her body shook violently for nearly a minute.

After the switch was flicked back to 'off' and Elsie had settled down, she was asked again: "Tell me again about your background ..."

"I lived in a palace with many servants ..."

Again the switch was flicked to 'on' and the electrical charge surged through her, producing another seizure.

After she had calmed down, once more, he asked her for a third time: "Tell me about your background ..."

"I was married in Lucknow to the Maharaja of Tikari and spoke Urdu during the ceremony, like ..."

This time the voltage dial was turned up before the 'on' switch was flicked. Elsie's limbs twitched violently for a minute against the strapping that held her down, as she had a third seizure.

Once calm had been restored, the chief psychiatrist tried for a fourth time, though on this occasion, all Elsie could do was cry.

"Take her back to her room!" he said, before recording in his notes:

21-1-49 Having ECT: Still very grandiose and in accents

ECT was continued regulary and in March she was put through a lengthy session that drained everybody involved, but Elsie insisted on speaking the truth, despite ten successive seizures being induced. The notes from that session read:

15-3-49 Finished after 10 seizures. She has euphoria... garrulous and almost pathologically charming.

Myrtle visited the next day and saw a shell of a woman. "Oh Elsie darling, what have they done to you?"

Elsie's face looked worn and tired, but there was still a fire within her beautiful eyes. "They can torture me as much as they like," she whispered, "but I am never going to deny that I am the Maharani of Tikari! They will not break me!"

Although neither knew it at the time, it would be the last occasion they would see each other for many years. Myrtle's mother had threatened to suicide if her daughter ever left her like she had done to go to Sydney. Now, even a casual local visit produced a tantrum.

Myrtle managed to drop in briefly on Friday 25 March, before heading home, but it was too late.

The day before, the chief psychiatrist had written a report for his director, which probably had at least one word missing:

24.3.49 Report to Director: Manic Depressive Insanity. At present grandiose delusions and euphoria. States she Maharajah Gopal Saran Narain Singh of Tikari. Garrulous, imperious and charming. Admits phases of depression when she is solitary. Self-absorbed and lachrymose.

Later that day, Thursday 24 March 1949, Royal Park Mental Hospital's Medical Superintendent, John K. Adey, signed a *M.H.1* form, declaring Elsie to be insane and ordering that she be transferred from the Royal Park Receiving House to Sunbury Lunatic Asylum, in Melbourne's north-west.

Chapter 99

The Sunbury Years

There are bugs within our bedding, and mashed maggots in our gruel
Our matron is a murderess, and more than half real cruel
They have their ways of torture, send you right around the bend
If you're not mad 'for Sunbury, you surely are by end.

Elsie was placed in the back of a locked van and driven the twenty-three miles from Royal Park in the Melbourne suburb of Parkville, to Sunbury Lunatic Asylum. It was just another one of Victoria's mental hospitals, though this one was for the certified insane.

As the van approached, turning up Circular Drive to the building's front entrance, Elsie thought the asylum looked anything but ordinary, for its three-storey frontage loomed large above the township of Sunbury, on Jackson's Hill.

Elsie's admission card to Sunbury on 24 March 1949, stated:

Diagnosis: *Manic Depressive Insanity*
Prognosis: *Favourable*
Mental and Physical Conditions   Physical: *Satisfactory*
Mental: Grandiose delusions, euphoric, garrulous, unreasoning. She admits phases of depression, tearful and solitary habits.

She was interviewed and inspected by staff before being taken to her new home: the large Ward F2, a room she shared with thirty-nine other female inmates, twenty beds along each wall with a corridor between. It was inevitable that her arrival would create a great deal of interest, and Elsie wondered if perhaps she should 'dumb herself down' to make herself more acceptable to those around her. That thought lasted just a few seconds, for, despite an acting background, Elsie was consistently her educated and cultured self.

"Hey, girls!" called out one inmate. "She has a posh voice!"

With that, the other women gathered around her, noting particularly her ageing beauty.

"You come down a bit, deary?" a woman missing a couple of front teeth asked.

Elsie was feeling uncomfortable and held out from telling the truth about her background until she had been in the ward for nearly a week.

"I was married to a maharaja," she said tentatively to Dulcie, the woman in the bed to her left, who had the disconcerting habit of knocking her head against the ward's green and cream-topped walls a few times each day.

"Sure!" responded Dulcie. "And I'm the Queen of Sheba!"

* * *

With Myrtle obliged to care for her mother, May Maxwell was the only friend who wrote to Elsie and with whom she corresponded, while in Sunbury Ward F2. May also visited when she could.

Elsie was delighted when May managed to come out to Sunbury on the train.

"Are they all mad in there, Elsie?" May asked.

"No, but if they are not mad when they arrive, they pretty soon will be! It is horrid, May! It is a wonder there are not regular suicides."

May and Elsie wrote frequently to each other. As a former journalist, May always typed her letters. By 1951, May was seventy-five years old, and relied more on letters than the occasional personal visit. She would often become concerned when she had no communication from Elsie. She would write to the matron at Sunbury and enquire about Elsie's welfare, as she did on 2 August 1951:

> A patient under your care Elsie Thompson (Sita Devi) is an old friend of mine, and I have had no news of her for the last few months.
>
> Since she has been at Sunbury she has written many times, but not of late. Every week I send her reading matter which I think would interest her, but she never responds.
>
> I know you must be a very busy woman but some day soon would you try and drop me a line about her. If a telephone call would be easier, my number is at the top of the page.

On 10 August, the Medical Superintendent of Sunbury wrote in response:

> In reply to your letter re Elsie THOMPSON, she has not been very well lately, and it is to be expected that she has been unable to reply to you. She will doubtless recover to some extent soon.

If, occasionally, Elsie was uncommunicative, this was not at all surprising. Between her initial admission to mental institutions at Royal Park in 1949 and late 1951, alone, she was subjected to Electroconvulsive Therapy (ECT) and brought to seizure on at least fifty-four separate days.

Again, on 3 December 1951, May followed up when there was no communication from Elsie, and received the following response from Sunbury:

> In reply to your letter, Mrs Thompson is in good health. Mentally she remains much the same as usual. She appears happy and contented. She is able to converse rationally. She is well enough to see you, and she would be pleased if you visit.

This pattern of communication between May Maxwell and Elsie (and Sunbury), continued for many years, as the two women aged. On 20 March 1957, May wrote to Matron Gilder, expressing her concern, once more:

> Would you be kind enough to let me know how my old friend Miss Elsie Thompson is faring. I know she is back in F.2 Ward but have had no letter from her for a few weeks. Generally she drops me a line regularly and somehow I have an uneasy feeling about her.
>
> I would be so grateful if you could give me a little news of her.
>
> Yours sincerely,
> May Maxwell
>
> Have enclosed a stamped and addressed envelope.

The response came from Sunbury's Medical Officer, J.R. Troussaint on 22 March:

Your letter to Miss Gilder about Miss Thompson has been referred to me. Miss Thompson's condition a short time ago prevented her from attending to correspondence. She has however now improved and says she will be writing to you shortly.

Once again, this time on 19 July 1961, May wrote stating that she had not heard from her 'very old friend' for some time. She enclosed a stamped self-addressed envelope. She received a response on 28 July 1961 from a person writing on behalf of Psychiatrist Superintendent Geoffrey Goding:

> Mrs Elsie Thompson is a cheerful old lady who is slowly getting on in years. She is feeble and does not work any more, but occupies her time with the occupational therapist.

May kept up her correspondence, often fretting that something had happened to Elsie. At the age of eighty-five she sent a letter dated 27 November 1961 to the Superintendent of Sunbury, on which handwritten notes were subsequently added by a Sunbury staff member:

Was married to maharajah

To the Superintendent

Dear Sir,

I would be very grateful if you would let me know about the condition of my old friend Elsie Thompson (Sita Devi). *Goddess – Lived in India*

It is months since I have had any news of her.

Soon I may have the opportunity of visiting Sunbury. Do you think she would be well enough to see me? *Yes*

Yours sincerely,
May Maxwell

* * *

All the while May Maxwell was trying to keep in contact with Elsie, the Public Trustee was looking after Elsie's affairs, including the 30 Fordholm Road house. In a letter of 30 April 1951, the Trustee's G Witcombe, wrote to Sunbury:

> The abovenamed patient's house at 30 Fordholm Road is now ready for occupation, and the Public Trustee would be pleased to learn when it is proposed to allow her on leave.
>
> The Public Trustee would need to approve of the conditions on which it is proposed to take some other person into the house, and you might advise on this matter, including particulars as to any proposal for payment of wages etc.
>
> You might note that the regular monthly allowance could not exceed 55 pounds, but there are accumulations of income out of which special payments could be made.

Just when there seemed a chance for Elsie to leave and return to live in Hawthorn, the Medical Superintendent responded in a letter of 7 May 1951:

> This patient has twice since my last communication relapsed into a bad mental state, on each occasion the outset of the relapse occurring when she was actually taking steps toward entering into occupation of her home. It is most probable, from our observations, that she is mentally unable to face the outside world, and that the whole question of trial leave will have to be left in abeyance for at least some months.

In a letter dated 9 January 1953, the Acting Medical Superintendent of Sunbury, wrote to The Public Trustee on behalf of Elsie:

> The above patient recently expressed concern over lack of news about her house. She wishes to know who is occupying the house at present and what is the present state of furniture and furnishings. Patient is also concerned over

the fate of her jewels (she mentioned emeralds and pearls) that were originally in her possession and deposited with Equity Trustees. She says a Mr Wood was dealing with these securities previously for her. Mr Wood apparently promised her beforehand to deal with the matter and let her know, but has not done so. As the patient is quite able to converse rationally and take reasonable interest in her affairs would you please let us know the relevant details so that we may be able to inform her accordingly.

In a letter dated 22 January 1953, Trust Officer K Glynn responded:

The Public Trustee acknowledges receipt of your letter of 9th January requesting information as to how the estate of the abovenamed patient stands.

The house is at present occupied by a Mr W Rae who has been allowed the use of part of the furniture. The rest is stored away. The jewellery mentioned by Miss Thompson is in the custody of the Public Trustee's bank and fully insured against loss etc. At the present time an amount of 1,847.2.8 pounds is held at this office on her account.

The Public Trustee tried once more to have Elsie returned to her house in Fordholm Road. On 3 November 1955, K Glynn wrote to the Sunbury's Psychiatrist Superintendent:

The Public Trustee advises that he has received a letter in which the patient states that she has fully recovered in health and will be leaving hospital shortly to return to her home. In the circumstances the Public Trustee enquires what are the patient's prospects of being discharged, or, alternatively, going on leave.

But each time the door was slammed shut, this time on 10 November 1955, with a letter from Psychiatrist Superintendent Geoffrey Goding:

I am afraid that this patient has by no means recovered and in fact it is considered unlikely that she will be discharged or allowed on trial in the reasonably near future.

Being persistent in managing Elsie's affairs, The Public Trustee wrote again on 26 April 1956:

The Public Trustee refers to previous correspondence and advises that the abovementioned's property at 30 Fordholm Road, Hawthorn, will become vacant on the 11th May. Before the Public Trustee decides on re-letting the property, would you please advise what are the patient's prospects of recovery or going on leave.

However, Elsie was being treated for her 'diagnosed' mania and depression with lithium salts, which by 1956 resulted in her suffering lithium-related toxicity. Geoffrey Goding replied by letter on 3 May 1956:

Unfortunately since our previous correspondence about this patient she has shown signs of toxicity on the dosage of Lithium medication which is necessary to keep her emotionally stable. It would appear from this that the chances of her being able to leave or remain out of Hospital are small, and therefore that she will be unlikely to need her house at any rate for some time.

* * *

Though she was in a lunatic asylum, Elsie was doing her best to lead as normal a life as possible. Her communication demonstrated that she remained lucid, articulate and polite. Elsie's clothes were a key interest for her as she demonstrated in a handwritten letter on 21 June 1952:

Ward F2
Sunbury Mental Hospital
"The Hill"
Sunbury, Victoria

21/6/52

To The Superintendent
The Office

Dear Sir,

Subject to Matron's approval—may I be granted credit and payment of accounts for goods sent to me by Sunbury merchants to whom I wish to tender my thanks for their courtesy.

Yours truly,
Elsie C Thompson
(Sita Devi)

Elsie appreciated that a princess could not dress in rags, though The Public Trustee became concerned that she was spending too much money on clothes. On 5 March 1956, they wrote to Sunbury:

The Public Trustee acknowledges receipt of your letter of 29 February, requesting that 35 pounds be made available to allow the abovenamed to purchase clothing.

The Public Trustee desires to bring your attention to the fact that over 260 pounds has been spent on clothing for this patient since July, 1953. As recently as three weeks ago 56 pounds was paid out to Endalls of Sunbury, for clothing purchased by the patient. A perusal of the dockets for these purchases shows that most of the clothing selected by the patient is most expensive and unsuitable. In the circumstances the Public Trustee does not feel that he should advance further funds with which clothing is to be purchased for the patient.

The Public Trustee would appreciate your comments on this matter and pending your reply, has written to Endalls Drapery advising that he will not be responsible for any future debts incurred by the patient.

713

It should be pointed out that the amount of 260 pounds mentioned above does not include quarterly allowance of 20 pounds nor the frequent extra allowances of 10 pounds sent by this office.

Geoffrey Goding replied on 8 March 1956, stating that Elsie was doing 'concert work' in the asylum:

I quite agree that the amount of money spent by this patient on her clothing does appear excessive. However her clothes and her concert work in the hospital are the main interests that Mrs Thompson has.

We were under the impression that Mrs Thompson had very considerable funds at her disposal and therefore felt that her indulgences in the matter of clothing were justifiable.

If Mrs Thompson's funds are in fact limited this will have to be explained to the patient especially in view of the fact that her mental state has improved to the point where if a suitable companion could be found for her she could perhaps live out of hospital. In the meantime I would appreciate advice from you as to what you consider would be a reasonable expenditure on clothing in view of the funds available.

Mrs Thompson's quarterly allowance barely covers the extra comforts she desires bearing in mind her standard of living prior to coming to hospital.

The performing princess now had a captive audience, and was once again, the star of the show.

In March 1959, at the age of seventy-five, Elsie was still sending handwritten letters to the clothing shop to maintain her wardrobe:

Ward F2
10th March 1959

Dear Miss Endall,

Please send me two warm dresses two

plain petticoats (black) two 'velnit' vests
(women's) and two warm bloomers O.S.

Yours truly,
E. C. Thompson

* * *

On 2 November 1962, Elsie, now aged seventy-nine, was transferred (after more than thirteen years) from Sunbury to Kew Mental Hospital (both having been forced to shed their 'Lunatic Asylum' titles under a 1959 Act). Kew was closer to the centre of Melbourne, and a grand, French Second Empire style edifice that Elsie would well have appreciated under different circumstances.

Chapter 100

The Coffin Cheaters

If you hear soprano singing 'cross Cheltenham Cemetery
A joke, a glint from violet eyes, recited poetry
Should you see a figure gliding in a swirling sari dress
It's just Elsie C. Thompson—first Australian princess.

Elsie's nursing notes for the day of her admission to Kew stated:

> Mental State: Pleasant and co-operative
> Phy State: Old op. scar on abdo.
> Social State: Clean
> Treat: Largactil 50 mgn B. D.

Three days later, her patient card at Kew carried the following typed diagnosis:

> 5/11/62   Manic-Depressive Psychosis—
> Manic Type (311)

In 1964, after her mother had died, Myrtle McLeod, who was now living in a housing commission flat, set out to search for Elsie and found her at Kew. A social worker (P.S.W.) at Kew made typed notes on her meetings with Myrtle:

P.S.W. had 2 interviews and several telephone conversations with friend Miss McLeod. On 6.8.64 and at other times Miss McLeod told PSW something of pts. background. She said she had known pt. for 38 years and had at one time lived with her. She had lost track of pt. for some time but had recently managed to trace her to this hospital. When previously she had phoned Sunbury she was told pt. had been dead for years. Pts. brother "dropped her" years ago.

Miss McLeod is quite sure that pt. is 82 and not 73 as in the hospital record. She gave the following information re pt. She had a good singing voice and was for a time "on the stage" as

"Mrs Stillwell". She eventually divorced her husband "gave up Christianity" married an Indian and went to live in India, where she was accorded the rank of princess. When she returned from India she sang again in the Sydney Town Hall. She appeared wearing 75,000 pounds worth of jewellery and "took the Town Hall by storm".

She left her Indian husband and lived with Mr Ivan Jones "the Jute King". Mr Jones died leaving her a lovely home in Fordholm Rd. for her lifetime and leaving her well provided for …

… At a later interview she told P.S.W. that she had obtained a copy of Mr Ivan Jones' will, which indicated that a large sum of money had been left to pt. and a life interest in the house. Miss McLeod feels sure the Public Trustee is not aware of all the money due to Pt. and mentioned a Solicitor who had information. P.S.W. urged Miss McLeod to write to the P.T. revealing all the sources of her information and asking him to look into the matter.

When Myrtle visited, Elsie would often talk about India and sometimes ask Myrtle to bring a dish of curried prawns. She would also quote Omar Khayyám as best as she could, though she had great trouble remembering the appropriate quatrain number.

On one particular day, she seemed very quiet and reflective before stating:

When you and I behind the Veil are past,
Oh, but the long, long while the World shall last,
    Which of our Coming and Departure heeds
As the Sea's self should heed a pebble-cast.

Even Myrtle could interpret this piece of the *Rubáiyát*. She reached over and gave Elsie a kiss, saying: "Well, I will always remember you, princess!"

As early as 1961, it was noted in Elsie's nursing notes that she was fond of laxatives. In August 1966, she complained of severe

constipation. Although it was not confirmed at the time, she
had bowel cancer.

On New Years Day 1967, a nurse wrote the following in Elsie's
nursing notes:

Elsie collapsed again, on Wednesday 22 November 1967 at
6.30 pm and matron called Myrtle, who said she would be in
first thing the next morning.

As Elsie's condition rapidly deteriorated, she was visited by a
Church of England minister. The fact that she was technically
a Hindu and that a Hindu priest and subsequent cremation
would have been more appropriate, would never have occurred
to 1960s Melbourne.

Elsie's nursing notes stated that:

When Myrtle arrived the next morning, it was too late—her
great friend had passed away.

Later that day—Thursday 23 November—Mont Park
Pathology Centre did an autopsy on Elsie. Their report stated:

THOMPSON Elsie Caroline – woman, from Mental Hospital,
Kew.

A body of a small, elderly woman in poor nutritional state
with a large abdomen and bilateral halluces valgi. There
was an old, low, abdominal paramedian scar. The arteries
of the basal cerebral area of the abdomen and the coronaries

showed moderate atheroma. One necessary spleen was found in the splinic helum. The liver had a nutmeg appearance. Both kidneys had fine, granular surfaces. The abdominal cavity contained large amounts of faecal fluid with few solid fragments. The serosa of the intestine was deeply injected and the cavity exuded an objectionable odour. Some areas were covered with sero-fibrinous deposit. A large tumour occupied the caecum and a portion of lower ascending colon. The cancerous modular mass was projecting into the lumen and obstructing the ileo-caecal valve. A small perforation was found on the later-posterior aspect of the caecum. The regional lymph node of the mesentery was enlarged but did not seem to contain tumour masses. There were many old adhesions of the peritoneum. The uterus was in situ.

Cause of death:	Obstructing carcinoma of the caecum with perforation.
	Peritonitis.
Other Findings:	Mesenteric lymphadenitis.
	Moderate generalized atherosclerosis.
	Nutmeg liver.
	Accessory spleen.
	Old abdominal operational scar.
	Halluces valgi.

No death notice appeared in Melbourne's *The Age* newspaper, but it did have a funeral notice on page twenty of its Friday 24 November issue:

THOMPSON – The Funeral of Miss ELSIE CAROLINE
THOMPSON will arrive at the New Cheltenham Cemetery,
Holloway Road, Sandringham, on MONDAY at 9 a.m.

SLEIGHT'S in conj. DRAYTON & GARSON. 69 4626.

Just before 8.45 am on the morning of Monday 27 November 1967, Myrtle McLeod was dropped off by a taxi at the New Cheltenham Cemetery office. Wearing a black raincoat, to guard against the forecast showers, Myrtle tapped on the window, to gain the attention of the older cemetery worker. He was giving a young assistant on his first day of work, the lowdown, while he polished a gold watch he had stolen from a freshly dead corpse.

"Excuse me, but I was wondering where the burial of Elsie Caroline Thompson will be?"

"Thompson?" the older man said, looking down at his listing for the day. "Take the second turn left, madam, then walk along to Section A. You will see the open grave!"

Myrtle headed off, mentally preparing to say goodbye to Elsie after over forty years. By the time the large black Sleights Funeral Directors hearse arrived, it was clear to Myrtle that she was the only mourner.

As a Public Trustee burial, Elsie had the cheapest coffin. Myrtle took a large pink rose that she had been wearing, pinned to her dress, kissed it and placed it on the centre of the coffin's lid.

Wiping tears away, she then stood back and said a silent prayer as the coffin was lowered, before taking a piece of paper out of her pocket. Her local librarian had helped her locate and select the piece she had transcribed. She wiped her nose and took a deep breath. She had practised this many times the evening before. Now she needed some of Elsie's courage and stage skills to realise any hope of 'doing her proud':

Strange is it not ? that of the myriads who
Before us pass'd the door of Darkness through,
   Not one returns to tell us of the Road,
Which to discover we must travel too.

"Rubáiyát of Omar Khayyám, Quatrain 64 ... goodbye princess!" she added, blowing her a kiss.

In the cemetery office, the farewell was not so fond.

"See that old duck up there? Well, there is nobody else, because nobody cares—except we do, 'cause that is a Public Trustee's job, and they will send us twenty dollars for a plaque, which we kindly donate to our drinkin' fund!"

"But, that is stealing!" the young man protested. "That would mean she is buried in an unmarked grave!"

"So? You got a lot to learn, son! 'Cause that is the way it will be!" his boss insisted, as he put the gold watch to his ear to check it was ticking. "Who the hell was she, any rate, this … Elsie Caroline Thompson?" he said, checking back to the listing in front of him. "A bloody nobody, who nobody cares about and nobody will ever remember!"

Epilogue

The Maharaja of Tikari did not make regular annuity payments to Elsie after September 1921, despite the Indian High Court in Patna ruling in 1928 that he must (in perpetuity) and the highest court under British Commonwealth legal dominion, the Privy Council, confirming this by dismissing Raji's appeal in 1931.

Raji's friends tried to excuse this behaviour by claiming that Elsie had subsequently married a rich man and that she 'didn't need the money'. Elsie had never remarried.

Raji died in May 1958, just a month after the passing of his lifelong great friend, John Guerney Wakefield. Raji's body was cremated on the steps of the Vishnupad Mandir, a Hindu temple by the banks of the Falgu River at Gaya.

Some time after Elsie's death in 1967, the Office of The Public Trustee in Melbourne began a search for her closest relatives, after Myrtle McLeod testified that she saw Elsie burn her will.

Myrtle knew that Elsie had three nieces, Marjorie, Elsie and Stella, though she had forgotten the name of the latter.

On 3 June 1970, The Public Trustee had a notice inserted on page 1,898 of the *Victoria Gazette*, appealing for any creditors or relatives who had claims on the estate of Elsie Caroline Thompson, widow, formerly of 30 Fordholm Road in Hawthorn, who died at Kew on 22 November 1967, to contact them.

In mid 1970, Myrtle managed to contact Emma Binstead, then aged eighty-five and a widow—Joe Binstead having died on 29 August 1969. Emma went to the former Walter Thompson family home at 21 Boundary Street, Roseville, but found no Thompson relatives.

This was not surprising. Walter had died on 13 April 1962. He never fully recovered from being run over by a car while crossing the Pacific Highway a year earlier. The three Thompson girls had long since left home. All eventually married.

Stella, the youngest, was the first to wed. She became a teacher and married a farmer in Wellington, western New South Wales in 1945. They had two children: a girl born in 1946, and a boy born in 1950.

The middle one of the Thompson sisters, Elsie (named after her aunt the Maharani), was a great friend of the writers Florence James and Dymphna Cusack, typing their manuscript for their 1947 book *Four Winds and a Family*. They went on to write the 1951 Australian classic *Come In Spinner*, which Dymphna said was, in part, about their collective experiences in Sydney.

Elsie enrolled at Sydney University and gained a Bachelor of Arts. After completing library examinations, she worked at Sydney's Mitchell Library where she met Dr Egon (Frank) Kunz, a Hungarian refugee who had arrived in Australia in 1949.

From their marriage in 1953, they lived in the downstairs rooms at 27 Wycombe Road, Neutral Bay, the home of the widow of Australia's famous wartime cameraman Damien Parer. Parer was the cinematographer for Australia's first Oscar-winning film, *Kokoda Front Line!* (1942). He was killed while filming with American forces in the Pacific in 1944.

* * *

Elizabeth Parer and her son, also called Damien, lived upstairs. It was while my parents were living in that house that my twin brother and I were born, in 1956.

The impending birth of a third Kunz baby, my younger brother, saw us move to Mosman from 1957, then from March 1968 to Canberra.

Marjorie, the eldest of the three Thompson sisters, worked for the Red Cross. She was the last to marry. She wed a sweetheart from her youth in 1974, when she was sixty-seven. They lived in a flat in Mosman, before moving to one in Chatswood.

A regular reader of the classifieds in *The Sydney Morning Herald*, Marjorie spotted The Public Trustee's August 1970 advertisement for the three nieces of Elsie Caroline Thompson, to contact them.

In Melbourne, my parents visited the Office of The Public Trustee at 168 Exhibition St. On the fourth floor, they were introduced to Mr Peverill, who became my mother's contact over the next few years, until Elsie Caroline Thompson's estate was resolved.

On 8 April 1971, Mr Peverill passed on a letter from Myrtle McLeod:

Flat 3, Block 11
538 New Street
Elsternwick
Melb. VIC Code 3185

Dear Miss Thompson,

I hope you will not think it impertinent of me writing to you. I have been a friend of your aunt since 1926 on her arrival here from India. I did pearl repair work for one of the leading jewellers here in Melbourne, and it was through this work that I met your aunt.

After some more visits to your aunt's home in Fordholm Rd, Hawthorn, we became fast friends, and when Mr Jones had to return to India on business, I stayed with your aunt until his return.

About 1931 Mr Jones had a heart attack in WA and died. It was then that your aunt ask me if I would live with her and be like a sister and companion to her. This I did.

A few years later I had an accident. I was put in hospital for plaster for my spine. After I got well I lived again with your aunt, but later had to return to my home to look after my mother who was ill. I went out to Hawthorn as often as I could.

I found your aunt had taken to drink. I tried hard to break the habit, but she by this time was mixed up with so called friends about Toorak. And we never found out, someone had rung the police, they took the poor dear to Royal Park and from there she was sent up to Sunbury.

Your aunt Miss Thompson was never a mental case. Had I my own home I could have taken her. I could not go to the Fordholm Rd home as that was left to your aunt as long as she lived.

In the mean time I had applied for a Housing Commission Flat, which I got. Had I taken your aunt back to Fordholm Rd home, and anything happened to her, I my self would have been turned out without a home over my head.

Your aunt always said she would never see me want, and right up to the week before she died, she wished she could buy a little home for us both, so as I could look after her, and she longed for her jewellery.

A few years ago, I got her into a Private Hospital near me. I visited her each day and looked after her as much as I could. Unfortunately, Matron ask if I could take her for a few weeks until they had a single ward. I was not able to take her here. I am in a Housing Commission Lone Person Flat and an Old Age Pensioner.

I phoned the hospital to take her. When I went to fetch her Matron had sent her back to Kew Mental Hospital. I was very up set over it. I went out whenever I could sometimes each week. She looked forward to my coming and I took coffee, chicken sandwhiches and always a piece of chicken for her next day lunch and some fruit.

Near her birthday I ask what she would

like she said oh Myrtle some curried prawns like I showed you we did in India, so you see she never forgot.

Your aunt always said that I was to have a piece of her lovely jewellery. It was a Black Onyx Pendant with a Diamond set Watch enclosed. I know it is valuable, but likewise so is all the other jewellery, which by the way the Public Trustees have in their Strong Room.

The day your aunt took very ill Matron rang me about 7 pm to tell me. I ask if they would send her to a hospital. I was told she was too ill to be moved. I said I would be out on the first bus next morning. By 6 am she had died.

I ask if I could have your aunt cremated with a rose tree over her ashes. I was told at my own expense. This I was not in a position to do. I had her buried in a lawn grave at Cheltenham. I was her only mourner.

It was a very sad time for me, when I buried my very dear friend. I knew she was in God's hands, free at last from sorrow and pain.

It was I who told the Trustees I thought there were three nieces, one Marjorie, also Elsie, but had forgotten the name of the other niece. I did try to find you people myself but was unable to do so.

If at any time you would care to get in touch with me or would like to know more of your aunt I would be pleased to hear from you or see you.

My mother typed up a copy of this letter and sent carbon copies to each of her sisters, asking what they should do. At that stage the estate had not been finalised as The Public Trustee still sought more information and assurances from the sisters.

On 8 August 1972, The Public Trustee asked the sisters to sign a counter indemnity document, just in case the Maharaja had not pre-deceased Elsie, or they had a child. This, the sisters were happy to do as they were sure neither situation occurred.

Finally, more than two and a half years after contact began, The Public Trustee sent each of the three sisters cheques for just short of $11,000. This was accumulated rental income from the occupation of 30 Fordholm Road over many years—the house that Ivan had left to Elsie to use as long as she lived.

There was no sign that any of the money in the estate had Indian origin.

There were however eight pieces of jewellery, all presumed to have been gifts from the Maharaja to Elsie. They had survived, thanks to Myrtle's dedication, from a larger group that had either been sold by Elsie when she ran short of money, or 'borrowed by her friends'.

The Office of The Public Trustee had asked a Melbourne jeweller to value each of the pieces. They must have thought that the Trustee was desperate to sell, because they valued the Black Onyx Diamond-studded Pendant Watch (with 120 small and 11 larger diamonds) at just $450.

My mother was keen to see Myrtle acknowledged in some way, though felt that it would be best to meet her first. This, my mother and father did. My mother subsequently wrote to her sisters. Having been trained as a secretary and typist in her youth, she found it quicker and easier to type. She slipped two sheets of carbon paper behind her original (as this was in the days before the ease of personal photocopying) and typed then posted the following:

Myrtle McLeod: Now don't scowl, the two of you!

All the while in Melbourne I felt it was terrible not to see whether she was alive or dead, so I got her address out of the file, and blow me down, if we had not passed it each morning going out to the Archives at Middle Brighton.

Because of your feelings I was very apprehensive going to see her, and right up to passing through the gate F. was half urging me, and half threatening me with dire consequences from you two.

She lives in an old person's single flat, in Block 11 of a huge complex facing a park. I knocked at Flat 3, a very broad figured, short woman with glasses came pleasantly to the door, and I said I was the niece of Elsie Thompson. She asked me in, and two neighbours with her vanished like the mist!

She just has a small kitchen, a messy bed-sittingroom and apparently some kind of bathroom. She kept on saying 'I see the resemblance!' F. said that the only possible likeness was my imperious manner as I sat on her window seat.

She was doing some work—threading pearls, kept on saying 'your Elsie'—but didn't ask me my name—where I lived— who F. was, or really any relevant questions.

I was prepared for a bedridden, frail old lady clutching my hand and begging for help, but she looks very well, says she was although 77 years old—seemed almost impossible.

I told her the Estate was not finalised, but that as I was passing through Melbourne I thought I would call. F. said my lady-muck-of-the-dustheap manner obviously fitted in with the mistress-servant-companion relationship she had had with

Auntie Elsie, but I was really scared stiff she would ask me some awkward questions.

But she just talked about Auntie Elsie, and also how some people around Melb.—big people she said—took advantage of her. I can imagine some of them wear her jewels, and some have beggar's bowls etc. Certainly Myrtle has no Indian pieces on display, that's why I wanted to call unexpectedly.

F. and I both got the impression that she was a genuine good body, and certainly if she had not had to leave Elsie to look after her own mother, she would have been just the solid type to keep Auntie Elsie in tow and stop her excesses.

She said she never knew who had her put in a mental hospital—she considered she was never mental, but she did drink and for this she blamed her 'Toorak friends'—obviously in a different social class than Myrtle.

Unless it is a terribly ugly piece, I think it would be useless to give her the onyx piece of jewellery she mentioned in the letter—during the visit she didn't mention the jewellery, money or remuneration—but I do think she warrants some token from the $33,000. I feel that $500 would be ok and I am willing to give it on my own if you should both consider she is impertinent.

I feel she really did serve Elsie. Of course she may have helped herself to jewellery or objects when the home was open to all, I suppose. Perhaps she did, perhaps she felt she had more right to things than possibly the absolute strangers who may have been around when Elsie was in Sunbury.

I suppose officers from the Public Trustee went out, but goodness knows how promptly and how thoroughly such things were done. However, I don't know any details, but I do feel my conscience tells me that she should have some acknowledgment.

She said how she had tried to find us and how Emma Binstead went to the old home in Roseville, but there were no Thompsons there. I asked how was Mrs Binstead and she said very frail; Mr Binstead died some years ago. Of course I always feel the Will may have been made in the Binsteads' favour. On the other hand, Mr Peverill had a photograph of two children, apparently grandchildren of a Captain Slocombe, and Auntie Elsie's gushing sentiments and writing was all over the photograph.

Well, better finish—think that's all and if I don't end you'll need a day's leave to read it!

Eventually, Myrtle was sent a cheque for $400, said to be from two of the sisters. My mother rang her to say the cheque had been posted and to inform her about the likelihood of a plaque. Myrtle replied:

Flat 3, Block 11
538 New Street
Elsternwick
Melb. VIC 3185
Tuesday 9th Oct

Dear Mrs Kunz,

Today I received your little letter together with a cheque for $400. I do want to thank you and your family ever so much for your generous gift to my self. It sure will help me in many ways.

The memory of your aunt will not be forgotten. I am only sorry I could not have helped her more during the last sad 20 years of her life.

I do feel so happy about the plaque and its wording. I think too, that Madame would of liked that.

I would of loved to have a beautiful rose put over her resting place. I think I told you in my letter the Public Trustees told

me at my own expense. I was not able to
do this.

In several weeks time I will be able to ask
my niece to take me out to Cheltenham.
She and her husband are coming back to
live at Lilydale. I shall send you a card if
the plaque has been placed to mark the
resting place.

Again, asking you to accept my sincere
thanks and best wishes,

Yours very sincerely,
Myrtle McLeod

All the jewellery pieces that came into our possession from
my great-aunt were subsequently sold.

A few days before Myrtle's thank you letter, my mother had
written to the Trustees of the Cheltenham Lawn Cemetery:

Mrs E. F. Kunz
10 Tivey Place
Hughes ACT 2605
October 4, 1973

The Trustees,
Cheltenham Lawn Cemetery,
Wangara Road,
Cheltenham VIC 3192

Dear Sirs,

I refer to Grave 26, Comp. K, Section A in which Elsie
Caroline Thompson was interred on the 27th November 1967.

Her Estate has now been finalised by the Public Trustees of
Victoria and I am writing to you as one of the beneficiaries.

Accounts from the Public Trust Office show that the sum of
$275.50 was paid to Sleights, funeral directors of High Street,

Glen Iris. (I am aware that Drayton & Garson took over Sleights' business but this fact is not relevant.)

It is known to me that on 27/11/67 the full price of a bronze plaque (then costing $20) was paid over by Sleights to you specifically for the purpose that you should provide a bronze plaque.

When I visited the cemetery I found that the grave was unmarked indicating that your Board had failed to carry out your obligation.

I therefore request you now to affix a plaque. What is required is the simplest bronze plaque, without any decoration or symbol and with the following wording:

SITA DEVI

MAHARANI OF TIKARI

born Elsie Caroline daughter of

James and Mary Ann Thompson

1883 – 1967

May I stress that as you accepted the amount of $20 in 1967 as full payment for the plaque but failed to fix it or return the sum to the Public Trustees and have apparently made unauthorised use of it since, you are not in a position to demand additional payment from the Public Trustee or from the beneficiaries on account of possible price rises.

The speed of your reply and your willingness to take corrective action will help me to assess whether this has been an isolated incidence of an unfortunate and explicable mistake, or perhaps only one instance of a profitable practice which warrants wider investigation by appropriate authorities.

Yours faithfully,
Elsie Kunz

It has been publicly stated (and no doubt, now generally accepted) that Raji's much-loved V16 Cadillac was 'a gift from the Maharaja of Patiala'. However, I have a copy of a 1965 letter from an Indian third party, who states that the car was "purchased new" by the late Maharaja of Tikari. It was, reputedly, the Maharaja's 152nd motor vehicle. It ended up being bought in the 1980s by one-time Lotus car designer, engineer and inventor of the Black & Decker Workbench, Ron Hickman. It was exhibited at many car shows and regularly won awards.

Ron and his wife Helen lived on the island of Jersey, and the car featured on a Jersey stamp in 1989. They invited my wife and me to stay with them in Jersey for a few days in 2009, on our way back from a visit to the Privy Council Office, in London.

Ron insisted that I drive the V16, something I did with some trepidation and great care, given its value. Raji would have been outraged if he had known that Elsie's great-nephew would one day drive one of his prized possessions.

We headed out on Route Orange on a beautiful June evening, Ron soon tooting the car's horn ostentatiously as we glided past people gathered outside La Pulente Restaurant. I held the steering wheel tightly as we thundered on, away from the setting sun. I have never driven a bus, but there could not have been too much difference.

Ron was commending me on how quickly I had adjusted to the gear changing, but I just wanted to stop before I crashed. He said that the car had one of the world's largest turning circles—and he was not kidding. I had to turn left into the car park of the Channel Islands Military Museum, manage to avoid the parked cars and pedestrians and sweep around its circumference, to end up facing the way we had come.

Eventually, I pulled the emerald and silver monster to a halt by the roadside, just relieved to be able to get out of the driver's seat.

While there, Ron mentioned that he had a handkerchief with the Maharaja's monogram. Raji had given it to a Bertine Teater, Ron said, who was formerly married to Cecil Kempster, Raji's ADC. She died on Jersey just after 2000.

* * *

Arthur Nelstone married a Gaiety Girl after his return to London. He had at least one child, a daughter called Marie, who later appeared in his comedy dance routine. He died in 1929.

George Stillwell is believed to have died in Manila in 1934.

Eugen Sandow, the strongman, died in London on 14 October 1925, at the age of fifty-eight. He was buried in an unmarked grave in Putney Vale Cemetery, according to his wife Blanche's direction. His muscled and posing figure has been immortalised in the Mr Olympia trophy—the prize for the winner of the international professional men's bodybuilding competition.

Grace Knighton is believed to have died in Chicago in the late 1970s. She was always proud of her link with Elsie.

Ranbir Singh of Jind died on 31 March 1948 after ruling for sixty-one years.

Joe Binstead, John (Jack) Proud and Bernard O'Reilly, all attended the erection of a stone memorial to James Westray, thirty-one years after the Stinson crash. Bernard died on 20 January 1975.

In 1987, a telemovie was aired called *The Riddle of the Stinson* starring Jack Thompson as Bernard. Bernard O'Reilly's guesthouse has been transformed into multi-venue accommodation called O'Reilly's in the rainforest of the western Lamington National Park, complete with its own memorial to the Stinson crash and Bernard's efforts. You can even journey with a guide to the Stinson crash site.

Emma Binstead died on 30 October 1977 in Balgowlah, Sydney, almost ten years after the passing of her former great friend Elsie.

Her daughter Sita, Elsie's goddaughter, married in 1944 and held many senior positions with the Anglican Church, working for decades on boards of hospitals and aged care facilities. The Sita Carter Day Centre for the aged and frail in Sydney's inner west, is named after her. On Australia Day in 1998, Sita was awarded the Order of Australia for service to the Anglican Deaconess Institution, Sydney and Hope Healthcare. She retired to the New South Wales Southern Highlands, where she died on 5 September 2008.

May (Masie) Maxwell was a one-time actress and comedienne, who became editor of the women's page in Melbourne's *The Herald* newspaper for twenty-four years from 1910, and later a freelance journalist. Given her background and fondness for opera and elocution, it is no surprise that she became a good friend of Elsie's. She was made a life member of the Australian Journalist's Association in 1960, and awarded the British Empire Medal in 1969 for services to the profession. She died on 24 July 1977 in Jolimont, Melbourne, at the age of one hundred, and was buried in Box Hill Cemetery.

As for Myrtle McLeod, she is believed to have died in 1982 at the age of eighty-five and cremated at The Necropolis Springvale, now called Springvale Botanical Cemetery, in Melbourne's south-east.

I only wish that I could have been able to thank both May and Myrtle personally for their many years of dedication to Elsie. It would have been so easy to walk away, as Elsie's brother—my grandfather—did. Though from very different backgrounds, they were both remarkable, determined and generous women. Clearly, they both believed a great injustice had occurred with Elsie's near nineteen years of incarceration.

* * *

So who, if anyone, had Elsie Caroline Thompson locked away—a very sad and traumatic end to the remarkable life of the first Australian princess.

Was it the Maharaja, who did not make regular perpetual annuity payments after 1921—payments that the Indian High Court and the Privy Council ruled he should? His great friend Wakefield may well have used his contacts in Australia to assist.

Was it the Jones family, who through their solicitor fought to gain control of the Fordholm Road house from Elsie once she was incarcerated?

Or was it Elsie's 'Toorak friends', who were then able to keep the jewels they had 'borrowed'? Or, was it in fact a combination of at least two of these three?

Yet, there exists the intriguing possibility of a fourth party's involvement.

From 1946, there was ongoing public discussion of the

likelihood of Lord Louis Mountbatten becoming Australia's next Governor-General. Mountbatten was a great grandson of Queen Victoria, and from November 1947, when his nephew Philip Mountbatten married Princess Elizabeth, he was 'Uncle Louis' to the heir to the British throne.

It is quite possible that Elsie mentioned to 'Toorak friends' with high-level contacts, that she had once had an intimate association with Mountbatten—in an age when the royal family was believed to be beyond reproach, and any questioning of their morality, was sacrilege.

Certainly, the clinical notes on Elsie made after her admission to Royal Park, have the psychiatrist recording 'married to Mountbatten'. This is likely to have been the recorder's euphemism for a sexual relationship, something thought impossible at the time. It was only years later that Lord Louis himself admitted he had an open marriage, and that he and his wife spent much of their time in other people's beds.

Irrespective, I shall leave readers to come to their own conclusion as to who was behind Elsie's incarceration.

What is however certain, is that if you visit Melbourne's Cheltenham Memorial Park, Harper Lawn, Section A-Row K-Grave 26, you will find the appropriately marked last resting place of 'the first Australian princess'. She was a woman of significant intelligence, talent, personality, and in her younger days, beauty, who led a remarkable life that few would have believed possible.

She was convinced that all Indians, particularly girls and women, deserved greater opportunity and education. As schools board president for Tikari Raj, she worked to improve the pupils' prospects and freedom. She argued the need for tertiary education in Bihar. Eventually, the state's first university was founded in Patna in 1917.

Elsie demonstrated in her marriages, friendships and learning of multiple languages, a broadmindedness and welcoming of people of varying cultures, irrespective of their colour, race and religion.

Sadly, Elsie was denied the freedom and opportunity she sought for others, spending most of her last two decades cruelly institutionalised in mental asylums, disbelieved and deserted by all but the faithful Myrtle McLeod and May Maxwell.